# LOVING, LIVING, PARTY GOING

Henry Green was the pen name of Henry Vincent Yorke. Born in 1905 near Tewkesbury in Gloucestershire, he was educated at Eton and Oxford and went on to become managing director of an engineering business, writing novels in his spare time. His first novel, *Blindness* (1926), was written whilst he was still at school and published while he was at Oxford. He married in 1929 and had one son, and during the Second World War served in the London Fire Brigade. Between 1926 and 1952 he wrote nine novels, *Blindness*, *Living*, *Party Going*, *Caught*, *Loving*, *Back*, *Concluding*, *Nothing* and *Doting*, and a memoir, *Pack My Bag*. Henry Green died in 1973.

ALSO BY HENRY GREEN

*Blindness*
*Caught*
*Back*
*Concluding*
*Nothing*
*Doting*
*Pack My Bag*

Henry Green

# LOVING, LIVING, PARTY GOING

### WITH AN INTRODUCTION BY
### Sebastian Faulks

VINTAGE

Published by Vintage 2005

2 4 6 8 10 9 7 5 3 1

Copyright © Henry Green 1929, 1939, 1945

Introduction copyright © Sebastian Faulks, 2005

*Living* first published in Great Britain in 1929 by The
Hogarth Press

*Party Going* first published in Great Britain in 1939 by
The Hogarth Press

*Loving* first published in Great Britain in 1945 by The
Hogarth Press

Vintage

Random House, 20 Vauxhall Bridge Road,
London SW1V 2SA

Random House Australia (Pty) Limited
20 Alfred Street, Milsons Point, Sydney,
New South Wales 2061, Australia

Random House New Zealand Limited
18 Poland Road, Glenfield,
Auckland 10, New Zealand

Random House (Pty) Limited
Endulini, 5A Jubilee Road, Parktown 2193,
South Africa

The Random House Group Limited Reg. No. 954009

www.randomhouse.co.uk/vintage

A CIP catalogue record for this book
is available from the British Library

ISBN 0 099 48147 2

Printed and bound in Great Britain by
Bookmarque Ltd, Croydon, Surrey

# CONTENTS

# INTRODUCTION

HENRY GREEN IS a writer who always seems to need 'introducing', like a stranger at a party: dark, louche, awkward. It is odd, this need for an outrider to go ahead and smooth his way, because in his life he had friends enough, while his novels were viewed by people of dependable judgement as being among the best – perhaps the very best – of their time. Is it just that to later generations he is a little too 'difficult'? Is it merely that Green requires a fraction more concentration than Greene? Perhaps so; but it is puzzling, this chronic shyness, when what his admirers are chiefly claiming for him is that he brings pleasure – a pleasure more intense, more original and more rewarding than that offered by any of his contemporaries.

Your first Green novel is in some ways your most memorable. I can still remember the incredulous pleasure with which I read *Living* in a battered library edition about thirty years ago. Here was a novelist who was doing something I had never experienced in fiction before. He seemed to have redrawn the familiar triangle between reader, writer and character, so that you somehow had the impression that you knew his characters better than he himself did. So real were they, so grand yet so fragile, that one felt protective of them – protective even against the plotting of the author whose skill had allowed one to know them in the first place.

*Living* is a story about people in a Birmingham iron foundry, most of them poor manual workers without much life beyond factory, family or a small terraced house. From the first page, the absence of certain common words from the prose brings us face to face with the concrete nature of their world: harsh, hard to mould, monotonous. Yet alongside this machine-age view of the 'masses', something underhand is going on. To begin with, it is in a kind of tenderness that Green allows to colour his descriptions; though when this feeling threatens to swell, he usually deflates it: sometimes our love for the people in the book seems unrequited – by them or by their author – and this can be painful. You vow not to fall so easily next time; yet soon the beguiling rhythms of the prose begin to seduce you once again, so that you long for emotional release, either within the fictional lives of the characters or in your unstable relationship with them. The inner shape of the novel in this way imitates our experience of living: it promises pattern, then withholds it, insisting on a formless banality; it describes intensity, but as part of a grudgingly accepted monotony; it glimpses poetry, but only from the corner of its eye.

Green came from a wealthy family, was educated at Eton and Oxford and knew many of the the people whose names are familiar from literary biographies of the period. His 'research' for *Living* was undertaken while he worked for his father's company, which made plumbing supplies and beer-bottling equipment in a factory similar to the one described in the book. His attentive, unpatronising attitude to the working-class characters in the novel was cause for comment at the time it came out, in 1929, as was his largely satirical treatment of their employers. Green, however, had grander interests than those of 'class'. Most of the workers are idle or conniving, and while the toffs are epitomised by a young man who can do tricks with a glass of water without spilling it on his dinner jacket, they also have their complications, their light and shade. Young Dupret, the factory owner's son, may be a secret nose-picker, but he does see beauty in the work the men do.

Green hardly ever gives psychological accounts of his characters, their motives, childhoods or formative experiences. (He beautifully mocks the attempt to do so in *Party Going*, when one character tries to explain the hapless Alex with an

8

unintentionally comic resumé of what he has 'been through'.)
In this respect Green seems to belong to the Modernist
movement, which preferred its depiction of reality broken up
into its constituent planes, like Picasso's, or fragmented, like
Eliot's. What makes Green distinctive, however, is that
despite following the manner of his time, he is able to convey,
in *Living* for instance, such a warm sense of what old Mr
Craigan, or the talented but shifty Tarver, or Lily Gates,
desperate to be a mother, is really like. One of the book's
greatest passages is the attempted elopement of Lily and Bert
Jones to Canada, which takes them no further than Liverpool.
In a scene that is comic and moving at the same time, one sees
these human fragments move from one urban mass to
another, then falter under the weight of their own insigni-
ficance. Even the story seems unable to bear it. 'What is a
town then, how do I know? What did they do?' asks the
narrative. Even at this self-consciously literary moment, one
never loses sight of Lily in her childish desire to escape, so
easily deflated, or Bert forced by his wounded bravado to
abandon his lover when he cannot even track down his own
parents in the sprawling, indifferent city of his birth.

Green wrote his first novel, *Blindness*, when he was
eighteen. It is a book of astonishing maturity for one so
young, yet it is *Living* that is the triumph of his precocity: a
near-masterpiece written at the age of twenty-four. Of the
three novels in this volume, *Party Going* (1939), though it has
proved a most fertile ground for critics and theorists of
narrative, is the one that is most likely to be problematic to
the non-academic reader. The reason is simple: nothing much
happens, and the characters are all more or less appalling.
Frank Kermode has written that the way most contemporary
readers see this novel is as 'an expression of disgust at the
conduct of the immature, ostentatious rich . . . and of admiration, even tenderness for the poor.'

Professor Kermode does not say that this is his own inter-
pretation, however, and I must say that this is not at all the
way that I read *Party Going*. Green was a naughty man in
some ways, and occasionally his naughtiness gets into the
books; usually it appears as a playful teasing of the reader (he

likes characters to be known by different names: Mrs Henderson is for no clear reason both Evelyn and Evelyna; Angela Crevy is known by both her names; in *Loving* two characters have the same forename, and so on). Generally one feels that his is an attitude like that of Shakespeare in his comedies: the world is an absurd mess, you cannot blame me if in our enchanted wood there are two men called Jacques. Green talked in interviews about getting a 'dig' in at various real people and at the aristocracy in general, and doubtless he took some small pleasure from exactly that (his stern father is guyed in the figure of old Dupret in *Living;* what Oedipal laughter must have rung in his head when he wrote the scene with the courtesan brought in the revive the old man!). But the artist in him was above the drab politics of twentieth-century class warfare. For Green is a plotter – not in the sense of someone full of narrative surprises, because in the fog-bound world of Victoria Station that is the setting of this novel the most exciting things that happen are that a rich young woman has a bath and a manservant gets a kiss – but in the manner of a spider with a web in which these flies are caught and then inspected.

*Party Going* is at pains to point out the shallowness of its characters ('Robin . . . wondered angrily how Angela could go with these revolting people'), but its artistic purpose is surely more ambitious than that of social criticism. Green, in his youth, was an addicted cinema-goer, and much has reason-ably been made of his cinematic technique: the short, flickering scenes, the jump-cuts and so on. However, it seems to me that a more helpful, if necessarily approximate, analogy is with music. *Living* must, I suppose, be a symphony by an 'avant-garde' Russian, though with more melody than that comparison perhaps suggests; *Loving* could be a collabor-ation between Britten and Vaughan Williams; but *Party Going* is pure chamber music. This is amoral virtuosity, unashamed, self-regarding in places, dizzy with its own patterns of invention.

Can you tell the difference between Angela and Claire and Julia and Evelyn? Does it matter? Isn't part of the point that such people are, ironically, just like the 'masses' outside on the station concourse: indistinguishable one from another? Does Max prefer Angela to Amabel or Julia to both? In fact, how can he be sure, when they are almost interchangeable? Who is this man with the mysteriously shifting accent who shuttles to and forth between the hotel barred against possible 'revolution' and the foggy underworld outside? Why are there two elderly nannies in attendance? What is the function of the dead pigeon and why does Miss Fellowes feel she has to wash it? Does it matter if the viola rather than the violin plays the next few bars?

In view of the abstract nature of these questions, Evelyn Waugh's literal-minded complaint that he can't understand why Miss Henderson has been entrusted with the tickets was perhaps even funnier than he intended. At times it seems that the people in *Party Going* are like characters from a Robbe-Grillet novel, from whom individuality has been withheld as a matter of literary dogma; and yet they do have individual characters, even if what distinguishes them (different amounts of money, different degrees of familiarity and affection for one another) is not profound. The climactic interchange of the book, it seems to me, is between the lovers Max and Amabel, who have been deceiving and avoiding one another through-out the action and continue to do so when face to face. She pulls at her handkerchief, threatening tears; but he 'hated tears, he never found them genuine'. Never! A few moments later, she 'made her eyes cloud over', and we do not know if she is truly sad or not – and neither, perhaps, does she. As real feeling eddies beneath the surface of brilliantly simulated emotion, Green begins to see what dialogue, unmediated by a narrator, can achieve; his interest in this technique was to take him in one of his later novels, *Nothing*, into a rather austere place, where fewer readers wanted to follow. Here, however, between Max and Amabel, the effects are sublimely minimal; it as though a scene from *Private Lives* has been revised by Samuel Beckett.

*Party Going* is not as easy to love as *Living* is, but it is impossible not to admire its artistry. Of these three novels, *Loving* (1945) is perhaps the most immediately sympathetic to a contemporary reader. We are in the aristocratic setting of

*Party Going*, but it is the servant class of *Living* who are the main characters in a largely below-stairs comedy of life in an Irish country house during the Second World War. The erotic manoeuvrings and duplicity of the servants are given to us with some of the stylistic quirks of *Living* – the ellipsis, the omissions of articles and so on – though here this quirky grammar serves to depict not a factory but a mansion of closed rooms and quiet corridors where people are often surprised by the unheard approach of others; stables where an idiot lampman lies asleep; and gardens where the damp air is rent by the screech of peacocks.

Another distinctive feature of *Loving* is that, in a quiet way, a great deal happens. In *Romancing*, his admirably concise, no-nonsense biography of Green, Jeremy Treglown's summary of the action runs over three pages. I also feel that the main characters in *Loving* are more fully developed psychologically than Bert, Lily, Craigan, or young Dupret in *Living*, or than any of the party-goers. Green still offers little in the way of 'back-story' and retains a distrust of 'motivation', but somehow we do become familiar with the nature of Charley Raunce, the venal, nervous head footman, surprisingly promoted to butler, and of Edith, the ravishing, gentle but conniving underhousemaid.

Green clearly loves this girl, and we can forgive him for doing so. The delicacy of her nature is beautifully given, in her consolation of the old head housemaid Miss Burch, in the modesty of her blushes, in the sensitivity that causes her to shriek then faint at the sight of a trapped mouse (though her faintness is perhaps also caused by the hysteria of her suppressed desire for Raunce) and in the natural and loving way that she plays with her employer's granddaughters, Miss Moira and Miss Evelyn. Indeed, the game of blind-man's buff between Edith and the children in an abandoned room of the old castle is one of the great lyrical scenes of the novel; others include Edith dancing with her fellow-housemaid Kate beneath the broken light of the chandelier in the deserted ballroom, 'the two girls, minute in purple, dancing, multiplied to eternity in those trembling pears of glass'; and the lamp-man asleep in the straw, beneath a cobweb in the sun, when 'it might have been almost that O'Conor's dreams were held by the gold binding his head beneath a vaulted roof on which the floor of cobbles reflected an old king's molten treasure from the bog'.

I have perhaps already quoted too much from the riches that await the reader. I would like to end by emphasising that these pleasures are not of the same kind as those provided by other novelists. This writer is unique. No fiction has ever thrilled me as the great moments in *Living* and *Loving*; I have been moved by Tolstoy, Lawrence, Proust and others, perhaps more so, but not in the same way. Interviewing him once, the American Terry Southern, while ostensibly writing about a number of internal inconsistencies in Green's plots, described this singular quality quite well, I think:

> The reader does not simply forget that there is an author behind the words, but because of some annoyance over a seeming 'discrepancy' in the story must, in fact, *remind* himself that there is one. This reminding is accompanied by an irritation with the author for these apparent oversights on his part, and his 'failings' to see the particular *significance* of certain happenings. The irritation gives way then to a feeling of pleasure and superiority in that he, the reader, sees *more* in the situation than the author does – so that all of this now belongs to *him*. And the author is dismissed, even perhaps with a slight contempt – and only the work remains, alone now with this reader who has to take over. Thus, in the spell of his own imagination the characters and story *come alive* in an almost incredible way, quite beyond anything achieved by conventional methods of writing.

Henry Green's writing life was sadly short. He drank too much, worried about money and found the effort of producing these complex, touching works of art too much to contemplate after middle age. He wrote an early memoir called *Pack My Bag*, published in 1940, when he was only thirty-five. In a passage that begins as no more than a reflection on the memoirist's difficulty in using the real names

13

of people he has known, he goes on to talk about what writing is, or should be. His definition is one that I – and, I expect, many other admirers – have long had pinned above the desk:

> Prose is not to be read aloud but to oneself alone at night, and it is not quick as poetry but rather a gathering web of insinuations . . . Prose should be a long intimacy between strangers with no direct appeal to what both may have known. It should slowly appeal to feelings unexpressed, it should in the end draw tears out of the stone . . .

Sebastian Faulks, 2005

# LOVING, LIVING, PARTY GOING

# Loving

Once upon a day an old butler called Eldon lay dying in his room attended by the head housemaid, Miss Agatha Burch. From time to time the other servants separately or in chorus gave expression to proper sentiments and then went on with what they had been doing.

One name he uttered over and over, 'Ellen.'

The pointed windows of Mr Eldon's room were naked glass with no blinds or curtains. For this was in Eire where there is no black-out.

Came a man's laugh. Miss Burch jerked, then the voice broke out again. Charley Raunce, head footman, was talking outside to Bert his yellow pantry boy. She recognized the voice but could not catch what was said.

'. . . on with what I was on with,' he spoke, 'you should clean your teeth before ever you have anything to do with a woman. That's a matter of personal hygiene. Because I take an interest in you for which you should be thankful. I'm sayin' you want to take it easy my lad, or you'll be the death of yourself.'

The lad looked sick.

'A spot of john barley corn is what you are in need of,' Raunce went on, but the boy was not having any.

'Not in there,' he said in answer, quavering, 'I couldn't.'

'How's that? You know where he keeps the decanter don't you? Surely you must do.'

'Not out of that room I couldn't.'

'Go ahead, don't let a little thing worry your guts,' Raunce said. He was a pale individual, paler now. 'The old man's on with his Ellen, 'e won't take notice.'

'But there's Miss Burch.'

'Is that so? Then why didn't you say in the first place? That's different. Now you get stuck into my knives and forks. I'll handle her.'

Raunce hesitated, then went in. The boy looked to listen as for a shriek. The door having been left ajar he could hear the way Raunce put it to her.

'This is my afternoon on in case they take it into their heads to punish the bell,' he told her. 'If you like I'll sit by him for a spell while you go get a breath of air.'

'Very good then,' she replied, 'I might.'

'That's the idea Miss Burch, you take yourself out for a stroll. It'll fetch your mind off.'

'I shan't be far. Not out of sight just round by the back. You'd call me, now, if he came in for a bad spell?'

Charley reassured her. She came away. Bert stood motionless his right hand stiff with wet knives. That door hung wide once more. Then, almost before Miss Burch was far enough to miss it, was a noise of the drawer being closed. Raunce came back, a cut-glass decanter warm with whisky in his hands. The door stayed gaping open.

'Go ahead, listen,' he said to Bert, 'it's meat and drink at your age, I know, an old man dying but this stuff is more than grub or wine to me That's what. Let's get us behind the old door.'

To do so had been ritual in Mr Eldon's day. There was cover between this other door, opened back, and a wall of the pantry Here they poured Mrs T 's whisky. 'Ellen,' came the voice again, 'Ellen.'

At a rustle Raunce stuck his head out while Bert, farther in because he was smallest, could do no more than peek the other way along a back passage, his eyes on a level with one of the door hinges Bert saw no one. But Charley eyed Edith, one of two underhousemaids.

She stood averted watching that first door which stayed swung back into Mr Eldon's room. Not until he had said, 'hello there,' did she turn. Only then could he see that she had stuck a peacock's feather above her lovely head, in her dark-folded hair. 'What have you?' he asked pushing the decanter out to the front edge so much as to say, 'look what I've found.'

In both hands she held a gauntlet glove by the wrist. He could tell that it was packed full of white unbroken eggs.

'Why you gave me a jump,' she said, not startled.

'Look what I've got us,' he answered, glancing at the decanter he held out. Then he turned his attention back where perhaps she expected, onto the feather in her hair.

'You take that off before they can set eyes on you,' he went on, 'and what's this? Eggs? What for?' he asked. Bert poked his head out under the decanter, putting on a kind of male child's grin for girls. With no change in expression, without warning, she began to blush. The slow tide frosted her dark eyes, endowed them with facets. 'You won't tell,' she pleaded and Charley was about to give back that it depended when a bell rang. The indicator board gave a chock. 'Oh all right,' Raunce said, coming out to see which room had rung. Bert followed sheepish.

Charley put two wet glasses into a wooden tub in the sink, shut that decanter away in a pantry drawer. 'Ellen,' the old man called faintly. This drew Edith's eyes back towards the butler's room. 'Now lad,' Raunce said to Bert, 'I'm relying on you mind to see Mrs Welch won't come out of her kitchen to knock the whisky off.' He did not get a laugh. Both younger ones must have been listening for Mr Eldon. The bell rang a second time. 'O K ,' Raunce said, 'I'm coming. And let me have that glove back,' he went on. 'I'll have to slap it on a salver to take in some time.'

'Yes Mr Raunce,' she replied

'Mister is it now,' he said, grinning as he put on his jacket. When he was gone she turned to Bert She was short with him She was no more than three months older, yet by the tone of voice she might have been his mother's sister.

'Well he'll be Mr Raunce when it's over,' she said.

'Will Mr Eldon die?' Bert asked, then swallowed.

'Why surely,' says she giving a shocked giggle, then passing a hand along her cheek.

Meantime Charley entered as Mrs Tennant yawned. She said to him,

'Oh yes I rang didn't I, Arthur,' she said and he was called by that name as every footman from the first had been called, whose name had really been Arthur, all the Toms, Harrys, Percys, Victors one after the other, all called Arthur. 'Have you seen a gardening glove of mine? One of a pair I brought back from London?'

'No Madam.'

'Ask if any of the other servants have come across it will you? Such a nuisance.'

'Yes Madam.'

'And, oh tell me, how is Eldon?'

'Much about the same I believe Madam.'

'Dear dear Yes thank you Arthur. That will be all. Listen though. I expect Doctor Connolly will be here directly.'

He went out, shutting the mahogany door without a sound. After twenty trained paces he closed a green baize door behind him. As it clicked he called out,

'Now me lad she wants that glove and don't forget.'

'What glove?'

'The old gardening glove Edith went birds'-nesting with,' Raunce replied. 'Holy Moses look at the clock,' he went on, 'ten to three and me not on me bed. Come on look slippy.' He whipped out the decanter while Bert provided those tumblers that had not yet been dried. 'God rest his soul,' Raunce added in a different tone of voice then carried on,

'Wet glasses? Where was you brought up? No we'll have two dry ones thank you,' he cried. 'Get crackin' now Behind the old door.' Upon this came yet another double pitiful appeal to Ellen. 'And there's another thing, Mrs T. she still calls me Arthur. But it will be Mr Raunce to you d'you hear?'

' 'E ain't dead yet.'

'Nor he ain't far to go before he will be. Oh dear. Yes and that reminds me. Did you ever notice where the old man kept that black book of his and the red one?'

'What d'you mean? I never touched 'em.'

'Don't be daft I never said you did did I? But he wouldn't trouble to watch himself in front of you. Times out of mind you must have seen.'

'Not me I never.'

'We shan't make anything out of you, that's one thing certain,' Raunce stated. 'There's occasions I despair altogether.' He went on, 'You mean to stand and tell me you've never so much as set eyes on 'em, not even to tell where they was kept.'

'What for Mr Raunce?'

'Well you can't help seeing when a thing's before your nose, though I'm getting so's I could believe any mortal idiotic stroke of yours, so help me.'

'I never.'

'So you never eh? You never what?' Raunce asked. 'Don't talk so sloppy. What I'm asking is can you call to mind his studying in a black or a red thrupenny notebook?'

'Study what?' Bert said, bolder by his tot now the glass he held was empty.

'All right. You've never seen those books then. That's all I wanted. But I ask you look at the clock. I'm going to get the old head down, it's me siesta. And don't forget to give us a call sharp on four thirty. You can't be trusted yet to lay the tea. Listen though. If that front door rings it will likely be the doctor. He's expected Show him straight in,' Raunce said, pointing with his thumb into the door agape He made off.

'What about Miss Burch?' the boy called.

'Shall I call her?' he shouted, desperate.

Raunce must have heard, but he gave no answer. Left alone young Albert began to shake.

In the morning room two days later Raunce stood before Mrs Tennant and showed part of his back to Violet her daughter-in-law.

'Might I speak to you for a moment Madam?'

'Yes Arthur what is it?'

'I'm sure I would not want to cause any inconvenience but I desire to give in my notice.'

She could not see Violet because he was in the way. So she glared at the last button but one of his waistcoat, on a level with her daughter-in-law's head behind him. He had been standing with arms loose at his sides and now a hand came uncertainly to find if he was done up and having found dropped back.

'What Arthur?' she asked. She seemed exasperated. 'Just when I'm like this when this has happened to Eldon?'

'The place won't be the same without him Madam.'

'Surely that's not a reason Well never mind. I daresay not but I simply can't run to another butler.'

'No Madam.'

'Things are not what they used to be you know. It's the war. And then there's taxation and everything. You must understand that.'

'I'm sure I have always tried to give every satisfaction Madam,' he replied.

At this she picked up a newspaper She put it down again She got to her feet. She walked over to one of six tall french windows with gothic arches 'Violet,' she said, 'I can't imagine what Michael thinks he is about with the grass court darling. Even from where I am I can see plantains like the tops of palm trees.'

Her daughter-in-law's silence seemed to imply that all effort was to butt one's head against wire netting. Charley stood firm. Mrs T. turned. With her back to the light he could not see her mouth and nose.

'Very well then,' she announced, 'I suppose we shall have to call you Raunce.'

'Thank you Madam.'

'Think it over will you?' She was smiling. 'Mind I've said nothing about more wages.' She dropped her eyes and in so doing she deepened her forehead on which once each month a hundred miles away in Dublin her white hair was washed in blue and waved and curled. She moved over to another table She pushed the ashtray with one long lacquered oyster nail across the black slab of polished marble supported by a dolphin layered in gold. Then she added as though confidentially,

'I feel we should all hang together in these detestable times.'

'Yes Madam.'

'We're really in enemy country here you know We simply must keep things up. With my boy away at the war. Just go and think it over.'

'Yes Madam.'

'We know we can rely on you you know Arthur.'

'Thank you Madam.'

'Then don't let me hear any more of this nonsense. Oh and I can't find one of my gloves I use for gardening. I can't find it anywhere.'

'I will make enquiries. Very good Madam.'

He shut the great door after. He almost swung his arms, he might have been said to step out for the thirty yards he had to go along that soft passage to the green baize door. Then he stopped. In one of the malachite vases, filled with daffodils, which stood on tall pedestals of gold naked male children without wings, he had seen a withered trumpet. He cut off the head with a pair of nail clippers He carried this head away in cupped hand from above thick pile carpet in black and white squares through onto linoleum which was bordered with a purple key pattern on white until, when he had shut that green door to open his kingdom, he punted the daffodil ahead like a rugger ball. It fell limp on the oiled parquet a yard beyond his pointed shoes.

He was kicking this flower into his pantry not more than thirty inches at a time when Miss Burch with no warning opened and came out of Mr Eldon's death chamber. She was snuffling. He picked it up off the floor quick. He said friendly,

'The stink of flowers always makes my eyes run.'

'And when may daffodils have had a perfume,' she asked, tart through tears.

'I seem to recollect they had a smell once,' he said.

'You're referring to musk, oh dear,' she answered making off, tearful But apparently he could not leave it alone.

'Then what about hay fever?' he almost shouted. 'That never comes with hay, or does it? There was a lady once at a place where I worked,' and then he stopped. Miss Burch had moved out of ear-shot. 'Well if you won't pay heed I can't force you,' he said out loud. He shut Mr Eldon's door, then stood with his back to it. He spoke to Bert.

'What time's the interment?' he asked. 'And how long to go before dinner?' not waiting for answers. 'See here my lad I've got something that needs must be attended to you know where ' He jangled keys in his pocket. Then instead of entering Mr Eldon's room he walked away to dispose of the daffodil in a bucket He coughed. He came back again. 'All right,' he said, 'give us a whistle if one of 'em shows up '

He slipped inside like an eel into its drainpipe. He closed the door so that Bert could not see. Within all was immeasurable stillness with the mass of daffodils on the bed. He stood face averted then hurried smooth and his quietest to the roll-top desk He held his breath. He had the top left-hand drawer open. He breathed again. And then Bert whistled.

Raunce snatched at those red and black notebooks He had them. He put them away in a hip pocket. They fitted. 'Close that drawer,' he said aloud. He did this. He fairly scrambled out again He shut the door after, leaving all immeasurably still within. He stood with his back to it, taking out a handkerchief, and looked about.

He saw Edith. She was just inside the pantry where Bert watched him open mouthed. Raunce eyed her very sharp. He seemed to appraise the dark eyes she sported which were warm and yet caught the light like plums dipped in cold water. He stayed absolutely quiet. At last she said quite calm,

'Would the dinner bell have gone yet?'

'My dinner,' he cried obviously putting on an act, 'holy smoke is it as late as that, and this lad of mine not taken up the nursery tray yet. Get going,' he said to Bert, 'look sharp.' The boy rushed out. 'God forgive me,' he remarked, 'but there's times I want to liquidate 'im. Come to father beautiful,' he said.

'Not me,' she replied amused.

'Well if you don't want I'm not one to insist. But did nobody never tell you about yourself?'

'Aren't you just awful,' she said apparently delighted.

'That's as may be,' he answered, 'but it's you we're speaking of. With those eyes you ought to be in pictures.'

'Oh yeah?'

"Come on,' he said, 'if we're going to be lucky with our dinner we'd best be going for it.'

'No, you don't,' she said slipping before him. And they came out through this pantry into the long high stone passage with a vaulted ceiling which led to the kitchen and their servants' hall.

'Now steady,' he said, as he caught up with her. 'What will Miss Burch say if she finds us chasing one after the other?' When they were walking side by side he asked,

'What made you come through my way to dinner?'

'Why you do need to know a lot,' she said.

'I know all I can my girl and that's never done me harm I got other things to think to besides love and kisses, did you know?'

'No I didn't, not from the way you go on I didn't.'

'The trouble with you girls is you take everything so solemn. Now all I was asking was why you looked in on us while you came down to dinner?'

'Thinkin' I came to see you I suppose,' she said. She turned to look at him. What she saw made her giggle mouth open and almost soundless. Then she slapped a hand across her teeth and ran on ahead He took no notice. With a swirl of the coloured skirt of her uniform she turned a corner in front along this high endless corridor. The tap of her shoes faded. He walked on He appeared to be thinking. He went so soft he might have been a ghost without a head. But as he made his way he repeated to himself, over and over,

'This time I'll take his old chair. I must.'

He arrived to find the household seated at table waiting, except for Mrs Welch and her two girls who ate in the kitchen and for Bert who was late. There was his place laid for Raunce next Miss Burch. Kate and Edith were drawn up ready. They sat with hands folded on laps before their knives, spoons and forks. At the head, empty, was the large chair from which Mr Eldon had been accustomed to preside. At the last and apart sat Paddy the lampman For this huge house, which was almost entirely shut up, had no electric light.

Charley went straight over to a red mahogany sideboard that was decorated with a swan at either end to support the top on each long curved neck. In the centre three ferns were niggardly growing in gold Worcester vases. He took out a knife, a spoon and a fork He sat down in Mr Eldon's chair, the one with arms. Seated, he laid his own place They all stared at him.

'What are we waiting for?' he said into the silence He took out a handkerchief again. Then he blew his nose as though nervous.

'Would you be in a draught?' Miss Burch enquired at last.

'Why no thank you,' he replied. The silence was pregnant.

'I thought perhaps you might be,' she said and sniffed.

At that he turned to see whether he had forgotten to close the door. It was shut all right. The way he looked made Kate choke.

'I heard no one venture a pleasantry,' Miss Burch announced at this girl.

'I thought I caught Paddy crack one of his jokes,' Raunce added with a sort of violence. A grin spread over this man's face as it always did when his name was mentioned. He was uncouth, in shirt-sleeves, barely coming up over the table he was so short. With a thick dark neck and face he had a thatch of hair which also sprouted grey from the nostrils His eyes were light blue as was one of Charley's, for Raunce had different coloured eyes, one dark one light which was arresting.

The girls looked down to their laps.

'Or maybe she swallowed the wrong way although there's nothing on the table and it's all growing cold in the kitchen,' Raunce continued He got no reply.

'Well what are we waiting on?' he asked.

'Why for your precious lad to fetch in our joint,' Miss Burch replied.

'I shouldn't wonder if the nursery hasn't detained him,' was Charley's answer.

'Then Kate had better bring it,' Miss Burch said. And they sat

26

without a word while she was gone. Twice Agatha made as though to speak, seated as he was for the first time in Mr Eldon's place, but she did not seem able to bring it to words. Her eyes, which before now had been dull, each sported a ripple of light from tears. Until, after Kate had returned laden Raunce cast a calculated look at Miss Burch as he stood to carve, saying,

'Nor I won't go Not even if it is to be Church of England I don't aim to watch them lower that coffin in the soil.'

At this Miss Burch pushed the plate away from in front of her to sit with closed eyes. He paused. Then as he handed a portion to Edith he went on,

'I don't reckon on that as the last I shall see of the man. It's nothing but superstition all that part.'

'And the wicked shall flourish even as a green bay tree,' Miss Burch announced in a loud voice as though something had her by the throat. Once more there was a pause. Then Raunce began again as he served Paddy. Because he had taken a roast potato into his mouth with the carving fork he spoke uneasy.

'Why will Mrs Welch have it that she must carve for the kitchen? Don't call her cook she don't like the name. There's not much I can do the way this joint's been started.'

The girls were busy with their food. O'Conor was noisy with the portion before him. Raunce settled down to his plate. Agatha still sat back.

'And how many months would it be since you went out?' she asked like vinegar.

'Let me think now. The last occasion must have been when I had to see Paddy here to the Park Gates that time he was "dronk" at Christmas.'

This man grinned although his mouth was watering in volume so that he had to swallow constantly.

'Careful now,' said Raunce.

Kate and Edith stopped eating to watch the Irishman open eyed. This man was their sport and to one of them he was even more than that. In spite of Miss Burch he looked so ludicrous that they had suddenly to choke back tremors of giggling.

'It was nearly my lot,' Raunce added.

'It couldn't hurt no one to show respect to the dead,' Miss Burch tremulously said. Charley answered in downright tones,

'Begging your pardon Miss Burch my feelings are my own and I daresay there's no one here but yourself misses him more than me. Only this morning I went to Mrs T., asked leave and told her,' but he did not at once continue. The silence in which he was received seemed to daunt him. With a clumsy manner he turned it off, saying,

'Yes, I remember when I came for my first interview she said I can't call you Charles, no she says "I'll call you Arthur. All the first footmen have been called Arthur ever since Arthur Weavell, a real jewel that man was," she said.'

He looked at Miss Burch to find that she had flushed.

'And now I make no doubt you are counting on her addressing you as Raunce,' Miss Burch said in real anger. 'With Mr Eldon not yet in the ground But I'll tell you one thing,' she continued, her voice rising, 'you'll never get a Mr out of me not ever, even if there is a war on.'

'What's the war got to do with it?' he asked, and he winked at Kate. 'Never mind let it go. Anyway I know now don't I.'

'No,' she said, having the last word, 'men like you never will appreciate or realize.'

Next morning Raunce chose to enter Mrs Jack's bedroom when Agatha Burch was at work on the Aubusson carpet.

He carried a large tray on which he had arranged three stacks of fresh blotting paper coloured pink, white and yellow, two saucers of Worcester china in which were knibs of bronze and gold plated, two bottles of red and blue ink with clean syringes to fill the inkwells, and piles of new stationery which matched those three shades of blotting paper.

He laid this down on a writing table. When he saw her face which was as it sometimes looked on her bad days so called, pale or blotchy as a shrimp before boiling, he cleared his throat. He watched her close but she did not regard him. He cleared his throat again. He spoke.

'Just the very person,' he said warmly.

'Oh yes,' was her answer.

'I had a bit of a shock this morning,' he went on, looking out of the window onto a glorious day, 'I moved down into the butler's apartment yesterday as will be known to you because one of your girls got the room ready.'

'I don't know how you had the heart,' she said.

'That's all right Miss Burch, everyone has their feelings, but I'm sure Mrs T. would not wish the strongroom left unguarded of a night time.'

'I hope everything was to your fancy,' she remarked.

'I slept very well thank you, mustn't grumble at all. Sheets nicely aired, a good night's sleep considerin'. But I had a bit of a shock when my tea was fetched me.'

'Tea! I never knew you took it first thing.'

'Oh yes I must have me cup of tea, and I'm not alone in that I believe. I couldn't start the day without.'

'And was it all right?' she asked, so cheerfully she might have thought she had the advantage of him. 'Had it been made with boiling water?'

'Yes,' he said weak, 'it was a good cup of tea.'

'Then they'll have warmed the pot. I'm glad, I am really. Because I'll tell you something,' and her voice rose. 'D'you know I can't get one for meself at that hour?'

'You can't? Is that so? There's a lot wrong there if you'll pardon me with all the girls you've got to serve you. I should say that wants to be looked into.'

'They've got their work to do same as I have,' she said in a voice charged with meaning.

'Yes I had a bit of a shock first thing,' he went on, ignoring this. 'It was nasty to tell the truth. That lad of mine Albert brought my tea.'

'You don't say. Why I didn't know he was up so prompt.'

'I'll guarantee you this,' Raunce said, his voice beginning to grate a trifle, 'he's up before anyone in the Castle.'

'I won't argue,' she announced.

'No but if you know any different you'll oblige by contradicting.'

'I never argue, I'm not that way,' she said.

'Nor me,' he answered, 'I never was one to contradict this or that. No, all I had in mind was the lad. It's his first place and he's a good obliging boy.'

'I'm not saying he's not '

'Then you don't deny it,' Raunce said on a rising tone.

'Deny what?' she replied. 'I'm denying nobody.'

'That's O.K. Miss Burch. It was only to make certain I understood like any man has a right. I may have misinterpreted. For if you must know it upset me to see that lad of mine Albert carry me my tea.'

'That was what he always used to do surely.'

'Yes, in Mr Eldon's day that's the way it used to be every morning,' Raunce admitted. Then he went on,

'But one of the girls always brought the old man's.'

'And now I suppose you won't be satisfied unless one of my girls brings you yours,' Miss Burch said with surprising bitterness. 'And I don't doubt she must be Kate,' she added.

'I can't seem to follow you,' he said.

'You can't? I'll ask you this then. How's the work to get done of a morning?'

'Well same as it always has I presume.'

'Now then,' she said taking up this last remark She drew a great breath and was about to loose it probably in a storm of angry sentences when Mrs T. entered.

The passage carpet was so thick you never could hear anyone coming.

'Oh Raunce,' she said using his new title for the second time, 'I've just come from nanny. Such a nuisance. I don't really know what we can do. Of course the children must come first but I'm sure everyone is doing their best. We shall simply all have to put our heads together.' At this point Miss Burch left Her back was stiff She seemed indignant. Mrs T. watched her go with no change in expression. Then turned back to Charley. 'Raunce,' she said, 'surely you aren't proposing to put that pink blotting paper in the Gold Bedroom.'

'This is the only shade they could send us Madam.'

She walked away and tried the mantelpiece with her finger which she then examined as though it was going to smell. He cleared his throat Having established there was no dust she rearranged the peacock's feathers that for years had stood in a famille rose vase which was as always on a woollen scarlet mat in the centre.

'You write to London for the blotting paper of course?'

'Yes Madam but this is all Mr Eldon could get. I believe he was going to speak about it '

'No, he never did,' she said, 'and naturally it would be hopeless trying to buy anything in this wretched country. But tell me why if

30

there are several pastel blues can they do only one shade of pink?'

'I believe it's the war Madam.'

She laughed and faced him. 'Oh yes the shops will be using that as an excuse for everything soon. Mind I'm not blaming anyone,' she said, 'but it's going to be hopeless. Now Raunce I'm so very worried about these nursery meals.'

'Yes Madam.'

She began to smile, as though pleading with him. 'I want your help. Everyone is being so very awkward. Nanny has complained that the food is quite cold by the time it gets to the nursery and Mrs Welch tells me it leaves the kitchen piping hot so what am I to believe?'

They looked long at each other. At last he smiled.

'I'm sure Albert carries the meals up soon as ever they are served,' he said. 'But if it would be of any assistance Madam I'll take them up myself for the next few days.'

'Oh thank you Raunce, yes that is good of you. Now I promised Michael I would go along, why was it he wanted me? Yes well that will be all.' She started off to the head gardener. She did not get far. Miss Burch stopped her in the Long Passage.

'Could I speak to you for a moment Madam?'

'Yes Agatha?'

Before going on Miss Burch waited until Raunce, who was leaving Mrs Jack's room, should be out of earshot.

'It's Kate Madam. I wouldn't bother you Madam only it does seem not right to me that a slip of a girl can take him his tea first thing while he lies in bed there.'

'Whose tea good heavens?'

'Arthur Madam.'

'We must call him Raunce now Agatha. It does sound absurd I know. What's more I don't like that name.' Her voice had taken a teasing note. 'I think we shall have to change it don't you?'

'And he would not go to the funeral. He even boasts about it Madam.'

'Well we wouldn't have wanted him there would we?' she said. Miss Burch seemed pleased. 'And now he's moved down to Eldon's room and wants his morning tea brought him?' Mrs Tennant went on. 'Yes well thanks very much for telling me. I suppose one of the girls used to carry Eldon his cup first thing?'

'Yes Madam but that was different.'

'I know Agatha but I fancy that's the difficulty you see.'

'Very good Madam,' Miss Burch said grim.

'Oh yes and I forgot, where is the man,' and she called for Raunce. There was no reply. 'He must have gone.' She rang the bell. 'I meant to tell you both,' she continued, 'it's about Mrs Welch. Her nephew is coming over to-morrow. Not for long mind, just a few weeks. He's old enough to look after himself. She'll do everything for the little chap.'

Miss Burch did not look delighted but she said, 'Yes Madam.'

'He's a dear boy I believe and it will be nice for the children to have someone to play with. His name is Albert. Why what a coincidence. Yes Albert what is it?'

'You rang, Madam.'

'Oh it's of no consequence it was Raunce I wanted. That's all thank you. There's nothing else I think I will see Raunce some other time. I've simply got to rush out now to Michael.'

The morning was almost over and that afternoon, as Raunce was in his new armchair putting his feet up to study those two notebooks Edith, upstairs in the attic she shared with Kate and half undressed, was filling into a jam jar those eggs she had been carrying in Mrs Tennant's glove and which she intended to preserve with waterglass.

'You're surely not ever goin' to put that dirtiness on your face and neck sometime Edie?'

'I am that. It's good.'

'But not peacocks. Edie for land's sake.'

'Peacocks is no use. They only screech.'

'I can't make you out at all.'

Edith explained. 'Their eggs've got to be lifted when there's not a soul to witness, you understand, an' they must be peacocks. I wouldn't know for why. But you just ask anyone. They are the valuablest birds, the rarest.'

'And what if you come out in the spots like they have stuck on their tails?'

Edie turned at this to face Kate and put a hand along her cheek. She was naked to the waist. In that light from the window overgrown with ivy her detached skin shone like the flower of white lilac under leaves.

'Oh dear,' she said.

'And who's it for?' Kate went on. 'Patrick?' and in one movement she jumped on her bed, lay back. But at the mention of a name and as though they had entered on a conspiracy Edith blocked even more light from that window by climbing on the sill. The sky drew a line of white round her mass of dark hair falling to shoulders which paled to blue lilac She laughed in her throat.

As they settled down Kate said:

'So Mrs Welch is to have her sister's little boy to visit Albert his name is.' Edith made no reply. 'That'll be more for us that will,' Kate added.

'He'll do his own work. He's old enough,' Edith said. 'And it'll be a change for the children,' she went on referring to Mrs Jack's girls. 'They don't get much out of forever playing on their own the sweet lambs.'

'I wish I was back 'ome the age they are Edie.'

'Hard work never done a girl any harm.'

'But doesn't Miss Burch keep us two girls at it dear. Oh my poor feet.'

'Take your stockings off Katie and I'll rub 'em for you.'

'Not in that old egg you won't.'

Edith jumped down off the sill. She took up a towel which she laid under Kate's feet. She turned back to the washbasin to wet her hands in cold water. Then leaning over Kate who had closed her eyes she began to stroke and knead the hot feet. Her hair fell forward. She was smiling as she ministered, all her bare skin above Kate's body stretched white as spring again.

'Clean your teeth before you have to do with a woman,' Edith said, 'what talk is that?'

'Have you gone out of your mind then?' Kate asked, murmuring. 'But whoever said?'

'Mr Raunce.'

'So it's Mr to you? I shan't ever. I couldn't, not after he's been Charley all this time. Oh honey is that easing my arches.'

'It's only right now he's got the position,' Edith said. 'I wish I had your ankles dear I do.'

'But why the teeth?' Kate asked.

'I expect it's smoking or something.'

'Does Patrick?'

'Oh he's got a lovely lot,' Edith said. 'But I can't say as I shall see

33

him even this evening. Talk of half days off in this rotten old country, why, there's nothing for a girl when your time is your own.'

'You're telling me,' said Kate.

Then Edith sat down on the side of the bed, and shook the hair back from off her face.

'Here we are,' she went on, 'the two of us on a Thursday and still inside, with nothing to move for. And the Germans across the water, that might invade any minute. Oh I shall have to journey back home. Why I'm browned off absolutely.'

Kate took her up. 'I don't think there's much in this talk about the Jerries. And if they did come over that's not saying they'd offer any impoliteness, they're ordinary working folk same as us. But speak of never going out why Charley Raunce hasn't shoved his head into the air these three years it must be.'

'Wrong side of the window is his name for it He should've grown up with us as children. Kate, my mother had every window open rain or shine and so they stayed all day.'

'He writes to his,' Kate said, 'not like you you bad girl. When did she get word from you last?'

'There's times I say that's the one thing keeps me here. I daresn't go back when I've kept silent such ages, while she's on every week writing for news.'

'Why, listen to those birds,' Kate said.

Edith looked out. A great distance beneath she saw Mrs Tennant and her daughter-in-law starting for a walk. The dogs raced about on the terrace yapping which made the six peacocks present scream. The two women set off negligent and well dressed behind their bounding pets to get an appetite for tea.

'Was it the beginning or the end of June Jack wrote that he expected to get leave?'

'Why I told you,' Mrs Jack answered sweet and low. 'Any time after the third week in May he said.'

'I'm so glad for you both. It's been such a long time. I expect you'll go to London of course.'

'Simply look at the daffodils,' her daughter-in-law exclaimed. 'There's masses of new ones out you know. Oh isn't it lovely. Yes it's a hopeless time of the year here isn't it? I mean there's no shooting or fishing yet. He'd get very restless poor dear.'

'D'you know what I thought last night?' said Mrs Tennant. 'As I got into bed? I shall probably be down at Merlow all the time and you won't see anything of me but I half made up my mind I would come over with you.'

'How lovely,' her daughter-in-law replied clear as a bell. 'Oh but then we must have an evening all together. Jack would be terribly disappointed.'

'Darling you've seen so little of each other with this war coming directly after the wedding. I do feel for your generation you know. Of course I'd love it. Still I don't mean to butt in. I mean the leave is precious, you must have all of him.'

There fell a silence.

'Really,' she added, 'I'm not sure what I'm saying,' and dared to look full at her son's wife. This young woman was poised with an object, it may have been the dry white bone of a bird that she was about to throw. She flung it a short distance. The dog faced in the wrong direction, ears cocked, whining, while attendant peacocks keenly dashed forward a few paces.

'Oh Badger,' she said and wiped her fingers on a frilled handkerchief, 'you are so dumb.'

'We could do a play together,' Mrs Tennant proposed.

'How lovely. The only thing is the children. I imagine it's all right leaving them. I mean nothing can happen can it?'

'I'd thought of that. I don't think so. We did before.'

'I know. Then that will be lovely.'

'When d'you think he'll let you know dear?'

Mrs Jack showed irritation. 'No Badger no,' she said. On being spoken to the dog made as if to leap up at her. 'Down damn you,' she said. 'Oh you know how it is,' she went on, 'the usual, three days notice at the most. On top of everything you've got to be looking your best as though you'd been in and out of the London shops all winter.'

'You won't have to worry your head over that,' Mrs Tennant archly told her. 'Oh by the way did I ever mention about Mrs Welch's nephew coming over to stay?'

'How old is he?'

'Just the right age Violet, nine next March. I thought it would be nice for the children that's why I bought his ticket. His father's the chauffeur to old Lord Cheltenham.'

'My dear have you broken it yet to nanny?'

'No darling to tell you the truth I didn't dare.'

'It is a bit of a facer isn't it?'

'You see I couldn't very well refuse,' Mrs Tennant said, 'and it will be so good for the children.'

'What's he like?'

'Oh Mrs Welch is a most superior woman. I'm sure he'll be perfect. I wouldn't mind if there were any possible children down in the village But even Michael's eldest boy at the Lodge Gates is dressed as a girl.'

'Do they really still believe the boys get carried off by fairies?'

'Well if they do they could expect fairies to see through the skirts. But couldn't you say the little chap's been ill?' she asked her daughter-in-law.

'Then she'd think she'll have to nurse him,' Mrs Jack objected.

'But couldn't you promise her that Mrs Welch won't let him out of sight Violet?'

'It is so difficult isn't it? And it's just what Evelyn and Moira have been wanting. Anyway bother nanny.' The two women smiled at one another, grew mischievous. 'I'll tell you what,' Mrs Jack went on, 'why don't we say it's Mrs Welch's illegitimate? Then she'll be so thrilled she'll look after him like one of her own.'

Mrs Tennant tee hee'd.

'Oh Violet you are naughty,' she said.

'Well I don't know why not. After all the worry they bring it would be a score to give them something to really chatter about.'

'And then we should have to find another cook and another nanny,' Mrs Tennant objected. 'It's quite bad enough having them die on one. Besides, Nanny Swift will think it out for herself. I shouldn't be a bit surprised if she didn't start throwing dark hints before the child has been here ten days.'

'D'you think it's true then?'

'My dear what do we know about the servants? Agatha took the trouble only this morning to let out some frightful double meanings in connection with Kate and Arthur. I must remember to call him Raunce.'

'Kate? I'd've thought it would be Edith. I wish I had that girl's skin.'

'Yes she's a lovely child isn't she? D'you know Violet I don't think I care what they do so long as they stay.'

'You poor dear,' Mrs Jack said. 'Why look,' she went on, 'there it is already.' And there it was close, on a low hill, surrounded by cypresses amongst which grew a palm tree, the marble pillars lying beside jagged cement topped walls against a blue sky with blue clouds 'D'you think we have to go right up this time?' she asked.

'I don't think we need to-day, do you?' her mother-in-law replied. Calling to the dogs they turned for home. They began a talk about underclothes.

But Kate and Edith were not to get out of the Castle without difficulty. As they came down their passage ready dressed for the afternoon they were halted by a broken noise of sobbing.

'Why listen,' Kate said, 'it must be the old girl herself. Now what do you say to that?'

'You go on dear,' Edith answered, 'don't wait for me.'

'Ah now come on Edie, half the day's gone already, you don't want to bother.'

'Why the poor soul,' Edith said and went in, shutting the door after.

Miss Burch lay on her bed wrapped in a huge blue crocheted shawl. She had taken off her wig and wore a lace mob cap which hung askew. With hands inside that shawl and face sideways on the pillow over a patch of wet Miss Burch seemed given over to despair and sobbed and shook and hiccuped.

Edith took off her beret, sat on the bedside shaking her hair free.

'Oh Burchie Burchie,' she said, 'why whatever's the matter?'

She got no other answer than a wail. Then Miss Burch rolled over face to the wall. The cap twisted off her head. Edith gently put it back and because her shiny skull was sideways on that pillow she could only place the cap so that it sat at right angles to Miss Burch's pinched nose, as someone lying in the open puts their hat to protect their face and terrible eyes.

'Now then,' Edith tried again, 'what's this?' She spoke soft.

'Oh I can't bear it,' Miss Burch cried out, 'I can't bear it.'

'Can't bear what dear?' But the sobbing started redoubled.

'Now Burchie don't take on so, you shouldn't,' Edith went on, searching over this cocoon with her hand for Miss Burch's where it lay wrapped warm to her side, 'listen to me dear, it can't be so bad. You let me bring you a nice cup of tea.'

'I can't bear it,' Miss Burch replied a trifle calmer.

'It wouldn't take me more than a minute to run down. No one would ever know, the kettle was nicely on the boil in the hall when I just left it. You see now if that mightn't do you good.'

'Nothing'll ever be the same,' was all Miss Burch said.

'Now don't talk so wild Burchie. You just go easy and let me fetch you a good cup of tea.'

'You're a good child.'

'Of course I am. There dear. Rest yourself.'

Miss Burch began to sniff, to show signs of coming round.

'It wouldn't take but a minute to nip down,' Edith went on but Miss Burch interrupted.

'No don't leave me, Edith,' she said.

'Then what is it now?' the girl asked, 'what's happened to upset you like you are?'

Then it came out much interrupted and in a confused flow after she had adjusted her cap. What Miss Burch felt so she said was that nothing would ever be the same, that after thirty-five years in service she could not look forward to being in a respectable house again where your work was respected and in which you could do your best. Yet with the same breath she told Edith that Kate and her were lucky to be in a place like this. She went on that there were not many girls in their position able to learn the trade as she was able to teach it, to pass on all she had acquired about the cleaning and ordering of a house, particularly when over at home they were all being sent in the army to be leapt on so she honestly believed by drunken soldiers in darkness. She said they were never to leave the Castle, that they didn't know their luck. But at the same time, with another burst of sobs, she repeated that nothing would ever be the same, that it was to throw away a life time's labour for her to go on here. She made no mention of Mr Eldon. In the end a cup of tea had finally quietened Miss Burch so that the two girls were at last able to set off down the back way which joined the main drive not far from Michael's Lodge Gate, cut in the ruined wall which shut this demesne from tumble-down country outside.

Another morning, as he had been warned that Captain Davenport and Mrs Tancy were coming over to luncheon, Charley went to his room, got out the red and black notebooks, consulted the index and looked these people up. He read:

'Davenport Captain Irish Rifles ret'd salmon trout Master Dermot first term. Wife passed away flu' 1937. Digs after the old kings in his bog' Then there was a long list of amounts with a date set against each. These possibly were tips. But Raunce noticed that Mr Eldon had touched the Captain for larger and larger amounts. At the last which was for a fiver Charley whistled. He said out loud, 'Now I wonder.'

Then he turned to the woman's page. 'Mrs Tancy her old Morris,' he found set down and the word Morris had been crossed out Mr Eldon had added above, 'her old pony male eleven years.' There came another long list of dates with unvaryingly small payments, not one larger than a shilling, the last in August.

Mr Eldon had always seen to opening the door himself so that when the Captain rang it was the first time that Raunce had received him.

'Well now if it isn't Arthur,' this man said hearty and also it appeared with distaste. He put up the cycle for himself. 'And what news of Eldon?'

After Raunce told him and he had expressed regret he stood there awkward so to speak. Charley took his chance.

'And how are the salmon trout running sir?' he asked.

'Salmon trout? No fishin' yet. Close season.'

'And Master Dermot sir?' Raunce enquired without a flicker.

'Very fit thank you very fit. He's in the eleven. I'll find me own way thank you Arthur.'

'Not a sausage, not a solitary sausage,' Raunce muttered at his back referring to the fact that he had not been tipped.

He waited for Mrs Tancy behind the closed door, presumably so as to have nothing to do with Michael who stood outside to take over this lady's pony and trap.

'I'm late,' she said when she did come. 'I'm late aren't I?' she said to them both. 'Could you?' she asked Michael handing him the reins. 'Oh Punch there now!'

For the cob with lifted tail was evacuating onto the gravelled drive. One hundred donkey cart loads of washed gravel from Michael's brother's pit had been ordered at Michael's suggestion to freshen the rutted drive where this turned inward across the ha-ha. Gravel sold by Michael's brother Patrick and carted by Danny his mother's other son who had thought to stop at the seventy-ninth

39

load the donkey being tired after it was understood that Mrs Tennant would be charged for the full hundred.

Michael ran forward to catch Punch's droppings before these could fall on the gravel which he had raked over that very morning.

'Asy,' he said as though in pain, 'asy.'

'The dear man he should not have bothered,' Mrs Tancy remarked in a momentary brogue.

With a pyramid steaming on his hands Michael glared about at the daffodil sprouted lawn Then he shambled off till he could scatter what he carried on the nearest border. Meantime Charley, looking his disgust, stood at the pony's hazy violet eyes. After a moment of withdrawal Punch began to nose about his pocket.

'The cob is looking well Madam,' he brought out.

'Isn't he, isn't he?' she said. 'Well thank you Arthur,' she said slipping a British threepenny bit into his hand and sailed past with not so much as a thank you for Michael.

When there were guests to lunch the servants had theirs afterwards. So it was not until ten past two that Raunce sat down in Mr Eldon's chair. He carved savagely like a head-hunter. They ate what he gave them in haste, silent for a time. Then Charley thought to ask,

'That Captain Davenport? Now where would I have heard he seeks after treasure in a bog?'

He got no answer.

'Do they dig for it,' he went on, 'or pry long sticks into the ground or what?' he mused aloud.

'Are you thinking you'll have a go?' Kate said.

'Now there was no cause to be pert my girl,' he said. 'Why goodness gracious me,' he remarked to Edith, 'whatever are you blushing for?'

She looked as though she was going to choke. If he had only known she was stricken by embarrassment. She knew very well that the last time the lady had been over to view the excavations Mrs Jack returned without her drawers. And it was with not a single word. They had vanished, there was not a trace. To turn it perhaps, she said to the lampman,

'What d'you know Paddy?'

'Why here we are sitting and we never thought of him,' Kate said. 'Come on now. You'd know Clancarty.'

He made no answer. But he laughed once, bent over his dish.

'Clancarty Paddy,' Kate tried again, 'Mr Raunce is asking you?'

Charley watched Edith. He said under his breath, 'it's funny the way she blushes but then she's only a kid.'

'Are they makin' a search?' Kate went on and she fixed her small eyes unwavering on Edith. The lampman made no reply. He seldom did.

Edith while she blushed hot was picturing that wet afternoon Mrs Jack had last been over to Clancarty. While Mrs T. and her daughter-in-law were on with their dinner Edith had been in the younger woman's room busily clearing up. She hung the thin coat and skirt of tweed which held the scent used, she put the folded web of shirt and stockings into drawers of rosewood. She laid the outdoor crocodile skin shoes ready to take down to Paddy. She tidied the towels then went to prepare that bed, boat-shaped black and gold with a gold oar at the foot. She moved softly gently as someone in devotion and handled the pink silk sheets like veils. The curtains were drawn. Then all that she had to do was done. Those oil lamps were lit. But she stuck a finger in her mouth, looked about as if she missed something. Then she searched, and faster. She had gone through everything that was put away faster and faster. When she was sure those drawers Mrs Jack had worn to go out were astray her great dark eyes had been hot to glowing.

'I'll wager they had everything of gold,' Raunce said, still on about the excavations.

'And wore silk on their legs,' said Edith, short of breath.

'Don't talk so silly,' Miss Burch took her up. 'They never put silk next to themselves in those days my girl. It wasn't discovered.'

'Did they have silk knickers then Paddy,' Kate asked giggling.

'I never heard such a thing,' Miss Burch replied. 'You'll oblige me by dropping the subject. Isn't it bad enough to have dinner late as it is,' she said 'You just leave the poor man alone. You let him be.'

Bert spoke. 'The nursery never had much of theirs,' he said. 'I must've took back the better part of what I carried up.'

'Oh dear,' cried Raunce in the high falsetto he put on whenever he referred to Nanny Swift.

'You should have seen 'er,' Bert added.

Both girls giggled softly while Charley still in falsetto asked whose face, holy smoke.

41

'Now that's quite enough of that,' Miss Burch said firm. There was a pause. 'I knew Mrs Welch had been upset,' she went on, 'and now I perceive why, not that I'm trying to excuse those potatoes she just gave us,' she said All of them listened. She seemed almost to be in good humour. 'They were never cooked,' she added, 'and I do believe that's why they put salt on spuds,' looking at Paddy, 'but I'll say this, those precious peacocks of yours would have spurned 'em.'

Right to the last meal Mr Eldon had taken in this room it had been his part to speak, to wind up as it were, almost to leave the impress of a bishop on his flock. This may have been what led Charley to echo in a serious tone,

'Miss Swift is a difficult woman whilst she's up in her nursery. But she can be nice as you please outside.'

'That's right,' Miss Burch said, 'and as I've often found, take someone out of their position in life and you find a different person altogether, yes.'

The two girls looked at one another, a waste of giggling behind their eyes again.

'But our potatoes this afternoon were not fit for the table,' Raunce said to Miss Burch.

'Thank you Mr Raunce,' she replied. In this way for the first time she seemed to recognize his place.

'Well look sharp my lad,' he said to Bert. He appeared to ooze authority. 'Holy Moses see what time it is.'

He hastened out like a man who does not know how long his new found luck will hold. Also he had to make his first entry in the red notebook, to record the first tip. He put the date under Mrs Tancy's name, and then '3d'. 'Wonder what happened in that six months gap,' he murmured to himself about Mr Eldon's last date, 'she's been over to lunch many a time since and he'll have had the old dropsy out of her. He was losing grip not entering it, that's what,' he added aloud. Then he laid the books aside.

He first addressed an envelope. 'To Mrs William Raunce,' he wrote in pencil, '396 May Road Peterboro' Yorks' and immediately afterwards traced this with a pen. Next he began on the letter, again in pencil.

'*Dear Mother*,' he wrote without hesitating, '*I hope you are well. I am. Mr Eldon's funeral was last Tuesday. The floral tributes were grand. He will be sadly missed. At present I am doing his work and mine. I am not getting any extra money which I have spoken of to Mrs Tennant. This war will make a big difference in every home.*

*'Mother I am very worried for you with the terrible bombing. Have you got a Anderson shelter yet? I ought to be over there with you Mother not here. But perhaps he will keep to London with his bombing. What will become of the old town.*

*'We are all in God's hands Mother dear. I am very perplexed with what is best to do whether to come over or stay. If I went away from here to be with you there would be the Labour Exchange and then the Army. They have not got to my age yet because I will be forty next June you remember. But I'm thinking they shall Mother and sooner than we look to. We must all hope for the best.*

*'With love Mother to my sister Bell I do hope she looks after you all right tell her. Your loving son, Charley.'*

Then he inked it in. As he licked the envelope flap after putting in the Money Order he squinted a bit wild, and this was shocking with his two different-coloured eyes. Lastly he laid his head down on his arms, went straight off to sleep.

There was often no real work went on in the Castle of an afternoon. Generally speaking this time was set aside so that Edith could sew or darn for Mrs Jack whom she looked after, and for Kate to see to the linen. But this afternoon as there had been guests they lent Bert a hand to clear away, then helped Mrs Welch's two girls Jane and Mary whose job it was to wash up everything except the tea things. The four of them chattered in Mrs Welch's scullery while this woman, seated in an armchair behind the closed door of her kitchen, stared grimly at her own black notebook.

'How is she?' Edith asked jerking her head and in a whisper.

'She's all right,' Mary whispered back, 'though we wondered a bit in the morning didn't we dear?' she said to Jane.

'I'll say we wondered.'

'But it was O.K. at the finish,' Mary went on. 'All's well that ends well as they say. There was practically nothing came back from the luncheon nor the nursery and you people do seem to've enjoyed your dinners.'

'Just old Aggie Burch as didn't like 'er spuds,' Kate said, 'but you don't want to take notice. I know I don't.'

'Doesn't this sink make your back ache,' Edith remarked. 'But there,' she said, 'I expect her nephew on his way over is bringing a big change in Mrs Welch. I shouldn't be surprised if she didn't have him on account of the bombing Isn't it dreadful?'

'The war's on now all right,' Kate said, 'and do these rotten Irish care? They make me sick.'

'What's the Irish got to do with it?' Jane asked. 'They're out aren't they? If they mean to stay out who's to blame 'em?'

'If it wasn't for the children the little angels I wouldn't ever remain. I couldn't really,' Edith announced. 'Look I'm going to dry, my back's broke. I could worship the ground they walks on. They're real little ladies. And how Mrs Jack dresses them. They've got everything so nice I cherish those kids.'

'Well they're goin' to have a boy to keep 'em company now,' Kate said with malice. 'Very nice too and so they should,' she added.

'But what will Miss Swift say to that?' asked Edith.

'Oh that's O K.,' Mary said, 'Miss Swift she come down to have a chat and Jane and me gets out of the light thinking there will be ructions but not a sound come past that closed door not one. We stayed here to see too didn't we love?' she said to Jane 'Then in the end they both came through proper buddies, Mrs Welch seein' 'er out as pleasant as you please and her saying "well I hope the air will do him good. It's like this with children Mrs Welch," she says. "One and all they're better for a change," she says. I was that surprised.'

'There now I'm very glad,' said Edith, 'I am, honest.'

'Now you girls hurry with that washing up,' said the dreadful voice, 'oh, I see you've some help There's quite a change come over this house I must admit. And don't you start a'wagging of those light tongues. But would you two young ladies like a glass of milk?'

It was Mrs Welch. It was almost unheard of that she should offer refreshment. Kate and Edith could only giggle.

'Mary,' she went on, 'you run and fetch that pitcher from the larder. What I've said over and over is at the age you are you girls don't get sufficient milk My sister writes it's short enough at home.'

'Might it be your sister's little boy who is coming to visit, Mrs Welch?'

'That's so Edith and his name is Albert, same as that Raunce's sick lad. One name less for Mrs T. to remember And if he had been christened Arthur we wouldn't understand what to think would we?

44

All the men in this place having to be of the same name, whoever heard of such stuff and nonsense.'

They laughed. Then when Edith and Kate had had their milk these two girls judged it best to be gone.

'You can't be sure of her, love,' Edith said as they made their way up the back stairs 'We did leave a bit for them yet but I'm positive she meant us to go really, calling us young ladies did you hear? You know what she is.'

'That's O.K. Edie an' if there were a few plates over it's not our work anyway. I got those sheets from the Gold Bedroom to mend. I wish the people they have to stay would cut their toenails or lie quiet one or the other.'

'Hush dear they'll hear,' Edith said and then went on: 'But have you ever seen such a change in anyone? Why she made herself quite pleasant.'

'Well what if she did the old nanny goat...'

'Hush love.'

'With that great beard she's got...'

'Oh Kate you are dreadful you are really. But do be careful, anyone could hear.'

'It's Miss Burch's afternoon out isn't it? Besides who would there be to come our way worse luck.' They had arrived at the door of their room. Kate flung it open. 'There,' she cried, 'look at the great boy you've got waiting inside.'

'What you don't mean Bert wouldn't presume,' said Edith going in. 'Why Kate you are silly there's no one. No,' she went on sitting down on her bed to take off shoes and stockings, 'it's her nephew coming over has softened 'er, that's what it is, love.'

Kate got down by Edith on her bed.

'What would you have said Edie if Bert had been in 'ere?'

'Why I'd've sent him packin'.'

'Would you Edie? Even if I hadn't been along?'

'How d'you mean? Kate, I never heard you speak so.'

Both girls giggled. The sky was overcast so that the light was dark as though under water. The afternoon was warm. It was the first afternoon to be warm since autumn. Though they could not see them the peacocks below were beginning to parade.

'And if it had've been Charley Edie?'

Edith gave a screech then slapped a hand over her mouth. A

peacock screamed beneath but they were so used to this they paid no notice.

'Kate Armstrong what d'you mean?'

'What I say stupid. Suppose you was come alone up here,' and her voice went rising, 'and found 'im waitin' on yer bed,' she ended, with a shriek of bed.

Both gave way at this, collapsed back across the eiderdown giggling. Edith pulled herself together first. 'No,' she said, 'for land's sake have a mind to the quilting Come on,' she added, 'we might as well be comfy' and they both got underneath, lay at ease with pillowed heads.

'Suppose it was Charley,' Kate said again.

'Why I daresn't even look at the man with his queer eyes. Each time I have sight of 'em I can't stop laughing,' Edith said. 'And the strange thing is I didn't ever properly take it in that they was a different colour till the other day. Not after two years and five months here, not till just the other day,' she added.

'You watch out Edie that's a sign.'

'A sign? A sign of what, I'd like to know?' she asked.

'Ah now you're asking,' Kate said. 'I wonder is she married or was she ever d'you reckon?'

'No dear she's only called Mrs like all cooks if you're referrin' to Mrs Welch Whatever made you say?'

'Why nothing. But I wish he was goin' to be older that's all.'

'Kate I'm getting too hot.'

'Take off some of your clothes then silly. Come on with you I'll help.'

'Quiet. There's Mrs Jack's stockings I've got to go over.'

'If you lie on your buttons I can't undo 'em at the back can I?' Kate said Then she tickled Edith to make her shift.

'Mercy stop it,' Edith screamed. 'Whatever are you doin'?'

'You said you was too warm. And struggling like you are will only make you warmer. There.'

'Kate Armstrong I thought I asked you. It tickles Why you aren't pulling the dress off my back surely? Whatever are you at?'

But she made it easier for Kate by moving her body here and there as was required.

'It's only your old uniform,' Kate said and soon Edith was lying almost naked.

46

'I'll stroke you dear if you like,' Kate said. 'Shut your eyes now.'

'I ought to be going over those silk stockings.'

'If you don't take good care I'll run over you like you was an old pair Edie and darn you in all sorts of places you wouldn't think.'

They giggled in shrieks again at this then quietened down. Kate began to stroke up and down the inside of Edith's arm from the hollow of her elbow to the wrist. Edith lay still with closed eyes. The room was dark as long weed in the lake.

'What if it had been Charley?' Kate asked.

'Why d'you want to go on at me about him?'

'But supposin' it was Edie?'

'Well how would you have acted?' said Edith.

'Me? He would never've had to ask me twice. Not the way I am these days.'

'Oh Kate you are dreadful.' But Edith's voice was low. Kate's stroking was beginning to make her drowse.

Then there was a real outcry from the peacocks. Kate slipped out of bed to look She saw Mrs Jack walking down the drive far beneath with Captain Davenport who was pushing his bike.

'What is it?' Edith asked.

'Just those two again.' Then Edith got up to look. The girls blocked their window, made night in the room.

'What two?' Edith. said her back to the darkness And answered herself. 'Oh Mrs Jack and the Captain. But won't the children be disappointed. I know they was counting on their mother taking them out the little loves.'

'Well they can count on summat else then and so can she very likely,' Kate said.

'Now Kate you've no call to say such a thing.' Edith's voice was truly indignant They could not hear their masters.

'It's not fair You could get one of these,' Davenport was saying.

'Now Dermot,' she replied, 'you've no right to be beastly.'

'But a bike's the only way to get about these days,' he said.

'Darling I've already told you,' she said.

'She couldn't surely object to your having a bike Violet after all.'

'Oh I can't go on like this behind her back,' she announced from an expressionless face but with tears coming into her blue, blue eyes that matched the curtains in her room, 'no I can't Dermot any longer.' She stopped. She stamped the ground. 'Oh darling,' she said, 'I do wish I could get you out of my system.'

'Now you're upset,' he began. 'By the way,' he went on, 'what's the matter with that footman you've got here? He asked me how the salmon trout were runnin'. I thought everyone in Old Ireland knew it was close season.'

'Dermot you don't mean he suspects anything?'

'Suspect anything? My dear girl I only mentioned it to change the conversation. Good Lord I only meant he seemed a funny sort.'

'And why d'you say you wanted to change the conversation?' she asked.

'Now you're all upset.'

'You don't understand,' she wailed.

'All I meant was I'd rather have him than Eldon,' the Captain said with bitterness. But it seemed that she was not thinking of the servants.

Charley now studied the black and red notebooks each afternoon. In the black he found Mr Eldon had written down peculiarities of those who were invited to Kinalty Castle with a note of the tips received on mentioning those peculiarities. But he did not as a rule spend long over this. There were not many people came to the Castle in wartime.

In the red Charley found Mr Eldon had kept a record of everything he drew under the petty cash account, which was presented monthly to Mrs Tennant. At one end was a copy of each account on which he had been paid. Against every item was an index number. At the other end of this red notebook the leaves were numbered and at least one whole sheet was given over entirely to copious notes on the item in question. Thus with a charge for sashcord of 7s 6d in March 1938 which reappeared in September of that year in an amount of 6s 8d and did not recur until July 1939 at 8s 9d, Raunce turned up the page on sashcord to find that hardly a yard had been bought or used in these last three years and that Mr Eldon was reminding himself to charge for more but had not lived to do it.

Once he had got the hang of things and had well studied the amount of corn bought for the peacocks at certain periods, Charley turned to that part which dealt only with the Cellar. By keeping open a Cellar Diary which had also to be shown each month to Mrs

Tennant and by comparing the two, he was able to refer from one to the other. Thus much that would otherwise have been obscure became plain.

For instance it was Mrs Tennant's custom to have on tap a cask of whisky, which had to be replenished at regular intervals by means of ten-gallon jars shipped from Scotland. Not only had Mr Eldon never credited her with the empties, that was straightforward enough, but he had left whole pages of calculations on the probable loss of the volatile spirit arising from evaporation in a confined space from which the outside atmosphere was excluded. He had gone into it thoroughly, had probably been prepared for almost any query. Charley appeared to find it suggestive because he whistled. There was also an encouraging note of recent date to say that no questions had been asked for years.

After the whisky had been blended in cask for a period at a calculable loss it was Mrs Tennant's custom to have her butler bottle it. Mr Eldon had charged her for new bottles every time. There was even a note of his about a rise in the cost of corks which he had not been able to use over again.

What this forenoon halted Charley in the study while on his weekly round rewinding clocks was a reminder in the red notebook to charge 10s 6d for a new spring to the weathervane. This was fixed on top of the tower and turned with a wind in the usual way. Where it differed from similar appliances was that Mr Tennant had had it connected to a pointer which was set to swing over a large map of the country round about elaborately painted over the mantelpiece. Raunce did not know yet how the thing worked. He stood and pondered and asked himself aloud where he could say he was going to fix the replacements if she asked him.

This map was peculiar. For instance Kinalty Church was represented by a miniature painting of its tower and steeple while the Castle, which was set right in the centre, was a fair sized caricature in exaggerated Gothic. There were no names against places.

As Charley stood there it so happened that the pointer was fixed unwavering E.S.E. with the arrow tip exactly on Clancarty, Clancarty which was indicated by two nude figures male and female recumbent in gold crowns. For the artist had been told the place was a home of the old kings.

Mrs Jack came in looking for a letter from Dermot. The carpets were so deep Raunce did not hear her. He was staring. She noticed he seemed obsessed by the weathervane and turned to find what in particular held him.

When she saw and thought she knew she drew breath with a hiss.

'Raunce,' she said and he had never heard her speak so sharp, 'what is it?'

He faced about, holding himself quite still.

'Why Madam I never heard you. The thing seems to have got stuck Madam.'

'Stuck? What d'you mean stuck?'

'It does not seem to be revolving Madam, and I'm sure the wind is not in that quarter.'

She reacted at once. She strode up to that arrow and gave it a wild tug presumably to drag the pointer away from those now disgusting people lying there in a position which, only before she had known Dermot, she had once or twice laughed at to her husband. The arrow snapped off in her hand. The vane up top might have been held in a stiff breeze or something could have jammed it.

Charley knew nothing as yet about Clancarty. 'It's the spring Madam,' he said cheerful as he took that broken piece from her. 'You noticed the arm did not have any give Madam?'

'Oh get on with your work,' she said appearing to lose control and half ran out. Shaking his head, grumbling to himself, Raunce made his way upstairs.

He made his way smooth down the Long Passage until he found one of the girls. It was Edith opposite Mrs Jack's chamber, doing out this lady's bathroom.

'Hello ducks,' he whispered.

'What brings you here?' she asked as soft.

'Who d'you think?' he answered.

'Get on with you,' she said.

'Look it's like this,' he began. 'This weathervane now. Where's the old works? I mean behind a little door or suchlike there must be a spring to do with some clockwork. At least that's what I'm led to understand.'

She looked disappointed.

'Behind a little door there's clockwork? Whatever's that?' she enquired.

'Don't ask me but Mr Eldon's left a book of directions which makes mention. Here,' he said, 'give us a kiss.' She said no as though she had been waiting to say this. She backed away against sweet primrose tiles. 'No,' she repeated quite loud and decided.

'Whatever's the matter with you these days?' he asked.

'I'm fed up I shouldn't wonder.'

'No need to take it out on me is there? What's up?'

'It's the war most likely,' she said pouting 'I shall have to get me out of this old place.'

'You don't want to talk like that my girl. Why we're on a good thing here all of us. Trust Uncle Charley, he's seen some. There's a war on, the other side. You don't want none of it do you? And there's the grub question. You got to consider that. About this weathervane now. I'll have to find the other one of you then, that's the only thing left for me to do.' He leered at her. 'Where is she?' he demanded.

Edith looked sideways as though embarrassed but she told him.

'Next door in Mrs Tennant's bathroom,' she said.

He whipped out and along that passage. He looked in the next open door. Against deep blue tiles Kate with her doll's face and tow hair was rearranging a scarlet bathrobe on the chromium towel horse. Edith had followed. But where he went in she stayed by the door, through which she watched as though reluctant.

He slipped up behind Kate, put his palms over her eyes.

'Guess baby,' he said, still whispering.

She gave a great screech beneath her breath, so discreetly she hardly made a sound.

'Why Charley you did give me a start.'

'I don't know,' he said, 'but I can't seem to bring it off these days. See here,' he went on, hands still over her eyes, 'where's there a kind of box in the wall with clockwork inside to do with that weathervane?'

She stood quiet, seemed almost to press her face into his palms. But she let out a giggle at the question.

'Oh my,' she said, 'what next?'

'Come on,' he said murmuring yet, 'give us a kiss,' as he turned her. And while he heartily kissed Kate's mouth her right eye winked at Edith under one of his outstanding ears.

Charley straightened himself at last, passed a forefinger over his lips. At once Edith said as though she could hear somebody. 'It's this way Mr Raunce.'

He came smoothly out, automatic. She led him along. Neither looked back. Soon she stopped at a panel with a button. She opened it. He put his head forward to peer. He saw two shafts which met to be joined by three gear wheels interlocked. And caught between those teeth, held by the leg was a live mouse.

At this Edith let a shriek with the full force of her lungs. A silence of horror fell.

Then even over the rustle of Kate hurrying up a paper-thin scream came as if in answer from between the wheels. And as Raunce looked for the person Edith said she had heard and except for Kate not a soul appeared, not one, Edith fainted slap into his arms.

After a moment Miss Burch came bustling towards them. 'What's this?' she asked, 'and what trick have you played on that poor girl now? Let go of her this instant goodness gracious whoever heard,' she said to Raunce and taking Edith, stretched her rather rough on the floor.

That same afternoon after dinner Miss Burch paid a call on Mrs Welch, slipping from the servants' hall out through the vast scullery straight into her kitchen.

'Come right in,' Mrs Welch welcomed from where she was seated concentrating over the opened notebook. 'Jane,' she called, 'Miss Burch will have a cup of tea.'

'Why thanking you,' Miss Burch said, 'and is this Albert?'

'Yes this is Albert,' Mrs Welch replied. 'Get up when you're spoken of,' she added and the boy stood He had been crying. 'Come to think of it,' she went on, 'run out now and don't get in the way of my girls at their work nor into any more trouble my word.'

'Trouble,' Miss Burch remarked once they were alone as she stirred with a teaspoon, 'trouble. This morning's just been one long worry an' what it's going to come to I don't know.' There was no reply. Miss Burch watched steam from off her tea.

'I don't know I'm sure,' she continued eventually, 'but it's him or me that's the long and short of the whole matter. We can't go on like it and that's a fact,' she said.

'A large big bird like that,' Mrs Welch insisted, 'and with a powerful wallop in each wing. Why 'e might've got killed the little terror.'

'Killed?' Miss Burch asked, giving way. 'I hope he's not gone and had an accident on his very first day at the Castle?'

'Children is all little 'Itlers these days,' Mrs Welch answered. 'D'you know what 'e done. Up and throttled one of them peacocks with 'is bare hands not 'alf an hour after he got in. Yes that's what,' she said.

'Oh dear,' Miss Burch said, 'one of the peacocks?'

'I got'm covered up in the larder,' Mrs Welch went on. 'I'll choose my time to bury'm away at dusk. He might've been killed easy. I 'adn't turned my back not above two minutes to get on with their luncheon when I heard a kind of squawking. I ran to that window and there 'e was with one in 'is two fists. Oh I screamed out but 'e 'ad it about finished the little storm trooper. There wasn't nothing left to do but 'ide the dead body away from that mad Irish Conor.'

'Yes he's taken up with the things that man,' Miss Burch agreed.

'As to that I've only to pluck it,' Mrs Welch said, 'and 'e won't never distinguish the bird from a chicken they're that ignorant the savages. Mrs Tennant can't miss just the one out of above two hundred. But I won't deny it give me a start.'

'There you are,' Miss Burch said, 'but listen to this. I was upstairs in the Long Gallery this morning to get on with my work when I heard a screech, why I thought one of the girls had come by some terrible accident, or had their necks broke with one of the sashcords going which are a proper deathtrap along the Passage out of the Gallery. Well what d'you think? I'll give you three guesses.'

'You heard me 'oller out very likely,' Mrs Welch replied, watching the door yet that Albert had shut behind him.

'It was Edith, and that Raunce had been after her,' Miss Burch said, 'that man who makes this place a deathly menace.'

'Excuse me a moment,' Mrs Welch remarked and got up. She moved painful across the kitchen dragging her feet. Opening the door between she looked into her scullery. Albert was seated over a cup of tea while Mary and Jane went on with their work.

'You stay there quiet,' she said to him. 'You've been trouble enough this morning my oath,' she said, 'without your plotting something fresh.' Her voice was thick with love. She shut the door.

'Oh these long spaces,' she exclaimed as she came back.

'This place won't ever be the same, not since Mr Eldon left us,' Miss Burch began again. 'I said it over his open grave and I don't care who hears me this minute. With Raunce let loose without check about the house there's no saying what we'll come to. And there's the trouble of his morning tea. He will insist on one of my girls fetching it. They won't even tell me which one of them it is but I keep watch. She's Edith though I told Mrs Tennant different by being mistaken at the time. What I say is who's to answer for it when he gets up to his games with her in the bedroom. Tormenting a girl till she faints will be child's play Mrs Welch.'

'It's the food,' Mrs Welch answered, 'though I do speak as shouldn't seein' as I occupy meself with the kitchen. They're starving over there my sister says in her letter she sent. If it wasn't for that I'd go tomorrer, I would straight. He's that thin.'

'Nothing'll be like it was,' Miss Burch repeated. 'I said so at the time.'

Mrs Welch had the last word. 'Not but what Albert makes a difference being a refugee like the Belgians we had in the last war,' she said. 'Yes 'e'll be a tie,' she ended, 'and he'll take feedin'.'

But not more than half an hour after Miss Burch had left there fell another blow. Mrs Welch went into the larder for a last look before going to her room. While fixing a cheese cloth in front to hide the plucked peacock she chanced to regard the great jar where she kept her waterglass. With arms upraised in the gesture of a woman hanging out smalls she watched that jar with pursed lips. She called Albert.

'Ever set eyes on that before?' she asked.

'No'm I ain't,' he replied in the manner of Raunce's lad.

'Ever been in this larder in your puff?'

'No'm.'

'You wouldn't tell me an untruth would yer?'

'Oh no'm.'

'Because what I 'ave to say to you is this: it's 'ighly dangerous that stuff is. A sup of that and it would be your lot d'you hear me?'

'Yes'm.'

'So you never seen it before?'

'No'm.'

'And you've not even been in this place? Is that right?'

'Yes'm.'

'All right then and I don't want to hear any more. But if you so much as breathes a word of what 'as just passed I'll tan the 'ide clean off your back you little poulterer you h'understand?'

'Yes'm.' He turned, ran out.

Then high shrieking giggles came faint with distance from without. Mrs Welch moved over to perforated iron which formed a wall of the larder, advanced one eye to a hole and grimly watched.

The back premises of this grey Castle were on a vast scale. What she saw afar was Kate and Edith with their backs to her in purple uniforms and caps the colour of a priest's cassock. They seemed to be waiting outside O'Conor's lamp room. This was two tall Gothic windows and a pointed iron-studded door in a long wall of other similar doors and windows topped by battlements above which was set back another wall with a greater number of windows which in its turn was terraced into the last storey that was almost all blind Gothic windows under a steep roof of slate. Mrs Welch after seeming to linger over the great shaft of golden sun which lighted these girls through parted cloud let a great gust of sigh and turned away saying,

'Well if Aggie Burch can't hold 'em in leash it's none of my business, the pair of two-legged mice, the thieves,' she added.

But as Edith reached for O'Conor's latch Kate screamed at her,

'And what if there's a mouse?' Then Edie, hands to the side over a swelling heart, gave back, 'Oh love you can't say that to me,' and leant against the door post. 'That you can't say love,' she said, dizzy once more all of a sudden.

'Aw come on I only meant it for a game.'

'Oh Kate.'

'You're soft that's what it is dear.'

'Not after what come to pass this very morning you didn't ought.'

'Why see who's brought 'erself to have a peek at him,' Kate said of a moulting peacock which head sideways was gazing up with one black white-rimmed eye. 'Get off,' she cried, 'I don't like none of you.'

'Quiet dear. It's likely his favourite.'

'Why what d'you know,' said Kate, 'she's not taken up with us at all at all, it's the buzzard above she's fixed on, would you believe.'

'A buzzard?'

'And if I said I didn't care.'

'No Kate you mustn't, don't strike her I said. You can't tell what might happen if he came to learn.'

'Oh Paddy,' Kate said, 'I'll bet he's well away after that dinner he ate. He'll never stir. But I shan't if you wouldn't rather.'

'She's his special I know,' Edith went on. 'I can't distinguish one from the other but there's something tells me. And who's to say if he is asleep in the dark?'

'You go on in to oblige me then,' Kate said.

'Not me I shan't. I couldn't.'

'Well I will at that.'

'Nor you won't either,' Edith said. 'You've made me frighted.'

'I will then,' Kate answered, raising the heavy latch. 'But love I'll never cause a sound even the smallest,' she said low. Edith plastered her mouth over with the palm of a hand.

'No,' she said muffled, 'no,' as O'Conor's life was opened, as Kate let the sun in and Edith bent to look.

What they saw was a saddleroom which dated back to the time when there had been guests out hunting from Kinalty. It was a place from which light was almost excluded now by cobwebs across its two windows and into which, with the door ajar, the shafted sun lay in a lengthened arch of blazing sovereigns Over a corn bin on which he had packed last autumn's ferns lay Paddy snoring between these windows, a web strung from one' lock of hair back onto the sill above and which rose and fell as he breathed. Caught in the reflection of spring sunlight this cobweb looked to be made of gold as did those others which by working long minutes spiders had drawn from spar to spar of the fern bedding on which his head rested. It might have been almost that O'Conor's dreams were held by hairs of gold binding his head beneath a vaulted roof on which the floor of cobbles reflected an old king's molten treasure from the bog.

'He won't wake now, only for tea,' Kate said. 'Because after he's had his he feeds the birds.'

'Oh Kate isn't he a sight and all.'

'Well come on we can't stand looking. What's next?'

'If I make a crown out of them ferns in the corner,' Edith said, 'will you fetch something he can hold?'

'You aim to make him a bishop? Well if I 'ad my way I'd strip those rags off to give that pelt of his a good rub over.'

'Don't talk so. You couldn't.'

'Who's doing all the talking?' O'Conor gave a loud snore. Both girls began to giggle.

'Oh do be quiet dear,' Edith said picking a handful of ferns and starting to twist them. Then they were arrested by movement in the sunset of that sidewall which reflected glare from the floor in its glass.

For most of one side of this room was taken up by a vast glass-fronted cupboard in which had once been kept the bits, the halters and bridles, and the martingales. At some time O'Conor had cut away wooden partitioning at the back to make a window into the next chamber, given over nowadays to his peacocks. This was where these birds sheltered in winter, nested in spring, and where they died of natural causes at the end. As though stuffed in a dusty case they showed themselves from time to time as one after another across the heavy days they came up to look at him. Now, through a veil of light reflected over this plate glass from beneath, Edith could dimly see, not hear, a number of peacocks driven into view by some disturbance on their side and hardly to be recognized in this sovereign light. For their eyes had changed to rubies, their plumage to orange as they bowed and scraped at each other against the equal danger. Then again they were gone with a beat of wings and in their room stood Charley Raunce, the skin of his pale face altered by refraction to red morocco leather.

The girls stood transfixed as if by arrows between the Irishman dead motionless asleep and the other intent and quiet behind a division. Then dropping everything they turned, they also fled.

Miss Swift was deaf and could not always hear her charges' words as along with Evelyn and Moira and Mrs Welch's Albert she came that afternoon to the dovecote round by the back. She groaned while she settled herself in the shady seat and the doves rose in a white cloud on softly clapping wings.

'What's troublin' 'er?' Albert asked.

'It's only nanny's rheumatism,' Miss Moira quoted.

'Why come to that I got an uncle 'as 'is joints boiled Tuesdays and Thursdays over at St Luke's down the old Bow Road.'

'Now shall poor old nanny tell you a story of the two white doves that didn't agree?'

Moira nudged Evelyn and pointed. A pair of these birds on a ledge were bowing beak to beak. The two girls copied them, nodding deeply one to the other as they sat on either side of Miss Swift. This woman rubbed a knee with both hands without looking at it. She had closed her eyes.

'Once upon a time there were six little doves lived in a nest,' she began and Raunce came out of an unused door in that Castle wall. The rusted hinges creaked. The two girls waved but Mrs Welch's Albert beyond Evelyn might almost have been said to cringe. Raunce put a finger to his lips. He was on his way back from the round he had made of the peacocks' corn bins and during which he startled Kate and Edith. Then Miss Evelyn and Miss Moira each put a finger to their mouths as they went on bowing to each other. Raunce made off. Miss Swift continued,

'Because they were so poor and hungry and cold in their thin feathers out there in the rain.' She opened her eyes. 'Children,' she said, 'stop those silly tricks' and the girls obeyed. 'But the sun came out to warm them,' she intoned.

'Jesus,' Albert muttered, 'look at that.'

This dovecote was a careful reproduction of the leaning tower of Pisa on a small scale. It had balconies to each tier of windows. Now that the birds had settled again they seemed to have taken up their affairs at the point where they had been interrupted So that all these balconies were crowded with doves and a heavy murmur of cooing throbbed the air though at one spot there seemed to be trouble.

'You're very very wicked boy,' said Evelyn to Albert looking where she thought he looked. What she saw was one dove driving another along a ledge backwards Each time it reached the end the driven one took flight and fluttered then settled back on that same ledge once more only to be driven back the other way to clatter into air again. This was being repeated tirelessly when from another balcony something fell.

'That's ripe that is,' Albert said.

'I didn't see,' Evelyn cried. 'I didn't really. What came about?'

'And then there was a time,' the nanny said from behind closed eyes and the wall of deafness, 'oh my dears your old nanny hardly knows how to tell you but the naughty unloyal dove I told of.

'It was a baby one,' Albert said.

'A baby dove. Oh do let me see.'

'I daresn't stir,' he said.

'Where did she fall then?' Evelyn asked.

'Quiet children,' Miss Swift said having opened her eyes, 'or I shan't finish the story you asked after, restless chicks,' she said. 'And then there came a time,' she went on, shutting her eyes again, hands folded.

'What? Where?' Moira whispered.

'It was a baby one,' Albert said, 'and nude. That big bastard pushed it.'

'The big what?' Evelyn asked. 'Oh but I mean oughtn't we to rescue the poor?'

'Where did she drop then?' Moira wanted to be told  But a rustle made them turn about on either side of Miss Swift who sat facing that dovecote shuteyed and deaf. They saw Kate and Edith in long purple uniforms bow swaying towards them in soft sunlight through the white budding branches, fingers over lips. Even little Albert copied the gesture back this time. All five began soundlessly giggling in the face of beauty.

'Did you see Mr Raunce?' Kate asked at last.

' 'E went that way,' Albert answered while the two girl children sat with forefingers still on their mouths.

'What did 'e come out of?' Kate asked.

'That door,' Albert said.

'And then they were in great peril every mortal one,' Miss Swift continued.

'And oh Edith,' Miss Evelyn announced, 'we've been watching the doves they are so funny.'

'I shouldn't pay attention if I was you dear.'

'Why shouldn't I pay attention?'

'Not if I was you I shouldn't.'

'Why shouldn't I?' Miss Evelyn asked.

'Because they're very rum them birds,' Kate said also whispering.

'Why are they rum?' Miss Moira asked.

'I'll say they're rum,' Albert announced. 'One of the old 'uns shoved a young bird and 'e fell down right on 'is nut.'

'Well I never,' Kate remarked to Edith. They watched that dovecote over the children's heads.

'Sssh,' said Edith watching rapt. The children turned. There were so many doves they hardly knew which way to look.

'And then there came a time when this wicked tempting bird came to her father to ask her hand,' Miss Swift said, passing a dry tongue over dry lips, shuteyed.

'It don't seem right not out in the open,' Kate mentioned casual.

'And again over there too and there,' said Edith.

'Where?' cried Miss Evelyn too loud though not sharp enough as she thought to interrupt Miss Swift. The nanny just put a hand on her arm while she droned.

'Oh what are they doing then?' Miss Moira cried.

'They're kissing love,' Kate answered low.

'Hush dear,' said Edith.

'But where Kate I don't see. Oh look at those two oh look she's got her head right down his beak, she's going to strangle him,' and Moira's voice rose 'Nanny nanny stop it quick.'

'Good gracious child what's this?'

But the children had got up and as they rose every dove was apart once more and on the wing, filling the air with sighing.

'Why now Edith and Kate whatever do you think you're about?'

'We've just finished our dinner,' Kate replied.

'Wandering all over the grounds where anyone might see. Who's ever heard?' the nanny said. 'Sit down children and you Albert. If you're going to stay with us you'll do as you're told.'

'Yes'm.'

'Well we're accustomed to let our dinner settle,' Kate said.

'And I make no doubt you use that to get away of an afternoon and let the work look after itself. You'll have Miss Burch after you.'

'Come away, dear,' Edith said to Kate.

'Doves kissing indeed,' Miss Swift called surprisingly after their backs, 'stuff and nonsense. That's the mother feeding her little one dears If you sit quiet enough you'll see for yourselves,' she said to the children. 'And now where was I?'

'You were at that bit where the kind old father says he can marry her 'cause he's getting too old to know better.'

'Well now that's right,' Miss Swift began once more and the

doves, spiralling down in the funnel made by trees which were coming out all over in a yellow green through chestnut sheaths the colour of a horse's coat, settled one after another each outside the door to his quarters and after strutting once or twice went on quarrelling, murdering and making love again. 'So then not knowing any better he let him have her hand,' the nanny said.

Breathless the children watched this leaning tower. Very soon one white dove was crouching with opened beak before another with stuck-out chest. Not long after that they were at it once more and the fat bird, grown thin now, had his head deep down the other's neck which was swallowing in frantic gulps that shook its crescent body. Elsewhere another bird trundled an egg to the edge. Yet another chased a fifth to a corner until it fluttered over behind where these two began again. In pairs they advanced and retreated. Then one more small mass fell without a thud, pink.

'There y'are,' said Albert.

'Where? I didn't see. Oh I've missed again,' Evelyn said. 'Did you?' to Moira.

'You're none of you listening you naughty children,' the nanny said. 'Here's poor nanny wasting her breath and you don't pay attention. We'd better get on with our walk if you ask me.'

'Why nanny?'

'Are you coming?'

'Yes'm.'

'But why nanny?'

'Because nanny says so. Come on now. We'll go down by the fish 'atchery,' and she made off, holding Evelyn by the hand. She dragged on her right leg.

'Tell you what,' Albert said to Moira as they loitered to follow, 'I'll bite 'is little 'ead off'n.'

'You'll what?'

'Like they did in the local where I was evacuated.'

'What's the local?'

'In the pub down in the country. There was a man there bit the 'eads off of mice for a pint. The lady I was evacuated with said so.'

'You shan't you wicked boy I'll call nanny.'

'I'll show yer,' he said darting sideways towards the base of that tower. 'You wait till I find'm,' he said and she burst out wailing.

Miss Swift came back, mopped the child's face. The others watched as though disinterested. She did not ask Albert. 'I'll tell Mrs Welch about you' was all she told him.

Later that same afternoon Raunce was in the pantry lending his lad a hand with the tea things. That is to say while his Albert washed the cups and saucers, the spoons and plates, Raunce held up a heavy silver tray like a cymbal to polish it. 'Ha' he went at the expanse of mirror metal, 'ha,' then he rubbed his breath away as he whistled through his teeth in time to the short strokes in the way a man will when grooming a horse, and squinting terribly the while.

Suddenly he spoke. Bert grew quiet at his voice. Raunce said,

'I could have laughed right in her face,' and stopped.

'When was that?' Albert enquired.

'Yes so I could and with you sitting there still as a mouse.'

The boy looked speechless at him.

'Oh get on with your work,' Raunce quoted from another context There was another lull while Albert redoubled his effort and the butler watched. 'It's not as if we had all night,' Raunce went on, 'which is to say I have not,' he said speaking genteely and he let a short guffaw, 'lucky Charley they call me, begorrah,' he added.

'Yes Mr Raunce,' mumbled Albert.

'It won't wash your acting the innocent my lad. The moment she come in that door between the scullery and where we was sitting over our tea I could tell you felt the draught.'

'I didn't feel nothing.'

'When Mrs Welch reported present on the steps there was something caused my eyes to settle on that cheese face of yours, something told me. And when she started about that waterglass of 'ers which is missing I says to myself Charley you don't have to look far, it's plain as my face in the mirror. What induced you to take the stuff?'

'I never.'

'Come on tell uncle.'

'I never took nothing.'

'You've no call to feel uneasy my lad. I've not made out I was any different from what I am now have I?'

'Mr Raunce I haven't so much as seen it.'

'Well, if you won't, then I will. I'll tell you. It's because you over-heard me say what my old mother had written that they was on the very brink of starvation over in London with the bombing. You must've idea'd you'd go get hold of some to send 'em a few eggs in.'

'Gawd's truth I did not Mr Raunce.'

'Don't stand there like a stuck pig my lad. Get down to it for the love of Moses. We aren't finished with the day's work by a long chalk. But you got your parents in London yet?' he went on. 'Haven't you?'

There was no reply except for the slop of sink water.

'Well haven't you?'

'Yes Mr Raunce.'

'All right then why make a mystery? You thought you might send 'em along an egg or two.'

'I tell you I never.'

'I'm not saying you did, all I'm telling you is you thought you might. There's times I despair of you my lad,' Raunce said. 'We'll not possibly make anything out of you that's one item dead certain. And another thing now. Once you can shine a bit of good silver up like this here you'll have learned a start of the trade that's took me many a long year to master. And I'm still learning.'

'I couldn't even name what that glass is for,' the boy uttered deep in his sink.

'D'you want me to fetch you one?'' Raunce shouted at once. 'Would you provoke me to strike you? No? Then don't attempt impudence again. There's the National Service Officer waiting the other side for growing lads such as you soon as you're of age.'

'Yessir,' the boy said as though galvanized.

'And don't call me sir,' Raunce said calmer, 'give a Mr when you address me that's all I ask. Well if you won't tell you won't. You may be right at that. See nothing know nothing as they say in the Army.'

Albert tried a furtive smile.

'I don't say I blame you,' Raunce went on after pondering a moment He was picking his teeth with a needle he had taken from underneath the lapel of his coat 'But one thing we will get straight here and now,' he said. 'Keep all of it to yourself if you wish. And clean your teeth of course before you have anything to do with a woman. Yet if I 'ave any more of that side from you there's one thing you can bet your life. A word to Mrs T. from me, just one little word and it's the Army for you my lad, old king and country and all the rest d'you understand.'

'Yes Mr Raunce.'

'Where'd those two girls of Miss Burch go working after tea did you happen to notice?'

'Over in the empty place.'

'Yes but what part?'

'I couldn't tell. I never 'eard. On my oath I don't bloody know.'

'O.K. O.K. what's all the excitement?' Raunce said. 'If you don't know you don't,' he said. 'That's all there is to it. But I got a message to give one or both of 'em see? Lucky Charley they call me. I chanced upon one of their little games this dinnertime. And if that bell was to go just you answer it. If they should want to know where I am say I'm down in the cellar d'you understand. All right? But I shan't be more'n a minute,' he said as he glided softly out softly whistling. The boy trembled.

As has been explained most of this great house was closed. It was for Kate and Edith once or twice each week to open various dust-sheeted rooms to let the air in. When Raunce after making his way up the Grand Staircase, going through the Long Gallery and past the Chapel came to a great sombre pair of doors which divided one part of this Castle from the other, he passed once he had opened these into yet another world. And in spite of his training they made a booming sound as he shut them behind him.

He stood to listen through a white-wrapped dimness. For what he heard was music. In a moment he knew he heard a waltz.

'What are they up to now?' he asked half under his breath. 'What's Edith after?' he repeated. He was grave all of a sudden.

He started on his way, then almost at once stopped by a large bowl which sat naked on a window ledge and which had a sheet of cardboard laid over. He picked this up, set it aside, then dipped his fingers in the rustle of potpourri which lay within. Walking on again he sniffed once at his fingers he had dabbled in the dry bones of roses and to do this was a habit with him the few times he was over in this part.

He went forward, still intently listening. To his left was a range of high windows muted by white blinds. On his right he passed objects sheeted in white and to which he had never raised the cloths. For this house that had yet to be burned down, and in particular that greater part of it which remained closed, was a shadowless castle of treasures. But he was following music. Also he went like the most silent cat after two white mice, and to tell them as well that what had been missing was now found to have been stolen by a rat.

The music came louder and louder as he progressed until at the white and gold ballroom doors it fairly thundered. He paused to look over his shoulder with his hand on a leaping salmon trout in gilt before pressing this lever to go in. There was no one. Nevertheless he spoke back the way he had come. 'They'll break it,' he said aloud as though in explanation, presumably referring to the gramophone which was one of the first luxury clockwork models. 'And in a war,' he added as he turned back to these portals, 'it would still fetch good money,' talking to himself against the thrust of music. 'The little bitches I'll show 'em,' he said and suddenly opened.

They were wheeling wheeling in each other's arms heedless at the far-end where they had drawn up one of the white blinds. Above from a rather low ceiling five great chandeliers swept one after the other almost to the waxed parquet floor reflecting in their hundred thousand drops the single sparkle of distant day, again and again red velvet panelled walls, and two girls, minute in purple, dancing multiplied to eternity in these trembling pears of glass.

'You're daft,' he called out They stopped with their arms about each other. Then as he walked up they disengaged to rearrange their hair and still the waltz thundered. He switched it off. The needle grated.

The girls said nothing. They stood with arms up rolling their curls and watched. He went over to the window, twitched down that blind. He came back. He spoke at last.

'Oh all right,' he said, 'I only happened to be passing O K.? Yes I know it's none of my business. Go on play it once more if you like.'

'Not now,' Kate said.

'It was only that one of them might hear you,' he explained.

'It's over now,' Edith answered him.

'And that reminds me,' he went on seeming to forget he had just given another reason for his presence. 'What I came to tell you girls was I found out about the waterglass. It's my lad has been and had some. Only a trifle, not enough to notice. He took what he did more out of curiosity than anything.'

'Albert?' Edith exclaimed.

'Fortunate 'e didn't try a taste,' Raunce continued. 'He's that sort. He'd never think twice if it came over him to see what the effects might be. He's a crank that's why. I know I've tried along of that lad but there's some you can't do anything with.'

Kate laughed. 'So it was Albert, Albert after all,' she said.

'I came special to mention the matter,' Raunce added and he had not left Edith with his eyes. 'Ever since Mrs Welch barged in like that at teatime I thought well you never know maybe these girls will take what she said wrong, think it was addressed to them.'

'That cap didn't fit, we never took no notice,' Kate announced.

'It's Edith here,' Raunce said, 'with her talk of she must get home and being dissatisfied.'

'Well thank you very much,' Edith replied as though astounded.

'Don't mention,' he said. 'And I must be off. Busy Charley that's me,' he wound up with what seemed an empty return to his old manner as he abruptly turned away. He went straight out not saying another word.

'Well would you believe that?' Edith murmured half giggling. But Kate was looking at her like she might have been a stranger and she stopped.

'All right come on,' Kate said vicious, 'we're not goin' to stay here all night are we? I reckon we've done what we can. Enough's enough,' she said and they set about leaving this end of the great room as they had found it. And then made their way back to the part that was inhabited, their day's work done.


It may have been a few days later that Miss Burch came in late for her elevenses. She looked worried. As she sat down she said,

'She's mislaid her big sapphire cluster.'

There was no need to ask whose ring that was Ever since the French maid went back to her own country Miss Burch had been in charge of Mrs Tennant's things. But Mrs T. was always finding what she had just lost, while she seldom bothered to announce that whatever it might be was no longer missing. Charley seriously said, and at the same time imitated Mrs Welch's nephew,

'Maybe she put'm down and forgot to pick'm up.'

Except for Miss Burch they none of them bothered. It could be assumed if she did not in good time come across the ring that she would get another of equal value out of the Company and better because it was fresh.

'Which reminds me,' Charley asked his lad, 'did you remember to take her back that glove? Now don't give me the old answer, don't say which glove?'

'It's in the pantry Mr Raunce,' Albert said.

'What is?'

'The gardening glove.'

'You'll excuse me it's not. I ought to know seeing that's my own pantry. Where is it then?'

'I put 'er glove in the cupboard,' Albert said, 'on the bottom shelf. I seen it only this morning.'

'Oh well if you've hidden the thing,' Raunce replied and they fell back on silence.

Edith looked up to find Kate watching her. She blushed.

'Land's sakes there she goes colouring again,' Raunce announced hearty. 'She should go and give one of them blood transfusions they are asking volunteers for, she's got too much,' he commented out of one side of his mouth to Miss Burch next him.

'Don't be disgusting,' was all this woman said.

But he had obviously recollected. Eggs must have made him think of waterglass. 'Wait a minute,' he cried. Kate watched. 'I've just remembered summat,' he went on. He paused, and his eyes were on Edith while her blushes flooded once more. 'I do believe I done you a real injustice,' he said to Albert perhaps. But he did not seem able to take his eyes off the girl while she looked at him melting as though at his mercy.

'We shall have to make them open up the drains for us that's all,' Miss Burch stated, still on about the ring.

'Oh forget it,' Charley said to Edith, probably meaning this remark for Albert. He lowered his eyes and an odd sort of bewilderment showed in his face. But Miss Burch must have understood that he was answering her for she objected,

'I can't forget,' and she spoke resigned. 'I'm sure I've looked every place and it was a beautiful ring, an antique,' she added.

At this moment Mrs Welch had an idea away in the kitchen. Leaving her black notebook she shuffled swift into the scullery where little Albert was at table over a cup of cocoa while the two girls prepared vegetables in one of six sinks.

'There's none of you girls go talking to the tradesmen?' she asked in a menacing voice and gave no warning.

'Oh no m'm.'

'There's not one of you so much as passes the time of day with that butcher?'

'No m'm truly.'

'Because remember what I said. Don't have nothing to do with them Irish or you'll likely bring our own blood on us. By reason of the I R.A. And never forget.'

'Yes m'm.'

'And where do they carry the victuals when they call?' Mrs Welch went on to ask.

'They leave 'em in the outside larder like you said.'

'Now when d'you fetch what they've left?'

'When they're gone,' the girls answered.

'That's right. Also I'll take up with those merchants what they've delivered short, what they owe me, on the blower, understand. Nor you 'aven't spoken with one of them?'

'No m'm.'

'And 'ow d'you know when they've been?'

'They ring the little bell as they're leavin'.'

'That's right. Then it can't be one of the tradesmen after all,' she said going back into the kitchen and there cried out loud to herself, 'Oh my waterglass.'

What she had lost still seemed uppermost on Mrs Welch's mind when after dinner that same day Miss Burch dropped in to have a word.

'I've been and measured'n again,' she greeted Agatha, 'and there's above a quart gone without trace. Mary bring Miss Burch a cup of tea.'

'I do miss Mr Eldon, I do miss that man,' Miss Burch said. 'No matter who couldn't happen to lay their hands on something he always imagined where to find it. He startled you that way.'

'Not what is short out of my jar he never could.'

'No matter where it was Mrs Tennant dropped whatever it might be,' Agatha went on regardless, 'he was on 'and to restore it. He

68

knew where things had lodged before they were rightly out of your fingers. There you are Mrs Welch it's a gift.'

'It's a gift right enough the way some is born sticky fingered.'

'Now I wouldn't say anyone had taken that ring, no I'd never go so far as that. I don't believe there's a soul in this Castle would do such a thing.'

'I've 'ad the matter over with my girls,' Mrs Welch said, 'right into things I've been, and I've given Albert a talkin' to my word. If 'e'd known the slightest bit I'd've had it out of 'im you can lay your oath on that.'

'It's a mystery.'

'A dark mystery's right,' Mrs Welch echoed. 'A ring will roll I grant, but don't tell me above a quart of waterglass will fly out of what it's in without a drop spilled on the floor, the diabolical stroke,' she added.

'I knew a woman once went down to Brighton for the Whitsun,' Miss Burch began, 'and her ring slipped in the sand. The next day she went back with her little nipper's wooden shovel, dug away where she'd been seated, and there it was after the tide had been over even.'

'You'll 'ave to get the plumbin' opened up that's all.'

'Just what I said with the cup of cocoa this morning,' Miss Burch replied. 'Of course I've got my girls searching this minute but they would never see the Crown jewels laying right before them they're so occupied looking over their shoulders for that Raunce.'

'I won't 'ave 'im in my kitchen.'

'Oh you're fortunate, you've a place you can call your own. Though he's improved the last few days, I will allow that. We may make something of him yet.'

''Ave they so much as glanced at those drains in the last twelve-month?' Mrs Welch enquired.

'They should be done out,' Miss Burch said. 'But the proper time will be when they both go over for Mr Jack's leave which will be any time now or so I'm led to believe.'

'I was goin' to speak to 'er myself on it,' Mrs Welch announced. 'It ain't 'ealthy in these old buildings that has a cesspool dug before sewers come to be invented. Not with children about that is.'

'And where would the little chap be this afternoon?'

'My Albert? Oh I sent 'im up to Miss Swift to get 'is run out.'

'That's right,' Miss Burch said. 'It's not right for them to be all day inside. Like Raunce is for instance.'

'Gawd 'elp us with the man when they do go over the other side for Mr Jack.' As she spoke Mrs Welch started to look wild again.

'You think so?' Miss Burch asked seeming at once to dread.

'It's not thinking, I'm certain sure. Well there's just the one thing for it,' Mrs Welch cried suddenly frantic, 'every mortal object must be under lock and key. There maun't be a drawer can be opened or a door they shall get in by. And as for my pots and pans I'll get me a padlock and chains and stake 'em down to me dresser,' she almost shouted pointing to the vast array of burnished copper and aluminium. 'And if I can't get a chain will go through them 'oles in the 'andles so 'elp me God I'll send to Berlin if I shouldn't find what'll suit in this poor law island.'

'To Berlin?' Miss Burch asked with a gasp.

'That's right,' Mrs Welch answered and seemed gratified. 'We're in a nootral country aren't we?'

'Bless me but I can't stay sitting here,' Miss Burch said getting up, 'I must do a bit more I suppose. I'm obliged to you for the cup of tea I was parched,' she added.

'You're welcome,' Mrs Welch replied as she reopened her black notebook.

Agatha walked stiffly through the back premises towards Mrs Tennant's bedroom which was being given a thorough turnout by her girls. She had made the loss of this ring an excuse to favour the room with a proper doing. But unusual sounds of activity in the pantry made her choose to go through this on the way upstairs. She found Raunce hard at it with silver out over green baize cloths across every table he could lay hands on and even into his bedroom. Saucers filled with a violet coloured polish, old toothbrushes, shammy leather and the long white soft-haired brushes were laid out for use among sauceboats, salvers, rose bowls and the silver candlesticks of all shapes and sizes. She passed Raunce and his lad in a silence which seemed to grant gracious approval.

'The old cow,' Charley remarked once she was out of earshot.

'You've said it,' the boy replied.

'You know Bert I sometimes marvel women can go sour like that. When you think of them young, soft and tender it doesn't 'ardly seem possible now the way they turn so that you would never hold a crab apple up to them they're so acid.'

'That's right,' the boy said as he worked.

'And what Mr Eldon could see in her is a mystery but then he was deep,' Raunce commented with admiration in his voice. 'He was deep if ever there was one.' At any pause in what he was saying he whistled between his teeth like a groom while he rubbed and polished. He was apparently in fine fettle.

'What day is it?' he asked.

'Why Saturday,' the boy answered.

'Holy smoke if we was to creep upstairs tomorrow after dinner and find those two slaves of hers laid out on their little beds where they'll be of a Sunday afternoon. What would you do eh?'

Albert stopped work and stared. He seemed astonished.

'After cleaning your teeth of course,' Charley added.

'Why what d'you mean?' Albert asked.

'What would you say to Kate? A lovely blonde? Now then take your hands out of those pockets and get on with the work or we'll be here all night. Have you ever had anything to do with a woman?'

The habitual look of obstinacy appeared on Albert's face. He did not answer.

'There's no call to be bashful,' Raunce said. 'Everyone's got to make a start one time or another. Have you or have you not? You won't answer. I don't blame you neither. Broadminded Charley that's what I'm known as. But one thing you can get into that thick skull of yours. You lay off Edith, understand. You can muck about with Kate all you please but Edith's close season, get me?'

'Yes Mr Raunce, whatever you say.'

'What d'you mean whatever I say? You be careful my lad else you'll be getting me upset in another minute. Strike me blind I don't for the life of me know why I'm talking to you. But I lie awake at night moithering about that lass. Have you ever lain awake at night?'

'No Mr Raunce.'

'Don't. It's not worth it. Tell me something. D'you shave?'

The boy's left hand went to his chin.

'Not yet I don't.'

'Then put it out of mind, she wouldn't think of you Kate might now. She's different. What say we go to their room to-morrow eh?'

'You wouldn't dare.'

'I wouldn't dare! Who d'you take me for? Let me tell you there was many an occasion I went up to Mamselle's boudoir to give her a long bongjour before she went back to France.'

'That's different,' the boy said and said under his breath, 'oh Christ help me.'

'What d'you mean that's different? They're all made the same aren't they an' that means they're built different from you and me doesn't it? What are you gettin' at talking so soft?'

'Then why ask me then?'

'Because you're sweet on 'er, that's why,' Raunce said in a sort of shout. 'Holy Moses I don't know why I allow myself to get put out,' he went on calmer. 'But there's a certain way you have of looking down that dam delicate snotty nose you sniff with that gets my goat. Gets my goat see?' he added in rising tones.

'Yes Mr Raunce.'

'That's all right then. Don't pay attention to uncle, at least not on every occasion. No you're going the wrong way about it with that toast rack,' he said as helpful as you please. 'Hand over and I'll show you.' And he proceeded to demonstrate.

Meantime Mrs Tennant and her daughter-in-law were making their way as usual to the ruined temple.

'Violet,' she said, 'Mrs Manton, poor Mother's old friend, has asked me to stay with her at Belchester on my way over.'

'Yes dear.'

'I thought I might. It would be a change.'

'Yes dear.'

'When did you say Jack was definitely getting his leave? The twenty-first isn't it? Well if I crossed over on the eighteenth that would give me three days with Hermione at Belchester before coming up to London. You wouldn't mind just forty-eight hours down here alone?'

Every part of the young woman's body except her Adam's apple was crying out the one word Dermot. She could not trust herself to speak.

'Because if you did,' Mrs Tennant went on in a doubtful voice, 'I could visit Hermione after Jack had gone back to his unit. Because I expect you will be staying on in London for a few days.'

'Don't you bother about little me,' Mrs Jack brought out at last 'I shall be all right.'

'Are you sure? Really I feel I would rather get away from this place for a bit. The servants are being so truly beastly. And then there was my lovely cluster ring Jack's Aunt Emily gave me. D'you know I haven't had a word of sympathy yet from one of them about it.'

'Darling it is a shame,' Mrs Jack said. 'Badger come here. Come here when I tell you.'

'I know it's an absurd thing to expect,' Mrs Tennant went on looking up into the sky, 'but Eldon with all his faults always had a word of comfort when there was a disaster. Oh isn't it really too dreadful? Violet dear what d'you think?'

'I think it'll turn up. I know they haven't found anything in your bedroom but it can't simply have disappeared.'

'That's why I think if I went away somehow the luck might change,' Mrs Tennant said. 'I know there's a voice tells me the minute I turn my back they'll find my ring.'

'But Raunce is a bit of a wet rag isn't he?' her daughter-in-law remarked.

'Wet blanket you mean,' Mrs Tennant said. 'Oh well what can you expect with servants nowadays.' She spoke much more cheerfully. 'Then that's settled,' she went on, 'I'll go over a day or two ahead and we'll all meet in London to try and give the dear boy a good time. But talking of Raunce,' she went on and Mrs Jack could have had no suspicion of what was coming, 'he brought me his book this morning. You know I hardly ever look at it but well this was the first time he'd presented the thing himself and I don't know why, I suppose it's the war, but four pounds seven and six for a new arm to the map in the study why I could hardly believe my eyes. Why darling whatever's the matter?' Because Mrs Jack was leaning helpless against a tree with her face averted.

'Nothing,' she murmured weak voiced.

Mrs Tennant asked herself under her breath if the child was going to have another baby, and counted up the months from when the darling had seen her husband last.

'Sit down. No it's damp. Lean on my arm,' she said, and then her lips shaped March April May.

'I shall be all right in a minute.'

'I should never have dragged you out like this you poor child,' Mrs Tennant said. 'You should have said you didn't feel quite the thing.'

'What did he say?' Mrs Jack enquired as though in spite of herself.

'What did who say? Here sit here. At least it's dry.'

'That man Raunce,' the younger woman answered.

'My dear really I shall always repeat what you've just asked as the most wonderful example of self possession that's ever come my way. I must say your generation's too extraordinary. Here you are you poor child nearly in a faint and yet you remember I was talking about the compass arm over the map in the study. Lean back against me now. And keep your head down.'

Her daughter-in-law made a great effort.

'Well you wouldn't want me to go on about my silly old tummy, would you?' she asked in stronger tones.

'Why my darling,' Mrs Tennant exclaimed in what was almost a fruity voice, obviously visualizing a third grandchild. 'Why darling . . .'

'No, it isn't that,' Mrs Jack said and the searing rage, which that very moment swept over her as she realized, showed in how loudly she spoke. 'I expect it's something I had for lunch,' she added subsiding, guilty.

'I'll speak to Mrs Welch.'

'Oh no don't, please don't,' her daughter-in-law implored. Mrs Tennant said no more but she had made up her mind. The pots and pans were not being kept clean. That was all, or was it?

Raunce also became the subject in Mrs Tennant's bedroom. Miss Burch had not stayed long. When they were alone, turning the place upside down, Edith tried without success to get Kate to talk. They took the covers off all the armchairs, removed every rug and stripped the bed but to each comment Edith made such as 'well it's not here,' or 'I can't see it love can you?' Kate made answer with a silence that might have begun to work on Edith. For at last this girl said,

'D'you think I did ought to have told Mr Raunce about that waterglass?'

'Ah you're a deep one you are,' Kate immediately replied.

'I'm not and I don't know what you're after,' Edith protested beating a monogrammed pillow edged with lace between the palms of her two hands. But Kate made no reply and Edith apparently did not want to leave the matter for she tried again.

'When all's said and done love it's not as if Albert was suspected. That's just Mr Raunce's way,' she said.

'What makes you give him a Mr?' Kate asked.

'Why he's got the position now surely?'

'But he's no different to what he was,' Kate objected.

'According to one way of takin' it he's not,' Edith said, 'but whichever way we regard him he sees himself the butler.'

'O.K. if that's how you look at it.'

'Now Kate what's come over you? You wouldn't wish to spite him surely?'

'Listen,' Kate said, 'it don't matter to me what he thinks we think. All he'll be to me is Charley same as he always has been.'

'All right,' said Edith, 'I'll call him Charley and drop the mister.'

'And blush right in 'is face?'

'Kate Armstrong I'm surprised.'

'You can be surprised all right. I should worry. No I'm disappointed in you Edie, I am that.'

They stood on either side of the bed looking at each other.

'Then you do think I should never have kept silent. What you say is I should have talked up at the first go off when Mrs Welch came in at teatime?' Edith spoke as though she had been running but Kate only smiled. Kate said,

'I wouldn't play the innocent if I was you, not with me. It don't come off and that's a fact.'

'Then what you're gettin' at, without you're having what it takes to tell, what you're tryin' to say is you think I'm after 'im when he's something to you? Is that right?'

'Christ 'e's nothing to me. Charley Raunce? I'd sooner be dead.'

'I'll bet you'd sooner be dead.'

'What d'you insinuate by that Edie? I don't have to tell you you can go so far and no farther where I'm concerned thank you.'

'All right then I'll learn you something,' Edith said and she panted and panted. 'I love Charley Raunce I love 'im I love 'im so there. I could open the veins of my right arm for that man,' she said, turned her back on Kate, walked out and left her.

'You needn't have told me. I knew, don't worry,' Kate said to the now empty room, but with a sort of satisfaction as it seemed in pain.

*

On the 18th Mrs Tennant left for England and Belchester. That same evening Captain Davenport dined at the Castle alone with Mrs Jack who had instructed Raunce that he need not wait up to see the Captain out.

There was nothing unusual in this to draw comment, and next morning Edith was rubbing her face, yawning like a child when it was time to call the lady. She gently knocked. She got no reply but then she never did. When she went in after knocking a second time the curtains which Miss Burch had already drawn back in the passage outside let sufficient light for Edith to see her way across the room. But she went soft, cautious so as not to stumble against the gold oar that stood out from the bed. Then she drew those curtains. She folded the shutters back into the wall. And Edith looked out on the morning, the soft bright morning that struck her dazzled dazzling eyes.

A movement over in the bed attracted her attention. She turned slow. She saw a quick stir beside the curls under which Mrs Jack's head lay asleep, she caught sight of someone else's hair as well, and it was retreating beneath silk sheets. A man. Her heart hammered fit to burst her veins. She gave a little gasp.

Then the dark head was altogether gone. But there were two humps of body, turf over graves under those pink bedclothes. And it was at this moment Mrs Jack jumped as if she had been pinched. Not properly awake she sat straight up. She was nude. Then no doubt remembering she said very quick, 'Oh Edith it's you it's quite all right I'll ring.' On which she must have recognized that she was naked With a sort of cry and crossing her lovely arms over that great brilliant upper part of her on which, wayward, were two dark upraised dry wounds shaking on her, she also slid entirely underneath.

When Edith came to herself she found she was outside in the Long Passage, that bedroom door shut after her and with Miss Burch halted staring at her face. She said, all come over faint,

'I don't know how I was able to find me way out.'

'How d'you mean Edith?'

'An' if I'd been a'carryin' her early tea I'd 'a' dropped it.'

'And so you might dashing into me as you did.'

'In there,' Edith added. She seemed at her last gasp.

'In where?' Miss Burch asked grim.

For two moments Edith struggled to get breath.

'A man,' she said at last.

'God save us a man,' Miss Burch muttered, knocked and went straight through, shutting the door after. Edith leant against the table, the one that had naked cupids inlaid with precious woods on its top. She bent her head. She seemed afraid she might be sick. But when Miss Burch came out again as she did at once Edith drew herself straight to hear the verdict.

' 'E's puttin' 'is shirt on,' was all Miss Burch said, shocked into dropping her aitches. Then she added as though truly broken-hearted,

'Come on away my girl. Let 'im get off h'out.'

Edith made no move, stayed gazing at her.

'Come will you,' Miss Burch repeated gentle, 'this is no place for us my dear,' she said drawing a hand across her mouth.

At that Edith took to her heels and ran. She ran. She went straight up the back stairs. And along their passage into the deep room she shared with Kate. This girl was doing her hair before she went down to breakfast. She was at variance with Edith yet, which may have been why she did not turn round at first. But Edith's panting made her look.

'Why whatever . . .?' she began.

'There 'e was,' Edith broke out between gasps, 'I seen the hair of 'is 'ead, large as life, you could 'a' knocked me down with a leaf,' she said.

'The what?' cried Kate arrested.

'A man,' Edith said.

'A I.R.A. man?' Kate asked, voice rising.

'The Captain,' Edith replied calmer, put a hand to her throat and swallowed. With obviously a great leap of her mind Kate got there.

'In your young lady's bed. Oh goody,' she shouted, at which both began to giggle helpless. 'Large as life,' one said, the other repeated, then the two of them giggled again. 'In her bed,' one said, the other echoed, and both shouted with laughter. 'All night?' shrieked Kate, and it seemed she forgot she had been at odds with Edith about Charley Raunce. 'All night,' Edith screamed back. Holding their sides they crowed with laughter.

'And 've you told old Mother Burch?' Kate asked when both were quieter.

'She seen him too,' Edith answered, as she dabbed the heel of her right hand at her eyes where these had been running.

'She did?' Kate echoed.

'She went in,' Edith called out with a high yell then fell back on the eiderdown and howled she laughed so much, faintly kicking with her legs.

Kate began to gasp as if she could not get enough air to speak.

'She went in?' she asked.

'And d'you know – what she said?' Edith said choking.

'What's that?'

'When she come out,' Edith went on by fits and starts, 'oh you'll never guess – no love you could never – oh I shall die – Katie it hurts my side – d'you know what she said?' – and by this time Kate as she stood in front of her was doubled up hands on knees in such shrieks that she was dribbling – 'she said' – and Edith fought to get the words out – 'oh she said why 'e's puttin' 'is shirt on.' At this Kate collapsed, fell back. Both girls howled. Between screeches Kate managed to get out, 'Take care I'll wet myself.' Edith calmed at once.

'Hush dear someone'll hear.'

'Just puttin' 'is shirt on,' Kate quoted sobering.

'That's what she said,' Edith answered.

'Well Edie I'd've given a week's wages to be there I would really. What did you do?' And at this Edith went into a long description of each thought she had and every step she took after so gently knocking on that bedroom.

'But then who was it dear?' Kate asked at last.

'Oh I never saw his face only the top of his head like I told you where he was going thin. It was the Captain make no mistake.'

They giggled a bit more at this then Kate wanted to know if she had not asked old Aggie Burch.

'Hush Kate she'll hear,' Edith said, 'but if you'd seen her face you could never've questioned her.'

'Look I'll just sluice some cold water over me and then I'll get down to the 'all,' Kate answered. 'I wouldn't miss the look she'll be wearin' for nothing in the world, not for a 'ug from an old ugly bastard of a tinker even,' she said.

'An old ugly what? Why Kate Armstrong whatever are you saying?'

'Forget it dearie. There,' she said throwing her towel down, 'I'm off.' And Edith had to rush so as not to be left out below. But where Kate made straight to the servants' hall Edith struck right-handed for the pantry. She was in luck, Raunce was there yet. The moment she saw him she seemed overjoyed. With for her an altogether extraordinary animation she fairly danced up. He stood as though embarrassed, fumbling his nose, squinting.

'Why Charley,' she laughed, 'what d'you know?'

'Yes,' he said solemn.

'Well then isn't this a knock out?' she asked. 'An' it happened to me,' she added. 'After all these years.'

'Now steady on lass there's my lad Bert to consider.'

'Bert?' she asked. 'Why 'e's getting our breakfast or should be at this hour. Why what about him?'

'That lad ain't of an age yet,' Mr Raunce replied but he spoke as though in apology. She quietened down, stopped rocking backwards and forwards and ceased almost pushing her flushed face into his.

'Well aren't you glad?' she went on after a minute, 'for me I mean,' she mocked.

'I can't make you out at all,' he answered.

'Why there's all those stories you've had, openin' this door and seeing that when you were in a place in Dorset and lookin' through the bathroom window down in Wales an' suchlike oh I've heard you or Kate has and now it's come to me. Right a'bed they was next to one another. Stuff that in your old smelly pipe and smoke it.' She began once more to force her body on his notice, getting right up to him then away again, as though pretending to dance. Then she turned herself completely round in front of his very eyes. He seemed ill at ease.

'But how would you know it was me?' she asked suddenly stopping.

'Miss Burch,' he replied. 'It come as a big surprise. I didn't guess she'd have the sense of right and wrong to acquaint me. But I shouldn't pay attention to this mess up if I was you.'

'What d'you mean pay no attention?' she asked and she spoke angry.

'What they see fit to do is no concern of our own,' he said still watching her as if ashamed and surprisingly he yawned.

'You mean you're going to make nothing of it just because I

found 'em? The Captain in Mrs Jack's bed?' She blushed, with anger perhaps. 'You're going to try and take that from me?'

'Take it from you how's that?' he asked.

'Take it away from me,' she repeated and her eyes filled beautifully with tears.

'Honey,' he said calling her this for the first time, 'you don't want to go and talk, see, or you'll likely lose your place?'

'Lose my place?' she echoed, 'I should worry in this lousy hole.'

'Without a reference,' he added, 'you mark what I say.'

'I should worry,' she repeated and for the moment looked as if she might burst out crying. He put on a grin. He looked appealing and upset.

'What they do is no concern of us,' he said again. 'And there's the National bloody Service Officer waitin' for you over on the other side.'

'Don't you swear at me of all people,' she answered. Turning on her heel she actually ran out in the direction of the servants' hall.

Breakfast that morning took place at first in utter silence. Even Kate looked down her nose. Raunce fidgeted and often glanced quickly at Edith who was hurried in everything she did. But as for Miss Burch she could not eat anything at all hardly. Her hand shook so she spilled the tea from out her cup. Only Paddy behaved as usual, concentrated on his food.

Before this meal was done Miss Burch hastened out by the scullery door. She passed through to the kitchen. But Mrs Welch sat adamant with little Albert and barely looked round to return Agatha's dark good morning. So Miss Burch went off to her room to be alone.

Meantime Charley spoke up in the hall. 'There's someone got to take the breakfast tray,' he said.

'Oh I couldn't,' Edith said at once, 'I'd spill it on that bed.' It was for her to answer because it was her duty each morning.

'There'll need be two trays,' Kate put in sly.

'There will not,' Raunce replied his eyes on Bert, 'the other party left the Castle first thing by pedal bicycle,' he said.

'The Captain?' Bert asked, 'I seen 'im as I was doin' the brass.' It was probably instinct made the lad continue as he did. 'What room did he occupy then?' he enquired.

'Ah you may well ask boy,' Raunce answered solemn. At that Edith broke out with, 'I'm surprised at you Mr Raunce I am really, that you should make a mystery out of nothing.' She seemed furious and Kate watched avidly. 'Listen Bert,' Edith went on, 'the Captain 'e spent the night in my lady's bed next 'er, an' she was nude I saw, only they overslept the two of them as I know from when I went to open the room in the morning. And don't you let anyone tell you different because it was me found it and called Aggie Burch so there.'

'I'll bet they overslept,' Kate announced while Raunce's lad gaped at Edith. Raunce could not let this pass.

'That's enough thank you my gel,' he said, 'I'll thank you...' he was going on when a great braying laugh started out of the lamp-man. It swelled. It filled the room. Raunce said, 'Look what you've done,' and in his turn began to laugh. Kate joined in. So at last did Edith. These two girls did not giggle this time, they both deeply laughed. Only Bert was left as if embarrassed, twisting a fork over and over on the table.

'Why?' Raunce threw out at the first pause and in Nanny Swift's falsetto. 'All night? And in the same bed as well? Oh dear.'

'And I hope she enjoyed it there,' Kate pronounced, become serious.

'Now Kate!' Edith said starting to blush. Raunce watched.

'I got nothing against 'er,' Kate went on. 'She's all right she is. Because it's not natural for a married woman with 'er 'usband away at the war. Not that Mr Jack ever was...' but at this Raunce interrupted loud.

'Now then,' he said, 'what d'you know about bein' a married woman?'

'Not that 'e ever was much to go on with,' Kate finished dogged.

'You can say what you please,' Edith replied scarlet and they could all see that she was truly angry still. 'But 'e tried to get me in a dark corner one morning just the same,' she said.

' 'E didn't,' Raunce broke out.

'Oh there's no call for you to fash yourself Mr Raunce, there was no harm done nor offence taken if you're so keen to learn.'

'I'm sure it's no concern of mine,' he said and seemed on tenterhooks.

'Now you mention it I wouldn't say he'd never made a grab at me,' Kate brought out in a small voice. With great calmness Raunce commented,

'You surprise me.'

'You don't like to say he'd never but you never have said he did,' Edith cried and seemed to accuse.

'O.K. dear O K. I know you found Mrs Jack and the Captain.'

'Of course I found 'em,' Edith remarked subsiding.

'Well now who's going to take her tray?' Raunce asked. 'Tell you what, I will.'

'But that would give 'er the idea you thought the Captain was up there yet,' Edith objected.

'Go on then I'll take the old tray,' Kate offered.

'Then she'll think I'm on to what she was doing last night,' said Edith.

'Well so she must if you did discover 'em.'

'All right dear I needs must then even if I should drop it,' Edith announced as she got up from table. She stood there and looked full at Raunce.

'It's not the job for a man, not this morning,' she said to him and went out.

'What d'you make of that Paddy?' Kate enquired but Raunce told her to shut her mouth with such sudden violence that she dropped her gimlet eyes. Then he went out to get the tray ready for Edith.

So it was left to Edith to carry up that breakfast which she did as though nothing had occurred. She found the mistress sitting in bed wearing her best nightdress and bedjacket. She did not look at Edith but said at once, collected,

'I'm going over to England by the night boat. Would you tell Raunce to get on the phone and reserve a cabin if he can? And ask the Nanny if she would come along to see me now?'

'To-day Madam?'

'Yes to-night I think. Not the day after to-morrow any longer. I've changed my plans.'

'Very good Madam.'

As Edith came into the passage outside and shut the door she found Miss Burch waiting white-lipped. This woman asked almost under her breath,

'Were you all right dear?'

'I was O.K.,' Edith whispered back. And then, 'She's leavin' to-night instead.'

'With him d'you wonder?'

'Oh no,' Edith replied serious, 'it stands out a mile she can't bring herself to face me. That's why.'

'There was nothing between the Captain and you was there my girl?'

'Are you crazy?' Edith broke out loud. Hearing this from inside the room Mrs Jack cowered, put a trembling hand over her lips, and pushed the tray to one side. 'Can you beat that?' Edith asked violent.

'Hush dear,' Miss Burch whispered. 'Very well then. We'll never mention what you saw again. You see I trust you. Never, you understand me?'

'Yes Miss Burch,' Edith replied. From her tone she was calming down. But as she went off to find the nanny she said to herself over and over, 'now would you believe it?' By the time she had got to the nursery she was repeating way down her throat, 'that's how they are at their age, they go funny.' And she gave Miss Swift the message as though to an enemy.

'This very moment?' this woman asked frantic.

'That's what she said.'

'Of all the times? And in the morning too? Then you'll oblige me by watching 'em till I'm back or they'll go dropping each other out to their deaths.'

While the nanny patted her hair, wiped her face with a handkerchief and then, after hesitating, was gone, Edith stood slack at one of the high windows and did not seem to see those bluebells already coming up between wind-stunted beeches which grew out of the Grove onto that part of the lawn till their tops were level with her eyes. Also there was a rainbow from the sun on a shower blowing in from the sea but you could safely say she took no notice. Nor paid heed to the shrieks next door of two little girls at a game.

Miss Swift had been Mrs Jack's nanny when this lady was a tiny tot so she addressed her as Miss Violet. When told of the journey which had been put forward Miss Swift did not beat about the bush. She said roundly there was one thing poor old nanny felt to the heart and that was forgetfulness. For this day was to have been her afternoon out. If Miss Violet was going who was there left to look after the children when nobody cared? Or would silly old nanny have to go to the wall?

'How could you when I'm not feeling well?' was Mrs Jack's answer, delivered in a little girl's whining voice and she added, 'Edith can look after them perfectly.'

'Then who's to pack for you? Not me with my back Miss Violet.'

'I'd never thought. But if I asked Agatha nicely?'

'You're pale Miss Violet, you want a pill,' was Miss Swift's answer.

'Want a pill?' and the young woman spoke sharp now as if to ask what was behind this.

'When you're that colour it means you're constipated. Even if you don't know I should who cared for you from the start. Right pale. You lie there. I won't be a minute.'

Mrs Jack possibly knew better than to argue. 'Tell Agatha I want her then,' was all she said.

Miss Swift came across Miss Burch at once. Agatha might almost have been said to be on guard in that Long Passage.

'She wants you in there,' Miss Swift told her barely civil.

'Me?' Miss Burch enquired, 'what for?'

'I couldn't say,' Miss Swift replied, 'I don't meddle in other's business.'

'Well I'm not going,' Miss Burch announced. 'Not again. Wild horses couldn't.'

'What's come over you?' Miss Swift asked coming to a halt some distance up the passage. 'First I get impertinence from one of your girls which I don't pay attention to because I know how it is at their age always worriting over men and now you cast Miss Violet in my face. What's this?'

'I don't mind what you tell her you can please yourself but I'm not going in,' and Miss Burch added under her breath, 'And I could tell you something about your lily would make you say poor me but I won't.'

'That's nice I must say,' Miss Swift in her innocence replied. 'You draw your monthly wage yet you're gettin' like your girls, you want this and that besides.'

'You can leave my girls out of your conversation thanking you Miss Swift. They have more to put up with than you'll ever learn I hope.'

'Now you're being nothing but ridiculous. Poor nanny,' Miss Swift added and her face seemed to wrinkle as though about to cast a skin.

'No thank you,' Miss Burch said inconsequent and turned her back.

The nanny appeared to take hold of herself. She started on her way once more. 'I don't know I'm sure,' she said over her shoulder, making off to the medicine cupboard. She left Miss Burch outside that bedroom door but when she was back with a glass of water and a flat box in her hands, she found Miss Burch inside saying, 'yes Madam, no Madam,' at the side of the bed after all, plainly ill at ease yet taking instructions about what and about what not to pack.

But Agatha did not seem able to keep her eyes from those other pillows on Mrs Jack's double bed. These had been well beaten and the clothes were pulled up smooth over where that man's body must have lain yet she stared on and off. It must have been she could not help herself. Until the young lady told her to go as soon as she had so to speak been reinforced by Miss Swift's return. And Agatha left with a stiff back Once she was gone,

'Now take a sip and swallow it right down,' the nanny said as she bustled. Then added, 'It's liver that's what it is dear. They won't trouble to give themselves a walk to loosen the bowels. They get fat on your food and cups of tea and with leaning on their brooms.'

'Who do?' Mrs Jack asked. She was probably unsure of everything and everyone.

'Why those that's paid to keep the Castle fit for us to live in,' the nanny replied.

'Oh I'm tired. Your little girl's not slept well,' Mrs Jack broke out.

'Now isn't that a shame? You just lie back and let that pill do its duty. I'll tell your angels you'll be wanting them around midday. You go on as your old nanny says and you'll have clear cheeks for the young man.'

On this she left. The lady fell back as though exhausted. But her breakfast tray was bare. She must have found strength in between to eat it all.

'Well I've got to take those little draggers out this afternoon,' Edith announced at dinner the same day. 'It's not fair I tell you.'

'Hey?' Raunce asked at his most serious, 'and you who has

always made a point they were your favourites?'

'How's the work goin' to be finished? I'll ask you that,' she said quoting Miss Burch.

'You're the one to talk when you're not going to do none,' Kate put in.

'There'll be all the more for me tomorrer then,' was Edith's answer. 'You're not a girl to take on another's share and there's no reason why you should.'

'Now then that's plenty,' Miss Burch appealed to both.

'But there's a thing I won't do,' Edith went on in a lower tone, obstinately. 'Mrs Welch's Albert. Now I won't take 'im with them.'

'Be quiet both of you please. Oh my poor head. I've got a sick headache,' Miss Burch explained to Charley Raunce at which Kate muttered, 'I wasn't sayin' nothin'.'

'Look,' Charley announced at Edith, 'if you choose I'll come along.'

'Well that's a real step forward,' Miss Burch said looking kindly. Then she added as though unable to help herself, 'It should do you a mort of good.'

In spite of the differences grown fast as mushrooms and their bad temper on this day of days, Kate and Edith glanced at each other, a waste of giggling beginning behind their eyes.

'A turn in the air might be just what your sick headache needs,' he offered still at his most courteous to Miss Burch.

'Me?' she asked, 'and with all the packin' still to be done? A aspirin is all I shall get of fresh air this afternoon.'

'Well Edith could see to that while you took the children out,' Kate said. Her little eyes sparkled.

'Why you could never expect Miss Burch to go trail after them children when she feels the way she does, with God knows what Mrs Welch's kid will get up to,' Raunce said. 'About half past two then,' he went on to Edith, speaking rather fast. 'I'll be in my room.'

Kate started to choke, Edith to blush. Miss Burch did not appear to notice.

'I think I'll go lie down for ten minutes,' she informed those present. And Edith got out of Kate's sight by rising to follow her to ask if she would care for a cup of tea.

Outside, at a quarter to three, they both wore raincoats and Charley had his bowler hat. As the little girls raced about behind,

86

Charley bent down, picked up two peacock's feathers which he offered to Edith.

'Whatever should I do with those?' she asked low.

'You wore one the week of the funeral,' he replied.

'Not now,' she said. They walked on with a space between.

'What's happened to all those blessed birds anyway?' he asked in a tired voice.

'It's the rain,' she answered. 'They don't like wet.' There was a silence.

'Tell you where they'd be then,' he began again. 'Away in the stable back of Paddy's room.' She made no comment. 'Should we go in that direction?'

'Not now,' she said.

'If you liked I could find you some eggs? I know where they lay.'

She laughed. 'Oh no thanks all the same. That kind's no use,' and crossed her fingers in the raincoat pocket, against this lie perhaps.

'What kind then?' he asked.

'Oh I couldn't say,' she said.

'I get you,' he answered in a doubtful voice. Once more they both fell silent.

Meantime Kate had slipped out to the lampman's where he kept corn for his peacocks. Paddy was awake. He showed no surprise when she entered.

'I wasn't goin' to carry on when nobody else was workin',' she announced.

He sat where he was and grunted.

'Not your baby,' she said, wandering about to inspect this and that. She seemed familiar with the place. It was certainly not the first time she had been alone with him.

'What this old dump needs is a good scrub out,' she said, 'only you're too Irish to give it.'

He spoke then. He spoke in English and quite free although his accent was such you could take a file to it. But she must have understood.

'Not me,' she replied. 'What d'you take me for? You do your own chores for yourself thanks. I don't want none.'

He laughed. His mouth was fringed with great brown teeth. His light eyes shone through the grey hair over them.

'Look at you,' she said coming up slow, swinging her hips. 'Have you got no pride?'

He laughed again but sat quiet. She turned away saying, 'Where did you put it then?' She made a search amongst oddments overlaid with dust upon a thick shelf. He followed with his eyes and did not turn his head. As a result for a full minute one pupil was swivelled almost back of the nose he had on him whilst the other was nearly behind a temple but he grinned the while. Then she turned up a dog's comb of tinned iron. She blew on this to dust it.

Lifting the piece of broken mirror glass off a wall from between four nails which held it at the edges she said,

'Take a load of yourself while I do yer.'

Standing at the back of him she began to comb his head. She worked like a simple woman that rakes a beanfield and jerked his head back with each pull. As the hair on his forehead was lifted it uncovered a line of dirt, a tidemark, along where the laid beans of his hair started grey and black. He tilted the glass he held to watch.

'Heed yerself and the state you're in,' she said. 'Give over watchin' me.'

He muttered something. For once she could not have understood. 'Say that again,' she asked.

He spoke rapid for about thirty seconds after placing the bit of mirror between his knees. He turned to face her.

'Well that's your look out,' she answered when he was done. Kate's arms lay along her purple uniformed sides. He smelled of peat smoke and she of carbolic. She added in a softer voice, 'You want to find one of your Irish women as'll see to you.'

He put out a paw like to sugar cake.

'No you don't,' she cried sharp and dodged back. 'What's more if you can't sit there quiet as gold I'll get me gone. I've got my share to do back in the Castle.'

He muttered. He faced the way he had been, picked up the glass again.

'That's right,' she said, 'though lord knows this is good labour wasted,' and began on his head once more.

Then she started to talk almost as though to herself.

' 'E's out, out in the air for a walk Mr Charley Raunce is, the first time since nobody can remember. Ah but she's deep our Edith, deep as the lake there. "Will I take the little angels out bless their little white hearts, sweetheart come too, along for the stroll." And if you don't believe you've only to risk a peek outside. Takin' 'is death he is. Round by the doves at the back I'll lay they are Paddy, billing an' all the rest. What d'you say to that you Irishman? Or they're over by the water. But what've you been at with your glory since I done it for you last? 'Ere,' she said, 'clear the combings off for yourself,' she said handing the comb back to him, 'I never made out I'd free the strakes for you into the bargain.'

Once her hands were disengaged she put these up to reroll her curls but halted before she touched. Then she sniffed at her fingers.

'Christ,' she said, 'what we girls have to put up with.' Then she added, 'You might give us a break and wash it occasionally.'

He said something.

'You got nowhere you mean?' she replied. 'Well I don't wonder they won't let you be free with their sink I must say. You've only to look at you. But what's wrong with a clean bucket? When Charley's little Bert has a mind to 'is boiler the water's O.K.,' she said and took the comb back. This time she began about his right ear. 'I'll give you a roll just 'ere exactly like the Captain. Oh the Captain,' and she laughed.

Paddy's enormous head began to show signs of order with parts of the tangle, which might have been laid by hail, starting to stand once more wildly on its own on his black beanfield of hair after a ground frost.

'But lord,' she remarked, 'whatever would my mother say to you Tarzan?'

'Look,' she announced, 'I'm fed up. You take hold and finish,' she told him handing back that comb.

'I'm fed up with you,' Mrs Welch said to her Albert at this precise moment as she sat him down at the kitchen table. 'So she wouldn't take you eh? Expect me to believe that eh?' She watched the boy with what appeared to be disfavour.

'That's what she said'm.'

'What did she say then?'

'When she come in the nursery I was like you said. I 'ad my coat zipped up and me 'at in me pocket. "No," she said, "not you Albert my little man, you go down in the kitchen," she says an' she give me a bit of toffee out of a bag.'

'Where is it?'

'I've ate it.'

'Is it in your pocket this minute along with your hat?'

'No'm.'

'Let me see if you're tellin' lies.' And Mrs Welch clambered to her feet, leaned right over that table. She felt in his coat.

'Is this it?' she asked bringing the thing out, a toffee in a screw of paper. She gingerly lowered herself back while she held this sweet out at arm's length, resting her bare arm along the table top. He made no reply.

'You wouldn't lie to me would yer?' she asked.

'No'm.'

'Then is this what she give you?'

He kept silent.

'You see what I'm goin' to do with this,' she went on, and unwrapped the sweet. Then she spat on it and threw the toffee into a can of ashes by the range. 'Now listen,' she continued, 'if ever I catch you taking what she offers I'll tan the 'ide right off you d'you h'understand?'

'Yes'm.'

'For why? Because she's a nasty little piece that considers we're not good enough for 'er, and very likely a thief into the bargain. With her precious Miss Moira this and little Miss Evelyn that. Never again no more. Right?'

'Yes'm.'

'And what are you goin' to do with yerself this afternoon of springtime that you can't go h'out with the others? I'll tell you. You're goin' to set to work my lad.'

The boy who had been gazing at the floor suddenly stared at her sharp.

'Yes,' she said, 'that comes as a bit of a surprise d'ain't it? Never you mind. You got to start some day. You won't always be runnin' around with gentry and their stuck-up maids. Now you see that saucepan, the one which's last on the left?'

He looked reluctant at three burnished rows hanging on the dresser, on nails through the holes in their steel handles.

'That's right,' she went on, 'the last on the left. You'll take that down so help me and you'll make a start scourin'. The young leddy was took faint. Took faint,' she repeated giving a short laugh as Kate had done. 'Yes. One time she was out with Mrs Tennant. "It's the pots and pans," Mrs T. says to me after. "You'll oblige me by casting a look on them Madam," I said. "I can't help it Mrs Welch," she says, "I'm certain there was something in that sole or its sauce." Sauce indeed. But she never listened. So now you're going to make a start scourin' them saucepans. Even if you bring all the tin off and they get copper poison. Get on then.'

The boy got up slow.

'And don't you go break that thread I've 'ad put through the handles,' she cried frantic all of a sudden. 'You'll find where it's tied there by the side. I'm gettin' me chains and a padlock,' she explained grim as grim.

Kate had left the comb stuck at an angle in Paddy's head. The lampman sat where he was on a corn bin while she wandered round again. She came up to that glass division and looked through.

'Can a person eat them eggs?' she asked. He answered excitely.

'That's all right,' she said. 'No need to get worked up. I only asked didn't I?'

He muttered something.

'Oh all right I know you set great store by the birds,' she replied, 'an' if you took one half the trouble over yourself as you do with their layin' why you'd be a different person altogether,' she explained.

He got up, made after her. 'No,' she said, 'no,' but she did not move as he came grinning. He reached round her middle and drank her in a kiss like a man home after a journey. He pressed her back against the glass that fronted that huge cabinet. Through the opening behind could be seen those peacocks getting up with a sort of chittering as though alarmed. She sank into him as her knees gave way yet both of them stayed decent.

Out in the demesne Raunce said to Edith,

'I got to sit me down.'

'You got to sit down?' she echoed as he looked dull about him.

'I've come over queer,' he said. Indeed his face was now the colour of the pantry boy Albert's.

'Why you're not goin' to faint right off like I did surely,' she exclaimed and clucked with concern. 'Sit yourself on this stone,' she said, 'it's dry for one thing.'

He sat. He put his new terrible face into his hands. They stayed silent. The two children came up, stood and watched him.

'Run along,' she told them gentle. 'Go find Michael.'

When they were alone Raunce spoke. 'It must be the air,' he said.

She stood awkward at his side as though she could not think what to do. Then she said, 'If we were inside I could fetch you a cup of tea.' She talked soft with concern. He groaned.

'It's me dyspepsia,' he said. 'It's coming away in the air 'as done it.'

'But you do go out,' she replied low, 'I saw you when we were by the doves that dinner time.'

'That was only for a minute,' was his answer. 'But this long stretch...' and he ended his sentence with a groan. By and by however he grew better while she stood helpless at his bowed shoulders. After a time he got up. Then they summoned the little girls, tenderly made their way back to the Castle.

'You should take more care,' she kept on repeating.

It was some days later they sat in the servants' hall talking with dread of the I R A. They were on their own now, with the lady and her daughter still over in England, and the feeling they had was that they stood in worse danger than ever.

Kate asked the lampman if he had heard any rumours. Paddy gabbled an answer. As he did so he did not meet their eyes in this low room of antlered heads along the walls, his back to the sideboard with red swans.

Raunce's neck was tied up in a white silk scarf of Mr Jack's. He seemed to turn his head with difficulty to ask Kate what the Irishman had said.

'He says not to believe all you're told.' 'I don't,' Raunce put in at once. 'And that they're not so busy by half as what they was,' Kate ended.

Edith anxiously regarded her Charley.

'I should hope not indeed,' Miss Burch informed the company. 'Though I will say for Mrs Welch she was dead right when she forbade her girls passing the time of day with those tradesmen. Just in case,' she added.

'And what about their afternoons off?' Mr Raunce enquired.

'What I always insist is that if you can't trust your girls,' Miss Burch replied, 'you might as soon give in your notice and go find yourself another place.' She turned to Edith. 'Now you never speak to none of the natives when you get outside?'

'Oh no Miss Burch,' they both replied, mum about Patrick with his fine set of teeth.

'That's right,' Raunce told them. 'You can't be too careful. There's a war on,' he said.

'Are you in a draught?' Edith asked him tenderly. 'You don't want to take risks.' And Kate looked as though she might start a giggle any minute.

'There is a draught,' Raunce answered grave. 'There's a draught in every corner of this room which is a danger to sit in.'

'Move over to the other side then,' Miss Burch suggested.

'Thank you,' he said, 'but it's the same whichever side you are. I don't know,' he went on, 'but with them away now I feel responsible.'

'And what about the Jerries?' Kate put in suddenly. 'What if they come over tell me that?'

'Kate Armstrong,' Edith cried, 'why I asked you that selfsame question not so long since and you said they were ordinary working folk same as us so wouldn't offer no incivilities.'

'And I'm not saying they would,' Kate answered, 'not that sort and kind. But it might go hard for a young girl in the first week perhaps.'

'Mercy on us you don't want to talk like that,' Miss Burch said. 'You think of nothing but men, there's the trouble. Though if it did happen it would naturally be the same for the older women. They're famished like a lion out in the desert them fighting men,' she announced.

'For land's sake,' Edith began but Paddy started to mouth something. It was so seldom he spoke at meals that all listened.

'What's he say?' Raunce asked when the lampman was done.

'He reckons the I R.A. would see to the Jerries,' Kate translated.

'Holy smoke but he'll be getting me annoyed in a minute. First he says there aren't none then 'e pretends they can sort out a panzer division. What with? Bows and arrows?'

Paddy muttered a bit.

'He says,' and Kate gave a laugh, 'they got more'n pikes like those Home Guard over at home.'

'If you can snigger at that you would laugh over anything my gel,'

Raunce announced with signs of temper. 'Why you've only to go down in Kinalty and see yourself. Every other house burned right out. Once they got started they'd be so occupied fightin' each other they'd never notice Jerry was in the hamlet even.'

Paddy gave a great braying laugh.

'Laugh?' Raunce shouted and sprang up. All except for Miss Burch wilted and his lad's jaw dropped. 'You would would you?' he went on but the lampman had returned to wooden silence and Raunce subsided back into his seat again. 'Well,' he went on, 'if it should ever come to it there's guns and ammo in the gunroom.'

Edith gave a cry and Kate looked serious. But Miss Burch displayed impatience.

'Whatever's come over you?' she asked. 'You're never thinking you could knock down one of the Mark something tanks as you would a rabbit with one of those shot guns they've got locked up here,' she said.

'What I had in mind was a cartridge each for you ladies,' he replied in a low voice. Utterly serious he was.

'Would you spare one for Mrs Welch?' Miss Burch enquired tart and Kate let out a yell of laughter. Edith laughed also and after a minute Raunce himself joined in shamefaced. Paddy stayed impassive.

'You want to go delicate you know,' Miss Burch went on, 'you've no game licence.'

'You mean you wouldn't hesitate...?' Edith began to ask him seriously but Charley interrupted her.

'I'd like to see 'em up in Dublin issue a permit over Mrs Welch as they do with the salmon trout,' he said to Miss Burch. At this they all laughed once more when Kate broke in with,

'Speakin' for myself I'd rather have the Jerry.'

'Under 'er bed,' Raunce made comment and even Miss Burch tee-hee'd wholehearted.

'There's the telephone,' Raunce announced. Bert got up to answer it away in the pantry.

Miss Burch fixed a stern eye on Kate so much as to say a minute or so ago just now you were about to be actually coarse.

'Well I don't aim to be shot dead. On no account I don't,' the girl explained.

'There's worse things than death my girl,' Miss Burch repeated.

'As anyone can tell you who remembers the last war.'

'I saw in the papers they behave themselves most correct towards the French people,' Edith said, still looking at Charley.

'What can you believe in these Irish rags?' Raunce asked.

'Well, there's one thing,' Miss Burch told him, 'they're neutral enough, they print what both sides say against one another.'

'Ah,' said Raunce, 'that's nothing but propaganda these days. It's human nature you've got to keep count of. Why it stands to reason with an invadin' army...' he was going on as Edith watched him open eyed when Albert came back.

'It was a wire for you,' he said to Raunce.

'Where is it then?' this man asked.

'Well there ain't no telegram,' was the answer he got. 'They read it out over the phone.'

''Ow many times have I told you never to take nothin' over that instrument without you write it down,' Raunce demanded in rising tones. 'Why I remember once at a place I was in, that very thing occasioned the death of a certain Mrs Harris. There you are. Killed her it did as if she had been blown in smithereens with a shotgun.'

'Go on,' the boy said respectful.

'Don't give me no go ons,' Raunce almost shouted at him. 'D'you know what you're about?'

'Yes Mr Raunce.'

'All right then.' The authority Raunce seemed to have acquired since Mr Eldon's death must have impressed them all. Even Kate gave him earnest attention. 'Now,' he went on, 'take your time. Don't rush it. What did the thing say?'

'Staying on for a few days Tennant, Mr Raunce.'

'Ho,' said Raunce, 'stayin' on a few days eh? That would be Mrs Tennant then. Mrs Jack she signs herself different. Staying over eh? Leavin' us to face the music that's about the long and short of it.'

'D'you consider there's something likely to occur then?' Edith asked.

'I feel responsible,' he replied.

'For two pins I'd give in my notice,' Kate told them.

'How would you do that?' Edith enquired, 'when they aren't here?'

'Why I'd send it by post or I'd put it on a post card if I was in the mood,' the girl answered and there was a pause. 'I'm game if you are Edie,' Kate added, giving Edith a look that seemed highly inquisitive. But long before she could get an answer Charley was speaking, had so to speak thrown himself into a breach to stop the rot.

'Here,' he cried, 'what's all this, tell me that, what is it? I know the name it could be given, runnin' away, that's two words for it make no mistake. We're British aren't we? Turn tail and flee?' he asked in a loud voice. He glanced in menacing fashion at the lampman.

'Is it running away to get back to your own country to lend a hand?' Miss Burch enquired almost with amusement.

'And block the roads getting there?' Raunce asked.

'Why certainly,' she said, 'and block the roads, why not? If it's in the path of the enemy,' she said.

'But suppose they wished to evacuate the Governor General? Or the gold in the Bank of Ireland?' Raunce objected.

Paddy murmured something.

'There 'e goes again,' Raunce said and looked at Kate. 'What is it this time?'

'He says the Governor General is an Irishman an' would never go to England.'

'That's a bloody lie,' Raunce announced with finality. 'There's always been a Britisher in that job. Excuse me,' he added to Miss Burch, 'I seem to have forgot myself. Well what d'you know?' he went on. 'There's that telephone again.' Bert left the room. This time they kept uneasy silence till he returned.

'Well?' Charley asked the lad when he got back. He was handed a scrap of paper. He examined it. 'I can't read this,' he said.

'You should write down the messages neatly on a proper bit of paper,' Miss Burch told Albert. Raunce sat staring at what he held. 'There's times I despair of you my lad,' he moaned. Kate winked at Albert. 'Well come on, don't stand there dumb,' Charley went on, 'I can tell it's from Mrs Jack an' that's all.'

'Not returning for few days Violet Tennant,' the lad recited.

A silence fell over them once more. Then Kate saw fit to comment with what seemed like satisfaction,

'And that's the last we shall see or even 'ear of her if you ask me.'

'Why Kate,' Edith said, 'I never heard such a thing.'

'It was uncalled for,' Miss Burch pronounced, 'and what's more I don't wish another word spoken,' she added very grim. Silence fell yet again. At last Raunce broke the spell.

'Left all on our own,' he said with genuine emotion, seeming to ignore the others. 'How do you like that?'

Edith appealed to the lampman,

'But the Irish would act the same as anyone surely?' she put it to him, 'they'd be busy looking after their own if Jerry came? They'd never bother to protect us. They wouldn't have the leisure?'

He made no reply. It was Charley gave her an answer.

'And what about the panzer grenadiers?' he asked. 'When they come through this tight little island like a dose of Epsom salts will they bother with those hovels, with two pennorth of cotton? Not on your life. They'll make tracks straight for great mansions like we're in my girl.'

'Mr Raunce,' Miss Burch reproved him.

'I'll ask you to excuse me Miss Burch,' he said. 'I got carried away for a moment. It's you ladies I can't get off my mind.'

'I know what I'd say if one of those dirty Germans offered me an impoliteness,' Edith said.

'And what good would that do if he didn't speak English?' Kate wanted to be told.

'This much,' Edith answered. 'He wouldn't be left in two minds even if he was only familiar with his own language.'

'Now look girl,' Raunce broke in gently, 'it's not only a question of one but of a whole company. Not just one individual but of above a score. Get me?'

'Oo a hundred,' Edith moaned. 'I ought to get away from here.'

Paddy spoke again indistinct as ever.

'Well what is it now?' Charley asked Kate.

' 'E says not to worry, they won't never come over.'

'I will not allow myself to get upset,' Raunce announced with what appeared to be excessive good humour, 'I've promised my lad here. But can anyone tell me what's to stop 'em,' he went on.

Paddy replied readily in sibilants and gutturals. Kate did not wait to be asked. She translated at once.

'Because the country's too poor to tempt an army he reckons, all bog and stones he says.'

'I'm going to lie down for a spell before I sit by Miss Swift,' Agatha announced as she got up to leave by way of the scullery. For the nanny had taken to her bed. No one paid attention. They all stared at the lampman.

'But let 'im satisfy me in this respect,' Raunce cried, 'what the condition of Ireland has to do with it? For one thing if it wasn't rotten land fit only for spuds we'd've been 'ere to this day, our government I mean. No we gave Ireland back because we didn't want it, or this part anyway. Nor Jerry doesn't want it. Then what is 'e after? I'll tell you. What he requires is a stepping stone to invade the old country with. Like crossin' a stream to keep your feet dry.'

'D'you really think so Mr Raunce?' Edith asked.

'I'm dead certain,' he answered.

'Then what are we waitin' for?' Kate wanted to know. 'If Michael drove us down this afternoon we could cross over on the night boat.'

'Hold hard a minute,' Raunce advised her, 'you're drawin' your wages. Right? You're gettin' what you thought was fair I presume or you wouldn't have come nor taken the place?'

'I wanted to get away from 'ome,' she interrupted.

'You wanted to leave home so you went into service,' he echoed. 'All right. You've been here 'ow long? Sixteen months O.K. All that period you ate their grub, took your wage, and didn't give more in return than would cover a tanner. I'm not blaming, mind, I've done the same. Now then when they're entitled to a month's notice you want to welsh no offence to cook. Don't call her cook she don't like it,' he added referring to Mrs Welch, and seemingly in high good humour.

'Forty quid a year and all found then to have a hundred Jerries after me no thank you,' she said.

'Kate Armstrong,' Edith cried out.

'Send in your notice then,' Raunce went on, 'there's nothing and nobody to stop you. But give them the four weeks that's coming to 'em. And be called up in the Army when you land on the other side.'

'What d'you mean get called up?'

'Didn't you know? They've Army police waitin' where the travellers come off the boat. You'll be took straight off to the depot.'

'I wouldn't go.'

'Then if you resist it's the glass 'ouse for you my girl.'

'The glass 'ouse? What's that?'

'Army Detention Barracks ducks It's rough in them places.'

'Well I don't know, you are cheerful aren't you,' Kate said.

'That's right you forget all about it,' he answered. He winked his bluest eye at Edith so Kate could not see him.

Looking round the corner into the great kitchen Miss Burch said, 'I was going to have a lie down for ten minutes but here I am.'

Mrs Welch was alone with her notebook. She did not look up. She called out,

'Jane a cup of tea for Miss Burch.'

Agatha sat down across the table from her. She did not speak again until the tea was brought. Then she came out almost tragically dramatic, in a very different tone to the one she had used in the servants' hall.

'They're not either of them coming back now,' she said. 'There's been a telegram. They're staying over.'

'Not ever?' Mrs Welch enquired sharp, drawing a tumbler of what appeared to be water towards her.

'Oh I don't go so far as that Mrs Welch,' Miss Burch replied, 'I wouldn't like to say they were never returning, but here we are now on our own and there's Raunce in there over his dinner upsetting my girls with his talk of the war and this I.R.A. worry.'

'I never let that man into my kitchen.'

'You're one of the lucky ones Mrs Welch. You've a place you can call your own.'

'Ah,' this woman answered, 'but run over by two-legged mice.'

'Can't keep nothing safe,' she went on after a silence, and took a gulp out of the glass. 'It's me kidneys,' she explained.

'I wonder you don't take that hot,' Miss Burch commented.

'Hot?' Mrs Welch cried. 'Not on your life not with...' and then she checked herself. 'It's not natural to sup what's been heated except when it's soup or broth,' she went on careful. Miss Burch eyed the tumbler. On which Mrs Welch put her head back and drank what was left at one go, as if in defiance. 'There you are,' she said to Agatha in a thicker voice.

'Very soon if he carries on in the way he's doing,' Miss Burch began again rather quickly, 'I'll remain to do the work alone. Even now with Miss Swift taken bad there's only Edith to look after the children.'

At this Mrs Welch without warning let out a shout of, 'Who took my waterglass tell me that,' and leaned right across the table.

'Bless me,' Miss Burch said, hurriedly drinking up her tea. 'But it's not as if it was any more trouble takin' your Albert out for the afternoons I'm sure. The girl's bringing a third along doesn't amount to nothing,' she said.

At this point, as Agatha was getting up to go, Mary the scullery maid came in the door.

'I spoke to the butcher'm,' she said.

There was a heavy silence. At last Mrs Welch replied unctuously, 'So you spoke in spite of what I said,' From her voice she might have been pleased.

''E said Captain Davenport had left for England sudden. Jane and me's wonderin' if per'aps they've learned something about this invasion.'

'Maybe there's something you don't know Mary,' Miss Burch said, 'and which has nothing to do with wars or rumours of wars.'

'I won't wear it,' Mrs Welch suddenly shouted out thumping the table. 'You'll get us all butchered in our beds that's what I tell you.'

'I was only out by the larder when he rang the bell'm an' I 'id behind the monument like you said but 'e must've catched sight of my dress for he came behind.'

'Did he?' Miss Burch announced with dignity. 'There's no end to it nowadays,' she said She stopped by the door, turned back towards Mrs Welch. 'And the Captain's gone over you say? I shall go and lie down.'

'Well don't stand there lookin' Mary, get on with your work,' Mrs Welch remarked as if exhausted and once she was alone got out the key, unlocked the cupboard, and poured another measure of gin.

'For why?' she asked herself aloud, 'because it ain't no use.'

When they broke up after dinner in the servants' hall Albert went to clear away in the nursery. Kate followed to help Paddy returned to his lamproom. This gave Raunce a chance to say to Edith quite formal,

'Have you seen the pictures in my room?'

She called him every day now with his early tea. So she said,

'What d'you mean?'

'Why the pictures I've hanged on the walls.'

She had done this bedroom out these last five weeks and had

carefully examined what he had put in place of Mr Eldon's Coronation likenesses of King Edward and his Danish Queen.

'What's that?' she asked.

'It's brought a big improvement you'll see,' he answered, leading the way. He said twice to himself, 'if I make it seem ordinary she'll follow,' and did not look round for he heard her come after. But his legs went shaky. Probably it was trying to counteract this that made him walk stiff.

'Mortal damp these passages are,' he remarked as their footfalls echoed.

'You want to take care with those swollen glands,' she replied.

'That's why I've got it well wrapped round,' he said. 'Trust little Charley.' It was not long before he was opening his door and entering in front of her.

'Well?' he asked, 'what d'you say to that? Brightens the old place up doesn't it?'

Making herself dainty she looked once more at the two colourful lithographs of Windsor Castle, and the late King George's Coronation Coach, a plain house photograph of Etonians including Mr Jack in tails, and the polychrome print of scarlet-coated soldiers marching in bearskins. The frames were black and matched.

'The British Grenadiers girl,' he said hearty. 'Grenadier Guardsmen they are,' he said. 'Finest soldiers in the world,' he added.

She let this pass, merely enquiring if the pictures were not out of Mr Jack's old playroom and if he did not think they would mind his taking them.

'I don't pay attention,' he announced.

'So I notice,' she said.

'Well what's the object?' he wanted to know. 'They can't remember what they've got.' He was getting almost brisk with her.

'No,' she replied, 'but that's not saying they would never recognize a picture which is hung on the wall.'

'All right,' he said, 'what then? They couldn't make out I'd took it could they when it's in the house all the time.'

'Oh I'm not talkin' of that old picture,' she replied, not looking at him. 'There's other matters I've noticed.'

'Really!' he asked as though he had not made up his mind whether or no to be sarcastic.

'Yes Mr Raunce,' she said.

'Aw come on now,' he objected, 'you don't need to call me Mr Raunce, not when we're like this. I'm Charley to you as we are.'

'All right, yes ... Charley,' she murmured.

'Listen dear you don't want to bother your head with what you see,' he began again.

'Me?' she answered. 'I'm not worrying.'

'Well then what is it you take exception to?'

'Oh nothing,' she said as if she did not care what he did.

'Should it be the lamp wicks now why they're just my perks since I come into the place,' he explained. 'I know old Aggie Burch reckons she tumbled something the other day and I don't doubt she's talked. But you needn't run away with the notion I put new wicks down in my book and then buy none. Why it's to get them a stock up. One day they might turn round to find there won't be wicks being made no more for the duration. If I didn't tell Mrs T. they were required I couldn't get any for 'er could I?'

'It'll be all right till they find you out.'

'No one ever found out Charley Raunce. Lucky Charley they call me.'

'It's the lucky ones have furthest to fall,' she said low.

'But what's it to you?' he asked as though challenging her. 'It's nothing to you,' he said.

'I do care,' she said and turned away abruptly.

'What's this?' he enquired chuckling, a light in his eyes. Coming up behind he laid hold of her shoulders. 'Here give us a little kiss,' he said. For answer she burst into noisy tears. 'Now girlie,' he cried as if stricken, dropped his hands and sat heavily down on the bed. He seized her wrist and began rubbing the knuckles.

'Oh I don't know,' she broke out keeping her head turned so he should not see and blowing her nose, 'it's all this talk of invasion – an' the Jerries an' the Irish – then what I witnessed when I called my young lady – an' you makin' out I never seen what I did – oh it's disgustin' that's what this old place is, it's horrible,' she said.

'Why whatever's up?' Raunce asked abashed, still rubbing the back of her hand.

'First you blow hot then you blow cold,' Edith said and snuffled.

'Blow hot then cold?'

'One minute you say the Jerries are comin' over,' she complained, 'and next you won't have a body try to get over home while there's time.'

He pulled gently on her arm. 'Come and sit by father,' he said.

'Me?' she said in a brighter voice. 'What d'you take me for?'

'That's better,' he said although she was still standing there. 'The trouble with you is you take everything so dead serious.'

'And how do you view things for the matter of that?' she enquired.

'Here,' he replied, 'we don't want you jumpin' on me into the bargain. No me,' he went on, 'I take things to 'eart.'

'Yes?' she said and sat down as though bemused.

'I take things right down inside me girl,' he said putting an arm lightly round her. 'When I feel whatever it is I feel it deep. I'm not like some,' he was going on when she turned her face so that he looked into her eyes which seemed now to have a curve of laughter in their brimming light.

'Oh baby,' he said, reached out with his face. He might have been about to kiss her. She twisted slightly, came out with a 'now then,' and he ceased. 'Look,' he went on and put his other arm round her waist so that he had her in a hoop of himself and was obliged to lean awkwardly to do this. 'Look,' he said again, 'it's what is to happen to you I can't get out of my system, that I think of all the time.'

'And so you should,' she said.

'What's that?' he asked and began to pull at her. She put one hand loose on his nearest arm, holding it between a small finger and thumb.

'Well,' she answered looking away at the rain through that pointed window so that he could not see her face which was smiling, 'the two ladies are gone. They're not coming back are they? We're all alone Charley. We've only you to look to, to know what's best.' He relaxed.

'And you'd rather have it that way, eh ducks?' he asked jovial. 'What can Mrs T. do for you?'

'She can ring up them green police can't she?' Edith said loud and sudden and pushed and shook his arms off while he stayed limp. One of his arms fell across her lap. He lifted it off at once. 'They'd never come for us, not them Irish,' she said.

'Come what for?' he asked confused.

'Why to protect us if the Germans took this place for their billets,' she said.

'You don't want to pay no attention,' he told her.

'Is that so? Then what do you need to go talkin' round it for?'

'It's you I'm concerned about,' he said.

Again she took a short look at him. This time it was as if he could not understand the flash of rage on her face. He put an arm through hers. As she turned her head away he said almost hoarse,

'Here, give us a kiss.'

'Lucky we left the door open wasn't it?' she said.

'Just a small one?' he asked.

She got up.

'Have you cleaned your teeth?' she enquired.

'Have I cleaned my what?'

'Oh nothing,' she said. She did not seem so pleasant.

'Why,' he remarked, 'I brush them every morning first thing.'

'Forget it,' she said and wandered over to that group photograph of Mr Jack which she peered into.

'I can't make you out at all,' he complained, getting up to follow her.

'You will,' she replied. 'You will when those Jerries come over and start murdering us or worse in our beds. When the police begin to fight one another like you said they would.'

He stood back making motions with his hands.

'But it's you I was concerned over love,' he said.

'Me?' she took him up. 'What have I got to lose by goin' home? I'll thank you to tell me that. While if I stay on here there's worse than death can come. It'll be too late then. I got my life still to live Mr Raunce. I'm not like many have had the best part of theirs.'

'Just lately I been wonderin' if my life weren't just starting.'

'Well even if you can't tell whether you're comin' or goin' I know the way I'm placed thank you.'

'Look dear I could fall for you in a big way,' he said and he saw her back stiffen as though she had begun to hear with intense attention. She said no word.

'I could,' he went on. 'For the matter of that I have.'

At this moment she flung round on him and his hangdog face was dazzled by the excitement and scorn which seemed to blaze from her. But all she said was,

'You tell that to them all Charley.'

He appeared to rally a trifle and was about to answer when she exclaimed,

'Why Badger you dirty thing whatever have you got then?'

He turned to find the greyhound wagging its tail at him, muddy nosed, and carrying a plucked carcass that stank.

'Get off out from my premises,' he cried at once, galvanized. 'No wait,' he said. 'What've you got there mate?' The dog wagged its tail.

'Why d'you bother?' she asked impatient. 'It's only one of them peacocks.'

'One of the peacocks?' he almost shouted. 'But there'll be murder over this. No,' he added, 'you're having me on.' He made a step towards the dog which started to growl.

'That's right,' she said, 'Mrs Welch buried it away where none should see.'

'You're crazy,' he said.

'I'll have you remember who you're speaking to Charley Raunce,' she broke out at him. 'Mrs Welch thinks nobody's learned but this bird aimed a peck at 'er Albert's little neck so the little chap upped and killed it. Then she buried it in such a way that no one shouldn't know. The children told me. But I wouldn't have that stinking thing lying around in my part no thank you. Badger,' she said, 'you be off you bad dog.'

On which the dog deposited this carcass at Raunce's feet.

'Holy Moses,' he said, 'the old cow.' 'Now then,' Edith interrupted. 'That's all right,' he went on, 'I'm thinkin' of you ducks. See?'

'No I don't.'

'Well she's got it in for you about that waterglass an' now we've something on her. Get me?'

A noise of high shrieks and the clapping of hands announced Miss Evelyn and Miss Moira, tearing along towards them down passages.

'For land's sake the children,' Edith exclaimed. 'Why I declare I forgot all about...'

Meantime Raunce had dashed out into the pantry snapping his fingers at the dog. It picked up the dead peacock and followed. Raunce shut that further door behind them both. For a moment

Edith was alone as those children raced towards her the other way. Then they had arrived. She was holding her breasts.

'Mercy,' Miss Evelyn exclaimed with a trace of Cockney accent, 'why Edith you do look thrilled at something.'

Raunce's Albert came out of the door Mr Raunce had closed. He shut it again after him, on the butler and the dog and its find it carried.

'Hello Bert,' Miss Moira said.

'Hullo Miss Moira,' he replied. He just stood looking pale and miserable.

'You coming with us?' Edith asked. 'It's your afternoon off isn't it?'

'Oh yes,' he said, and a smile broke over his wan face.

'I got to get ready,' she announced. 'I'll race you two all the way up to my hide out One three go,' she shouted and they were gone. The boy got out a handkerchief, blew his nose. His weak eyes shone.

As the three of them ran the front way through all the magnificence and the gilt of that Castle Miss Evelyn looked back. She cried,

'Why couldn't Bert race with us?'

'Because he's too old,' Edith called back panting, and steadied herself round a turn of the Grand Staircase by holding the black hand of a life-sized negro boy of cast iron in a great red turban and in gold-painted clothes.

Albert went behind the door to the cellar, unhooked his mackintosh and put on the rubber boots he kept there. It was not long before the others were back ready dressed to meet showers. Edith's head was in a silk scarf Mrs Jack had given her which was red and which had for decoration the words 'I love you I love you' written all over in black longhand with rounded letters.

Albert stayed silent while the rest argued where to go. At last they decided on that walk to the temple. Miss Evelyn had a bag of scraps to feed the peacocks When they went through Raunce's pantry to reach the back door this man and the dog were gone without trace.

But as soon as they were outside rain began to come down so thick that they hesitated. Edith said not unkind,

'That's a silly thing Bert to come without a hat.'

He looked back speechless and plastered his long streaming yellow hair down one cheek with a hand. While those two little girls

106

argued where they should go next to get out of the wet Edith looked at the lad derisively. She added as if in answer to a question,

'Oh it does mine good, the soft water curls my hair.'

Then while he regarded her, and he was yearning in the rain, Miss Evelyn announced they'd decided that they'd go play in the Skull-pier Gallery.

'All right if you want,' Edith replied, 'but not through the old premises or we'll dirty 'em wet as we are,' for this Gallery was built on to the far portion of the Castle beyond the part that was shut up. So they ran along a path round by the back past the dovecote and any number of doors set in the Castle's long high walls pierced with tall Gothic windows. Running they flashed along like in the reflection of a river on a grey day, and smashed through white puddles which spurted.

Squat under this great Gothic pile lay the complete copy of a Greek temple roofed, windowed and with two green bronze doors for entrance. The children dashed through an iron turnstile, which clicked into another darker daylight, into a vast hall lit by rain and dark skylights and which was filled with marble bronze and plaster statuary in rows.

'What shall we play?' the Misses Evelyn and Moira cried. Their sharp voices echoed, echoed. The place was damp. Albert kept his mackintosh on. Edith took off her scarf. She was brilliant, she glowed as she rang her curls like bells without a note.

'Blind man's buff,' she said. 'Oh let's,' the girls cried. It was plain this was what they had expected.

'You won't have no difficulty telling it's me,' Albert brought out as if he held a grievance, 'it's me,' the walls repeated.

'You stay mum or we'd never have invited you. We're not playing for you,' Edith told him.

On this there came a kind of faint mewing from the back. Albert started but stayed where he was while those others went hand in hand to see. Away in the depths, out from behind a group of robed men kneeling with heads and arms raised to heaven something small minced out into half light. It was a peacock which had come in to get out of the wet. 'You see her off these premises,' Edith told Albert, 'we don't aim to catch her when we're blindfolded. We don't want another death, the sauce,' she explained. But it took Albert some time to get the creature out. He had to make it hop over that turnstile which caused it to squawk spinsterish. 'You'll have Paddy after you,' Edith called to him at the noise.

When he came back he found Miss Moira had been chosen, had had her eyes bound with the sopping 'I love you.' She stumbled about in flat spirals under a half-dressed lady that held a wreath at the end of her two long arms. Stifled with giggling Edith and Evelyn moved quiet on the outside circle while Albert stood numb. So that it was he was caught.

'Mr Raunce's Albert,' Miss Moira announced without hesitation, her short arms round his thighs. 'Kiss me,' she commanded. 'Kiss me,' the walls said back.

He bent down. His bang of yellow hair fell at right angles to his nose. He kissed her wet forehead over the scarf. Her child's skin was electric hot under a film of water.

Then it was his turn. There was only Edith tall enough to tie him and as 'I love you I love you' was knotted over his eyes he quietly drew a great breath perhaps to find out if Edith had left anything on this piece of stuff. He drew and drew again cautious as if he might be after a deep draught of her, of her skin, of herself. He was puffed already when his arms went out to go round and round and round her. But she was not there and for answer he had a storm of giggles which he could not tell one from the other and which went ricochetting from stone cold bosoms to damp streaming marble bellies, to and from huge oyster niches in the walls in which boys fought giant boas or idled with a flute, and which volleyed under green skylights empty in the ceiling. He went slow. He could hear feet slither. Then he turned in a flash. He had Edith. He stood awkward one hand on her stomach the other on the small of her back.

'Guess then,' he heard Miss Evelyn tell him out of sudden silence. 'Edith,' he said low.

'Kiss her then,' they shrieked disinterested, 'kiss her,' they shrieked again. In a tumult of these words re-echoed over and over from above from below and from all sides his hands began to grope awkward, not feeling at her body but more as if he wished to find his distance. 'Kiss her.'

'Come on then,' she said brisk. She stepped for the first time into his arms. Blinded as he was by those words knotted wet on his eyes he must have more than witnessed her as his head without direction went nuzzling to where hers came at him in a short contact, and in spite of being so short more brilliant more soft and warm perhaps than his thousand dreams.

'Crikey,' he said and took the scarf off in one piece. He seemed absolutely dazzled although it had become almost too dark to see his face.

'You tie it dear,' she said kneeling down to Miss Moira. 'He's that awkward,' she said in a cold voice.

But there was an interruption. As Edith knelt before the child a door in the wall opened with a grinding shriek of rusty hinge and Raunce entered upon a scene which this noise and perhaps also his presence had instantly turned to more stone.

'I figured this was where you could be found,' he said advancing smooth on Edith. She had raised a hand to her eyes as though to lift the scarf but she let her arm drop and faced him when he spoke, blind as any statue.

'Yes?' she said. 'What is it?'

'Won't you play Mr Raunce?' Miss Evelyn asked.

'Playin' eh?' he remarked to Albert.

'It's Thursday isn't it?' Edith enquired sharp. 'That's his half day off or always was. What's up?'

'Nothin',' he replied, 'only I just wondered how you might be getting along.'

'Is that all?' was her comment. At which Albert spoke for himself.

'We was havin' a game of blind man's buff,' he said.

'So I perceive Albert,' the butler remarked.

'Oh do come on do,' one of the little girls pleaded but Edith chose this moment to take that scarf off her eyes.

'You surely didn't pass through all that old part alone?' she asked.

'And why not?'

'Oh Charley I never could not in a month of Sundays. Not on my own.'

'Is that so?'

'You are pleasant I must say aren't you?' she said.

'Thanking you,' Raunce answered.

'Oh please come on Mr Raunce please,' the child entreated. 'Edith'll give you up her turn.'

'I'm past the age and that's a fact Miss Evelyn,' Raunce said almost nasty. 'For the matter of that I chucked this blind man's buff before I'd lived as many years as my lad here. In my time if we had nothing better to do than lark about on a half day we got on with our work.'

'Here,' Edith said, 'just a minute.' She led him aside. 'What's up Charley?'

'Nothing's up. What makes you ask?'

'You act so strange. Whatever's the matter then?'

'Oh honey,' he suddenly said low and urgent, 'I never seem to see you these days.'

'That's not a reason,' she objected. 'You know I've got to look after them with Miss Swift sick as she is.'

'Yes,' he said. 'There's always something or other in the way each time.'

'How's your neck dear?' she asked as she strolled away. She gradually led him nearer and nearer the door he had come in by.

'Oh it's bad,' he said. 'It hurts so Edith.'

'Well you shouldn't stand about in a damp place like here,' she replied. 'For land's sake I don't know how you managed those passages alone. They give me the creeps. And what's become of Badger with the peacock?'

'I gave that dog the slip. All the brains he's got is in his jaw. Once he's dropped anything 'e's lost that dog is. I put it away where they'll find it in the outside larder.'

She slapped a hand across her mouth. 'You hung it in the outside larder?'

He smiled for the first time. 'That's right,' he said.

'Lord,' she remarked, 'what'll old Mother Welch say when Jane or Mary tells 'er?' She began to giggle.

'Don't call 'er cook she don't like it,' Raunce replied broadly smiling.

'Now look you mustn't stay here Charley with that neck of yours. You get back out of this damp. I'll see if I can't manage to slip down after tea.'

'O K ducks. Give us a kiss.'

'Don't be daft,' she said, 'what in front of all of them?'

'O K. then,' he ended, 'I'll be seeing you.' And he shut that door soft although the hinges shrieked and groaned. Then he came in once more, stared at the mechanism. 'Wants a drop of oil that does,' he remarked, winked and was gone again. As he walked off into grey dust-sheeted twilight he said two or three times to himself, 'How she has come on. You'd never know it was the same girlie,' he repeated.

'At last,' Miss Moira called out back in the Gallery, 'I thought we'd never get rid of him. Kneel Edith,' she said pulling that scarf out of Edith's pocket.

Once Edith was blinded the little girls let out piercing shrieks and dodged as in laughter she moved her arms as though swimming towards them. Their cries reverberated round the Gallery. Miss Evelyn hopped on one leg pressing her snub nose upwards with the palm of a hand When Edith came near, Miss Moira would turn and slip by Edith's blind wrists looking round over a shoulder ready to dodge again after Miss Evelyn had ducked under. But Albert stood like a statue and must have hoped he would be found. As he was. Yet when her fingers knew him which they did at once she murmured 'I don't want you,' and to shrieks from the others of 'You'll never catch us,' this immemorial game went on before witnesses in bronze in marble and plaster, echoed up and down over and over again.

Back in his room Raunce unlocked the drawer in which he kept the red and black notebooks. He verified that they were there. Then he drew pencil and paper towards him, laboriously made out the date and the address then settled down to write to his mother.

'*Dear Mother,*' he began, '*I hope you are well. I am. There has been nothing fresh here. Mrs Tennant has gone to England to stay. While she is over she hopes to see Mr Jack who is on leave just at present. Mrs Jack has also gone to be with them. So we are on our own here now and will be for a bit I expect.*

'*Mother I am very worried over this bombing for you. Don't wait until he comes to get your Anderson shelter fixed. Get it done now Mother dear and it will be something off my mind.*

'*I often wish I was with you dear but you know the way I'm placed. Once I should leave this country then I'm in their power over there. There's the Labour Exchange with the Army waiting. It's hard to know what to do best.*

'*Mother what would you say to your coming here. Who knows but there might be a change in my situation one of these days.*

*You've often said it was time I settled down. But not a word to anyone dear, there's nothing said yet. But I've my eye on a nice little place in the park what the married butler before Mr Eldon had. Think of it will you Mother. And mind not a word not even to my sister Bell.*

'Well, I must close now. But I certainly am worried about you with all this bombing. Tell her, that's Bell I mean, to be sure and look after you all right. Your loving son Charley.'

Then he inked it in. And he wrote the address with his pencil and then inked that. Finally he slipped in the Money Order. After he had stamped the envelope he laid his head down on his arms and dropped off to sleep at once.

When a few days later as she lay in bed Miss Swift was paid a call by Miss Burch she was able to cut short the thanks having expressed what was necessary on the first of two visits of sympathy Miss Burch had already paid. But on the subject of her symptoms she left nothing out.

'I wonder you don't ask Doctor Connolly to put his rule over you,' Miss Burch remarked at last.

'Poor nanny,' Miss Swift exclaimed. 'That man?' she added as if injured.

'There's not another within reaching distance only the native doctors and we won't speak about them. Now they've taken their petrol away that is.'

'You'd never expect me to see him, Miss Burch, after what we witnessed every one of us with Mr Eldon. Why it was no more than a crime if I'm to put a name to it.'

'Mr Eldon he died of a broken heart Miss Swift. There was a lot he told nobody.'

'I'm sure I trembled for him as he lay there Miss Burch but then you see I knew. What training I've had was the best even if I've never served with a hospital. I could tell you things. There was a place I was in, I had him from a baby. The doctors gave him up, gave him up dear and they had two in from Harley Street. It was simple enough really. There he was such a good little chap. Lancelot his name was, his mother was Lady Mercy Swinley. Well one night when they were all gone I was watching for I never left his side, day and night I watched him yes, so I leant forward and looked into his little face and I could see he was going before my very eyes. It was all or nothing Miss Burch. So I took him up and I shook him. Yes and I slapped hard. My heart was in my mouth but he gave a kind of convulsive heave of his whole body and brought it all up. I'd known all along there was something stuck in his gullet but there they wouldn't listen. He brought it up. It was black as pitch. Then after I'd changed his bed things he fell into such a sweet sleep. Something made me do it there you are. But I shook so afterwards I dropped the cup when I poured myself a cup of tea. That hospital nurse couldn't fathom it once she came back. But I knew better.'

'Well,' said Miss Burch. 'But wasn't that the lady I read about the other day, the mother I mean?'

'Yes,' the nanny answered, 'times are hard for a number of them now, there's big changes under way. I shouldn't wonder if things were never the same say what you will. But don't mistake me. I wouldn't put myself above a doctor. Though we can all bear witness about Mr Eldon how that poor man lay calling on a name and Doctor Connolly no more than paid him a call every so often, when we all know what we had under our very eyes with him growing weaker each day that passed, I don't say but someone might have taken matters into their own hands. And I'm sure they could have made free with my medicine cupboard and welcome.'

'You'll excuse me,' Agatha gently said, 'but that's a topic I can't mention.'

'Why certainly,' Miss Swift said bright. 'You don't want to take notice. The truth is,' she said frank, 'I'm an old woman and I'm growing simple.'

'Now Miss Swift . . .'

'Thank you,' the nanny interrupted rather breathless, 'and perhaps it's understandable. After all there's not a woman after a life spent with her charges but doesn't get an eye for illness. It may start as no more than a snivel when you put 'em to bed and then before you've time to adjust yourself you're right in the middle of it, day and night nurses under your feet with oxygen bottles and all that flummery. Prevention is better than cure I say. And there's many a one I've saved when those others in stiff cuffs had their backs turned.'

'I dare hazard it's no different to what I am with a floor,' Miss Burch said conversationally. 'Take a good polished parquet, now, that they've let go. With my experience I can tell at a glance, tell at a glance,' she said.

'There you are,' the nanny exclaimed and lay back grey about the lips. She was wrapped round in the huge crocheted shawl Miss Burch had lent her on the first visit.

'And there's some won't learn their lesson,' Agatha went on. 'Take Raunce. There's a man gone forty, been in good places all his life but his silver's a disgrace. I know of houses, houses I've worked in mind, where he could never have lasted seven days.'

'I won't have Arthur in my nursery.'

'Mrs Welch won't let him enter her kitchen. But then you've both of you a place you can call your own. Not like me with no more than a door opening into the sink and a bit of a cupboard in all this mansion. Now there's one woman been very different lately. Hardly the same at all. Mrs Welch.'

'Time was I wouldn't even venture into her scullery,' the nanny said, 'but since her little Albert's been over there's a noticeable change. He's a sweet child if he may be a bit of a monkey.'

'I suspicion whether it's all the child Miss Swift.'

'I've seen so many,' Miss Swift said, 'oh dear such a number I've looked after and not one but has a soft spot in their hearts for old nanny.'

'I shouldn't wonder if it wasn't the gin again,' Miss Burch said grim.

'Oh dear oh no I wouldn't wish to listen. Why fancy. Oh no I'm an old woman. I've seen things you'd never believe but I wouldn't wish to hear such a thing.'

'It's true for all that,' Miss Burch announced with what seemed to be satisfaction.

'There now I've forgotten every bit of it poor nanny,' Miss Swift replied. 'I don't know I'm sure but you gave me quite a shock with what you just said. But there, I've forgotten all about it. Bless me yes.'

'There's things I wish I could forget,' Agatha said in a far-off voice.

Miss Swift squirmed in bed.

'Take Raunce,' Miss Burch began, then stopped.

'You think I should be told?' the nanny asked.

'You'd never guess what he's been up to now,' Miss Burch went on adamant.

'I'm not strong, leastways that's how I've felt lately, weak,' the nanny muttered.

'He's took that peacock little Albert killed, which Mrs Welch hid away, and he's hung it in the outside larder. Swarming with maggots over our meat. How do you like that Miss Swift? It's wicked or worse it is.'

'Little Albert killed?' the nanny cried with a sort of wail.

'No. One of the peacocks crossed 'is path so he up and killed the thing. That's a flea bite, there's plenty more of the creatures. But from what I can make out Mrs Welch must have took umbrage. And who is there to say she was mistaken if she thought her life in peril even with that mad Irishman with his ear to every keyhole? So she put it back of a piece of cheese cloth away in her kitchen. Then she thought she'd dispose of the thing after, one way or another, but the carcass turned up again in such a fashion as Raunce could get hold of it. Crawling with maggots all over which is what my girl Kate tells me. Can you imagine the like Miss Swift? Infecting all our food.'

'Oh dear,' the nanny said come over limp. 'Arthur. I see yes, Arthur.'

'But that's a trifle,' Miss Burch continued placid yet firm, her eyes on her knitting. 'Now I went into the Red Library after dinner to see to the fire. Mrs Tennant will have fires lit to keep the rooms right for the pictures. And d'you know what I found. Why Edith and that man, the impudence, sat back in the armchairs they'd drawn to the fender. As if they owned the Castle.'

'Oh dear,' Miss Swift moaned.

'"Why whatever's this," I said,' Miss Burch went on. '"It's my neck," he answered me. "Your cheek my man," I said and then Edith she did have the grace to get up on her two feet after that. But he went on sitting there. "What's it to you?" he asked though I could see he was ashamed for both of them. "Just this," I said so he couldn't be in doubt upon it. "There's right and wrong," I says, "and there's no two ways about which this is," I said.'

'His neck?' Miss Swift asked faint. 'You never can tell. Oh dear perhaps if I could have a glance.'

'He's kept his neck wrapped up the last two weeks,' Miss Burch announced, 'he makes out the glands are enlarged. But it's his whole head has swelled.'

'They can be dangerous swollen glands can,' the nanny said firmer.

'Well if you ask me things will go from bad to worse if Mrs Tennant won't come home soon. And I love that girl of mine Edith, I love that child Miss Swift.'

'She's a good girl Miss Burch. The children will do anything for her.'

'There it is Miss Swift, she's had her eyes on him a long time and wishing's not likely to make things different. But I'm afraid for her with that man. He's up to no good,' Miss Burch pronounced and then paused.

The nanny did not seem anxious for more. She merely repeated once again, 'She's a good girl Edith is.'

'I've never had a better,' Miss Burch began afresh. 'There, I'll go so far as that, never a better under me,' she said. 'In this great rambling place we have a week's cleaning to do each day. But you can depend on her. And that's something can't be said of the other, Kate. Sometimes I even wish with that one I'd been given an Irish girl to train up instead.'

'No Roman Catholics thank you,' Miss Swift said sharp.

'Yes,' Miss Burch agreed, 'we don't want those fat priests about confessin' people or taking snuff.' She stared from her knitting at Miss Swift for a moment 'Are you feeling quite well?' she asked.

'Me?' the nanny said in a quavering voice. 'Thank you I'm sure. Poor nanny...' she began as if about to continue but Agatha broke in, 'Then that's all right. But I'm sorry for the girls nowadays,' she announced. 'It puts me in mind of the South Africa war. They see the men going out to get killed and it makes them restless. I remember how it was with me at the time. Then they look at us old women and they say to themselves they don't wish to end up like us. I was the same at their age. It's only after they've lived a few years longer that they'll come to realize there's worse than sleeping alone in your own bed, with a fresh joint down in the larder for dinner every day.'

'And a pension at the end, not just the old age,' Miss Swift put in quite bright once more. 'It was a weight off poor old nanny's mind I can tell you when they asked nanny to come back to Miss Violet after she'd done for her from a baby. To take on her own child's sweet babies the little angels.'

'Ah Mrs Jack,' Miss Burch announced in a voice of doom.

Miss Swift looked askance. She hurriedly went on, 'And two of the best behaved little girls as ever I've had in my charge,' she said, 'so loving with their pretty little ways the lambs. There's but one thing I could wish which is that there were more children round about for them to play with. You know Miss Burch it's not right at the age they are and with their position in life to have none but themselves. I was right glad when Mrs Jack told me about this Albert ' She paused for breath.

'Ah Mrs Jack,' Miss Burch put in as though sorrowing.

The nanny set off again, more breathless still. 'Of course it's the times,' she said. 'Now even after the last war they would never have entertained it, the very idea. Why a boy like Albert, the cook's own nephew, dear me no. Never in your life. But it's come about. It's the shortage. Having no petrol,' she ended and lay back, blue about the lips.

'What was revealed came as a great shock to me,' Miss Burch said and paused to pick up a dropped stitch. The nanny rested herself with closed eyes. There was a silence. 'A great shock,' Miss Burch repeated getting up speed once more with her knitting. Miss Swift did not utter.

'They can do what they like after all,' Miss Burch went on, 'there's little or nothing we can say will make any difference when all's told. Yet I've got to consider my girls. It's not so much the example. Enough goes on in any farm yard. But there's the upset to a girl of Edith's age coming from a good home. I'm afraid for her.'

'She's a strong girl,' Miss Swift said faint, 'I can tell.'

'That's as may be,' Miss Burch replied, 'but going to call the lady and then to turn round after drawing those curtains to find the Captain Davenport in her bed as well why ...' Miss Burch said and pursed her lips. There was no response so she looked up full at Miss Swift. This woman was lying back eyes closed or rather screwed shut in a wild look of alarm.

'There,' Agatha added and returned to her knitting, 'I never meant to tell you. It slipped out. These last days I've been afraid it would throw my Edith right off her balance. It's her I mind for.'

'They imagine things that's how it is,' the nanny murmured. 'I remember when I was a girl. Always imagining I was till I didn't rightly know.'

'I saw him don't worry,' Miss Burch said in a loud voice. 'Why I thought she was going to faint away into my arms when she came out. Of course the moment she told me I went straight in. And there she lay the young lady naked as the day she was born with him just putting his shirt on. It didn't take me long to come away again I can tell you.'

'She was all the time the sweetest child,' the nanny said in a stronger voice. Miss Burch looked at her quickly, saw her face was smooth now, that she seemed peaceful. 'Miss Violet had such lovely golden hair,' Miss Swift went on, 'the only child I knew to keep it always. On her wedding day it was the same, oh dear. What a number of years that is to be sure.'

'So I told Edith, Miss Swift, how she'd best be off out of it. The less said the better I told her. And the next time we were alone I insisted she shouldn't pay attention, that what they did was no concern of ours. But she's took it to heart. I know. There's times I feel desperate.'

'Such a picture in white when she come up the aisle. Dear me it's a strange thing but I feel quite tired. I fancy I'll take a little nap.'

'Are you sure there's nothing you'd like, a cup of tea or something?'

'No thank you Miss Burch all the same.'

Agatha got her knitting together. She cast another glance at Miss Swift who was very blue about the lips.

'You're sure there's nothing now?' she said once more. 'You wouldn't like me to change your hot-water bottle?'

'No I'm quite comfortable,' the nanny answered. 'I just wonder if I won't have a little nap that's all.' So Miss Burch left. As she closed the door she said to herself, 'Well she never thanked me for coming but then I shouldn't have let my tongue run on. But she never took it in even. We're both getting old women,' she repeated aloud as she went along the white linoleum in that corridor and walked to one side over the purple key pattern border.

Miss Burch never told the nanny that her protest to Raunce and Edith had been without effect. Edith it is true had risen to her feet when she left them but Charley had not stirred. And now as Agatha went slowly to her room with a pounding heart, Edith down in the Red Library was back in what used to be Mr Tennant's special easy chair. She hardly seemed comfortable however for she was protesting,

'. . . and, well, I don't like it.'

'Now ducks,' he said.

'I don't want to set her against me Charley. It's me has to work with her. Not you after all.'

'She's got nothing on us,' he replied, 'no one has.' At that a silence fell between them. Then she let out careless in a low voice,

'Charley I found the ring.'

'What ring?' he asked as though talking of daisy chains.

'Why,' she explained with sudden excitement, 'Mrs T's ring she mislaid before she went away. I chanced on it the other afternoon.'

'She's always losin' valuables,' he remarked casual, 'the wonder is she gets them back so often.'

'That's what I mean,' she said.

'I don't get you.'

'Suppose she didn't get this ring back?'

'Well you're goin' to give it her surely? You don't want to hand it over to our Agatha so she claims all the credit. Stand up for yourself love. You found the object. You hand it back and gather the reward though I'm afraid you'll be unlucky there you know.'

'What I was wondering was suppose I never offered the old ring back?'

'Here,' he said, 'easy on. Knock the ring off you mean?'

'Keep it,' she agreed. She seemed overexcited.

'Where is it?' he asked.

'Hid here in the lining,' she replied and got up. She forked the thing out of a tear with her finger. Her hands trembled.

'Let's have a look,' he said. 'You know you want to go steady with suggestions like the one you've just put forward. See,' he said holding the ring on a level with his chin. It winked and glittered at him. He smiled on it. 'Christ,' he said low.

'Well Charley what d'you say?'

'I tell you this won't do,' he answered. 'Put'm back where you found'm.'

'Put it back where I found it,' she echoed as though dumbfounded.

'Yes so they can't discover the old loot on you and call that stealing by finding. Go on,' he said, 'I hate to do this but put'm back.'

'An' then what?' she wanted to know and pouted.

'The minute Mrs T. returns you go up to her and say you came by it as you were doing this room out.'

'I thought you'd have a better use for it than that,' she said.

'I don't follow you,' he said extremely cautious.

'What d'you keep writin' in those notebooks then?' she asked.

'I have to make up my accounts I put before Mrs Tennant each month,' he replied in an educated voice.

'Oh yeah?' she said.

'You've got to understand,' he said.

'It'll take a lot of understandin', Charley.'

'Listen I'm not makin' out I can be accurate down to the last cork or that when someone comes to stay they don't forget to put back a pencil they've taken off one of the tables.'

'You're telling me,' she said.

'But there's no place for valuables like this object,' he went on. 'You've got to see that dear. Why you'd gum up the whole works.'

'I can't fathom you,' she said. 'Here's a ring may be worth hundreds. It's been missed. It's lost and you want me to hand it back. There's no sense in a thing like that.'

'What would you do then?'

'I'd sell it an' save the money for a rainy day,' and she gave him a look as if to say the sky always rained at weddings.

'You're crazy,' he said.

'I'm crazy am I,' she cried, 'right then I'll act like I was,' and snatching that ring from his fingers she threw it in the fire.

'Now look what you've done,' he said going down on his knees. He fished it out with a pair of tongs. 'That'll need cleanin' that will. You leave me.'

'Leave what to you not very likely,' she said as though beside herself. 'I wouldn't trust you no further than that fender. Give here.' She grabbed the ring back again.

'Ouch it's hot,' she said dropping the thing on the rug. They stood looking down and from the droop of her shoulders it could be assumed that her rage had subsided.

'For land's sake I do feel awful,' she brought out.

'Now honey you don't want to take things so awkward,' he said putting an arm round her shoulders. 'There's nothing to get wrought up over,' he explained. 'I was only goin' to give it a rub so that when you gave it back to Mrs T. she wouldn't notice the difference. And look,' he said, 'you've no sense of proportion. If I make me a few shillings each week fiddlin' the monthly books that don't mean I can go and knock off valuables. That's dangerous that is. Besides what I'm on to is steady, ducks, get me? While I hold down this job I can put by something all the time.'

'What do you put by?' she asked not looking at him. There was a short silence during which she seemed to listen intently.

'Why a bit here and a bit there,' he said.

'And I don't suppose it's worth the small risk there is in it,' she broke out sudden.

'I don't know love but maybe there's two or three hundred a year one way or another all told.'

'Pounds?' she asked making her eyes big.

'Lovely British Bradbury's,' he answered.

'Oh Charley,' she said in admiration, 'so that's what you're on to?'

'And that's a sight less than old Eldon drew. But he was at the receiving end of some very special money.'

'What d'you mean?'

'He'd kept his eyes open. He wasn't so slow. Tell you the truth I never did give him credit till I come upon it the other day. He'd got your Captain weighed up.'

'The Captain?' she asked eyes shining.

'Those were my words.'

'But I mean that's worse than takin' a ring ain't it Charley?'

'Depends how you mean worse,' he replied. 'All I know is it's secure.'

'D'you stand there an' tell me Mr Eldon had come upon them some time? Just as I did? That she sat up in bed with her fronts bobblin' at him like a pair of geese the way she did to me? Is that what you're sayin'?' She was so excited again that she fairly danced before him.

'Oh I don't know,' he replied cautious and as if he was shy.

'There she sits up at me ...' Edith ran on, eyes sparkling. And he had to listen to the whole thing again, and with embellishments that he had never heard, that even he must have doubted.

Raunce's Albert, Edith, Kate, the little girls and Mrs Welch's lad chose for their picnic a place just off the beach. While those children ran screaming down to where great rollers diminished to fans of milk new from the udder upon pressed sand, Albert laid himself under a hedge all over which red fuchsia bells swung without a note in the wind the sure travelling sea brought with its low heavy swell. He could watch the light blue heave between their donkey Peter's legs and his ears were crowded with the thunder of the ocean.

'Fat lot of use you are,' Kate shouted to him as she began to unstow the panniers on Peter's back.

'Ain't there a glare,' he called.

'For land's sake you're not goin' sick on me surely like Charley did when I brought him out?'

'Don't he look pale?' Kate echoed Edith.

'Never mind let him be,' Edith went on, 'and we'll allow he may light the Primus.' She laughed, probably because it would never start up without a deal of coaxing.

'Did you remember your matches?' Kate yelled. On which he got to his feet to bring out a packet of cigarettes.

'Lawks we've took a man along,' Kate mocked. He offered them round. As he cupped his hands to shield the flame and Edith bent her lovely head he lowered his yellow one over hers. She giggled which blew the match out. 'One thing at a time thank you,' she remarked looking him in the eye from close. He blushed painfully. Then the wind sent her hair over her vast double-surfaced eyes with their two depths. As she watched him thus, he might have felt this was how she could wear herself in bed for him, screened but open, open terribly.

'Come on,' she said, 'snap out of it.'

Then all three huddled round as if over a live bird sat between his palms till their fags were lit. He collapsed back onto the ground.

'You wouldn't be looking up our legs by any chance now would you?' Kate enquired in an educated voice. For answer he rolled over onto his stomach and faced inland, all Ireland flat on a level with his clouded eyes.

'Let him be,' Edith said again. The wind blew a sickle of black hair down the opening of her dress.

'It tickles,' she said giggling, and swung her head back to let that breeze carry the curls off. 'Oh this wind,' she added. And it drove the girls' dresses onto them like statues as they lifted rectangles of white cartridge paper tied in string out of the panniers to lay these where sand joined that moss short grass. Then Edith stopped to gently pull Peter's ears.

'Aw come on,' Kate called to Albert, 'you don't want to go sulking away there. Why I daresay she'd never've minded if you had of 'ad a peep.'

'Now Kate,' Edith repeated, 'why can't you let him alone.'

'I never,' the lad cried turning over to face them, 'honest I never.'

'Well then don't act like you wished you did.'

'Katie,' Edith said and bent down to kiss the donkey's nose. She seemed altogether indifferent. At this moment little Albert interrupted.

'Can I take the shrimpin' net'm. There's 'undreds down there in that pool we're at.'

And so the long afternoon started. Then when they had had cup after cup of tea Albert in lighting Kate another cigarette set fire to a thin curl of her fair hair. She took this in good part, did no more than exclaim at the smell.

' 'Er peacock didn't half cause a stink,' he told them. The wind had dropped. They no longer had to shout. But the roar of that Atlantic swell was heavy.

'What peacock?' she asked.

'Why the one old Charley put back in the outside larder. Mrs Welch must've bided her time when there was nobody in the pantry so as to slip down and stuff 'im in my boiler.'

'In your boiler?' Edith shrieked. 'Whoever's heard?'

'Didn't you smell it at that?' the lad enquired.

'It's the first I've known,' Kate said.

'He created something alarming Charley did,' his lad continued. 'He said there was enough to give us asthma and 'e went about coughin' for two days.'

'She's up to a lark then,' Edith said seemingly delighted. 'Bless us,' she added, 'look what he's after now,' she exclaimed. All three saw little Albert hopping round and round with a fair-sized crab fastened onto a toe of his sandshoes. The excited shrieks that came back from the children blanketed a screaming from gulls fighting over the waste food which they had thrown away although Raunce's Albert still had some scraps in a paper bag.

'Let 'em,' Kate said and closed her eyes again. 'I've got what I've had to digest yet,' she added. Then just as Edith was about to get up to help that crab fell off. The children began to stone it, driving it blow upon blow into a grave its own shape in the sand. At which Peter put his ears back and snatched the scraps out of Albert's hand, swallowed them bag and all.

'Why you ugly bastard,' Albert said scrambling out of the way.

'Now Albert,' Edith remarked indifferent.

'I thought 'e was asleep,' the boy explained.

'Which is what I would be if you'd only shut down,' Kate said from behind closed eyes. Her eyelids were pink. The sun warm.

As he was about to settle again Edith invited him to use part of the mackintosh on which she was seated adding that he would only spoil his indoor suit. He was dressed in the blue serge double-breasted outfit a livery tailor had made him on Mrs Tennant's instructions.

'You do look a sight,' was her comment, 'got up as you are like you were goin' in Hyde Park.'

He lay down at her side while she sat bolt upright to keep an eye on the children.

'I got a sister over at home,' he said low.

'What's that?' she asked careless. 'I can't hear you with the sea.'

'I got a sister works in an airplane factory,' he began. If she heard him she gave no indication. 'Madge we call her. They's terrible the hours she puts in.'

He lay on his stomach facing inland while Edith watched the ocean.

'I've only her and mum left now,' he went on. 'Dad, 'e died a month or two afore I came here. He worked in a fruiterer's in Albany Place. It was a cancer took 'im.'

When he broke off the heavy Atlantic reverberated in their ears.

'Now Mr Raunce writes to his,' he continued, 'and can't never get a reply. And there's me writes to mine, every week I do since this terrible bombing started but I don't ever seem to receive no answers though every time 'e comes over I'm afeared mum an' sis must've got theirs. To read the papers you wouldn't think there was anything left of the old town.'

'That young Albert,' Edith yelled against the sea, 'I regret we took him along.'

Raunce's Albert looked over his shoulder on the side away from Edith but could not see how his namesake was misbehaving.

'You see with dad gone I feel responsible,' he tried again loud. 'I know I'm only young but I'm earnin' and there's times I consider I ought to be back to look after them. Not that I don't send the best part of me wages each week. I do that of course.'

A silence fell.

'What did you say your sister's name was?' Edith asked.

'Mum had her christened Madge,' the lad replied. He tried a glance at Edith but she was not regarding him. 'To tell you the truth,' he continued, 'I did wonder what's the right thing? I thought maybe you could advise me?' He looked at her again. This time she was indeed contemplating him though he could not make out the expression in her enormous eyes behind the black yew branch of windblown hair.

He turned away once more. He spoke in what seemed to be bitterness.

'Of course I'm only young I know,' he said.

'Well it's not as if they'd written for you is it?' she announced, on which he turned over and lay on his side to face her. She was looking out to sea again.

'No but then they're like that. Mum always reckoned she'd rather scrub the house out than take a pen. Madge's the same. It's 'ard to know what's for the best,' he ended.

'I should stay put,' she said, speaking impartially. 'You're learnin' a trade after all. If they should ever come for you into the Army you could be an officer's servant. We're all right here.'

'Then you don't reckon there's much in what they say about this invasion? If there's one thing I don't aim at it's being interned by the Jerries.'

'Oh that's all a lot of talk in my opinion,' she answered. 'You don't want to pay no attention. Oh me oh my,' she said, 'but isn't it slow for a picnic. Here,' and at this she leant over him, 'let's see if we can't set old Kate goin'.'

She picked up a stray bit of spent straw which was lying on his other side then lowered all the upper part of her body down onto his, resting her elbow between him and the sleeping girl. Her mouth was open in a soundless laugh so that he could see the wet scarlet roof as she reached over to tickle Kate's sand-coloured eyebrows.

Kate's face twitched. Her arm that was stretched white palm upwards along deep green moss struggled to lift itself as though caught on the surface of a morass. Then still asleep she turned away abrupt till the other cheek showed dented with what she was lain on. She muttered once out loud 'Paddy.'

At this Edith burst into giggles bringing her hand still with its bit of straw up to her mouth as, eyes welling, she looked direct into Albert's below her. He lay quiet and yellow in a simper. This brought her up sharp.

'Can't you even have a joke?' she asked.

'Well you're a pretty pair no mistake,' Kate said and yawned. They found she was sitting to rearrange her tow locks.

'Not so comical as you, you believe me,' Edith answered removing herself from off Albert. He turned over onto his stomach again, facing Ireland.

'What have I done now then?' Kate wanted to know. 'Can't a girl treat herself a nap?'

'Forget it dear,' Edith told her.

'I don't know as I want to forget,' Kate replied. 'It's not nice finding people makin' fun of you when you're asleep.'

'It's only what you brought out love,' Edith sweetly said.

'What was that then?'

'You called a name.'

'Is that all,' Kate announced and blushed, which was unusual with her. 'Why from the fuss you two made lain right in each other's arms you'd imagine it might be something serious.'

'We wasn't,' Albert said sharp, twisting his head towards her. His eyes did not seem to see.

'Oh all right let it pass,' Kate replied. Her blush had gone. 'But you can take it from me what I witnessed was sufficient to make them precious children look twice if they'd noticed.'

'Just let 'im be,' Edith said indifferent.

'There's one thing I won't have,' Kate quoted looking with malice at Edith, 'an' that is the children bein' worried by it the little lambs.'

Edith gave a short laugh.

'Why who said that?' Albert asked.

'Miss Swift.'

'What for?' he enquired.

'And I say she's an old duck stickin' up for them,' Edith interrupted. 'They don't want to be bothered with what I witnessed, not yet awhiles any old how. They got plenty of time to learn.'

'You mean what you saw when you called Mrs Jack?' the lad said scornful. 'That old tale?'

' 'E won't believe it yet,' Kate announced as if delighted.

'Call it a tale if you will,' Edith answered. 'There's many a time I've wished I hadn't been the one. But you ask Agatha Burch if you disbelieve me. Stark naked she sat up in bed as the day she was born.'

'Get out?' Albert politely said.

'Well she's right Miss Swift is,' Edith added above the boy's head. 'Their mother's everything to them I should hope? Nor you'd never get 'em to believe if you did tell them. Not like you and someone I could mention.'

'That's enough,' Kate said violent. 'I've had all I can stomach from . . .'

'Land's sakes,' Edith called scrambling to her feet, 'will you just look what they're at now all three,' she cried making off at a run down to the ocean.

'Come on,' Kate said, 'give us a kiss when she's not lookin'.'

But he would not, did not even bother to reply. Yet the moment Edith came back he rolled over to ask if she had forgotten she had still to return him that gauntlet glove.

'What glove?' she asked as she sat down once more.

'Why the one you had full of eggs it must be six weeks since.'

'I got one or two things of hers when Mrs T. arrives,' she said.

'How's that Edie?' Kate asked opening her gimlet eyes.

'Oh nothing dear, nothing which is to say that concerns you,' Edith sweetly answered. 'It's only that she will leave things lying idle.'

'Like her ring,' Kate commented shrewd. 'Which was worth more than an old king's ransom I'll be bound.'

'Which ring?' the lad enquired.

'Why Albert I will admit you're chronic,' Edith said. 'You mean to lie there and tell us you never heard of Mrs Tennant's ring that was mislaid.'

'I never heard nothing.'

'No more he would,' Kate announced. "He's simple that's all.'

'Well,' Edith said, 'I made sure you must have. It was only that she's lost another valuable, a ring this time. But I chanced to come upon it the other day.'

'You did?' Kate exclaimed sitting up, 'an' you never told me.'

'Oh I've got it hid away trust little Edith,' Edith announced dully. 'They're never goin' to pin a thing on me they can call stealing by findin'. Once she gets back I'll tell her just where she'll come upon it,' she said.

'An object like that,' was Kate's comment.

'It's hid well away. There's only Miss Moira I've showed to an' she'd never tell. I worship that child,' Edith said.

'There you go again,' Kate exclaimed, 'when she's right under the thumb of Mrs Welch's precious lad. They both are. After what 'e done to that peacock one or two sapphires in a ring would be mincemeat for 'im.'

'So you've seen it,' Edith asked suddenly intense.

'Me?' Kate wanted to be told. 'Not me I never.'

'How do you come to know it was a sapphire ring then?'

'Because I've got eyes in my head, silly. I've seen 'er wear it.'

'Oh if that's all,' Edith pronounced turning away again. 'From the way you talked I thought you must've known.'

'So you 'id the ring away then?' Albert said.

'Well what else could I do, use your sense do. I didn't want to hand that over to Agatha Burch so she could get the credit did I?'

'She'd've told you were the person that came across it.'

'That's what you think Albert. You talk like one of these Irishmen you're so innocent but then there's more behind what they say than they let on to If you want to know they're an improvement.'

'Edie,' Kate said in an admiring voice, 'you've changed.'

'Too true I have,' Edith answered, 'but there you are you see. Circumstances alter cases,' she said.

'Over at Clancarty,' Kate began, 'that Captain Davenport strips 'is men naked when their day's work diggin' is done to see they don't take nothing. Paddy says the priest 'as taken the matter up.'

'I bet you wishes you was there,' Albert surprisingly remarked.

In reply Kate fetched him a swipe with the back of her hand across his cheek. He scrambled up while she sat on fists clenched, ready to fight and get the better of him. But he walked off and did not say a word. The dejected donkey followed at his heels. Against the everlastingly hurrying ocean with its bright glare from the beginning of the world, he wandered with the donkey drooped to his tracks as if he was a journeying choirboy.

'The sauce,' Kate said.

' 'E's only a kid,' Edith remarked and lay back along the sand after spreading out 'I love you' for her head. She looked straight up at the sky without wrinkling the skin about her eyes.

'There's times I could go scatty in this old country,' Kate announced calm as though nothing had occurred, 'I could really. Come on let's have one of them talks like we used to. Now what about you for a start? You tell your own girl what it's like to be loved.'

'Kate you are awful.'

'Come on now there's no one to hear with this sea. Your boy friend is in the sulks along of 'is precious donkey. You tell your Kate.'

'Oh him,' Edith said, 'you want to go easy with him. What you let slip when we woke you upset Bert.'

'What d'you mean?'

'Oh I wasn't referring to that name you mentioned.'

'Then what you're gettin' at Edie is my poking fun at you lyin' over 'im to reach me?'

'That's right. You see Kate 'e's touchy. It's calf love.'

'Don't make me laugh,' Kate said scornful. 'Calf love you call that? Why you talk like you was your young lady. We got no time for calf love dear as you call it. We're ordinary workin' folk. 'E'll be going off in a faint next.'

'Just because when I see a mouse caught by its little leg in a wheel and he opens a great mouth at me ...'

'Now then,' Kate interrupted, ' 'old on. I wasn't gettin' at you. I don't know why we can't be like we used to I'm sure but nowadays we don't seem able ever to do anything but go sarky at one another.'

Edith turned away from her once more. 'O.K. let it pass,' she said.

'But surely you don't intend to permit that lad to go moonin' after you like a drowned duck?'

'Well what d'you want me to do then?' Edith asked her.

'You should've seen 'is face when you was leant over. It was enough to make me bring up my dinner. And you lookin' down into his eyes as though you liked it.'

'If he'd so much as touched me I'd've shown him dear I can tell you,' Edith said. 'I'd've given a lesson he'd remember all his life,' she added.

'Well if you want my advice that's what I'd learn the kid before this day is done.'

'Why,' asked Edith, 'you don't suppose I relish his goin' mushy surely? A child like that? He wants his old mother, that's his trouble. But live an' let live is what I always say.'

'Then don't you keep on about me and you know who,' Kate said.

'O K. dear. Now let's have a nap,' said Edith.

And in no time both were well away. The children got wet through.

Raunce's Albert crept back followed by the donkey that he could not rid himself of. He sat down by Edith. He never took his eyes off her body.

Edith found out that Agatha had a cup of tea most days with Mrs Welch. So she persuaded Miss Burch to put forward a claim to tea all round after dinner, a privilege not enjoyed by the others since before the war. Everyone was surprised when the cook agreed But that was not all. Edith feared for Raunce's neck. She said those draughts in the servant's hall might harm him. Now coal was so short it was only a small peat fire she could lay each morning in the butler's room, and she insisted that the grate Raunce had was too narrow for peat. This no doubt could be her excuse to get him to take his cup along with her to one of the living rooms where huge fires were kept stoked all day to condition the old masters.

So it came about next afternoon that Charley and Edith had drawn up deep leather armchairs of purple in the Red Library. A ledge of more purple leather on the fender supported Raunce's heels next his you-and-me in a gold Worcester cup and saucer. Pointed french windows were open onto the lawn about which peacocks stood pat in the dry as though enchanted. A light summer air played in from over massed geraniums, toyed with Edith's curls a trifle. Between the books the walls were covered cool in green silk. But she seemed to have no thought to the draught.

'You ever noticed that little place this side of the East Gate?' he was asking.

'Well I can't say I've looked over it if that's what you're after,' she replied. He hooked a finger into the bandage round his throat as though to ease himself.

'Next time you pass that way you have a look, see.'

'Why Charley?'

'It's empty that's why.'

'It's empty is it?' she echoed dull but with a sharp glance.

'The married butlers used to live there at one time,' he explained. Then he lied. 'Yesterday mornin',' he went on canny, 'Michael stopped me as he came out of the kitchen. You'll never guess what he was onto.'

'Not something for one of his family again?' she enquired.

'That's right,' he said. 'It was only he's goin' to ask Mrs. T. for it when she gets back, that's all. The roof of their pig sty of a hovel 'as gone an' fallen on 'is blessed sister-in-law's head and's crushed a finger of one of their kids.'

'The cheek,' she exclaimed.

'A horrid liar the man is,' Charley commented. 'But it's not the truth that matters. It's what's believed,' he added.

'You think she'll credit such a tale?' Edith wanted to know.

'Now love,' he began then paused. He was dressed in black trousers and a stiff shirt with no jacket, the only colour being in his footman's livery waistcoat of pink and white stripes. He wore no collar on account of his neck. Lying back he squinted into the blushing rose of that huge turf fire as it glowed, his bluer eye azure on which was a crescent rose reflection. 'Love,' he went on toneless, 'what about you an' me getting married? There I've said it.'

'That'll want thinking over Charley,' she replied at once Her eyes left his face and with what seemed a quadrupling in depth came following his to rest on those rectangles of warmth alive like blood. From this peat light her great eyes became invested with rose incandescence that was soft and soft and soft.

'There's none of this love nonsense,' he began again appearing to strain so as not to look at her. 'It's logical dear that's what. You see I thought to get my old mother over out of the bombers.'

'And quite right too,' she answered prompt.

'I'm glad you see it my way,' he took her up. 'Oh honey you don't know what that means.'

'I've always said a wife that can't make a home for her man's mother doesn't merit a place of her own,' she announced gentle.

'Then you don't say no?' he asked glancing her way at last. His white face was shot with green from the lawn.

'I haven't said yes have I?' she countered and looked straight at him, her heart opening about her lips. Seated as she was back to the light he could see only a blinding space for her head framed in dark hair and inhabited by those great eyes on her, fathoms deep.

'No that's right,' he murmured obviously lost.

'I'll need to think over it,' she gently said. Folding hands she returned her gaze into the peat fire.

'She's a good woman,' Raunce began again. 'She worked hard to raise us when dad died. There were six in our family. She had a struggle.'

Edith sat on quiet.

'Now we're scattered all over,' he went on. 'There's only my sister Bell with the old lady these days. There's her to consider,' he said.

'The one working in the gun factory?' she asked.

'That's right,' he replied. Then he waited.

'Well I don't know as she'd need to come to Ireland,' Edith said at last. 'She's got her job all right? I'd hardly reckon to make the change myself if I was in her position.'

'You have it any way you want,' Raunce explained. 'I thought to just mention her that's all. Mrs Charley Raunce,' he announced in educated accents. 'There you are eh?' He seemed to be gathering confidence.

She suddenly got up half turned from him.

'I'm not sayin' one way or the other, Charley. Not yet awhile.'

'But it's not no for a start,' he said, also rising.

'No,' she replied. She began to blush. Seeing this he grinned with an absurd look of sweet pain. 'No,' she went on, 'I don't say I couldn't.' And all at once her mood appeared to change. She whirled about and made a dive at the cushion of the chair she had been using.

'What's more I'll wear this old ring for the engagement,' she crowed, 'oh let me it won't only be for a minute.' He approached doltish while she hooked with her finger in the tear. 'That's funny,' she said. 'Why it can't have,' she murmured. 'But it has,' she announced drawing herself up to look him in the face. 'It's gone,' she said.

'What's gone?'

'Mrs Tennant's ring,' she said.

'It can't have,' he objected. 'Give here,' and he took that cushion, ripped the seam open. 'Must've slipped inside that's about the long and short of it,' he said as he worked.

'I don't know about can't have gone,' she said looking intently at him with something in her voice, 'but it's not there that's all.'

He felt round the edges.

'You're right,' he pronounced, 'there's nothing.'

'Yet a ring wouldn't have wings now would it?' she said meaningly.

'Edie,' he said, 'if you think I took that you must consider me worse than the lowest thing which crawls.'

'No,' she murmured, 'I don't,' and leant over to give him a light kiss.

'Then you ain't never found nothing, see,' he said putting his arms round her. 'Oh honey...' he began when both heard a car turn towards the Castle over the ha-ha.

'Look sharp,' he brought out as if she had been kissing him. 'That must be Mrs Tancy,' he said and turned to go. 'Holy smoke,' he added, 'but I can't answer the door dressed as I am.' While Raunce hastened out she went on her knees it might be to make believe she was only in the room to do the fire.

His training probably induced Charley to close the door soft after him and it was not until he had reached his quarters, when he was out of earshot, that he began to yell for Bert. So nobody saw this car drive up but Edith. She noted in it not the lady above referred to but a stranger, a man, a grey homburg hat.

His boy came running in a green baize apron. At that moment the bell rang. 'The front door,' Raunce said as the indicator chocked, 'I'm wrongly dressed. Put 'er in the Red Library an' don't leave till I come or something might go missing. Not like that,' he almost shouted as Albert made off tied in green, 'let's 'ave that down,' he cried as he twitched at the bow it was knotted with, 'an' where's your jacket?' Raunce got the lad away at last discreetly clad, calling out to him, 'I won't be a minute while I dress.'

So it was Albert received Michael Mathewson at the entrance, who took this man's business card when he asked for Mrs Tennant. The lad held it upsidedown. In consequence he could not read the name or the line in Irish below, underneath which came a translation between brackets which went, 'Irish Regina Assurance.' There was finally a Dublin address in the right-hand corner.

'This way please,' Albert said the way he had been taught. He led the man over the chequered marble floor. Mike Mathewson followed fat and short and bald with blue spats.

'That's to say they're not here,' the boy piped over his shoulder.

'It'th O.K. thon,' Mike lisped.

So it was Albert showed him in where Edith was still on her knees after a proposal of marriage, as if tidying. As Mathewson passed Albert probably remembered twice for he sang out again. 'This way please.'

'Thankth thon,' the man replied. Edith turned away from them and began a fit of giggling.

'Nithe plathe you've got,' he remarked bright in her direction. Albert closed the door gently, stood so it seemed unobserved and ill at ease. He licked a palm of his hand then smarmed his yellow hair.

'The familieth away?' Mr Mathewson enquired picking up the paper-knife with the agate handle.

'Yes sir,' Edith made answer  She looked for a second time full at him seriously with her raving beauty.

'That'th all right girlie,' he brought out and goggled a trifle. Then he put that paper-knife down. He came near.

'I'll do thomething for you,' he announced soft, 'I'll put you in the way to make a fool out of Mike. That'th me. There'th my bithneth card he holdth. It'th thith way. We'll maybe have a little bet on thith. I'll wager thixpenth you can never gueth my bithneth.'

On this she rose to her feet, back to the fire. Her eyes were large as she smoothed her dress. He turned round as though to give her time.

'You're in on thith thon,' he called urgent, soft, but the lad made no move.

'It's Mr Raunce you want,' she interrupted.

'That'th all right,' he answered, 'I'm not thelling anything. I gave up thelling when trade got thlack. I'm an enquiry agent,' he brought out sharp, turning to her close.

'What?' she muttered and began to blush.

'Yeth that'th a thurprithe ain't it,' he went on seemingly delighted.

'Now you'd never have guethed ith'nt that right without you'd theen my bithneth card. Mike Mathewthonth the name. Jutht had a tooth out that'th why I thpeak like thith,' he excused then laid a hand genteel across his mouth. He took it away at once to finger the spotted tie. He was now very near indeed. He smelled of acid of violets.

'I come down when they claim a loss,' he brought out sharp, not lisping.

'Oh,' she said faint.

'I reprethent the Inthuranth Company,' he explained again.

At this precise moment out by the dovecote little Albert was with Mrs Jack's little girls. He knelt down while Miss Evelyn and Miss Moira stood dappled by leaf sunshine. The lad himself was shaded by that pierced tower of Pisa inside which a hundred ruby eyes were round.

'You're not ever goin' to bury it Bert?' Miss Evelyn enquired.

'Naw,' he replied picking up half an empty eggshell.

The sisters squatted. Opening his fist he displayed the ring, a small blaze of blue. He scooped it into that eggshell which he then placed with the unbroken end upwards, a pale bell over the jewel, under a tuft of sharp grass.

'You won't leave that out in the open?' Miss Moira asked.

'It's on account of them birds pinch rings,' he answered. 'If Mr Raunce come to find'm then we don't know a thing, the pigeons took'm see.'

'But doves don't steal rings Albert, you mean jackdaws.'

'Don't be so soft,' he said. 'Everyone knows doves will,' he ended.

'You'll lose it,' Miss Evelyn announced wondering.

'Rings don't walk,' he said, 'an' this shell's so them birds won't rout'm out,' he explained. 'They'd never think to turn an egg that's broken.'

'Well you are clever,' Miss Moira told him and meant it.

'I'm smart don't fear,' he said, 'only I didn't ought to let you girls in on this. You'd never keep a secret. So you'll 'ave to take a oath see.'

'An oath?'

'That's right. You're to swear you won't never tell. It'll be special. This is 'ow it goes. While I break a cock's egg over your mouth you say, "My lips is sealed may I drop dead."'

'Cock's eggs?'

'Peacock's softy. I'll fetch me a couple.' As he ran off to that door he had seen Raunce come out of an another occasion he called back as he stumbled with urgency, 'Don't you stir from where you be.' He had picked up countrified expressions when he was evacuated.

'Well it's wicked I know,' Miss Moira said with satisfaction.

'How will you swear so the egg doesn't get in your mouth?' Miss Evelyn asked.

But they waited. In almost no time the lad was back. Then one of the girls objected. She said she wasn't going to stand for having that filthy sticky stuff on her face. The other wanted to know who she considered she was to think she couldn't, when Edith had hundreds of these eggs put away in waterglass against the time she might want them for her skin. And little Albert heard. And then made them both go through with it. They seemed delighted.

Meantime the assessor had been asking questions. Edith did not know so she said. Or she could not tell for certain she was sure. Mike Mathewson was getting nowhere. Albert kept silence. Then Raunce at last arrived, in his dark suit and without the bandage. He came quiet and Mike Mathewson did not hear him. He had to clear his throat to make this man turn round.

'Yes sir?' Charley asked.

'That'th all right my man,' Mike answered. 'Making a few enquirieth that'th all.'

It might have been Raunce thought Edith looked upset. Not moving from the door he took a line.

'I'm sure Mrs Tennant would not wish for questions asked,' he said.

'Precithely why I wath thent,' Mr Mathewson replied, a green high light following out his nose.

'I'm afraid we can't have this,' Charley said firm. 'Mrs Tennant would never allow it.'

'Is it so?' Mike said grim, not lisping.

'I will have to ask you to leave that's all,' Charley went on and did not call him sir.

'But I have been thent.'

'Who by?'

Then Edith must have forgot herself. She interrupted.

'It's about the ring,' she said in a small voice.

'What ring?' Raunce wanted to know without a sign of any kind.

'Let'th thee,' Mike suggested. 'When Mr Tennant wath alive you uthed to be hith man I take it.'

'No I was not.'

'And you never heard of a ring being gone?' Mike asked in menacing fashion.

''Ow d'you mean?' Raunce enquired in a less educated voice.

'That'th thtrange,' Mathewson said almost genial, 'nobody theemth to know nothing.'

'What's strange about that?' Charley asked and began to squint. 'Come on you tell me. Who might you be for a start?'

'You're the butler?'

'What's that got to do with you? It's you we're talkin' about. Who're you?'

Edith broke in again.

'He's come about the insurance,' she explained and appealed.

'Nobody asked you,' her Charley said sharp but with a soft glance in her direction. 'You don't know nothing,' he added.

'Know nothing?' Mr Mathewson echoed. 'Mark what I'm thaying now. I never inthinuated thith young lady knew anything.' He spoke gently as if to ingratiate.

'In – what?' Charley asked.

'Inferred,' Mike Mathewson explained and now he spoke sharp. 'Don't try and be thmart with me. You'll find it don't work.'

'I wouldn't know what you're referrin' to,' Raunce said a bit daunted.

'The ring,' the assessor replied soft. 'The thapphire cluthter my company inthured on.'

'Is Mrs Tennant acquainted with you?' Raunce asked.

'She called us in,' the man said very sharp, again without lisping. 'Now is that sufficient?'

'She called you in?' Raunce echoed.

'You do know about the ring then?'

'Know about it? I've 'eard Mrs Tennant mislaid one.'

'Then why tell me jutht now you never did,' Mike asked him very quiet.

Raunce began to bluster. 'Me?' he cried, 'me tell you that? I never made any such statement and this girl and my lad here's my witnesses. What I very likely said was I didn't know your business an' I say I don't know it now any more than I did at the start. There you are.' He glanced as though for support at Edith. She was gazing at the seat of the armchair. She seemed distracted.

'Will you anthwer a fair quethtion?' Mr Mathewson began again. 'That'th above board ain't-it?' he said almost friendly.

'Reply to a question? Well I don't know before you ask me do I?' Raunce replied.

'Then you won't anthwer?'

'I never said that. What are you tryin'? To trap someone?'

'Who mentioned a trap? I'm here to trathe a ring.'

'What's that got to do with me?' Raunce enquired.

'I don't know yet,' Mike replied gentle.

'Well get this then. I don't know nothin' an' I'm not sayin' nothin' without Mrs Tennant gives permission. So now have you got that straight?'

They stared at each other. Edith went down on her knees again. She began to polish the bright steel fire irons with a leather. Catching Charley's eye behind Mike's back she shook her head urgent at him. Albert stood as though transfixed.

'Mithith Tennant thent for me to come over before she got back,' Mr Mathewson began again. This time he appeared to speak to Albert.

'Mrs Tennant's comin' back?' Raunce cried.

'Tho I'm led to underthtand.'

'Then thank God for that,' Raunce said relieved. 'She can clear a whole lot up Mrs Tennant can. But if she don't all I'll say is she can have my notice. Arriving down 'ere to bully the girls, then treatin' me like I was a criminal.'

'Lithen,' Mike began again as if tired. 'A ring'th been mithed. A very valuable thapphire cluthter. My company'th been called on to dithburthe. I've come down to invethtigate. I've driven a hundred mileth. Now do you underthtand?'

'O.K.,' Raunce answered. 'And now you can tell me something. What's all this to do with me?'

'I'm asking you that's all,' the assessor said with sudden venom.

Again they stood and stared at one another. Then Raunce's Albert spoke.

'I got it,' he confessed.

'You what?' Raunce shouted. Edith jumped to her feet. Raunce swallowed three times and began an, 'I tell you,' when Mike Mathewson brought him up sharp, fairly hissing.

'I've had about enough d'you hear me? Now then my lad we're getting placeth. You got it?'

Albert was trembling but he stood his ground.

'Come on then,' Mike continued. 'Nothing to be afraid of. Where've you got what?'

The boy was silent in a palsy. There was a sort of lull. Edith went over and knelt by him, arms by her sides, as though he was very small and was to tie the scarf over her eyes. Until she turned on the assessor, blushing dark.

'He got an idea he meant an' who may you be to come scarin' honest folk that earn a living?' She spoke loud. 'You get off h'out, there's the best place for you. We don't want none of your sort here, frightenin' his wits out of the lad. How should we care about her old ring? If I was a man I'd show him off the premises,' she said panting to Raunce.

'That's an idea,' this man replied. He began to move slowly over to the assessor who started to say, 'What idea did the young chap have?' Only to break off with a 'now then,' as he moved backwards to the open french windows away from Charley.

'Plantin' words into people's mouths like it was evidence,' Raunce almost chanted as he advanced. 'When a lad says he got an idea makin' out he got the ring.'

'Well what wath the idea?'

'It's a disgrace that's all,' Charley said, now very close. 'You go on off see?'

'All right I'm on my way,' Mr Mathewson announced. Then he had the last word. 'But get this. We're not paying,' he said and went.

'Wait till 'e's gone,' Raunce warned the others.

And Mike Mathewson drove off quick.

As soon as the car had cleared the ha-ha Raunce rounded on Albert. He was shouting in passion, dead white with a wild squint.

'So you got it,' he yelled, 'you got what? I got it,' he shrieked in falsetto. 'And you can have at that. 'Ere you are then 'and over.' He came at Albert who seemed paralysed. 'Where is it then?' he cried like an epileptic as he shook him 'Where is it?' Albert's head swung back and forth, his yellow shock of hair flopping But the lad kept silent.

'That's enough Charley,' Edith said. 'He's never had it.'

'But 'e might 'ave,' Raunce answered desisting. His rages never lasted. ' 'E's capable of anything that lad is. Why there was none spoke to 'im. I don't suppose there was one of us in this room remembered 'is presence. An' then what must 'e go an' do. Why bless my soul if 'e doesn't feel the need to sing out 'e's got the miserable object  Holy Moses,' Charley ended, apparently in better humour. 'But that was smart of you love to think that one up. It was you had the idea all right. Now don't start snivellin',' he said to Albert who began to cry in the painful way boys do when they are too old for tears.

'Charley,' she said, 'what did that mean when 'e said his company wouldn't even pay.'

Mr Raunce explained. Albert's sobs grew louder but they paid no attention.

'Then that's awkward Charley. I mean it may come back on Mrs Tennant.'

'Well she's lost so much, girl, I shouldn't wonder if the Insurance Company would never take her on a second time. Once one refuses her I don't suppose she'll get any to insure her jewellery again. That's the way it goes.'

'Yes but look here then that's serious that is Charley.'

'Serious you bet the thing is serious,' he replied. 'But you wait until I get this lad of mine to meself. Just give me two minutes alone with him.'

'Oh him,' she said indifferent, 'don't trouble your mind over him.'

'And why wouldn't I when 'e knows? My God what an afternoon.'

'He never took it,' she told him without so much as a glance at Albert. 'He did what he done for me. He thought that inspector was makin' out I'd had it.'

'He what?'

'He was,' she said. Albert sobbed suddenly unrestrained as though somehow he had come unstoppered. 'You don't understand these things, I do,' she said. Then she bent down. Before Raunce's eyes she kissed the lad's cheek. 'There, thanks kid,' she said. But Albert, not looking, made a move to strike her away without however hitting her.

'Did you see what 'e done then?' Raunce asked low. 'I'll learn 'im.'

'Let him be dearest,' she advised and the boy ran out. Raunce shut the door Albert had left open.

'Well I don't know,' he began, taking her by the shoulders. She looked into his face. 'The dirty tyke,' he said. 'But we got to find it.'

'All right,' she replied, 'an' I'm goin' to start with my Miss Moira. You go off, I'll handle this best alone. And don't you lay hands on that Albert. It's the other I have my suspicions of,' she ended.

When Raunce was gone she went to the window. She called the child.

The little girl came running, stood moist in the sun before Edith.

'Where've you been Miss Moira?' She asked sweet.

'Why out by the dovecote Edith.'

'Look at you then,' Edith scolded gently and squatted down. 'Just see the state you're in. You'll be landin' me in such trouble if you don't take good care when your grandma gets back.'

'Is grandma coming?'

'She is that,' Edith said smiling as she began to clear up the child's glowing face with her own grubby handkerchief.

'Is mummy too?'

'I couldn't say love. Whatever've you been at to get in such a state?'

'I hope mummy doesn't come.'

'Hark at you,' Edith said letting it go.

'I do. 'Cos that Captain Davenport will be over all the time when she does.'

'Hush dear,' Edith said sharp, 'someone'll hear. And you shouldn't mention such a thing even to your own Edith.'

'I don't like him.'

'It's not for us to like or not like. You're too little.'

'Darling Edith why are you looking so excited?'

Edith giggled. 'Am I?' she asked, wiping away at stains on Miss Moira's deep blue skirt.

'You should see yourself.'

'Well I expect I've had a day and a half. But what've you been up to? That's what I want to be told thanks.'

'Edith why are you?'

'Can you keep secrets ducky?' Edith asked in reply.

'A secret oo how lovely,' Miss Moira exclaimed.

'I don't suppose you know how.'

'Oh I promise. Let my lips be sealed,' the child said. May I drop dead she added to herself.

'Well then. Only don't breathe to nobody mind. Your Edith's had a proposal.'

'Oh Edith has Albert at last? And are you going to marry him?'
Edith put the handkerchief away and kissed her.

'There that's better,' she said.

'Do tell,' the child pleaded warm.

'One secret for another,' Edith announced. 'You say what you've been along of.'

'Will you marry him then?'

'Look I've told you my secret. Now you come out with yours. Fair's fair,' Edith said.

'We've been with Albert.'

'That's no secret.'

'It was.'

'What's dark about that then?' Edith wanted to know.

'He's got my grandma's ring. The one she lost.'

'Has he so? And what's he done with it?' Edith enquired casual.

'I don't know,' the little girl lied, on account of dropping dead perhaps.

'Which Albert, yours or mine?' Edith asked soft.

'Mine,' Miss Moira answered. 'Oh I do love him.'

'Are you goin' to be married?'

'Of course.'

'Isn't that lovely,' Edith said. 'But what's he been up to with that ring meantime?' she went on carefully disinterested.

'I don't know, honest I don't,' the child lied once more. And Edith let it go. And the day laden with sunshine, with the noise of bees broke in upon their silence. There was a sharp smell of geraniums.

'Well I must be off now,' Miss Moira said. She ran away stepping high.

'I don't know,' Charley grumbled good natured again at Albert in the pantry as the lad washed his face, 'I don't rightly know what to make of you an' that's a fact. Speakin' out of turn like you did. There's times I ask myself if you'll ever learn.'

'I'm sorry Mr Raunce.'

'That's O K. my lad,' said Charley unexpectedly mild. 'To-day of all days I wouldn't wish to have a disagreement with nobody. But you must use your best endeavours. 'Owever hard it may seem to keep mum for 'eaven's sake keep mum. That's your place and in a manner of speakin' it's mine. You've no knowledge of this ring, nor I have, we none of us know. What's more it's no concern of ours. When Mrs T. made a rumpus soon as she first lost it well then it was up to anyone she spoke to to make a search. She's always puttin' things down where she can't find 'em. But after the first upset let sleepin' dogs lie. D'you get me?'

'Yes Mr Raunce.'

'It did your heart credit to speak up when you did, mind. But you'll discover it don't pay to have a heart on most occasions. Anyway not with a man of his stamp. Where did 'e say 'e come from? What's 'is trade card?'

Albert picked up the man's bit of pasteboard and handed it to Charley.

'Not with wet fingers,' Mr Raunce began again. ''Ow many times do I have to tell you, wipe your hands when you pass anything and clean your teeth before you have to do with a woman. Holy Jesus', he sang out without warning, 'holy Moses,' he corrected himself, 'what's this?'

'What's the matter Mr Raunce?'

'Why the Insurance Company. I knew it all along. See 'ere. "Irish Regina Assurance." Don't you read that the way I do.'

'No Mr Raunce.'

'Why spell me out those letters. Irish Regina Assurance. I.R.A. boy. So 'e was one of their scouts, must a' been.'

'I.R A.?'

'Where's my girl?' Raunce asked and dashed out.

*

A few days passed. Then one morning while they were at their dinner in the servants' hall that telephone began to ring away in the pantry. Albert came back with a message he had written out in block letters.

'Returning Monday, Tennant,' Raunce read aloud into a silence. 'Well thank God for it,' he added, 'and about time if you ask me.'

'I never knew you so keen to start work again,' Agatha remarked malicious.

'That's all right Miss Burch,' he said.

'There's more in this than meets the eye,' she suggested.

'Why I've not said a word,' he began as Edith watched him anxiously and as though disapproving. Then he went on, 'I've not let on about it because I wouldn't have you bothered. We've all of us got our worries with this bombin' over the other side to mention just the one item. So I thought I'll keep it to meself. Your own back's broad enough I said.'

'Thanks I'm sure,' Miss Burch announced, putting a small slice of potato dainty into her mouth. Then she raised a crooked finger as if to scratch under the wig but thought better perhaps for she picked up the fork again.

'There's things occur which you'd never believe,' he went on.

'Now Charley,' Edith said. It was the first time, as Kate's eyes showed, that the girl had called him in public by his christian name. 'You don't want to bring all that up,' she ended weak.

'Well we're all one family in this place, there's how I see the situation,' he started. Kate began to giggle. But she got no encouragement from Edith. 'We can share,' he continued, still sentimental. 'Now Mrs T. is comin' back she can clear this little matter up. It was something occurred not more than five days ago.'

'No Charley,' Edith interrupted.

'Bless me,' Miss Burch said staring at her, 'if it's known to another it should be known to me I hope.'

'She couldn't help herself,' Raunce put in. 'She was present when 'e called along with my Albert here.'

'Who called?' Miss Burch enquired.

'The I.R.A. man,' Raunce announced as though with an ultimatum.

'Mercy,' Miss Burch exclaimed, 'and are we going to have that old nonsense all over again?'

'Nonsense it may be to you Miss Burch but you'll excuse me, I know different,' he said.

'Then I'd best learn more,' she suggested.

'It was about the ring,' Edith put in.

'That was 'is pretext right enough,' Raunce said, 'that was how he got past Albert here at the door. It was my bandage,' he explained. 'I couldn't answer the bell dressed as I was. So I sent the lad. If it had been me opened the door to him then with my experience I'd've told within a second, like in the twinklin' of an eye,' he said serious.

'Mrs Tennant's ring she mislaid?' Agatha enquired.

'That was no more than the way he chose to put it,' Charley began again when Miss Burch surprisingly broke out as follows.

'Then they'll needs must dig the drains up,' she cried in what seemed to be great agitation, 'I've said so all along now haven't I?'

'Come, come,' Raunce said, 'there's no call to take things that far,' he said and frowned. 'She's always mislayin' possessions.'

Paddy spoke.

'What's 'e say?' Raunce asked.

'He says that weren't no I.R.A. man if 'e came to the front door,' translated Kate. 'They only use the back entrance those gentry he reckons.'

'Hark at 'im,' Raunce announced.

'Well how d'you know he's mistaken?' Kate wanted to be told.

'Now then,' Raunce said to her. 'We don't want none o' your backchat my gel thank you.'

'You leave my girls out of it,' Miss Burch ordered but in a weak voice as though about to faint.

'I told you,' Edith said to her Charley.

'I don't know,' Charley said, 'there's times I can't fathom any one of you an' that's a fact. What is all this?'

'What is all this?' Miss Burch echoed in a shrill voice. 'You ask me that? When you're telling us we've had a I.R.A. man actually call at the Castle?'

'But I thought you were on about the drains.'

'Oh you men,' Miss Burch replied faint once more, 'you will never understand even the simplest thing.'

'It was only an insurance inspector came about the ring,' Edith explained. 'I don't know where Mr Raunce got it he was from the I.R.A. I'm sure,' she said.

'You mean he said that ring was stolen?' Miss Burch cried, plainly beside herself again.

'Not on your life,' Charley took her up. 'You ladies will always jump at conclusions.'

'Well what was he here for then?' Miss Burch enquired.

'Why to see 'ow much his Insurance Company could do about it,' Raunce replied. But Miss Burch, who seemed really agitated, was not having any.

'You said just now he was an I.R A. man,' she objected quavering.

'Well maybe he was both,' Raunce said. 'They've got to live like everyone else when all's said and done.'

'And we never had the drains up,' Miss Burch wailed. 'Oh dear. Now Mrs Tennant's coming back when it will be too late. Only the other day Mrs Welch was tellin' me they should be dug on account of the children. She's nervous for her Albert.'

'The drains?' Edith asked.

'The drains?' Charley echoed. 'You'll pardon me but you don't dig drains again.'

'Well clean them out then, do whatever you do with the things,' Miss Burch answered a trifle sharper. 'They're unhealthy as they are now if they aren't worse.'

'We're livin' under a shadow these days,' Raunce announced, 'that's the way it is with all of us. There's matters you mightn't take account of in normal times get you down now.'

Kate began to giggle cautious and looked for support to Edith. Edith however appeared grave. So did Albert who was watching her. Then Edith said to Raunce,

'I don't know, I can't seem to take any account of it,' she said.

'Oh you're young,' Miss Burch told her.

'She's gone and hit the nail right on the head Miss Burch has,' Raunce announced agitated in his turn. 'An I R A. man now. An inspector from the Insurance Company. Then the drains an' all on top of all this bombing not to mention the invasion with Jerry set to cross over with drawn swords, it's plenty to get anyone down.'

At this point Albert spoke. His face was dead white.

'Well I'm crossing over the other side to enlist,' he said.

'What?' Edith sighed.

'Oh?' Raunce shouted. 'Enlist? You at your age? Enlist in what will you oblige me?'

'I'm goin' to be a air gunner,' the lad said.

'An air gunner eh?' Raunce chortled but you could tell he was distracted. 'But you aren't of an age boy. Besides that's the most dangerous of all bloody jobs boy. You'll be killed.'

Edith and Kate had gone pale. Miss Burch's eyes filled with tears. They all stared at Albert except Paddy who went on with his food. Edith said,

'But what about your mum Bert?'

'Sis'll look after her and I'll be home while I'm waiting till I'm old enough. I wish to get me out of here, then go an' fight,' he said. Miss Burch burst into tears.

'Why you poor dear,' Edith murmured going round the table to her.

'Now look what you done,' Raunce said.

'I'm sorry Mr Raunce I never intended . . .' the lad mumbled.

'You've no thought for others that's the trouble,' Raunce complained his eyes anxious on Agatha, 'speaking up like you did, sayin' this that and the other. But there it's your age.'

'You let me fetch you a nice cup of tea,' Edith was telling Miss Burch who sat bowed with her face in her hands. 'Oh dear oh dear,' Agatha moaned.

'Gawd strewth look what you done,' Raunce said once more at which Albert got to his feet, moved over to the door. He stood for a moment before he went out.

'I'm sorry Miss Burch I'm sure. I'm goin' to be a air gunner,' he said white, as though defiant.

When the door was shut Miss Burch looked up between her fingers.

'How old would he be?' she asked.

'My Albert?' Raunce replied. 'Not above sixteen I'll be bound.'

'He's eighteen,' Edith said.

'Eighteen?' Raunce cried. 'Why you've only to look at 'im. No girl, I've got it somewhere in my desk, the letter 'e come with I mean, he can't be a day more than I just said.'

'He's eighteen. That was his birthday the other week,' Edith insisted calmly.

'Oh this war,' Miss Burch wailed, then hid her face again.

'You run and carry her a cup of tea,' Edith asked Kate.

'All right I'll go,' the girl replied unwilling.

But Miss Burch would not stay. She said she had best lie down for a spell. So Edith slipped out to the kitchen to ask Kate to fetch that cup to Agatha's room. When she got back in the hall she found Raunce seated on his own there. Paddy had probably gone back to his peacocks. So she sat down alongside him although this must have seemed rather noticeable, seeing that it was nearly time to start work.

Charley barely glanced at her. 'Eighteen?' he muttered. 'Is he that much? I could've sworn he was two year younger.'

'Well dear,' she said, 'you did put your foot right in it.'

'In what way?' he asked.

'I'll say you opened your mouth. That ring's not found yet even if I do fancy I know who's got it.'

'It's you honey,' he explained. 'I was worried over you. Then when I received the wire I thought to myself now everything will come right once Mrs T. gets back. It seemed to loose my tongue,' he said.

'Something loosed it dear. But there's nothing gained by speakin' of that ring until we hold it safe.'

'You never took the ring,' he said reaching over for her hand. 'You found a valuable yes but you put that back right where you came across it. And what else could you do? Tell me? You've no lock up Of course there's the strongroom back in my quarters. But we can't have that shut all day and the things which are kept in it might as well be laid out on the drive for all the safety they're in of a daytime in this barracks of a hole. So you couldn't count on the old strongroom. Then what did you do? You put it back where for all you could speak to Mrs Tennant had hid the thing in security. In the finish someone or other pinched it from there. That's all.'

'What's on your mind then Charley?'

'Nothing,' he answered not looking at her.

'Oh yes there is. I can tell,' she returned. 'Besides you said just now you was worried over me.'

'Oh honey,' he broke out sudden, 'I do love you so.'

'Of course,' she replied bright.

'Give us a kiss dear please.'

'What here?' she asked. 'Where someone will come in any minute?'

'I didn't realize I could love anyone the way I love you. I thought I'd lived too long.'

'You thought you'd lived too long?' and she laughed in her throat.

'I can't properly see myself these days,' Raunce went on looking sideways past her at the red eye of a deer's stuffed head. 'Why I'm altogether changed,' he said. 'But look love, no man's younger than his age. There's more'n twenty years between us.'

'I like a man that's a man and not a lad,' she murmured.

'Yes but the years fly fast,' he answered. 'To think of Albert old enough to enlist.'

'He's upset you your lad has isn't that right?'

'Yes Edie,' Raunce said wondering. 'It did give me a turn I must confess.'

'Why?' she asked grim.

'Well it looks like we're out of it over in Eire as we are or whatever they call this country of savages. D'you get me? I can't seem able to express myself but there you are. Away from it somehow.'

'That's what we want to be surely?'

'Yes dear.'

'I mean you're too old. They'd never take you could they?'

'They'd never take me over here. Not if de Valera keeps 'em out '

'Well we're not crossin' over to the other side are we?' She looked sharp at him. He seemed dreamy.

'No,' he answered, 'we're not. Not so long as we can find that ring,' he said. 'And keep the house from bein' burned down over our heads. Or Mrs Jack from running off with the Captain so Mrs Tennant goes over for good to England.'

'Why Charley,' she objected soft, 'there's other places.'

'Not without we find that ring,' he said.

'But I thought you was bringing your mother across,' she said and seemed bitter. She was about to go on when Kate stuck her head in at the door.

'Ho,' this girl announced, 'so you're still 'ere. An' what about the work?' she asked Edith. 'I'm not carryin' on alone let me tell you.'

'I won't be a minute,' Edith answered.

'I know your minutes. I've 'ad some,' Kate remarked.

'And there's the children,' Edith said remembering. 'They'll want their walk.'

'Then I fancy I'll lay me down on my bed. I feel faint,' Kate suggested in Agatha's voice.

'What?' Raunce asked as though confused. 'And with Mrs Tennant returning the day after to-morrow?'

'Oh go drown yourself,' Kate said and slammed the door.

'Holy smoke look what we're coming to,' Raunce muttered under his breath.

But Edith laughed. 'Come on slow coach,' she invited giving him a light kiss on his forehead as she got up. 'Here wait a tick,' he cried as if waking. 'Come to father beautiful,' he called. Only by the time he was on his feet she was gone.

He began to clear away the dinner things for his lad Albert. He surprised himself doing it.

When later that afternoon Edith came into Raunce's room to find him unconscious with his feet on the other chair, he awoke with a start. 'Why me love here I am,' he remarked as if to say you see I don't come out of a good sleep bad-tempered.

'It's me that's worried now all right,' she announced.

'How's that?' he asked.

'They won't tell where they've hid the ring.'

He was wide awake at once.

'You're certain they've got it?'

'I know that for sure,' she answered, 'Miss Moira wouldn't lie to me.'

'You give me just five minutes alone with young Albert.'

'No dear,' she said, 'we don't want more trouble with Mrs Welch.'

'Just five minutes. That's all I need.'

'It won't do dear. If only I had more time. But she'll be back Monday.'

'Mrs Tennant you mean?' he asked. 'Well all I can say is if 'er own grandchildren have took it the little thieves I don't see what she can say to us.'

'Then what were you on about when you came out at dinnertime that if we couldn't discover the ring we'd never get another place in Ireland?'

'Did I say that?'

'You did dear,' she told him. 'An' you went on that they'd clap you in the Army soon as ever you stepped off the boat over in Britain.'

'Look,' he said, 'don't you worry your head. We'll think of a way. Of course it would be best if we found where they've 'id it particularly after the visit we've been paid. That's what I must've intended. It has made things more awkward that man turning up. And then Albert sayin' what 'e did. And now he wants to go and be killed just to get his own back for speaking out of turn I shouldn't wonder.'

'No Charley you don't understand.'

'I don't. That's a fact. I never will I shouldn't be surprised. But I'll say this. You'll live to regret having a kid like that fallen in love over you.'

'He's not,' she lied, it may have been to protect the lad.

'And they say nothing gets past a woman,' Raunce said heavy. 'Why it stands out a mile he is.'

'You're imaginin' Charley,' she said soft.

'Imagining my eye,' he replied. 'But if 'e just wanted to fight for the old country I could agree with the lad.'

She sat up.

'You mean to say you're even considerin' such a step?' she asked.

He answered in a low voice. 'I'm bewitched and bewildered I am really,' he said. 'I don't know what I'm after.'

'Thanks I'm sure,' was her bitter comment.

'Here wait a minute, not so fast,' he exclaimed and leaning forward he got hold of one of her hands on the arm of the other chair. 'Don't get me wrong,' he said. 'That's dam all to do with you an' me.'

'And your old mother you were so keen to get over?' Edith wanted to know.

'Oh her,' Raunce answered.

There was a miserable pause. Then Edith began again,

'Then what did you intend a week or two back when you made out our place was where we are now and Miss Burch said that about blocking the roads? The time Paddy got the wrong side of you?'

'I expect I had in mind what they told us in the newspapers about stayin' put where you happen to be in an invasion.'

'You don't sound very sure,' she said.

'It's Albert,' he explained. 'My Albert to want to do a thing like that. Why it's almost as if 'e was me own son.'

151

'I wish he could hear you now after the way you bawl him out.'

'Me?' Raunce said, 'Why I just give him the rough side of my tongue on occasion so that he'll learn a trade,' he said. 'Here give us a kiss,' he added smiling at last.

This time she actually got up in haste and did no less than sit on his knee.

'You don't love me,' she murmured. When he kissed her she kissed him back with such passion, all of her hard as a board, that he flopped back flabbergasted, having caught a glimpse of what was in her waiting for him.

When the other Albert came to the kitchen for his tea that same afternoon he found Mrs Welch asleep with her head on the massive table. Labouring she lifted heavy bloodshot eyes in his direction.

'Well?' she asked.

'I been out,' he answered sly.

'Out where?'

'We was round the back,' he said.

'And who's we?' she wanted to know as she scratched a vast soft thigh. She gave a wide yawn.

'The young leddies,' he replied. He passed a hand over his forehead as if he could tidy his hair with that one gesture and came to sit quiet opposite auntie.

'Not with that Edith?' she enquired sharp.

'Oh no'm.'

'You're positive?' and Mrs Welch leant across. 'For you know what I told you?'

'Yes'm.'

'What was that then?'

'That I weren't to have nothing more to do with 'er ever,' the boy repeated.

'That's right,' Mrs Welch rejoined. She leant back again and left her arms straight out from her bosom resting on closed fists upon the kitchen table. Her dark hair straggled across her face. 'You wouldn't lie to me?' she asked.

'Oh no'm.'

'Because I daren't abandon this kitchen day or night, not till I go to me bed when day is done that is and then I double lock the door. On guard I am,' she announced in a loud voice. 'Because that Edith's no more'n a thief I tell you an' my girls are hand in glove with 'er, I don't need to be told.' She came to a stop and although glaring at him she seemed rather at a loss.

'Yes'm,' he said respectful.

'An' they're in league with the tradesmen, the I.R.A. merchants, the whole lot are,' she went on a bit wild. 'You mark my words,' she finished and closed anguished eyes.

There was a pause. Then he asked a question with such a glance of malice as must have frightened her if she had caught it.

'What's a I.R.A. man auntie?' he enquired.

'Thieves and murderers,' she said half under her breath as though her thoughts were elsewhere.

'Blimey,' he said. If she had looked she would have seen he mocked.

'Makin' out she's too good to have anything to do with us,' Mrs Welch began again. She opened her eyes. 'Sayin' she won't take you along of Miss Moira and Miss Evelyn.' Mrs Welch heaved herself back to the table, propping her head on the palms of her hands. 'The lousy bitch,' she said soft, 'runnin' in double 'arness with that Raunce into the bargain. Oh,' she suddenly yelled, 'if I catch you I'll tan the 'ide right off of you d'you understand?'

Out in the scullery Jane and Mary nodded at one another, at the rise and fall of this thick voice.

'Tan the 'ide off me what for?' the lad asked.

'What for you bastard imp?' she shouted and lumbering while still on her seat she made a slow grab which he easily dodged.

'I ain't done nothing,' he pretended to whine.

'Ah they're in a society with them tradesmen,' she cried out. 'Don't I know it. Why only the other day Jane was got be'ind the monument by one. I made out I never noticed when she told me,' Mrs Welch explained lowering her voice, 'but I marked it well. And I shan't forget,' she added although she seemed short of breath, 'I weren't born yesterday,' she said.

'Can I 'ave my tea'm?' he requested.

'Can you 'ave your tea?' she replied with scorn and made no move. 'Yes,' she went on dark, 'I've watched their thievin'. Raunce an' that Edith. Not to mention Kate with what she gets up to.... As I've witnessed times without number from me larder windows. So don't you never 'ave nothin' to do with any one of 'em see. 'Ave you got that straight?' she asked hoarse, glaring right through him.

Without waiting for an answer she called out, 'Jane, Master Albert's tea.' She was perfectly serious.

'And may your ladyship's heart be asy on her to get back to the Castle,' Michael said from the driver's seat as obviously excited, grinning in his idiot way, he at once drove off to the stables leaving Mrs Tennant dumped down in front of her own front door surrounded by the luggage.

'Michael,' she called after him to a wisp of blue smoke.

Then she reached for the latch which was a bullock's horn bound in bronze. But these great portals were barred. She gave the ordinary bell a vicious jab.

'What's this Arthur I mean Raunce?' she asked when Charley opened.

'I am very sorry I'm sure Madam. I had no idea the boat would be punctual. I was just putting on my coat to come to look out for you Madam.'

'But why the locked door?' she asked as she entered.

'We had an unwelcome visitor Madam,' he replied, a suitcase already in each hand.

'What do you mean Raunce? Really do try and talk sense. Such a trying journey which it always is now one can't fly and then this.' Charley's Albert came hurrying for the other bags. Mrs Tennant seemed to watch the lad. Raunce had his eye cautious on her.

'Is nobody even going to say good afternoon to me then?' she enquired without warning. 'Raunce I'm sure you don't mean to be unfriendly but when one comes home one does expect a little something. Eldon when he was alive always had a word of welcome.'

'Well all I can say is Madam thank God you are back,' Raunce burst out.

'I suppose that means you've all been at each other's throats again? Very well put those bags of mine down and tell me about it. I might have known,' she added as she went into the Red Library. He followed after.

She sat down where he had rested his heels a day or so before. She took off her gloves.

'Have you had much rain here?' she enquired.

'Hardly any at all Madam.'

154

'I do hope the wells don't run dry then. Now Raunce what is all this?'

'Well Madam we had an unwelcome visitor on the Saturday.' There he stopped short although she could tell from his manner that he had thoroughly prepared what he meant to say.

'So you said a minute ago,' was Mrs Tennant's comment.

'It was about your ring Madam,' he went on taking his time. He gazed at her as though hypnotized.

'Good heavens had he found it?'

'No Madam. To tell you the truth he came to enquire if we had come across the ring.'

'Well has anyone?'

'No Madam, we haven't and that's a fact.'

'It is a shame. It was rather a beautiful one too,' she said. 'And d'you know Raunce I've never had a word of sympathy from any of you? Just a single word would have made all the difference.'

'I'm very sorry Madam. We were all very disturbed when you lost the ring I'm sure.'

'Very well then. Now what has made you so thankful that I'm back?'

'It was not very pleasant Madam. Indeed this individual seemed to take the attitude one of us might have had the ring.'

'You can go now Albert,' Mrs Tennant sang out to the lad through the open door. 'This doesn't concern you. Just take my bags up for Agatha to unpack do you mind?'

'I regret to inform you Miss Burch is indisposed Madam. And Miss Swift is no better I'm sorry to add,' Raunce told her.

'What's the matter with Agatha then?'

'I couldn't say I'm sure but I don't think she has anything serious Madam.'

'All right then. I don't want to be difficult. I'll unpack for myself. Now you surely aren't going to tell me that an insurance inspector calling to make the usual enquiries has set the household at sixes and sevens?'

'Well this was not exactly a pleasant experience Madam. More like the third degree Madam. And it seemed to throw my boy Albert right off his balance, Madam.'

'Raunce may I say something?'

'Yes Madam.'

'Don't Madam me quite as much as you do. Put in one now and again for politeness but repeating a thing over and over rather seems to take away from the value,' and she gave him a sweet smile really.

'Very good Madam.'

'Well go on.'

'It seemed as I say to put my lad right off his balance. I was astounded Madam there is no other word. The first thing anyone knew while this individual was making his enquiries was that Albert said he had it.'

'Had what?'

'Well I suppose the ring Madam.'

'Albert has it?' Mrs Tennant echoed brightly. 'Why on earth doesn't he hand over then?'

'Oh no Madam I'm sure he's never even seen the ring. It was only he completely lost his head Madam.'

'Stuff and nonsense Raunce if the boy said he had it and you heard him, very well then he's had it and he's a miserable little thief isn't he?'

'I do assure you Madam Albert could never do such a thing.'

'But you told me yourself he'd said he had it. You heard him.'

'That was the inspector from the insurance people.'

'All right then what on earth did the insurance man say to make Albert go out of his mind? Because this is what you're asking me to believe isn't it, that Albert's had a breakdown or what?'

Raunce answered with what appeared to be reluctance.

'He said the company would not meet the claim I'm sorry to tell Madam.'

'Not meet the claim? Really Raunce this is too detestable. Are you sure?'

'Yes Madam.'

'It's not the money I'm worried about, the thing had memories for me that money couldn't buy. No what I'm thinking is that I shan't get any insurance company to insure me if we don't get this cleared up. Oh how aggravating you all of you are. Why the whole thing's distasteful. Here am I have got to suffer because you can't control your pantry boy. You do see that don't you Raunce? Then tell me this. What on earth would you advise me to do now?'

'Well Madam if I may say so Albert is a good lad. In fact I can't believe he can know the least thing. If you would give me another few days Madam I'm positive I can sift to the bottom of it for you.'

However Mrs Tennant decided that she must see Albert for herself. As Raunce went to fetch the lad she called him back.

'But what are you thanking God for that I'm here if things are in the state they're in?' she asked.

'It's the uncertainty,' he replied straight out and went.

Mrs Tennant did not have a satisfactory little talk with Bert. He readily explained that he had told the assessor he'd got it but he would not admit to her that he had the ring. He just stood there upright and yellow, refusing to answer most of the time. She told him it was despicable to take refuge in silence but this had no effect, any more than it did when she meaningly said she would have to think it over. Indeed he chose that moment to say he wished to give in his notice.

'I won't accept it,' she said at once.

He could not have thought of this for his jaw dropped in a ludicrous look of surprise.

'It wouldn't be fair to you Albert, not with this hanging over you.'

'I want to be a air gunner'm,' he blurted out.

'Stuff and nonsense. Speak to Raunce and ask him to get some sense into you. I'm very displeased. I'm very displeased indeed and I shall have to consider what I'm going to do. Run along at once. You've stolen a ring and now you want to be a hero. Yes that's all. Run along.'

He did not cry as he went to the servants' hall, he shook with rage. He was repeating to himself 'I won't ever speak to one of 'em in this bloody 'ouse not ever again.'

Meantime Raunce had hurried back to his room where Edith was waiting. 'Any sign yet?' he asked urgent. She shook her head. She was biting her nails.

'Why don't you change your mind an' let me 'ave a go at that precious lad?' he appealed. 'Honest Edie dear we've no time. Mrs T.'s just sent for my Albert. There's no tellin' what 'e'll say. He's just a bundle of nerves that kid. Because if we don't find the ring this afternoon we'll be in a proper pickle.'

'I tell you you'll never get anything out of them children by fright. I understand them and you don't.'

'That's all fine and dandy,' Raunce answered, 'but there's nothing come of your method these last two days and now I warn you it's desperate dear,' he appealed. 'Lord but I do wish you'd never found the object.'

'What lies on your mind so Charley?' she asked. 'You're that nervous you've got me upset. You tell me this then you tell me the other till I'm all confused.'

'Look this is the way I see the situation,' he explained. 'I must've been crazy not to tumble it in the first place. The minute Mrs Welch's Albert goes to cash in on that ring an' they ask the kid where he got a valuable like it, all 'e'll say is that 'e found what you'd hid away. He'll drag you in see?'

'But listen,' she objected, 'the young ladies'd never allow him.'

'Allow him?' Raunce echoed intense, 'but how could they prevent it? There's one thing about evacuees,' he said. 'No matter what the homes are they've come from they're like fiends straight up from hell honey after they've been a month or more down in the country districts. And comin' as 'e does from that woman's sister before 'e even left London, – well what else can you expect? There's only one language those little merchants understand an' that's a kind of morse spelt out with a belt on their backsides.'

'No Charley,' she appealed looking up at him round-eyed from where she sat in his chair, 'you leave me my own way till nightfall at any rate. Because I know Miss Evelyn and Miss Moira like I've read them in a book. If they get frighted then there's nothing in this world will make them say a word.' Came a knock on the door. 'This is it.' And Miss Moira entered.

'Oh hullo Mr Raunce,' the child said, standing as though uncertain.

'Hullo Miss Moira,' he said very loud.

'Are you come about our secret?' Edith asked. The little girl nodded. 'Then you can tell in front of Mr Raunce, he's in it along with us,' she explained. But Miss Moira stood hands behind her back, shifting from one foot to the other, and looked from Raunce to Edith then back again.

'Tell Edith,' the maid gently persuaded.

'I got it,' Miss Moira piped at last.

'You got what darlin'?' Edith asked through Raunce's heavy breathing.

'Why your wedding present of course,' the child replied. 'Just what you said you wanted. But from me, not from Evelyn or Albert. It's my special present,' she explained.

'Oh isn't that kind,' Edith exclaimed softly. 'When can I see it?'

'Here,' the child said. And she whipped out another of Mrs Tennant's rings heavy with uncut rubies worth perhaps two hundred pounds.

'Christ,' Raunce muttered half under his breath. Edith let the thing drop through her fingers and began to cry. Her crying was genuine, even became noisy.

'Now Miss Moira if I was you I'd run along,' Raunce began, stepping awkwardly up to Edith. But Edith clutched his arm in such a grip he took it for a warning. Then she held her arms out blind to the child who ran into them.

'Why darling Edith don't cry,' she said, 'darling don't, darling.'

'It's Albert,' Edith wailed, 'Albert and me'd set our hearts on the blue one.'

'Then why ever didn't you say?' Miss Moira asked with her lips at Edith's ear. 'I won't be a minute.'

'You'll take this one back,' Edith said beginning to recover. 'You won't let your grandma know it's been missed.'

Miss Moira grabbed the ruby ring. 'Of course not,' she said.

'She's about this minute, Miss Moira. You'll never let her catch sight of you?' Raunce asked. Edith clutched his arm again so that he kept silent.

'You do fuss so,' the child pouted. 'Goodbye for now.'

'And you'll let me have my blue one?' Edith begged. 'We've made our minds up to have that, honest we have dear.'

'Don't be so terribly impatient,' Miss Moira replied reproving. 'I told you I won't be a minute. And it's a great lot to do for anyone even if it is a wedding present,' she added as though bitter, and then was gone.

'Oh my Christ,' Raunce uttered, 'did you ever know the like?'

'Hush dear don't swear everything'll come right in a jiffy,' Edith answered as she began to dry her face. 'But where did the child come across those rubies?'

'Where else but in Mrs T.'s room,' Raunce answered gloomy. 'Even when she goes over to London they lie there open in a drawer. Will that child bring the blue one d'you suppose?'

'It's all right now don't worry,' Edith said.

'I hope,' he said. 'An' so that's what you told Miss Moira,' he went on. 'You're deep you are. Which Albert is it you're goin' to be wife to? Mine or Mrs Welch's?'

'Don't be silly it was yours I told her of course.'

'I don't get that,' he pointed out. 'I mean I don't see the reason.'

'I had to so she could understand. I've been obliged to do a lot I didn't like.'

'Women are deep,' he said. He bent down and kissed her. She put her arms slack about his neck. She did not kiss him. He straightened up.

'And now where are we?' he asked beginning to pace up and down. 'Before we're much older we'll be caught with all her bloody jewellery in this room red 'anded.'

'Be quiet,' Edith said. 'Ring or no ring I don't aim for Mrs Tennant to find me if she thought to come through this way to the kitchen. But it'll be all right now you'll see. Miss Moira'll fetch the right ring this time. I worship that child,' she added. Raunce halted when he heard this. He looked at her almost in alarm.

After she had done with Charley's Albert Mrs Tennant went straight upstairs, took off her hat, washed her hands, murmured to herself 'better get it over,' came down again and went to the kitchen by a way which did not lead through the pantry.

The cook lumbered to her feet on Mrs Tennant's entry.

'Well mum I do 'ope you had a enjoyable visit and that the young gentleman was in good health as well as in good spirits in spite of this terrible war,' Mrs Welch said.

'You are a dear, Mrs Welch,' Mrs T. replied. 'D'you know you're the first person has greeted me since I got back as though they had ever seen me before, not counting Michael. I don't count him. You can't believe these Irishmen can you?'

Mrs Welch let out a deep, cavernous chuckle. She behaved like an established favourite.

'Gawd save us from 'em, they're foreigners after all,' she announced. 'What's more I won't allow my girls to have nothing to do with 'em,' she announced, beginning to grow mysterious.

'I'm sure you're right,' Mrs Tennant agreed brightly.

'Now it's strange your mentioning that mum but I had an example only the other day,' Mrs Welch went on fast. 'I happened to be stood by the larder windows when I 'ad a terrible stench of drains very sudden. Quite took my breath away. Just like those Irish I said to myself as I stood there, never to clean a thing out.'

'You don't imagine...?' Mrs Tennant began to ask. She sat down on a kitchen chair.

'A terrible stench of drains,' Mrs Welch repeated. 'And me that had thought we were goin' to have them all up while you was away with Mrs Jack.'

'The drains?' Mrs Tennant echoed.

'That's what was said,' Mrs Welch insisted.

'Who said? I never gave orders.'

'No mum I'd be the last to say you did seein' you knew nothing. Only when that lovely cluster ring you had was lost, an' what a terrible thing to 'appen, there was one or two did mention that takin' 'em up was the only thing.'

'Down the drain?' Mrs Tennant cried. 'How fantastic.'

'Ah I could've told them they'd never get away with that,' Mrs Welch rejoined as though triumphant. 'Fantastic's the word beggin' your pardon. Down the plumbin' indeed when it was all the time right where I'll be bound it is this moment if it's not already been come upon.'

'No,' Mrs Tennant said guarded, 'there's no trace.'

'Ah there you are,' Mrs Welch replied profound.

'Now Mrs Welch I don't think we shall get anywhere like this,' Mrs Tennant gently expostulated.

'Just as you please mum,' the cook answered calm. 'And what would you fancy for your luncheon?'

'That is to say what I really came for was to ask your advice,' Mrs Tennant countered, looking again to make sure the kitchen door was shut.

'I shouldn't think twice about the stench of drains,' Mrs Welch put in, 'that was likely nothin' really. Probably the way the wind lay or something.'

'I haven't had you with me all these years without getting to know when I'm to take you seriously,' Mrs Tennant replied. 'No it's about Albert'

'Albert?' Mrs Welch echoed with a set look on her face. ''Ave they been on to you about Albert?'

'Well you know he's admitted it.'

161

'Admitted what I'd like to be told?' cried Mrs Welch.

'Why he did to me only a quarter of an hour ago.'

'What about?' Mrs Welch asked grim.

'Well what we've been discussing, my sapphire cluster ring,' Mrs Tennant answered.

'Your lovely sapphire cluster,' Mrs Welch echoed anguished. 'Why the lyin' lot of ... no I won't say it, that would be too good for 'em.'

'D'you think the others have had a part in this then?'

'I don't think. I know mum,' Mrs Welch announced.

'But they would hardly have told him what to say to incriminate himself?'

'Criminal?' Mrs Welch replied, her voice rising. 'That's just it mum. For this is what those two are, that Raunce and his Edith. I don't say nothin' about their being lain all day in each other's arms, and the best part of the night too very likely though I can't speak to the night time, I must take my rest on guard and watch as I am while it's light outside, lain right in each other's arms,' she resumed, 'the almighty lovers they make out they are but no more than fornicators when all's said and done if you'll excuse the expression, where was I? Yes. "Love" this an' "dear" that, so they go on day and night yet they're no better than a pair of thieves mum, misappropriatin' your goods behind your back.'

'Mrs Welch,' Mrs T. protested rising to her feet with a deep look of distaste. 'I won't listen,' she was going on but the cook interrupted.

'I'm sorry mum but you must allow me my say. There's been insinuations made and it's only right I should have the privilege to cast 'em back in the teeth of those that's made it. They're like a pair of squirrels before the winter layin' in a store with your property mum against their marriage if they ever find a parson to be joined in matrimony which I take leave to doubt. And it's not your ring alone. Did you ever look to the cellar mum? Why you hadn't been gone over into England more than a few hours when I chanced to look into that jar where I keep my waterglass. I was just goin' over my stores as I do regular every so often. Believe it or not there was above a quart gone. So I made my enquiry. You'll never credit this'm. It seems that Edith has been makin' away with the peacock's eggs to store them. There you are. But that's child's play. Listen to this.'

'Peacock's eggs? Whatever for?'

'Because they're starvin' over the other side the ordinary common people are begging your pardon mum.'

'Really Mrs Welch,' Mrs Tennant began again peremptory.

'I'm sorry I'm sure,' the cook insisted, 'but a few dozen eggs and a gallon or two of that stuff is child's play. Take the dead peacock. Stuffed 'im in my larder Raunce did all a'crawlin' with maggots over the lovely bit of meat I'd got for their supper. And what for you'll ask? As well you might. Ah you'd never believe their wickedness. It's to set that I R A, man Conor against me, that devil everyone's afeared for their life of in this place. And they're in it the two of them over your corn that's fed to the birds, Raunce an' that mad Irishman is. Like it was over the gravel between Raunce again an' Michael. The diabolical plunderers,' she said and paused to take breath, her face a dark purple.

'I'm not going to listen. I shall leave you till you're in a fit state. ...' Mrs Tennant insisted wearily but Mrs Welch cut her short by shambling forward between her mistress and the door.

'Yet when they grow bold to come forward with their lying tales,' she went on, and grew hoarse, 'when they say cruel lies about the innocent, their fingers winkin' with your rings once your back is turned, then the honest shan't stay silent. If I should let myself dwell on what they told you, that my Albert, my sister's own son, so much as set eyes on that ring of yours or anything which belongs to you an' you don't know how to look after, then that's slander and libel, that there is, which is punishable by law.'

'All this is too absurd,' Mrs Tennant said cold. 'What's more I shouldn't be a bit surprised if you hadn't been drinking. I've wondered now for some time. In any case it never was a question of your Albert but of the pantry boy.'

'Gin?' Mrs Welch cried, 'I've not come upon any yet in this be-nighted island and you'll excuse me mum but I know who was intended, which Albert ...'

'Now then,' Mrs Tennant cut her short in a voice that carried Jane and Mary went crimson outside, began to giggle. 'Out of my way.' Mrs Welch leant back against the dresser. Her face was congested. She was in difficulty with her breathing.

'An' my pots and pans,' she began once more but this time in a mutter.

'We won't say any more about this,' Mrs Tennant went on, 'but if I ever find you like it another time you'll go on the next boat d'you hear me, even if I have to cook for the whole lot of you myself. Good mornin' to you. Oh I forgot what I really came about,' she added turning back. 'Mr Jack's been given embarkation leave now so Mrs Jack is bringing him home by the day boat to-morrow.' And on that she left.

As she came out of that swing door which bounded Mrs Welch's kingdom she found Raunce waiting bent forward in obvious suspense and excitement.

'It's been recovered Madam,' he announced.

'What has Arthur?'

'Why your sapphire ring Madam.'

'Thank you,' she said as though she had not heard. Taking it from him she slipped it on a finger. As she walked away she said half under her breath but loud enough for him to hear,

'And now perhaps you'll tell me what I'm to say to the Insurance Company?'

He was absolutely stunned. His jaw hung open.

'Oh Raunce,' she called over her shoulder. He stood up straight. Perhaps he simply could not make a sound.

'Who found it?' she asked.

He seemed to pull himself together.

'It was Edith,' he answered at random and probably forgot at once whom he had named.

Even then she had the last word. She turned round when she was some way off down the passage.

'Oh Raunce,' she said, 'I'm afraid your luncheon to-day may be burned,' gave a short laugh, then was gone.

Young Mrs Tennant came into the Red Library where her mother-in-law was seated at the desk which had a flat sloping top of rhinoceros hide supported on gold fluted pillars of wood.

'Where's Jack?' she asked.

'Fishing of course dear.'

'I shouldn't have thought there was enough water in the river.'

'Oh Violet,' Mrs Tennant replied, 'that reminds me. Ask to-morrow if I've told Raunce the servants can't have any more baths, so that I shan't forget. Or not more than one a week anyway until we can be sure the wells won't go dry.'

'I will. Was he always as fond of fishing?'

'Always. But tell me Violet. Oughtn't we to do something about him in the evenings? Get someone over I mean. Another man so that he needn't sit over his port alone.'

'But who is there now they've stopped the petrol?' the young woman asked. 'Anyway I'd have thought a girl would have been better.'

'Oh no we don't want anything like that do we? In any case they're all Roman Catholics. No I was thinking of Captain Davenport?'

'Not him,' Mrs Jack answered too quickly.

'Why not Violet? He used to be such a companion of yours?'

'Well I don't think Jack likes him.'

'Oh I shouldn't pay any attention,' Mrs Tennant said vaguely. 'I've so often noticed that if they can talk salmon trout they never go as far as disliking one another. Ring him up.'

'You're sure? I mean I don't want to crowd the house out just when you've got Jack home.'

'Oh really Violet,' her mother-in-law replied. 'That's perfectly sweet of you but in this great barn of a place with the servants simply eating their heads off it's a breath of fresh air to see someone new. Oh the servants, Violet darling,' Mrs Tennant said in tragic tones. She turned her leather Spanish stool round to face the younger woman.

'Have they been tiresome again?'

'Did I tell you I'd got my ring back?' Mrs Tennant enquired.

'No. How splendid.'

'My dear it was quite fantastic. When I arrived I found all the servants up in arms about it with not a trace of the ring. They were going round in small circles accusing each other.'

'Good lord,' her daughter-in-law remarked looking almost rudely out of the open window on the edge of which she was perched.

'Whether it's never having been educated or whether it's just plain downright stupidity I don't know,' the elder Mrs Tennant went on, 'but there's been the most detestable muddle about my sapphire ring.'

'Your sapphire cluster ring?'

'Yes I lost it just before we crossed over for Jack's leave. You know I told you. I was wearing the thing one day and the next I knew it was gone. I must have taken it off to wash my hands. Anyway suddenly it had disappeared into thin air. Such a lovely one too that Jack's Aunt Emily gave me.'

'You never said,' Mrs Jack complained limp.

'Didn't I darling? Well there it is. And the moment I got inside the house three days ago I found Raunce crossing and uncrossing his fingers obviously most terribly nervous about something. Well I let him get it off his chest and what d'you think? It seems that when the insurance inspector came down after I'd reported the loss the pantry Albert all at once went mad and said he'd got it whatever that means. What would you say?'

'Why I suppose he'd picked the thing up somewhere.'

'My dear that's just what I thought at the time. But not at all. Oh no Raunce took the trouble to explain the boy had never even seen my ring. In the meantime of course the inspector had gone back to Dublin and I received a rather odd letter from them, everything considered, and only this morning to say that in view of the circumstances they could not regard the thing as lost. Well that's quite right because I'm wearing it now. But what I can't and shall never understand is what the boy thought he had or had got, whichever it was. Now d'you think I ought to take all this further?'

'It's so complicated,' Mrs Jack complained.

'Would you advise me to have Raunce in and get to the bottom of things I mean?'

At this question the younger woman suddenly displayed unusual animation. She got up, stood with her back to the light, and began to smooth her skirts.

'Not if I were you,' she said. 'Let sleeping dogs lie.'

This answer probably made Mrs Tennant obstinate. 'But I should at least like to know where it was found,' she cried. 'Why there is Edith. Edith,' she summoned her shrilly, 'come here a moment I want you.'

The girl came modest through the open portals. She did not look at Mrs Jack.

'Where did you find my sapphire ring in the end Edith?'

'Me Madam?' she replied almost sharp, 'I never found your ring Madam.'

'But Raunce told me you did when he gave it back.'

'Not me Madam,' Edith said looking at the floor.

'Then who did find it then?'

'I couldn't say Madam.'

'Oh why is there all this mystery Edith? The whole thing's most unsatisfactory.'

The housemaid stayed silent, calm and composed.

'Yes that's all how you can go,' Mrs Tennant said as though exasperated. 'Shut the door will you please?'

When they were alone again Mrs Tennant raised a hand to her ear which she tugged.

'Well there you are Violet. What d'you think?'

'I expect you heard wrong. Perhaps Raunce said someone else.'

'Oh no I'm not deaf yet. I know he named Edith.'

'Darling,' Mrs Jack entreated, 'I'm sure you're not. At all events you've got your ring back haven't you?'

'Yes but I don't like having things hang over me.'

'Hanging over you?'

'When there's something unexplained. Don't you ever feel somehow that you must get whatever it is cleared up? And then I don't think I can afford to keep the insurance going. It comes so frightfully expensive these days. But if I feel that there is someone not quite honest who perhaps was caught out by the servants and made to give the thing back then I do think it would be madness to let the insurance drop. Violet don't you find that everything now is the most frightful dilemma always? But I don't suppose you do. You're so wonderfully calm all the time dear.'

'I'm not if you only knew. But you've got so many worries with everything you have to manage.'

'That's just it. And when you feel there's someone in the house you can't trust matters become almost impossible.'

'Someone you can't trust?' the young woman asked in an agitated voice so that Mrs Tennant looked but could not see her expression, standing as she was against the light.

'Why yes,' Mrs Tennant said, 'because that ring must have been somewhere to have been found.'

'Oh of course.'

'Then Violet you don't really consider I need do any more?'

'Well I don't see why. I'd let sleeping dogs rest,' the young woman repeated.

'Well perhaps you're right. Oh and darling Violet there's this other thing. You know Agatha is ill now so that with Nanny Swift that makes two trays for every meal. As a matter of fact Jane and Mary are being very good and I've been able to ease things for the pantry by telling Raunce to discontinue the fires now it's so much warmer. The pictures won't come to any harm for the weather really is quite hot. At the same time it makes rather a lot for Edith when she has to take the children out. There's all the cleaning still to be done as usual. So I was wondering Violet darling if you could possibly take on the children a bit more after Jack's leave is up but only in the afternoons of course.'

As soon as the children were mentioned the younger woman relaxed, sat down again. There came over her face the expression of a spoiled child.

'Why of course,' she said. 'I was going to anyway.'

'You are a brick Violet. One knows one can always rely on you. Things are really becoming detestable in these big houses. I must have a word with Doctor Connolly. It's all very well I shall tell him his killing off poor Eldon but he must be more careful over Agatha,' and Mrs Tennant tittered at herself. 'We simply can't afford to lose her I shall tell him. Or nanny for that matter, though of course if there was anyone to take her place she would almost be pensionable now.'

'Oh I think she's still very good,' Mrs Jack objected. Miss Swift was her own servant.

'She's excellent Violet, quite excellent. I only meant she was getting older as I am. But that's the dilemma nowadays. Whether to have matters out with the servants and then to see them all give notice, or to carry on anyhow so to speak with the existing staff and have some idea in the back of one's mind that things may change for the better? What would you do?'

'My dear I think you manage wonderfully,' Mrs Jack said in a reassuring voice.

'Well I don't know about that,' Mrs Tennant replied. 'It seems we're living pretty well from hand to mouth when I hardly dare ask anyone over to a meal even for fear one or more of the creatures will give notice. You will remember to ring up that Captain Davenport won't you? But in a way I regard this as my war work, maintaining the place I mean. Because we're practically in enemy country here you know and I do consider it so important from the morale point of view to keep up appearances. This country has been ruined by people who did not live on their estates. It might be different if de Valera had a use for places of the kind. Why he doesn't offer Ireland as a hospital base I can't imagine. Then one could hand over a house like this with an easy conscience. Because after all as I always say there are the children to consider. I look on myself simply as a steward. We could shut Kinalty up to-morrow and go and live in one of the cottages. But if I once did that would your darlings ever be able to live here again? I wonder.'

'Did Jack's stepfather live here much before he died?'

'Edward would never be away from the place when he first rented it,' Mrs Tennant replied. 'But once he bought outright he seemed to tire. Still he was a sick man then and most of the time he stayed in London to be near the doctors.'

'Well anyway I think you are doing a perfectly marvellous job,' Mrs Jack murmured.

'Thank you darling. You are a great comfort. I love this house. It's my life now. If only there wasn't this feeling of distrust hanging over one.'

'Distrust?' Mrs Jack enquired rather sharply again.

'This business about my ring,' her mother-in-law replied. 'What I always say is, if one can't trust the people about you where is one?'

'Oh but I'm sure you can? Of course Edith's very much in love with Raunce, we all know that, which makes her a bit funny and imaginative sometimes. Still I'm sure she's absolutely reliable otherwise.'

'Imaginative my dear?'

'Well you know how it is. She's trying to land Raunce. My God that man's a cold fish. I'm glad it isn't me.'

'Let them marry, let them live in sin if they like so long as we keep them but my dear,' the elder Mrs Tennant said, 'what do we know about the servants? Why,' she added, 'there's Jack. Whatever can be the matter to make him leave the river at this hour? Hullo Jack,' she called, 'done any good?' She had moved over to the open window with this man's wife and stuck her rather astounding head with its blue-washed silver hair out into the day as though she were a parrot embarrassed at finding itself not tied to a perch and which had turned its back on the cage. He waved. He came over. He was in grey flannel trousers with an open red-and-white checked shirt. He looked too young for service in a war.

'I ran out of fags,' he explained looking mildly at his wife who smiled faintly indulgent at him.

'Oh Jack,' his mother said, 'we're asking Captain Davenport, do you remember him, over for dinner to-night?'

'Him?' the young man asked. 'Has he got back then?'

'I didn't know he'd been away,' Mrs Tennant said. Her daughter-in-law stayed very quiet.

'Oh we saw quite a lot of him in London this time didn't we Doll,' he remarked casually to his wife.

'Well there's no one else in this desert of a place so you'll simply have to see him again that's all,' Mrs Tennant said sharp but cheerful and all three drifted off on their separate ways without another word.

The evenings were fast lengthening. Charley and Edith slipped out after supper that same day to be with each other on the very seat by the dovecote where Miss Swift that first afternoon of spring had told her charges a fairy story while they watched the birds love-making. These, up in the air in declining light, were all now engaged on a last turn round before going back inside the leaning tower to hood their eyes in feathers.

Edith laid her lovely head on Raunce's nearest shoulder and above them, above the great shadows laid by trees those white birds wheeled in a sky of eggshell blue and pink with a remote sound of applause as, circling, they clapped their stretched, starched wings in flight.

That side of Edith's face open to the reflection of the sky was a deep red.

'She passed my books all right this mornin',' he murmured.

'What books?' she asked low and sleepy.

'Me monthly accounts,' he replied.

'Did she?' Edith sighed content. They fell silent. At some distance peacocks called to one another, shriek upon far shriek.

'That'll mean a bit more put away for when we are together,' he went on and pressed her arm. She settled closer to him.

170

'You're wonderful,' she said so low he hardly heard.

'I love you,' he answered.

Her left hand came up to lie against his cheek.

'An' did you ask about our little house we're going to have?' she enquired.

'I did that. But Mrs T. couldn't seem to take it in. She said yes and no and went on about Michael being tiresome. But of course I didn't come straight out about it's being for us dear.'

'You wouldn't,' she made comment dreamily.

'Ah you want to move too fast in some things you do. Slow but sure that's me,' and he chuckled. 'I get 'em so they think it's their idea.'

'You're smart!' she murmured in admiration.

'Clever Charley's the name,' he echoed and kissed her forehead. 'You see girl you want to go soft. A bit at a time.'

'What's it worth to you?' she wanted to know, the hand she had against his cheek stiffening up his face. 'This job I mean,' she added.

'Why you know the money I draw dear? I've made no secret.'

'Yes but the extra on the books?'

'Oh maybe two or three quid a week.'

'Here,' she said drawing her face slightly away, 'it was more like five or six pounds when you told me a week or two back.'

'Not on your life,' he said in a louder voice. 'You've got it wrong. I couldn't have.'

'You did,' she insisted.

'All you women are the same,' he announced calm, 'you ask so many questions you get a man tied in knots. Then you never forget but bring it up later. Why it couldn't have been that much dear. Mrs T. would notice. She's not short-sighted let me tell you.'

'You wouldn't hold out on me would you Charley?' Edith asked sweet, but looking at him.

'Come off it,' he murmured and kissed her mouth.

'I don't know but I do love you,' she said when she could.

After a time he rather unexpectedly tried her out with some news, sitting back as though to watch the effect.

'The Captain was at dinner,' he said.

'Captain Davenport? Oh him,' and she laughed.

'What's comical about that?' he enquired. 'I thought you might consider it a trifle strange so soon after you know what.'

171

She just lay on him without replying.

'A bit thick it looked to me after he'd followed her right over to England,' he went on.

'Captain Davenport?' she repeated. 'You just put that silliness out of your mind.'

'Can you beat it? With all the rumpus you made at the time,' he announced. For answer she turned her face up and kissed him.

'Women are a mystery,' he added. He kissed her avidly.

Some minutes later he spoke once more. 'Was that right what you said about Mr Jack taking liberties?' he asked.

'Wouldn't you like to know,' she replied.

'No girl,' he objected drawing a bit away from her again, 'I got the right to learn now I hope.'

'You don't have to worry your head about him either,' she said.

'I'm the best judge of that,' he muttered.

'Why Charley you're not ever goin' to be jealous of a stuck-up useless card like him surely?'

'You've got such peculiar notions,' he said. 'It'd be hard to tell what you consider is right or wrong.'

'Say that a second time,' she demanded.

'Now sweet'eart,' he said, 'don't go ridin' your high horse.'

'I'm not ridin' nothing.'

'Then what's it all about?' he asked.

'Seems to me you're trying to make out I gave that boy encouragement.'

'Yes they do take 'em young for the army,' he replied.

'Were you?' she went on. 'Because I won't stand for it Charley.' But she was only grumbling.

'Who me?' he said. 'Not on your life. You wouldn't reply to my question.'

'What girl would?' she enquired sweet.

'I'd have thought any woman could give a straight answer if she was asked whether a certain individual had offered ... well offered ...' and he seemed at a loss.

'Offered what?' she murmured obviously amused.

'Well all right then, tried to kiss her?' he ended.

'An' I should never've thought there was a man breathing would be so easy as to expect he'd be told the truth.'

'Oho so that's the old game,' he laughed. 'Keeping me on a string is it, to leave me to picture this that and the other to do with you and him?'

'If you can bring your imagination to such a level you're to be pitied,' she answered tart.

'All I did was to ask,' he objected.

'You're free to picture what you please,' she replied. 'I've got no hold on your old imagination, not yet I haven't.'

'What d'you mean not yet?'

'I mean after we're married,' she whispered, her voice gone husky. 'After we're married I'll see to it that you don't have no imagination. I'll make everything you want of me now so much more than you ever dreamed that you'll be quit imaginin' for the rest of your life.'

'Oh honey,' he said in a sort of cry and kissed her passionately. But a rustling noise interrupted them.

'What's that?' he asked violent.

'Hush dear,' she said, 'it'th only the peacockth.'

And indeed a line of these birds one after the other and hardly visible in this dusk was making tracks back to the stables.

'Whatever brought you to think of that cow son at a time like this,' he asked awkward.

'There'th a lot you'd like to know ithn't there,' she answered.

'Oh give us a kiss do,' he begged.

'If you behave yourthelf,' she said.


After tea one afternoon Edith went up to her room to lie down. She was tired. Agatha and Miss Swift were still confined to bed. The extra work this caused was hard.

She found Kate stretched out already. The rain pattered on ivy round their opened window.

'I'm dead beat I am,' this girl said to Edith who answered,

'Well I don't suppose hard work ever did anyone any harm.'

'But don't it keep pilin' up against you dear all the time,' Kate remarked. Then she added as Edith sat to roll down her stockings. 'There's one thing we still get you can't buy the other side.'

'What's that?'

'Silk stockings,' Kate explained.

'It certainly is a change to hear you have a good word for this place,' Edith said.

Kate let it pass. 'Why don't we have the talks we used to Edie?' she asked.

'Land's sakes I expect it's we're too tired for anything when we do get up in the old room,' Edith answered.

'We used to have some lovely talks Edie.'

'Maybe we've got past talkin'.'

'What d'you mean by that?'

'Well things is different now Kate.'

'If you're referring to the fact that you've an understandin' with Mr Raunce that's no reason to tell me nothing about you, or about him for that matter, is it?'

Edith laughed at this.

'O.K. dear,' she said, 'you win. You go on asking then?'

'You are going to be married Edie?'

'We are that,' Edith said, lying down full length. Both girls looked up at the ceiling, stretched out on their backs airing their feet.

'Well I wish you all I could wish meself,' Kate said in a low voice.

'Thanks love,' Edith replied matter of fact.

'When's it going to be?'

'As soon as I've got me a few pretties together I shouldn't wonder,' Edith answered.

At this a sort of snorting sob came from the other bed. Edith rolled to look, then sat up. 'Why you're crying,' she exclaimed. She came across and sat on the edge of Kate's eiderdown.

'Whatever for? You are silly,' she added gentle. 'Here,' she said, 'look at you right on top of the quilting. Let's get you comfortable.' She began to roll Kate across to one side to get the eiderdown from underneath her. Kate was limp. 'Oh Edie' she wailed and started to cry noisily.

'Hush dear,' Edith murmured, 'someone'll hear.' She began to ease Kate's clothes off.

'Oh Edie,' Kate moaned. Edith stopped to wipe the girl's face which was damp with tears.

'There,' Edith said. 'Now don't you pay attention love. They're nothin' but an old lot of muddlers every one.' She covered Kate's greenish body up.

Kate's violent crying passed to hiccups.

'Why,' she asked turning so that she could watch Edith, 'has one of them spoken about me?'

'No not a word.'

'I got the hiccups,' Kate announced, almost started a giggle. She brightened. ''Cause you'd've known what to tell 'em if they had?'

'Of course I would dear,' Edith was stroking the nape of Kate's neck.

'Oh that's nice love,' this girl said. She blew her nose on the handkerchief Edith had left ready to hand. 'You don't know what a lot of good that's doin'.'

'And so it should,' Edith answered.

'Thanks duck. And now we're like we used to be isn't that right?'

'That's right.'

'I can't make out what came over me,' Kate went on. 'Honest I can't.'

'It's a hard bloody world.'

'Why Edith I never thought to hear you swear of all people, I didn't that.'

'It's the truth Kate just the same.'

'You're right it is,' Kate said. 'Look I've got rid of my 'iccups. That's one good thing. Yes there's times I could bust right out with it all. It gets you down. An' then your tellin' me about you an' Mr Raunce.'

'I thought you said once you'd never give him a Mr.'

'Oh Edie that's different. Now you're to be married I must show my respect.'

'I don't know dear. I'm sure you can call him Charley for all I care.'

'Have it any way you want,' said Kate peaceably. 'An' where will you live? Are you planning to stay in Kinalty?'

'Yes we got our eye on that little place in the demesne.'

'Oh isn't that lovely.'

'And we're thinking of gettin' his mother to come over to be with us so she will be out of the bombin'.'

'Oh isn't that nice,' Kate said and seemed to choke. She began to cry silently again, great tears welling from her shut eyes.

'Why love,' Edith asked, 'is anything the matter?'

'No,' Kate wailed.

'You're sure now?' Edith went on. Then she asked, 'There's nothing going to happen to you is there?'

'Me?' Kate echoed, suddenly quiet. 'You mean on account of Paddy don't you?'

'Then there is,' Edith said. Her eyes opened wide.

'Why Edie,' Kate replied serious, 'you wouldn't ever believe that surely?'

'That's all right then.'

'Never in your life,' Kate went on. 'So you guessed?'

'It was Albert told my young ladies. That little bastard had it from Mrs Welch. There's no other word to describe the lad.'

'She calls 'im that 'erself so Jane told me. She heard her.'

'Would you believe it?' Edith murmured.

'But Paddy's not what you suppose dear,' Kate said as if she had given Edith's last remark a certain meaning. 'You've no need to bother yourself about that between Paddy an' me. I'm not goin' to have nothing don't worry. No it was everything got me down all of a sudden.'

'You weren't thinkin' of him in such a way then?'

'Well there's not much else to think of is there Edie?'

'Why he's a Roman.'

'That don't make no difference.'

'I don't suppose it should. But these Irish are not like us.'

'Once I get Paddy smartened up you'd never recognize him for one.'

'But what about his speech, Kate?'

'Yes I know that's a problem. It'll be the hardest thing to alter.'

'So you are considering him?' Edith asked.

'There's nobody else. A girl gets lonely,' Kate answered beginning to cry once more. 'And I think you're not bein' gracious about it,' she added.

'There dear,' Edith said, 'you're upset.'

'Don't go,' Kate muttered between sobs.

'I'm not goin' love. You quiet yourself. Life's not easy.'

'You're tellin' me,' Kate agreed and pulled herself together to blow her nose. 'Now d'you know what's come about?'

'What's that?' Edith asked as she began to stroke her again.

'He's in a terrible state about them eggs.'

'What eggs?'

'Why the eggs you put away under waterglass in this very room,' Kate answered.

'But that was months ago. However did he come to learn?'

'It was young Albert again who else? I promise I never told 'im nothin'. I wouldn't do such a thing. And then in addition Mr Raunce went and informed about that peacock Mrs Welch had in the larder. Oh Edie 'e got in such a state. I was frighted.'

'I'll speak of this to Charley,' Edith said grim.

'It's as you like,' Kate replied, 'but 'e worships the birds, there you are love, he fair worships 'em. There's nothing I can do. And what he's just learned has made 'im act so strange. I don't know what to think, honest I don't.'

'Then what does he say he'll do?' Edith enquired.

'Why 'e talks as if 'e was goin' to lock 'em up and never let the things out any more. Can you tell me how Mrs Tennant'll see that?'

'I'd forgotten all about those old eggs,' Edith said. Then she added in a wondering voice, 'I suppose it was me knowin' I had no more use for 'em.'

'What d'you mean no more use? You used to reckon they'd still be good for your skin even if they had been stood in that stuff.'

'Yes,' Edith said, 'it's not that I've no need any more for my face which'll still come in handy I don't doubt. But the fact is now Raunce an' me's come to an understanding I got no time for charms.'

'I shouldn't wonder if he didn't find time for yours even if you shouldn't,' Kate remarked archly.

Edith blushed.

'Look,' Kate cried and seemed far more cheery, 'you're blushin'.'

'It's not that kind you mention,' Edith said. 'I meant like crossing a gipsy's palm with silver at the fair. A charm to make you seem different,' she explained.

'Would they do the same for me d'you suppose?'

'I don't know Kate seein' I've never tried.'

'But if 'e came upon it Edie 'e'd strangle me.'

'Like little Albert did to one of his peacocks?' Edith was smiling.

'You don't know 'im Edie, there's no one could tell what action 'e'd take.'

'Why should he ever learn?' Edith asked.

'There's not much is kept mum in this house love.'

'O.K. then. But it's only the children after all, Kate, as we've found since little Albert came. They'll never discover. I shan't tell.'

'But d'you think it's real what you believed about the things?'

'There's this to it Kate. He loves the birds, you've just said so. If you used their eggs and he was ignorant then it might do something to him.'

'Just imagine me smarming that muck over my face and chest to please. What we girls do have to put up with.'

'Go on,' Edith said, 'that's nothing,' Both began to giggle. Edith put the heel of her hand up to cover her mouth. 'For land's sake,' she cried.

'And when they come at you...' Kate began then stopped. She started laughing helplessly all of a sudden. Edith joined in. Within a minute they were exchanging breathless and indistinct accounts of the antics men get up to, in between shrieks of giggling.

Later that afternoon came over dark with a storm outside. Edith had filled a polished copper jug and was hurrying down the Long Passage to lay the hot water in Mrs Jack's washbasin when she saw something move in an open doorway into the dressing room next door. She stopped dead, raised her free hand to her heart. But it was Raunce.

'You Charley,' she said low when she saw him, 'why I nearly spilled it.'

'Sorry ducks,' he answered, whispering also, 'I was only puttin' out his things.'

'Whatever for?' she asked. 'You don't do that so early do you?'

'Well if you're speaking of the hour I'll wager this hot water you're carryin' will go cold before she comes to use it.'

'There's a cover I put over the jug stupid,' she replied. 'Are you goin' to tell me you didn't know that after all the years you've been here?'

'I don't like to let you out of my sight.'

'Why Charley,' she said warm, 'you don't mean to say you've got him on your mind again?'

'Well it's not right when he might come across you in his own bedroom.'

'Have you ever heard?' she muttered in a delighted voice and went inside Mrs Jack's room. He followed after.

'I don't know,' he said, 'but I gave you a bit of a start. I saw.'

'Oh these jugs,' she began, 'they will tarnish. And when we're shorthanded like we are.'

'You give'm to me in the morning an' I'll rub'm up for you.'

'Not if you set Albert to it I won't.'

'Where did you get that notion?' he enquired. He was looking at her as he usually did nowadays, like a spaniel dog.

'I move around,' she answered.

'No. What I do for you I do for you,' he announced. 'Who'd you take me for?'

'Take you for? You're not so easily mistaken for anyone.'

'Just now,' he explained, 'you thought I was someone else.'

'You do want to know a great deal.' She was smiling. They stood close to each other. Then she reached up to finger a button on his coat. She poked at it as though at a bell. He did not seem to dare touching her.

'I'll have to be on hand each time you come up that's all,' he said.

'But what about your work?'

'Only when it's like now, when there's none of us about dear,' he appealed.

'You are silly,' she replied and gave him a quick kiss.

'But did he ever?' he asked still rigid.

'See here,' she said, 'you may have your Albert to do everything for you but I've not, I'm on my own.' She crossed over to the bed. 'Look,' she said. She took a black silk transparent nightdress out of its embroidered case. 'What d'you say to that Charley?'

He gazed, obviously struck dumb. She held it up in front of her. She put a hand in at the neck so that he could see the veiled skin. He began to breathe heavy.

'It's wicked that's all,' he announced at last while she watched.

'What?' she echoed. 'Not more than it was with mam'selle surely?'

''Ow d'you mean Edie?'

'"There's many a time I'd give her a long bong jour,"' she quoted.

'I never,' he said and took a step forward.

'That's you men all over,' she went on.

'Her?' he protested. He had gone quite white. 'Why you're crackers. That two pennorth of French sweat rag?'

'Now you're being disgustin' dear.'

'I can't make you out,' he said coming towards her.

'No,' she cried, 'you stop where you are. I'm goin' to punish you. What d'you say if we took this for when we are married? How would I look eh Charley?' And she held that nightdress before her face.

'Punishment eh?' he laughed. If it had been a spell then he seemed to be out of it for the moment. 'That's all you girls think of. Why holy Moses,' he added as if trying to appear gay, 'that piece of cobweb ain't for us.'

'Don't you reckon I'd look nice in it then?' She lowered the nightdress till he could see she was pouting.

'You'd appear like a bloody tart,' he said, then broadly smiled. She stamped her foot.

'Don't you swear at me of all people Charley.'

'O.K.,' he said.

'Why,' she went on, returning to the charge, 'not above a minute or two ago you were puffin' like a grampus.'

'What's a grampus honey?' he asked and looked a bit daunted.

'Wouldn't you like to know?' she teased him.

'I can't make out why you want all this mystification,' he said. 'Honest you've got me so I'm anyhow.'

'An' so you should be Charley dearest.'

'Oh Edie,' he gasped moving forward. The room had grown immeasurably dark from the storm massed outside. Their two bodies flowed into one as he put his arms about her. The shape they made was crowned with his head, on top of a white sharp curved neck, dominating and cruel over the blur that was her mass of hair through which her lips sucked at him warm and heady.

'Edie,' he muttered breaking away only to drive his face down into hers once more. But he was pressing her back into a bow shape. 'Edie,' he called again.

With a violent shove and twist she pushed him off. As she wiped her mouth on the back of a hand she remarked as though wondering,

'You aren't like this first thing are you?'

This must have been a reference to the fact that when she called him with a cup of tea in the mornings he never kissed her then as he lay in bed. Or he must have understood it as such because, standing as he was like he had been drained of blood, he actually moaned.

'Why,' he said, 'that wouldn't be right.'

180

'Don't you love me in the early hours then?'

'Sweetheart,' he protested.

'With me carryin' you a cup of tea and all?'

'Well it's usually half cold at that,' he said, seeming to pull himself together.

'Oho,' she cried and began to do her hair with Mrs Jack's comb. 'Then I won't bring no more.'

'I'd been intending to speak to you about that very point,' he began shamefaced. 'I don't know that you should continue with the practice. It might lead to talk,' he said.

'Charley you don't say I'm not to,' she appealed and seemed really hurt. 'Why, don't you like me fetchin' your tea?'

'It's not that dear.'

She turned vast reproachful eyes on him.

'I was kidding myself you would fancy me above any other to open your eyes on first thing,' she repeated softly grumbling.

'It's the rest,' he moaned.

'Just because I'm keeping myself for you on our wedding night you reckon they'd think you're free with me?' she asked as though he had hit her.

'Well that's what would happen isn't it, being as they are?' he enquired.

'Oh Charley,' she went on gentle but reproachful, 'that's cowardly so it is?'

'You know I love you don't you?' he entreated and took hold of her hands. She was limp.

'Yes.'

'Well then,' he went on, 'we don't want no chitter chatter do we?'

'You mean no one shouldn't know in case you change your mind about our being married?' she asked. There was laughter now in her voice.

'What's comical in that when you've just spoken a lie?' he demanded.

'All right then I'll not bring your old tea again that's all.' She laid her arms round his neck and gave him a powerful kiss. Putting his hands against her shoulders he pushed her away.

'You said yourself we were on a good thing an' didn't want to lose this place,' he explained.

'I never imagined you could do without me pulling your curtains.

So the first you set eyes on every new day should be me.'

'I love you that's why honey,' he said.

'O.K.,' she said, 'but you're to do the explainin' with Mother Burch mind.'

'That's a good girl. Holy smoke,' he exclaimed, 'an' there's my lad forgotten to lay their table I'll be bound. I'll be seeing you,' he said. He fairly stumbled out.

Some days later Mrs Jack unexpectedly entered the Blue Drawing Room to find her mother-in-law in tears beneath a vaulted roof painted to represent the evening sky at dusk. Mrs Tennant immediately turned her face away to hide her state. She was seated forlorn, plumb centre of this chamber, on an antique Gothic imitation of a hammock slung between four black marble columns and cunningly fashioned out of gold wire. But she had not concealed her tears in time. Mrs Jack saw. She went across at once.

'Why you poor thing,' she said rubbing the point of Mrs Tennant's shoulder with the palm of a hand.

'I'm sorry to make such a fool of myself Violet,' this older woman said from between gritted teeth and got out a handkerchief.

'I think you've been perfectly wonderful dear,' Mrs Jack suggested.

'Really I don't know how your generation bears it,' Mrs Tennant went on. She blew her nose while Mrs Jack stood ill at ease.

As she rubbed the shoulder of her husband's mother she was surrounded by milking stools, pails, clogs, the cow byre furniture all in gilded wood which was disposed around to create the most celebrated eighteenth-century folly in Eire that had still to be burned down.

'You've been absolutely magnificent Violet,' Mrs T. continued. 'Here he's been gone three days God knows where on active service if he hasn't already sailed. There's been not a whimper out of you once.'

'Don't,' his wife said sharp and gripped that shoulder in such a way as to hurt the older woman.

'No you must let me,' Mrs Tennant began again but calmer as though the pain was what she needed. 'It's so hard for my generation to talk to yours about the things one really feels. I never seem to have the chance to speak up over the great admiration I hold you in my dear.'

'You mustn't.'

Her mother-in-law ignored this though she must have recognized that it had been uttered in anguish. 'I grant you,' she went on, looking straight in front of her, 'your contemporaries have all got this amazing control of yourselves. Never showing I mean. So I just wanted to say once more if I never say it again. Violet dear I think you are perfectly wonderful and Jack's a very lucky man.'

Violet stood as if frozen. Mrs Tennant used her handkerchief.

'There,' Mrs T. said, 'I feel better for that. I'm sorry I've been such an idiot. Oh and Violet could you let go of me. You are hurting rather.'

'Good heavens,' the young woman exclaimed gazing at the impression her nails had made on Mrs Tennant's shirt and with trembling lips.

'It's my fault entirely Violet because I invaded your privacy,' Mrs Tennant said with a positive note of satisfaction in her voice. 'Oh your generation's hard,' she added.

'But he'll be all right you'll see,' Mrs Jack began, then did not seem able to go on while she smoothed the silk where her nails had dug in. 'He'll come back,' she said finally.

'Of course he will,' Mrs Tennant agreed at once, all of a sudden brisk with assurance. But under her breath with an agony of shame the younger woman was repeating I will write to Dermot and say my darling I must never see you again never in my life my darling.

'You must forgive me for just now Violet,' the older woman said not in the least apologetic.

My darling my darling my darling, her daughter-in-law prayed in her heart to the Captain, never ever again.

'I think everything's partly to do with the servants.' Mrs Tennant announced as if drawing a logical conclusion.

'The servants?' Mrs Jack echoed, it might have been from a great distance.

'Well one gets no rest. It's always on one's mind Violet.' She got up. She began to search for dust, smelling her wetted forefinger as though there could be a smell. 'This last trouble over my cluster ring now. I spoke to Raunce again but it was most unsatisfactory.'

'I shouldn't have,' Mrs Jack murmured a trifle louder.

'I know Violet. But you do see one can't stand things hanging over one? This hateful business round the pantry boy. There's no

183

two ways about it. Either you can trust people or you can't and if you can't then they're distasteful to live with.'

'Yes,' Mrs Jack agreed simply. All at once she seemed to recollect. 'What d'you mean quite?' she asked sharp almost in spite of herself.

'Well he said he had it, he told Raunce so.'

'Had what?' Mrs Jack demanded suddenly frantic.

Mrs Tennant swung round to face her daughter-in-law who did not raise her blue eyes. There was something hard and glittering beyond the stone of age in that other pair below the blue waved tresses. And then Mrs Tennant turned away once more.

'Why my cluster ring Violet,' she said going over to an imitation pint measure also in gilded wood and in which peacock's feathers were arranged. She lifted this off the white marble mantelpiece that was a triumph of sculptured reliefs depicting on small plaques various unlikely animals, even in one instance a snake, sucking milk out of full udders and then she blew at it delicately through pursed lips.

'Besides there's another thing,' Mrs Tennant went on, moving around amongst the historic pieces which made up this fabulous dairy of a drawing room. 'The peacocks,' she said. 'Now yesterday was perfectly dry without a drop of rain yet I couldn't see one of the birds all morning.'

'Perhaps they thought it was going to rain,' Mrs Jack proposed and drifted over to the windows. 'They don't like getting wet.'

'My dear Violet please tell me when does it ever not threaten rain in this climate? No I made enquiries. Like everything else in this house it was quite different. Not the natural explanation at all. Just as I'd feared. Because I had Raunce in and I asked him. Of course he pretended to know nothing as the servants always do,' and at this Mrs Jack winced, 'but I can't stand lies. D'you know what he wanted me to believe?'

'You said he was lying?' Mrs Jack asked faint over her shoulder.

'Well he must have been my dear. Now look at this pitchfork or lamp standard or whatever they call it.' Mrs Tennant was halted before a gold instrument cunningly fixed as so to appear leant against the wall and which had been adapted to take an oil lamp between its prongs. 'The damp has settled on the metal part which is all peeling. In spite of the fire I have kept up on account of the Cuyps. Isn't that provoking? And of course it's a museum piece. Or that's what they say when they come down. They simply exclaim out loud when they see this room.' But her daughter-in-law did not look. 'It's all French you know,' Mrs Tennant continued, 'they say it came from France, which is why I try to impress it on the servants that they really must be careful. There'll be so little left when this war's finished. But Raunce is hopeless. D'you know what he said to me?'

'No?'

'Well Violet I'd asked him to have a word with O'Conor. You know how extremely difficult that man is. Then it came out,' and Mrs Jack drew her breath sharp, 'or not everything, just a bit probably. You see he said O'Conor had locked the peacocks up in their quarters as he termed it. Now that's very unsatisfactory of course. After all they are my peacocks as I pointed out to Raunce. I have a right to see them I should hope. They're a part of the decoration of the place. But he told me he thought O'Conor was afraid of something or other.'

'How ridiculous,' Mrs Jack exclaimed. She turned to face her mother-in-law with a look which appeared stiff with apprehension. But if Mrs Tennant noticed this she gave no sign.

'Exactly,' she said. 'Frightened of what I'd like to know? I put it to Raunce. But he couldn't or wouldn't say.'

'Which is just like the man,' the younger woman interrupted. 'Always hinting.'

'But that wasn't the lie,' Mrs Tennant said soft. 'When it came it was much more direct than that. You see as I said before I asked him to speak to O'Conor. D'you know what he answered? Sheer impertinence really. He had the cheek to stand where you are now and tell me that it was no use his going to interrogate the lampman, can't you hear him, because he couldn't understand a word he said.'

'I don't quite see,' Mrs Jack put in livelier. 'I can't catch what he says myself.'

'No more can I. That's why I wanted someone else to go. But my dear it's not for us to understand O'Conor,' Mrs Tennant explained as she replaced into its niche a fly-whisk carved out of a block of sandalwood, the handle enamelled with a reddish silver. 'We don't have to live with the servants. Not yet. It's they who condescend to stay with us nowadays. No but you're not telling me that they pass all their huge meals in utter silence. He eats with them you know. Of course Raunce was lying. He understands perfectly what O'Conor says. There's something behind all this Violet. It's detestable.'

'Raunce told you that O'Conor shut the peacocks up? But that's too extraordinary,' Mrs Jack remarked in a confident voice. She was tracing patterns on the window-pane with a purple finger nail.

'I shall get to the bottom of it,' Mrs Tennant announced. For an instant she sent a grim smile at her daughter-in-law's back. 'I shall bide my time though,' she said, then quietly left that chamber the walls of which were hung with blue silk. Mrs Jack swung round but the room was empty.

That night the servants all sat down to supper together. Mrs Welch had asked for and been granted leave to stay in Dublin overnight to consult a doctor. Her Albert had been sent to bed. By this time he was probably running naked on the steeply sloping roofs high up. Mrs Jack now looked after her children who ate with their mother and the grandparent while Miss Swift died inch by inch in the bedroom off the nursery. And because Miss Burch was still indisposed Edith as though by right took this woman's place at table.

'Well what are we waiting for?' she asked quite natural in Agatha's manner.

'Bert's just bringing in the cold joint,' Mary replied. 'Jane's lending a hand. My,' she went on, 'this certainly is nice for us girls to have company. It's a thought we both of us appreciate Mr Raunce to be invited to your supper.'

'You're welcome,' the man replied as he sharpened his carving knife against a fork. He spoke moodily.

'Come on Bert do,' Edith remarked keen to the lad when, followed by Jane carrying vegetables in Worcester dishes, he came struggling under a great weight of best beef. He cast a reproachful look in her direction but made no reply.

'If it wasn't for O'Conor being absent this could be termed a reunion,' Raunce announced pompous. 'With Miss Swift and Miss Burch confined to their quarters as they are by sickness we won't count them. Nor Mrs Welch thanks be with her 'ardening of the kidneys.'

'Charley,' Edith remonstrated.

'Pardon,' he said. He sent her a glance that seemed saturated with despair.

'I'm sure we're very happy to have you with us,' Edith said in Jane's direction. Kate watched. Her gimlet eyes narrowed.

'Because if Paddy turns up I've been charged to speak to him,' Raunce began heavy as he set about carving the joint.

'Well you know right well where he is the sad soul,' Kate replied. 'Locked up with them birds 'e's been the past ten days and only gettin' what I fetch out. Not that I defend it,' she ended.

'We can excuse him. I'd be the very last to question 'is motives,' Raunce answered who without doubt had his own reasons for leaving Paddy alone if only that he cannot have been anxious to implicate Edith in the affair of the eggs. 'Matter of that,' he continued, 'Mrs Tennant's got a lot she wants me to say and not to our friend alone. Oh no,' he said. 'For she's on about her ring still.'

'And how would that be Mr Raunce since she got it back didn't she?' Mary enquired.

'There you are,' he answered with as good reasons perhaps for not pursuing this one either. 'There you are you've said it,' he repeated rather lamely.

'It was only that man who came down upset her,' Edith explained while Albert watched. 'And you can't wonder after all. Setting everyone about the place at sixes and sevens as he did. But all's well that ends well,' she concluded.

'If it has ended,' Raunce remarked. 'A sewer rat like him should never be permitted to harass honest folk. Is that right or isn't it? What'th that you thay. Lithping like a tothpot,' he added in a wild and sudden good humour.

'Charley,' Edith called. She began to go red.

'You should have seen the expression you wore,' he said complacent, 'you should really. When he had the impudence to ask you if you'd theen a thertain thomething. D'you recollect?'

'I certainly don't,' Edith said and pouted.

But Kate took this up. 'You don't thay he thpoke like thith thurely,' she asked letting out a shriek of amusement. All of them started to laugh or giggle except Edith and Raunce's Albert.

'It's a lot of foolishness,' Edith reproved them.

'Foolithneth perhapth,' Raunce said roguish. 'But you're dead right. Whatever it may have been it was uncalled for.'

'Why Charley,' Edith went on, 'you're not going to starve yourself again. You will have your supper to-night surely?'

'No girl,' he answered but with a soft look. 'Truth is I don't feel equal to it.'

'The spuds are nice. I cooked 'em myself,' Jane explained and the girls all clucked with sympathy at him except Kate who went on with the lisping.

'If he'd 'a lithped at me I'm dead thure I'd 'a lithped back. I couldn't help mythelf.' Mary giggled. 'Oh Kate you don't thay tho,' she cried.

'Holy thmoke but you've got me goin' now,' Raunce laughed. They all began giggling once more, even Edith. But Albert simpered.

'The whole thing'th too dithtathteful,' Raunce quoted. ' 'Ere I can't get my tongue round it. Dithtasteful,' he tried again. 'No that won't do.' In a moment most of them were attempting this.

'Detethtable,' he shouted out into the hubbub then doubled up with laughter.

'Hush dear they'll hear you,' Edith giggled.

'And what do I care?' he asked. 'Now if you'd said "Huth" I might've harkened. But detethtable's right. It is detestable and distasteful if you like, to have been put through what we've been as if we were criminals,' he said.

'What d'you mean Mr Raunce?' Mary asked.

'Why over this ring she mislaid. Had an investigator sent down and all she did,' he explained. 'Got hold of my lad here then drove 'im half out of his mind with the cunning queries he put till there was Bert sayin' the first thing that came into 'is head. Proper upset you didn't he?' Raunce said to the boy who kept quiet. 'No, but it's wrong,' Raunce told the others, 'it didn't ought to be allowed. Why matters went so far he got 'im talkin' of joining up to get killed. There you are. Not but what we'd all be better off over on the other side.'

'Charley,' Edith called as though he had turned his back on her.

'Upset me too that merchant did. There's been something wrong with my interior from that day to this. I can't seem able to digest my food.'

'You want to take care,' Jane chipped in solicitous. 'Now if I was to put you together a nice bowl of hot broth,' she suggested.

'Thank you,' Raunce replied lordly. 'Thank you but I'd best give my economy a half holiday. It's me dyspepsia,' he explained. 'Dyth-pepthia,' he added gay on a sudden.

'Don't be disgusting,' Edith reproved him. 'And I'll do all the looking after you need,' she said glancing jealous at Jane.

Kate began to blush deeply.

'Holy Motheth,' Raunce crowed, 'now see what you've been and done Edie. You've set our Kate goin'.'

'Things is getting out of hand if you ask me.' Edith remarked. She looked desperate. At that Kate rose, left the room absolutely scarlet.

'Why whatever's the matter with her then?' Mary asked but if Charley was about to reply he never managed it because he was taken by a violent fit of coughing. Edith went to his side. A volley of suggestions was directed at him. Only Albert sat back apart.

'I choked,' he excused himself when he had recovered. 'I don't feel very grand. But you'll agree it's not good enough. It's not right this cross questionin'. Men entering the house without leave and then every sort and kind of question asked. I know she lost a valuable,' he went on, 'but it was not worth that much, couldn't have been, or she would never have gone over to England.' Then he corrected himself. 'Well I don't know,' he said. 'It's a fact Jack had his week's leave right enough but that's not to say she should permit this individual to come nosing round. Conditions are bad enough as it is with all the buzzes and rumours over the invasion,' and all this time the others listened to Raunce with deference, 'not to mention talk of the I.R.A. Because we're at the mercy of any 'ooligan, German or Irish, situated as we are. With Mrs Tennant away we've no influence none whatever.' He paused to couch, not so violently. 'For two pins I'd throw the place up. And one reason is I got a feelin' I'm not appreciated. My work I mean.'

'I don't suppose she was in a position to help herself,' Edith pointed out reasonably. 'Once she claimed on her insurance it would be a thing the company in Dublin would do in the ordinary run, to send down and investigate.'

'I'm not disputing that,' Raunce countered, 'but what I say is Mrs T. should've been here to receive 'im. We're plain honest folk we are. This is not the first position of trust we've held down. We've come out of our places with a good reference each time or she would never have engaged us. No,' he insisted with authority, 'there's a right and a wrong way to go about matters of this sort. There you are, it's 'ighly dithtrething,' he ended as though, having noticed

Edith's expression, he now intended to turn all this off into a joke. If that was his intention it was immediately successful. Like a class at school when given the signal to break up they all with one accord burst out lisping, with the exception of Raunce's Albert. In no time their hilarity had grown until each effort was received with shrieks, Edith's this time amongst the loudest.

Charley began to laugh unrestrained as he held his side which seemed to pain him. Yet he let himself go.

'There'th a tanner in thith for you altho,' he shouted to Edith above the din, quoting her description of Mike Mathewson's proceedings.

'Thankth thon,' she called back. He doubled up again.

'Well thith evening'th a big differenth I mutht thay,' Jane shrieked to Mary. 'Not what we uthually have to look forward to duckth, ith it?' she yelled. At this Kate who had slipped back again began to laugh so much she dribbled. 'Mith Burthch,' she squealed, 'Mitheth Welcheth,' Mary screamed, 'oh Burcheth Welhech,' Raunce echoed and pandemonium reigned. But in his convulsions of laughter Charley was noticeably paler even. For the past fortnight he had been looking very ill. 'Landth thakes Mith Thwift,' howled Edith. By now everyone bar Albert was crying. All wore a look of agony, or as though they were in a close finish to a race over a hundred yards. 'Jethuth,' Raunce moaned.

'Hush dear,' Edith said at once. 'That's not comical dear,' and they began to sober down.

'Moses,' he corrected himself.

'There,' Jane announced between gasps, 'I feel like I'd been emptied.'

'What of duckth?' Kate asked and there blew up another gust of giggling. 'Oh me,' someone remarked weak. 'It's my side,' another said. Then they quietened.

'Well nobody can say we don't have our fun on occasions,' Edith made comment as she dabbed at her great eyes.

'It'd be all right if we was like this every night,' Jane murmured.

'Oh it's not so bad after all.'

'I don't know Edith,' Mary answered. 'You've not got Mrs Welch although I shouldn't mention names.'

'We ain't got her Albert,' Raunce put in.

'It's not him so much,' Jane explained. 'He's well enough conducted indoors in the kitchen,' she said. 'It's Mrs Welch is the matter. Oh I know I shouldn't but she drinks. All the time she drinks. She's only gone in to Dublin to get another crate. She's like the wells, she's runnin' dry. There you are. That's right isn't it Mary or isn't it?'

'It's the honest truth,' Mary said.

'Go on,' Raunce objected, 'but then 'ow does she get the stuff delivered will you oblige me with that? Because I don't need to tell you she's not drawin' a drop out of my cellar. I don't hold with this fiddling like you'll come across in some households.'

'Why,' Jane disclosed in a hushed voice, 'it's the tradesmen. You know she won't 'ave one of us pass the time of day with 'em even. Well you'd never guess what's behind it. I tell you they drop a case of the stuff with the meat and another with the groceries. And the price all included in the monthly books, isn't that so Mary?'

'That's right,' this girl replied.

'The artful old cow,' Raunce exclaimed.

'Charley,' Edith said firm.

'Pardon I'm sure,' he answered gravely, 'but did you ever hear anything to touch this? Fiddlin' 'er monthly books. No. You know that's serious this is.' He was solemn.

'You're tellin' me,' Kate muttered.

'What?' he asked at once and sharp. 'Bless me my gel but you seem to grow more and more sarky every day which passes. What's come over you?'

'Nothin' Mr Raunce.'

'You let her be, Charley,' Edith reproved him. 'She was only agreein'.'

'No offence intended I'm sure,' he assured her. 'But is that what Mrs Welch is up to? Would you believe it?' he enquired of all and sundry in an astounded tone of voice.

'The wickedness there is in this world,' Mary said.

'The wickedness?' he asked gentle but with a sharp look.

'Because that's thievin' that is,' Jane concluded like a little girl put through her catechism.

'You've said it,' Raunce agreed and relaxed. It had plainly been the right answer. 'That's the very word.' Then he quoted Miss Burch with solemnity. 'And the wicked shall flourish even as a green bay tree,' he intoned. Everyone bar Albert seemed to approve.

A few days afterwards Edith entered Charley's room as she was coming on her way from tea in the servants' hall.

'Come on out and feed the peacockth,' she proposed, for Paddy had at last consented to free these birds again. She waved a bag she had filled with scraps.

'Steady,' he replied. 'That's no light matter.'

'Why what's up Charley?'

'Nothing,' he answered.

'I know there is,' she said.

'I'm not right,' he went on. 'I vomited this morning another time.'

'Oh dear that's bad,' she said lightly.

'I shouldn't wonder if you made fun of this as you've done before but I love you so much my stomach's all upset an' there you are.'

'So it should be,' she countered as though determined not to worry.

'Yes but what's to be the end?' he asked low. 'I can't go on the way I am. I'm in bad shape. Honest, dear.'

'You wait till we're married love. I'll take care you're never sick then.'

'Oh the worry of it all,' he broke out.

'Now just you come along with me,' she said. 'Getting out in the air for a while will do you more good than any other thing.'

'I've no time.'

'No time Charley? How's that?'

'I must lay the dinner dear. Now my Albert's left, everything falls back on me you know.'

'But surely you've never forgotten how they're over to Clancarty for dinner with the Captain. Why you've a free evenin'.'

'There I go again,' he said bewildered. 'It had clean slipped my memory. Well perhaps I will at that.'

'That's right Charley,' she coaxed as she took his arm. She laid her body up against his shoulder. 'We'll sit us down by the old dovecote so you can rest. It will do you ever such a lot of good you'll see.'

When they were established there after she had conducted him as

192

though he was an old man and he had sat himself down heavily he remarked,

'It come as a big shock to me my Albert leavin' the way he did.'

'But you knew he'd given in his notice love,' she objected.

'Of course I knew,' he replied querulous, 'but I never thought he meant to go, any more than Mrs Tennant took it that he did. As she told me.'

'I can't say I considered it was other than talk,' she agreed.

'To walk in just like that an' say look my month's up I must be off the way he did. I never guessed that bloodless abortion 'ad the guts,' he said with a return to his old manner.

'You never could abide him could you?' she remarked.

'That dam kid's attitude was what got my goat,' Mr Raunce explained. 'The high falutin' love he laid claim to, the suffering looks he darted, 'is faintin' snotty ways.'

Edith gave a single deep laugh.

'Yes go on and laugh,' Raunce said.

'No you made yourself awkward with that lad.'

'That's as may be,' he answered and seemed despondent. 'Yet there's only the one method to learn them kids a trade. It's no earthly good kissin' 'em as you did.'

'Me?' she cried. 'I never.'

'You did that and in front of the investigator johnny into the bargain.'

'Oh well,' she said.

'Have it your own way,' he replied. He relapsed into silence.

'What is it dear?' she asked.

'I'm worried,' he answered.

'What's worrying you then?'

'Nothing.'

'It's not about the old ring any more is it?' she enquired.

'Well Albert's goin' did set 'er mind on it once again. Seems that she'd told him she couldn't accept his notice while he was under suspicion, or so she made out to me. I thought we'd better make an end to that talk. "Look Madam," I said to her, "you can't deny you have the ring back so where's the evidence," I said. She says to me, "But it's what I suspect Raunce, that's where the shoe pinches," or some such phrase. "I can't guarantee it won't happen a second time

Madam," I told her, "an' if anything should, then you report it to me Madam an' I'll see you don't have any more trouble. There's things I didn't know then that I know now," I says. "I see Raunce," she said. "Then you don't wish for me to do another thing and I can sleep quiet into the bargain?" "You silly old cow you can do just that," I said to her only I didn't.'

'Charley that's not very nice,' Edith objected.

'But we've 'ad about enough surely? There's more going on in the world these days than a little crazy bastard of a cook's nephew having the laugh on us. Secreted it right here too didn't he? I shouldn't mind if I never set eyes on these blasted white pigeons again,' he ended.

'Why,' she said, 'your pain you've got's upset you.'

'You're dead right it has,' he replied.

'You don't benefit by your night's rest,' she went on.

He appeared to warm to this description of his symptoms. 'That's exactly it,' he agreed. 'I sometimes just seem to do nothin' but turn over.'

'And d'you always think of me?' she asked taking tighter hold of the arm she had hung on to.

'You bet I do,' he answered. 'More'n you ever realize.'

'That's right,' she said, 'then you won't come by much harm.'

'I do love you Edie.'

'Do you?'

'D'you know I sometimes wonder if the air in these parts hadn't a lot to do with my stomach,' he began again. 'I couldn't say if it's too weak or too strong but there's something about these sea breezes might be harmful to a delicate constitution. What d'you say?' He was dead serious.

'No that's good for you.'

'Then what d'you reckon can be the matter with me Edie?'

It was plain she was not worried. 'D'you think Mrs Welch is slipping a pinch of something in your food?' she asked maliciously, hardly paying attention.

'I wouldn't put that past her,' he replied. 'But she's too set on keepin' young Albert over on this side of the water to start a game like it. Why if I had proof I'd choke the life out of 'er by pokin' a peacock down that great gullet she has.' Edith laughed. 'I would straight,' he assured her in a strong voice. 'And that's a death would

194

be too good for the woman, the diabolical mason.'

'Women can't be masons. They aren't accepted.'

'Can't they,' he retorted. 'That's all you know then.'

'It takes all sorts to make a world,' she remarked.

'You're telling me,' he said. Holding one of her hands in his he shut his eyes and appeared to want to rest. 'I'd tear the 'eart right out of 'er,' he added in a weak voice.

'I had a look over that little house Charley,' she murmured soft after a moment.

'You what?'

'Where we're goin' to live when we're married,' she explained.

'So you did·did you?' he said stirring in his seat.

'Why whatever's the matter now?' she asked. 'You wished me to surely?'

'I shouldn't wonder if my ideas hadn't changed,' he said cautious. 'About where we plan to find a home together,' he added.

'What's come over you Charley?' she enquired. She began at last to show signs of alarm.

'What experience I've had, and I've 'ad some mind, has gone to show that it's no manner of use hanging on in a place where you're not valued,' he said.

'But there are the little extras,' she cried. 'That two or three quid a week you speak about.'

'Oh well,' he answered, 'it's no more'n can be picked up in any butler's job if you know the ropes. No, what's goin' on over in Britain is what bothers me. The way things are shapin' it wouldn't come as a surprise if places such as this weren't doomed to a natural death so to say.'

'Go on with you,' she replied. 'Why if Mrs Tennant loses all her dough there'll always be those that took it. Don't you tell me there isn't good pickings to be had in service long after our children have said thank you madam for the first bawlin' out over nothing at all that they'll receive.' She was beginning to speak like him.

'That's as may be girl,' he countered, 'but from all accounts there's some lovely money going in munitions.'

'Yes and then once this old war's over it's out on your ear with no work.'

'Yet you've just argued that there'll be jobs in service we can go back to,' he complained.

'Stay in what you know, that's what I always maintain,' Edith announced although she had never before expressed an opinion one way or the other.

'Well you may be right but it's this country gets me down.'

'You're fed up, Charley, on account of your stomach.'

'It's too bloody neutral this country is.'

'Too neutral?' she echoed.

'Well there's danger in being a neutral in this war,' he said, 'you've only to read the newspapers to appreciate that.'

'I thought you'd given up listenin' to such talk,' she complained.

'And then my lad going over to give 'imself up, to enlist.'

'What's that to do with you an' me?' she grumbled,

'I'm unsettled. There you are. This has unsettled me Edie.'

'Charley what's the matter? You tell. Nothing serious is it dear?'

'I received a letter this morning.'

'You've had bad news?'

'Not exactly,' he admitted.

'Then who was it from?' she asked.

'My mum wrote me.'

'Your old mother? Well what did she say?'

'She's not comin' over mate, that's what."

'Not coming over?' she repeated in quite a loud voice. 'Why then we can have the little house all to ourselves dearest.'

'If we want to live there in the end,' he said.

'Whatever are you saying?' she cried really disturbed at last.

'I wrote to 'er see,' Raunce explained with some embarrassment, 'and what I said was I'd like to have her out of that awful air raid business. I know he's never been over Peterboro' yet but the way he's going it might be any minute now. I said she could do worse than come here and told 'er what you and I had thought of. It would be a weight off my mind I said and how you would look after 'er better than my sister Bell ever did.'

'Well what did she say?'

'I got the letter here,' he said. 'She writes she reckons that would be cowardly or something.'

'Can I see it?' she requested serious.

'No I won't show it to you,' he answered.

'Then there's matters disobligin' about me in it,' she cried.

'To tell you the truth there's no mention of you at all.'

'Well whoever's heard,' she exclaimed.

'I can't understand that part,' he went on. 'I said as clear as clear we were thinkin' of getting married but it's just as if she'd never bothered to read to the bottom.'

'Well I never,' Edith said cautious.

'It's that bit about being afraid that gets me,' he muttered.

'Afraid to marry me she means?'

'Not on your life. I told you she never mentioned you Edie. No she reckons we're 'iding ourselves away in this neutral country.'

'Here let me read it.'

'No mate I don't want you to get a wrong impression of the old lady, seeing that we're to be man and wife.'

'Your sister's put her up to it,' she said.

'My sister Bell?' he laughed. 'You wait till you meet.'

'You don't love me,' she wailed.

'Oh honey,' he said with a sigh, 'you'll never know how much I do.' But he made no move towards her. She had gone quite white. She chanced a quick look at him, noted that he seemed exhausted.

'Why dearest,' she exclaimed, 'd'you feel all right?'

'It's our plans,' he said. 'We'd just about got everything settled when this comes along.'

'But we could live here without your mother,' she pleaded. 'Oh you don't realize how I'll look after you,' she went on, 'and by this means I'll have twice the time to do it. Because I was never aiming to give up work at the Castle. Mrs Tennant can't get help. She'll be glad to have me over six days a week only the seventh I must keep for our washin'.'

He leant over to kiss her. She allowed it. Then she interrupted him.

'No Charley,' she said, 'we got to discuss this.'

'She's funny that way,' he remarked as though in a dream.

'What are you getting at?' she asked sharp.

'She's obstinate mother is. Always was. I remember when the old man wanted to chuck his job on the railway because 'e'd been made a good offer I can't exactly remember where now but I know it would've meant more money. Well she wouldn't 'ear of it, wouldn't even let it be mentioned twice. They had a rare argument at the time. I was only a kid but I can hear them now. But she got her way. He stayed where 'e was. And I couldn't say that he lost by so doing.'

'Yet she wishes us to throw this place up.'

'Yes Edie, but it's different this time.'

'I'm that bewildered,' she said.

'Now love,' he said in a voice that was weak with exhaustion, 'you're not to worry.'

'But we'd laid all our plans,' she objected and seemed to be fighting back the tears. Then she gave way. 'Oh our little 'ouse,' she sobbed. She turned to him like a child, and held out her arms. With a quick movement she got onto his knees. She merged into him and copiously wept.

'There sweet'eart there,' he comforted. She was crying noisily. He appeared to grope for words. 'Don't take on love,' he said. He shifted his legs as though the weight was beginning to tell. 'This would occur just when I'm not quite up to the mark,' he exclaimed. She gave no sign of having heard. 'There's other places,' he tried to appease her. 'We'll find you a lovely home,' he ended, and fell silent.

'Don't stop,' she sobbed into his ear.

'Why,' he said, 'I love you more than I thought I was capable. I'm surprised at myself, honest I am. If my old mother could see her Charley now she'd never recognize 'im,' he murmured.

She at once got off his knees. She started blowing her nose and cleaning up. He leant forward, gazed awkward into her face. 'I never seen anything like your eyes they're so 'uge not in all my experience,' he announced soft. 'Yet for eighteen months I didn't so much as notice them. Can you explain that?' Then, perhaps to distract her attention, he invited her to witness what he saw, the peacocks that had been attracted. For these most greedy of all birds had collected in twos about and behind the lilac trees, on the scrounge for tit-bits.

'Oh those,' she answered. 'It's wicked the way they spy on you.'

'They've been raised in a good school,' he remarked.

'There,' she said giving her face a last dab. She did not look at him. 'I'm sorry I did that. Well then Charley what's next?'

'You mustn't blame this on my old lady ducks,' he replied. 'She gets pig'eaded at times the way all old people do. But that's not to say she hasn't wounded me because she has and where a man feels it most, right in my pride in myself,' he explained. 'She knows I'm barely an age for this war, yet awhiles anyhow, yet she seems to think I'm not in it all I might be, d'you get me?'

Edith stayed silent.

'Oh this pain,' he suddenly groaned. 'It will nag a man.'

'I got some bicarbonate indoors will soon see to that,' she said.

'I was wonderin' if you could just nip over and fetch us some,' he suggested green in the face.

'We haven't finished,' she answered grim. 'There's a lot I want to get straight first.'

'What's that love?' he asked.

'What are we goin' to do then?' Edith continued. She spoke calm.

Raunce leant forward. In an effort to pull himself together perhaps, he squinted terribly.

'We got to get out of here,' he said.

'Leave this place?' she asked.

'There's nothing else for it sweetheart,' he replied.

'And go to the Agency in Dublin to find us another Charley?'

'No dear. We've just been in to all that. We'd best clear right out.'

'What and go to America somewhere Charley?'

'Not on your life,' he answered. 'It's back to the old country for you an' me my love.'

'And have me took up as I step from off the ship which brought us across by one of those women police waiting on the dockside to put me in the A.T.S.? 'Ave you gone out of your mind then?'

'Steady on Edie where did you get that from? They don't act in such a fashion, not yet they don't.'

'Out of your very lips and not so long since either. You sat at dinner and frightened my Kate out of her mind almost, so she shouldn't go.'

'Why it was only a tale,' he pleaded.

'How d'you know? You said so Charley.'

'You've got no diplomacy love, that's what's the matter. I didn't want you left with all her work or some dirty Irish judy brought in to help who you'd have to go round after all the time. Sure I pitched 'er a tale. Mind you they'll be forced to it in the end before this war's over, when the casualties start an' they get real short of labour. You mark my words we'll all be in uniform then. But just at present there's nothing of the sort I tell you.'

'And you're certain this ain't just your idea to get rid of me?' she asked tearfully once more.

He put an arm round her shoulders.

''Ere,' he said, 'what's up all of a sudden? It's not like you to have nightmares or see shadows followin' you round.'

'I'm that bewildered,' she explained again, settling her cheek against his.

'Now don't you fret,' he comforted. 'You leave all the brain work to your old man. Lucky Charley they call him,' he said in a thread-bare return to his usual manner. 'We want to get out of this country and when once we've made up our minds we want to get out fast.'

'Elope?' she cried delighted all of a sudden.

'Elope,' he agreed grave.

She gave him a big kiss. 'Why Charley,' she said, seemingly more and more delighted, 'that's romantic.'

'It's what we're going to do whatever the name you give it,' he replied.

'But don't you see that's a wonderful thing to do,' she went on.

'Maybe so,' he said soft into her ear, 'but it's what we're doing.'

'Oh I can love you for this,' she murmured. 'There I've said it now haven't I? You were always on at me to say. But go on.'

'That's all,' he announced. 'Only once I get hold of Michael we'd best get away out to-morrow.'

'Wait a minute,' she cried in a disappointed voice. 'And how about our month's notice?'

'We shan't hand it in mate that's all. We'll flit.'

'Oh but Charley that would be wrong,' she said in a low voice.

'Right or wrong it's what we'll do. We could get Kate to come along if you was to feel awkward.'

'Awkward?' she asked. 'How d'you mean?'

'Well,' he replied shyly. 'We can't get married before we've put the banns up a full three weeks on the other side. I was just askin' myself if you'd feel it was right our travelling without we were man and wife.'

She laughed. 'D'you reckon I can't protect myself from you after all this time?' she enquired gentle.

'I know you can right enough,' he replied, 'but I couldn't tell the way you'd see it.'

She did not answer this. She said,

'Kate would never come with us, not now.'

'How's that Edie?'

'On account of her Paddy.'

'Go on with that for a tale.'

'I thought you knew dear,' she said.

'Well I did in a manner of speaking but not to place any reliance on it.'

'It's true right enough. She says he needs 'er.'

'Then all I can say is that's disgusting, downright disgusting.'

'Dithtrething and dithtathteful?' she asked.

'No mate it's no joking matter. Why a big, grown girl like her an' that ape out of a Zoo.'

'There's the way things are Charley.'

'But how did this come about?'

'She was lonely,' Edith explained, 'an' she watched us.'

' 'Ere,' he said, 'don't go layin' Paddy at my door. Why it's unnatural.'

'Well she's made her bed an' she needs must lie on it.'

'All the more reason then for us to get quick out of here,' was his comment.

'And not say goodbye to a soul?' she now asked in an excited voice.

'Not to anyone,' he replied narrowly watching her.

'Oh I couldn't,' she cried as though all at once she had despaired. 'I must tell Miss Evelyn and Miss Moira.'

'That's been the cause of half the trouble in this place. Once they get hold of something it's taken right out of control.'

'But it wouldn't be right. Why they're innocent.'

' 'Ow d'you mean innocent?' he enquired. 'There's a lot we could lay to their door.'

'They're not grown up,' she explained. 'They've got their lives to live yet. They mightn't understand if I was to go off without a word.'

'They'll forget soon enough dearest,' he said.

'No Charley,' she insisted and appeared distressed, 'you don't know. It would be wicked that's all. D'you mean to say we've not got to say one word?'

'That's right mate.'

'But what about Miss Burch? How will she take it? Can you tell me? Or Miss Swift who's trusted me with the young ladies?'

He put his arms about her. He held her close.

'Look my own love,' he said, 'it's like this. Once we let it get about that we're goin' then they'll all of them begin to talk. Mrs Tennant will pay a call on Mrs Welch who will send for old Agatha out of her bed. Miss Swift'll 'ave 'ysterics an' the Captain will receive a phone call from Mrs Jack to stop you an' me on the boat. Michael will be threatened with the sack. They'll even tell the garage in Kinalty they mustn't hire to us.'

He could feel her trembling.

'But Charley dear,' she protested, 'this is a free country surely to goodness?'

'It's priest-ridden love,' he replied.

'But Mrs Tennant's got no right to stop someones, not if we give her a month's wages.'

'A month's wages my eye. That's a fine way to start bein' married, to throw good money down the drain.'

'All right then Charley. You know best I expect.'

'No,' he went on, 'it's on account of that ring. She's got her suspicions you see love. She let Albert find his way but with us she'd raise holy Cain, making out I was carryin' you off.'

'But that's what you are doin' surely dear,' Edith announced. She settled deeper in his arms.

'It's you cartin' me off body and soul more likely,' he answered. He fastened on to her mouth. His face was very white and green and grey.

When he lifted his lips from hers he asked,

'Then you will to-morrow, without a word said to anyone?'

'I expect so,' she replied.

'You don't sound very certain,' he remarked.

'Oh I will, I will,' she cried very loud and wildly kissed him.

'You could tell Kate if you wished,' he said when he had a chance.

'I'll not say a word to a soul,' she promised.

At this he began to flush. The colour spread until his face had become an alarming ugly purple.

'Why I do declare you're blushin',' she cried delightedly. 'You who never have.' Then as he leant himself back, obviously stretched and tested by what he experienced, she said nervous again.

'What's up with you? You're not goin' sick on me are you?'

'I'll be O.K.,' he said faint.

'Not just when we've got this great journey?' she added.

'It was only that I feared you'd never consent,' he explained in a weak voice, with closed eyes. 'If I know anything it's that they'll keep us here one way or the other if we let a word out. Oh sweet'eart darlin' I'd hardly liked to think you'd see it my way.' He closed his eyes. An arm was limp over her shoulders. 'We'll go straight to Peterboro' where my mum'll have a bed for you. Arthur Sanders the sergeant of police I was at school with will put me up at his place till we can have the ceremony. And we must find us a room for a start.'

'Yes,' she said. She kissed the inside of his hand.

'Why look who's here,' she exclaimed. He opened his eyes and found Badger wagging his tail so hard that he was screwed right round into a crescent. The dog seemed deeply ashamed of something.

'You go on out of it,' Raunce ordered. 'This no place for you when you're only after one of those pigeon to knock off.' The hound left, looking back twice as he went. And once he turned to stand with pricked ears, with a wild yearning look of grief.

'That dog's more trouble than he's worth,' Raunce muttered. He let his eyelids shut down over his eyes. 'He'd never catch a mouse that had lost all its legs not now he wouldn't,' he added in a voice of deep content.

'Well this is a fine elopement,' she remarked amused. 'I didn't gamble on you going to sleep on me I must say.'

'It's me dyspepsia,' he excused himself from behind shut eyes. 'That's a condition don't let up on you however you're placed.'

'You rest yourself dearest,' she answered then murmured happily to herself that in another minute she would have forgotten what they had come out for.

Accordingly she picked up the bag of scraps. She began to feed the peacocks. They came forward until they had her surrounded. Then a company of doves flew down on the seat to be fed. They settled all over her. And their fluttering disturbed Raunce who re-opened his eyes. What he saw then he watched so that it could be guessed that he was in pain with his great delight. For what with the peacocks bowing at her purple skirts, the white doves nodding on her shoulders round her brilliant cheeks and her great eyes that blinked tears of happiness, it made a picture.

'Edie,' he appealed soft, probably not daring to move or speak too sharp for fear he might disturb it all. Yet he used exactly that tone Mr Eldon had employed at the last when calling his Ellen. 'Edie,' he moaned.

The next day Raunce and Edith left without a word of warning. Over in England they were married and lived happily ever after.

# Living

for Dig

'As these birds would go
where so where would this child go?'

# 1

Bridesley, Birmingham.

Two o'clock. Thousands came back from dinner along streets.

'What we want is go, push,' said works manager to son of Mr Dupret. 'What I say to them is – let's get on with it, let's get the stuff out.'

Thousands came back to factories they worked in from their dinners.

'I'm always at them but they know me. They know I'm a father and mother to them. If they're in trouble they've but to come to me. And they turn out beautiful work, beautiful work. I'd do anything for 'em and they know it.'

Noise of lathes working began again in this factory. Hundreds went along road outside, men and girls. Some turned in to Dupret factory.

Some had stayed in iron foundry shop in this factory for dinner. They sat round brazier in a circle.

'And I was standing by the stores in the doorway with me back to the door into the pipe shop with a false nose on and green whiskers. Albert inside was laughin' and laughin' again when 'Tis 'im comes in through the pipe shop and I sees Albert draw up but I didn't take much notice till I heard, 'Ain't you got nothin' better to do Gates but to make a fool of yourself?' And 'e says to Albert, 'What would you be standin' there for Milligan?' And I was too surprised to take the nose off, it was so sudden. I shan't ever forget that.'

'And that was all that 'e said to you Joe?'

'Not by a mile and a bit. 'E went on about my being as old as he was, and 'ow 'e'd given up that sort of thing when 'e was a kid, and he told on me to Joe Brown that was foreman in this shop at that time, but 'e didn't take much notice I reckon. Yer know I couldn't take that nose off, I was kinder paralysed. And it was just the same when I see old Tupe fall at me feet this morning, I was that glad I couldn't move one way or t'other to pick 'im up.'

'What does 'e want to go fallin' about for at his age?'

'That's what I told him. I said "You'll go hurtin' yourself falling about one of these days" I said, "and when you do it won't only be but your deserts. It's a judgment on you" I said "to be tumbling at my feet, you dirty old man" I said "for all the things you've said about me and my mate." There were several there. They heard it. Then he started cussin'. I laughed! It 'urt the cheeks in me face.'

'I can't see 'em.'

'You silly bleeder and 'ow does your little bit like it when you come 'ome and lay yer head up against hers on the pillow and her 'as only been married to you three months and as can't be used to the dirt.'

'All right with yer has 'as's, all right.'

'But I'd like to see that Tupe dead and I don't mind who knows it. So 'e will be if 'e goes on fallin' about. Every bloody thing that 'appens straightaway 'e goes and tells 'Tis 'im. I shouldn't wonder if 'e hadn't fetched him when I 'ad the green whiskers on me face. And that was six years ago now. Dirty sod.'

'Ah. He's not like the one you work with Joe. 'E tells too much, Tupe does, always nosing into other people's doings.'


'Tis 'im, who was works manager, and Mr Dupret's son were going about this factory. They went through engineer's shop. Sparrows flew by belts that ran from lathes on floor up to shafting above by skylights. The men had thrown crumbs for them on floor. Works manager said they were in the way, it made him mad, he said, to see them about, 'the men watch them Mr Dupret while God knows what may be up with the job on the lathe. I say to them – don't throw crumbs to sparrows on the floor, one of these days you'll get hurt from not watching your job. We pay them while they bet on these sparrows. And you can't stop it. You can't keep the sparrows out. I've had a man on the roof three weeks now patching holes they come in by. But they find a way.'

Works manager and Mr Dupret's son went through sliding doors and works manager said this was the iron foundry. Black sand made the floor. Men knelt in it. Young man passed by Mr Dupret and works manager.

'What a beautiful face.'

'What? Eh? Well I don't know. He works for that moulder over in the corner. He's getting an old man now but there's no one can beat him for his work. The best moulder in Birmingham Mr Dupret. And he's a worry. That's his labourer there by him now. That man gets on my nerves. I'd have sacked him years ago but I didn't dare. Joe Gates 'is name is. I've seen that man make paper aeroplanes and float them about the shop and I couldn't do anything for fear I might put Craigan in a rage. He won't work with no one else Mr Dupret and he's the best moulder in Birmingham. But then the best engineer I ever met couldn't see you to talk business with you but he 'ad his pet spaniel on a chair by him. There's no accounting for it, none.'

Foreman came up and works manager asked him about stamping frames he would be casting that evening and they talked and Mr Dupret looked at the foundry. He walked over nearer to where Craigan worked. This man scooped gently at great shape cut down in black sand in great iron box. He was grimed with the black sand.

Mr Gates was talking to storekeeper, Albert Milligan. 'And the old man fell at me toes and I wasn't goin' to stretch out me 'and, "lie there" I said to him, "and serve you right you dirty old man" I said, "that has no right to be falling about at your age. Ye'll fall once too often," I said.'

'Ah, he'll kill himself one o' these days. It'll be a judgment on 'im. Everything that goes on 'Tis 'im hears of it through him. But as to falling it ain't healthy for 'im, there was an old chap in 'ospital that had done just the same.'

'That's what I said to 'im. But 'ow would you be feelin' now Albert?'

'Middlin' Joe. I 'ad it bad again yesterday. I said to myself if you sit yourself down you'll grow morbid. So I kept on. It worked off in the end. Yes there was a feller opposite my bed that had lengths cut out of his belly and when they brought 'im in again, an' he come to after the operation, they told him 'e could eat anything that took 'is fancy. So he said a poached egg on toast would suit 'im for a start but when they took it to 'im 'e brought it up. Black it was. And, everything they took him after he brought it up just the same till they were givin' 'im port, then brandy and champagne at the end.'

'Ah.'

'And one day I couldn't stick it no longer and I said to the sister, 'I want to go 'ome.' And she said "but you can't." And I said "I want to go 'ome" and she said "but it would kill you Mr Milligan." And I said I didn't mind, "I want to go 'ome" I said. So at last they sent the matron to me. She came and sat by the bed. She could do anything with you, and she said "What's the trouble Mr Milligan?" and I said "I want to go 'ome, I want to sleep in my own bed." And she said "but it'll kill you" and I asked if there weren't an ambulance as could take me. "I can't stick it with that poor feller over there" I said, "what's the matter with 'im that 'e can't keep nothing down. He'll die soon, won't 'e?" And she said "we can't keep them 'ere as God wants to take to himself Mr Milligan." I reckon that was a fine woman. Well I stayed and I seemed to do better after that. And the next day the chap next me said, "What was the matter with you yesterday Albert that you got jumpy like you did? Stick it, you'll be out soon." And I said "yes, I'll stick it," and we shook 'ands on that. But I wouldn't go back.'

'Well you can't expect to get right in a day not after anythin' like what you 'ad. Any road yer looking as fat as an egg now, old sow pig.'

'Out yer go. I got more to do than stand talking to foundry rats. Gor glomey ain't 'Tis 'im about with the governor's son. Come out now, go on back to yer old man. 'E'll be 'owling for yer. But 'ere. Joe, you might've given the old bleeder a 'and up, there was one or two came in here this morning that didn't like your standin' by Tupey and not doin' nothing. And there was no one else but you about for a few moments. Though I'm not saying I shouldn't 've done the same.'

' 'Elp 'im, I'd be dead before. Look what 'e's done to others, what 'e's said along 'o their private lives. Give 'im a hand, might as well 'elp the devil shovel coals.'

'Ah. Well so long Joe.'

' 'Elp that carcase. It was as much as I could do not to wipe me boots on 'is lying mouth. I'll be — before I 'elp 'is kind.'

'And that'll come to you one of these days.'

Mr Gates went back to foundry with chaplets he had fetched from stores shouting against storekeeper's dirty mind, and laughing, but noise of lathes working made it so what he said could not be heard.

Standing in foundry shop son of Mr Dupret thought in mind and it seemed to him that these iron castings were beautiful and he reached out fingers to them, he touched them; he thought and only in machinery it seemed to him was savagery left now for in the country, in summer, trees were like sheep while here men created what you could touch, wild shapes, soft like silk, which would last and would be working in great factories, they made them with their hands. He felt more certain and he said to himself it was wild incidental beauty in these things where engineers had thought only of the use put to them. He thought, he declaimed to himself this was the life to lead, making useful things which were beautiful, and the gladness to make them, which you could touch; but when he was most sure he remembered, he remembered it had been said before and he said to himself, 'Ruskin built a road which went nowhere with the help of undergraduates and in so doing said the last word on that.' And then what had been so plain, stiff and bursting inside him like soda fountains, this died as a small wind goes out, and he felt embarrassed standing as he did in fine clothes.

Works manager gave up talking to foreman of iron foundry shop and said Mr Dupret must be tired of seeing iron foundry now and they must get on. 'It's all beautiful work we do Mr Dupret, beautiful work. And we turn it out' he said.

As Mr Dupret and Bridges walked through the shops Mr Tarver followed them. This man was chief designer in Birmingham factory. He was very clever man at his work.

As they went round he followed, like a poacher, for he had no business to be following them. But above all things he wanted to speak to young Mr Dupret because he was afraid he was being forgotten.

Mr Dupret and works manager came to outside assembling shop. Old man stopped them there, it was Tupe, and told Mr Bridges how he fell that morning. As they talked Mr Dupret began to notice man signalling from behind a big cylinder which had been machined. This man beckoned and waved arm at him, it was Tarver. Mr Dupret turned to works manager but Tupe had got hold of that one's coat and was passionately saying, '—and there was one there as dain't make no move to 'elp me.'

But Mr Dupret interrupted them.

'Mr Bridges I think there's someone wants to see you,' he said, 'that man behind that thing over there.'

'Where?' said Mr Bridges. Tarver had disappeared. Then he saw Mr Tarver walking off behind. 'Oh that's Tarver,' he said, ''e can see me any time.' But Bridges took Mr Dupret away at once, and young Mr Dupret wondered why Bridges seemed displeased.

Afterwards Mr Tarver saw his opportunity. Bridges was called away to look at something and then he came up. He brought it all out in a rush: 'Mr Dupret sir,' he said, 'could I trouble you for a few words with me sir. I figured it out in my own mind that it was my duty and I'll put it to you in this way sir – would you think it right that any works manager, I don't mean especially Mr Bridges there, but any works manager in any factory would let you see none but 'im. Look here Mr Dupret,' he said and went on about how all of them were old men in this firm except Dupret and he, was no punch in what they did, 'no shoulder behind it sir,' he said. Luckily he took strong line with Mr Dupret who at first was surprised, then was beginning to be impressed when works manager came back again.

'That's all right John' said Mr Bridges, 'you get along now. This way Mr Dupret. Don't you listen to 'im, your dad knows 'im. I keep 'em from you, those like 'im. Ah they're a worry to me. He's a good man mind you, your dad's got a great opinion of 'im and there it is. But 'e's a worry to me' said Mr Bridges and led young Mr Dupret away.

Mr Alf Smith and Mr Jones worked on bench. They were vice hands in the tool room. Both were young men.

Mr Jones said what was the time. Mr Smith went out to where by bending down he could see clock on the wall in shop next to them.

'It wants a $\frac{1}{4}$ to 4 Bert.'

'Then I'll go and have a sit down,' said Mr Jones.

He went out of their shop but at the door he knocked against Tupe who was struggling with a trolley.

'Look out' he said, 'you nearly 'ad me over then.'

'Over,' cried Tupe, 'over, ah an' I wish you was over an' all. Ah, and talkin' of that, why this morning I tripped over meself. Bang on me 'ead I went and there was Craigan's nose-wiper by me, Joe Gates, but 'e dain't stir, no, 'e watched me lie. But then he's tired, 'e is. Soon as 'e gets 'ome – on with 'is pinney an' 'e does the 'ousework for 'is daughter, her makes 'im. 'Is gaffer's slops an' 'ers. 'E don't get much rest in the night time neither as 'e's reading fairy stories for the old gaffer to get to sleep by. 'E's a wretched poor sort of a man. 'E ain't no more'n my age. Where'll I pull this 'igh speed stuff Bert?'

'You'll go hurtin' yourself one of these days, you know, falling about at your age. Blimey,' said Mr Jones, 'if we picked you up every time one of you old chaps fell down we'd be wore out, regular wore out.'

'Ssh!' said Mr Tupe, 'I ain't a young wench. In course you wouldn't pick 'er up where she'd laid 'erself down. An' that reminds me I seen you out with 'is daughter, only I was forgetting just now. But she ain't destinated your road. Craigan 'as picked 'is young mate for 'er, Jim Dale.'

'So he may pick for all I'm bothering. Come on now, put them rods in 'ere and get out of my road.'

'Where would you be off to then, hurry?' said Mr Tupe. 'Ain't any tarts in this factory, you know, the more's the pity' he said. 'But you ain't a bad young feller so you did ought to look 'igher than Lily Gates. Fly 'igh' he said, 'and you'll see the birds circling up to yer, the darling little tarts. Then you can pick the 'ighest as comes to yer fancy.'

Evening. In their house works manager sat with his wife. He said a hard day it had been, with the young fellow down. It wasn't that he did not mean well young Mr Dupret, 'but they live different to you and me' he said. 'I've worked over forty years. I 'ave been fifteen years manager for Mr Dupret. Then 'e sends his son down, presumably. I say to myself "where am I?" He's good intentioned but 'e's soft. He never took much notice of the works but then he wouldn't do, not having been through the shops. Work with the men, do what they have to do or you'll never be a salesman, I look at it that way. All he wanted was to let our men know the profits. What'd that help them but unsettle them. They wouldn't understand. They'd not draw more money than it. I've worked for 'is father fifteen years. Ten with the O.K. gas plant before. What's he send his son for throwing educated stuff at me? He didn't interfere before. And all through today them others, like crows after sheep's eyes, trying to get 'old of 'im and tell lies. I'm tired. Tired. Takes the use out of you.'

Evening. Was spring. Heavy blue clouds stayed over above. In

213

small back garden of villa small tree was with yellow buds. On table in back room daffodils, faded, were between ferns in a vase. Later she spoke of these saying she must buy new ones and how nice were first spring flowers.

# 2

Mr Bert Jones with Mr Herbert Tomson, who smoked cigarette, walked along street. They did not speak. Then blowing ash from cigarette end he said:

'I'm going off.'

'Where to? Down the road?'

'I'm going off. I'm fed up. In this country it's nothin' doin' all the time. I'm going to Orstrylia.'

'What d'you want to go there for?'

'You can't get on in this country. You'll never get out of that tool room an'll be lucky if you stay there, just the same as I shan't never get off the bench in the engineers but be there all my life. I'm goin' to get off while there's nothin' keepin' me. You can get somewhere out in Orstrylia.'

'And what'll you do when you get there?'

'I got an aunt out there.'

'I got you fixed in me mind's eye tucking away lamb with mint sauce.'

'I wouldn't go ranching not me but in the shops out there where you've got a chance not like 'ere where you're lucky if you keep the job.'

'Well they say there's a lot of unemployment out there.'

'It's those that don't want a day's work I'm for getting on.'

'There won't be no job for you 'Erbert. Take my tip, don't you go, not for nothing. They'll only ship you back again and where'll you be then?'

'I'll 'ave 'ad the trip any road.'

'No but honest are you going?'

'Honest.'

Craigan sat at head of table in his house. His mate Mr Gates sat with him to supper and his mate's daughter brought over shepherd's pie from range and the young fellow also was at table who worked with him also in the foundry, Jim Dale.

She laid dish on the table. She wiped red, wet hands on dishcloth. She said:

'Mr Craigan Mrs Eames that's next door, her sister says a job's going with the packers at Waley's.'

'None o' the womenfolk go to work from the house I inhabit' he said.

'Don't get thinking crazy Lily' her father said to her and she wiped fingers white. She carried dirty plates to the sink then.

She came back to table and ate of the shepherd's pie. She took big helping. Her father swallowed mouthful and said:

'You got a appetite' he said. 'You didn't ought to eat that much. Yer mother was sparin'.'

Craigan said: 'Who'd think anybody was the worser off for eatin' a stomach-full at her age.'

Weather was hot. They lived back of a street and kitchen which they ate in was on to their garden. Range made kitchen hotter. A man next door to them kept racing pigeon and these were in slow air. They ate in shirt sleeves. Plump she was. They did not say much.

Baby howled till mother there lifted him from bed to breast and sighed most parts asleep in darkness. Gluttonously baby sucked. Then he choked for a moment. Then he slept. Mrs Eames held baby and slept again.

Later woke Mr Eames. Sun shone in room and Mrs woke.

'Oh dear' he cried. He sneezed.

'What makes you always sneeze at the sun I don't know' she said most parts asleep and he said 'another day.' She now was not quite woke up and said you wouldn't believe, she was so happy now.

'Dear me' he murmured sliding back into sleep.

They slept.

Later alarm clock sounded next door. They woke. She began to get out of bed and he put on his spectacles. 'Another day' he said after he sneezed. She said was one thing to these houses with narrow walls it saved buying alarm clocks; 'they're ten and six now if they're a tanner and it's wonderful to me old Craigan let his folk buy one.' Rod of iron he ruled with in that house she said, pulling on stockings, 'or more likely a huge great poker. That poor girl' she said, 'and not even his daughter but 'e won't let 'er go out to work, nor out of the House Hardly'; and he said, quite awake, 'Oho, listen to your haitches.'

Lily Gates and Jim Dale, who was Mr Craigan's young mate in iron foundry, stood in queue outside cinema on Friday night. They said nothing to each other. Later they got in and found seats. Light rain had been falling, so when these two acting on screen walked by summer night down leafy lane, hair over her ears left wet on his cheek as she leant head, when they on screen stopped and looked at each other. Boys at school had been singing outside schoolroom on screen, had been singing at stars, and these two heard them and kissed in boskage deep low in this lane and band played softly, women in audience crooning. Lily Gates sank lower over arm of her seat. Mr Dale did not move.

Play on screen went on and this girl who was acting had married another man now. She had children now. But her husband thought she still loved other man because when they had first started on the honeymoon this other man had taken his new wife away in the motor car. They had spent night together leaving husband alone in America. But she had gone back to him. They had children now. Still he wasn't sure.

Lily Gates was sitting up now and she told Jim Dale to take arm off arm of her chair; 'you might give me room to move myself in' she said, and he said 'sorry.'

Then this play ended and Lily Gates thought this girl on screen still loved both men though it was meant she should love only her husband. 'She loves the first one still in her heart and then she loves the father of 'er children' she said to herself. Mr Dale spoke and mumbling said band had not played so well tonight and she said he mumbled so you could not tell what he said. Before he could speak again she said he was kill-joy taking the pleasant out of the evening, not that it was not a bad film she said, by saying he thought band had played badly when they had played better than she had known for three months. Then she said she could not understand what he came to cinemas for, to listen to the band and not watch the picture, she liked the stories.

Later her head was leaning on his shoulder again, like hanging clouds against hills every head in this theatre tumbled without hats against another, leaning everywhere.

Eight o'clock of morning. Thousands came up the road to work and few turned in to Mr Dupret's factory. Sirens were sounded, very sad.

Then road was empty, only one or two were running and bicyclist, bent over handle bars, drove his legs fast as he could.

Later office people began to come up road. And man, Mr Tarver, who had spoken to Mr Dupret's son outside brass foundry came along with a man in drawing office, Mr Bumpus, and talked to him. 'Tis 'im, he said, could be decent at times almost or it wasn't decent rather but the pretence and that did not take him in. He and the wife had gone with 'Tis 'im and the wife 'Tis 'er out on motor ride to a ruined abbey 'and you know the style 'e throws himself about in a tea-room well 'e put the napkin under 'is chin which is what the wife won't stand for and while I was talking to his wife there was the wife snatching 'is napkin down each time 'e put it up. It wasn't fair on 'er to behave that way before everyone. You know what womenfolk are. I 'ad a time with 'er that night for taking her but as I put it to 'er I said: "How could I tell 'e was going to indulge himself in what 'e learned in Wales." ' They stood now by works office doors and Mr Bridges came in and said:

'How are you, John?'

And he said, speaking refinedly, 'Top hole. What about you Colonel?'

'I'm fine. Come in John. Take a cigar.'

'I'm sure I don't mind, sir.'

'Eh it's a fine leaf, a great smoke. John, I don't know what's the matter with me but I feel like someone had given me a cut over the brow with a five-eighth spanner. Worry, I've 'ad enough of that washing about in my head to drown a dolphin. If another bit comes along it'll displace the brains. Yes there won't be room, something'll have to go. Anyone else'd be dead now in my place. Ah, so it goes on, every day, and then one day it breaks, the blood comes running out of your nose as you might be a fish has got a knock on the snout. Till you drop dead. I'll have to get right away, go right away for a bit.'

They talked. John and Mr Bridges' faces grew red with companionship and Bridges waved cigar and John got smoke once in lungs and coughed; – they shouted together and held each other by the arm.

This girl Lily Gates went shopping with basket and by fruiterer's she met Mrs Eames who stood to watch potatoes on trestle table there. Mrs Eames carried her baby. Lily Gates said why Mrs Eames and oh the lovely baby the little lump. She said she saw prices was going up again. She put finger into baby's hand and sang goo-goo. Then she said to Mrs Eames who had not said much up till then how the old man would not let her try for job at Waley's though she knew her father would not think twice about that if it was for him to decide, who thought only of money. Mrs Eames said to listen at her, talking like that of her own dad. But Lily Gates said it was so lonely doing house all day with the food and everything that it put her all wrong, and Mrs Eames said she would be in rooms of her own not so very long now. Most likely with a husband.

'Well I don't know much about that.'

'That's what you all say. And when you 'ave children's when you'll find your hands full my girl.'

Baby in her arms lay mass of flesh, no bones, eyes open to the sky. Lily Gates sang goo-goo at baby.

Craigan household was at supper. Mr Craigan, Dale his young mate, Joe Gates and his daughter Lily, sat eating rhubarb tart there. Mr Gates asked Mr Craigan if he had ever taken rhubarb wine and that it was very strong, he had had it once. Mr Craigan did not speak. Mr Gates said but after all was nothing to touch good old beer and they could say who liked that water was what lions drank. His daughter Lily broke in saying would he get the beer tonight for she was going to the movies, and he said didn't he fetch it every night and work to buy food for her stomach all day and every. She answered him that she could just change and only be in time for second performance now. He said he'd never go. This time was once too many he said. But Craigan told him to go and fetching down the jug from dresser he stood by mantelpiece. Then why didn't they both go off now both of them he said if they were in so much hurry;

but Dale said he was not going. Lily Gates opened door and went out quickly then. Mr Craigan asked slowly who was she going to pictures with; Dale said she had told him it was Bert Jones, who would be the one working with Alf Smith on the bench in tool room. Mr Craigan said nothing and Joe Gates thought Mr Craigan did not mind Lily going out with Bert Jones so he said how when he was young chap his dad would never have let his girls go, but that now things were different. Mr Craigan said nothing so he went out with the jug.

Soon after Lily Gates came quickly out of house and went quickly up the street.

Then when Joe Gates came back with the beer and he and Mr Craigan sat on kitchen chairs and Dale on a box, at back of house before garden, he said he met a man in the public who had told him one or two good tales. Then for some time then Joe Gates told dirty stories. He spoke of tarts and birds. 'An' speakin' of birds' he said, 'look there's a bird caught in the window.' (Window was open and a sparrow was caught between upper and lower window frames.) He went over and began to push up upper frame to free this bird. But it fluttered and seemed as though it would be crushed. Mr Dale said, 'don't push 'er up so Joe, you'll crush it,' and he went over to the window. Mr Dale said he would put his hand in between the two frames, which he did, but bird fluttered more and pecked at his finger. 'Don't go 'urting it Jim don't be so rough with the little bleeder' Joe Gates said and Dale answered him 'ain't they got sharp beaks to 'em.' Joe Gates now took over and raised upper frame again, and gently. This bird only fluttered the more. At this time Mr Craigan came over and took fork and said to leave it to him. Very gently he pushed up upper frame and put fork under the bird and very gently tried to force the bird up but the bird got away from this fork and fluttered. Then all three together moithered round the window and then they all drew back and watched and the bird was still. Then Craigan said to fetch Mrs Eames and Dale went. Mr Craigan and Joe Gates stood and said nothing, watching, and now still the bird was quiet.

Mrs Eames came and she lowered upper frame and put hand in and gathered this bird up and gently carefully lifted it out and opened hand and it flew away and was gone. Mr Gates asked to strike him dead. Mr Dale said it looked easy the way she done it, and Mr Craigan, dignified and courtly, said they had to thank Mrs Eames for what three men could not do. She said, 'Where's Lily then?' and Mr Dale said she had gone out. Mrs Eames said what a fine evening it was to be sure but Craigan was saying no more though Mr Gates began talking at once to Mrs Eames; this happening of the bird put him in mind of some stories, he said, and not long after Mrs Eames had gone, offended. Dale said she did not like Joe's stories and Joe Gates answered that anyone could see it and he knew it before but he wanted to wake her up he said. Mr Craigan did not speak and looked to be troubled in his mind. He sat outside in the last light of sun which had shone all day.

In the evening Gates went to public house. He went alone, which he did not do often. Every Monday night Mr Craigan and he went together to their public house but this was Friday so he went further up Coventry Road to house he did not often visit. Tupe was there. At first they did not speak. Mr Gates looked at tiled lower part of wall (pattern on the tiles was like beetles with backs open and three white lilies in each of these) and he looked at rows of bottles on shelves against mirror glass which was above these tiles and at paper doylies which now again regularly were under bottles there and hung down in triangles from the shelves. (Orange coloured roses with a few curly green leaves were round corner of these which hung down.) Then Tupe shouted across saying was no use in saying nothing and what would he have and Mr Gates said another half of mild and he was obliged he said. Soon they were sitting next each her and they told dirty stories one after the other to each other and Gates laughed and drank and got a little drunk.

Soon then Mr Tupe made him begin laughing at old Craigan. Mr Gates never used to laugh about that man. Soon he told Tupe Lily had gone out with Bert Jones and left Dale at home. Tupe said didn't the old man mean Lily to marry Jim Dale and Mr Gates said Craigan was mad at her going. Tupe said wasn't Joe Gates her father and wasn't a father's word enough in arranging for his daughter and Gates said but Craigan hadn't dared speak to her about having gone out like that. He had said you put a girl wrong with you nowadays and like too independent minded if you talk to her straight away. Tupe said wasn't Joe Gates her father and wasn't what a father said and thought enough for his girl without another interfering. And soon Mr Gates was saying it was and never again would he let himself be bossed in his family, not ever again, no, not he, said he.

Joe Gates stood by tap in factory, drinking water, and Mr Tupe came by wheeling barrow of coke. 'What'll you 'ave' Tupe cried and Mr Gates answered him 'a pint of mild.' 'It's strange to see you drinkin' water' and Gates said he could hardly believe it of himself but they had been casting in their shop and running metal made their shop warm in such weather. Maybe Aaron Connolly had the only cool job, he said, up on travelling crane in the machine shop among draughts; but it was cold up there in winter. Tupe said perhaps that was why he was so mingy, not a penny coming from his pocket without his making a groan. But he had been paid out for it. Had Joe Gates heard, he asked, about the other night, and reason for Aaron Connolly's black eye next morning. He had told his son it wasn't right him paying so little in at end of the week at home, 'not as if Aaron drew more'n labourer's wages though he be on the crane,' Tupe said. 'But 'is son up and knocked him spark out, and he done a good job that night.' Mr Gates laughed and said that would teach him. 'Ah and his missus' said Tupe 'dropped the chamber pot on his head not so long ago when 'e was at her for buying a 'aporth of salt, her being on the landing as he were coming upstairs.' They walked through machine shop, Joe Gates laughing with Mr Tupe when five-eighth spanner fell from above close to them. They looked up and saw the crane but they could see no one on the crane. 'Hi Aaron' bawled Mr Tupe and Mr Connolly's face came out over side of it, 'Hi Aaron you'll be killin' people next dropping things, bein' like palsied from 'oldin' too tight on to yer money.' 'In 'ell they will stoke the coke on your tongue babble baby' he answered and several men laughing at Tupe, Gates also, he went off with his barrow load. Mr Gates went to the stores.

   Just then in iron foundry shop Craigan look up from big cylinder he was making and beckoned to boy who was one of the boys making cores. This one came up. Craigan said how would he like piece of cake and while boy ate piece of cake he said it was easier for boys in foundries now than when he started. Boy said it may have been but all the same wouldn't have been a misery like Craigan in any iron foundry, not to touch him, not since they started. Mr Craigan said in his young days you could never have said that to a moulder when you were core boy. 'You would say worse' boy said and Craigan said this one would never make a moulder. 'And your mate' boy said '"as been laughin' with old Tupey this last 'alf 'our, I seen 'em' boy said earnestly. Craigan answered him 'Clear off my lad and don't tell tales.'

Mr Milligan who was storekeeper told Joe Gates about his health. But soon he came back to iron foundry and Dale told him to look out against Mr Craigan.

# 3

'What will we do with him? Beauty, when you grow to be a man, eh, what will we do with you?'

Waking, Mr Eames turned over. Rain came down outside.

'When you grows to be a man, a man.' She put her face up against his. 'Maybe like your dad you'll be a turner when you're a man. Beauty!' She sighed. She fed him. She felt cold, and he was warm.

His father said: 'a turner like his dad?' and she answered for him saying: 'Yes and so long as 'is lathe goes round he'll be there, earning 'is money like 'is dad.'

Mr Eames said it always did rain in this town though garden would benefit.

'When you're grown you'll be a turner, lovely, when you're grown up. We shan't be up to much work not when you've been a man for long so you'll look to our comfort when we'll have worked to see you come to strength. Beauty, ma's cold but if she draws up the clothes you'll stifle seeing you're still at me.'

Mr Eames sneezed again.

'And when you're grown you'll marry and we shall lose you and you'll 'ave kiddies of your own and a 'ouse of your own, love, we'll be out in the cold. (Ain't it chill this morning?) Why do we bring kids into the world, they leave you so soon as they're grown, eh? But you don't know one of these things yet. But sure as anything you'll leave us when you're a man, and who'll we 'ave then, eh cruel? Sons and daughters why do we bring them into the world?'

She was laughing. 'Because, because' she said laughing and then lay smiling and then yawned.

' "Yes I'm goin' to Orstrylia" 'e said' said Aaron Connolly to Mr Eames, ' "I'm goin' to Orstrylia, don't care what no one says but I'm goin'," 'e said. And I told 'im not to be 'asty but to bide 'is time, that's what I told 'im – "it am a grand country for one that 'as some money," I said, "but it am a 'ard bleeder for one that ain't." '

'That's right,' said Mr Eames.

'It am right' said Mr Connolly. 'I told 'im right but 'e wouldn't listen. "It am a grand country" 'e said to me, "this be a poor sodding place for a poor bleeder," 'e said. "I'm for going'." I said "don't be a fool 'erbert, sure as your name's Tomson you'll be back within the year without you go Christmas time and where'll you be then?" I said. 'E laughed and made out 'e'd 'ave this trip any road and I told 'im 'e'd be laffing tother side of 'is mug when 'e got back, "for what d'you get for nothin' not since the war?" I said. "Time was they'd give pint and a 'alf measure when you asked for the usual, but now they put publicans in jug if so 'appen they give yer a smell over the pint." '

These two were in lavatory. Mr Eames went so soon as he was done but Connolly waited there. He smoked pipe against the rules. Mr Bert Jones came in.

Aaron told him how Mr Tomson said he was going to Australia and Bert Jones said he had been the one to tell Aaron himself. 'Well now' said Aaron Connolly 'but 'e told me I'll be positive.' It seemed crazy notion anyway you looked at it said Mr Jones, why not go to Canada he said, though it was fool's game to go at all. Tupe looked in then. At once he went away. After Aaron Connolly said how he was glad always to see backside of that man's head he said Eames was poor sort of a chap, most likely ginger pop was all he could stomach, and Bert Jones lit cigarette. They gossiped. Mr Bridges came in then. He caught them smoking, both of them. He was very angry. 'Discipline,' he shouted, 'keep the shops going, I got to do it. When I come in, here I find you smoking. It's our bread burning away. I got to stop smoking. I don't come in 'ere once but I find someone miking. Firm'll be ruined. Debtor prison. Siam. Bankrupt.' He gave each fortnight's holiday after shouting much more.

When he was gone Bert Jones said Father had not been in for over twelve month. Aaron Connolly spat and said, 'It am Tupe done it. It am Tupe. Nor it won't be spanners I'll drop next time.'

They were in cinema. Band played tune tum tum did dee dee. She hugged Dale's arm. She jumped her knees to the time.

Couple on screen danced in ballroom there. She did not see them. Dee dee did da.

Tum tum tum tum tum. Dale did not budge. Dee dee de did dee. She hummed now. She rolled his arm between her palms. Da da did dee – did dee dee tum, ta.

'I do love this tune' she said.

'Ah' he said.

Did dee dee tum ta. Tune was over. She clapped hands and clapped. Applause was general. But film did not stop oh no heroine's knickers slipped down slinky legs in full floor.

eeeee Lily Gates screamed.

OOEEE the audience.

And band took encore then. Tum tum ti tumpy tum.

Lily arranged her hair. Dum dum di dumpy dum.

She hummed then. She moved her knees in time. Heroine's father struggled with policeman now in full ballroom. She did not watch but jumped her knees now. Da da did DEE – (what a pause!) – did dee dee tum ta. Great clapping of hands. Attendant moved up gangway and shouted 'Order please.' He moved down. Lily Gates said to young Mr Dale he didn't take much interest in nothing did he? 'Why not take a bit of fun Jim when it comes your way?' she softly said. He said 'I can't enjoy the music when I'm not in the mood.' 'Why you funny' she said ' 'ave a mood then.' He said 'Don't call me your names Lil when there's so many can 'ear you.'

'Why they're all listenin' to the music.' She was whispering 'Jim!'

She hummed tune band was now playing whey widdle o.

'It's 'ot in 'ere' he said.

'H.O.T. warm' she said.

'Why they're playin' it again' she said. She looked at screen. She saw heroine's knickers again were coming down, now in young man's bedroom.

ooeee she screamed.

EEEEE the audience.

The band played that tune. Tum tum ti tumpy tum. Dum dum di dumpy dum. She jumped her knees to time. Da da DID DEE – (it wasn't her knickers after all) – did dee dee tum ta.

In Dupret factory man had now been put on guard over the lavatory door. He had to clock men in and out.

'Seein'' we're animals 'e's got to treat us as animals' Mr Bentley cried very much excited. 'Put a man on at the lavatory door, it ain't decent,' seven minutes every day ain't long enough for a man to do what nature demands of 'is time, stop 'im a quarter 'our of 'is pay if 'e's a minute over why 'e ain't allowed to do it by law, I'm raisin' the question in the Club tonight, and if I was out o' work for three years I wouldn't take on a job of that description. It's plum against the laws of this land, checking men in and out o' lavatories and only seven minutes for each man. Why in kennels even they don't do it.'

'You go and see Tupe about it, Bob, 'e brought it on.'

'I know nowt against Tupe. There's no proof 'e went to Bridges when 'e saw Aaron here and Bert smoking. It ain't justice 'im sending Bert off for a fortnight and having Aaron stay back – no offence to you mate.'

'It am a bleeder. "Aaron" 'e says to me "Aaron I got no one but you to work that crane in your shop. But man" 'e said, "the next time and you're sacked and out you go." It am a bleeder.'

Joe Gates was saying as much to Mr Craigan in iron foundry shop. And Dale asked him why he went round with Tupe then and Mr Gates said me never and Dale said he seen him and Joe Gates answered it might have been once. (They were ramming.) Gates said Tupe should have tongue cut and why didn't some of the shop go and dig his grave in his back garden to show him. When he smiled it rained, Mr Gates said of him, and he'd be glad when he was dead: 'glad, more'n glad, I'll go straight into the boozer and 'ave one.'

'Think you'll live to see 'is 'earse?' Dale asked him.

'Me' cried Mr Gates 'with my clean life and 'is dirty living, me?' cried Mr Gates.

# 4

Mrs Dupret and her son, (who had walked round factory with Mr Bridges) these two were in drawing-room of the London house; each had engagement book, hers she had laid on her knees, he held his up close to his nose, so she would not see him picking his nose.

She said: 'Tuesday fortnight then is the first evening I've got free.'

Slowly he turned pages.

'No I can't manage Tuesday fortnight I'm dining with the Masons for their dance.'

Mr Tarver came home.

'The old man's been at it again' he said to wife. 'Been and sacked my best fitter.' 'Jim!' said Mrs Tarver. 'Yes sacked 'im, said 'e was faking his time on the outdoor jobs but it's spite, that's it go and sack the only man who can put up my work and then expect me to carry on.' 'It's low' said Mrs Tarver. 'Low' said Mr Tarver, 'low' he said 'but when Walters comes down Wednesday from the London office I'll speak straight out to him, but it's crazy, 'ow can you do your work conscientiously and be 'eld up like this and a pistol put to your heart. It is a firm. It's a policy of obstruction. Do you know what 'e did today on top of that, 'e caught two men lounging about and gave one a fortnight's holiday and let the other johnny off. Well you can't do things like that. You can't run a factory on those lines, one rule for one and none for the other. I'll go raving mad. Then my fitter.' 'It's downright low' said Mrs Tarver. 'Whitacre was the only man I could trust,' he said, 'the others would put a spanner into the job and wreck it to please 'im, or they didn't know the difference between a nut and a washer. It's no wonder we're the laughing stock of every firm in Brummagen. If I 'ad a better chance I'd go this minute. But I got nothing to show for it, 'e's seen to that, 'olding my stuff up in the shops and in the end, after you've 'owled to get it, turning out a job a dog wouldn't sniff. Then 'e says it's the design, while 'e can't read a drawing. Why if you asked 'im the principle underlying the simple bolt and nut 'e couldn't tell you. It's sickening. I'm wearing away the best years of my life. Walters's in league with him, 'e's backed 'im up all along. There's only Archer on my side. I'll write to Mr Dupret, that's what I'll do. I saw 'is son but 'e's a schoolboy, 'e didn't take it in. That's what I'll do. I'll write to Mr Dupret.'

'You write to Mr Dupret, John, and act by what your conscience tells you and he'll see you're a honest man.'

'That's right, I'll do it. What is there for supper? I'll write after I've 'ad a feed. I'll put it to 'im this way, I'll say . . .'

He wrote to Mr Archer, chief accountant in London office, instead.


Mr Bridges picked up letter in his office.

'Ah these cylinders, they're a worry' he said to Miss Alexander, typist. 'In business there's always something wrong, I've had my share of it. These big cylinders, you never can depend on them. And 'ere's Simson howling for delivery and Walters been shouting for 'em from London. I said to 'im on the telephone, "What can I do?" Can never depend on a foundry, same job same men and perhaps they'll go three months without a waster and then they'll get a run of seven that are scrap and a loss to the firm. It's enough to drive you crazy, eh?'

'Yes Mr Bridges.'

'Tarver sent those drawings down?'

'Not yet Mr Bridges.'

'Then why the devil not eh? Here I am, been waiting for 'em six weeks now. What's up with the man?'

'He's been very excited lately ay think.'

'I can't understand Tarver. What's the matter with him anyway. I can't live with that fellow about, my life's no pleasure to me. And I take him with his wife out in the car, there's nothing I don't do, keeping everyone happy.'

'Yes and grateful you'd hardly believe' said Miss Alexander, 'ay don't think he knows the meaning of a long word layke that, why he said you were crazy only yesterday Mr Bridges.'

'What? Eh? What d'you mean? How do you know about that any way?'

'He said it to my face.'

'Did 'e? In front of you. It's a comedy ain't it? What's 'e mean. Crazy am I? You see who'll be in Siam first, him or me. That's what it is, you work with a man, you make things difficult for yourself to be pleasant and easy, and then 'e rounds on you. Spits in your face.

It's dis'eartening. Walters knows how things are and 'e can't abide the man no more than me. I'll see him. I'm through. Done up. Who's manager here, perhaps 'e can tell me, Mr lord Tarver? Yes, who's boss here? Said it to your face? I'll wait till tomorrow though. I might raise my 'ands to 'im if I saw 'im now. Yes there's no knowing what I might do to him, so his mammy wouldn't know 'im.'

Four o'clock. And now men in iron foundry in Mr Dupret's factory straightened their backs for the fan had been started which gave draught in cupola in which the iron was melted. They stood by, two by two, holding ladles, or waiting. Craigan and Joe Gates and Dale stood by their box ready weighted for pouring and in which was mould of one of those cylinders. They said nothing. They had worked all day. The foreman stood near by. They waited. Gates was tired. Foreman stood near by. Mr Craigan threw spade to ground then which had been in his hand. He went up to foreman.

'I know there's been three wasters off this job better'n nobody. But man I'll tell you this'ns a good un.'

'Right you are Phil' foreman said and moved away. 'I can't sleep at night for those cylinders' he told himself again, 'I can't sleep at night. I took tablets last night' he told himself 'but did I sleep, no I did not. No I didn't sleep,' he said to himself, moving away.

'Dirty bleeder, what call 'as 'e to stand waiting for?' said Mr Gates muttering.

'You talk more'n is natural in a man' Mr Craigan said and then no word was said between them not while their eight ton of metal was carried them in a ladle by the crane or after when they fed their casting, lifting their rods up in the risers and letting them down, and again and again.

Later moulder going home, his boxes cast, called to Gates saying: 'is it a good one this time Joeie?' and Mr Gates answered him it would be if his sweat was what it used to be.

In the foundry was now sharp smell of burnt sand. Steam rose from the boxes round about. On these, in the running gates and risers, metal shone out red where it set. On Mr Craigan's huge box in which was his casting Mr Craigan and Jim Dale stood. They raised and lowered long rods into metal in the risers so as to keep the metal molten. Steam rose up round them so their legs were wet and heat from the molten metal under them made balls of sweat roll down them. Arc lamps above threw their shadows out sprawling along over the floor and as they worked rhythmically their rods up and down só their shadows worked. Mr Craigan called to Gates to take his place. He got down off the box. He sat himself on a sieve and wiped his face. And all this time as the metal set and contracted down in casting so metal which they kept molten by disturbing it with their rods, sank in the risers down to the casting. So their strength ebbed after the hard day. Mr Craigan's face was striped with black dust which had stuck to his face and which the sweat, in running down his face, had made in stripes. He put hands up over his face and laid weight of his head on them, resting elbows on his knees.

Continuing conversation Mrs Dupret said to her son well she was sorry it could not be then, she had so wanted they should have one quiet evening together, well it would have to be another time. He said some other time. Immediately he thought: 'When I am with her I echo as a landscape by Claude echoes.' She yawned. She said it was so boring discussing engagements and he answered he thought planning the evenings most important part of the day. Immediately, as was his custom, he analysed this and thought very clever what he had said, and correct.

She yawned and said she was tired, season was so busy.

He said he was tired, last night had been late.

'Whose dance dear?'

'The White's. I was back at four. And tonight it will be late again,' he said. 'I take Mary on to Prince's after Mrs James' dance.'

They went in to dinner, Mrs Dupret and her son. Butler and footman brought soup to them.

'James' said Mrs Dupret after searching 'I left my handkerchief upstairs' and footman went to get this.

'Now this is very unexpected' she said to son, 'Emily threw me over and here you are when I thought we were never going to have our quiet evening together.'

'Dolly chucked me. I'm tired. It's so tiring in the train.'

'Yes trains are very uncomfortable now. You went to the works at Birmingham today didn't you? Tell me about it.'

'Well there's nothing to tell really. I'd never been before you know. It was all grimy and tiring. It was so dirty there that I had to have a bath as soon as I was back before going out to tea somewhere. Where did I go for tea now? But no matter, yes, the works, yes you know there's a kind of romance about it or perhaps it's only romantic. In the iron foundry the castings, they call them, were very moving. And there was a fellow there who had a beautiful face, really beautiful, he was about my age...'

(He went on talking and she thought how true when she had told Grizel he was really so appreciative.)

'... but it was pretty boring on the whole.'

'Tell me' she said with fish before her, 'are you still happy in the London office?'

'It's all right, but of course I can't do anything. You can't shift Father, he's set in his ways and the others are like him, you've no idea of it, they've had no fresh blood in the show for years. Look at Bridges the manager at Birmingham, he's an old man, so's Walters our head man in London, they all are. A man came up to me in the works just now and said as much, he'd be Tarver I expect, he's about the only coming younger chap in the place. You see Father's all right in his way only he's slow, but he hasn't the time with all his other business.' And while he talked she thought what a success it had turned out, putting him into business.

'What we want in the place is some go and push' he said 'but it's what none of them seem to realize.'

She smiled and had occasion to sniff. 'Where can James have got to' she cried, breaking into his argument 'I sent him for a handkerchief while we were at the soup, and here we are in the middle of the fish.'

She pushed button of bell; this was in onyx. She laid hand by it on table and diamonds on her rings glittered together with white metal round onyx button under the electric light. Electric light was like stone. He was cut short by her. He was hurt at it. He kept silence then.

'Pringle,' she said to butler 'would you mind going up to see what has become of James?'

Mr Walters was saying in Mr Bridges' office at Birmingham factory if you took average profits of all engineering firms in the country you found it was but three per cent. Mr Bridges said 'that's right, that's right.' Mr Walters went on saying were no profits anywhere, why look if they quoted for one of their big cylinders their price was double what those Belgians asked. 'It is' said Mr Bridges.

'It's wonderful isn't it?' said Mr Walters.

'You've got it' said Mr Bridges. 'Not as if' he said 'there isn't worry every minute either, it wasn't as if we sat still and did nothing. And you can't keep your men' he shouted. 'Whitacre now, one of the best fitters I've taught, what's he do? He goes and fakes his time. He's on a job outside and takes three days off and charges it on the firm. Says he was working. But I've got the letter here, from their manager, complaining 'e wouldn't stay on the job. I sacked him, had to. What can you do? Then I go into the latrines, what do I run into, more trouble two robbers sitting on the seat, without even their trousers off, smoking. I said to them 'You might as well go straight to the chief's back pocket and take the money from it.' That's right isn't it? I'm going to put a honest man on at the door to clock 'em in and out, seven minutes each man. And one of them was the crane driver in the machine shop, a key man. Then when I sack that Whitacre Tarver comes to me and says I did it to spite 'imself. To spite him! Said he was the only one could do his work. But I never get his work, that's where it is, I never get it down from the drawing office, I've been standing my thumbs tied for a drawing seven weeks now. What can you do, eh? 'E's no good.'

'I don't know Arthur, we've got to be careful. Young Mr Dupret thinks well of him, and his father does.'

'What's the young chap know of it?'

'I know but don't you forget he's the one the old man sees most often. If he was in his pram I'd still treat him like a lord. What do you know he tells the old man about us, the old man don't come into the office often now. He's getting shaky, he might be run into by a bus, with this circular traffic you're lucky if you get away with it crossing the street. He'll leave it all to his son soon.'

'And I've served 'im faithfully for fifteen years. It's a nightmare. Where am I, eh? Where do I stand then, tell me that.'

Mrs Eames put cold new potato into her mouth.

'Ain't they good' said she.

'They are' he said.

'Better'n what you could get up the road or if you took a tram up into town.'

'There's none like your own.'

So for a time they ate supper. She sat on then looking out of window. When she turned and put hands on table to get up and clear away supper she noticed those flowers.

'Why look' said she 'you brought 'em back from the garden only yesterday and I put them in that pot, and now all their faces've turned to the sun.'

# 5

Water dripped from tap on wall into basin and into water there. Sun. Water drops made rings in clear coloured water. Sun in there shook on the walls and ceiling. As rings went out round trembling over the water shadows of light from sun in these trembled on walls. On the ceiling.

They came back from work. Mr Joe Gates was speaking.

'Ah and didn't I tell that foreman only a month or two back it would go, silly cow keeping on using it till it went. "It's dangerous" I said to 'im "it's dangerous it'll go one of these days" I said "you see, it's all wore away that wire rope is and the block too, look at it, being lopsided like that, it ain't safe." And he said "What business is it of yourn?" and I said "Ain't my life my business with a daughter to keep at 'ome" and 'e said one of these days 'ed get on a line about me so I sheered off then, it doesn't serve no purpose to lose a job through just talking, might as well lose it for something better'n that, knock 'is bloody 'ead off.'

Mr Craigan washed first in basin. Lily Gates came in then.

'D'you know what nearly came to pass Lily, it were nearly all up with 'im, ah, the wire rope parted when they were pulling out the trolley with it from the core stove. Ah and it dain't miss 'im but by inches.'

Lily Gates went to basin and stood there by Mr Craigan.

'Why grandad!' she said.

'Ah and when I sees 'im standin' there I thought to meself it ain't safe standin' there, now if it went now it would get anyone as was standin' there as 'e was. Then it parted. It dain't miss 'im but by inches.'

Mr Craigan dried face and hands. Joe Gates put head under the water in basin.

'It weren't far off' Mr Dale said.

'You mightn't have come back?' Lily Gates picked piece of cotton off his sleeve.

'Don't do that my wench' Mr Craigan said 'I can still do that for meself.'

'It didn't ought to be' said Mr Gates, drying face.

'They did ought to look to them things and not wait till you complain to 'em about it and then do nothing. With that trolley gear and with the boxes you've got to wait for 'em to go before they change them and when a box breaks when the crane's carrying it the feller underneath, why think of it, flat, when I was working at Grey's I seen a feller catch a six by four box on top of 'im and when they lifted it it was just like they'd mangled 'im, 'orrible, like as if they'd mangled 'im, like they'd put a steam roller on to 'im. It's a funny thing to get a living by ain't it?'

Once she had said to Mrs Eames she had said it made you ridiculous she had said walking with Jim, yes she had said that to Mrs Eames, when he looked odd like that, daft you might say, she had gone far as that even, dafty with his eyes yes, she had said, yes and with the girls tittering behind him it made you feel awkward to be with him and Mrs Eames had said she shouldn't be so touchy, not she meant you shouldn't be particular so she said, but touchy it only brought you trouble in this world so your life wasn't your own, that's how she thought so she had said. Now walking with Dale Lily thought that. Girls tittering behind not that he was posh. Not as if they would like to be with him, but for his being strange.

She wasn't the giggling sort. No.

So it wasn't hardly respectable going up the street with him, drawing so much notice.

(He had on bowler hat, high, high crown. Thousands walked along broad pavements of this big street in bowler hats with high, high crowns, in sun, in evening.)

He didn't ever speak either.

(She walked with him, arm round his arm. Party in front, four girls four young men, the girls on one pavement men on the other side, two parties but one at same time, these did Charleston dance along pavements.)

'What d'you think of that?' she said.

'Ah' said he.

'It mightn't be a public place where they can see you for all they take notice of' she said 'be'aving as if they was in their favourite dance 'all; it's funny what people are coming to these days' she said.

They walked on, said no more. He was pale. Many were laughing, screeching, not at him really, perhaps partly, but it was Friday night.

She then had to sneeze. As she sneezed Mr Dale called out: 'Ello.'

She said: 'Yes it's me sneezing, I know that thank you.'

'Ello' he said to Mr Bert Jones who had come up.

'Oh' she said.

''Ow do Jim, I hear your old man very near 'ad a nasty accident last night.'

'Ah and it was a near go and all. 'Ow d'you come to 'ear?'

'Oh someone round at the club. So you 'eard about my being suspended for a fortnight.'

'It's the talk of the shops. By the way you know Miss Gates would you? This is Bert Jones from our place.' Lily Gates shook hands, holding limply out hand, looking down her nose.

'I believe we've met before' said Mr Jones. He had on plum coloured suit, trousers were cone-shaped.

'And it was Jim here introduced us' said Miss Gates furiously.

'Now I come to think on it it would be' Mr Dale said.

'I remembered right enough' said Mr Jones.

'Did you?'

'It's the talk of the shops' Mr Dale said. 'Giving you a fortnight's 'oliday and not doing the same by Aaron.'

'Ah it's a firm ain't it. Twisting, twisting all the time. And by all I 'ear what nearly made your old man a goner was the fault of their never getting new equipment. It's the same old tale, in our shop anyway.'

'You're right. I don't know if you knows your way about a foundry but we 'as to dry some moulds before the metal can be poured into 'em. They're put on a trolley, see, and the crane pulls it into the stove with a wire rope. Well the wire rope give. Ah, it parted right at the top, mate, right by the eye and whipped out not above a foot away from our old man. It's wicked I reckon.'

'No, they don't give you a square deal. If you work for them they ought to see you can do it with a decent amount of safety.'

'Yes' said Lily Gates. 'I think it's a shame, yes, I do.'

'That's right. And you can't get a job outside, that's where it is. So we've got to put up with it and there it is. But you know 'erbert Tomson, well 'e's going to Australia,' but Mr Dale was not listening. ' 'E's a feller that works in the fitters. I don't know. They tell me there's not a great many jobs going there.'

' 'Ere you don't mind' Dale said suddenly. 'See you in the park' he said pointing across road and quickly went off.

'Well that's a bit sudden.'

'It's his digestion you see' said Miss Gates.

'Ah.'

'It comes over him all of a sudden, yes, no matter where 'e may be' she said furiously.

'But that's a bad bit of news about your old man.'

'Yes' she said. 'There'd still've been breadwinners in the house,' she said, 'but where we'd've been without 'im I don't know at all. We all live by Mr Craigan.'

'All the men in the place respect 'im.'

' 'E's been like a father to me. And now I shan't lie quiet in my bed at night for thinking harm'll come to 'im.'

'Ah.'

They stood silent.

'Look 'ere' he said 'shall we go across the road into the park' he said 'and wait for Jim there?'

'Oh! I shouldn't like to.'

'Go on. I got nothing on tonight.'

'I don't like to bother you like that. You go on, I'll wait here.'

'Get out. It's a pleasure.'

'Oh well it's nicer in the park isn't it?'

They crossed the road.

'We went to the Lickeys Sunday' she said.

'It's nice there isn't it.'

'Yes, and don't they keep the roads beautiful with the grass in between them and the trams going one road and cars t'other. Yes it's a pleasure to be there of a Sunday afternoon. I'd say I saw quite seven from our street up there. And only a 6d bus ride.'

'Ah, it's worth a tanner every time.'

'Yes it is. Yes we all went there last Sunday. Mr Craigan said 'e'd like a bit of fresh air after all the hot weather we've been 'aving so we packed up and went. I cut steps of bread and cheese that we took with us, oh we did 'ave a time.'

'I reckon it was a good thing when the Corporation took it over, giving the people somewhere to go on a Sunday.'

'Yes because you can get right out into the country and get the fresh air. You know where we live there's a factory where they make phosphor bronze they call it, I don't mean they make only that but when they're making it the fumes come down into our 'ouse when the winds is one way and the fumes is awful. I wonder the poor fellows can stick it inside.'

'It's terrible stuff by all accounts.'

'Yes. Of course we could live in a better part than we do now but Mr Craigan won't live in another man's house, yes that's what he says isn't it funny, and 'e bought this one years back and he wouldn't change now for love nor money. I keep 'ouse for them. Of course it's very lonely sometimes, there being no one much to talk to while they're all out at work. Yes sometimes I wish I could go outside into a factory but Mr Craigan won't hear of it, yes, isn't it funny. He won't 'ear of it. Still I get along I suppose like we all do.'

'It must be lonely at times.'

'It isn't as if you don't soon get used to that though, don't you.'

'I'm glad that accident didn't turn out any worse for 'im. Did 'e seem at all affected by it.'

'No but 'e'd never show you you know. But isn't it a shame about your being suspended, well I never.'

'I thought I'd lose you' Mr Dale said coming up 'seeing it's dark in this park. Lil' he said 'we ought to be going 'ome or the old man won't like it.'

'I'd better be getting along' said Mr Jones and they said goodnight then and went their ways.

'Where'd you go?' she said. 'There ain't no public lavatory for miles round 'ere.'

'In the Horse and Lion.'

*

'Well what about it?'

'What about what?'

'Work.'

'How's that?'

So began Mr Bridges to Tarver, so Tarver answered him. That's how he answers me thought Bridges. Then Mr Bridges said he didn't see Tarver got through anything, couldn't go on like that, here he'd been six weeks for those drawings, and Tarver said what about Bumpus was it his fault he'd gone to bed and not got up since. Mr Bridges said couldn't he do work without Bumpus and Tarver said what did he mean.

'I mean what I speak.'

'What's that?'

Bridges said Tarver not to be gay with him, he was general manager, people could think they were fine, fine, but he was general manager, was no one disputed that, and what he said was what went through in this firm. Mr Tarver said what he had meant was he hadn't heard. Bridges went on not listening that he'd soon see who stuck himself up against him, whatever friends that one had in London office, he and his friends he'd see who was general manager, while Tarver speaking at same time said what he'd meant saying was pardon me, I could not hear you, girls in office make such noise giggling.

Later Mr Tarver was saying 'Yes sir' and Father said 'my boy' often then.

Bentley came up to where Mr Eames worked on his allotment garden.

'That's a fine crop of apples you'll pick off that tree of yours' he said and said was no tree in all the gardens like it there.

'Yes' said Mr Eames 'I don't remember its bearing so well in years, it's a picture. When the blossom was out the missus and I came along and sat under it of a Sunday with the baby.'

'There'll be a pound or two off it when they're ripe.' Changing tone he said he had seen Bert Jones back at work in factory that morning.

Mr Eames said he had not noticed him yet.

'Ah he's back and 'e ought never to've gone away.'

' 'E didn't 'ave any choice.'

'I didn't mean it lay with him, what I meant was they 'ad no right to send one away and do nothing to t'other when it was the same offence.'

'Well I suppose they can do as they like doing.'

'That's where you're wrong Fred, there's the law of England. And the pity of it is they ain't forbidden to go on as they do, one man a favourite and nothing too bad for the next.'

'Well they 'aven't trespassed against the law.'

'I'm not so sure they ain't. But leaving that as may be 'ad they any right to treat young Alfred Parker the way they did eight months back?'

'I ain't got nothing to say for that.'

'Now I'm asking you a straight question, 'ad they any right?'

'No, they 'ad no business to do it.'

'It's wicked, that's what it is. And look at that feller Whitacre. 'E was 30/– short in his money when they sent it to 'im so 'e writes to 'em about it and by the next post they tell 'im they're done with 'im and 'e can go tramp over England looking for another job. 'E wrote for 'is money again what 'e'd earned by labour but didn't get an answer. Is that straight?'

'Why don't he take it to the Courts?'

'What would they do? 'E'd get 'is marching orders quick enough. They'd 'ave a lawyer, so's the firm shouldn't get a bad name and 'e'd be tied into knots in no time. I shouldn't wonder if it ended in 'is being tried for perjury.'

'Well I don't know anything about that but what you just said there – it ain't anything but 'is story is it?'

'I can't say I've seen 'im personally to talk to, but 'e's a truthful feller mind you. But you ain't going to believe their tale are you?'

'I don't see myself believing either of 'em.'

'Twisters that's all they are, dirty twisters. And I'm waiting for 'em, I know the laws of England and once they step over on the wrong side I'll bring 'em into court, I'll sue them with me own money. They'll see soon enough. Why with the lavatories as they're now it ain't decent for a woman to come through the works.'

'I ain't seen one of the girls from the office come through in seven months. I shouldn't like a woman to do it with the language some use.'

'No nor should I. But the lavatories ain't made it any better for 'em.'

'Why?'

'Well it's not decent a man timing you in and out, it's contrary to nature. Any road I ain't told the wife about it. Besides she 'as 'ardships enough keeping her and me alive on our money without me telling 'er the pinpricks you get all the time at our place.'

Bentley filled pipe.

'It's downright wicked' he said going on.

He lit pipe. Smoke from it went slowly up through bars of sunlight here and there which came between leaves of apple tree.

'Ah it's a fine crop' Mr Bentley said, changing tone, 'and it's a good thing for a man to get away in the evenings out into the air.'


As they went downstairs in to dinner he had been shouting to one in front – this was only but nervousness because her he was taking in was so pretty – so when they sat down and he turned to her it was first time he had spoken to her.

'Didn't we meet at dinner with the Masons about a fortnight ago before going on to somebody's dance' he said.

'Probably, I expect so.'

'Whose dance was it, I can't remember, I'm so bad at names. Anyway I know I've got to go on tonight to Lady Randolph's afterwards to pick someone up.'

'Isn't it Lady Radolph's we're going to?'

'Isn't that lucky? Think of it, going to the dance one's going on to.'

'But it may be boring, and boring waiting on so long.'

He thought why couldn't she say 'you' may be bored: flattery, he thought, flattery, you could count on fingers of two hands only the girls who flattered you at dinner and that surely he thought was next most important after champagne at dinner parties. Was danger these people they were dining with would not give champagne, he saw glasses did not look like champagne.

'Brilliant' he said letting no break in conversation, 'brilliant' thinking more of himself 'of course it will be ghastly waiting, and it was for two o'clock when we were going on to a little place I know of' he said. 'But of course I can go away and come back again: you don't think that's rude do you?'

She thought what a priggish boy and hadn't heard more of what he said than his little place he knew of. Why speak like a serial she asked in her mind.

'It's done a great deal' he said after waiting for her 'I've done it but perhaps it's rude.'

She thinks it rude he thought, she's half witted and why not take up his quotation 'a little place I wot of' he cried in his mind.

'D'you go much to the dog races?' he said changing conversation.

'Yes I do.'

'Isn't it astounding the crowds that go there.'

'Crowds' she said.

'And all you hear about the lower classes not being able to live decently when you see ten's of thousands there every night.'

'Perhaps that's why.'

'No I can't allow that' he said. 'If they really couldn't afford it they wouldn't go' he said.

'I don't know.'

'Well we've got a factory in Birmingham and I know if you really can't afford it there you don't go.'

He didn't know but why had she taken him up and he was desperate.

'Are you in business then?' she said.

'Yes I am worse luck.'

'Everyone's in business or in the Guards now' she said and, satisfied, he leaned back in chair and said to himself what incredible, incredible things you heard, he would tell it to Mary when they went on to Princes, she would laugh.

'Another thing I can't understand about the lower classes' he said 'is this business by which they pay 1d per week for all their lives and get a whopping £60 funeral at their end.'

'Well they tell me it's because they don't like their families to pay for it, you see, as it's hard on them after they're dead.'

Why be well informed at dinner he said to himself. And would be no champagne; it was claret. Would he tell her what wrong it was not giving champagne at dinner, but was she the hostess' daughter, anyway what was her name. Not even cards on the table he said to himself looking round, and saw she was talking now to next door neighbour and he turned to his left but that one talked also to neighbour next door, and he refused claret then, asked for lemonade, took water, was no lemonade in house.

Monday night Mr Craigan and Mr Gates in bowler hats went along

Coventry Road to public house. Mr Tupe saw them. He said to young man he was with was no man so deceitful as man he could see walking on other side of road if he looked. No man like it for deceit. And didn't he think a deal of himself for never saying much when that was easy as picking a tart up in this street. 'I could hold my gob for a day and a year if I so wanted' he said. 'Pity was they hadn't killed him when they nearly did.' Wire rope breaking had nearly caught him day or two ago. You never heard such a hulla-balloo as there was over him. It might have been the gaffer himself that had been burnt alive in the boilers. He'd gone about with a look on his dial days after like 'hold it up where it hurts and let mammy kiss it.' 'Deceitful old bleeder' he said. 'Enough to make you go bald'eaded just seeing 'im go up the street.'

Tarver went down to tennis club. 'Hello Captain.' 'How are you Colonel, how's it going?'

Mr Tarver had in him feeling of expectation this evening, sinking feeling in his stomach. Standing behind row of deck chairs from which people watched the tennis he made violent swings with his racket. 'I say look out,' one man said 'Tarver's in form, men.' 'Boy' said Mr Tarver, imitating American slang he saw at the movies, 'if that old ball was our old manager, well, he wouldn't have much shape after I'd finished with him.' Then he went on, but spoke to himself, that already the old devil looked a bit lopsided already. No you couldn't go on like the old man went on, was some justice had got to overtake you. You couldn't victimize the people under you for ever and always, not you. That was a bright lad, Archer. That letter he'd got from Archer was a peach of a letter, a peach.

When these four finished who had been playing he went on the court next with three others. Man served to Tarver. Tarver full of anger and victory against Mr Bridges leapt at the ball as it came and sent it back faster yet. He stood still and watched where it went and this man who had served ran after it, but he won't get to it said Mr Tarver. But this man did get to it, though he could only return it high and soft, like a harmonic.

'What' said Mr Tarver and rushed at this return and smashed it. Indeed his shot went so fast over the net that those two opponents against him in this game could only stand and watch, it came by so fast. They clapped hands who sat on chairs. Mr Tarver looked round triumphant in young manhood. Bridges, he sang in his mind, what could Bridges do against him in the long run, he sang. You can't keep a good man down. You can fill him with pins-like a pincushion but he will come up again. And at this moment ball came past him and he was not ready for it – he did not even know they had begun to play again. He could only stand and watch. 'Oh Mr Tarver!' said his partner and Mr Tarver said damn. One of the ladies heard that. 'Careful, ladies present y'know,' she said to him, archly smiling, and he blushed for shame, who was so careful always in his expressions.

Lily Gates was saying half smiling to Jim Dale it gave her creeps Mr Craigan always sitting at home of an evening. He listened to the wireless every night of the week except Mondays. And look what Sunday was, was as much as they could do to get him out to the Lickeys she said. No when you asked he said he would not come, and what for? all the morning listening to preachers in foreign countries, why when you didn't know the language she couldn't see what was in it, and the afternoon and the evening the same, right till he went to his room, she said.

And when it wasn't the wireless he was reading the works of Dickens, over and over again. 'Don't you ever read any but the works of Dickens?' she'd asked him once. 'No why should I?' he'd said. Always the same books, she was fond of a book now and again, but she couldn't do that. He was a wonderful old man.

' 'E's like the deep sea' she was saying, half smiling.


# 6

Mr Dupret 'pater' indeed had fallen on his shoulder after slipping on dog's mess and was in bed now: pretty young nurse read out of *The Field* to him lying in bed, and doctors had said he would be six weeks in bed seeing what he had done at his age. So he had said to his wife, 'Get me a pretty young nurse.'

At the club they said 'Dupret has fallen on his shoulder, that sort of thing is a perpetual menace at our age': at the works they said, 'the gaffer's fallen on 'is shoulder so they say, at 'is time of life you don't get over it so easy as that,' and two men had quarrelled at dinner hour over his age.

So young Mr Dupret was left in charge of business. He came to the London offices early every morning and made great trouble with those who were late. Was all the others let him do. And he signed the cheques also.

Yet Mr Archer had in his pocket letter from Mr Tarver about Whitacre his fitter and this told also of one man suspended for two weeks while the other had nothing done to him though he was as guilty. This was the opportunity. The old man had fallen on his shoulder, young Mr Dupret would be wanting to do something, to assert himself. Now he would work in with young Mr Dupret, now young Mr Dupret could splash about, would want to. Would be rows when the old man came back over what had been done but it could be managed so to fall back on Tarver. Tarver was a fool and did not see whatever row he made was sure to come back on him. Also on young Mr Dupret. So Mr Archer thought and planned.

But he was sincere in his thinking the old place wanted a rouser and in his thinking he was always building, always building in his thinking.

' 'Ow you goin' Albert' Tupe asked storekeeper.

'Rotten, I'm all any'ow today.'

'I 'eard a good one yesterday Albert, there was a chap died, see, and when 'e was dead 'e went to 'eaven. Well after a day or two 'e went to the side like and looked to see if 'e could see any of 'is acquaintance down in 'ell. 'E sees one that 'e used to be friendly with and 'e calls down to 'im " 'Ow do Ben, 'ow be you goin'?" "Fine thanks Jim." "There wouldn't be no way of my getting down to where you works Ben would there" 'e says. " 'Ow's that Jim?" " 'Ow many hours d'you reckon to work down where you are Ben?" "Four-and-a-half with the weekends off." "Yus," 'e says, "and it's ten with us up in 'eaven, Sundays and all, there being so few on us to run the place on" that's why 'e wanted to change eh?'

'Yes' she said to Bert Jones 'yes when 'e said 'e was going to the concert in the City Hall' she breathed on H in Hall 'I said let you go and so 'ere we are again, the city orchestra 'ave begun for another season and now I'll be on my own again, Friday nights. I said to

243

'im, "Yes. But don't consider" I said, "that I'll be a stay at 'ome even if I 'ave to go out alone, no I can go and take myself out for a walk and get a mouthful of fresh air for myself thank you." Still who would've thought it, meeting you in the road like that, I don't know I'm sure.'

'The world's a small place.'

'Yes' she said 'me walking down the road and there you are. Well!'

'I did use to be going out with a young lady but 'er parents 'ave just moved to London where her dad's found a job so she's up there now.'

'So we're both in the same boat, as they say.'

'Ah and it's a lonely kind of a boat ain't it? But you wouldn't be affected really seeing the orchestra only plays Friday nights.'

'Yes, but I got no use for someone that goes off at a moment's notice when I was just looking forward to the pictures for this evening. There's not many in front of us, we'll be inside within a half hour.'

'It kind of puts you out.'

'Yes it does, yes I like to know what I'm going to do of an evening. So when 'e went I said it's no use your sitting moping indoors alone, you go out to the pictures anyway, even if it is alone.'

'But wasn't there anyone in where you live?'

'No you see Mr Craigan was gone with Jim to the concert, 'e says girls can't understand music though I'm very fond of it myself, yes I am, and my dad was out of the 'ouse before you could say knife, soon as Mr Craigan was off to the concert.'

'It makes the evenings long when there's no one in the 'ouse.'

'Yes it does doesn't it. Yes the minutes seem like hours.'

'I like a bit of music myself. And it's pretty fair the music in this movie 'ouse.'

Why she said when they did get in, wasn't that strange what would've happened to the lights and girl in front turned round to her saying they had been up ever since she'd been in. Lily said with the film going on and all, wasn't it hard on the eyes she said and Mr Jones said he didn't understand it, he'd never known it before like this. Yes man in front said turning back to him, yes all the evening but people in front cried ssh: band was playing softly, softly.

A great number were in cinema, many standing, battalions were in cinemas over all the country, young Mr Dupret was in a cinema, over above up into the sky their feeling panted up supported by each other's feeling, away away, Europe and America, mass on mass their feeling united supporting, renewed their sky.

'They're always playing this tune 'ere' she said looking for opening in conversation.

'They are' he said carefully.

'D'you come to this one often then?'

'Before my young lady went up to London.'

'I think the music's lovely 'ere.'

Later they found seats. Sweetness of agitation in her, both her and he sitting bolt upright. So they continued sitting. And film came round again, that one, to where it was when they first came in.

'Shall we stay on a bit now the band's back again?' he said.

'I don't mind I'm sure.'

So still upright. But she tired.

'We might as well go' she said trembling. He did not see this.

He walked her home, neither said much to other. She no longer trembled and indeed was bored now. In the street they met Gates that was a little drunk. He wheezed, out of breath.

'They're only takin' those that are short of breath up in 'eaven now' he said 'they run short of trumpets there, 'arps is all the go now' he said.

'I'll wager that was Tupe you got that from' she said.

' 'Ow'd you know' said he.


'Everyone is in the Guards now or in business' repeated he to himself coming in to one of the private rooms in London office. He thought if she had said that as last night she had well then he need not be so humiliated. But he was, oh yes. Last night had been one of those nights, clearly had he seen then extent of tomorrow's humiliation. Aye and clearly had seen himself throwing up bastions around citadel of his personality now all of it retreated back, in state of siege, behind 'everyone now is a Guardee or in business'.

He threw away cigarette.

It was because, all of it, because she was so beautiful, he repeated to himself, so beautiful.

After all I work, repeated he to himself, I work, here I am in London offices of Dupret & Son, general engineers.

Why had they not brought the correspondence? He rang.

'Why hasn't Mr Sewell brought in this morning's letters?'

'He hasn't come yet Mr Dupret.'

'He hasn't come' he said echo echo to Miss Wilbraham. That dreadful night he thought. Mary had been late – that other with fellows twirling small moustaches round about her, she laughing – and Mary, when she had come, furious, he could not find why. May have been she'd bought new hat. Bother bother. And here was whole day stretching out in front. What had been her name? A – a – Anne – Anya – Nunk – HANNAH GLOSSOP.

'It is not' Archer was saying 'it is not a thing I want to bring officially before you Mr Dupret, for instance I would never contemplate putting the facts before your father, sir, but I would like to bring it to your notice in a semi-official manner. Of course in your position you want to know everything that is going on and I know that you are already "au fay" with everything that goes on. I know that you have already noticed in the short time, comparatively short time you have been in the business that all is not well at Birmingham. I mean this that it is not running smoothly. I always look on a business as a kind of machine Mr Dupret, one unit, I shall never forget my old employer old Mr March drawing my attention to that aspect of trade, and of course when one part is not running smoothly, wants oiling shall we say, then that machine or unit is not functioning to its full productive capacity. Well a few days ago I received this letter Mr Dupret which I should like to place before you. Of course before you read it I must say that the writer never intended it to be read by anyone but myself, Tarver is not the man to do anything behind another man's back, but in my opinion, for what it is worth, I am sure he is one of the most promising younger men in the Birmingham side. Of course this letter is in the strictest confidence sir, I'm sure Tarver would be most upset if he knew I was giving it to you to read and yet I am certain I would be failing in my duty if I didn't bring it to your notice.'

More frightful trouble Mr Dupret said to himself and took the letter.

Intrigue he cried in his mind, still sitting in private room in London office, intrigue and how horrible people are. Of course Archer was working against old Bridges for Bridges ignored Mr Archer and only dealt with him through old Walters. Both these were old, old. How horrible they all were and everyone too for that matter, loathsome the people in buses, worse in trams of course – he faintly smiled.

And when you went out anywhere, he went on in his mind about people, how rude everyone, and they did not laugh at your jokes. And when you sat sweating here in daytime when you might be dodging enemies in the Park or receiving rudeness impassively there, here you were dying of it, the badly managed intrigues, another's mistake so ignorantly exploited, mismanaged. They were like children in their intrigues, like little children, cried he in his mind and then casting back to Hannah Glossop, what figure must he have cut when she did not see point in 'a little place I know of.' He might have said 'I wot of' and so it would have been worse, one should never be, he thought, facetious in conversation with a stranger. Still it would have been 'I know of,' yes must have been.

So stupid are they he said still going on, that there is no doing with them, and there his mind stopped and only kept on repeating then, 'no doing with them.'

Later temper began to come up gorgon-headed within him, he flagellated it, words hung across his mind – stupidity, and then – angry, and then – old men. We shall be ruined cried he in his mind, business will go bankrupt, 'to Siam, Siam,' 'not functioning to its full capacity for production': the old men are smashing it, he cried, something has got to be done, must.

'Who would it be?' Mrs Eames said, holding baby.

'Bentley 'is name is' said Mr Eames.

'So that's what you do when you go up to the garden, you stand talking to that class. You ought to 'ave more respect for your child.'

'Well I didn't tell 'im he was right did I?'

'And what's coming to the garden when you're standing there gossiping all the time?'

'It's staying there.'

'Oh gor blimey, you men it's enough to drive us women mad.'

'Well it is staying there isn't it?'

'You hadn't ought to stand listening to a man of 'is kind.'

'I'll do as I please' he said taking off spectacles to wipe them 'and

I'm not saying a good deal of what 'e said weren't true.'

'Lord I can't keep mad at you when you take your specs off. You 'ave a look about you of the lamp post outside.'

'I'm not saying a lot of what 'e touched on 'e wasn't justified in saying. To my way of thinking they didn't ought to keep the tackle in the way they do. The crane in our shop ain't safe now and Aaron Connolly driving it don't make it any safer.'

The lathes he said were all anyhow and any time now he said glass roof might fall in if gale of wind came.

'You'll give me fits' she said.

'And the government inspector's meant to look to all that but there's a woman comes to our place mostly and what can she know about it. And there ain't a girl in the whole factory. Old Bentley didn't mention that no nor did I for I thought 'e might never stop if I went suggesting things to 'im.'

'That's right' she said 'don't get into argument with that sort.'

' 'E's a decent enough feller all right.'

'Don't you go talking with them.'

'Why shouldn't I?'

'It ain't going to do no good to your wife or child.'

'What ain't. You talk too much that's what it is. If Eve hadn't've started off clacking the serpent wouldn't 'ave caught 'er in his trap.'

'Oo began it, the serpent or her, tell me that.'

'Well I don't know if I remember for sure which of 'em it was.'

'You don't know the Bible, that's what's the matter with you my man.'

'Well what if I don't know, where's the Bible come into it anyway?'

'Never you mind.'

'What's Adam and Eve got to do with Bentley?'

'You begun that, I don't know.'

'I did not.'

'Why you know you did.'

'I did not.'

'I don't know I'm sure,' she said, 'but you did, I know that. Well anyway what's the use in arguing. I'm going to bed.'

'I'm about ready too.'

Halfway upstairs she turned round and said to remember to lock front door for turning then to baby in her arms 'love' she said 'they might come in the night and steal you away. And what would we do then, and what would we do then?'

'Well when are you going to let us have some of that Bryson order?' asked Mr Walters.

'In a twelve month' darkly said Mr Bridges.

'Someone at it again?'

'The day I got the specifications from London I sent them to the drawing office and now I can't get anything. Everything's done that I can do. Seven days they've had 'em and not a thing on paper yet.'

'What's Tarver up to then?'

'I don't know' cried Mr Bridges 'don't ask me. But 'is nails take a long time paring.'

'We've got to have them' (Walters' voice today was dull as felt).

'You can't get drawings out of him, everyone in this place knows how I've tried to get on with 'im. I could go up there and cry my eyes out but dirty Shylock he's like stone, and he'd leave the place straightaway, quick as knife, if anyone went into his place. If I went in he'd knock me on the head. I never go near him, just to keep him in a good temper I daren't do it, he goes up in smoke if you so much as look at 'im.'

'What are we to do then?'

'Don't ask me I'm telling you.'

'I'd better see him.'

'Only a week or two ago I had to have a word with him over that Smithson plant he was seven weeks with, only a week ago. He said Bumpus had been ill and he wanted another man as well. Where's the money going to come from to pay that extra man, eh, tell me that? If we can't keep overheads down where are we? And still there's not everyone could do so nice a job when 'e's in the mood. But we'll be out of business before he's done. It's all fine enough to be pleased with yourself as punch but there's others can do the job just as good and in half the time. That's what it is in business now, they take any job so long as you do it quick.'

'I'll see him, Arthur.'

'You look out what you're doing. Something's up, you haven't got to be blind to see that. I gave 'im something to chew that other day and had 'im on his knees before my chair there where you're sitting.

He was sick as if I'd been Mussolini and given him cod liver oil. And then he looked so perked up a day or two after I didn't know what to make of it. Now the young fellow's coming down. What's there in all this?'

'Archer and young Mr Dupret have been a lot together lately' said Mr Walters with muted drama and called through to office for Miss Maisie Alexander to get Mr Tarver.

'Have they eh? And d'you know what Tarver said I was to Maisie, said I was off it, crazy. Can you work with a man like that, and when he's old enough to be your son. What are you going to say to 'im?'

'You leave it to me Arthur.'

Then Tarver came in.

'How are you Mr Tarver? Keeping fit?'

'I'm fine thanks Colonel. Feeling on top of the world.'

'That's good. Is the wife well?'

'Fit as she can be.'

'That's good. Look here about that Bryson order, they telephoned me yesterday—'

'Yesterday? How's that?'

'They're expecting that jacket right away.'

'Why I only got the rough drawings three days ago.'

'Three days ago' cried Mr Bridges.

'Three days ago' said Mr Tarver.

'What's that?' said Mr Walters.

'I don't know when anyone else got 'em' said Mr Tarver 'but we got the specifications Tuesday in our office.'

Then they lied for some time all of them.

Was no record of when specifications went from office of works manager to drawing office and Walters said perhaps they had been lying about in cost office before they had gone through to Tarver, but Bridges and this one did not listen. One waved newspaper, other clenched fist over rolled up handkerchief in his hand and bit at ends of it.

Gradually they got quieter.

'What we want' said Mr Bridges 'is the work to go through.'

'That's what we are all trying to do in our different ways' said Mr Walters and Mr Tarver said 'We're working just for that and nothing else.'

'Of course it's got to be a good job, an engineer's job' Bridges said.

'We've got the best name in the trade for the quality of the work we turn out' Walters said.

'But how'd you expect anyone to turn it out in three days, that's what I can't get hold of' Tarver said.

'But as you were saying just now Arthur' Mr Walters murmured as if he had not heard Mr Tarver 'the whole trend of modern business is that they don't care how it is so long as they get the job quick.'

'What d'you mean three days' said Bridges to Tarver, 'more like three weeks, and that's not guess work it's observation, I haven't sat watching you these days and days with what I've seen going in at one eye and out of the next.'

'Where'd you get three weeks. It was the day before yesterday when I got those measurements.'

'Day before yesterday, Thursday, Wednesday, d'you hear that Tom' to Mr Walters ' 'e's on a new talk now, it was six days I remember him telling us not three minutes back.'

'It was not.'

'I'm not saying any more' Mr Bridges said 'you go on and talk it out between you if talking helped anyone ever.' He went out.

'There goes a fine man' said Mr Walters. 'Look here' he said speaking like as of earthquake or the deluge 'look here we're all Brummagem men all three of us let's face up to this, John, like fellow citizens. I know and you know Arthur's hard to work with when he's got one of his tantrums on him, I've had some times with him, my word, but you know he's got a lot better in the last few years. But in the old days my word, it's nothing to what it used to be. And of course you're a young man and this place will seem to you a dead alive sort of hole but you've got to take into account mind you that there's not more than ten per cent of the engineering firms in this country making above three per cent profits.'

'That's all they declare' said Mr Tarver.

'I don't know, that's a big thing to say. In London you get a pretty good view of the whole thing and from what I've been told I say it's that myself. Now look here John you won't find another firm that'll give you so much scope, you haven't got much to do, you get time here to work out your ideas and put 'em on paper. Let's get down to it and live in peace. Why when I was with Watsons you were lucky if you got away with it of a morning without someone about the place resigning or getting the sack. There was no time to work or know whether you were on your head or not. But here you've got your own office pretty well, and there isn't all that amount to do.'

'That's just what there is. I can't get through it with Bumpus bad on and off like 'e is. We've got to do something, though it'll take two years to do it in this place. And I must have another draughtsman because as it is now he' nodding to door 'he's on at me the whole time like a can with a stone in it at the end of a dog's tail so that I can't do anything for worry three parts of the time. You can't work with him.'

'I've had terrible times with him myself, terrible times, don't I know it. But I've stuck it out and I've done better for myself in this firm than I could in most others. Though you might see eye to eye with him, he's a fine man, you can't help respecting him. There's not everyone could have done what he's done for himself.'

'But what's 'e do for the firm?'

'He's done more than anyone for it except myself John.'

'Oh well I'll say this, squire, I've got nothing against him personally.'

'No that's right—' and so Mr Walters quieted Mr Tarver and the door opened minutes later.

'That bed-plate' said Mr Bridges coming in, 'it's a worry, every time I go into the works and go by it I could go crazy. Crazy' he said remembering Miss Alexander, 'crazy, of course you can't expect much of a man that's crazy especially when he's manager. Little things like dates you can't expect him to remember that.'

'What's wrong with the bed-plate Arthur?' Mr Walters said.

'It's cracked, you can put the blade of your knife in a full quarter of an inch. I'm having them fake it up but there it is there, they've only got to spot it and the money's gone.'

'You cement it and no one will notice.'

'The vibration of the engine when it's set up will crack it right across' said Mr Tarver.

'Oho' said Mr Bridges 'but when you've seen as many bed-plates as I have my lad you'll tell a different tale to your grandmother. Why I remember one bed-plate I saw at the H.B.S. and the moulder put his trowel right down into it and it's working now on a liner.'

Mr Tarver was smiling.

'Well that's all Tarver for the moment' said Mr Walters but as soon as he was gone Mr Bridges cried out ''ave you seen anything like it, smilin' like a mandarin, what's 'e got up his sleeve? And he talks about engineering, why if it came down to drawing a door knob 'e couldn't do it. That's what we're coming to, eh, cubs like 'im and 'is little master trying to teach us. And I've given all I know to this firm, you know it, we all know it, I've worked my heart out. It makes you want to hang yourself by the window cord from the window. Years of work and now this.'

'The chief isn't dead yet' said Mr Walters 'and now he's fallen down in the street maybe he won't be so fond of walking across them as he was before, so he'll add another ten years to his life. You can't do it now unless you're a young man' said Mr Walters to Mr Bridges and soon he was talking of the difference in Birmingham and London streets and by much talking of such things friendly to both of them he dressed Mr Bridges' wounds.

'That bed-plate' said Mr Bridges – 'come along John as you're there. They were at me this morning on the 'phone calling me names, I might have been anything, a urinal, anything.'

'Their man said he'd put his walking stick into the one we sent him, he knows how he did it I don't, it was a wee crack, I could only put my knife in a bare eighth. What's he want with a walking stick in a factory eh, d'you call that business. It beats me how he's the cheek to say that over a public service like the telephone.'

Bridges and Tarver hurried down through works to iron foundry.

'It's going to cost a fortune, eh, we've got to cut the old one up and this one to replace it will take two men and a boy five days to ram up and six-and-a-half to finish, then it's got to be dried. We can't stand it. It's a worry.'

They came to iron foundry.

'They've put Craigan on it then' said Mr Tarver when he had seen what, as he told Bumpus later, he had not believed when he was told.

'I told him (meaning foreman) to do that. Craigan may be a bit slow now but he's sure. It'll be a fine job when he's done with it' Bridges was singing with sureness almost. 'We can't afford to have another like the last one.' His mood changing 'By God' he cried 'but look at the land it's taking.'

We can't afford to have them at all thought Mr Tarver. But I'm not saying anything yet awhile he said to himself.

'Get on with that bed-plate man' Bridges said rushing threateningly on foundry foreman Philpots.

'Yessir' foreman said 'they're tearing into it.'

Tearing into it thought Mr Tarver, two old age pension men and one young feller which looks like girl!

'We're doing over on it' said Philpots, foundry foreman.

There you are said Tarver to himself overtime and so much more on the job and one that I wouldn't answer their enquiry if I was manager. You can bet, he thought, they had to circularize all the old county to find a fool big enough to try and cast a thing that shape and manage to make a good one. Robbery, just robbery.

'It's robbery, dirty robbery in daylight, making us do another' said Mr Bridges to Philpots, 'I put my knife in that crack and it was a bare quarter yet they sent it back. But we can't afford to quarrel with them. Don't you leave it day or night Andrew' foreman's name was Andrew Philpots, 'it's worth your job to you, and mine to myself. The chief'd soon have me chasing if this happened twice in a year.'

'There they are' Joe Gates said of Mr Bridges and Tarver to Dale and Mr Craigan, ramming. Gates shovelled sand.

'More sand' Dale said.

They worked fast for another hour.

'Hold on' said Mr Craigan and then straightened backs. His eyes were like black stones with anger.

Later that evening, when they were home he said again he was getting to be old man. Lily and Jim Dale separately worried about his saying this, Joe Gates was too tired. He had never said that before, either said in his own mind.


# 7

They had taken bus. They had gone Saturday afternoon to Mr Jones' uncle and aunt that were lodge-keepers at gate of big house one mile out from bus terminus.

They had taken bus and had walked out. They had come in time for tea. They had stayed for supper. Lily Gates took pleasure in feeding chickens, it was infinitely amusing for her, and she had on new dress.

After supper they had started back for bus terminus towards ten o'clock. They had talked. Lily thought Bert Jones was great on talking. She had said what kind of a life did they live up in the big house which his uncle was gatekeeper of and he said there was three young ladies, daughters of the house, but were no sons, father employed a lot of men in Birmingham he said. She said when they married, those three, would the eldest come with her 'usband to live in the house so it would stay in the family, and he said he couldn't tell and she said she wondered what kind of lives they did live there.

She said it seemed a pity there wasn't a man the house wouldn't come to though girls were as good as men but still. She said they'd go out to dances every night probably and have a high old time. He said perhaps he kept his daughters in and didn't let them out much but she said that class never did that, the girls were free as the fishes in the sea and as slippery, using words her father would have used. And more than that she said, she had asked his aunt and she'd seen them come out of an evening scores of times, so she said.

From joking with him and from the long day talking with him her laughing went out all at once into confidences. Coming closer to him she began to tell what she had not meant to tell anyone, as if he had taken her will from her. She said how low Mr Craigan was often now in his self, and that once when he came back from work some time since she had thought he was finished.

''E's the man in our house really too you see' she said 'and he ain't never said it out like that before. When he an' dad gets too old for work I don't know what'll 'appen. I know I don't.'

'Well, of course,' Mr Jones said, 'he wouldn't be so young now' he said and was moved at her confiding in him.

She pressed closer to him.

'No, that's right, he ain't. But he loves his work. What'll come to us when he an' dad gets too old for it I don't know. Grandad won't know where he is. Yes I often lie awake o' nights thinking 'ow 'e'll manage. And how us'll get on, dad and the rest,' she said and was silent. As they walked, then Mr Jones had rush of feeling. He saw everything one way. 'Us working people we got to work for our living,' he said passionately, 'till we're too old. It's no manner of use

255

thinking about it, it's like that, right on till we're too old for them to use us. Then our children'll make provision for us,' he said and stopped and suddenly he kissed her for the first time. She pressed up to his face, her eyes shining. Then for a long time they kissed each other, murmuring and not hearing what they murmured, behind cattle shed in field they had been crossing.

He sat at home alone in a chair picking his nose.

'The other day I met a girl called Glossop' he said in his mind. He remembered he had asked Mary about her and she had known her by sight, had seen her at dances. Then how had he not seen her? But sometimes in reading, he thought, you will find word you do not know and when you learn the meaning then for a few days you come again and again upon that word. So perhaps he only noticed same people at dances. He thought you made a little circle and yours reflects other circles. Death, death, sackcloth and ashes.

When Lily wakes, her eyelids fold up and her two eyes soft, brutal with sleep blink out on what is too bright for them at first. She stirs a little in the warmness of bed. Then, eyes waking, she sees clearly about her and stretches. She brings arms up above her head and takes hold on one of those parallel bars up behind pillow, and pulls her heavy thighs and legs out straight. Till she brings head up against that bar and till it forces head down on her breast, so she pulls. This done, she sits up, awake.

She saw in images in her mind how Mr Dale was to her like being on the verge of sleep, in safe bed. She laughed and stretched again. She turned to thinking of this new day and what she would have to get for the house today. Then she laughed again for she saw that was how she was with Bert Jones; with Jim she forgot, but with Bert she remembered. When she was with Bert it was like she had just stretched, then waked, then was full of purposes. But with Jim, it was like end of the day with him. Yes, she said, Bert's someone to work for, yes there's something in him she said in feeling and jumped out of bed.

Now Miss Gates and Mr Jones went out often together.

When they were out together once, after that, she saw clearly how

256

unjust her life at home was to her, staying in all day, 'I never see another girl but over the garden fence and all the housework to do, yes, sometimes I could sit down and cry. And look at old Craigan now,' she said, 'I get black looks from him every time I come in after being out with you, he wants me to go out with Jim you see. But women aren't what they were, I'm not going to stay in an 'arem of his making, we're educated now. Yes he's made it pretty plain he wants Jim and me to be married but 'e can keep me in all day if he likes but he won't pick my husband. You've no idea, the 'ouse has got to be shining, there can't be a speck of dust or he'll say "what's this my wench?" Yes, that's what he says.'

'He won't let you go out to work?'

'No, he won't 'ear of it, I've got to stay in and wear away the linoleum by scrubbing,' and she said she did not know how she'd stood it up to then. She went on talking when he, more to draw her sympathy on him, said wasn't all that much enjoyment in factories.

'Oh yes, and how would you like to stay in all day by yourself and keep a place tidy, you're like all men, and then when they give you the 'ouse-keeping money Friday night to have nothing but black looks,' and seeing all this clearly in her mind she was scornful with him. He too, then, began to be angry.

'But when we're married, won't...' he began but she sprang at his face and then it was like so many other of their walks over again.

Later, still exalted, she drew back from him and said, whispering, surely he would not expect her to be like those other women, 'you won't be like dad,' she said, 'that had never any idea of bettering himself. You wouldn't want me to slave all my life till I was a bag of bones.' She said she was not afraid of the work, yes she was used to that looking after three men, but she couldn't do it if she didn't believe there was nothing better coming, 'we shan't be like the others Bert?' and he said of course they wouldn't be, at the works he was a picked man already.

'Come on then,' she cried jumping up, holding out arms to him, 'I can't sit still.' He jumped up and she ran backwards at that, her head held back and her arms now behind her back. But running forward to catch her he fell full length, cutting his forehead slightly.

She sat cross-legged and making resting place for his head in her lap she spat on handkerchief and wiped cut on his forehead, disconsolate, wiping blood off his forehead. Then he was happier than he had ever been before.

They came into front room after supper.

'Have you caught a chill or something?' Mrs Tarver said to her husband.

'I don't know. I don't think I feel well.'

'You ought to be in bed.'

'The young chap came down today.'

'What young chap's that?'

'Where's your mind? Why, young Dupret. Doris' he said to only child, 'what have we got there?'

'Young Mr Dupret,' breathed Mrs Tarver and moved her chair nearer his. 'Darling' she said to the child, 'don't worry daddy now.'

'Don't talk to her like that mother, you'll upset the child. What's that you've got in your hands, answer your daddy.'

'It's only a toy ukulele she got at Mrs Smith's party, dear. What did he say to you? You ain't going to say he didn't see at once who was right, and the wrong.'

'I don't know. Here, Doris, come and sit on daddie's knee and show him the ukulele. Well, ain't you a ukulele lady now!'

'I am!'

'Johnikins you don't say you couldn't see him so's to get your word in first.'

'Yes I saw him.'

'What did he say?'

'He didn't say anything.'

'Didn't say anything? D'you mean to say.... Then what did he do?'

'Nothing. Well he did this. He took the man off they'd put by the lavatory door checking the men in and out.'

'Daddy, don't you like my uku – uku – ukulele?'

'Was that all he did?'

'Don't you like my ukulele, daddy?'

'Don't worry daddy now dear. Go and play over there and put the doll to bed. What did he do that for?'

'To please himself I suppose.'

'And didn't he give you another draughtsman?'

'No.'

'What did he say to you, then?'

'He had a lot of this educated jargon, I didn't understand much of it, though I got a bit nearer to it than old Bridges. He went on about what a fine looking chap – beautiful, that's the word he used – a man in the iron foundry was. I don't know how an iron moulder can be beautiful but there you are.'

'He must be a dandy though if that's all he thinks of in the works. I suppose he 'as ladies trailing round him once he gets home, and a lot of good they'll do him.'

'He's soft.'

'But did you go through the works with him?'

'No, I was coming through the iron foundry from the fettling shop when I ran into him and the old man.'

'And didn't you speak to him?'

'Of course I spoke to him, what d'you think I am?'

'Johnikins, why don't you tell me something?'

'What can I tell you? I was there for about five minutes and he went back to the offices and turned round to me – "I'll come along and see you before I go" lardida he said and went into the old man's room. So I waited for him in my department and the next thing I knew was the noise of him going off in 'is Bentley.'

'Then how d'you think it was him who took the man away from there?'

'Ah that's where I come in. I sent down Bumpus to get some stamps in the outside office and to look about him and make eyes at the girls when all of a sudden out bursts the old squire right up in the air and behind him was the young fellow saying – "but come Mr Bridges it's nothing very terrible" (fancy saying that to the old squire!) "it's nothing very terrible, surely, such a small thing, lavatories..." and then he banged the door right in the young chap's face and went off. Bumpus comes back to tell me and the first thing I did was to get up to go and catch him in there with the old devil out of the way, when I hear the noise of his car. I run to the window and there's the young chap driving himself away.'

'Did he? What d'you say to that?'

'I don't know.'

'So he didn't come up and see you after all?'

'Doris, come and play to Daddy on your ukulele, daddie's tired.'

'Leave the child alone, do, you'll be the death of her. What d'you think? Didn't he say nothing about another draughtsman?'

'Not a word.'

'Well he's crossed old Bridges in one thing, and that's to the good, the old scarecrow.'

'Yes, but what do we know went on else. He was there some time, must have been. And if he'd crossed the old man before then the old scarecrow would have been out of the room before that and Bumpus would have seen him. You can depend on his always rushing out when he's crossed.'

'I see they've took the man off from there,' nodding to lavatory door said Mr Tupe to Mr Bentley.

'They had to.'

'Why's that?'

'They were made to' Bentley heavily said. 'As soon as ever I saw a man put on there I said that's a thing a woman won't stand. I 'ad that factory inspector in me mind's eye. I thought to myself she'd never stand for it. And she didn't, that's why he's suspended.'

'But she 'asn't been through, not since that man was put on. 'Er angel feet've not crossed our thres-bloody-'old.'

'She must've 'eard then.'

'Well if you wan't to know, the young feller took 'm off. And the more's the pity I say.'

'Young Dupret?'

'That's 'im. Now it'll be the old story again, 'alf an hour's work and then twenty-one minutes in there for a smoke and a chat. They've got no conscience to the firm or to theirselves.'

'As the fly said to the spider. Of all the dirty swine – excuse my saying so – you're one of them. And if it was young Dupret 'e was made to.'

' 'E wasn't, 'e did it on 'is own from what I can 'ear of it. Probably 'e was 'alf witted enough to suppose 'e was pleasing mangy young Russian tykes like you.'

'I wonder at a man of your age swallowing what you swallow.'

'Speaking of beer' Mr Tupe said genially 'I could get down twice what you'd had after you couldn't drink no more, when your head was communing with the stars: if you'd care to try any night, you paying the drinks?'

*

'My poor old man, how are you?' Mrs Dupret said coming into sick room, 'how do you feel in yourself?'

Mr Dupret lay propped up on pillows. He related how his nurse had told him that he was 'naughty to ring so often and should be spanked.' Courageously he made a comedy out of it.

Mrs Dupret asked what tip should be given to this nurse when she had packed her things, for her one line of original research was into the question of tips. Mr Dupret decided at once and when his wife said surely not so little, since Archie, when he was ill, and had had a nurse for about the same period, had given her quite six shillings more he said no, he would give her that amount and no less. She said how very interesting that was to her. He said she would call him mean perhaps but she said not the least bit in the world, only it was so fascinating what tips people gave. The most absurd person of course was Proust, she said – her voice hazed with wonder. He had given enormous tips, big, huge, it was fantastic, she said sitting down by the bed, he had thought nothing of giving 200 francs to a waiter who brought his, his – well any little thing, but then he was not a gentleman she murmured, enviously almost. For what she wanted most in the world sometimes was to give huge tips but had never dared, she thought the waiter might take her for an actress. (She was of that generation of women which still feared actresses.)

Mr Dupret said Jews had brought the Continent to a ridiculous state with extravagant tipping, that was why he would never go abroad. 'I know dear,' she said. But he went on that it was really to spare her the anxiety of having to give them, he said she knew she never slept the night before moving out of a hotel abroad, and to spare her the disappointment when ten per cent was added to the bill so that there were no tips.

'I've got such a clever book here for you dear' she said, 'it's called *Lenin and Gandhi*. You ought to read it.' He put it down by the side of the bed.

'There's a thing in it which I thought so amusing darling,' she said 'which is where he says the Brahmins or Hindus, one of those people I don't know which, sit for whole half hours saying the same word over and over again. Of course it's very unkind, but it's so like Dickie when he's in love.' She said didn't he know that Dickie was starting another affair and Mr Dupret said another one? and she said yes, a girl called Glossop, a very nice girl from all she could make out, 'but very dull, I'm afraid, like all Dick's young ladies.' There was a certain stage in all his affairs when he sat and repeated to himself over and over again darling, darling, darling, like that, so like those old men squatting on the mountains. Mr Dupret laughed 'ho, ho!' Then he asked how she knew. 'Why the darling' she said 'he always tells me in spite of himself all those things like that about his girls. Then he has to go and make out a reason for his having told me so he shan't seem to have given himself away without meaning to. He is rather a darling, isn't he, Jack?'

'He's a nice boy but he's very silly still' said Mr Dupret. 'He's got no head.'

Mrs Dupret said she thought he wouldn't marry for another nine years at least but now her husband was bored and began to give instructions, summoning people and sending them off, all on business, and he dismissed Mrs Dupret. Going away she thought how nice it had been and still was while he lay ill though he wasn't really ill now any more of course, he was just pretending and it was high time he got about again. But how nice it had been, she had seen so much more of him since he had hurt his shoulder, usually he was working when he wasn't asleep. He worked all day.

She marvelled at the correctness of the tip he had decided on for that nurse, and to decide at once like that, he had a genius for tips, she thought. She went to get ready before going out.

But still, poor old man she thought, there was something about it which she didn't altogether like. His staying in bed like that made her uneasy. And when the doctors said there was nothing the matter with him now, why didn't he get up?

Again, some other morning, she was in his bedroom and they were talking about young Mr Dupret, Dick, and she said how she had seen this girl Hannah Glossop several times again and that she was giving a dinner party for her soon, though of course the party was not to look as though it were hers; Hannah – from talking about her to Dickie she called her Hannah now – would just, to all appearances, be one of the other girls.

Mr Dupret was listless and asked how Dick was getting on with the Dupret and son business and his wife said she thought he was so interested. Why was it, she asked him, that all this time he had not once asked after that 'side' when he had been managing all his other interests from his bed. He answered that he had decided to give him a free run of the place till he got back to work again, 'there is nothing like the actual experience for teaching you' he said and that when he got back he intended altering every single alteration the boy had made 'just to show him.'

Wasn't that rather cruel Mrs Dupret said, and he said no, of course not. For one thing, if he had done anything it was almost bound to be wrong, and then if you let them have all their own way, young men lost their keenness. After that he sank into a greater apathy and although he did not send her away, which was in itself, she thought, a sign that he was not right, she could hardly get anything out of him.

After Sunday dinner, when Lily Gates had cleared table and had put back on it bowl in which Mr Craigan kept tobacco, she said to those three what were they going to do that Sunday afternoon.

'Where are you goin'?' said Mr Dale.

'I'm not going anywhere.

'Aren't you goin' out?'

'I'm not goin' anywhere without you go.'

'Don't trouble about me' Mr Dale said. 'I'm used to that.'

'I didn't mean you particular, I meant all on you.'

'I'm stayin' in with me pipe,' Gates said half asleep. 'You go and get the beer.' Mr Craigan reached out and took wireless headphones which he fitted about his head.

'I thought you couldn't mean me,' said Mr Dale.

'No, I should think I couldn't.'

'But don't you put yourself out for us. You go on out.'

'I got nowhere to go.'

'What, ain't 'e waitin' for you at the corner?'

'Who's that?'

'Who's that!!' he said.

'Well what business is it of yours if 'e is?'

'I wouldn't keep 'im waitin'.'

'I tell you I'm not going out this afternoon.'

'Then what's it all about. 'Ad a lover's quarrel or what?'

She smiled at him and said what business was it of his and her smiling made him shout that most likely he had to take most of his time keeping his other loves quiet. Dropping voice he said people of that sort which took other people's girls from them, were not content with one only, they had several, wife in every port and married women some of them most likely, he said, voice rising. Still she smiled when, jumping up, he said he would give her smack across that smile. Craigan took off headphones then and said 'you go and get the beer Lil.' When she had shut door behind her he said to Dale to leave her alone. Mr Gates slept noisily in chair.

Mr Dale sat down. He leant towards fire which made room thick hot. They said nothing for a time. He looked up then towards Mr Craigan and said:

'I've been thinkin' I'd better change my lodgings.'

'You'll do nothing of the kind' Craigan said.

Again was silence.

'It makes it awkward for me' he said 'staying 'ere.'

Mr Craigan said nothing. Dale kicked Joe Gates: 'Joe' he said 'I've been thinkin' I ought to look out for other lodgings. Our wench and me don't seem to 'it it off any more, Joe.'

Mr Gates looked at Mr Craigan. Craigan said:

'You'll stay 'ere Jim.'

Dale kicked fender and upset poker which clattered and crashed on floor.

'I won't stand by and see 'er marry Bert Jones.'

'I can't stand by and see that feller go off with Lil' he said later. 'If her likes 'im better'n me well then let 'er 'ave 'im but I'm not goin' to be there to watch it.'

'I'm telling you she'll not marry Bert Jones' said Mr Craigan and again was silence and furtively Mr Gates watched Mr Craigan. Then Craigan said to Mr Dale: 'You go on off out, Jim, don't sit moping inside.'

'That's right' said Joe Gates. 'Lord love me, you ain't jealous of 'im are you? 'Im?!! Why 'e's nothing more than something to look at, though 'e's as ugly as your backside. But 'e's got no use to 'imself. You didn't ought to worry yourself about him. An' talkin' about women, the times I 'ad with 'er mother before we was married. Why if any dago stopped in the street her was after 'im.'

Taking hat Mr Dale went out of the house. He took a different way from where she had gone to fetch beer. Those two sat and said nothing. Then Gates said:

'I've a mind to 'ave it out with 'er.'

'You sit still.'

'She wants a good clout. You do it then.'

'If you touch 'er I'll break the poker 'cross yer legs.'

Mr Gates stayed silent then and Mr Craigan said no more. But he did not put headphones back on his head so later Gates said:

'Without meanin' any offence, what d'you think on it?' but Craigan did not answer and little later Mr Gates slept again. Mr Craigan sat on. With thinking he forgot what was to have been greatest treat, concert from Berlin.

Then, one morning in iron foundry, Arthur Jones began singing. He did not often sing. When he began the men looked up from work and at each other and stayed quiet. In machine shop, which was next iron foundry, they said it was Arthur singing and stayed quiet also. He sang all morning.

He was Welsh and sang in Welsh. His voice had a great soft yell in it. It rose and rose and fell then rose again and, when the crane was quiet for a moment, then his voice came out from behind noise of the crane in passionate singing. Soon each one in this factory heard that Arthur had begun and, if he had two moments, came by iron foundry shop to listen. So all through that morning, as he went on, was a little group of men standing by door in the machine shop, always different men. His singing made all of them sad. Everything in iron foundries is black with the burnt sand and here was his silver voice yelling like bells. The black grimed men bent over their black boxes.

When he came to end of a song or something in his work kept him from singing, men would call out to him with names of English songs but he would not sing these. So his morning was going on. And Mr Craigan was glad, work seemed light to him this morning who had only three months before he got old age pension, he ought to work at his voice he said of him in his mind and kept Joe Gates from humming tune of Arthur's songs.

Every one looked forward to Arthur's singing, each one was glad when he sang, only, this morning, Jim Dale had bitterness inside him like girders and when Arthur began singing his music was like acid to that man and it was like that girder was being melted and bitterness and anger decrystallized, up rising up in him till he was full and would have broken out – when he put on coat and walked off and went into town and drank. Mr Craigan did not know he was gone till he saw he did not come back.

Still Arthur sang and it might be months before he sang again. And no one else sang that day, but all listened to his singing. That night son had been born to him.

And now time is passing.

Mr Dupret had fallen into a greater apathy, nor was there anything which pleased him now. Nor was he ever angry.

Nothing interested him. Mr Dupret had sent for his friends. Those who came he recognized and they talked to him but he could find no answer to their questions or anything in their conversation which would rouse him.

The days come and then the evening, morning papers are hawked about, last editions of the evening papers are sold in the night while men sit writing morning papers. It rained. The summer was passing. Young Dupret would go into the sick room but while old Mr Dupret recognized him and once or twice thought of what he could say, he never arrived at wishing him more than good morning. If he came in the evening as soon as he was in the room old Mr Dupret said 'goodnight' and if he ignored this then the old man would lie with eyelids shut over his eyes. And his wife was treated in the same way.

Then Mrs Dupret had him moved to the house in the country. Young Mr Dupret used to come down for the weekends. Doctors came and went. Electrical treatment was given him, many other remedies were tried, even the most strikingly beautiful nurses were found to tend him, once a well-known courtesan was hired for the night, but the old man still showed no interest and little irritation; he said good-morning to his wife, son, doctors and nurses, good-night to the harlot.

Lines came out on his wife's face. He never mentioned the City or his interests, whenever he spoke it was about the needs of his body. He spoke of no more than these to the nurses, it is not known for certain if he spoke to the harlot. No one could find the face to be present when she was introduced into his room. He had constantly, before his illness, betrayed his wife and she had known it. Nothing really was simpler for her or more natural in such an emergency

266

than to arrange for the lady to come down, what was odd was the doctor of that particular moment allowing it. Mrs Dupret could have no official knowledge of her coming, she could not see her and had to invent many ruses that the servants might not know.

Richard had to receive this lady and show her to the bedroom, and he stood outside with the doctor and one of the nurses. The doctor insisted on standing close to the door as he said he feared 'the possible effects' upon a man of Mr Dupret's age, but his son stood further away, lost in embarrassment, particularly as the nurse seemed nervous and insisted on standing by him. After thirty minutes the lady reappeared. She lit a cigarette. The doctor said 'well' in a threatening voice and she answered that nothing has passed between them, she had done everything in her power, had done her utmost, she was ready to try again although she had packed up her things in her suitcase and if they liked they could go in with her and see for themselves, (she was plainly intimidated by the doctor and cast imploring glances at young Dupret), but she insisted that all he had said was goodnight and then he had shut eyelids over his eyes, 'the good baby' she said.

Some time passed before young Mr Dupret could recover from his surprise at this visit. To his friends in London he talked with horror about the cynical attitude of older women towards sex. There was so much horror in the tone of his voice that his friends asked themselves what could have happened to him and talked of it to each other. But while he soon recovered his old assurance it was some time before he could go into his father's room. Secretly he was annoyed that his mother had not asked him for his opinion, and for the rest of his life he spoke with venom of doctors.

So nobody knew what the old man thought, though everyone was certain that his brain was still working. A submarine is rammed and sinks. It lies for days upon the bed of the ocean and divers tap out messages to it and the survivors tap out answers to the divers, asking for oxygen and food. Above, on the surface of the ocean men work frantically but the day grows on into the evening, night falls, there is another day, another night, and as everyone realizes gradually that they cannot hope to raise the submarine in time, their efforts are not so frantic, they take a little longer over what they do. In the same way fresh doctors were still fetched to Mr Dupret, but no daring experiments were expected of them. They all said very much the same, that his frame was worn out and that only complete rest might bring him out of his illness. More they did not say and Mrs Dupret though she had never been very fond of him, was now thinking how very fond of him she was.

It was hot and it had been hot all day. Mr Gates had gone out, quite often now alone he went out, and Jim Dale had gone out.

When Lily had tea things put away she came with some darning to back door which opened onto the garden. This evening Mr Craigan sat there.

He smoked pipe. She brought chair and sat on it. She began darning.

Almost whispering he said:

'I'm getting to be an old man.'

'Why grandad, you're not.'

'I am.'

'It's the heat of the day's tired you.'

'It's been very hot.'

She darned his socks.

'I bought those socks three years ago,' he said and she said was another twelve months' wear in them yet. She asked in her mind what he was talking for, and was he going to talk to her about it? She waited.

'My mother' he said then, 'knitted socks that wore longer'n that, and they came farther up the leg. They was very good socks.'

She waited.

'This day' he said 'brought me to mind of the days I was in the fields there and the cider we 'ad. The farmer was bound to give us cider. It was good cider, but it's not such a drink as beer.'

So much talk from him frightened her.

'I mind' he said 'yer Aunt Ellie well.' He spoke cheerfully. 'She was older by nine years than your mother. She married a drover by name of Curley. I remember their getting married. I was in the choir.'

'Was you in the choir grandad?' Lily said from nervousness.

'Ah, I sang in the choir. I ain't been in a church since. Nor I shall go even if I 'ave to bury one of my own.'

'Wouldn't you go the funeral.'

'I would not. Yes I sang when them were married. They made a

268

fine show. I ate myself sick at the dinner there was after. She went to live with 'em up t'other end of the village. We lived next door to yer mother's parents so I didn't see much of 'er after that. But you'd say she was contented if you'd seen 'er. Curley was a nice young chap by what I can remember of 'im and yer aunt was a great upstanding woman. But she 'adn't the looks your ma had when she grew to be a woman. Any road she ran away from 'im three years after. No one knew where she'd went, she just gone out through the garden and down the road.'

'Didn't they put the police onto 'er?'

'No, Curley was frightened to do that. She went off. I ain't never 'eard of 'er since, nor nobody ain't.'

'And didn't you go away grandad?' She was trembling.

'Yes. Her going off like she did, that worked on me, and I thought I'd try my luck. And it was years after when I was settled in this town and earning good money that I wrote to yer father – I'd been pals with him though younger'n me – to find out 'ow my old folks was getting on. And when 'e read in my letter 'ow I was doing 'e brought your ma and you over to Brummagem. You was a baby then. But I'd've been better where I was. I wouldn't 'ave got the money but I broke the old people's hearts and where am I now, with no one of my own about me? I got no home and the streets is a poor place after the fields.'

'But you got me, and there's Dad, and Jim.'

'You'll be marrying.'

'Well, if I do we'll live in this 'ouse if you'd let us.'

'Would 'e like it? Maybe while you couldn't get a 'ouse of yer own. But not after.'

Neither spoke.

'Ah,' he said, 'she left 'er man and went off with a flashy sort of card, 'e was a groom to some hunting people that lived a mile off. And I left my people soon after without a word to tell them I was going, thinking it was a fine thing to do. I wanted to make my way up in the world. But I'm no more'n a moulder, a sand rat, and will be till they think I'm too old for work. Three pounds a week and lucky to get it. I'd rather be in the country on twenty-five shillings. And what's 'appened to yer Aunt Ellie? D'you suppose 'e's kept her? That sort never do.'

Lily was crying. She feared and loved Mr Craigan.

'No that sort never do' he said, and smoked pipe and did not watch her crying. He got up and went inside and listened in to the wireless.

In morning Mr Dupret came to office. Soon Mr Archer came into his office.

He said good-morning sir and said how was the Chief and Mr Dupret said they hoped to move him into country tomorrow after-noon. Archer said change was bound to do him good and when he got to country home he would be different man altogether and would come back nine years younger.

'In the meantime' he said 'I think we are carrying on very nicely with you at the helm Mr Dupret. It's being a most interesting time for all of us, sir, working together as the team we shall be when you take over the old ship.'

Mr Dupret said crew would be very different when he was captain, would be more able seamen in it, and he could not help laughing at this and Mr Archer tittered.

Then he looked serious and said: 'Look here, Archer,' and Archer said yes sir, 'you know I didn't touch on the subject of Tarver's having another draughtsman when I was last in Birming-ham three months ago but I think we ought to see how the land lies about it now.'

Archer said he thought time was ripe. Mr Dupret said he did not want to go too far with old Bridges, after all, he said, Tarver is still subordinate to the old man and must be while Bridges is still works manager, but that was no reason why Tarver should not have one, he said.

'We've lost several orders through it, Mr Dupret.'

Of course, Mr Dupret said, Tarver can't get his drawings out when he's understaffed. But Bridges must not be offended, or rather must be offended as little as possible. What did Archer think Walters thought about it?

'Of course' said Mr Archer, 'Mr Walters is a first class engineer, or was, and you know as well as I Mr Dupret that he's probably done more for the old firm than anyone – always excepting your father, sir. But I cannot get on with him, heaven knows I've tried, but his methods are not mine, his slowness grates on a nature like mine Mr Dupret. I should certainly not like to try sounding him on the matter.'

'No, I haven't asked you to.'

'Precisely, precisely, but I was afraid perhaps you were expecting me—'

Mr Walters came in. He was loud-voiced this morning.

'Good-morning Dick, how's your father?'

Why should he call me Dick, young Mr Dupret said in his mind, his familiarity was jovial but then he went on thinking any joviality was offensively familiar and was smiling at that while he answered Mr Walters his father was being taken down to country day after tomorrow.

Walters said they were all looking forward to seeing Mr Dupret back amongst them, which angered young Mr Dupret. Then they talked about business. Soon Walters began looking at Archer, expecting him to go and later Walters was glaring at him, but still Archer stayed on, very self conscious, till Mr Walters went off and was first to leave.

Young Mr Dupret saw this and dismissed Archer and was miserable and annoyed at both of them.

Another day and he was talking to Mr Archer about how Bridges would take idea of another draughtsman for Mr Tarver. He said he was not afraid of old Bridges and had taken man off lavatory door just to show Mr Bridges only that. And was also another reason. He thought it had interfered with reasonable liberty of men in the works. He said he thought they would work better for being left alone with as far as possible. After all, he said, it was comfortable factory and the shops were as safe as they could be.

Mr Archer replied yes, they had been very lucky in matter of accidents, but for the one they had had in iron foundry some months back.

'What accident?' said Mr Dupret sharply.

'Why, sir, a wire rope parted and one end in coming down narrowly missed a man.'

'When was this? Why wasn't I told?' Mr Dupret rose from out of chair.

'Three months ago I think sir. I only heard the other day and I didn't mention it to you as of course I thought Mr Bridges would have reported it to you.'

'This is disgraceful, I didn't even know of it!' Mr Dupret was furious. 'What happened?'

'The wire rope parted, sir, and nearly caught an iron moulder called Craigan. Of course it would have killed the man if he had met it.'

'Of course, yes. Why didn't Bridges tell me?'

'Mr Bridges certainly should have reported the matter. I did not mention it as I felt he was sure to have done so.'

'I suppose he thinks I'm a back number and mustn't be told what's going on. What if he'd killed what's-his-name?'

'He is getting an old man now I'm afraid, Mr Dupret, and he doesn't go round to see for himself that things are in a proper condition.'

He thought to himself yes, yes that was it, hush it up and think he wouldn't get to hear of it, incompetent old loafer, he'd see who was the boss, he'd teach him. Where was Walters? He'd let him see what he thought. He'd show them in their dotage they weren't still kings of old castle and they couldn't impose on him as they'd done on his father. Where was Walters? But perhaps he had better wait till he had calmed down. Yes, he would wait till tomorrow.

'All right, Archer,' he said, and Archer went out delighted.

Had anyone ever heard anything like it, young Mr Dupret shouted to himself, serious accident and no word about it said to head of the business. That swine Bridges. Damn them.

Soon as hooters in these factories sounded for dinner hour young man took his dinner over to where Mr Craigan sat every dinner hour eating bread and meat. This young man was in great state of agitation. He spoke quickly and was saying Andrew (foreman in iron foundry shop) had been at him again, it was persecution, Andrew had said he was used to getting eight of those brackets he was doing now to the five he was getting from him. But he knew, he said, Andrew was lying there as last time any had been off that pattern Will, who was in thick with Andrew, had done not more than four with no word spoke to him. He was saying to Mr Craigan Andrew was dead against him, lord if was another job going he'd go to it quick enough, and he'd like to see Andrew do eight off that

272

pattern himself, he'd have eight wasters, you'd see, when they came to be cast. Anyroad, he said, if it was possible for a man to do eight it was a day work job anyway, was no bonus or piece work on that job. It wasn't right, he kept on saying, it wasn't right.

Mr Craigan said to go back and do what the foreman told him. When you were young you had to go about and into different shops to learn the trade, but he had not been in this foundry long, which was good shop for experience in general work. Besides that, Mr Craigan said, was no work going just now, and he didn't want to be out of a job, surely.

'You go back and do what the foreman tells you,' he said, and soon this young man said well he would see how it was going to turn out, and if Andrew had in mind to go on dogging him and making it misery for him to work under him or no.

'You go on back,' Mr Craigan said, 'in my time foremen 'ave asked me to do a number more than eight off patterns similar to what you're workin' off.' He said no more and then this young man went away.

Mr Craigan sat there all the hour as he did always and when hooters sounded once more in these factories to tell men was only five minutes before work, he went to gate to put his check in, which he did. He went over then to drinking water tap. It happened Tupe was there. Stream of men was coming through gate. They put in their checks. Tupe was very angry. He had no money left for beer and it angered him to drink water. No one would lend him money. Mr Craigan waited till he was done and then took white enamelled cup which hung down from nail on the wall and which Tupe had been drinking from. He rinsed it out. Mr Tupe saw this and for benefit of men who were coming in he began joking about Mr Craigan rinsing cup out. But he hated Mr Craigan, and, from crowd of men being about, anger rose in him and he made personal injury to himself out of Mr Craigan's rinsing cup out. Then veil passed on his eyes and he shouted insults though he did not mention Mr Craigan's family. Men stood round. Mr Craigan meantime was drinking water. When he was done he rinsed cup out and went away. As he went through the door into factory he said 'ow do to one who was standing with other men there. When he was gone all turned backs on Tupe.

*

Mr Dupret, after he had waited three days, dictated letter to Mr Bridges in Birmingham. He dictated with many pauses for he was not used to it, but he wanted all London office to know what he had put in this letter.

'Dear Mr Bridges,' it was, 'I have just learned of an accident which happened in the iron foundry some months back which might have caused serious injury or cost the life of a moulder named, I think, Craigan. I am sorry that you should not have notified me re this matter. In future I would be glad if you sent me a full report in the event of similar occurrences. Yrs faithfully,' and he signed name after that and had office girl to type managing director under signature. He was pleased with letter as being very restrained.

So soon as Mr Bridges read it he telephoned to Mr Walters in London. When Mr Walters came to telephone he asked him had he heard anything about letter which he had just got from young Dupret and Walters said no. What tomfoolery was it now, Mr Walters asked? Mr Bridges said it wasn't tomfoolery, news of today was that he was resigning. Mr Walters said come now Arthur. Mr Bridges said he was and Mr Walters said what, Dick? and Bridges said no, Arthur Bridges was sending for his cards after fifty-four years' work. Walters said what was it for God's sake, and Mr Bridges said listen to this and read young Mr Dupret's letter to him. 'Managing director, d'you get that rightly' screamed he down telephone. Mr Walters said bloody cheek. He said he would speak to young fool now about it and rang off then, leaving Bridges wildly talking.

Saturday afternoon. Lily Gates and Bert Jones went out together.

'Old Mr Craigan was on at me' she said, 'the other night about our going out together.'

'On at you was 'e? What did he say about me?'

' 'E didn't say anything about you. It was all about my Auntie Ellie.'

'What did she do?'

'She ran away with a groom, yes, when she was married.'

'What's that got to do with you and me? Are you going to run off with some other chap when we're married?'

They kissed then.

'Go on' he said, 'don't listen to that old cuckoo.'

' 'E's been like a father to me Bert.'

'Is that any reason why 'e should 'ave you all to 'imself?'

'D'you really want to 'ave me?'

They kissed.

'Yes,' she said. She drew a little back from him. ' 'E said some terrible things.'

'What did he say then?'

'I don't know, not what you might like put into words. But to one who knowed him!'

' 'Ow old are you? Are you still a kid?'

'What d'you mean?'

'D'you mean to tell me 'e can frighten you into trembles just by talking about something else to you?'

' 'E never says much in the ordinary way of things you see.'

'You're a girl' he said, 'I suppose that's how it is. But we're respectable. I don't see what 'e's got against me. If my father and mother lived in Birmingham I'd 've taken you to see 'em long before now. We've been out to take tea with my mother's sister. And I've often said, often 'aven't I now, that I'd like you to come to Liverpool to see the ma and dad. I'd better go and see your old man, shall I?'

'No, Bert, no you mustn't go and see 'im.'

'Well what about your father?'

'Oh dad, 'e does what Mr Craigan tells 'im.'

'And so do you from what I can see of it.'

Moodily together they walked. Revolt gathered in her.

Later she was saying, exalted:

'Yes we're different to what we were, we've a right now to know things and choose for ourselves. Time was when a girl did just what her parents told 'er and thought herself lucky to do it, yes but we're different now. Why shouldn't I go out with you and 'ave a good time on me own? 'E's gettıng old, that's what it is. Of course I'm fond of 'im, 'e's been like a father and mother to me since my mother died when I was born so to speak, but I've worked for 'im ever since I was old enough, yes I've earned the right to think for myself. I cooks for all of them, 'im and dad and Jim Dale that lives with us as a boarder.'

'Well, I mean, you're a 'uman being aren't you?'

'Yes, girls now can pick for themselves. It's not like it was in the old days. Yes, I've chosen and 'e can say what 'e likes.'

Under this hedge again they kissed. Later again she was saying: 'Oh Bert we shan't be like the others shall we dear,' and he said if Duprets didn't appreciate him he would move some place where he was appreciated. And was a place he had written to, had got friend when they were boys together from Liverpool there, who would put in word for him and was more chance there, for Duprets was old fashioned, you couldn't get on in it. And when 'flu had been so bad January they had sent him out to that very firm with a fitter to put job up and manager there had said kind things to him, 'you should 'ave 'eard 'im,' said he. Lily Gates, listening, saw him as being foreman one day soon.

Old Mr Dupret lay in bed and as, day by day, he said a little more, so the hopes of each one in his house were raised little by little. Mrs Dupret even was becoming her old helpless self again. In the past he had always done all her thinking for her, then, while he had been so ill, she had been forced into being practical to a certain degree, and now, as he seemed to become daily more and more competent to deal with what was about him, so her sanity, what there was of it, so it ebbed and she was drifting back again to the gentle undulations of her spirit which heaved regularly with her breathing like the sea, and was as commonplace.

One day even he called for his letters. Of the first six letters they opened for him one was from Walters, one of his weekly reports. After describing the progress of several orders Walters went on to say how well Dick was doing, only that he had slightly overstepped the bounds of his authority when he had told Bridges to take that man off the lavatory door. But perhaps Mr Walters wrote, Mr Dupret himself had authorized it. After reading this Mr Dupret sent for Walters and a stenographer.

He was never so well again.

The next day Walters arrived and Mr Dupret had strength enough to dictate and sign a letter in which he ordered a different man to be put on at the lavatory door to check the men in and out. He whispered to Walters, when he had signed, that Dick's having done that must have made Bridges very angry, 'who is so young for his sixty years,' Mr Dupret whispered with a sly smile and then lay back and shut eyelids over his eyes. Thus Mr Walters was unable to tell him of the letter his son had written to Bridges because the old man was so visibly exhausted. Even if the doctor had not come in at that moment and ordered him out, he would have crept out then.

Walters went back to London, by Birmingham. He called at works on his way. He gave Bridges that letter from the chief and told him old man was very bad, he said it looked to him he might be dead any time now. Bridges said nonsense. His father, he said, had gone that way, but would be about again soon like his father had been, you'd see. And that letter was just what he wanted, said he, this would show young chap he wasn't cock of the roost yet. Had he told him about young chap's last effort, Mr Bridges asked, but Walters, eyes dimmed, said no, what manner of use was in talking of that to a dying man. 'He was a grand fine man,' Mr Walters said, 'a grand man,' in his dull voice. 'Is 'e as sick as that?' said Mr Bridges.

# 8

She lay, above town, with Jones. Autumn. Light from sky grew dark over town.

She half opened eyelids from her eyes, showing whites. She saw in feeling. She saw in every house was woman with her child. In all streets, in clumps, were children.

Here factories were and more there, in clumps. She saw in her feeling, she saw men working there, all the men, and girls and the two were divided, men from women. Racketing noise burst on her. They worked there with speed. And then over all town sound of hooters broke out. Men and women thickly came from, now together mixed, and they went like tongues along licking the streets.

Then children went into houses from streets along with these men and girls. Women gave them to eat. Were only sparrows now in streets. But on roads ceaselessly cars came in from country, or they went out into it, in, out.

Smell of food pressed on her. All were eating. All was black with smoke, here even, by her, cows went soot-covered and the sheep grey. She saw milk taken out from them, grey the surface of it. Yes, and blackbird fled across that town flying crying and made noise like noise made by ratchet. Yes and in every house was mother with her child and that was grey and that fluttered hands and then that died, in every house died those children to women. Was low wailing low in her ears.

Then clocks in that town all over town struck three and bells in churches there ringing started rushing sound of bells like wings tearing under roof of sky, so these bells rang. But women stood, reached up children drooping to sky, sharp boned, these women wailed and their noise rose and ate the noise of bells ringing.

But roaring sound came in her ears and a sun, dark half cold, pressed onto her face. Bert kissed her. She woke. She heard tinkling sound of a pebble in a can which boy was dragging along path. Till all women she remembered, to each one a child, and she clung to man and said she had dreamed, had dreamed, dreamed.

And then in bed, after, rigid, she cried in her, I, I am I.

I am I, why do I do work of this house, unloved work, why but they cannot find other woman to do this work.

Why may I not have children, feed them with my milk. Why may I not kiss their eyes, lick their skin, softness to softness, why not I? I have no man, my work is for others, not for mine.

Why may I not work for mine?

Why mayn't they laugh at my coming in to them. Why is there nothing that lives by me. And I would do everything by my child in the morning and at evening, why haven't I one? I would work for him who made child with me, oh day and night I'd be working for them, and get up in the night to feed him and in morning to get father's tea. I would be his mother, he his father, why have I no child?

Lord give me a child that I might wash him, feed him, give him life. Yes let him be a boy. Give him blue eyes, let him cling to me with his hands and never be loosed from me. Give him me to love that I'm always kissing him and working for him. I've had nothing of my own. Give him me and let him be mine, oh, oh give me a life to work for, and give me the love of him, and his father's.

Young Mr Dupret sat in their country house picking nose.

Why, he said in mind, why could not the old man die? Of course was gratitude and all that of sons to fathers but, old mummy, why couldn't he die. He had made mother's life misery to her, he had never done anything for him but to pull him up, all the time, taking him away from school, and again, little things, whole time. Then to pretend collapse, question was if he wasn't just shamming, when dinner party for Hannah was to come off, so it had to be cancelled. And how did fathers expect sons to learn business without making mistakes? Now after what had been done he couldn't go back to Birmingham. He couldn't look Bridges face to face.

How pleased Bridges would be.

He wasn't, he said again in his mind, going back to business till old man thought better of it. Besides mother wanted him. And what picture she had made of him and herself and of father with that ridiculous harlot. To put her into bedroom where he lay and all of them waiting outside – disgusting, filthy, revolting. He'd made that plain to her and it seemed to be telling on her. She mustn't do that again, or something like it. Pity was the old man did not get rush of blood to head and die of it, malicious old figure head.

Doctors said was no hope for him now. He felt he could go up now to room and say 'die, old fool, die.' Trouble was of course he was not an old fool, but clever like the devil.


Mr Bridges went down through works in Birmingham till Tupe he found.

'What about that Craigan?' Mr Bridges said.

'What about 'im?' Tupe said.

'What I want to get at is' said Mr Bridges, 'is what happened when that wire rope gave some time back.'

'Nothin' didn't 'appen.'

'Didn't it come down somewhere by Craigan?'

'I know it daint,' Mr Tupe said. 'It broke sure enough but there weren't much strain on it that moment and it wouldn't've bruised 'is arse if it 'ad fetched 'im one. But God strike me 'andsome if 'e didn't raise 'is ugly old dial an' start blubberin' an' made such a 'ullaballoo as if 'e might be dead, or the only one in the shop. That's 'im all over.'

'So it wasn't nearly all over with 'im.'

'All over with 'im? No! But it would've been a good thing for this factory if it'd caught 'im and so killed 'im. There's only one man in that shop by 'is way of looking at it and that's 'im. There's always trouble between 'im and Andrew (that was foreman in iron foundry shop in this factory). You listen to me, sir, the men'll go to 'im before they go to the foreman, it's God's truth I'm telling you. There'd be 'alf as much more work done again in there if 'e weren't in there. 'E's a trouble maker, like you find in all factories, but there ain't been a place I've worked in where there's been the like of 'im.'

'E's the best moulder I've got. I'd give £100 for another like him.'

' 'E may be a good enough moulder, Mr Bridges, but look 'ow slow 'e is. 'E works to suit 'is own convenience, not the firm's.'

Mr Bridges was moving off.

' 'Ow's the gaffer, sir, if you don't mind me asking you,' Mr Tupe said to change subject of conversation and because he could not abide seeing Bridges going away.

'He's pretty bad. The young chap is down there with 'im, and aint been to work this week. It looks bad.'

'Well, I don't know,' said Tupe, cunning, 'that dandy 'e daint ever go to work, do 'e!' Mr Tupe said and Bridges, laughing, went away.

'I knows what the old man likes, it's butter, not margarine, an' I gives it to 'im,' Tupe said, in his mind, rejoicing.

Later Mr Bridges sat in chair in his office.

Mr Bridges in his thinking and in most of his living was all theatre. Words were exciting to him, they made more words in him and wilder thinking.

Sometimes liquid metal foundrymen are pouring into moulding box will find hole in this, at the joint perhaps, and pour out. Sometimes stream of metal pouring out will fall on patch of wet sand or on cold iron, then it will shower out off in flying drops of liquid metal. To see this once or twice perhaps is exciting. But after twice, or once even, you just go to stop hole up where metal from box is pouring.

So with Mr Bridges.

You were to him speaking, and he began quietly answering, then, suddenly, he was acting, sincere in feeling, but acting, and words were out pouring, fine sentiments fine. At first you said, 'fine old man' in your mind, at last you were thinking only how to plug him. And with him this was not only with his talking, it was also in his silent thinking.

So in his thinking he thought now Mr Dupret is dying. He thought how he'd worked fifteen years for Mr Dupret. 'And never a cross word between us.' He began now in his thinking. He made Mr Dupret into angel beaming from sky, he saw Mrs Dupret and all their servants weeping in front parlour. He saw slavey bring Mrs Dupret cup of tea from the kitchen, 'from humblest to the highest' he was saying in his thinking, without her ever having asked for a cup. He was seeing doctors, great surgeons going in and out of room where the Chief was lying. Inside he for life was fighting. Mr Bridges thought then how all had to come to it, 'great and small, King and navvy.' He thought one day he would die, the wife would die.

And he thought then, sobering, he was too old to get another job and what would happen when young Dupret was head of business? And he couldn't afford to retire, wife had made him spend all the salary, were hardly no savings. What would happen to them? But then he thought the Chief was sure to put someone older as partner to young chap, or adviser, or trustee. You couldn't put kid like that at head of business, government wouldn't allow it. No, he thought, forgetting grieving.

Young Mr Dupret sat at bottom of garden down by where flowed river Thames. Autumn was about. Down this river leaves came floating on the water, yellow leaves, and with each coming of the wind yellow leaves left trees and came floating down on to the water, quietly settling on the Thames. So now thoughts settled three by three in his mind and soon he thought no more but as river Thames slipped away to the sea so drifted into sleeping.

Sunshine was pale. So drifted into sleep. Yet came party from Maidenhead in launch up the river, men and women, a silver launch. Laughter came like birds from women in it. It came on slowly and he opened eyes and it went by, this laughter reaching him. He stretched and watched it go. Laughter from it fluttered back to him and then in wide circle launch turned leisurely and came back past him and he thought why did they turn it there. Why did they turn it there he thought and then man on launch played dance tune from the wireless they had on it and it went on down with stream till he could see them no more but still hear them, then he could not hear them any more.

Women were on that launch, he envied the men. They would be back at Maidenhead for tea, he thought.

He thought and saw in his mind was no good his staying here with father getting no better nor any worse, and he saw what he most needed now was the company of women, like on that silver launch. Hannah. He thought he would go back to London. Also mother needed rest, he would try and bring her with him.

Again he thought was no use in struggling against that one defeat with Bridges. He would go back to work, and if Bridges and Walters mentioned man being put on at lavatory door he would tell them just what he thought. It was hollow triumph of theirs he thought and he would show them just how hollow. It would not be long now before he showed them.

He shook afternoon from off him and went back into house.

Still flowed river Thames and still the leaves were disturbed, then were loosed, and came down on to water and went by London where he was going, by there and out into the sea.

Mr Craigan with Joe Gates and Dale that was his mate in iron foundry, these sat at supper and Lily brought food in to them. Happiness moved with her where she went. Yet Bert was not going out with her that night, he had business. Yet in all she did showed happiness.

Dale wanted a knife, but, getting up from table, for himself fetched it.

And Gates asked to pass bread. Lily stretched for this, but Mr Dale leaned, he pushed bread forward over to him.

When plate of meat was eaten he handed plate to her and Craigan's that was next him.

When supper was over he fetched beer. The two old men had settled in chairs and were smoking. He said then to Miss Gates if she was going out tonight. She said not tonight. He said would she care to go to the movies? She said she didn't mind. They went off.

When they had got seats even at cinema he said nothing, like he always did say nothing. She for this was grateful and sat apart from him in her seat in glory of secret happiness. He felt this and he was miserable. She was so grateful to him and he said nothing and she hardly watched film, she thought so of Bert.

So.

# 9

Hannah Glossop.

Her father also had been sick and she had gone home, in country, over the weekend. Doctor had motored down from London to see her father. That night his chauffeur had been watching machinery which made electric light for this house in country. He watched too close, caught in fly-wheel he was killed.

She had never seen him but when she heard she cried. She cried all the weekend. Nothing had ever been near her before. No one had ever been badly hurt near her.

They said: 'darling, but you never saw the poor man.'

She said: 'I know,' and cried.

They said: 'darling, the doctor's providing for his family.'

She said: 'I know,' and cried.

'You never saw him, he can mean nothing to you,' they said to her, and she said again and again, 'to think of his dying!'

She cried all weekend, and she got quite weak. Doctor became quite worried over her. At last he told her mother was nothing physical the matter with her he was sure. What really was wanted he said was for something to do to be found for her, some work for her to do he said.

Her mother said work? What work could she do? It was true, she said, she had enjoyed enormously General Strike when she had carried plates from one hut to another all day, that was true enough, but what work could she do? Doctor said of course to be married would be the best thing for her but 'in the interim' he thought some kind of work was what she wanted, and he went away with hired chauffeur.

Another night. She had cleared table after supper. She went off out.

Jim Dale stayed a little, then he got up.

'Where you goin' Jim?' Mr Gates said.

'To the boozer,' and he went off out.

'Goin' to the boozer, did you 'ear that?' said Gates to Mr Craigan, 'that's what she's doing, she's drivin' a good lad to go and wet 'is troubles. 'E daint ever use to go before. And 'e's a good lad. Why can't I give 'er a clout?'

Mr Craigan was silent.

'It's wicked I reckon,' Mr Gates said. 'Ah and she gave him a short week the other week, that day when Arthur was singing and he put on his coat and went out. An' she don't wash up of an evening even, but leaves it till morning. She's got too much money, that's what it is, and you can wager she pays for Bert Jones into the movies.'

Mr Craigan put wireless earphones over his head.

'You and yer wireless,' Gates softly said, 'it's enough to make anyone that lives with you light 'eaded, listening like you might be a adder to the music. I'll go and 'ave one,' he said. He got up, 'I'll go to the boozer and 'ave one.'

Mr Gates went to public, to public where Tupe was.

Tupe drank with Gates and Gates with Tupe. 'Yes,' said Mr Tupe finishing story, ' 'e said to her, them are one and nine.'

'Them are one and nine, 'e said to 'er,' Gates chimed, and this story was done. He drank of his beer in pot.

'Ah,' he said easing trousers, 'that's the 'ang of 'em. Females is like that right enough. Take our wench. What do she do with the money?'

' 'Ow much d'you give 'er Friday nights?'

Mr Gates drank again.

'Mind, I'm not askin' as some would,' confidentially Mr Tupe said, 'I'm not Paul bloody Pry.'

Because Mr Gates was a little drunk, he leaned, he whispered.

'Strike!' Tupe said, 'You give 'er all that much?'

'Ah!' said Mr Gates flattered, 'we daint ever stint in our 'ouse.'

'Stint!' said Mr Tupe, 'I wonder 'er wouldn't choke you with grub on that money.'

'I never did hold with stintin' the grub, nor Craigan daint.'

'Nor I do. But on that money my old woman'd keep three kids as well and them'd ave more'n enough to eat. It's wicked, Joe, 'er's twistin' yer.'

'Twistin' is 'er?'

'All that money and 'er says it goes in grub. You can bet it daint. I give our old woman three bob less'n that and there's enough an' more to eat in our 'ouse, an' 'er gets 'er own clothes and anything for the 'ouse.'

Mr Gates banged fist then on table.

'I'll wager she pays for Bert Jones into the movie.'

'Why in course she do. Look 'ere Joe, what's Craigan at in your 'ouse.'

'It ain't my 'ouse, it's 'is'n.'

'What's 'e at, anyroad.'

In another public Mr Dale alone sat about, not drinking.

'What d'you mean, what's 'e at?'

'Do 'im pay 'er Friday nights,' Mr Tupe said.

'I think e' do,' said Mr Gates. They talked and Gates confided more in Tupe who got mysterious more and more. Each spoke in broader country accent they had come from to Birmingham, speaking louder.

Getting more drunk Gates forgot seriousness and said what good thing that Dale went to pub, which he did not do before, it would anger Mr Craigan. He was good lad, Gates said, he did not expect you to do your own and three others' work, like some expected. A drop of beer would do him good, say who would water was lion's drink. But Craigan now, if you looked up two moments at work he was down your throat, and then in evenings, in their house it was like being in a hearse with wireless to it: 'Dirty ice-faced 'ermit,' Gates said, holding sides, he was laughing at own image in a glass, ' 'e'd listen to the weather reports so long that 'e wouldn't tell what it was doin' outside, rainin', snowing or sleet.'

Few young men go to public houses in Birmingham, then, only when they are married. So when Mr Dale went he was alone, nor did he want to talk.

Mr Gibbon said after he had done the Holy Roman Empire he felt great relief and then sadness at old companion done with. Mr Dale wanted to feel relief but felt only as if part of him was not with him, and sadness of a vacuum.

Griping sorrow was in void in him, but felt he could draw into him all winds of air for sympathy with him, that he must take hold on someone and clutch him so he would not go away and say all the sadness that was in his heart to him, and suck the sympathy back from that one.

But then he could not do all that (what would people think of him?) so he went to where was warmth and noise, were many people and talking, nor did he drink but sat over pot of beer hoping to be distracted.

– This is substance of what he wanted, though he did not know what he wanted.

Also young Mr Dupret was restless so he came to London, and Miss Glossop also came to be distracted.

They met at dinner party. They sat next each other. She did not remember him but soon they were talking. And from their mouths this time went words that seemed like to sink into each other's eyes.

Soon he was saying what trouble parents were to their children and she got very interested.

(She thought mother was real cause of her not getting married. She would not let her do anything, when she enjoyed washing up – which she had never done but three times at picnics and the General Strike. She blamed mother for uselessness feeling she had just now, and but for that useless feeling she would not have cried when chauffeur was killed. So she got very interested.)

Then he said how his father was dying now, and how sad it was. How he had had to drag mother up here away for a rest. He said the doctors told them would be months before he died yet. Now bending her face to his she shone out feeling over him.

'It's so awful,' she said, 'I can't get used to the feeling of death. A doctor came to stay with us last week. His chauffeur got caught up in the thing that makes our electric light. He was killed. Poor man, he was dead at once and its so awful to think that it can happen to anyone. Of course its different for old people because they're old, but young people like us, we might go and die any time.'

They talked so, all through dinner, and hostess noticed. She thought in her mind young people didn't play the game nowadays but talked only on one side of them from soup till dessert if they were interested. 'Mr Dupret has talked to Hannah all through dinner,' she said in her mind, 'and there's poor Di next him absolutely starved. All she can do poor child is to listen to what's going on across the grapes over on the other side of the table. Henry's just as bad as the other boy, he won't speak to her either.'

So he talked to her throughout dinner and when ladies went and port was sent round he did not join in conversation then, he did not talk because he was still finding more in feeling to say to her. When they got into cars to go on to this dance, they went in different cars. He sat silent thinking of presently when they sat out.

As she sat in car misery came back over her, he was so clever she thought, and she must have seemed so silly talking to him all dinner when it hadn't been much, not worth all the notice it attracted, their talk. Also she felt fat.

When he came out of cloakroom he waited for her at foot of stairs in crowd of people. When she came out of cloakroom she looked happy as happy. Why, thought he, can this be for me? He pressed forward to her. She let him take her upstairs.

She hardly knew he was there, truth to tell!! As they had got out of motor-car, there, in doorway, just going in, Tom Tyler, back from Siam. Tom Tyler!! 'Tom!' she had screamed, 'Annie!' He was here!

As they went upstairs, so the music came nearer to them from room was dancing in.

Chandelier hung from ceiling on a level with half way upstairs. It was like bell-shaped, and crystal, cut in all manners, formed it. As they went up he looked at chandelier. Chatter of people going up and down past him and he thought this great brilliant thing, you are like her only she is not so cold, but how like you are, he thought, all these people ascending, descending, and then, as first tones of dance music came down through chatter about, chandelier thrilled all through and light tumbled down along it, like it was a bell and notes trembling from the clapper.

So, as they went upstairs, and she had put her arm on his (she did not know it), so happiness tumbled down his spine. They went slowly, were many people. All these were talking as these two went further so dance music got much louder and louder, and so she glided up into bliss:

Your eyes are my eyes
My heart looks through

sang the band: bliss again to be in London, and Tom Tyler being here, just think of it, bliss, and she said to notes of xylophone, darlings, she said, darlings.

And again, this was to be lucky night, was no one to receive them and they danced straight out into the room, marvellous band, Roberts, and she was thinking Dick was Tom Tyler.

Your eyes, sang they again,

287

Your eyes are my eyes
My heart looks through

'Oh' she whispered, 'Oh' and he felt quite transported.

Just then Mr Dupret in sleep, died, in sleep.

''Ow are ye Albert?'

'Middlin' Aaron. The sweat was dropping from off me again last night from the pain.'

'Them,' said Mr Connolly nodding to group of men, (it was lunch hour in Dupret factory and men sat about) 'them tell me the old gaffer am dead.'

'Ah, he died in 'is sleep. I can't say it makes a deal of difference to me, I ain't ever seen 'im only the once. How old would 'e be in your estimation?'

Mr Connolly said he had had fine innings and then they talked of young Dupret's age. They said he was twenty-six and didn't the old chap have him late on in life, seeing he was seventy-eight when he died.

'It's the food and the comfortable life,' said Mr Milligan.

'It am' said Mr Connolly.

'Ah' Mr Milligan said, 'the young chap's no older than Bert Jones there that is just turned twenty-six.'

When Mr Dupret came back to office in London Mr Archer went in to him.

'Mr Dupret, sir' he said, 'the office have asked me to come on behalf of them all to convey their condolences in your bereavement, which is also ours, sir, but to a smaller degree of course. It is an honour I very much appreciate, if I may say so, in that I did not have the – the honour to work under him as long as some who have been in this office all their lives. But every day we were here we were learning from him sir, every day, I am sure no one knows that better than I do. It was a pleasure to work for him Mr Richard, always a kind word for everyone. I remember once as I happened to be sharpening a pencil he came up behind me without I heard him. He put his hand on my shoulder and said, "Archer, go on as you are going on now and you will be all right!" I don't think I shall ever forget that, Mr Dupret, as long as it pleases our common father to spare me. The Lord giveth and the Lord taketh away, sir.'

Mr Dupret, embarrassed, said wreath they had sent looked very beautiful on the coffin. Archer went away delighted.

Mr Dupret thought how like father to say that to Archer and make joke for himself out of it in a wry way, knowing Archer would never see barbed end of it. How like too, to be always mistaken in his best men, good men like Tarver he thought nothing of while men like Bridges he exalted in his own manner, though without ever praising them.

'Well, Arthur, he's dead,'

'Yes' said Mr Bridges to Mr Walters.

'They weren't there when it happened,' said Mr Walters, 'he died all of a sudden with none of his own to hold 'is 'and.'

'Where was the young chap then? Wastin' up in town?'

'He took his mother up there, Arthur, to give her a change.'

'Yes, he's dead,' said Bridges.

'There was a fine man,' Mr Walters said, 'loyal to those under him, you knew where you were with him.'

'Yes,' cried Mr Bridges, 'yes and now we might be like in the desert with a pack of wolves as escort and at night when we lie down scorpions,' he cried, 'poisoned snakes for pillows.'

'Not so loud Arthur.'

'I don't care who 'ears me,' shouted Bridges clinging on to mantelpiece. 'I'd like to call 'em all in and say to 'em, we are like a flock that 'as lost its shepherd with the night coming on. I loved that man. Why, I'd 'ave laid down my life for 'im. And now where are we, tell me that? 'Ere, I'll tell you what he'll say. He'll say we're too old for our jobs. That gang in your office up there will be at 'im all the time, and what am I to do, I got nothing put by, if I can't 'old this job I'll have to go on the streets with the wife and die like any dog in a 'ole.'

'Arthur!' said Mr Walters.

'Aye,' Bridges was out of himself, 'aye and since I came 'ere I've built this side up stone by stone and made a job of it. Waller, of the O.K., said to me only a week ago standing where you are now, he said you turn out better work here than I've seen in the trade. Now there's a man of experience, mayn't I take part of that on myself?

No, it's now as I might be a 'orse or a dog turned off because their old man 'as died, or like an Indian widder woman that is burned beside 'er dead 'usband.'

'Well, there's other firms.'

'They wouldn't take us on at our age.'

Walters quietly said he would work for young Mr Dupret as he had worked for father.

'And so will I,' Mr Bridges said, abating, 'but you see what's coming to us, 'e's gone out of 'is way to make me a fool before my own men, you'll see,' (rising again) 'he'll bide 'is time till 'e can get us off without a pension, forcing us out of a living. And that's what comes to a man that 'as worked all 'is life for another. My bones in my body they ache all day now but when I've worn 'em out in 'is service 'e'll sell 'em as scrap to the rag and bone. That's 'ow it will be.'

'You ought to take a day or two off Arthur.' Then Mr Bridges began again at that, saying did he want him to starve right away. Suddenly he covered face in hands, he burst out into sobbing, and Walters sent for brandy.

Miss Gates went out in afternoon to buy food in shops and now was last sunshine of winter on the streets. She came into high road and trams went by her rocking, roaring sound came from them and sound of their bell like metals. Along line of shops which were on each side of this road women in dark clothes went in and out of them.

She passed by and black man passed by her. She had in mind to turn back and look at him. But she saw chest of tea in shop window. She stopped by it. She thought of film she had seen which was advertisement of a tea firm, she had seen in it black women that gathered the tea, and how delicate she had thought them and she remembered now, how delicate their arms and hands which did not seem touched by the hard labouring.

Were tins of pineapple in that shop window and she wondered and languor fell on her like in a mist as when the warm air comes down on cold earth; in images she saw in her heart sun countries, sun, and the infinite ease of warmth.

'Well, Albert,' said Mr Gates, who came to fetch chaplets, to Mr Milligan storekeeper, ' 'ow are you feeling?'

'Middlin', Joe.'

'Ah, and the old man's looking ill and all.'

'What – 'Tis 'im? Ah, 'e came by the other day and I said to myself, I said, that man 'as the shade of death on his face.'

'I said as much to Jim, when 'e went past. It's a shame there couldn't be a double funeral, the old gaffer and 'im.'

Mr Milligan laughed.

'Well, there's double weddings, ain't there,' cried Mr Gates 'and double beds bless my 'eart,' he said, 'all for the enjoyment of mankind, so why shouldn't we see two dirty sods put underground at one go off.'

'They buried the old gaffer some time back. I don't say I 'ad anything against the man. But it's marvellous the state these worryers get into, I don't reckon I'll be far out when I said Mr Bridges is done for.'

'Ah, and look at our foreman, Andrew there, 'e takes it 'ome with 'im. I'll wager 'is missus is a good moulder. I'll wager 'er 'as to listen to 'is troubles every night, 'ow this job blowed and that'n run out.'

'That's right. But, come to look at it, wouldn't Bridges and Tupe be all right in a 'earse together.'

Mr Gates did not relish this.

'I'd like 'im dead,' Mr Gates said carelessly. He meant Mr Bridges. He meant to keep off topic of Mr Tupe.

Milligan said indeed Tupe should be in a grave and Mr Gates asked for chaplets. When Mr Milligan came back he said to mark his words and that would be big changes in this factory soon. Yes, he said, they would see a lot different, whether for better or worse he couldn't say.

Well, Mr Walters said in his mind, I must try and like the young chap, and he came into Mr Richard's private office.

'Good morning, Dick.'

'Good morning' Mr Dupret said cordially. 'I hope you're well.'

'Pretty well thanks. But it's marvellous what the weather's been doing to people.'

'Yes, two or three of my friends are down with the 'flu. It's a wonder we're alive, Mr Walters.'

'Yes, it is that, and I'm worried about Mr Bridges, Dick. He's not as well as he ought to be, not by a long way. Everything seems to have got right on his mind lately. I shouldn't wonder if he didn't have a breakdown one of these days.'

'A breakdown?'

'Yes, he's right down on his luck. A good deal of it was your father dying as he did – (as he did? wondered young Mr Dupret) – and then he takes everything to heart very much. I think we ought to send him on a holiday.'

Mr Dupret said he was sorry to hear that and who would take over if he did go away.

'Cummings will take over.'

'What about Tarver, Mr Walters?'

'Cummings is senior to Tarver, Dick, it wouldn't do to put the younger man over the older one.'

'Wouldn't it give him a useful experience of running the works. After all, Tarver is our coming man isn't he, Walters?'

'Well Mr Dupret,' said Mr Walters, rage rising in him, 'I don't know that Tarver's got the all round knowledge necessary for a works manager.'

'What sort of a man is Cummings?'

'He's a real good man. He came to us as a lad and has been with us ever since. Mr Bridges has been bringing him on ever since he came here.'

'Then what sort of age is he?'

'He'd be round about fifty.'

'Rather a long time to be bringing along, isn't it Mr Walters?'

'Engineering isn't learnt in a day.'

'Well,' Mr Richard said importantly, 'I think I'll go down to the works for a day or two to see how things stand. I'm all for Mr Bridges going for a holiday but I don't quite see my way clear yet about his temporary successor.'

Hoity toity Mr Walters thought and why wouldn't he give him handle to his name, call a man 'Walters' who was old enough to be his father!

Mr Dupret picked up a letter.

'Why haven't these people had delivery yet?'

'There's been a heap of trouble in the iron foundry over that job, Dick. It's an awkward job, but they've pretty well got it weighed up now since I went down there and saw it.'

'Damn that iron foundry,' Mr Dupret said.

'Yes, I've said that many a time,' said Mr Walters. One sentence, like a bell, knolled in Mr Richard's mind, 'Cummings will take over,' sentence said confidently.

Lily came to go and meet Bert. She took short cut that was over piece of waste ground.

Night. Street lamps were lit over where she was going to. She walked across. She had done shopping and men had been fed at evening, now work was done and like as when gulls come and settle on the water so her spirit folded wings, so walked in quietness.

Night was mauve about her, mauve and cold. She only felt warmer.

So, wings folded, as the gull takes on motion of the sea, night flowed over her then in her.

Gathering coat she hugged arms round body and folded in night and buried face in it, in fur of her collar. And so containing it warmness rose in her, drowsed her mind, and came in little ball of warmth top of throat, behind her nose, breathed through her there, till she was drunk, and all of her was dyed in night.

She came nearer street lamps and then stumbled a little. Looking up she saw them, light sticking out from them, and as she came nearer so night left, excitement effervescing in her she put coat straight, and felt cold. When she stepped into cone of light of this lamp, night was outside and it might not have been night-time.

She met Bert at corner.

They kissed. Her warmth and his, their bodies straining against each other, became one warmth. Walking, his arm round her enclosed her warmth and his. So it came from his veins flowing into hers, so they were joined.

They walked from cone of light into darkness and then again into lamplight, nor, so their feeling lulled them, was light or dark, only their feeling of both of them which was one warmth, infinitely greater.

Tom Tyler was the life of the house-party. Before dinner he stood on his head; put a pin in the back of a chair and sitting on the chair leaned round it, bending his body into an arc and took the pin out in his mouth. Then when some other man did this, only not so quickly of course, Tom sent for a tumbler and filling this with water he put it on his forehead. He knelt down, he bent his body back in an arc from the knees, and soon was lying flat on his back with not a drop of water spilled, nor had he steadied the tumbler with his hands at any stage in the course of this delicate operation. No one could do it after him, many got soused with water in trying to do it, which only added to the general hilarity.

Hannah got quite hysterical with excitement.

Then he put an armchair in the middle of the floor and cushions at a little distance at the back of it, and he took a running leap and dived into the chair, turned a somersault on his head in it and landed with the chair onto the cushions. The chair was broken. That was a very good joke. Then they all played hunt the slipper.

All this was good clean fun. If anyone touched anyone it brought a bruise.

So it was all good clean fun. And when they were bored with hunt the slipper they sat in a circle, (Tom Tyler directed all this), and someone, man or woman was put in the middle and kept themselves very stiff and everyone, each one theoretically being for himself, everyone I say tried to push the person in the middle onto one of the others who were sitting. When that happened, amid screams, the person fallen on had to go in the middle. So boys fell across girls and then perhaps took a little time to get up, but it is quite true to say that there was nothing dirty in all this.

Hannah, for instance, did not even long for Tom to be pushed over her, nor did she even think of it, it was all – how shall I say, – all was like the clearness of an empty glass, with the transparency of light. Yet not transparent. You look into crystal globe and its round emptiness makes a core in it you can't see through, there is nothing there only the transparency is confused. That was like Hannah Glossop when someone wasn't talking to her, inoculating ideas.

When she went to dress for dinner she told maid she had never laughed so much in all her life.

Mr Bridges, on his leave, sat in sitting room of a lodging house at Weston. He was writing letter to Mr Walters. He looked up and onto the sea, grey under dark sky, incessantly moving, spotted with gulls. He had just written: What I won't wear about this place is seeing a big ship go down and then when you're sitting in the same place with nothing to do and not even a dog to speak to you see the same boat come back up again an hour later. There's times I could go loony wondering what it was up to.

What were they doing at Works, he thought? Young chap would be down there now, and most likely he had only given him the week off so he might play hell with the place while he was away. Some fathers had awkward children by God and to hand the whole show over to them when you were dead, it was like cutting the throat of a whole crowd of people.

What would Tarver be at?

Mrs Bridges came in then.

'She says it's sixpence for a bath!' she said.

'Sixpence, eh?' said Mr Bridges. 'You go tell her she's in competition. Tell her I can get a wash for nothing in the sea there and if she don't cut her prices she'll lose the order.'

'Oh, yes, you bathing in this cold.'

'You tell her I've bathed every Christmas Day since ever I could swim.'

'Why it aint November yet and you can't swim, you know you can't.'

'How'll she know that, eh? If it's going to cost us a tanner for a bath I'll wait till I get back to Brum before I wash the dust off me of this bloody 'ouse.'

Women, he thought, would you believe it, they'd ruin you. Yes, thought Mrs Bridges, and little he'd think of it if it was for a pint.

Cummings, he went on in mind, was a good man, he'd taught him all he knew, but he didn't like leaving works with him, not with Tarver and those sharks about. And he couldn't ring up again, he'd rung up twice this morning already. The waiting till you got back, that was the rub of it, was like having your arteries cut and watching the life blood spouting out.

Richard Dupret came late to that house-party. He arrived in middle of fish course at dinner. He had warned hostess was only train he could come by, having to work late that day in London; but yet, as he passed by open door of dining room to go and dress and saw brilliance of lights there and clash and glitter of women's dresses, and heard their laughing, he had a sickening in stomach.

Older woman asked hostess who was that young man that was arriving? and she said Richard Dupret.

'Sylvia Dupret's son?'

'Yes my dear. It was her husband who died not so very long ago.'

'Wasn't he very rich?'

'Yes very. Poor Sylvia it was quite dreadful for her, she was at the Embassy with a party when they telephoned through and Ian Lampson had to break it to her. Of course it wasn't altogether unexpected but the doctors had said he might linger on for months.'

'Didn't she stay by him at all then?'

'Oh yes, but she came up for a change.'

'She oughtn't to have left him, a woman shouldn't do a thing like that Grizel. It looks so bad.'

'Oh no, it's very unkind when you say a thing like that Katie dear. It was unfortunate I admit but I don't see how she could have helped it. He had been no more alive than a log for months.'

'Did he regain consciousness before the end?'

'Dear Katie, I don't know whether he did or not.' And they talked of something else, man sitting between them changed topic of conversation. But that woman thought obviously he had regained consciousness and that Grizel hadn't liked to admit it.

When our Richard came down, others had finished. The men even had done with the port. He ate alone, nervousness growing in him and served by footman that was anxious to get to his meal, so hurried Mr Dupret through his courses. Why did she have no flowers on table? thought he in interval of nervousness. When he had had glass of port footman announced him into the room where now all houseparty was concentrated. Shutting door behind him footman yawned in the passage and went quickly to supper. Now dinner table lay in empty room like a grave that has dead flowers on it.

Small hush was as Mr Dupret went to greet hostess. He shook hands with older people. Mary came up and then he was in midst of his contemporaries, was introduced to two or three, and then saw Hannah Glossop.

Mr Tyler went on with his plan of a game. It was like 'prisoner's base' only played in darkness and Mary, whose house this was, said they would take over the North Wing and turn out all lights, and play there.

All younger people went off. Walking with Miss Glossop Mr
Dupret had now lost feeling of nervousness.

After breakfast assembled women in one room, men in another.

Older man was saying he had only seen woodcock on the ground
once, which was by great bit of good fortune as he did not know
what made him look in that direction but there it was, on the
ground, twenty yards from him. He was saying this to Tom Tyler,
who upheld that conversation.

Mr Dupret thought that was how it was, once he had been going
upstairs with Hannah at a dance and chandelier which hung there
had trembled as it might be at sound of the band which was beginning to play, so light on that chandelier was beginning to move.
What difference is there, thought he, between my chandelier and his
woodcock, one or the other moved one of us? And yet how much
better if he could be excited at sight of woodcock on the ground for
excitement over chandelier was at light moving over it, caused
probably by someone stamping on the floor above. The woodcock
was on ground by no agency of man, its being there was a natural
phenomenon, and he thought his chandelier and how it moved him
was a spurious emotion.

He thought this was a parable. Darkness he thought was merely
opportunity for Tyler and Miss Glossop to play a game in, where to
him it would be another thing. That seemed centre of it all to him.
For in their games they sublimated all passions, all beliefs. That
was why Tom Tyler cut him out with Miss Glossop, who did not
care to talk. And so he saw these games they were always playing to
be charades of the passions. So was there no other way to her heart?

# 10

Leaving house-party Mr Dupret went to Birmingham. When he
heard Mr Bridges was already gone on leave he was glad. He did
not want to see Mr Bridges. Indeed, now he knew it was not for him
but Tom Tyler that Miss Glossop smiled and lilted, heart was out of
him.

So when he came he sent for Mr Cummings and just said he hoped everything was all right. Mr Cummings made no impression on his mind. When he had gone Mr Dupret sat on in office. He thought, and slowly tried to gather up energy inside him. At last he went up into Mr Tarver's office.

'Very glad to see you sir!'

'I'm sorry Mr Bridges is ill!'

'Yes, it's a shame he's bad.' (Mr Tarver was in great spirits this morning) 'But you mark my words squire,' he said, 'they'll all go together.'

'What on earth do you mean, they'll all go together?'

'Well you see Mr Dupret' said Tarver and he went red, 'I meant they were getting on, you can't be sixty-one and expect to feel on top of the world.'

'I don't want any intrigue Tarver,' Mr Dupret said in tired voice, 'we've all got to pull together or we'll be nowhere in no time.'

'You mustn't take what I say wrong, sir, we all work for the good of the firm, we all pull together, though we're all sorts and different sizes.'

'That's it,' said Mr Dupret, and felt like he was nurse at school for infants and surely this man Tarver was mad. Why did he call you squire?

'Mr Tarver, I thought when Mr Bridges came back I would suggest to him your having another draughtsman. And really if Bumpus is always getting ill like this we had better part with him.'

'Don't take Bumpus from me,' Mr Tarver said dangerously. He rose from his chair. 'I couldn't do without him, Mr Dupret, for God's sake.'

This one was pleased. The man had spirit. 'Right you are,' said he, 'I didn't know if you thought a lot of him, that's all. And I promise to get you another. Or rather you and Bumpus, and of course Mr Bridges will have to choose a further draughtsman between you.'

'It's been needed, I only said to the wife the other night I didn't see how I could go on short-handed like this with the new machine I'm bringing out. But with another man we'll eat it up colonel.'

Beaming he came up and shook Dupret by the hand.

Mr Dupret thought perhaps he was mad after all but enthusiastic anyway, not all words like old Bridges, and he was a young man,

Arthur thought well of him. Yes, damn it, he would show them and give Tarver pat on the back. So he asked Tarver if he was coming round works with him, and together they went round, Tarver visibly glad.

As they went round works, Mr Dupret and Mr Tarver, behind them was Cummings. He dodged behind machinery and everything they did he noticed, every time they stopped to look at something he took it to be complaints.

Mr Milligan, standing in gateway of stores department, saw him following and said in his mind who would believe it who did not know? Who would be in position of authority now, even to be storekeeper? You had to be strong man, nerves of steel, or it was more than your health would stand.

Didn't they make themselves ridiculous the way they behaved, look at Cummings, everyone in the place laughing at him so soon as he was gone by. That must have been a knock for him the young chap going round with Tarver. Yes, and their health couldn't stand it, some of them. Andrew, foreman in iron foundry, many a time worry was too much for him and he'd go off and sit in a corner where none could see him with his hands over his face. Was many would not believe that but with delivery, delivery always being shouted at you, in tricky work like iron founding were many foremen took their lives and those that didn't take them had their lives shortened by the worry. Andrew had been looking done up just lately, Mr Milligan said in his mind, and thought of when he himself was last in hospital.

Mr Dupret and Tarver came to iron foundry shop. 'Have they had many wasters here recently, Mr Tarver?'

'No, we've been very free of them for the last week or two. But they're slow in this shop colonel, terribly slow.'

'Well I suppose that's all right as long as they don't make bad ones.'

'You're right there Mr Dupret, but they ought to make sound castings quicker, like they do in other foundries.'

'Sometimes these people don't seem to be able to make good ones quick or slow. Do you remember a few weeks back—' and they talked of job which had given trouble. Dupret used what he thought was Mr Tarver's language.

'What d'you put it down to Tarver, ought we to have another

foreman?' nodding to Philpots who was busy and yet watching them, in corner of foundry shop.

'Andrew's all right,' said Mr Tarver, 'no it's the men he has to work with. You can't get old men to work fast squire, that's natural, and old men like Craigan keep the weight down.'

'Then why do we keep him on?'

'Mr Bridges says he couldn't do without him.'

'Well,' said Mr Dupret, 'I suppose Mr Bridges has his reasons,' and they moved off and into machine shop.

Mr Cummings darted into iron foundry. He went to Andrew Philpots.

'Did 'e say nothing to you Andy?'

'I didn't like to go and speak to 'im, I waited 'ere till 'e should come to me if 'e 'ad anything to say.'

Mr Cummings went off. What are they up to he asked in his mind. What is it?

'Well dear' Mrs Dupret said, 'did you go down to Birmingham today?'

'Yes,' said Mr Dupret.

'What's the matter, Dick, aren't you feeling well?'

'No, I'm feeling quite all right' said Mr Dupret lying, 'but the works are so depressing, it's all so incompetent. They are all such awful people.'

'Well from now on it's your own fault, darling, if you don't like them, isn't it? I mean you're head of the business now. When your father was alive you had to do things more or less under his super-vision but you are your own master now, aren't you dear? Still I expect the more you look into it you'll find your father right.'

'Yes. But it's not altogether the works. The fact is, I've gone crazy over a girl again.'

After Mrs Dupret had said what was fit and appreciative and had let him tell her that it was Hannah Glossop – he had told her some months ago only he'd forgotten that – he described Tom Tyler and the way she did not seem to notice anyone else.

Mrs Dupret comforted.

Mrs Dupret said that sort of man exercised a fascination over girls which soon wore off. 'He is young and fresh looking and full of spirits,' she said 'but they soon see there is nothing much in him after all.' She told him to keep away from Hannah a bit, above all not to run after her just now, and she proposed that they should have that little dinner party for her which they were to have had before his father fell ill. Hearing little of what she said, he went on about how the thought of her was perpetually running through his mind, and sometimes the thought of her came in spasms upon him, it made him feel quite ill, physically ill. Mrs Dupret said, 'poor darling,' and 'we'll see if we can't get her to dinner, shall we?'

Miss Gates. Now, as has been said, evenings were drawing in, now they could no longer go out in the evening, winter, or at most they allowed themselves one cinema in the week.

So it was often that she stayed indoors and Mr Jones began going to technical school where she sent him. Sitting at home with the family she darned their socks and mended clothes in the evenings, and Mr Craigan with her father and Jim Dale were there. Now again it seemed for Craigan like times when Lily had kept company with Jim. Their evenings were as they had been and that was comfortable for him.

She had begun saving and she made Mr Jones save. This was why she was so much quieter, but Dale thought perhaps those two were tiring of each other and soon they might quarrel, then she would come back to him again. So he took heart and went no more out in the evenings nor gave her much attention now he began to feel sure of her again, only Gates went more and more out and was often seen with Mr Tupe.

Mr Bridges put back receiver on its hook. He went back into sitting room of the lodging house at Weston. His wife asked him about the news. He said the young chap had just left works, he had had Cummings on the 'phone. Mrs Bridges asked if he had done anything?

'No, not a thing.'

'Well that's a bit off my mind.'

'How's that?'

'You know how I mean.'

'It's not what he does, he don't do anything, it's what 'e means to do Janie. And now the father's dead what's to stop him doing it.'

'How do you know what he means to do?'

'You can see it in 'is eye. He looks at me now and again with a look as if I'd murdered 'is best girl or got her be'ind a hedge.'

'You!'

'It's a vindictive somehow. That's why I shouldn't ever've come here. You'll see he'll use it some way against me.'

'But didn't Mr Cummings tell you nothing else just now?'

'Cummings? Ah, I was keeping the best for the end. The young chap wouldn't go round with Cummings, wasn't good enough for 'im, no he 'ad to go round the place with Tarver for everyone to see. What d'you make of that eh?'

Mrs Bridges shook head over that.

'Cummings said 'e went round after them but couldn't make out they'd said anything particular. That's a good man, Cummings. I wouldn't take £1,000 for 'im, not if I 'ad the choice. That's where it is. I ain't got the choice of me own men, I have to be told now if a man's a engineer or not.'

'Don't get talking so, Phil, young Mr Dupret ain't done nothing to you yet.'

'Ah, but what's 'e going to do? There's nothing that comes I can't see coming, all my life or I shouldn't be where I am. And Tarver? Aren't I as nice and easy with him as a man could be, cooing like a dove to 'im, yes, and I'd turn somersaults like other pigeons if that's what he preferred. Ah Janie I'm glad we're leaving for old Brum tomorrow. It's got on my nerves sitting here. But there's this to it, I feel grand, grand after this ten days.'

He went over and gave wife sounding kiss. She laughed: 'you get 'is girl behind a hedge!' she said.


# 11

Hannah Glossop stayed over into next day when rest of house-party had gone. All the men had gone back to offices but Tom Tyler, who was on leave from Siam. So she had him all to herself.

All afternoon went they for a walk across fields and she asked him what his life was. He was unpaid adjunct to British resident at Siam. He told about shooting they had and how you could get a game of squash racquets there. He said how once the resident's wife came down to official dinner with her dress back to front, and the difficulty he had had to let her know. The way he had done it was to turn his plate upside down and being a clever woman she had understood. Dropping suddenly to the intimate he said evenings there were marvellous, and between them they had got together quite a good little dance band at the country club.

He was bored with this walk because she made him do all the talking and was serious, but she – as sometimes on a ship when is sun and spray so do you see rainbows everywhere, on the deck, on wavecrests, so as he spoke wonder was round about all he said for her.

As soon as Mr Bridges had gotten back he went round works. ' 'Tis 'im' the men said when they saw him. He went round. He thought in his mind it was fine, fine to be back. 'The men have but to come to me when they're in trouble, I'm a father and mother to them,' he cried in his heart, 'aye, I am that.'

He talked long with Tupe, very hearty with him. Cummings came up then to greet him for Mr Bridges had gone straight into works when he was back. Loudly Mr Bridges met him. He said he felt fine, fine. He asked how things were and Mr Cummings said everything was going on all right. Then moving a few yards away so Tupe could not hear above the noise of lathes working in this shop Mr Bridges asked what about young chap? As heads of these two moved towards each other at that, men on lathes winked one to another, while Mr Cummings grew mysterious look on his face. He said he had only just heard, Tarver had come boasting to him he said, boasting the young chap was giving him another draughtsman. 'Our overheads won't stand it sir,' he said, though he did not know much about such charges.

Mr Bridges said: 'There's a grand thing to welcome you back.'

He stood silent.

'Another draughtsman, eh?' he said. He swore.

At last he said why couldn't Tarver have come and said a word to him when he got back, (forgetting he was but just arrived) no bit of friendliness in that man anywhere, it made life misery for you, why if you'd been so nearly dead you'd had a chat with Peter at the gate Tarver wouldn't say a word when you got back.

'Isn't 'e a beauty?' Mr Bridges said.

\*

That evening Mr Bridges went through works on the look out for trouble. Mr Tarver had not come to see him or ask him how he was. Bridges went through works on chance of finding someone to vent anger on.

That day Mr Bert Jones had one of his spells on him. Were days when he could not work, his mind was not in it. It was not that he couldn't concentrate because he was thinking of something else, but rather as if his mind was satiated by the trade he worked at, as if he had reached saturation point as day by day, year by year he did very much the same things with almost identical movements of arms and legs. So sometimes when you are working daze comes over you and your brain lies back, it rocks like the sea, and as commonplace.

So he stopped working.

'What's the matter with you Bert?'

'There aint nothing the matter?'

'Well come on then.'

But Mr Bridges came up behind. He made a row. Only that, he did not suspend him. But he relieved choking feeling he had in his chest. He went away satisfied.

Mr Jones worked for rest of evening without stopping. He felt like quite desperate.

That evening, half past five, and thousands came out of factories, the syrens sounding, and went home.

Mr Craigan, with Gates and Jim Dale, went out of Dupret factory together, when Mr Tupe came up with them. He walked with them. He said:

' 'Ow do you think the old man's lookin'?'

Mr Gates said holiday didn't seem to have done him much good. Anger rose in Mr Craigan at Tupe's coming up to them.

'Aint it a bloody shame' said Tupe, 'the way they try and drive a man of 'is age to the mad'ouse. Did you 'appen to see Tarver and young 'opeful goin' round together not above a week back? Well and now Tarver won't come and bid the old man good day when 'e gets back after goin' away for 'is 'ealth.'

' 'Ow d'you know, know all,' Mr Dale said.

'I knows young feller because 'e told me 'imself.'

'O he did, did 'e?'

'Ah, 'e did, and I don't reckon they've any right to treat an old man the way they're doin'. 'E's told me things. When a man gets on in years they should respect 'is age I reckon, what d'you say?' said he, turning to Mr Craigan. This one made no answer to him.

'Yes by rights that's what they should do' Mr Gates said, nervous.

'Ah, and 'e 'ad a row with young Jones, which wasn't nothing but those others trying to down 'im, that bein' a good lad' said maliciously Mr Tupe. Dale asked eagerly if he had suspended him. 'Suspend 'im' said Tupe, 'suspend a fine chap like that, not on yer life, 'e does the work of three in that shop.'

'Well 'e was suspended in the summer wasn't 'e?'

'Yes, 'e were suspended' said Mr Gates hoping to close conversation.

'Ah,' Mr Tupe said, 'and what was that but Aaron Connolly, I know the man, nothing's too low for 'im, I saw 'im go and tell Bridges 'imself Bert was in there, and being as it might be in front of witnesses, the old man 'ad no choice.' Here Mr Tupe had inspiration. 'That was why 'e daint suspend Aaron' he said triumphantly.

Mr Craigan went then to other side of the street and Dale followed him. Then at last Mr Gates followed them, because he feared Mr Craigan. Yet was he ashamed at leaving Tupe.

So came they home at evening. They went in to the house, they washed, and Lily had evening meal ready for them. Mr Dale was excited in his mind. He thought if Bert Jones was sacked chances were he would find no other job in Birmingham. Then he would leave the town, would have to, and go back to that home he said he had in Liverpool. Thought of this put Mr Dale in a good temper.

Lily began saying how Eames' child next door had grown. Mr Gates said Eames was poor sort of a man. But subject of the works was in Mr Dale's mind and he asked how much truth was there in this talk about old Bridges being crowded out.

'I don't know what 'e's told Tupey' said Mr Gates, 'but there's only men of 'is age and young men in that place, so trouble's bound to be between 'em, the younger lot trying to push the older out of the light. There's none that comes between 'em, speakin' of age. And the young chap's crazy like any lamb in the field.'

'He's not so crazy as some,' Mr Dale said, 'now take "our" Bert, that's the second time 'e's been suspended in four months.'

'Suspended! Where did you 'ear he'd been suspended? The old man daint suspend 'im' said Mr Gates.

Lily smiled. But Mr Craigan broke into conversation. He said:

'If I 'ad a son I wouldn't educate 'im above the station 'e was born in. It's hard enough to be a moulder and 'ave the worry of the job forty-seven hours in the week but to be on the staff, or foreman even, with the man above you doggin' at you and them under you never satisfied, like the young chaps never am nowadays, it aint like living at all. In course they're getting rid of Bridges like they'll get rid of me, seein' I'm an old man now. Another month and we'll be getting the old age pension Joe, and we'll get the sack then. Like Bridges will get the sack, seein' 'e's getting an old man, same as we.'

That same evening Lily Gates went out to meet Bert Jones.

When they met she saw for the first time white, cutting anger in him. He said they must get away, he said that! who had always been the one to draw back. They must go right off at once he said and anxiously she asked what the trouble was, for she knew him that he was not dependable worker. He said trouble? He said what was the matter with her who was so keen on their going and now, when he said they must go directly, wanted to know why?

'Aren't you on a line!' she said pleasantly.

He told her about Bridges, but she thought when they were married he would be quieter, it would be the responsibility would make him so. She told him he must not worry about that. Indirectly then they talked of their going like it might be tomorrow, yet both questioned in their hearts if they would ever go. Then she quieted him. They kissed. She made him talk of other things. Soon she felt him contented again. So again they let their time slip by.

Mr Craigan felt he must act. Tupe now was so thick with Joe – it looked bad his having the face to come up and talk to them – and Lily with her Bert Jones. All this in images appeared in his mind before him.

Home was sacred thing to him. Everything, his self-respect was built on home. If he had no home to go back into an evening then he would have to move to another town where none knew him. As it was shame for the Hebrew women to be barren so in his mind was it desolation not to have people about him in his house, though he had never married.

He also had noticed Lily seemed quieter and while he saw in his mind it was winter kept them indoors, yet, because he wanted to, he saw Lily did not look so enchanted, she had talked more, she had not lately always been waiting, waiting till moment came to put on her clothes and meet Bert Jones.

So when Mr Gates had gone out, as he did every evening now leaving Jim Dale and he alone, he called Jim and said to him why must he be chipping Lily about Jones, why not leave her alone more? If you spoke to a female nowadays he said they made grievance out of it and took care to go another way to yours, whether it was their way or not, only to spite you. 'And females,' he said, 'like to think you're thinking of them, and afraid for 'em, and once they know you're that way they try and keep you at it.' He said Jim's talking of Jones would give that man importance in Lily's mind which he did not deserve 'being like 9,000 other wasters in this town. Let her forget 'im.' Mr Dale did not answer.

Mr Gates went to public house, where already Tupe was.

'It made I laugh,' Tupe said, 'to see the look just now your old man give me when I come up. 'E daint like it, did 'e? No, we're not good enough for 'im, Joe.'

Gates was relieved that Mr Tupe had not taken it wrong, his crossing the street and leaving him for Craigan.

'That's the truth,' he said 'us ain't.'

'But I got in a good one, eh, when I said that about Aaron Connolly? There's a dirty sneakin' 'ound for you. Anyroads 'e ain't no better'n a peasant, you can tell it by 'is speech.'

'I don't know I got anything against Aaron.'

'Well Joe, you're a marvel. It's no wonder to me you're put upon. Got nothin' against Aaron Connolly? I know what you mean but that's the lie of it, 'e daint ever let no one see t'other side of 'is face. I know 'im. No there ain't nothin' above board about 'im, that's just it.'

Later Mr Gates repeated what Craigan had said about how, soon as they had old age pension coming to them, they would be stopped off. Mr Tupe ridiculed idea of that. He said it was done at Thatcher's but in old fashioned place like Duprets you could bet your live they'd never do anything of that kind. Then he gave all the old arguments for old men being better than young. Soon came in more friends of his, all labourers like Tupe himself. (This was loss of caste for Gates to be perpetually with them, as he was step above a labourer.) They sat drinking.

This was time of year when people that did not shoot came back from Scotland to watch shooters shooting pheasant instead of watching grouse-shooting. Also hunt balls were beginning. Now for Hannah Glossop, and Mr Tyler too, it was party after party in country houses, and they met at many of them.

Almost at once Mr Tyler began kissing Hannah when they were alone together, goodness she did like it. She made little rules about this for herself, one was she must not kiss him too often but let him kiss her. So when he kissed her, in little ecstasies she closed eyelids over eyes. He could not see of course that she rolled eyeballs under the lids when he kissed her. Yet she feared he would feel that in her lips so she did not often let him kiss her mouth, coy, coy, and did not often kiss him – well bred kissing.

Soon, after one or two more houseparties, he kissed her no more, though almost she stood about in dark places. He thought it was disgusting to kiss her who was so dumb then, and yearning.

Then he was rude to her.

Miss Glossop asked Tom to stay and he would not come.

Leaving house, going into the garden 'he does not care' she said aloud.

She walked in misery. She tried not to think of him. But as sometimes, coming across the sea from a cold country to the tropics and the sky is dull so the sea is like any other sea, so as you are coming tropical birds of exquisite colours settle to rest on the deck, unexpected, infinitely beautiful, so things she remembered of him came one by one back to her mind. And as the ship beat by beat draws nearer to that warmth the birds come from, so her feeling was being encompassed then by the memory of him and it was so warm she sat down on the wet ground and cried.

# 12

Mr Jones came back to his lodgings after work.

Man and woman who owned the house sat down to evening meal with him.

Their name was Johns. Mrs Johns said to him: 'What's the matter Bert? You've been that restless these last two days.'

'What's up with 'im?' husband said. 'It's nothing but one of you women've got hold on 'im.'

'Then what's your young lady been sayin' to you?' asked Mrs Johns smiling.

'It's what 'e said to her' cried Mr Johns, 'that's what 'as caused the rumpus. You women can't never take a thing right.'

'Yes I dare say but then men never could tell which was right or wrong. But I'm not talking to you, I've spoke enough to you these thirty years, I'm talking to Bert and I don't like to see 'im low like 'e is.'

'Take a tip from me young feller, don't do it, don't go and marry. I know.'

'Marry, why shouldn't 'e marry?'

'That's it, go on, ten bob down and fifty bob a week for the rest of your life, nothing wrong with that is there? That's why women are so keen on marrying, and I don't blame 'em seein' men is such fools. But I don't know where all the money goes.'

'I'd like to see you managing this 'ouse.'

'Oh well' he said winking, 'I aint never regretted it when I married you.'

''Ave some sugar candy,' Mrs Johns said to Mr Jones, 'oh my listen to my 'usband.' Husband and wife laughed but they both looked at Mr Jones who did not laugh, and they grew serious.

'I don't reckon to meddle in any man's business' said Mr Johns 'but seein' you've been 'ere some years you won't take it wrong if I ask 'as anything bad 'appened.'

'No it aint nothing that you can call bad, but I'm fed up, that's all.'

'Fed up, are yer? Yes, we've all been fed up in our time, and it's not a thing that gets any better as you grow older either. 'Ad a set-to with the foreman?'

'No, it was this way. I 'adn't put down the six inch file I was using about twenty seconds, just time to blow my nose and the old man –

we call 'im 'Tis 'im in our place – was all over me and threatens to suspend me. Well that's not treatin' you right. I tell you I'd like to get out of that place. It's old fashioned and there's no getting on in places like that. Tell you the truth I'd been thinking of clearin' out into a new country.'

'They aint no places for a woman' said Mrs Johns.

'She's more keen on going even than what I am.'

'Ah, that's all very well,' said Mr Johns, 'but what if she wants to come back after a month or two out there. Females is funny things.'

'You don't know 'er,' Mr Jones said. He spoke like he was sorry Lil was as she was.

'Women'll tell you there's nothin' they want more but then when it comes to doin' it they won't 'ave it.'

'Oh yes' said Mrs Johns, 'but who eats the 'ouse up, tell me that.'

'I'd go alone if I was you,' said Mr Johns, 'and then 'ave 'er come out after if you've fell on yer pins.'

'That's what I'll do' said Mr Jones triumphantly.

' 'E don't seem any too sorry to get away from 'er,' said Mr Johns to wife who said : 'but when's this comin' off, not any too soon is it? I mean we shall 'ave you stayin' on here a month or two yet, will we? We don't want to lose you, you know.'

'No, missus, it won't be for a month or two.'

'Where would you be thinkin' of going if I might ask,' said Mr Johns.

'Well she, I don't rightly know yet,' he said and Mr Johns looked at wife and winked. Jones went on to say Mr Herbert Tomson had gone out to Australia and just because he had not found job there except on the land, which he was not taking, it was no argument why you mightn't go to Canada. Then for a time they fell to talking how wrong it was to expect men who had worked in factories to go back to work on the land.

'It aint fair on the females,' Mr Johns was saying.

'No, my young lady wouldn't stand that,' Jones said.

Later, when they were alone, Mr Johns said Bert would never go out and to look at way he told Lily Gates he went to technical school in evenings when he never went after first three times. Mrs Johns said no, he would never go. He hadn't the stuff in him, she said.

*

When they had had supper and again Mr Craigan was reading Dickens and Joe Gates was gone out, Dale stared at Lily washing up. (She washed up now because this was not evening for going out with Bert Jones.)

Mr Craigan smoked pipe, already room was blurred by smoke from it and by steam from hot water in the sink. She swilled water over the plates and electric light caught in shining waves of water which rushed off plates as she held them, and then light caught on wet plates in moons. She dried these. One by one then she put them up into the rack on wall above her, and as she stretched up so her movements pulled all ways at his heart, so beautiful she seemed to him. Mr Craigan would never have windows opened at evening so was a haze in that room, like to Dale's feeling. When she had done and was drying red hands, he said would she care to go to the movies with him again. He was so humble, and then Bert and she were saving, Jim would pay for her into movie, why yes why not, she had had hard day's work, (it had been washing day), yes she would go. 'I don't mind,' she said, and went to change her clothes.

He thought of her face shining from the steam, and if it were his to touch it. Feeling of confidence rising in him he thought he would bite it. Yet when they came to cinema again helplessness came over him. Sitting next her in intimacy of the dark and music yet she was far from him.

This film was of the tropics and again as when she had seen that black man in the streets all her muscles softened under the influence of dreams and imagination of that warmth. She felt in her heart it must be a soft thing, not the cruel beating heat it is.

And he did not understand her, and how sitting beside felt her hard and cruel, and hating him. He did not see she was all dreams, all her own dreams.

But Mr Craigan saw this. *Little Dorrit* laid on his knee, he thought it was selfishness that was all of Miss Gates, like it had been with her Aunt Ellie. He began talking aloud to himself. 'Yet she's a good wench,' he said, 'there's not many of her age would keep the house so clean.' Was a silence. 'An' she aint been out so often with Bert Jones,' he said. He fell to picking at his coat. Then he held up finger and squinted at it. He chuckled. 'Her blubbered when I told 'er of her Aunt Ellie' he said in whisper. 'Ah' he said 'but as the tree leans so the branches is inclined.'

Suddenly he broke out into loud voice: 'I wouldn't educate my son above the station 'e was born in,' he said and then whispering 'what is there in it, old Dupret 'ad to work twelve hours a day to keep 'is money I'll be bound 'e did.' Was a silence. 'An' a motor-car, aint we better on the feet our mothers bore us.' No, he thought, she was good girl, and this trouble would go by. She'd see Jones hadn't the making in him to work. She would go back to Dale that was an honest lad.

And indeed, now tropic film was over, she said two words to Dale. She was grateful to him again, this time again for keeping quiet. Kindness in her voice bewildered Mr Dale.

'Well if we do go' he said in a bad temper, 'where'll we go to.'

'If that's the tone of voice you're using, Bert, to think of our goin' away in, well then,' she said, 'we'd better talk of it some other day.'

Sunday. They were walking out along road into the country. Air was warm and moist. Silence was between them then.

'Go on, dear,' she said. 'I didn't mean any 'urt.'

'It's this weather gets on my nerves.'

'Yes, I'm sure when I came out I didn't know what to wear yes I didn't at all. But I brought the old gamp,' she said and made a little wave with umbrella at clouds above.

'Don't you like our goin' to Canada?'

She said yes in undetermined sort of way.

'Yes or no,' he said.

'Aint I said yes. I don't know what's been the matter with you lately I'm sure, no I don't.'

They squabbled then a little and she dragged gamp behind her more and more, most mournful thing to see. Her face paled to sicklish colour. Her mouth grew stiff and grim like that umbrella looked. He said didn't she want to come, was she going to draw back, was she afraid of work he said. She smiled. 'Work,' she said, 'why you're a wonderful worker to be suspended twice in six months.'

He got very angry. He said he hadn't been suspended but the once and didn't he go to technical school so many nights a week, was it his fault he'd been suspended it being all along of Tupe, that her father went about with now. If she didn't want to come he didn't want her.

'You don't want me,' she said and she went paler. 'Don't want me,' she said and she began crying. Large tears came down from eyes down her still face. He turned. He saw these and as the sun comes out from behind clouds then birds whistle again for the sun, so love came out in his eyes (at the victory, at making her cry) and he whispered things senseless as whistling birds. Lastly he said, 'and what would I do if you weren't coming!' She clung to him – aching tenderness – and she thought how could he be so cruel.

Mrs Eames said to husband had he noticed Lily wore woollen stockings quite often now and he said no did she? Lily was in love, Mrs Eames said; she knew, she knew. Then it would be Jim Dale Mr Eames said, and Mrs laughed at him. 'Observant, lord save us!' she said and went on about Bert Jones saying he was the one Lily was after and he worked in Dupret factory. 'Works at our place?' said Mr Eames, 'ah, I know the one you mean. Given up silk stockings for 'im? Well that's not many of 'em would do that nowadays, goin' to work of a morning you don't see nothing but these art silk stockings.'

'No, I don't reckon you would! Yet what these girls put all their money on their legs for I don't know,' she said, 'seeing how some are made.'

'It's a bloody marvel to me they're alive all of 'em, getting their legs wet coming to work and going back of an evening.'

'Don't you go thinking about things like that my man. You've never told me about getting my feet wet. But what I like about Lily is she's got the spirit to do what's in 'er mind.' Mrs Eames said were not many girls would have courage to go out in woollen stockings and not paint her face, to go against the tide like she did to save money. Real pity was she did not dance, Lily, she said, had met too few men. What's this Bert Jones like? she said.

'I can't say I've spoken to 'im more than two or three times in the last year. 'E seems like a lot of the other young chaps, you know, he don't seem to 'ave much interest in nothing. But 'e's good at his job I've been told. 'E's one of them that are always smoking cigarettes.'

Mrs Eames said she would laugh if Lily married him instead of Jim Dale as old Craigan intended.

''Ow's that? Jim's all right, there's nothing wrong with Jim, he's as steady a man as any woman could wish.'

Mrs Eames said she would like to see the laugh on old Craigan. Mr said so that was it was it, but what had she got against Mr Craigan who was most respected man in the works. He never interfered in anyone's affairs and there was nobody didn't like him. Well, said Mrs Eames, it was Joe Gates really. She didn't like that man. Once a bird had got caught between windows over at their house and they had sent for her to come over. It was one of first times Lily had been out with Bert Jones. Well after she got tired out, that Gates had started telling her dirty stories like she wasn't respectable.

'I'll go over an' 'ave a bit of a talk with Joe Gates now,' he said.

'Now don't you go and get quarrelling. There ain't nothing in it to be worrying over, or to act foolish, it was all months ago.'

Mr Eames was angry. But at last, when she told him it was really nothing, he said he never could cotton to Joe Gates. 'I don't like the way he goes about with Tupe,' he said, 'who's no better than a low down spy of Bridges'. And seeing he lives in Craigan's 'ouse 'e's no business to go about with Tupe. There's no love beggin' between old Mr Craigan and 'im. The dirty 'ound, the names he's called 'im before now, and to his face.'

'Oh well I expect you know the old man best. But what's 'e keep that girl shut up for like he does?'

'It's none of my business what 'e does,' said Mr Eames, 'but if I 'ad a daughter of her age I don't say I wouldn't do the same.'

'Then you'd be a fool, my lad.'

'Maybe I would but I wouldn't 'ave things going on in my family like there is in houses no farther'n this street.'

'Listen to you!' cried Mrs Eames. 'Well, and d'you know what's goin' to 'appen to them all. You listen to me and I'll tell you. She's going to marry Bert Jones and Craigan'll go and live with 'em, while Gates goes off and lives with Tupe most likely.'

'Most likely the best place 'e could be,' said Mr Eames. 'but what exactly did you say 'e'd said to you.'

# 13

'What's in your mind then about where we're going to?' he said to Lily, on their Sunday walk, later. She rubbed his arm between palms of her hands. She said was nothing particular only instead of this Canada 'e was always talking about why couldn't they go East. He said what did she mean by that? She told him then of film she had seen.

'A tea plantation?'

'Yes,' she said, 'a tea place, a place where tea grows.' He said would not likely be any factories there to work in. She answered him he would have to give up his trade. What chances were in engineering now she said. If they went to Canada it might only be out of the frying pan into fire. 'There's no money in that trade and won't be for years. You chuck it up, Bert.'

'Well if we did go out where'd we get the passage money from. It's not like Canada, you'd have to pay the train fare to those places.'

'Mr Dupret would lend it you.'

'Oh would he, 'ow'd you know? I 'aven't been at his place more than three years. Anyway what's the hours and wages in a tea plantation.'

'I don't know for sure, but it'll be more than in factories.'

'Yes, but I don't know the trade.'

'They'd learn you. You see Bert there's not so many white men out there, here there's too many, that's what keeps wages low. I say go out to where a working chap's wanted, not where there's too many already.'

'Well and if we did go out, what about the 'eat. Could you stand the 'eat. It's the tropics where tea grows you know.'

'Oh yes I could stand it, yes I like it where it's warm.'

'Ah, but it's hot out there. How'd you know you could?'

'H.O.T. – warm,' she said and rubbed arm between palms of her hand. 'I know I could dear,' she said and he kissed her while she laughed at him. 'Crazyhead' he kept on saying to her then.

Miss Glossop was downcast. We have seen her feeling, when she thought of Tom Tyler, had been like a tropical ocean with an infinite variety of colour. As her boat came near dry land you could see coral reefs and the seaweed where in and out went bright fishes,

315

as her thoughts turned to him so you could see all these in her eyes. Further out, in the deep sea, in her deeper feeling about him when he was away, now and again dolphins came up to feed on the surface of that ocean. And in her passage she disturbed shoals of flying fish. These were the orchestration of her feelings, so transparently her feeling lapped him and her thoughts, in shoals, fed on the top, or hung poised for two moments in the shallows.

All this was so when he had come back only more so – the dolphins played more often and her boat, thrusting along, disturbed more flying fish. In the shallows was a greater activity, halcyon weather. Every day shone the sun, every day the sea took on new values. And every day at that time there was a look about her eyes of an excited stupefaction at these things.

Then, as we know, it was taken away. When he repulsed her it seemed she was on a boat surveying that discoloured feeling, that desolation in the sea when sky is grey and dark. And always the boat was circling round that land. Then, as we have seen, tropical birds came out and rested on this ship. One by one they reminded her she was on a particular sea, and near land very particular to her. Weeping, weeping, when she was reminded in this way of how bright her conceits had been, weeping she added to an ocean made up, as she was then thinking, of tears shed at the perfidy of man.

Her mother, seeing this, insisted that she must go out often, to be distracted. So when she came to dinner with the Duprets, that dinner which had so often been put off, she was still circling round her memory of Tom Tyler, only each day she circled a little wider, a little farther off.

But stretch this simile, and, having given Tom Tyler one island, make archipelago about him – though each day she circled farther from Mr Tyler yet she did not draw any nearer to where Dick lay. Nor any nearer to her mother's island.

Mrs Dupret had told son she too had heard Miss Glossop was in love with Mr Tyler but that he was not in love with her. She told him he would catch the girl on the rebound. So when at last Miss Glossop came to dinner this moment seemed of great importance to him.

When she came into room he dared not look at her. At the same time he could not answer girl he was talking to so she thought

316

sudden blankness in him must be because of pains in his stomach. Mrs Dupret called out: 'Dick, where are your manners, darling? Here is Hannah,' and he went over. Then girl he had been talking to saw just how it all was, that he was in love. He went over. He shook Miss Glossop by the hand. He could not find anything to say to her. At last he said in despair: 'What have you been doing? I haven't seen you for ages.' She said something about country house-parties and hunt balls and he thought 'Oh if she could have said – I have been in love and have been thrown over then oh then he would have said – I am in love, but my love is not returned!' Then would they have talked of this, each sympathizing with the other and then gradually he would have taught her it was she he was in love with. Then she would have seen what miserable sort of man was Mr Tyler.

As it was she said nothing and was another silence between them. Then he said he wished they would hurry up with dinner and she answered she was sorry she was so dull that he must long for escape to a meal. 'Not at all, no, no, it's only that I'm hungry. Heavens, I didn't mean ...'

'Oh all right, all right. Don't let's go on with that,' she said and said no more. He moved off feeling if he could shoot himself he would do then.

Very disturbed he went to his mother and drew her aside. He said she must change places at dinner, he could not sit next to Hannah. Mrs Dupret became helpless. She said what was the matter? and he answered Hannah was angry with him, would not speak to him.

'But how can I change all the places now dear. Look here comes Pringle now.'

'Dinner is served madam.'

'No dear, you must sit next her, it's too late now. And I don't suppose she is angry with you, darling. How can I change all the places now. I can't, can I?'

Terribly disturbed he took her down to dinner. People on either side of them began talking away from them, they were left high and dry.

When party went he stayed on over – was nothing for him to do in London, the business ran itself, nothing to do but sign cheques on Thursday and this was Tuesday. He took boat and rowed on the

317

river. What a new year, he thought in mind, what a new year, father dead and now Miss Glossop was over, that was done with!

River was brown and flowed rapidly down to the sea. On either side the violet land under this grey sky. Trees on either side graciously inclined this way and that, leaning on his oars he watched these and rooks that out of the sky came peaceably down on fields.

He thought in his mind here was end of another chapter, another episode done with (Miss Glossop had been rude to him whenever she could be rude.) He thought his mistake had been at all to mix with these people, he had no place here, he was like father in that who had never really mixed but had led his own life. Why, he asked in mind, should you leave your life lying about to be cut in pieces by Miss Glossop. And, when it was cut to ribbons, for other Miss Glossops to watch it lying there and be diverted by it. One should go away he thought.

One might go to foreign countries but what was in these but nausea of travelling, hotels, trains, languages you did not know, Americans? Besides it was work he wanted.

So gradually he decided he would go to Birmingham. Hadn't mother told him it was his own fault now if works were not satisfactory. He would take Walters and Archer and they would spend a week or two there. They would have a grand clear out, Tarver was not having a square deal – an early spring cleaning. Work, that was it, he would work.

# 14

Tuesday afternoon Mr Dupret went to London. He went to offices. He found Mr Walters and said he wanted him to come down also to factory tomorrow. Mr Walters said he was too busy, and what did he want him for? Mr Dupret said he was going to make thorough study of the place, such as he could not do when father was alive. He said he was taking Archer with him. Walters asked why he wanted to take Archer?

'Because I want to!'

'Right you are, Dick. How long will you be down there?'

Mr Dupret said he did not know yet. When Walters was gone he was very angry with him. He thought Mr Walters couldn't be bothered to come down could he, and oh yes Walters ran the business didn't he! Well, Mr Dupret was going to run business now.

Meanwhile Mr Archer was telephoning Tarver that they were coming down, he did not know what for.

Meanwhile Mr Craigan was in bed. He was coming to work in morning and a shower had caught him, had wetted his clothes through, and all day he had worked in wet clothes so that next morning he stayed in bed with a fever. His hands trembled, trembled at the bed-clothes. Lily was very frightened.

What was most on the old man's mind was thought of Bert Jones. He felt pretty certain Dupret factory would not turn him off when he got old age pension, when he had said they would it was only because he was depressed, yet you could not go on always working and he looked forward to living in Dale's house, with Lily his wife, till the end. They were both grateful to him, he had saved, and was more money in their house than in any on the street. But if she married Jones then those two would go off, Gates would leave him, he would be alone as he was when he first came to Birmingham.

Year after year Lily had grown to be his daughter, not Gates' daughter. Craigan was fonder of her now than if she had been his own. And Bert he knew, he knew was no good, he would never bring regular money to the house.

Lily came in then. Mr Craigan suddenly began talking and before he knew when or how, he was having it out with her.

He spoke calmly. He said Jones was a decent living man but that was it, he was too quiet a man he said, he knew the sort. They would never stay long in the same job that kind, he said, and what a woman wanted was man who brought in the money regular. Then look at his trade, were too many in it. He said he had worked for years and years now, best part of half a century, and he had learned it was not governments nor good times or bad that raised wages, but the demand for men. She had also thought of that.

'Take foundry work,' he said, 'the young chaps won't 'ave it now, it's too dirty for 'em and too hard, you can't get lads to start in foundries nowadays. In a few years there won't 'ardly be any moulders left and those that can do a clean job then will get any money, any amount o' money!'

He said she ought to think it over. 'Love's all right for them that 'as Rolls Royces' he said, 'but for the wives of working men it's the money that comes in regular at the end of the week that tells.' He went on, unfortunately, saying didn't she have any gratitude towards him? What sort of life would she have had with her father, didn't she think he, Craigan, deserved a home when he was too old for work.

'Why, grandad,' she said, 'you ain't too old for work, there's years in you yet' she said and loved him. Going away she thought of these things. She thought how faithful Dale was to her. And all this time heart had been sinking a little before adventure of going away. (Mr Craigan of course did not know they planned to go away.) She thought more of Jim Dale. He was more practical. And as Mr Craigan said it was the practical that tells. But really it was most practical to go away.

At cinema.

'It's like this Lil,' Mr Jones said in whispers, 'when I get out to Canada I may not get a job straight off. I may 'ave to look about a bit and with no money coming in I expect we'll 'ave a tightish time of it to start with. It stands to reason we shall. Then what's the good in your coming out with me just at first. You wait till I get settled in and I'll send word to you.'

'Yes then yes, then you don't want to 'ave me,' said Miss Gates in a calm voice.

'Get out, of course I do.' He tried to kiss her but she turned face away.

'Yes, that's it, off you'll go and leave no address and I'll never have another word of you.'

'I tell you I'll send for you, of course I will.'

'Will you?'

'Crazyhead.' He kissed her. She drew back.

'But I'll go out along with you, thank you my man,' she said. 'It may make two mouths to feed, yes, but there'll be four hands instead of two. They say there's any amount of work for girls out there.'

'Well I 'adn't thought of that. There's something in that Lil.'

'In course there is, silly. I know you're trying to get away from me. But just you try it on. Yes you were.'

'Crazyhead,' he said, but nearly all spontaneity had gone of their relations to each other.

'Oh Bert I wish your dad and mother did live in Brummagem and not in Liverpool. It's costly when we want a talk and it's raining and we 'ave to go to the movies to be out of the wet. 'Ow's your technical school going?'

He lied. He said it was interesting, that he had not missed any classes.

Walters had telephoned Mr Bridges to say Mr Dupret was coming down. The line had been bad, Bridges had not heard what time he was coming or how long he was staying. So when he arrived Mr Bridges was still making last minute inspection of the factory.

When Mr Dupret arrived he went with Archer straight to Mr Tarver's office. Cummings found Bridges and told him Mr Dupret had just got in with Archer with him, and had gone to Tarver. Mr Bridges stood still and then, at hearing this, an arrow as it might be pierced him, transfixed his heart. Mr Dupret comes into Tarver's office, Mr Archer with him.

'Good-morning Tarver, how are we this morning,' said Mr Richard, hearty, thinking he was using Mr Tarver's language.

'Why squire' Mr Tarver said. He pretended to be surprised, 'Come in sir, come in. The fact is we've not much work in but we're always busy in this department. How are you Archer? As a matter of fact I believe Mr Bridges is going to start the men on short time tomorrow. But this is a bit of a surprise isn't it. Fancy seeing you down 'ere he said to Mr Archer.

'Short time, that's a pity' said Mr Dupret. Why wasn't I told he said in mind?

'Yes here we are on a little expedition down into the provinces' said Mr Archer, 'isn't that so sir? We've left the gay metropolis to pay you a little visit John.'

'Didn't you know we were coming?' said Mr Dupret.

'No sir, I didn't hear a word.'

'That's funny' Mr Dupret said, 'I heard Mr Walters telephone the general manager, I thought he would have told you.'

'Mr Bridges didn't say anything about it,' Tarver said and thought he would say it was just like him not to say a word, but he remembered then how he had said similar things to Mr Dupret

321

before and it had not come off. So he thought he would let silences speak for themselves.

'Didn't he?' said Mr Dupret and Archer winked at Tarver, Tarver winked back.

Was a silence and then was loud noise on the stairs. Mr Bridges came in. Effusively he greeted young Mr Richard. Then he saw Archer.

'Why dammit it's Archer' he said shaking hands violently. 'What are you doing down 'ere?'

'Holiday-making,' said Mr Archer, 'holiday-making.'

'Well he won't get much of a holiday down here will 'e John, if that's what he's come for, it's work down here by God, work all the time.'

'When you don't put the place on short time,' Mr Dupret said.

'Ah, I hate to do it, I hate to see the men not drawing their full money at the end of the week. But what can you do? There's no place in all Brummagem that isn't the same. There's no money about, there's nobody buying now, they make do with the old stuff till times get better. But come along to my room will you Mr Dupret.'

As they were going out of the door Mr Bridges said he was sorry he had not been there when they had arrived, but he had been in the shops. 'What train are you catching back to town so I can order the car.'

'Well we shan't be going back tonight,' said Mr Dupret, 'we've come down to have a thorough look round the place. We'll be five or six days here.'

'That's grand,' said Mr Bridges and asked in his mind – what was it now, what was it? Why hadn't Walters told him, he cried in his mind, not that he had anything to hide, but just so as to know to be able to keep him from Tarver and so forth.

Mr Dale was very solitary kind of man. So when Thursday came and was no work at Dupret's, (for it was first day of the short time that was starting now) being a fine day he went walking into country.

This day he was bad-tempered. He was young man and he knew he could get work in another foundry he knew of where was better money to be picked up on piece work, for in Dupret foundry was

322

only day work. He was young man, the hard piece-work would not hurt him and again he ought to work in as many shops as he could to learn his trade, as all foundries have different ways of working. And now Dupret's were on short time, he was getting still less money. But he was grateful to Mr Craigan, he could not leave the old man, who was too slow now to work on his own.

Craigan had private money. Mr Dale was more comfortable in Mr Craigan's house than he would be elsewhere and he had to give Lily less money than he would a landlady because in their house were three wage-earners and but four mouths. If he went to work in another foundry he thought Craigan would not let him stay on.

And was Lily.

He was half hoping he would come across them walking, he knew they were out this way together. Just now he hated her. It was she was keeping him back and on low wages, gratitude or not he would have left Craigan if it hadn't been for her. And he would look at no other girl.

Just then he came across them. It was at crossroads and they came from behind houses there, walking together very close.

Lily was excited at short time being started in Dupret factory. Eagerly she and Mr Jones had talked of this. More and more she wanted now to go away. She called to Jim to come and talk with them, to discuss how long this three day week would last at Dupret's. But Mr Dale made as if he did not hear.

She called again, much louder. Then Mr Dale, anger bursting over in him, picked up small stone and threw it at them, as a boy might, and at once he walked away.

Mr Jones to make show of dignity shouted hey, hey, no more than hey because the stone had not come near them, but Dale went off.

That day Mr Dupret sat alone with Bridges in his office. He was very calm, he hated all of them now in a bored way.

'Mr Bridges,' said he 'we've got to have what the French call a little explanation.'

The Froggies, Mr Bridges said in mind, nerves on edge, the Froggies what have they got to do with it damn 'em.

'The point is this, I'm head of this business now and everything must go through me. You see it's only fair, all the money that's put into it is mine.'

'Of course it's yours,' said Mr Bridges 'and...'

'No, let me do the talking. The point is that my father with all the whole lot of interests he had hadn't the time to go into everything. Well I'm not on any boards, this is practically the only concern I'm in, and I want you and Walters to get out of the habit of doing things above my head and without my knowing it.'

'What d'you mean? I...'

'I mean this, that you and Walters for better or worse, and quite naturally, pretty well ran this business on your own before my father died. But it's different now, I want to take a hand in it.'

'If that's all you know about your father my lad...'

'God damn it Bridges will you listen to what I say? The point is this, from now on I'm going to run the whole show myself, or rather it's going to be run through me. Take the question of the men being put on short time. I didn't hear a word about it. Well in future I am going to hear. I'm not saying that it shouldn't have been done but it's only fair I should be told.'

'I think we'd better talk another time. I can see you're in a temper now...'

'No, we're going to talk now. The point is this, when I say we're going to talk we're going to talk, from now on.'

'Well you ain't going to make me talk,' Mr Bridges said and walked out.

Eleven o'clock. Mrs Eames had done house. She stood in their bedroom she had just tidied and their son pulled at her skirts.

'Ain't you gettin' active on your feet!' she said to him. She picked him up. She kissed him.

Thought came in her to call on the Craigans. Mr Craigan was still in bed. She thought he had got old very quickly and danger was with that sort if they stayed in bed for more than three weeks they might never get up again. She tidied hair. Then taking son she went next door and knocked. No answer. She knocked. She went in.

'Lily,' she cried, 'Lily.'

'Who might you be?' said Craigan from bed upstairs.

'It's Mrs Eames Mr Craigan, I thought I'd ask after you 'ow you were.'

'I'll bother you to come up missus, seein' I'm in bed. Lily shall be back directly.'

Always Mr Craigan had prided himself on not lengthily talking. 'Many a man 'as lost everything by it,' he was fond of saying. But more and more now he felt a need to talk and seeing this in himself he said in mind that he was getting old.

'Come in if you'll excuse my lyin' here in bed.'

She said again she'd called to ask how he was feeling, and to excuse her bringing son in with her but was no-one in their house, she could not leave him. He said he was not well and when you had got to his age you did not easily get over fevers like the one he had had.

'Where's Lily then?' said Mrs Eames.

He said she'd gone out for a spell and said Mrs Eames, what, to leave you alone like that! But he said she was a good wench, more than daughter to him. She had some crazy notions perhaps but were not many of her age would keep house in such good shape as it was now, or keep him so comfortable.

'An' you've got another coming if I see right,' he said looking at Mrs Eames' belly.

'Yes in three weeks' time.'

He said if it was like her boy there it would be a fine kid. Mrs Eames loved him, he had that way with women. She began trying to persuade him to get up. But he would not.

He would not get up because now he felt everything slipping away from him. Dale was dissatisfied at this short time they were working in Dupret factory and no one knew better than Mr Craigan he should get experience in other shops. Gates now went with no one else but Tupe in evenings. And Lily. What had she gone out for just now? He did not know what was in her heart. Everything was slipping away from him.


# 15

Friday and Mr Bridges talked to Mr Dupret in the office. 'It's like this Dick,' he said, 'Walters telephoned me to say you were coming down but the wire was so bad I couldn't for the life of me hear all he had to tell me. Well when he had had his say I told 'im I thought of putting the men on short time, but the wire being as it was, 'e didn't hear it. That's how you didn't come to know. The fact is we're right up to the quota that your dad laid down was safe to carry stock to. And as there's very little coming in you can't keep the men and 'ave nothing for 'em to do.'

'No of course not. But in future I'd be grateful if you would write a letter to go through our files. What I mean is it looks better if we seem to have a say in it,' Mr Dupret said smiling.

'There's no dirty work going on here, Dick.'

'No, no I know there's not. I didn't mean that. Only you must spare our feelings up there Mr Bridges, you must make us feel a little more important than we are perhaps.'

He was not being sarcastic. They had made up differences and Mr Bridges had said he liked a man who spoke out. But they were quite ready, both of them, to break out again. Indeed Bridges had said to wife, dramatizing, that he only stayed on still out of loyalty to the memory of the chief.

'Well you see Dick, this is how it was. We start our working week Wednesdays. It was simpler to start short time on Thursday or the books would get cockeyed. And I was watching the quota like a cat watches a mouse, watching it all the time. As soon as ever we were right up to it I came down and put the whole show on short time till we could get more orders.'

'Exactly. Well now it's all straight in my mind. But you'll remember about next time. I'm not sure we couldn't carry more stock but still I don't want to bring that up. How are the men taking it Mr Bridges?'

'That's the rub, that's the rub. If we have to work short more'n a week or two all our best men will be leaving us. I got a good team together, it'd break my heart if it was broken up.'

'I suppose it's only the young men will go?'

'Yes, it's the young chaps that'll send for their cards.'

'That's the disaster, to my mind. You're always telling me how difficult it is to get fully trained younger men. And of course the old men will hang on and be a millstone round our necks.'

'Ah I know you,' cried Mr Bridges and hit Mr Dupret on the back with palm of his hand.

'For God's sake don't hit me' said Mr Dupret.

'Sorry' said Mr Bridges, 'but the old men ain't so 'opeless as you young fellers would like to think. In the iron foundry now there's one or two older men I wouldn't part with for love or money. And the crane driver in the engineers, Aaron Connolly, rising seventy, I wouldn't part with him for love or money.'

'The iron foundry is just one of the things I wanted to talk to you about.'

'Go ahead' Mr Bridges said complacently.

'Well you've always told me there's no money to be made in iron founding but – you know, I'm not trying to be quarrelsome – isn't that rather a defeatist policy?'

'Diabetes?' said Mr Bridges.

'No I meant isn't that lying down before you're hit? If we can't make money in that horrible foundry can't we lose a little less at the very least.'

'That's just what I'm working for the whole time, I'm always after that place. But there's not one in all Brummagem but doesn't lose more money than we do.'

'Well look here, I've been talking it over' – talking it over eh? Mr Bridges cried in mind, 'and I think we ought to change our policy. What we do now as I understand it is to let the men work comparatively slow so as to be sure each job is a good one and not a waster.'

'They don't idle Dick,' said Mr Bridges.

'No, I don't mean they work idly but since we are all agreed we can't put them on piece work owing to the nature of the work what I want is that we should get rid of the old men, give the others a bit of extra money, and drive them a bit, taking our chance on the wasters. The point is that the old men keep production down with the tone they give the shop.'

'Taking our chance on the wasters eh?' said Mr Bridges. He laughed. 'No lad it won't do. I remember they tried that at the O.K. when I was with 'em. D'you know what 'appened, they went down on production by fifteen per cent.'

'What sort of a manager did they have?'

'They 'ad a man. 'E wasn't a fairy.'

'Well opinions differ, that's all I can say.'

'Who doesn't think so?' Mr Bridges said defiantly.

'Your subordinates don't.'

'What, Cummings?' Bridges thought he had made Mr Richard give away Tarver.

'Cummings? I'd rather ask Lot's wife what she thought of salt,' said Mr Dupret and was so pleased with that, it seemed to him so in the Bridges tradition, he thought he would go away on it.

'Well, it's lunch time,' he said pleasantly and went out.

Mr Bridges did not laugh.

Friday morning. While Mrs Eames visited Mr Craigan Miss Gates was walking back from Labour Exchange where she had got pamphlets on Canada.

She felt now they must be practical. No longer now she thought of tea plantations.

She thought how Mr Craigan had said it was the demand for men raised wages, only that. It was most practical to go where men were wanted.

They would be married in Liverpool, where his parents were. Then they would go.

But she loved Mr Craigan. She thought then he had been father to her for years and years. Now he was old and he was ill, she didn't ought to leave him, not now. 'But us workin' people, we got to work for our living, yes we have,' she cried out in mind, quoting Mr Jones, 'and go out to find the work.'

She thought how Mr Craigan was rich enough, was no need for him to work with the money he had put by. He would not be comfortable as she had made him but he could pay for comfort.

Mr Gates. She owed him nothing, nothing at all.

(She had forgotten Mr Dale.)

Mr Dupret walked down the street Lily was walking down.

He thought it was not poverty you saw in this quarter, the artisan class lived here, but a kind of terrible respectability on too little money. And what was in all this, he said as he was feeling now, or in any walk of life – you were born, you went to school, you worked, you married, you worked harder, you had children, you went on working, with a good deal of trouble your children grew up, then they married. What had you before you died? Grandchildren? The satisfaction of breeding the glorious Anglo Saxon breed?

He thought how he would sit in office chairs for another forty years, gradually taking to golf at the week-ends or the cultivation of gardenias. All because of Miss Glossop.

But these people, how much worse it was, he at least, he thought, had money. These people had music of course, but second-hand music. Still they had really only marriage and growing old. Every day in the year, every year, if they were lucky they went to work all through daylight. That is, the men did. Time passed quickly for them, in a rhythm. But it was the monotony, as one had said to him.

Coming to a recreation ground he walked into it and made to go across. At the gate he passed Lily and did not notice her, she was so like the others. Here, because it was mid-morning, some mothers had brought out their children too young still to walk. Cold winter sunshine. They stood about in groups while older children with cries ran about, like trying to catch their cries in the air, the boys at football, the girls at some game of their own. Passing through this he shuddered, a sense of foreboding gathered in him. What will they grow up to he thought in mind – they'll work, they'll marry, they'll work harder, have children and go on working, they'll die. He shuddered. Then he forgot all about them and thought about himself.

But Lily coming through the gate saw children running and those mothers and she stood and watched them, feeling out of it. 'I must have babies,' she said then, looking at baby in mother's arms. She was not excited when she said it. Just now she was being very practical.

Going down road after this, to Mr Craigan, excitement took hold on her. Every woman she passed, were mostly women in the streets now, every woman she looked at like she was a queen, they her subjects, was an eagle in her eyes.

What were they to her, they were like sheep and would always be here, was no kind of independence in them she thought in image in her mind, like lettuces in a row they were, yes, separate from one another but in one teeny plot of land.

Ashamed at so much imagining she thought then oh if I could break out now and run, yes and run in to grandad and scream to him I've got them, I got the things about Canada.

But thought of him being against it quietened her. So like any other girl there, only she had no shopping basket, she walked down the street only if you looked it was all over her face, what she was feeling.

*

Lily went home to get Mr Craigan his midday meal. She did not speak much to him and again he wondered at her. So it was only when she had washed the plates up afterwards that she sat down and read about Canada.

Then she took some clothes that were to be mended. Putting away the leaflets in her dress she went to window of the kitchen, and sat there where she could look over garden at the back and not be seen. In her senses she felt golden light covering a golden land, that was how she saw it from what she had been reading, and she thought how she always did love darning – and what it would be to her when she was mending for someone more particular, or her own child. Something fluttered at her fingers. (How can you darn when as it might be a bird is in your hand, fluttering between thumb and fingers.) Panting she laid her needle down. That's funny, she thought, my not being able to darn, and why, I'm all out of breath.

Now, for first time that year, day lingered noticeably in sky as the hour grew later, clouds were blown away or melted, I don't know, only all of a sudden spring nodded from a clear sky and most beautifully that clear light hung there far into evening. She folded hands in her lap. Everywhere round became suddenly quiet. Then syrens in the factories began sounding, mournful sound.

When she heard the syrens she rose from chair and put bread and cheese on the table, for other than bread and cheese no supper was put out on Fridays. She went upstairs to Mr Craigan to see if he wanted anything but he did not. She hardly noticed him. Now, the syrens having sounded, she was disappointed.

Now also in Mr Dupret's factory the men were being paid week's wages. Every pay envelope had at least £1 less in it as this had been a short week. Mr Gates and Mr Dale came back home silent. Joe was in bad temper because he had less money and because he had been put to work with another man who had more to do than Mr Craigan. Mr Dale was desperate because he had been put onto small work after Craigan's being ill had broken up the gang they worked in, all three of them.

When Mr Gates had finished washing he looked at bread and cheese on the table and spat. Lily said not to spit on the floor but into the grate if he had to spit. He did not listen to what she told him but said you got tired of the women never keeping any money to end of a week, and wasn't he entitled to a hot supper who had worked to fill her mouth. She said it always had been the custom with them to go out to a fish and chip on Friday nights. He said oil they fried the fish in was machine oil. She said particular wasn't he all at once and what about her who had to clean it up when he spat on floor. He said: 'Well, if it's been the custom to go out for a bit of fish Friday nights then it's all along of the same custom that I spit on the floor and spit I do,' he said and spat again.

Mr Dale sat and ate bread and cheese. They had had a short week yet he did not dare to give her less money than he always gave. One day, he thought so to speak, she must remember my goodness, that I would be a good husband to her, bringing the money back regular at end of the week. And if he gave less money than he always gave he did not dare to face her reproaches. He must risk nothing now that might offend Miss Gates. So when Mr Gates' back was turned to the bread and cheese he said here was his money for her housekeeping. Row with her father had made her forget short time they had been working and without saying a word she took it and put it in her dress. She asked Mr Gates what about him? He said here you are and puts down money on the table. She says what, only that much? He says yes and if that isn't enough well she doesn't have any, and snatches it back again.

She said that was half what Mr Craigan had said they should all give. He says well wasn't it a short week and why should he pay for Bert Jones into the movies with money he gave for housekeeping money. Why should he pay for Bert Jones into cinemas at all he says. She began to cry. He mimicked her, he was old, it was terrible the way he did it.

When, after that, in height of their argument Mr Gates hit his daughter she went upstairs to get hat and coat and then left the house. Mr Dale was very angry. He said to Joe to get out of it before the old man heard, Lily he said was gone up now to tell him. Mr Gates did go but he said ever since Craigan had been sick he had felt a new man. He was the girl's father, when she asked for a clout he'd give her one. What business was it of the old man's he said if he had kicked his daughter where it would hurt her most, and that's what he would do next time. He went and, greatly daring, he tried to drink all the money that night he had taken for a week's work, thing he had not done since he was a lad.

Mr Dale went upstairs to Mr Craigan. He thought he would find

Lily there but Craigan told him she had not been in after they had come in from work. He was sorry. He had hoped to benefit when he found her womanlike, as he thought, in tears beside Mr Craigan's bed. Or he hoped to make all that might be said about it felt, as she was not one to take being hit quietly and what had happened made him afraid.

'Joe hit 'er.'

'Joe did?'

'Ah.'

'What did 'e 'it 'er for?'

'Why 'e wouldn't give 'er the money, seeing we've had a short week.'

'Where would 'er be now?' Mr Craigan said.

'I don't know where she would be,' said Mr Dale, 'now you say she's gone outside.'

# 16

Miss Gates left house, dressed, so quickly that she was before almost the last of Mr Gates could be seen in their street where he went to Tupe and public houses. She walked firmly, quickly. She went to where Mr Jones lodged.

As she clapped the door knocker she thought for first time how he would be now at his evening class. Not used to think at all except about prices of things she was now quickly thinking. When Mrs Johns opened door to her she said with drama, and at once, she was that young lady Mr Bert Jones kept company with and she would leave a note for him if Mrs Johns did not mind. This one said to come in, Bert would be back in two ticks, and would she sit down in the front parlour. Then, as if she wanted to explain asking her into the front parlour, (formal entertaining of so young a girl compared with Mrs Johns) then she said 'You see dear you 'aven't been down our way before 'ave you,' and she says Bert Jones is as son to her in her heart, never having had children of her own. Miss Gates said she would write a letter to him if Mrs Johns wouldn't mind being bothered for paper and ink. This one said wasn't she in a hurry, why he'd only gone down the road to the post office, 'been writing a letter

332

to 'is mum and dad,' said Mrs Johns 'trying to find 'em.' But Lily noticed nothing in this, that he should not be at evening class or that he should be trying to find parents, not even when Mrs Johns went on to say that was why she felt so particular about him, being childless as she was. Lily Gates was now at bow window: ' 'Ere 'e is, 'e's coming,' cried she, and Mrs Johns left parlour saying to make herself at home please, though she knew the room wasn't up to much! This last Miss Gates did not notice either, indeed she was not noticing anything. This haste seemed indecent to Mrs Johns, and not to bring her manners with her, first time the girl came to his house, this shocked Mrs Johns. She went to front door to tell him not to trouble to come in by the back for Lily was in the front room, and to see what was on his face or if he knew about it whatever it was.

When Mr Jones came in she went back to kitchen where sat Mr Johns. She told him the story and said she gone herself to the front door to see if Bert's face wore any kind of look on it. But no, she says, he doesn't know anything about nothing whatever it is, and when she'd told him who was waiting for him he'd seemed like frightened.

'Time was when I said 'e 'adn't the stuffing in him to go out and shift for 'imself like, but now I seen 'is young lady, that girl could take a man anywheres, men being what they are.'

'That's bad,' said Mr Johns.

'Yes, and that girl's not 'appy at 'ome,' said Mrs Johns. 'I'll lay there's been some trouble at 'er 'ouse and she's come round to tell 'im about it. If I wasn't what I was, but like some I knows on, I'd be listening at that key 'ole this very minute.'

'You think 'e'll go then?'

'I'm afraid for 'im,' said Mrs Johns, 'such a nice lad that 'e is. That's what comes of taking up with foundry people,' she said.

Meanwhile, in other room, Lily was saying like as if everything had been knocked out of her now she was with Mr Jones.

'He struck me!'

' 'E 'it you? What did 'e hit you with?'

'With 'is fist, yes, I fell down, couldn't help myself 'e 'it out so hard.'

'Striking a woman,' said Mr Jones, 'that's about as low a thing as 'e could do.'

' 'E's my father you see Bert. Yes 'e's got a right to, one way you look at it. But I can't stay in that 'ouse,' she said and they talked of what they would do. Mr Jones fell more and more silent as this went on, and her temper rose till she said she would see him tomorrow and with that she went. She was afraid she might say something to him about himself which would bring quarrels between them, for now of all times she wanted him for her life.

And now for Mr Jones his position was this: that as it might be foreman had given him a job out of which, if he did it right and it was not easy to do, would come advancement and satisfaction for him.

Foreman set up the job on lathe and stood by then to see if he could do it. Others in the shop looked on from their places, maliciously, some enviously, and others hoped it would come out right for him. So he, Mr Jones, began on first part of what he had to do, and this part was easy for him. With all senses fixed on it yet in a sense he played with the job.

So he completed first stages of what had to be done. He looked at his work and it was right. But this part was not the test. Final, more difficult work on it was coming, foreman began to smile with anticipation at the difficulties that were before him.

If Mr Jones did not want to go on those others watching him, and the foreman, made it into confession of failure to draw back. Also he realized now, what he had not thought of before, that he had indeed begun – bit of metal he was using was scored now, partly used, and if he gave up they might not be able to bring it in for some other job. Also he might never have the chance again and suddenly it seemed so desirable to him that 'I'll have a try,' he said in mind and threw belt of his lathe over into gear.

Now the job, revolving so many turns each second, now it had a stillness more beautiful than when actually it had been still. On the small surface of it was sheen of light still and quiet, for noise of his lathe could not be heard above noise of other lathes working about him. And pace of events bearing on his life quickened so that for two moments their speed had appearance of stillness. Also the foreman and others that were looking on openly by now, had now his appearance and features. He said in mind he had to go on and do the job right. He poised before it, tool in his hand and it might be the sense of power he had and which he felt for the first time, to make waster of that bit of steel or a good job out of it, it might be that kept him still undecided.

Mr Dupret talked with Walters in Mr Bridges' office. He said they had to do something, they could not go on as they were now. If they got into rut of losing money they would never get out of it. He said while he had been down here this last week or two he had seen many more elderly men working than he had thought possible. 'It's not fair on the younger men Walters,' he said, thinking just now like a journalist, 'you can't get away from the fact that younger men work the harder.'

(Walters had been sent for as last resort to deal with Mr Dupret. Bridges now took everything as a joke. But Mr Dupret said constantly in his mind, 'I must work, work.' After Miss Glossop it was most necessary for him to do something tangible violently, and in this Mr Archer, and Tarver also, egged him on.)

Mr Walters saw that no argument would be heard by Mr Dupret and as he was actuated really by a devotion to Dupret's father he forgot about his pride. He thought no great harm would come of this, he would let the boy do it, and then he thought he could not prevent him if he wanted to, and smiled. If he threatened to resign, for instance, probability was his resignation would be accepted. And as all his life he had worked in this business he saw it as his own creation, and did not care to think of that work undone through Tarver's inexperience.

So it was decided that all men within six months of their old age pension (what would it mean, thought Mr Walters, nothing, twelve men at the most) all these would get their cards on Saturday. Mr Bridges had come in by then and smiling he said to make it Wednesday, Wednesday was end of every working week. Mr Dupret said no, tomorrow Saturday, for God's sake do get something done and walked out.

(Mr Archer was in course of being disappointed. Mr Dupret thinking over what had been said, thought afterwards these two had behaved very well and shown a real will to help.)

# 17

Lily stood in hat and coat by kitchen window quickly cutting stairs of bread. When she had stack of these by her she reached to tin of beef that was by the loaf and in stretching she raised head and saw man in garden next theirs digging in his garden. Behind him was line of chimney pots, for next street to theirs in that direction was beneath, hidden by swell of gardens back of their street. This man, then, leant on his spade and was like another chimney pot, dark against dark low clouds in the sky. Here pigeon quickly turned rising in spirals, grey, when clock in the church tower struck the quarter and away, away the pigeon fell from this noise in a diagonal from where church was built and that man who leant on his spade. Like hatchets they came towards Lily, down at her till when they were close to window they stopped, each clapped his wings then flew away slowly all of them, to the left. She had drawn back to full height. Then again she looked at that man and he also had been watching the pigeon. He again began to dig but the clock striking had told her she had time yet and she wondered at him digging in that unfruitful earth and that he was out of work and most likely would be for most of the rest of his days. There he was digging land which was worn out.

She reached to the beef and cut thin slices off it. One slice she put between two stairs of bread and when the sandwiches were all made she wrapped them up into a parcel. She looked once more at man digging and went out into the streets. At a corner some way from their house she waited for Mr Jones.

While she stood there waiting for Bert Jones clock struck the half hour and noise of it came faintly to her from where she had come. Just afterwards the syrens sounded and in Dupret factory. Mr Gates came out of iron foundry with the others and joined in long crowd of other men going out. All were animated at thought of the week-end though many talked still of how that morning nine men had been turned off for age. Laughing, and one man would shout to another ten yards in front of him in the crowd and some boys, separated from each other, threw balls of rolled up paper at each other above heads of these men. Day was dark and white paper balls were thrown above this dark crowd quickly moving to the gate and darkly Mr Gates went with them by side of Mr Tupe. He said his stomach felt like that lathe was working on end of it and he said this day was bitterest he would ever remember, a black day. Mr Tupe did not listen then, he also had got his cards and indeed, from moment that morning when they had been turned off both of them he had no use for Gates any more. By his being suspended he would be short of money so he would have to crawl to Gates now when he wanted a drink, (Mr Craigan was said to have money put by), instead of Gates making up to him for his company. Also this had been great shock to him, he had felt secure as Mr Bridges' spy.

Bentley came up outside gate and tried to shake hands with Gates, saying how bad he felt about their being turned off but Mr Gates would have nothing to do with him, his mind was all on himself. Bentley went off with Tupe. One thing only cheered Mr Gates. He had Craigan's cards in his pocket, now he had only to go on living in that house and Craigan would keep him to end of his days. And he would bring the wench to reason, if she married Dale then they were set right till they should die.

As he walked back along streets to Mr Craigan's house he thought how Tupe had made him the goat for all others in public house last night and he thought he was all square with Tupe now, being in the better position. But also he felt hopeless for he saw how he would be always under the dominion of Mr Craigan, and that made him savage with that hang-over he had, and being suspended being on his mind.

When he came into their house he found Dale was before him there. He went into kitchen.

'Where's Lil?' Dale said.

' 'Ow do I know where she is?' said Mr Gates.

'She ain't laid the dinner,' he said and Gates looked and swore. It was bare except for loaf of bread and the tinned beef so he picked up tinned beef and would have thrown it up chimney with histrionic gesture but he remembered he was now on Craigan's charity. He put it back on table.

'Maybe she's up with the old man,' he said and went to wash.

Mr Dale went upstairs. By time Mr Gates had done washing he calls down from top of the stairs to say she hasn't been up there since half past ten. Carefully putting Mr Craigan's cards in middle of kitchen table Mr Gates went out, bursting to get drunk.

(He had money he had earned from Wednesday to Saturday and

still had some of his last Friday's money which he had not been able to drink away all of it.)

Mr Dale went back to Craigan where he lay in bed. He said Lily was gone and Craigan said gone? Mr Dale said yes and she had not laid any dinner for them, hadn't cooked anything. Craigan said he was sorry for that, and this was first time he had ever apologized to Mr Dale, perhaps he could go cut himself some bread and cheese he said. But Mr Dale sat down on chair at side of the bed and Craigan, after looking at his face which was expressionless, began complaining. He said, and lately he had talked more and more, here he lay looking out of his window on the city with nothing but his thoughts by him. When you were old was little else to do but think, people same age as you died and you could not always expect young people to come and talk to you. And somehow, he said, he had lost the taste for Dickens, times were different now to when that man lived – it was funny he said that he should wait till he was this age to grow restless. Then again wireless was no longer what it had been and it got monotonous looking out down on the town hour after hour with days growing longer as they were.

Mr Dale looked past him out of the window and saw the shapes of factories and looked down streets down there below them. He picked out Parker's and out beyond was the Selwyn Motor Co. and over there was Beales and over there was Pullins. Then again picture of Lily running off with Bert Jones came before his mind and he looked down at floor again.

Town beneath them was a deep blue, like the Gulf Stream, with channels which were the roads cutting it up, appearing, being hidden, and they the colour of steel when it has been machined. Above it factory chimneys were built, the nearest rose up almost to level of where they were in bedroom only way away, and others further away came not so high. Rain had fallen ninety minutes before and this wet was now drying off the roofs. But these still glowed with white cold that steel has when it has been machined, and the streets also.

Mr Dale spoke out then. He said maybe she had run off with Bert Jones. But Craigan said why should it bother him her going for a walk with Jones and most likely she had not had dinner ready for them because she had been wild with her father at his clouting her.

338

He said Dale should not worry about things like that, because he was a young man, and to wait till he got to his, Craigan's, age, then was time to worry when was no longer time for anything, when life began to draw away from you.

So Craigan's voice droned on his complaint and Mr Dale thought how much more reason he had to complain and how the old man was losing grip, not to see Lily meant running off with Jones. But Mr Craigan did not want to see and when Dale went off he lay back and looked at the ceiling.

Mr Dale went up to centre of the town, to the Bull Ring and he wandered through markets there and through the Rag Market, joining in the crowds, drifting where they went. Mr Craigan lay on his back in his bed. He did not want to realize, even that he no longer worked at Dupret's (for Mr Dale had told him when first he came in) till turning his head his face rolled over opposite to the window. Sun had come out and showed between two rolls of cloud. Shining on the streets, points of the factory chimneys also caught some of it, and the wet roofs also that were on a path between him and the sun struck out at his eyes with brilliance. Mr Craigan turned his face from it.

Mr Craigan had gone to work when he was nine and every day he had worked through most of daylight till now, when he was going to get old age pension. So you will hear men who have worked like this talk of monotony of their lives, but when they grow to be old they are more glad to have work and this monotony has grown so great that they have forgotten it. Like on a train which goes through night smoothly and at an even pace – so monotony of noise made by the wheels bumping over joints between the rails becomes rhythm – so this monotony of hours grows to be the habit and regulation on which we grow old. And as women who have had nits in their hair over a long period collapse when these are killed, feeling so badly removal of that violent irritation which has become stimulus for them, so when men who have worked these regular hours are now deprived of work, so, often, their lives come to be like puddles on the beach where tide no longer reaches. But his time being up at Dupret factory woke Mr Craigan. At first, lying in bed after Mr Dale had gone, he was bitter. But when fully he saw that his working days were done he thought it was right he should be discharged, being an old man like he was. He began thinking again about Lily Gates.

When he had lain in bed, when he should have been at work, then rhythm had stopped for him and he had no motive, as rhythm was stopped, to get out of bed. Like as if train had stopped outside a station but now it draws in where he must get out and see to motorbike he rides on from now on. So this woke Mr Craigan, and he saw Lily was indispensable to his being now he had to sit about. Turning head on his pillow he saw shower was gathering over beyond the town and he was pleased. He thought that would drive them in if indeed they were out together.

Miss Gates walked with Mr Jones through streets and she was leading him to field where first he had kissed her.

She stopped him by yard of a monumental sculptor and they looked at tombstones there, both saying nothing and both dark with the white marble. One small stone had 'Reunited' only carved in middle of it and she wondered there should be no name and then wondered how much families got off price of headstones when they let them be shown lettered in the yard. All were recent – to memory of so-and-so 1927 and another, January, 1928.

When we think – it might be flock of pigeons flying in the sky so many things go to make our thought, the number of pigeons, and they don't fly straight. Now one pigeon will fly away from the greater number, now another: sometimes half the flock will follow one, half the other till they join again. So she thought about tombstones and how sculptor made it pay showing so many spoiled ones in his window as it might be. Till she dismissed this from her mind, thinking he would make it pay handsomely and well in any case.

When they came to that field they sat under hedge and he spread mackintosh he was carrying for them to sit on. At once she came to the point. She said they had waited too long...

She went on with arguments for their going which we have heard and he. Soon passionate scene was being enacted, as they say. Shower came on, rain welted down on them but neither noticed till at last, as she pushed her face into his yet again, suddenly her arms round his clothes felt his nerves go slack and he said they would go tomorrow.

So, as pigeon when she had watched out of kitchen window had flown diagonally down in a wedge and then recovered themselves, as each one had clapped his wings and gone slowly away, so she drew back from him, her mind unbound, and said to him: 'Why look it's raining.'

It was raining – it's coming on to rain decided Mr Craigan when he noticed it. He thought this would drive them in and he must see her face when first she came in from being with him, if indeed they had been out together.

With great care he got out of bed and went on his knees. He crawled to cupboard where his clothes were. This he had thought out, considering that his legs after three weeks in bed would be too weak to support his body, and he did not want to risk falls. Shapeless hump in his nightshirt he crawled along the floor. He dressed. His fingers trembled. Now and again he doubted if he had been discharged from Dupret factory. He knew he was best moulder in the shop.

With very great care he went downstairs. When he was down he stood at the foot to take breath. Well, he thought, he was down and this evening he would sit in the front room. He opened door into it and like all these front rooms air in it was stagnant but as he looked round for something out of its place, or as it should not be, he was satisfied by it. Was nothing but what was right. Well, he thought, whatever you might say against her the wench kept house clean as a whistle.

She would not keep it so clean if she had some light-witted notion in her head, so he thought and he was wrong for in this case Miss Gates was half ashamed at what she planned and had tried to justify herself in her own mind by doing more on the house than she had done before. But Mr Craigan was growing old, so more easily to be reassured. Still, picking out *Little Dorrit* from the bookshelf, he sat down in his best suit in the best chair and thought of what he would say to her that evening when she came in. Most likely she would be late if she had been with him and that would be added chance of saying something.

He sat. And he was so satisfied at how he had found the house after his time in bed, and above all so satisfied with his legs that had not given way as he went downstairs, as he had feared they would, that he fell into doze over open book.

He slept.

Round about seven Miss Gates came in. Taking off hat and coat she put them on a chair. She pressed palms of hands to her cheeks. Then she began to put out things for supper and to get food out of the cupboard. Her moving about in the next room woke Mr Craigan. He got out of his chair and carefully went to the door. He came in. As he came in she put his cards down which she had just seen on kitchen table. Her face wore guilty look as if he had surprised her prying into his life. She said:

'So you're down.' He was expecting to be first to speak and this put him off his guard but also he had recognized them as his cards which she had been holding, and now what had been uneasy feeling about losing his job was big as a slag heap before him.

'Ah. I'm down.'

She said no more to this and went on getting things out for supper. He was hurt she should take no more notice of his being downstairs, now of all times. But he was not going to talk about his being finished at Dupret's, he was not going to be first to open that. He thought of what to say:

'Maybe that's so much labour wasted o' your'n my gal,' he said, 'maybe they won't come in for supper after there weren't any dinner for 'em.'

'Maybe they will, maybe they won't but it'll be there for them, yes, on the kitchen table.'

This was so unlike her that Mr Craigan thought must have been more in her bawl out with her father than Jim had told him. For more you came to think on it more unlikely it was that she thought to run away from him. Where would they go? She hadn't got the banns out or he'd have heard. And his Lil would never stand for rooms, married or not. And there were his cards on the table.

'What made you not put dinner on for 'em?'

She did not answer him.

'Surely,' he said, 'you can't be mopin' like a pup that your dad 'it you?'

He waited to hear her sniff. Time was when anything from him had made her cry. Irritated, he expounded one of the great principles he lived by:

'In this 'ouse,' he said, 'the wage earners must 'ave hot meals every night bar Fridays, if they don't come back midday for it. And on Saturdays there is to be two 'ot meals, and one on Sunday.'

'Well ain't this going to be a 'ot meal?' she said.

He turned and went back into front room. In two minutes he felt he would be complaining to her of his health, instead of taking her to task. Again he said in mind he felt now to be an old man. Yes, and then, he thought, they took first chance they had to deprive you of work. Thinking he would have it out with her Sunday night, not now, not just now, he turned all his anger on to subject of Dupret factory, against his better judgment.

She was so excited anything she handled seemed to be alive. Bert had surprised her, yes, out of all knowledge. Once he'd said he would go he'd let out he'd looked up trains, he'd been so masterful, yes, it was now or never.

Neither Mr Dale nor Gates came in to supper. She waited for them. When still they did not come she put up the hot dish and took some sewing into front room where Mr Craigan sat. He said hadn't they come in and she said no. He said how was that? 'they 'ave no right not to come in when their supper's ready for 'em,' and she was pleased at that and thought her coming in had taken all suspicion from his mind.

She sat in a tumult, trying to keep fingers steady on her sewing.

Mr Dale came in then. She went into the kitchen and brought him his supper. When all had been put before him she said was anything he wanted? but he said no. She said something about bed and went upstairs. Craigan thought it was that she did not want to come face to face with Gates, when he would make her say to Joe she was wrong before all of them. Mr Dale ate and then came into front room where Craigan was. They sat in silence. Then at last Craigan began complaining. Gates being out gave him pretext for his complaint, how Gates was always out and now that they were finished at Dupret's they would not be able to afford boozers. Mr Dale also thought if it weren't for Lily he could go out and see the world now, travelling up and down England. But he would say goodbye to more than that for Lily. Some years of his life had been staked on her, like impaled, he could not think to let them go for nothing, the years and all he had said to her. (He had spoken little or nothing to her all that time.)

Just then Mr Gates came out of public house. He was drunk and in state of righteous indignation. Mr Tupe came out after him. He was in same state as Mr Gates. He said to find her out, to go and give her a good thraipin', ah, to make her give up all these mad thoughts and to marry decent and regular, to a respectable man, to Mr Dale, he said, that everyone in factory respected along with Mr Craigan. This he meant and he was sincere in this for he saw many free drinks in money Joe would get from that old man. But misfortune was following him like a dog for Mr Gates at that moment suddenly became aware to full extent of his own misfortunes come upon him this day. He broke loudly into long recitation of all the oaths known to him. This was more than what policeman on the corner would stand for and this one ran him in, took him to police station, locked Joe up.

# 18

When Lily got to station, bag in hand, she was so tired with strain of walking through streets seeing in each man or woman she passed someone who would ask her where she was going off to with a bag on Sunday morning, and at the first, leaving home like she had – all those lies and the way she crept downstairs had so tired her that she could hardly see who were standing on the platform. Whether were any there she knew. She said in mind she was in such a state now she did not mind if there was someone who'd see her. She put bag down and there, when she looked up again, was Mr Jones. In his hand was bouquet of tulips.

'Why, what 'ave you got there?'

'I stopped by the cemetery and bought 'em.'

'Whatever did you bring those for?' she said, 'Yes, what for?' growing hysterical. 'Why I nearly fainted away. Oh Bert, 'ow could you?'

'Why, what's the matter? I thought...'

'And me thinkin' 'ow I could make myself less conspicuous, yes, and then there you are with a great bunch of flowers on the station platform, why whatever will they think?'

'Think? Oo'll think? What's it matter what they think?'

'You stand where you are while I 'ave a look round your shoulder.'

Trembling, breathing deeply, she peered round his shoulder at those who were to travel with them. She stood by shoulder of the arm below which hung the tulips, his head bent over hers as she peered round and this movement repeated in her knee which was bent over heads of the tulips as they hung. She had on silk stockings today.

She gave up looking at the travellers. She looked now at the tulips.

'Where'll you put them?'

'Where will I put them?' He raised them up till they were upright as they grew.

'Do not!' she said and snatched at his wrist and turned them upside down.

'Oo's being conspicuous now?'

'You go and leave them in the Gentlemen.'

'Leave 'em in the lavatory?'

'Yes, what are you lookin' at me for, we can't take them with us what's come over you, yes, leave 'em in there. Why, at every station the train stopped we'd 'ave porters lookin' in at the window and wondering.'

'Well what's it matter if they do wonder, what do they know?'

'O Bert I do wish I 'adn't come.'

'All right,' he said, 'if that's the way you feel I'll leave 'em there.' He went off to do this. Looking at her shoes she thought in mind why you see they'd telegraph back, telegraphs being free between themselves so to speak, they'd telegraph back along the line – seen a young lady with a boy and tulips, something's up evidently, do the police want 'em, like that, yes, O why had he bought them? Look at those people on the platform now watching him going – but they were not watching him, being too disgusted at having to travel on a Sunday to notice anything but themselves.

When he came back without the tulips she breathed easier for it and began to feel for her hair under brim of hat. He was bewildered.

But they were not long without their tulips. Like old stage joke they were brought to them by lavatory attendant. As he gave them to Mr Jones, who did not resist, he said:

'You'm be by the banks of the river Nile, mister,' he said. 'I sees you forget 'em out of the corner of me eye from where I was in the office, and I daint stay longer'n to put me coat on before I was after you.'

Miss Gates turned and walked off to end of platform furthest from where other passengers stood.

'You'll 'ave the missus create at you my lad,' he said, 'if you go hon forgetting.' He turned and started back. 'Maybe, again, you'll forget 'erself,' he said, more to himself than to Mr Jones, turning prophetic. Mr Jones went after Miss Gates. Now again tulips hung down bobbing along, thumping against calves of his legs under plum coloured suit he wore. When he got to her she said:

'I come over bad.'

'Sit on the seat then.'

They sat there.

'Give 'em to me dear,' she said then, suddenly reckless, 'I don't care and it's a shame to hold 'em the way you are,' and she took them and rocked them in her arms. He smiled and for a moment had great relief. (For he wanted badly to go to the lavatory and having to leave the tulips had not given him time to have one. Now he could not go back, because of the lavatory attendant. His mind was fixed on possibility of train being corridor train.) At this moment train came in.

As on platform suddenly then she had stopped being afraid to meet someone she knew, now in the compartment, empty but for themselves – and, being Sunday, it was not corridor train – she put tulips on the rack and they did not worry her any more. Now one or two, their heads drooping through meshes of the rack, wobbled at them when train drew out of station.

They sat side by side. Now it was all over she folded eyelids down over her eyes. He thought Derby would be the next stop where there'd be any wait worth calling by the name. Other stations they'd just stop, look out, and be off again.

Tulips, tulips she remembered time of infinite happiness in a cinema when a film was on about tulips. Not about tulips, but tulips came in.

This train stopped at next station. Man came into their compartment. He was working man. They both looked at him, not speaking, and he looked at them and all three turned eyes away from each other's eyes. Then he looked again at Mr Jones and when train started again he said 'Excuse me won' cher but would your name be Pinks?' Mr Jones said no, his name weren't Pinks. This man said Pinks had a double in him then, they might be twin brothers for all you could tell the difference between them. 'Excuse my asking you like that,' he said and he noticed suddenly tulips on rack above his head – (he was sitting opposite to them). He had to lean his head back to see them properly and when he did Lily winked at Mr Jones. Then, bringing his face down to them, again all three turned eyes away from each other's eyes.

Lily looked to see if that man should smile but he did not and she thought it unobservant in him not to smile at meaning of those tulips. Then she was surprised because Mr Jones had winked at this man and jerked with his head to other side of the compartment. Both of them went over there, leaving her by herself, and Bert began whispering to him. Miss Gates did not know what to make of it.

They came into next station and stopped. This man got out. As he got out she heard him say to Mr Jones no, he wouldn't get real chance before Derby. As he went away she plainly heard him say well he hoped it would come out all right for him. She was amazed.

'What'll come out all right for you?' she said and Bert said it was nothing.

'You didn't take 'im into the corner away from me for nothing.'

'I just wanted to ask 'im something.'

'O it's something now is it, instead of being nothin? Ain't I supposed to know.'

'Well no, you ain't, that is . . .'

'Why ain't I supposed to know?'

'There weren't anything in it Lil, it was only I . . . I won't tell yer.'

'You will!'

'I won't.'

But she looked so miserable then that he explained. He went red in the face when she began to laugh at him. 'Ah, but I'm not laughing,' he said and she laughed and discussed ways and means with him. They could find no way out. 'Kiss me Bert,' she said but that was no good as he said he could not, the way he was feeling now. Somehow this delighted her. Their journey, at last, was beginning. Every minute they were further from Birmingham and everything harassing was away behind them now. And they were getting near to Derby.

When train drew into Derby station he ran out of the train and she leant out of the window. When he came back all smiles she opened door for him from where she was on the inside, and once he was in she put hands on his shoulders and pushed him down onto the seat. She sat down across his legs and kissed him.

Then she got down and sat by his side. Train started again. Now at last, she thought in mind, this journey is begun. He kissed her.

But it's not like that. While she expected to be happy she was not and Mr Jones could only think of what they would do when they got to Liverpool.

For as racing pigeon fly in the sky, always they go round above house which provides for them or, if loosed at a distance from that house then they fly straight there, so her thoughts would not point away long from house which had provided for her.

With us it is not only food, as possibly it is for pigeon, but if we are for any length of time among those who love us and whom we love too, then those people become part of ourselves.

As, in Yorkshire, the housewives on a Sunday will go out, in their aprons, carrying a pigeon and throw this one up and it will climb in spirals up in the air, then, when it has reached a sufficient height it will drop down plumb into the apron she holds out for it, so Miss Gates, in her thoughts and when these ever threatened to climb up in air, was always coming bump back again to Mr Craigan. And again, as when we set off impetuously sometimes then all at once we have to stop as suddenly just how little we are rushing off for becomes apparent to us, so, now first excitement was over, for first time it was plain to her just what she was after. She wanted to better herself and she wanted a kid.

At home was Mr Craigan with no more work in him, and her father, and Mr Dale. For some years Mr Dale's life had been part of hers and she thought in mind how she was mostly Mr Dale's life.

We do not want a thing so very badly all the time: just now she didn't, now she came to think on it, particularly want children.

Mr Craigan, what would he do without her? And in his illness, who'd look after him? And wasn't a bird in hand worth two in the bush? Who'd say if they'd be any better off wherever they were going.

Mr Jones jogged at her arm. What was she thinking of, he thought, she was so silent now? Nodding to window, he said:

'Black Country.'

She looked out of window. It was the Black Country. Now series of little hills followed one on the heels of another. Small houses. Lots of smoke.

Train began to slow down. She did hate the country anyway really. You couldn't say anything for this bit but that were lots of towns in it.

Mr Jones then said, wondering still what she could be thinking about.

'Black Country courtship.'

She looked out at once. When she had heard word 'courtship' just now and for some time past heart had tugged at her breathing.

She saw man and girl walking up winding path which had been made up a slag heap. Man was dressed in dark suit with a white stock for collar and wore bowler hat, high crowned. But it was the girl's clothes interested Miss Gates.

Her clothes were so much exactly what she liked that seeing her walking there, it might have been her twin. Not that she could see her face, but it was just what Miss Gates liked in clothes. And she who had been saving to go to Canada where they wore those things you saw in movie pictures, wide hats and blue shirts! Though the older women did dress more ordinary. But O it was so safe and comfortable what that girl was wearing. Temptation clutched at her. She put forefinger to her mouth. She hoped for train to go on. Train stopped. She could not take eyes away from looking at those two, O it was so safe and comfortable to be walking on this slag heap. For where was she going herself? Where would they walk themselves when they got out there. Miss Gates felt she didn't want to walk any place where she hadn't walked before. Or to wear any clothes but what that girl and she liked, and that only where would be others who liked those clothes looking out of train windows or from the roads, wherever they might be.

Looking at her Mr Jones saw she was dreaming. He thought this was a funny way to start off on life's journey, but then women, he thought in mind, were funny things. He relapsed back into his own worries. Fact was his parents had not written to him for three years. They'd be able to put her up for a night or two till he got the licence and he and Lily got married before they went off. Why hadn't Lily liked to get married in Brum. Anyway was no hanky panky about her, it was marry or nothing with her, and that's the way any responsible chap looks at it he thought in mind.

But that was the trouble, suppose he could not find parents. He knew they had changed shop they had managed, and lived over, for another. They had written to say they would write from their new address, but they never had. Suppose the people at the old address did not know where his home had gone. It made you bad to think of it. And his aunt, her who was wife of the lodge-keeper not far from tram terminus, she hadn't had word of them, not since long before he had. He hadn't told Lily, had kept it from her. He'd have to tell her, it wouldn't be right if he didn't tell her. He'd say, just as they were drawing into Liverpool, how he didn't know their address just yet as they'd changed houses and he'd lost letter when they'd written to tell him, but he and she would go to the old address and ask. Made you look foolish when you told all that was on your mind and then there was nothing in it. Yes, that's what he'd say and besides, they'd find them, the people who'd taken over their shop would be bound to know where they'd gone.

Now everything which before had seemed terrible to her, like how if she stayed in Birmingham she would get like all the other women, and Bert the same as all other men, never any better off – only poorer, now this to her put on appearance of the great comfort. But now at the same time she put this from her mind. Wheeling turning her thoughts took on formation ducks have or aeroplanes when they are flying, both of them. She had come so far. She could not go back. 'Yes, I can't go back now,' she said in mind. Blindly her hand stumbled to get in crook of his arm, (for she did not look at him), and crept through like water seeping and round his arm. He turned and kissed her. Then he turned back and watched those two on the slag heap.

They sat. The train was still. She looked at shoes on her feet, he at those two standing on the slag heap above. Her arm was round his arm. She put head on his shoulder, their hair whispered together, both had yellow hair. Train moved on now, smoothly, like water the land glided past outside. He rested his head on hers where it rested on his shoulder. So their heads inclined one to the other, so their breathing fell in one with the other, so they took breath together in one breath as they had been, once before in night. Her arm through his arm felt his body breathe with hers and then her life was deep and strong to her like she couldn't remember feeling before. He did not notice, for he worried yet.

Mr Craigan took headphones off his head.

Perhaps he could have a sleep. He leant back in chair.

He interlocked fingers of his hand across his belly. He crossed his feet. He closed eyes.

No he could not sleep.

He made movement as if to pick up *Little Dorrit* which lay on the table.

No he knew he could not read.

He drew back his hand and picked bits of fluff and cotton off his trousers.

He unbuttoned one more button of his shirt.

His fingers worried then at button of his waistcoat. Then he buttoned that button up again on his shirt, with difficulty, his fingers were swollen.

He thought what was it doing outside? He got up. He went to window and drew aside lace curtains. It looked like rain. He thought if it rained it might drive them in. If they weren't under cover this time.

Coming back to his chair which was by fireplace he saw again photograph of her aunt Ellie. What happened of her. What did her come to?

He knew if he went upstairs he'd know one way or t'other but that's just what he couldn't bring himself to do just now. When a thing's done it's done. When a job's scabbed it's scabbed. He'd talk to her tonight when she came back, her'd know, when she came back. If she did come back.

He sat down again. He looked into grate which had pink paper fan in it. Was clean as a whistle. Her didn't stint her work. If her took on a job you could wager she'd go right through with it, not just play with it. But there, that was it. He blamed himself. He shouldn't have put off bawling her out last night.

He'd see what they were doing now in Berlin. He put headphones on his head. As he did this he remembered again how, out of corner of his eye, he'd seen she go past this door out to the street with something in her hand, might have been a bag. It was no use. He took headphones off his head. He sat for a moment. Then he got up out of chair and made for the stairs. He climbed them. He went into her room.

They sat in railway carriage side by side. Now she had drawn back from him.

He was so sure they would find his parents when they got to Liverpool that he was making plans now of what they would do in Canada, of how well they would do. Again was first day outside, another fine evening. They stopped at station and he let down the window to let country air in onto air they had brought with them from Birmingham, but Lily asked him to close it. He thought how nervous she seemed but then it was only natural in a woman starting on life's journey.

Miss Gates was very nervous. She kept herself by force now, as it might be, from thinking of Mr Craigan. She was now wondering how she could ever happen to be in this railway carriage. Bert seemed like stranger to her, and in these strange stations. And the night air that was coming up, it couldn't be healthy in these parts. But she was frightened, O yes. Night was coming in, she was frightened of this night. In strange house. Not in her own bed. Her underclothes she was now wearing were strange to her, she had made them for this. No, they couldn't have had that window open, it wasn't safe.

Then – he was so confident he brought it out by the way like – he told her how he did not know his parents' address. He told her what they would do.

'Why did you tell me?'

'I 'ad to tell you, love. I wouldn't 'ave been right.'

'But we'll find them shan't we Bert?'

'Of course we will.'

'Then why put ideas into my 'ead. Now I feel frightened,' she said.

He put his arms about her shoulders. He poked his face blindly round in her hair. Strength of his arms about her made her feel safer but all the same her thoughts turned round and round this new thing now, in images. She lay limp against him. She saw them in streets, it getting darker, and they walking and walking till there'd be nowhere they could go. Being with his parents, well it was decent, it wasn't the last word on what they were going to do, she could still then go back to Birmingham, she hadn't burnt her boats as they say. But being alone with him, well there you were. She wondered if she could yet go back, even if his people were in Liverpool. She thought they'd just got to be in Liverpool.

Just then train came into a station and stopped. Mr Jones took arms from off her and looked out of window. Noise of loud voices came from towards them along platform, one man said ''Ere Charley this'd do,' another, 'No Ed let's go farther along.' Terrified Miss Gates watched bit of platform through the window and wooden paling behind it on which was nailed advertisement for Pears Soap. Next that was advertisement for Liverpool paper. Behind road outside was pink house and the sky in bars of red and black. She watched this space most intently. Nine men came into it. They looked into this carriage, she saw one man with white face who had bright green muffler. That was bad luck about, seeing green like that. They went by, she heard 'ere you are – get in 'ere Sid – of course there ain't no bloody corridor one said. Good thing there wasn't a corridor now, even if it had caused a bit of a bother before. Then she remembered these men had been carrying musical instrument cases. She thought what would they have been up to on a Sunday, think, on a Sunday. She did feel so nervous. Porter ran up laughing and said through window to these men how he hoped they were all right. Then he said, walking along by side of train which was now moving, how he did not think the folks down this way would forget them coming for some time yet. The men were all laughing.

This dance band had been hired by vicar to play hymn tunes in church service, for every Sunday now his church was empty and he would do anything to have it full. He had given them tea and while he had gone off to take his evening service and to find the church quite full again, not even standing room, these nine men had come and caught this train back to Liverpool where they lived and worked.

This Sunday had been unusual Sunday for them, by now they were quite worked up. Three sat in racks, six about on the seats. One said to come on and have a tune. As he took saxophone out of case this turned red in sunset light. Pianist said what'll I do? Someone said he could raise his ugly voice. As they got instruments out of the cases they laughed each one to himself, alone, they played a

353

little separately to tune these instruments. Then they all looked at one man. This one did not seem to move yet all at once suddenly they all slipped into playing, all nine of them, pianist played on cushions of the seat, they were one, no more nine of them, one now.

What more could have been wanted to fit in so with Mr Jones' happy feelings? In wonderment he listened. He got up. Forgetting Lily he opened window to listen better to them and hung head out.

'Bert' screamed Miss Gates. She jumped up and pulled at his shoulders.

When he came in again she said: 'whatever were you doing that for? Why a bridge might 'ave come and cut your head off and where would I be then?'

Sharp air of evening rushed in on them. She pulled window up. He sat down and when window was up he drew her down onto his knees. He said had she been scared? He kissed her. But she got down from his knees. She listened to tune they were playing with distrust. She trembled.

As he listened beat of that music, so together, made everything in the world brother to him. As he listened and they played he expanded in his feeling and looking back in his memory for something he might express this by he put arms round Lily. He said:

'In our iron foundry at our place there was a chap used to sing. 'E 'ad a wonderful voice, what you might call a really fine voice, you know love what I mean. Last time I 'eard him sing 'e went on all day. D'you know what it was? 'Is wife 'ad given 'im a son the night before.' He kissed Miss Gates. 'All the chaps used to come round when he sang.'

Again she lay limp in his arms, distraught. Kids, I don't want 'em she cried in mind.

Pianist sang. He was tenor. He sang:

Your eyes are my eyes
My heart looks through

Horror. She looked past Mr Jones' head which was pressing against her head and there was Liverpool beginning. She hated it. Factories. Poor quarters. More and more of them.

She got up and tidied herself by the glass. Her face even frightened her.

So when they got into station and got out she said in mind it was all she could do to walk.

'Aren't you going to take the flowers,' he said laughing.

'What are you talking of?' she said. 'Leave 'em in there for Christ's sake.'

# 19

What is a town then, how do I know? What did they do? They went by lamps, lamps, lamps, each one with light and dark strung up on it each with streets these were in. Houses made the streets, people made the houses. People lived in them, thousands millions of lives. Each life dully lived and the life next it, pitched together, walls between built, dully these lives went out onto streets promenaded dullness there. Ugly clothes, people, houses. They went along through these, strangers to it, she did not recognize her own form of ugliness in it.

Thousands of lamps, hundreds of streets, each house had generally a mother and complacent father, procreation, breeding, this was only natural thing there in that miserable thing home, natural to them because it was domesticated. Procreating was like having a dog, in particular spaniels. Fido who I'm so grateful to. Miserable people. Clerks dregs lowest of people these not fat and meat but like bellied fish or schoolmasters, in particular cod.

Sunday is worst day in the world. You can go out Sunday and come back in everything sucked out of you by inquisitiveness in eyes in residential districts, from clerk's fleshlessness. At night they all stay in, most of all Sundays, after a little fiddling walk for the wife to show off clothes after showing them off through a little bit of fiddling church service. Some of them have little jolly card parties with a few jolly fellows. They may be coming walking back from it. But for them, no one about. Getting dark now, each lamp has light and dark to it. By gad didn't know it was so late well better be getting along now or the wife won't have it eh, think I'm up to some of the old games what well old chap I'll say goodnight now oh I say no I say old man did you see your wife give me a kiss well perhaps it was a good thing you didn't what, Gracie you're the sweetest little woman, with another of course oh, that well dash it all that ever was. Well goodnight and God bless you all – well and my goodness now if he wasn't wiping a little wet wetness out of the corner of his little yellow little eyeballs God bless us.

Or is it the young sweetheart saying goodnight at the gate of the eight by four front garden to the girl chosen for him, her arch as her photographs. And her kiss has lit such a little light in him, like a little flaming candle, he'll warm himself over it all night yes he will. Inside the old people draw up nearer to the fire, out at the garden gate, Mary, when we were young what a glorious thing life was, Mary, glorious youth – but there's life in these old bones yet he said thinking Fido, only Fido wasn't biting.

They had come on tram to outskirts of Liverpool. They were walking in the direction back in now. They looked for address of shop. Mr Jones knew his way. Smell of the sea was at her, forcing itself on her.

They had been on edge of the Residential District. They were coming now to blinded shops. Roads were broader, lighter by a little. Here was dropsical fatness of shopkeepers' paunches, when they got to address they were looking for they knocked one up. Early to bed early to rise this one's motto. In nightshirt he came to window above. He leaned paunch out over window frame, he let his weight sink on it, bulging. If they'd wait two minutes he would get address for them where their parents had moved and in his place at window showed curling papers like bobbins. Whining voice came from inside of that room – 'what is it ma? Ma, ma, who's there ma, what is it?' His wife poked her nose over window frame. Lily saw nose, one eye, curling papers.

'Well now' said fat shopkeeper they met afterwards squirming along in shadows of the street looking for a bit of fun – these courting couples in the doorways y'know, y'know you can see a bit o' fun o' nights – 'well now' he said, 'it's Mulgrave Street you want is it?' He told them, shopkeeper they had knocked up hadn't been able to tell them way to address he had given them and Mr Jones did not know that part of town it was in. Dropsically fat, hatpin little eyes, shopkeeper watched Miss Gates as he told them. Something up here. That gal looked frightened out of her life. But that young chap was up to a bit o' fun. Didn't know how to start with 'er, that's 'ow it looked. Yum yum he felt in huge belly, um yum.

Now first that feeling which had soaked all through about Mr Jones, how everything, everything was wonderful, she was the sweetest girl in the world and wouldn't the old people be glad to see her, now first that feeling ebbed and died in him. He was afraid for her as now they were going into poorer quarter of the town, streets were getting now to be the streets of ports, darkness of waters looked now to be flowing over into these streets. He did not know the way, but he knew they were going towards the docks. He had seen in his mind their coming to that shop and those there telling him to go back the way he had come with Miss Gates, to go back in direction of the Residential District. In his heart picture had warmed him of his bringing Lily to quiet respectable shop in a quiet decent street. He had thought out two ways of turning off her surprise and admiration when she saw so much prosperity. 'It's simple,' was one thing he was going to say, 'it's simple but the old folks knows what's comfortable.' One thing he had always feared, and that was effect his father would have on Miss Gates and now, as they walked further, and the streets were poorer and poorer streets, it was his father he suspected as having thrown his ma's prosperity away.

Ship's syren sounded, wailing, and with a great pang Miss Gates thought a factory buzzer at this time of the night, it couldn't be nightshift at this time of the night, O she did feel afraid. And that man they had asked their way of, his eyes! How dark it was getting! Well she just wouldn't look any more if it only made her shivery, she just wouldn't notice anything more. But it didn't happen often, did it, that all you thought of worst came to pass. But then she thought it wasn't quite so bad, they'd not expected to find them first go off. All the same, these streets! Well, she wouldn't look that's all.

At this time Mr Craigan and Mr Dale sat in kitchen.

'Well I'll tell you, which is more'n she did,' Mr Dale said, 'I'm going off.'

'Yes,' Mr Craigan said in low voice, 'when 'er cooked the Sunday dinner I dain't think she was goin' after. Her even doesn't wait to wash up but off she goes like that.'

'I ain't goin' to stay in this 'ouse, I'm goin'' said Mr Dale.

'What's that?'

'I'm not goin' to stay 'ere when she's gone.'

'Eh?'

'I say I'm not going to stay here, I'm off too.'

'Ah, tonight.'

'What for?'

'I ain't goin' to stay in this 'ouse.'

'Where will you go to?'

'I don't know, I'll find a place.'

'Better you stay the night here Jim.'

'No, I'm goin' off.'

'But what's in your mind, leavin' me like this?'

Mr Dale did not answer.

'First her goes then you goes,' Mr Craigan said, looking away from him.

Mr Dale did not answer.

'Maybe her'll come back tonight,' Mr Craigan said.

'Oh ah, so she takes 'er sleeping things for the afternoon like she 'as.'

Rain kept on falling. A drip made sound like hammer striking on thick piece of iron, light tap, repeating, repeating.

'Where would you go then,' said Mr Craigan, 'if you be goin?'

'I dunno,' said Mr Dale.

'Don't you go. I might come over bad and then who'd be there to see to me.'

Someone knocked on front door.

' 'Tis 'er,' Mr Craigan said and got up quickly.

Trembling he went out and stopped in front of door and heart in his mouth, holding to the wall – his hands were sweating and dampness on them sucked to it – he said who was it. If it was Lily he would not let her in at first, so he intended. But Mrs Eames answered him and said if Lily had bit of cheese she might borrow. Mr Craigan stood for three minutes then he said no. No.

'No cheese? Not just a little bit?'

'No,' said Mr Craigan.

'Sorry to 'ave troubled you I'm sure,' said Mrs Eames with meaning in her voice, not that she guessed Lily was away at all, only that she knew they kept cheese in their house. She went back in and said to Mr they were bad neighbours, she'd always thought it, how anybody could live with the old man, being as mean as he was, she didn't know. Mr Eames said Joe Gates was locked up for swearing and that would be on old Craigan's mind. Also Craigan had got the sack, along with Joe, for old age. Mrs said if she'd known she wouldn't 'ave gone, why hadn't he told her. 'I wanted a bit of cheese,' he said. 'What a shame on old Craigan,' said Mrs Eames 'that always kept himself so respectable and then his mate goes and gets himself locked up.' 'Well you know what I always did think about 'im,' she said, 'Well now I wouldn't like to say what I think, not now,' she said.

But Mr Dale saw in his mind when he knew it was not her knocking, he saw he could not stay in this house and not see her any more, he could not stay and not see her any more, any more. When he had told Craigan he was going he had not really meant it but waiting to know who was knocking them up had torn only one way at his heart this time. Time was when her movements, it might be her putting plates up on the rack, they had torn all ways at his heart and he hadn't known what way he felt towards her. But now, as formerly he'd wanted to be comforted by a woman for just going on and on every day, every day, now especially he wanted to be comforted for her not coming back. He saw he would get no sympathy in this house. So he went.

Now Mr Craigan raised no objections. He saw Dale really meant to go this time.


So Miss Gates did not look at anything. She just followed Mr Jones.

They went by public house. Man played on instrument, which was kind of xylophone, laid flat in the doorway. As the air sweats on metal so little balls of notes this man made hung on smell of stale beer which was like a slab outside the door. Man playing on this instrument was on his knees, and trunk of his body bent over it, head almost touched ground on other side of this flat instrument. Mr Jones saw position that man was in. He'd never seen one like it. Feeling of uneasiness grew up in him.

They were now in working class streets. Doors stood open. Miss Gates heard voices talking dialect strange to her. But she shut her ears to this, though it gave her slight feeling of comfort. She was so tired with walking. She got more and more blank.

Mr Jones took tighter grip on bag he was carrying, (his own he had left at railway station). They were getting into the dockers' quarter. He did not like it. But this was Mulgrave St. And this was no. 439. He knocked on the door. Miss Gates stood, she did not look up. He knocked. Door was opened by man in his shirt sleeves. He was a stranger to Mr Jones. He told them where his parents had gone was a half-mile further on and then they'd shifted from there so he'd heard though he couldn't say where they'd gone. He'd better go there, he said, and the people there might tell him. Miss Gates heard this and did not think at all, except she thought once it would have to finish some time. Mr Jones was frightened now. Man shut door on him and he stood frightened. Street was dark.

Street was dark. Miss Gates felt something in the street looking out, looking out then it was gone. Then it was back again. Where was Bert, had he gone? She looked up quickly but of course he was there. But street was dark. She got much more frightened and was rigid with it for two moments. Again something looked and was gone. And again. She felt no, after looking up to see if Bert was there she wouldn't look up again to see what that was. There it was. She had to look. No she wouldn't. She had to, so she looked. It was searchlight from the lighthouse, it stroked over sky and was gone. With great pang she wondered what that was doing there. Then she decided that was what came from looking up. She would not look up again. They began walking again. She was blank, blank. Again it came along the sky.

Mr Jones watched, watched everything but Lil. He did not like to look at her. He thought of his parents, what could have brought them to this part? He was ashamed. What they would do now he couldn't say. What would come of it if the next address didn't know where they'd gone. What'd he do with Lil.

Once before when their relations one with the other had come to a point, he had seen it like he was setting job up on a lathe, the foreman looking on and others in the shop watching him. Job was difficult, he'd been in two minds to begin or not. Now he was alone, lathe was stopped, he was alone. Job was going wrong. If he went now, and he would never come back, chances were they could work that bit in again for now he thought this ending was like the finish of all what you might call dreams. Anything a bit out of the way and he couldn't do it. He blamed himself. What was the good in trying to better yourself when you couldn't hold a better job. Now if he went on with this bit on the lathe he would hopelessly spoil it. Now, he thought, if he went on with Lily, and his parents weren't there or in a bad way, he couldn't ask her to take on any wife's life in this town, the ordinary kind of life anywhere, when she'd come out to get on in the world. Better she went back to Mr Craigan which had money of his own.

For if he could not find father and mother who then would give them money for their passage. Besides it was like taking Lil on false pretences to take her to this. Smelling of the sea like this street did, it wasn't respectable, apart from the people that lived in it. He was afraid then she might not be able to go on, who had walked so far already this evening. He hardly dared look at her. Dragging a little behind, face turned down towards the ground, he thought she looked all one way, skint. He thought it was no wonder, but then this would be the address.

He stopped. Lily stopped. Door of this house was open, man he did not know sat on chair just by it. Mr Jones said in low voice so Lily would not hear, did a man called Jones live here at one time? This man said yes but he and his wife had gone and had left no address. 'Would you be connected with the family?' he said. Mr Jones said 'Yes.' 'Well then,' this man said, he believed there'd been a bit of trouble but he couldn't say for sure and said goodnight to Mr Jones. For looking at Lily he took her for daft, and he decided he did not want to be mixed up in this, for it looked funny to his mind's eye.

Mr Jones said, 'it ain't much further to go now Lil,' and went off again. She followed a little behind. He was so ashamed he did not like to come near her to help her. He only went slower as he was afraid her strength might give up any time now. He thought her blankness he saw to look at her, was her hating him.

He had remembered great tall street which should be near to them to the west. Trams ran down it. He leads her there.

They get there. It is bright with street lamps. He was sure now was nothing but to leave her get home, if he went with her it might all begin again, he might not be able to let her alone. Here they were in this tall street. He stopped by lamp post where trams stopped. She stopped. Then he sees she is crying quietly. He comes close to her and she leans a little on him. He stood so for a bit then he said, 'Lil, here's your bag.' Without thinking, she was all blank, she reached down to pick it up. She looks up to him then. But he was running away down this street. She picked up bag and began to run after him, still not realizing and like obediently, like small children run, in steps, not strides. She put forefinger in her mouth. She could not see distinctly so did not see him turn down alley way. (When he got into dark court at end of this alley he crouches down in a corner beyond cone of light which falls in front of it.) He looks back over his shoulder but she had not seen him turn, she is still trotting. Tear drops off her chin. Then she saw a policeman and no Bert. She stopped. Tram drew up there which was another stopping place for trams. Woman that was there and had seen her face said quickly come in on the tram dear. She got on. Policeman turned away.

# 20

Mr Craigan sat by bed at their home in Birmingham in which was Miss Gates.

'Dear heart,' he said, 'don't grieve so.'

Sobs tore her.

He put hand over her eyes, her eyes, tears would not come from them. Sobs seemed as though they would split her. 'Quiet, quiet,' he said. Her troubles stood up in her feeling like plinths to her. Sobs in spasms retched through body. Tear ran down by his nose then another, then from under his hand tears came from her eyes. Her body sank into the bed, down. Then she did not retch any more and tears came to her parched mouth and softened lips there and she opened them and sucked tears in. Her tears came more freely and she turned face into the pillow and they made wet patch on this.

Then, as after rain so the sky shines and again birds rise up into sky and turn there with still movements so her sorrow folded wings, so gently crying she sank deeper into the bed and was quieted. He still kept hand over her eyes, but she was quieted.

Sweat poured out from all her body now.

Miss Gates was still sleeping. Mr Craigan coming into room saw mass of her shapeless in the bed. Out of this her hair was like short golden rivers. When he came in she woke up and jumped round in bed.

He was carrying in his two hands – (in his two hands for his one hand would have spilt it, they trembled so, he was old,) – he carried cup of tea. Sleep still lay on her, from up on her elbows she watched him. He came up to the bed and looked to see where he would put down the tea. He put the cup on floor. He brought chair up. With difficulty he bent down and put the cup of tea onto chair. She thought when she saw him do this oh not on the chair, not that way, look at him, he would spill it. When he had safely put it down she thought how kind of him, how kind, how kind he was.

Year after year, every day after every day, she had brought him cup of tea in the morning.

She made to get up. He pushed her onto her back again.

'I brought you a cup o' tea.'

'You oughtn't, no, you oughtn't.'

'Lie you back, my wench, you'll stay where you is today.'

'But what about Jim's tea?'

' 'E's gone.'

'Gone?' Miss Gates said. Mr Craigan did not answer. Oh dear, oh dear but she thought she better not say anything.

'There's Joe,' she said.

' 'E's gone too.'

'Joe gone too?' She began crying. 'Oh dear, Joe gone too.'

'Was you about then all the time I was away?'

'You drink up that tea.'

She cried. She began drinking tea. She cried. Between catching her breaths she had sip of tea.

'You lie there all today,' he said, 'an' I'll get you a bite to eat. You must be wore out.'

He went downstairs and sat on chair in kitchen. She went to sleep again.

Later when he came up again she was still sleeping. He did not wake her.

Later she woke. He'd said for her to stay in bed, so she'd better stay. She looked at empty tea cup. Then she lay over on her back and looked at ceiling.

She thought now her father would have told everyone she'd gone when he left the house. What had he gone for? All the street would know. But they didn't make no difference to her, she'd behave like she didn't notice them. What they said didn't touch her.

Downstairs Craigan thought it was likely nobody didn't know. She hadn't mixed much ever with the other women, only thing was Mrs Eames calling round like she had night before last. And as it was Liverpool they'd gone to, so she'd told him when she got in last night, it wasn't likely there'd be anyone knew her in Liverpool. And it was likely Mrs Eames came just by chance. Anyroad she hadn't asked after her. But what had they been up to when they got to Liverpool?

Lily was now thinking she couldn't abide their eyes on her. She couldn't stand the way they'd look at her. No she thought she'd never be able to stand face to face with them, no never, never again, it was awful. Mr Craigan came up. He came into her room. He went over to chair at side of her bed and put the cup and saucer onto mantelpiece, then he sat on the chair.

'Let's 'ave it from start to finish,' he said.

She lay on her back in bed and her face on pillow was away from him so all he could see was her cheek and one side of her nose.

'I don't know,' she said, 'we walked an' walked.'

'Begin at the beginnin',' he said.

'Well I wonder you didn't notice me makin' all those clothes and all, yes, but I didn't think you would. You were only men all of you so I didn't trouble, I just made 'em under your noses. Then goin' out with my bag like that, you'd 've thought you'd 'ave stopped me, but no not a word and there I went with all the street watching me, the eyes nearly dropping out of their 'eads I expect. But it was funny,' Miss Gates said forgetting to be defiant and now getting interested, 'it was funny but I didn't meet no one. Except at the corner of James Road and Hobmore Lane I made sure there was Mrs Ludd but no I didn't meet no one all the way to the station. And there was 'im on the station platform with a bunch of tulips in 'is right 'and, yes, but oh well, well we got into the train and it went off. It was all right for a bit but then 'e 'ad to get out at Derby and then after that I don't know but nothing seemed to go right.'

'Wasn't that train slow,' said Miss Gates continuing after gulping. Now she lay looking up to the ceiling. She frowned a little. 'And we couldn't get anything to eat. I couldn't eat any dinner that morning only you didn't notice none of you, but I 'ad too much on me mind and we didn't like to nip out of the train to buy something, it might

364

'ave gone on you see and left one of us behind. O it was slow. Then we went on and on and it got like darker and darker, we was very quiet, and I got frightened. You see it was him bringing them tulips give me a turn at the start and then—' she turned face over away from him again, 'O I did wish I was back 'ere.'

She stopped. He did not say anything. He looked at his slippers. Then she went on:

'Well then, it seemed like hours and hours, and then we got to a little station and there was nine men on the platform, I counted them, and they all got in an' once the train started they began playing, it was a band. On a Sunday! One of them 'ad a green muffler on and soon as I saw it I said to myself there's a bad luck for you. Then after that there was that black that 'ad a green muffler when we was walking, that was in Liverpool. We come to a place in the road where they 'ad arc lamps up. They 'ad a crane there. There was three men right up on it doing somethin' and a great crowd of people below, I was frightened.'

Here again she stopped.

'When we got to Liverpool,' she said, 'it was night time and I knew I wouldn't like the town. But he took me to a posh place on the platform, not just a ordinary tea room and we 'ad a bite to eat there. That kind of put 'eart into me but that's what it was,' she said, 'yes, I 'ad too much heart, I didn't ought to 'ave been there at all. Then we got on a tram an' I didn't like the looks of that town, yes I thought I'll never be happy 'ere and then 'e took me off it, and we went to the first address. You see he didn't know where 'is people lived exactly, they'd changed addresses, O yes it's true, I know that by the way 'e left me. Well then we went from place to place. There was those arc lamps and the black, O it's like a dream and the ships 'ooting, I couldn't make out what that was at first. And then you see we couldn't find them. By the time it came to that I was too tired to take notice, we'd come so far. Then 'e took me to a road where the trams went and I thought we was just going on again but I was crying then and no wonder and there, he said,' said she extemporizing but she believed now he had said it, which he never had, ' "well Lil it's goodbye now" he says, "I ain't no good, you'd better go 'ome." '

Here Miss Gates cried.

'Was that all?' Mr Craigan said.

'Oh I don't know 'ow I found the train. Next thing I remember was being sick, oh dear I didn't sleep at all an' being sick gave me black eyes. And when we got to Birmingham I couldn't come back home by daylight, you see someone might spot me. So I waited about till it was dark. And then I came, when you let me in.'

Here she was so grateful to him for letting her back that she grew small again and her eyes looking at him were warm, adoring. Was silence. She drew out her arm from under bedclothes and laid it over his hands. He opened his hands and her forearm lay in over open palms. Was silence.

'Aye, he weren't much of a man,' he said.

'No grandad he was. Things is different now to what they were in your day.'

'Then you daint pass the night with 'im?'

'No grandad.'

'You would 'ave done when I was a lad.'

'Yes but things is different now you see, yes, they are really. Yes we didn't go for that.'

'What for then?'

'We went to better ourselves, and grandad I do wish we 'adn't gone.'

'You were dreamin'.'

'Yes grandad.'

'Nothin' ever come of dreams like them kind,' he said. 'Nothin' dain't ever come of dreams, I could 'ave told yer but that wouldn't be of no use, you 'ad to find out of yourselves and so you 'ave,' he said.

That morning Mr Craigan went out to buy food for both of them and Mrs Eames took it into her head to call on Miss Gates. Mrs Eames had not seen Lily about for some days. She had met Mr Craigan as he went out that morning to buy food and he had said Lily had a fever when Mrs Eames had asked after her. So Mrs Eames called in, thinking for a moment in her mind men did not know how to care for anybody when they were sick and it would be neighbourly in her to call round.

When Mrs Eames came up Lily of course was frightened with her at first. Then she began to make allusions to Liverpool. These Mrs Eames did not notice. She was too full of her child which was due any time now. She had now in her feeling contempt for this girl which had never had kids. Yet she felt kindly towards her because she thought Lily had man of her own, Mr Jones, and so was to be respected.

Both now had longing to talk of their own affairs. Mrs Eames hung back from speaking openly about herself, (she spoke now in sighs), not openly because she had in her feeling of superiority, Lily because she was frightened. Lily saw in mind Mrs Eames believing she had a kid coming in nine months time and her superiority, which Lily guessed at, was because hers would be bastard and Mrs Eames' legitimate. But she wasn't going to have a child, she'd had no chance to get one, but they'd never believe that, oh dear. When the nine months was up and she still didn't have one they'd only say she was one of the lucky ones or careful ones. But Mrs Eames was not thinking of Miss Gates, even if she were she had no call to be suspicious of her.

Is nothing wonderful in migrating birds but when we see them we become muddled in our feeling, we think it so romantic they should go so far, far. Is nothing wonderful in a woman carrying but Mrs Eames was muddled in her feeling by it. As these birds would go where so where would this child go? She thought this and Lily in her thinking now was simpler still, as she had done wrong so she had to suffer for it, thought she. Both sat intent, not saying anything now. Their relation one with the other was like two separate triangles. Till strain of that silence worked on Miss Gates till she broke it, so scattering her intentness. She said when you had done wrong you had to suffer for it. When she had gone to Liverpool it had been wrong in her to go she said. Mrs Eames said she'd gone to Liverpool? With Bert Jones then? Lily said hadn't she heard, why she'd thought all the street would know but Mrs Eames, with fine return said she'd had all day been gossiping lately but hadn't heard a word.

'Your time's coming?'

'Yes, 'e or she'll be bawling to the world in a day or two now.'

'Then you hadn't 'eard.'

'No, not a breath of it. Then you've come back,' said Mrs Eames. Lily was shocked at so little feeling in Mrs Eames. When she had expanded, had burst into admitting, so her intentness had scattered and now it crystallized in her again.

'Don't nobody know?'

Mrs Eames shook her head, looking now at Lily who was a bit disappointed at first.

'No, nobody,' Mrs Eames said, 'and I don't want to 'ear, not now anyway, I got too much on me mind with 'er coming – 'cos she'll be a gal won't you, love. I'm praying she won't sneeze every time the sun goes out like 'er dad but then,' she said, from charity perhaps, 'I certainly didn't know about you. Don't you worry your 'ead about it dear, stick by old Craigan now you're back. I suppose you 'aven't a kid coming?'

'No.'

'Certain.'

'Yes I know I 'aven't' said Miss Gates with irritation and bitterness.

'Well I'm sure I'm surprised at 'earing what you just told me,' Mrs Eames said and then said the doctors told you against going out too much, she'd better be going back and went back home.

This decided Miss Gates to get up. She felt she must get to work on the house to still her thoughts. She thought we got no one but ourselves, you learn that, yes, you do.

Some days later, when his ten days were up, Mr Gates came back. It was in morning, when Lily had gone out to buy food. Gates came into kitchen and found Mr Craigan in shirt sleeves again and his slippers.

'' 'Ere we am,' said Gates with forced sort of joviality.

'Lil's back, but it makes I laugh to see you,' Mr Craigan said. 'Aint you a lumpin' sort of young fool. By Christ as if that time fifteen year ago weren't enough, ah and almost to a day, but you go and 'as to get run in again.'

'I'll get back on that copper if it takes me my 'ealth. But did you say Lil was back.'

'You won't,' said Mr Craigan. He groped for something to say to him. But he was old now. He felt he should bawl him out over it. But he could not find anything to say to him except '' 'ah 'er's come back.'

Then quickly he brought out what he had planned.

'I got a job for you.'

'At Pullins?'

'No but you'll go to Prescotts and when they come out at end of the day you'll stop Jim and bring 'im back 'ere to board like 'e used to.'

'What, did 'e go too?'

'Yes an' I'm tellin' yer if you don't bring 'im back then you mightn't come back at all, yes my lad you'll 'ave to find someone else to feed you because I'm through with you.'

'After twenty year.'

'I got no money.'

'After twenty year together.'

'I'm finished.'

'Don't talk silly.'

'It's you will look silly.'

'Look 'ere' said Mr Gates – he had discovered this in prison, 'don't you be too sure of that. It'd be a pretty thing for a man like you, not too old oh no, to be living with a young wench that bears no relation to yer.' Mr Gates thought what luck she should be back for as he had thought in prison if only she had been home he would be all right. Now she was back. Things did not often happen that way. Indeed he was all right. Craigan was imprisoned by his love for Lily, he was tied down by it. Miss Gates chained him to her father and this he had never seen. So when Mr Gates spoke out Craigan seemed to shrink and now for ever, except for one time later, his old authority was gone. At last he said weakly.

'You go and get Jim.'

'I ain't got no money,' said Mr Gates with confidence. Craigan sat silent for a long time then. At last he thought was no help for it.

''Ere's a bob then,' said he. That's what comes of talking he thought in mind, blackmail and all through a word dropped edgeways, many a man 'as lost everything by it. It's a funny kind of world, he said in mind, first you work with a man for twenty years and then he tries to blackmail you. 'And 'e's got me but what do I care,' he said in mind.

As pigeon never fly far from house which provides for them (except when they are taken off then they fly back there), as they might be tied by piece of string to that house, so Mr Craigan's eyes did not leave off from Lily where she went. We are imprisoned by that person whom we love. In the same way as pigeon have an almost irritating knack of homing so our thoughts are coming back. And as the fancier soon forgets to wonder at their sure return so we forget to notice, as we get used to it, which way our thoughts are turned. And which way our eyes.

For now, wherever Miss Gates went there Mr Craigan followed with his eyes. As her hand fell so his eyes dropped, when she got up his eyes rose up to her from where he sat in chair. He was not watching, it was like these pigeons, that flying in a circle always keep that house in sight, so we are imprisoned, with that kind of liberty tied down.

Uncertainty also gripped Mr Craigan, or rather a certainty. He thought when she wasn't many days older, strong hearty wench as her would soon find another man and they would be married this time, she would see to that, he thought. And then what would he do, would they have him? Where would he live?

That was very much, from his position, what Mr Gates was thinking. He thought if Lily didn't marry Dale and married someone else then he was nowhere. A man can't live on the old age pension, 10/– a week won't feed you and keep a roof over you. If you don't sleep under a roof then they put you in prison. He was too old to get another job, nobody would take him in but this house where he was now, he was too old to tramp. Only thing was, he thought, was to prevent her ever marrying again.

So at this first dinner after he had been let out, he made no mention of her having gone away and she did not speak to him of where he had been. He even tried to compliment her and found one to say which he thought good and which also reminded her he was her father. He said it had always gladdened him she was not cleg handed like her mother had been.

Then he thought and later he said why didn't she eat more, she didn't eat enough, not sufficient to feed a pigeon, he said.

Soon he was only thinking how he could stop Mr Dale from coming here to live when he went to ask him back this evening.

# 21

Later, that evening, turned half-past five, he came into yard of Prescott's foundry. In that shop they were casting now and blast in the cupola roared and made air buzz all round him. From being used to this he took no notice but he did move away from where he had stopped from not watching his step. Because he had halted close to three great coffin shaped lumps of metal sunk in the ground. He thought Alf Igginbotham would be in one of those three, other two did it before no one could remember. With Alf the management had tried to make the men cast with molten metal Alf had suicided in, but of course the men didn't have that, they dug his coffin for him here, like had been done for those other two and poured into it the metal he was in. (The great heat there would have utterly done away with him.) There he was in that lump of metal, thirty ton to a penny, but then likely as not he'd risen in dross to top of the metal, and like dross does when you ain't casting, it'd stuck to the sides of the ladle or gone back to the bottom as they poured the metal out. So Alf had got out of it after all, though in different shape to what he'd gone in he thought and Joe chuckled. An' that's about all that man ever was, or any on 'em – dirt, he said in mind.

One or two men that had done pouring their jobs came out through open doorway of the foundry. As they went past Mr Gates they greeted him, as most ironmoulders know one another by sight in Birmingham. Joe asked them if Jim Dale were working in their shop now and they said he was and would be out directly, he was still pouring they said.

Mr Gates looked up to top of the cupola to that intermittent glare which came from it. He thought of all that heat here, where Alf had thrown himself in. He felt cold. He came in closer to that centre of the roar and buzz. More moulders came out, their work done. One asked him had he come for a job as the foreman would be out directly, they was just going to shut off the fan now. After Joe and this man shouted together in midst of the violent vibration they went on, they left Joe. He watched them. He thought all that now is over for me, coming out at night from the shop – and then at that moment the fan was stopped and that roar and buzz stopped. Mr Gates heard voices now inside the foundry. 'Yes,' he said in mind, 'and look at the way they walk, splay-footed bleeders, we always did walk slower an' more awkward than any other trade. Ah there's no more of that for me and God bless me,' he said aloud now, 'aint I glad to get shut on it.'

Then Mr Dale came out.

''Ow do Jim?' said Mr Gates.

'O it's you is it?' Mr Dale said, not stopping.

'Ah, it's I,' said Mr Gates, 'the old man sent me.'

'Well I don't want to 'ave nothing to do with you.'

Mr Dale walked so fast Gates almost trotted to keep up with him.

'Lil's come back Jim.'

Mr Dale stopped. 'Is Lil back?' he said.

'Ah 'er's back and the old man sent me to see if you wouldn't come back to lodge at our 'ouse.'

Mr Dale was silent. Then, 'where 'ave you been then?' he said to gain time.

Gates was afraid Mr Dale meant to come now, yet he was afraid to discourage him lest Craigan hear of it.

'I got pinched,' he said.

'What for?'

'For raising me eyebrow at a copper, beetlebrow.'

'What d'you mean,' said Mr Dale ominously, ''oo's beetlebrow, me or you?'

'Don't you take no notice of what I say, it's me 'ave got to take back 'ome what you says. Are you comin' or is you not?'

'I'm through with you, not on yer life I'm not coming.'

Mr Gates said nothing, delighted.

''Er's made a fool of me,' said Mr Dale, 'I ain't a'coming back and it's all along of you,' he said walking quicker.

''Ow's that Jim?' Gates said, hoping to find out so as to use it afterwards if he could.

'Dirty old waster,' Mr Dale said, having no words again. 'I aint a'coming back, no I never would, not for money.' Then he turned round suddenly. 'Get out before I 'its you,' he said, 'clear off quick, I mightn't know what I was doing in two minutes time.'

Gates almost ran away. When he was at a distance and could see Mr Dale still standing there under lamplight, when he saw Mr Dale was kicking the wall up at side of the footway he contemplated shouting – ''ave a good cry, cry your 'eart out dovvy wovvy,' but then he thought Mr Dale could run faster than him and could catch him. So he went off. But when he was quite half mile off he turned and let off one great laugh, for a gesture.

Monday night and Mr Craigan with Joe Gates went out to public house.

So they began again as they had been before Mr Craigan had fallen ill, Lily gone off, and Gates locked up. You might think they were very different now to what they had been, but they weren't, they were only quieter. Once Mr Craigan had really lost grip he never tried to get it back again, he grew remote in the memory of his young days. For the moment he had all power necessary, the money to feed them, so, once his grip was gone, he did not trouble to try any other authority over them. Gates was only too thankful anything he had said might be forgotten. Lily asked for herself that anything she had done might be forgotten, now she sat very quiet at home through evenings. She was like anyone getting better after long sickness who has taken ship. She cruised across that well charted ocean towards that land from which birds landed on her decks. She thought Mr Jones leaving her like he had done was more and more right and proper, only she was not now interested in him – she was sure she would never set eyes on him again. That land round which she steamed was every inch of it her own, her case still enchanted her as she kept watch on it. And Mr Craigan's youth, where he had to go looking through the lanes to find Lily in her aunt Ellie as they both of them had once been, enchanted him like noise of bells.

In evenings, all three were so thankful to be back together where they had been that they couldn't find two words to say of what they'd done when they were on their own. Perhaps Mr Craigan was sad, but Gates wasn't, nor his daughter. Mr Gates could never be sad. Even now, as he tapped on the bar with florin Craigan had given him, he yelled and laughed. For bar tender, with histrionic gesture, and from some earlier reason with tears of laughing running down his cheeks, snatched up a spade he had hidden there and made to cleave Mr Gates in two if he should go on tapping on the bar.

'That'll land you where I just come from,' said Mr Gates, delighted.

' 'Ow did you find it in there, Joe?' said bar tender.

'They didn't 'ave no beer in there,' Mr Gates said 'and I said to the superintendent I says I can't understand your not having no beer, water's what lions an' gorillas, rhinocerosses, donkeys, birds, tarts and eagles drinks, but moulders must 'ave beer I said. Two 'alves Reuben, I brought my mate along with me tonight.'

Bar tender called out good evening to Mr Craigan who nodded to him. Craigan sat by himself, his eyes on the floor. Bar tender said to Joe how his mate had aged in the last month or two, since he'd been in last, and Joe said ah, old man had been ill, he said.

Mr Connolly came in then.

'An' what about your team, Aaron,' cried Mr Gates, for Aaron was very keen on football.

'I sent me shilling last Saturday Joe, I dain't go.'

'No, you dain't like to go, that was it, not the way they're playing now. Villa supporter! You ain't no more'n a newspaper supporter shoutin' goal at the page.'

'It am a bleeder,' Mr Connolly said, 'I be frighted to go down to the Villa ground, I can't abide to see 'em beaten, not a grand team like they used to be. Why if it ain't Mr Craigan' he cried, 'and 'ow would you be feelin' now mister?' he said to him.

'It passed Aaron' said Mr Craigan.

'What ailed you?'

'It were a chill I reckon Aaron.'

'Well it am a grand sight to see you back,' Mr Connolly said. His cheerfulness was forced.

'Did they give you the sack too?' said Mr Craigan.

'Ah' Gates said, 'they give us all the sack.'

'It weren't Bridges,' said Mr Craigan, 'who was it then?'

'Why, the young chap of course,' said Mr Gates and Craigan said that he'd give something to know what went on in his mind. Then all three were silent till bar tender took it up, asking if it was true, and Mr Gates took that up, with oaths, and answered him.

Door opened and Tupe stood in doorway, holding door open.

'This way sir, come in sir,' cried he.

Who was it but Mr Bridges?

Gates, when he saw Tupe, came from where he was standing by the bar and sat down by Mr Craigan. Mr Connolly stood by the bar.

' 'Ow do Aaron,' Tupe said.

Mr Connolly took no notice of him.

Mr Bridges then took no notice of Connolly, remembering he'd had trouble with him and Jones. Bridges was quiet. He was poorly dressed. Then he saw Mr Craigan. He moved across through crowd of people standing about and said ' 'ow d'you do Craigan?' Mr

374

Craigan nodded merely, though Gates smiled and said 'you'll 'ave a drink with me sir later in the evening.' Mr Bridges was about answering this when up came Tupe with two glasses.

''Ere you are, sir, 'ere we are then,' cried he. 'Well if it ain't Joe.'

'You got someone again as'll pay for you I see,' Mr Craigan said. He hated Tupe so, it made him feel younger. Mr Gates took hint.

'Did 'e sack you as well, strike, what's the world coming to?' said Mr Gates.

Mr Connolly came up to them then and as he passed by Tupe he jogged his arm like accidentally. 'Sorry' said he.

'That's all right mate' Tupe said to him 'accidental is as accidental does.'

'Mate' screamed Mr Gates, 'God strike, did you 'ear that. Why what is 'e but a man what snatches the bread from other people's mouths. And 'e's not content with that, oh no, 'e gets them pinched with provocating them.'

'Now then, now then what's this?' said Mr Bridges.

'Would you still be working for 'em?' said Mr Craigan to Tupe nodding his head back towards factory.

'No.'

Mr Craigan laughed.

Then Craigan looked Bridges in his eyes. Mr Bridges felt like he was being hauled up before someone and when Mr Craigan looked at him he stepped forward like he was the next now. He felt frightened even.

'An' 'ave they sacked you?' Mr Craigan said, his eyes on his eyes.

'Yes,' said Bridges 'ten years at the O.K. gas plant, fifteen years with his father, but 'e 'ad no more use for me more'n a bit of shit on 'is shoe,' he screamed and noticed Craigan was laughing at him. He stopped and drew in breath for long speech he would make now, but Joe Gates was before him.

''Tis 'im, 'tis 'im,' cried Mr Gates, crowing. 'To listen to 'im you'd think 'e was the only one in the world, but there's more'n 'im thrown out 'omeless, penniless, ah, more'n 'im by a million.' He jumped up. Then he began screaming. 'Listen to me,' shrieked he, 'listen to me.'

And Joe was about to draw attention of all the world to Mr Bridges, and bar tender was already saying with appeal Joe, Joe when Craigan got up and butted him in the stomach with his head. Both being so old this looked very silly, Mr Gates more so where he lay trying to get back his wind.

Mr Craigan turned round then and laughed and grinned at Bridges. This one put down his glass of beer and went away out of public house, with Tupe trotting after him. Mr Connolly went and talked in low voice to bar tender. Rest of those in this public house turned round now to each other as if nothing had happened.

Mr Craigan took up glass of beer which Bridges had left half drunk.

'You get this for nowt' he said to Joe who was sitting up now, 'what 'e left won't cost you nothin'. But what d'you want to go and get excited for,' he said 'you'm no better than Tupe and you knows it.'

'It weren't Tupe, it's that Bridges.'

'Well what about 'im?' said Mr Craigan. 'No it was Tupe you was after. Come along back Joe,' Mr Craigan said. When they were outside they looked older still as they walked back slowly.

'To 'ave the coppers come in an' take you for disorderly be'aviour, and when you ain't even tight, it's loony, Joe. But you'm be getting quite a lad as you gets older,' said Mr Craigan, strangely pleased.

And now time is passing now.

Mr Craigan had gone to bed again. He did not get out of bed any more, and gave no reason for it.

Joe Gates was always out again now. He could not drink because he had no money. He stood about in high streets, on the corners.

So Miss Gates was alone when she sat down, with housework done, and sewed. Often she sat upstairs with Mr Craigan. After going to that public house he had altogether sunk again into himself. She did not notice he was there as she sat by his bed. She noticed him only when Mrs Eames' new baby cried next door. Walls between their houses were thin and she would wonder then if baby's crying did not worry grandad. When it was angry, which it always seemed to be at first, it raucously cried out with loud rasping shrieks, only Mr Craigan did not seem to take much notice. Then after three weeks or so it began sometimes to be amused and sound would come through the wall of its strange burbling.

When she sat sewing, always thinking of her mistake, then sometimes this baby would be amused. Sound it made then was like the fluttering of the hands, palms out, which Charleston dancers used to make, or like cymbals, in her heart. Because she was young. Because he was old, thought she, that meant nothing to him.

She never went out, why should I go out, she said in mind, who have done so wrong, so all through her days and nights she heard all the noises Mrs Eames' daughter made. Even when now and again the sun showed out she now listened to hear if it would begin to sneeze like Mr Eames did at the sun. Only what she did not like at first was Mrs Eames making noises to her baby, this was too near to her, but gradually, she had feeling of guilt about it, she came to listening for them too.

Sitting at window-sill of her grandad's window she overlooked Birmingham and the sky over it. This was filled with pigeon flocks. Thousands of pigeon wavered there in the sky, and that baby's raucous cry would come to her now and again. So day after day and slowly her feelings began to waver too and make expeditions away from herself, though like on a string. And disturbed her hands at sewing.

Friday evening and Miss Gates was sitting by Mr Craigan's bed. She was sewing. Then getting up on elbow he fetched out purse from under his pillows. He took 6d from it and said for her to go to the movies. She said what alone, and to leave him! He said she'd better go, she was in too much he said. So that night she went.

Saturday morning Gates was sitting downstairs when Mr Connolly called in. He explained he had called to ask after Mr Craigan. Lily heard their voices in kitchen so she came downstairs from where she was, she sat on chair opposite to Mr Connolly and answered his questions for Mr Craigan. She said yes he'd been to bed before, for a week or two, and now he was gone back there again and wouldn't see a doctor. Yes it was silly in him, she said, but it did seem difficult with people as they got older to move them from what they decided on. Yes he'd said so to speak in his mind to himself, yes I won't get up, I'll stay in bed. In a man of his age, she said, you couldn't go and tell him to get up, yes and there might be something the matter with him, really.

'It am a bleeder,' said Mr Connolly, 'an' when 'e went for you in

377

the boozer that night I thought to myself well 'e am back to what 'e were when 'e was secretary of the Club. D'you mind Joe the road 'e used to manage 'em meetings, 'e were a proper business man.'

'Ah,' Mr Gates said.

'Well if you'll excuse me,' said Miss Gates, 'I'll go an' do a bit more as they say.'

'Yes missus, a woman's work am never done,' said Mr Connolly and she said yes that's right and went out. She had glowing feeling over her for someone had called and had been sociable, to sympathize over Mr Craigan's illness.

Connolly and Gates sat. Mr Connolly picked his teeth.

'Would the Villa be at 'ome today Aaron?' Mr Gates said.

'They am.'

'I ain't been down to the Villa ground in years,' Mr Gates said. Was silence.

'Cardiff they'll 'ave against them today Joe.'

'It'll be glorious football,' Mr Gates said, like he was musing.

'They am the best two teams in the League, and those two with the finest record,' said Mr Connolly.

Was silence.

'Only being out o' work—' said Mr Connolly.

'That's right,' said Mr Gates.

'Without I get a couple o' bob out of the old man,' said Mr Gates, audacious. ' 'E sent our wench to the movies last night.'

'I dain't mean that Joe,' said Mr Connolly, 'you knows I dain't.'

'That's all right mate, that's all right, no need to worry your 'ead about that. Why, if he 'as the doings well then it's right enough ain't it?'

'I don't like it.'

'What don't you like? Gor blimey, you a Villa supporter and won't take the loan of a bob to see 'em play. I don't know 'ow it is but some'ow today I don't feel I will rest easy till I seen the Villa play.'

Miss Gates came in then. She was thinking in mind what if Mr Connolly should stay to dinner, why she hadn't anything in, nor the money to buy it with. Yes he couldn't stay she thought.

'Lil,' said Mr Gates, 'come 'ere, there's something I wants to ask yer. Would you reckon the old man'll lend us a couple o' bob to go an' see the Villa play?'

'Well I don't know,' said Miss Gates, serious 'you'd better go an' try 'im.'

'Will you come with me then?'

'All right, I'll come.'

They went upstairs. She went behind her father. She laughed at idea of this, like two kids, her dad and her, going to ask grandad for two shillings.

Mr Craigan gave it to Gates.

Mr Connolly did not stay to dinner and so afterwards, when Gates had gone out to meet him and she had washed up, from relief at Mr Connolly not staying and from the cinema she had been to she laughed and smiled to herself, standing by kitchen window. She thought in feeling of that band, which was playing now in her heart, in the cinema, and even without a pang now she thought of band in that railway train. And at the cinema last night, what a good band that was.

Then Miss Gates remembered words Mr Connolly had spoken this morning. He had been speaking of baby he knew, a little girl – a little wench he called her, she smiled, how nice their old way of talking was she thought in mind, yes, speaking like that made that baby grown up like in time she would be. There was some said 'it' to babies. She laughed, 'the ignorance,' she said in mind. Then she heard Mrs Eames' baby next door and she thought today she'd go and see her. She hadn't been yet but now she would go. She ran upstairs to Mr Craigan and said she was just going to pay a call on Mrs Eames, she'd be back directly she said. Mr Craigan mumbled she didn't want to sit moping indoors, nor nobody wanted her to.

So she ran round to Mrs Eames.

As Gates and Mr Connolly walked more and more men came out from other roads into street they were walking down to the Villa ground. These formed on each side of street long lines of men walking, many of them still in blue overalls. Day was dark, rain had fallen just before and the roadway was still wet with this and the sky dark, so it dully shone like iron, this time, when it has been machined. The lines of men were dark coloured.

Everyone is very quiet. They walk quickly and quietly. It is early yet. These lines of men come to big red building, they pass in quickly through turnstiles onto the stands. Numbers of policemen. Trams with FOOTBALL SPECIAL showing instead of their numbers draw up every moment and more men get out of them. Men stand about selling the Villa News, always being pushed down along the street by weight of the numbers of men coming down on them. Others sell the teams' colours in rosettes. Hawkers are selling sweets and the crowd eddies round the barrows. And here, close to the gates, everyone walks faster. Quickly, quietly they pass in onto the stands through turnstiles.

Gates and Connolly pass in and stand on the mound, they go to behind the goalposts and lean against rail there. Silver band in dark blue overcoats is playing in middle of the green, green pitch. Everything but the grass is black with smoke, only thin blue waves of smoke coming up from the dark crowds already waiting gives any colour, and the pink brick.

Band plays and always, at the gates, men are coming in, lines of them coming in are thicker and thicker. Man with a rattle lets this off suddenly, then suddenly stops. Drunk man begins shouting at this. Now as this mound is filling up you see nothing but faces, lozenges, against black shoulders. As time gets nearer so more rattles are let off, part of the crowd begins singing. The drunk man, who has a great voice, roars and shouts and near him hundreds of faces are turned to look at him. The band packs up, it moves off, then over at further corner the whole vast crowd that begins roaring, the Villa team comes out, then everyone is shouting. On face of the two mounds great swaying, like corn before wind, is made down towards the ground, frantic excitement, Gates wailed and sobbed for now his voice had left him. The Villa, the Villa, come on the Villa. Mr Connolly stood like transfixed with passion and 30,000 people waved and shrieked and swayed and clamoured at eleven men who play the best football in the world. These took no notice of the crowd, no notice.

Mr Craigan lay in bed in his house. He thought in mind. He thought in mind how he had gone to work when he was eight. He had worked on till no one would give him work. He thought what had he got out of fifty-seven years' work? Nothing. He thought of Lily. He thought what was there now for him? Nothing, nothing. He lay.

But Miss Gates was not that way inclined. Everything, so she felt, was beginning for her again. Niece of Mrs Eames was there, girl of her own age, and they talked about this baby before its mother in rapturous voices. Then this niece had a story about the likeness to parents in their babies. Miss Gates listened with intentness and knew she would be great friends with her.

'And then I said to them,' said niece of Mrs Eames, 'I said, "well you're a wonder you are, there's a child, your own flesh and blood in the manner of speaking, and you can say that, why" I said, "Mrs Pye, how can you, the poor little lamb."'

'Yes I should think so!' said Miss Gates, while Mrs Eames said nothing, being all taken up with her daughter.

'"Well" so she said "you won't never understand dear till you've 'ad one of your own" and I said "maybe I won't but that doesn't stop me from knowing what's right from what's wrong. No," I said, "taking that road won't persuade me from thinking you love the little mite more than," – and then I couldn't think of nothing, you know the words kind of left me, well I said "more than anything, your 'usband or nothing." She 'adn't a word to say to that.'

At that moment Mr Eames came in with his son.

''Ullo mother,' he said and greeted Miss Gates and his niece. Then he said why shouldn't they take baby out between the showers, 'shall us' he said and Miss Gates and her new friend were enthusiastic over this. 'Yes and take the new-old pram for a ride,' said Mrs Eames who took gaily to this idea.

When Mrs Eames was dressed, her coat was plum coloured, and they started out she let Miss Gates push the pram. She went on ahead with husband and left her niece with Lily. Her niece was great talker, she was saying:

'So I said to him "well I declare," I said, "and would you call that a nice way to speak to anyone, with your mouth full and all, what's the world coming to these days" I said, "but some boys are the dirtiest horrible things in the world." That's what I told him,' she said, and now the story was at an end.

'Yes,' Miss Gates said indistinctly. She was torn between listening to what her new friend had to say and at sight of baby blowing bubbles on her mouth. This was moment of utter bliss for her. She was like dazed by it. Then as they walked, Miss Gates exalted, friend of Mr Eames called to him out of alley way which led to his house back of the street. He invited them all in. Lily pushed the pram down alley way and they turned into small yard which was this man's, who was pigeon fancier. Mr Eames was already talking to this man about them, and both whistled to the pigeon. These were strutting on roof of outhouse in the yard. Baby now woke up and began to make waves at the pigeon with its arms and legs. 'Why the little love, look at 'er' cried Mrs Eames.

'You wait a second, missis, and we'll give 'er a closer sight of 'em,' said the pigeon fancier, and hoping to sell a few pigeon to Mr Eames he disappeared into outhouse to fetch some grain.

When he came back he put grain onto hood of the pram and one by one pigeon fluttered off the roof onto hood of this pram. As they did so they fluttered round heads of those people in the yard, who kept heads very still. Then the fancier put grain onto apron of the pram in front of the baby and one pigeon hopped from hood down onto the apron right in front of the baby. This baby made wave with its arm at the pigeon which waddled out of reach. Mrs Eames looked at its fierce red eye and said would it peck at her daughter but fancier said not on your life. Soon all were laughing at way this one pigeon, which alone dared to come onto apron, dodged the baby which laughed and crowed and grabbed at it. Soon also they were bored and went all of them into his house, only Mrs Eames did not go, nor her son who held her skirt. And Lily did not go, but stood like fascinated.

Suddenly with loud raucous cry she rushed at the baby, and with clatter of wings all the pigeon lifted and flew away, she rushed at baby to kiss it. Mrs Eames hid her son's face in her hand, laughing:

'You're too young, that's too old for you' she said.

# Party Going

Fog was so dense, bird that had been disturbed went flat into a balustrade and slowly fell, dead, at her feet.

There it lay and Miss Fellowes looked up to where that pall of fog was twenty foot above and out of which it had fallen, turning over once. She bent down and took a wing then entered a tunnel in front of her, and this had DEPARTURES lit up over it, carrying her dead pigeon.

No one paid attention, all were intent and everyone hurried, nobody looked back. Her dead pigeon then lay sideways, wings outspread as she held it, its dead head down towards the ground. She turned and she went back to where it had fallen and again looked up to where it must have died for it was still warm and, everything unexplained, she turned once more into the tunnel back to the station.

She thought it must be dirty with all that fog and wondered if it might not be, now it was dead, that it had fleas and they would come out on the feathers of its head but she did not like to look as there might have been blood. She remembered she had seen that with rabbits' ears when they had been shot and she remembered that swallows were most verminous of all birds – how could it have died she wondered and then decided that it must be washed.

As Miss Fellowes penetrated through at leisure and at last stepped out under a huge vault of glass – and here people hurriedly crossed her path and shuttled past on either side – Miss Crevy and her young man drove up outside and getting out were at once part of all that movement. And this affected them, for if they also had to engage in one of those tunnels to get to where they were going it was not for them simply to pick up dead birds and then wander through slowly. Miss Crevy had hat-boxes and bags and if her young man was only there to see her off and hate her for going and if Miss Fellowes had no more to do than kiss her niece and wave good-bye, Miss Angela Crevy must find porters and connect with Evelyn Henderson, who was also going and who had all the tickets.

People were gathering everywhere then at this time and making their way to the station.

Of their party two more had also arrived who like Miss Fellowes had only come to wave good-bye; two nannies dressed in granite with black straw hats and white hair. They were just now going downstairs in the centre of an open space and those stairs had LADIES lit up over them.

Meantime Miss Crevy's young man said:

'This porter here says the fog outside is appalling, Angela darling.' He went on to say it was common knowledge with all the porters that no more trains would go out that evening, it was four-thirty now, it would soon be dark, then so much worse. But she said now they had got a porter it would be silly to go away and certainly she must see the others first. Besides she knew Robin did not want her to go and though she did not mind she wondered how much he wanted her to stay. Anyway, nothing on earth would prevent her going. Their porter then made difficulties and did not want to come with them; he would only offer to put her things in the cloakroom, so her young man, Robin, had to tip him in advance and so at last they too went in under into one of those tunnels.

Descending underground, down fifty steps, these two nannies saw beneath them a quarter-opened door and beyond, in electric light, another old woman who must be the guardian of this place; it might have been one of their sisters, looking upstairs at them. As they came down she looked over behind her and then back at them.

For Miss Fellowes, as they soon saw, had drawn up her sleeves and on the now dirty water with a thin wreath or two of blood, feathers puffed up and its head sideways, drowned along one wing, lay her dead pigeon. Air just above it was dizzy with a little steam, for she was doing what she felt must be done with hot water, turning her fingers to the colour of its legs and blood.

No word passed. The attendant watched the two nannies who stood in a corner. In one hand she gripped her Lysol bottle, her other was in her pocket and held a two-shilling piece that Miss Fellowes had slipped her. She whispered to them:

'She won't be long,' and turning she watched her stairs again, uneasy lest there should be more witnesses.

At this moment Mr Wray was telling how his niece Miss Julia Wray and party would be travelling by the boat train and 'Roberts,' he said over the telephone, 'get on to the station master's office, will you, and tell him to look out for her.' Mr Wray was a director of the line. Mr Roberts said they would be delighted to look out for Miss Wray and that they were only too glad to be of service to Mr Wray at any time. Mr Wray said 'So that's all right then,' and rang off just when Mr Roberts was going on to explain how thick the fog was, not down to the ground right here but two miles out it was as bad as any could remember: 'impenetrable, Mr Wray – why he must have hung up on me.'

'What I want now is some brown paper and a piece of string,' Miss Fellowes quite firmly said and all that attendant could get out was, 'Well, I never did.' Not so loud though that Miss Fellowes could hear; it was on account of those two nannies that she minded, not realizing that they knew Miss Fellowes, sister to one of their employers. They did not say anything to this. They did not care to retire as that might seem as if they were embarrassed by what they were seeing, speak they could not as they had not been spoken to, nor could they pass remarks with this attendant out of loyalty to homes they were pensioners of and of which Miss Fellowes was a part.

And as Miss Fellowes considered it was a private act she was performing and thought it was a bore their being there, for she saw who they were, when she went out she ignored them and it was not their place to look up at her.

Now Miss Fellowes did not feel well, so, when she got to the top of those steps she rested there leaning on a handrail. Miss Crevy and her young man came by, Miss Fellowes saw them and they saw her, they hesitated and then greeted each other, Miss Crevy being extremely sweet. So was she going on this trip, too, Miss Fellowes asked, wondering if she were going to faint after all, and Miss Crevy said she was and had Miss Fellowes met Mr Robin Adams? Miss Fellowes said which was the platform, did she know, on which Miss Crevy's young man broke in with 'I shouldn't bother about that, there'll be no train for hours with this fog.'

'Then aren't you going with them all?' and saying this she took an extra grip on that handrail and said to herself that it was coming over her now and when it did come would she fall over backwards and down those stairs and she smiled vaguely over clenched teeth. 'O what a pity,' she said. Below those two nannies poked out their heads together to see if all was clear but when they saw her still there they withdrew. And now Miss Crevy was telling her who was coming with them. 'The Hignams,' she pronounced Hinnem, 'Robert and your niece Claire, Evelyn Henderson, who has all our tickets, Julia, Alex Alexander and Max Adey.'

'Is that the young man I hear so much about nowadays?' she said and then felt worse. She felt that if she were going to faint then she would not do it in front of this rude young man and in despair she turned to him and said: 'I wonder if you would mind throwing this parcel away in the first wastepaper basket.' He took it and went off. She felt better at once, it began to go off and relief came over her in a glow following out her weakness.

'Do you mean Max?' Miss Crevy asked self-consciously.

'Yes, he goes about a great deal, doesn't he?'

She was reviving and her eyes moved away from a fixed spot just beyond Miss Crevy and, taking in what was round about, spotted Mr Adams coming back.

'How kind of him,' she said and to herself she thought how wonderful it's gone, I feel quite strong again, what an awful day it's been and how idiotic to be here. 'Then you won't be even numbers, dear, will you?'

'No, you see no one quite knew whether Max would come or not.'

As she had not thanked him yet Adams thought he would try to get something out of this old woman, so he said:

'I put your parcel away for you.'

'Oh, did you find somewhere to put it, how very kind of you. I wonder if you would show me which one you put it in,' and when he had shown her she made excuses and broke away, asking Miss Crevy to tell Julia she would be on the platform later. Once free of them she went to where he had shown her and, partly because she felt so much better now, she retrieved her dead pigeon done up in brown paper.

The main office district of London centred round this station and now innumerable people, male and female, after thinking about getting home, were yawning, stretching, having another look at their clocks, putting files away and closing books, some were signing their last letters almost without reading what they had dictated and licking the flaps where earlier on they would have wetted their fingers and taken time.

Now they came out in ones and threes and now a flood was

coming out and spreading into streets round; but while traffic might be going in any direction there was no one on foot who was not making his way home and that meant for most by way of the station.

As pavements swelled out under this dark flood so that if you had been ensconced in that pall of fog looking down below at twenty foot deep of night illuminated by street lamps, these crowded pavements would have looked to you as if for all the world they might have been conduits.

While these others walked all in one direction, the traffic was motionless for long and then longer periods. Fog was down to ground level outside London, no cars could penetrate there so that if you had been seven thousand feet up and could have seen through you would have been amused at blocked main roads in solid lines and, on the pavements within two miles of this station, crawling worms on either side.

In ones and threes they came into the station by way of those tunnels, then out under that huge vault of glass. As they filed in, Miss Fellowes, who was looking round for a porter to ask him which platform was hers, thought every porter had deserted. But as it happened what few there were had been obscured.

At this moment Mr Roberts, ensconced in his office where he could see hundreds below, for his windows overlooked the station, was telephoning for police reinforcements. 'There are hundreds here now, Mr Clarke,' he said, 'in another quarter of an hour these hundreds will be thousands. They tell me no buses are running and "this must be one of those nights you'll be glad you live over your work," ' he said. Then they talked for some time about who was to pay for all this – as railways have to keep their own police – and they enjoyed quoting Acts of Parliament to each other.

One then of legion when she had left her uncle's house, Miss Julia Wray left where she lived saying she would rather walk. With all this fog she felt certain she would get to the station before her luggage.

As she stepped out into this darkness of fog above and left warm rooms with bells and servants and her uncle who was one of Mr Roberts' directors – a rich important man – she lost her name and was all at once anonymous; if it had not been for her rich coat she might have been any typist making her way home.

Or she might have been a poisoner, anything. Few people passed her and they did not look up, as if they also were guilty. As each and every one went about their business they were divided by this gloom and were nervous, and as she herself turned into the Green Park it was so dim she was sorry she had not gone by car.

Air she breathed was harsh, and here where there were no lamps or what few there were shone at greater distances, it was like night with fog as a ceiling shutting out the sky, lying below tops of trees.

Where hundreds of thousands she could not see were now going home, their day done, she was only starting out and there was this difference that where she had been nervous of her journey and of starting, so that she had said she would rather go on foot to the station to walk it off, she was frightened now. As a path she was following turned this way and that round bushes and shrubs that hid from her what she would find she felt she would next come upon this fog dropped suddenly down to the ground, when she would be lost.

Then at another turn she was on more open ground. Headlights of cars above turning into a road as they swept round hooting swept their light above where she walked, illuminating lower branches of trees. As she hurried she started at each blaring horn and each time she would look up to make sure that noise heralded a light and then was reassured to see leaves brilliantly green veined like marble with wet dirt and these veins reflecting each light back for a moment then it would be gone out beyond her and then was altogether gone and there was another.

These lights would come like thoughts in darkness, in a stream; a flash and then each was away. Looking round, and she was always glancing back, she would now and then see loving couples dimly two by two; in flashes their faces and anything white in their clothes picked up what light was at moments reflected down on them.

What a fuss and trouble it had been, and how terrible it all was she thought of Max, and then it was a stretch of water she was going by and lights still curved overhead as drivers sounded horns and birds, deceived by darkness, woken by these lights, stirred in their sleep, mesmerized in darkness.

It was so wrong, so unfair of Max not to say whether he was really coming, not to be in when she rang up, leaving that man of his, Edwards, to say he had gone out, leaving it like that to the last so that none of them knew if he was going to come or not. She imagined she met him now on this path looking particularly dark and how she would stop him and ask him why he was here, why wasn't he at the station? He would only ask her what she was doing herself. Then she would not be able to tell him she was frightened because he would think it silly. She would hardly admit to herself that she was only walking to try and calm herself, she was so certain he would not come after all.

It was so strange and dreadful to be walking here in darkness when it was only half-past four, so unlucky they had ever discussed all going off together though he had been the first to suggest it. How did people manage when they said they would do something and then did not do it? How silly she had been ever to say she would be of this party for now she would have to go with them, she could not go home now she was packed, they would not understand. But how could people be vague about going abroad what with passports and travelling? He had her at a hopeless disadvantage, he could gad about London with her gone and go to bed with every girl.

She realized that she was quite alone, no cars were passing and by the faint glow of a lamp she was near she could see no lovers, even, under trees.

It came to her then that she might not have packed her charms, that her maid had left them out and this would explain why things were so wrong. There they were, she could see them, on the table by her bed, her egg with the elephants in it, her wooden pistol and her little painted top. She could not remember them being put in. She turned round, facing the other way. She looked in her bag though she never carried them there. It would be hopeless to go without them, she must hurry back. Oh why had she not gone in the taxi with her things?

And as she turned back Thomson went by with her luggage, light from his taxi curving over her head. She did not know, and he did not know she was there, he was taken up in his mind with how difficult it was going to be for him to find Miss Henderson and how most likely he would miss his tea.

Meantime, as he was letting himself into his flat, Max was wondering if he would go after all. It would mean leaving Amabel. Blinds were drawn, there was a fire. He could not leave Amabel. Edwards, his manservant, came in to say that Mrs Hignam had rung up and would he please ring her back. He did not like to leave Amabel. He asked Edwards if his things were packed and he was told they nearly were. Well if his bags were ready then he might as well leave Amabel.

Julia, crossing a footbridge, was so struck by misery she had to stand still, and she looked down at stagnant water beneath. Then three seagulls flew through that span on which she stood and that is what had happened one of the times she first met him, doves had flown under a bridge where she had been standing when she had stayed away last summer. She thought those gulls were for the sea they were to cross that evening.

Mr and Mrs Hignam were on their way, crawling along, continually in traffic blocks so that their driver was always folding his arms over the wheel and resting his head.

Claire Hignam was talking hard and fast. First she told her husband Robert she had rung Max up to say they were just off and to ask him why he was not already on his way. He had told her he was not packed yet but she had known enough of him not to believe that. Edwards was too good a servant to leave things so late and anyway Max could not give straight answers.

'D'you suppose we shall see Nannie on the platform, it's so touching really how she always comes to see me off.'

As he did not reply she went on to ask him if he had seen that Edward Cumberland was dead, so young. He paid no attention for he was thinking of something he had forgotten. She explained she had been in too much of a rush to tell him before and he then said tell him what? At this she said he was maddening, didn't he realize this boy had died when he was only twenty-six? He said what of? She did not know and what on earth did it matter anyway, wasn't the awful thing that he was dead and at twenty-six? She went on that she would live till she was eighty-four. He made no answer. Then she said this dead man was a cousin of Embassy Richard's, what did he know about that?

(It appears that a young fellow, Richard Cumberland, was so fond of going out that, like many others, he often went to parties uninvited. A Foreign Embassy was entertaining its Prince who was paying visits in this country and someone had stolen some sheets of Cumberland's note-paper and had sent to every newspaper in London asking them to put the following in their Court Columns: Mr Richard Cumberland regrets that he was unavoidably prevented by indisposition from accepting His Excellency the Ambassador's invitation to meet his Prince Royal. This notice had duly appeared and the Ambassador, thinking to strike out for a host's right to have what guests he chose, had written to the Press pointing out that he had never invited Mr Cumberland and that this gentleman was unknown to him. The whole subject was now being discussed at length everywhere and in two solicitors' offices and in correspondence columns in the Press.)

He could not tell her anything that she did not already know but he thought perhaps they might hear some news when they got to the station.

'If we ever get there,' she said. 'Really it is too awful trying to get round London nowadays. We've been fifteen minutes already, block after block like this it's too frightful.'

Even then she had no train fever, she was confident their train would not go without her. But Miss Evelyn Henderson, who had been urging her driver on and telling him every moment of short cuts to take which he knew would delay them, was in a great rush and bother when she was driven up. Fumbling to pay him off in her bag bulging with the others' tickets she told her porter they were certain to be separated, they must meet where luggage was registered, under the clock. He said which one, there were three. Under the clock she said and then they were gone.

Inside, dolled up in his top hat, the station master came out under that huge vault of green he called his roof, smelled fog which disabled all his trains, looked about at fog-coloured people, his travellers who scurried though now and again they stood swaying and he thought that the air, his atmosphere, was wonderfully clear considering, although everyone did seem smudged by fog. And how was he going to find Miss Julia Wray he asked, whom he did not know by sight, and when by rights he should be in his office.

Miss Fellowes also considered how she was to find her niece. She did feel better but not yet altogether safe, if her faintness had left her she was not confident it would not return. She decided that it would be better for her to sit down.

Those two nannies were already over cups of tea when they saw her come in and look round for somewhere to sit. She saw an oval counter behind which two sweating females served and round it, one row deep, were chromium-painted stools, like chrysanthemums with chromium-plated stalks. Each one of these was occupied but there were some other seats of canvas with chromium plate again so that, associating them with deck chairs, for an instant she indulged herself with plans of sea voyages and the South of France. All these were also taken except one and on this she sat down, holding her dead pigeon wrapped up on her lap and waiting to be served.

As time went by and no one came to take her order she knew how tired she was. Although this was her first time out today she thought she might have been through long illnesses she felt so weak. She saw there was only one waitress to serve customers beyond that counter and as she was still waiting she understood at last that it was for her to fetch what she wanted. Leaving the pigeon in her place, and asking a man next her to keep it, she went to see.

At first all those two nannies noticed was that Miss Fellowes had gone up to the counter and they did not doubt but what she was ordering tea. They were not surprised when she was not served as they themselves had been kept waiting. But as they watched her they soon saw that thin-lipped flush which, with their experience, told them that for Miss Fellowes all this was getting past all bearing. They knew what it meant and they could have warned her it was useless to give girls like these a chance to answer back. You had to be thankful if you were served and it only made things worse to complain as she was doing.

Then they realized that words were passing, but what shocked them most, when it was over and Miss Fellowes was walking back to her seat, was to see that it was not tea she had ordered, what she was carrying back was whisky. They were sorry to see her order and sorry again for all this had drawn attention to her. One rough-looking customer in particular eyed her rather close.

Miss Fellowes did not care, she could dismiss things of that kind from her mind and entirely ignore at will anything unpleasant or what she called rude behaviour, so long as this was from servants. It had been a fancy to order whisky and she was trying to remember what her father's brand had been called which was always laid out for them years ago when they got back from hunting. He said it was good for everyone after a hard day and you drank it, went to have your bath and then sat down to high tea. And now how extraordinary she should be here, drinking in tea rooms with all these extraordinary looking people. And there was that poor bird. One had seen so many killed out shooting, but any dead animal shocked one in London, even birds, though of course they had easy living in towns. She remembered how her father had shot his dog when she was small and how much they had cried. There was that poor boy Cumberland, his uncle had been one of her dancing partners, what had he died of so young? One did not seem to expect it when one was cooped up in London and then to fall like that dead at her feet. It did seem only a pious thing to pick it up, though it was going to be a nuisance even now it was wrapped up in paper. But she had been right she felt, she could not have left it there and besides someone might have stepped on it and that would have been disgusting. She was glad she had washed it.

The man who had eyed her, spoke.

'Them girls is terrible I reckon,' he said. 'Trouble enough many of us 'ave had to get here without they refuse to serve you.'

'Yes,' she said, 'it's quite all right now, thank you,' and hoped he was not going to be a nuisance. She wondered whether she had been wise to choose spirits, she really did not feel well, they did not seem to have done her any good.

Meantime Claire and Evelyn had met and were greeting each other in the Hall for registering luggage with cries not unlike more seagulls. Robert was taking off his hat and saying, 'Why hullo Evelyna,' and she was asking them where everyone was and telling them she had seen Thomson with Julia's luggage who said Julia had started out on foot, could anyone imagine anything so like her? Where on earth was Angela, or Max and Alex? Did anyone know if Max meant to come? Claire said she had telephoned and that she thought he would. 'Anyway,' said Evelyn, 'I've got their tickets here. Now Robert, you and Thomson had better go and try and find them all, will you please at once? Thomson go with Mr Hignam and see if you can bring Miss Crevy and the others back here will you? You haven't seen anything of Edwards I suppose? No, then just do that, will you Robert, we must be all together. Now dear,' she said turning to Claire, 'we can sit on our things and have a good chat.' They then sat down on their luggage to discuss indifferent subjects very calmly while porters, leaning on their upended barrows, went to sleep standing up. So calm was Evelyna she made one wonder if, now those two men had gone, she was not more at ease.

They had been addressed in much the same tone of voice as if both had been in service and Robert Hignam remarked to Thomson that it looked like the hell of a job this time. 'It's not going to be easy.' 'No sir, it's not,' and on that they separated and were at once engulfed in swarming ponds of humanity most of them at this particular spot gazing at a vast board with DEPARTURES OF TRAINS lit up over it. This showed no train due to leave after half past two, or two hours earlier, or, in other words, confusion.

Miss Crevy and her young man were standing in the main crowd. She was very pretty and dressed well, her hands were ridiculously white and her face had an expression so bland, so magnificently untouched and calm she might never have been more than amused and as though nothing had ever been more than tiresome. His expression was of intolerance.

Like two lilies in a pond, romantically part of it but infinitely remote, surrounded, supported, floating in it if you will, but projected by being different on to another plane, though there was so much water you could not see these flowers or were liable to miss them, stood Miss Crevy and her young man, apparently serene, envied for their obviously easy circumstances and Angela coveted for her looks by all those water beetles if you like, by those people standing round.

Surrounded as they were on every side yet they talked so loud they might have been alone.

'Well, whatever you say I must go and find the others.'

'But Angela, I've told you it can't be done in this crowd.'

'I know you have, but how else am I going to get my tickets?'

'What d'you want tickets for now? I tell you they'll never get trains out of here.'

'But Robin, it's been paid for. And I want to go, don't you see.'

At this someone pushed by them, saying he was sorry and that finished it.

'Well,' he said, 'I must go, good-bye, enjoy yourself,' and then it was all so unjust he added, although it made him feel a fool, 'I don't ever want to see you again.' She kissed him on his nose as he was turning away, conscious that she was behaving well, and then he was gone.

If that swarm of people could be likened to a pond for her lily

then you could not see her like, and certainly not her kind, anywhere about her, nor was her likeness mirrored in their faces.
Electric lights had been lit by now, fog still came in by the open end
of this station, below that vast green vault of glass roof with every
third person smoking it might all have looked to Mr Roberts,
ensconced in his office away above, like November sun striking
through mist rising off water.

Mostly dressed in dark clothes, women in low green or mustard
colours, their faces were pale and showed, when not too tired, a sort
of desperate good humour. There was almost no noise and yet, if
you were to make yourself heard, it was necessary to speak up, you
found so many people were talking. Having never been so surrounded before, and with what was before her, she felt excited. She
felt she must get to the side and was surprised to find she had been
in quite a small crowd for here almost at once were fewer people.

Coming up to her the station master asked if she could by any
chance be Miss Julia Wray, and, taken aback, she could only say
no, she had not seen her. As he passed majestically on, murmuring
regrets, she wondered whether she ought not to run after him to say
she was in her party, but then that seemed absurd, Julia was sure to
be where their luggage was to be registered, she could tell her then.

And as Miss Crevy made her way to this place, Claire and Evelyna had arrived at that stage in their conversation when they were
discussing what clothes they were bringing. Both exclaimed aloud at
the beauty and appropriateness of the other's choice, but it was as
though two old men were swapping jokes, they did not listen to each
other they were so anxious to explain. Already both had been made
to regret they had left such and such a dress behind and it was
because he felt it impossible to leave things as they were with
Angela, it was too ludicrous that she should go off on that note, that
kiss on his nose, he must explain, that Robin came back to apolo-
gize.

He found her quite soon and not so far away. She did not seem
surprised at his turning up again and told him about the station
master. He did not see what this had to do with it and plunged into
how sorry he was, he had had an awful time coming up with her
again, would she forgive him? He thought what had done it was her
ancient friend giving him that parcel to get rid of and then, as soon
as he had carried that out, sending him to get it back for her. This

made Angela quite cross, she told him he had been very rude, and that he had better stay away if he was going to be tiresome.

Julia had been back to her room and had not found her charms. It had been bare as though she had never lived there. Her curtains were down, they were being sent to be cleaned, her mattress had gone and her pillow cases were humps under dustsheets in the middle of her bed. Thinking it unlucky to stay and see more and besides Jemima swore that everything was packed in the cabin trunk, she called them her toys, Julia had fled by taxi this time.

Feeling rather faint she hurried through tunnels, made her way dazedly through crowds which she only noticed, to ask herself what she would do if she could not find the others and was surprised to find Claire and Evelyn where they were sitting on their luggage.

She asked how were they, darlings, and they asked her, and they kissed and all sat down again. She wanted to know where everyone had got to and saw poor Evelyna was in a great fuss which made her feel calmer in that she now felt resigned. And indeed Evelyn considered that she must do something, she told herself that if she did not deal with this situation they would be sitting here till domesday and that without her not one of this party would catch their train. So she said it must be a waste of time to try and register luggage with all the piles of it waiting in front of theirs, and she would try to find out something about their train. With that she was gone.

Used to having everything done for them, Julia and Claire settled down to wait. Soon Julia asked if Claire had seen Max and was told about their telephone conversation. She tried to make out whether this had been before she had imagined meeting him in the Green Park and took some comfort from deciding that it must have been. But she did not feel reassured. She tried to discuss how other travellers were dressed, where they could be seen at intervals standing about, many of them almost hidden by their luggage. She never mentioned Max. There was a silence and at last she coughed and said :

'Really he's hopeless, isn't he, don't you think?'

Max was still in his flat. He was also drinking whisky and soda. His arm-chair was covered with thick fake Spanish brocade, all the coverings were of this material with walls to match, fake Spanish tables with ironwork, silver ashtrays, everything heavy and thick, all of it fake, although he thought it genuine, and it was expensive in proportion. That is to say that if all these things had been authentic he would not have had to pay more, anyone less well off could have bought museum pieces cheaper.

He answered the telephone after he had let it ring for some time. Amabel said:

'Is that you, Max?'

'Who is it speaking?'

'Oh, Max, are you really going?'

'Why?' said he.

'I mean must you really go?'

'Just hang on a moment will you, there's something here,' and he put the receiver by and taking his glass he shot his whisky and soda into the fire. It went up in steam with a hiss. He stood still for twenty seconds then he went and mixed himself another. When he came back to the telephone she said:

'Have you got someone else there?'

'No. Why?'

'I thought I heard you shushing someone. What were you doing then?'

'I was putting water on the fire, soda water if you want to know.'

'People don't put soda water on fires.'

'I did. My paper caught alight and I had to put it out.'

'Max, I must see you. Supposing I came round now if I promised to be good.'

'What?'

'I said I could come round now if I swore to you I wouldn't be silly? Oh, Max.'

'But what is it about?'

'I won't have you go, that's all. I can't bear it.'

'I didn't say I was going.'

'It's unfair, we've had such a marvellous time together, I do love you so, darling love. Why can't we be as we were? I swear to you I won't be tiresome again. You must believe me, darling.'

'I rang you up yesterday.'

'Did you?'

'You weren't in.'

'I expect I was having my hair done. I was there all afternoon.

Max, who have you got with you, I heard them whispering just now?'

'And what were you at last night?'

'What was I at? How can you say things like that? Max, darling, what has come over you lately?'

'I rang up about half past nine.'

'I was lying down, you know all this has made me quite ill and I had such a business getting on to Dr Godley, his line was engaged all the time, I expect I was ringing him up.'

'I didn't get the engaged signal.'

'Max, my darling, I shan't argue, you have only to ask Marjorie, she was with me later. I wish you would get on to her, my dear, she could tell you the state she found me in. She was horrified.'

'I'm sorry.'

'Max, my darling, I'm so bewildered and miserable I really don't know where I am. What has happened to make everything different, it was all so perfect before and now here we are like a couple of old washerwomen slanging away at each other whenever we meet? Darling, really the whole thing is making me ill. Dr Godley says the best thing for me to do would be to go away to the sun out of this frightful fog for a month or two to give my system time to right itself. He says my whole system is out of gear and wants toning up.'

'Well, look here, are you doing anything this evening?'

And as she was saying no she was not, Edwards, his manservant, came in to say his bags were packed.

'Just a moment, Am,' he said. 'What's that?'

'Your bags are all ready, sir.'

'Who was that, darling?'

'It's only Edwards asking if I wanted any tea.'

'Ask him from me if his little boy is any better, will you?'

'I will.'

'What were you going to say?'

'Look here, supposing you came round about half past nine, we could go out and have dinner somewhere.'

'Oh, darling, that would be perfect, you are an angel, so you are not going after all?'

He said, 'That's settled then,' and rang off.

'Is the car round?'

'Yes, sir.'

'My bags in? Yes, then come on, I'm in a hurry.' Edwards put on a black bowler hat, Max had no hat at all and he drove his rich car off at speed.

He drove hard, by back streets to avoid traffic blocks, swinging his big car round corners too sharp for it and driving too fast. Edwards said it was bad weather for getting about in, was there not one air service operating and he said no, and there wouldn't be to-day of all days.

'I doubt if your boat train will run, sir.'

'That's not the point, I've got to go.'

So what made him drive faster, and taxi drivers and others drew up their cars and shouted after him, was that he felt he was treating her badly. If he must get away then it was not right to leave her by asking her round to find him gone. He was sick and tired of it. All the same it was bad to ask her round to find he'd gone, that was all there was to it.

Accordingly when they drew up at the station, where at once a little crowd collected to admire his car, he put it to himself that what he wanted was a drink, so he told Edwards to get his luggage registered, Miss Henderson would have the tickets, and that he would be along later. Then he went in under into a larger tunnel that had HOTEL ENTRANCE lit up over it.

He engaged a sitting-room which had a bedroom off, for when he told them what he wanted they explained they had no sitting-rooms without bedrooms and that he would have to engage both. This was typical of his whole style of living, he was always being sold more than he need buy and he did not question prices. Once in this room, with his drink ordered, he rang up Amabel. His trouble was inexperience, he could not let good lies stand.

'Why, darling, it's you again,' she said.

'About this evening. Look here, don't come after all.'

'Whyever not?'

'It won't be any good.'

'But you said I might.'

'I shan't be there.'

As she did not reply, he said he could not be there.

'You mean to tell me you are going after all?'

'Yes, I'm at the Airport now,' he said, and because she must not find him here, she would make a scene, he rang off before she had found anything to say. He gave up his room at once.

Meantime Alexander was on his way, bowling along in his taxi the length of cricket pitches at a time, from block to block, one red light to another, or shimmering policemen dressed in rubber. Humming, he likened what he saw to being dead and thought of himself as a ghost driving through streets of the living, this darkness or that veil between him and what he saw a difference between being alive and death. Streets he went through were wet as though that fog twenty foot up had deposited water, and reflections which lights slapped over the roadways suggested to him he might be a Zulu, in the Zulu's hell of ice, seated in his taxi in the part of Umslopogaas with his axe, skin beating over the hole in his temple, on his way to see She, or better still Leo.

He did not know where he was, it was impossible to recognize streets, fog at moments collapsed on traffic from its ceiling. One moment you were in dirty cotton wool saturated with iced water and then out of it into ravines of cold sweating granite with cave-dwellers' windows and entrances – some of which he began to feel he had seen before till he realized he was in Max's street.

He thought he had told his driver to go to the station but when they drew up outside Max's block of flats he realized he must have given this address, probably because he had been wondering if Max had really meant to come. He was then all at once completely given over to train fever, his driver did not know what time it was, he rushed into the lift, rang Max's bell, asked Franklin what time it was, found Max had already gone and that it was much later than he thought, ran downstairs because he thought it would be quicker, and, lying back panting, trembling, said to his driver,

'Hurry, hurry.'

'Where to?'

'To the station of course.'

'Which station?'

'For France, stupid.'

As he climbed into his cab his driver said:

'Another bloody one of those.'

All this time Julia and Claire had been sitting by their trunks. They had not spoken of Max again, and this is where Edwards came upon them as he followed Max's luggage. Julia sprang up.

'Oh, Edwards, there you are,' she said. 'Where is Mr Adey?'

'I couldn't say, Miss.'

'Didn't he come with you?'

'Yes, Miss.'

(Edwards had learned never to give information about his gentleman to ladies.)

'Then isn't he in the station?'

'I couldn't say, Miss.'

Claire then took her turn, 'Where did he go when he left you?' she asked him.

'He told me to meet him here, Madam.'

Both girls, as though by consent, dropped it and left well alone. It had come to both of them that where he was now of course was in the lavatory.

Alex drove up, still haunted by how late he was. Getting out he screamed for porters and, when he found one, he told him they must meet again at the registration place, he had no time, he must fly and he rushed off, forgetting to pay his taxi. The driver was at once hysterically angry, called out warnings to everyone near about Alex, said to that porter, 'Wait for me, mate,' drove his taxi nine feet forward to where he thought it would cause more obstruction, said, 'Where's a bloody copper?' and with Alex's luggage, and his porter, also went in under into one of those tunnels and was gone.

So now at last all of this party is in one place, and, even if they have not yet all of them come across each other, their baggage is collected in the Registration Hall. Where, earlier, hundreds had made their way to this station thousands were coming in now, it was the end of a day for them, the beginning of a time for our party.


Anyone who found herself alone with Julia could not help feeling they had been left in charge. Again there was so much luggage round about in piles like an exaggerated grave yard, with the owners of it and their porters like mourners with the undertakers' men, and so much agitation on one hand with subdued respectful indifference on the other that this uneasiness had at last been passed on to Claire. Several other passengers were nearly in hysterics. And as she was used to leaving all her worries to her husband, who had to do everything for her, this was one of those moments when she missed him. She felt almost cross with Julia for being so helpless.

She said to Julia there did not seem to be much point in waiting for Evelyn to come back, they might try to get some of their luggage registered now, it would be such a rush when they did begin with all the mountains of stuff already waiting. Looking up from where she sat she put this to her porter drooping over his barrow. He told her nothing was being accepted for registration on account of there being no trains running as she could see for herself; he seemed pleased, he spat, and then became more despondent.

When once she had put her anxiety into words it was as though she had screamed after having tried not to for some time, when in pain. She might easily have got into the state that woman was in there, whose hat had all but fallen over her face, when she saw Alex waving, waving and smiling to them while making his way. He kissed them both while she was still saying 'why, here's Alex.' He asked where was Max, not here he supposed, and they said of course not. Claire explained how appalling it was they would not register any luggage, but already her fears had left her and she was joking and he laughed and said they never would if they could possibly avoid it, and they all laughed, too, and spoke at once. 'Anyway,' he said, 'they can't surely expect us to sleep here.'

'Alex darling, what is it about this fog, there isn't any where we are, isn't it rather tiresome of them?'

'They say it's down to the ground outside London, you see, Julia, and they can't get through, why, I can't imagine.'

'But do you think they're really doing anything about it?'

He said they must be and then described his adventures while on his way to them. They laughed again. Then he asked if they had heard the latest about Embassy Richard, he had been told the postmark on that letter was St John's Wood, which must mean Charlie Troupe had sent it. Claire said that if he meant the letter enclosing his advertisement for *The Times* then she had heard from someone in that office there had been no postmark at all, it had come unstamped. Alex said that if it did not have a stamp then it would have had one of those things which show you what you have to pay, and that must have been postmarked. Usually anything that had not been stamped was covered with postmarks, and even times of posting, and they rang your bell to tell you. 'It's rather like travelling on trains,' he said, 'without your ticket. They make you pay and write you out one, putting down where you got on and where you are going to.' Claire said yes, but you could not ask letters where they had been posted, and so this argument might have gone on if Miss Henderson had not returned. She was quite sure any un-stamped letter would have two postmarks.

Edwards asked Julia, who had not been paying attention, what was to be done about all this luggage. She said she did not know and wasn't it awful. 'You'd better ask Miss Henderson, she has just been to try and find out.'

Now what Evelyn Henderson had in mind was this: she had most of their party in one place and it would be best to keep them here until all were assembled whatever their chances of getting a train later. She was not sure any trains would run ever again, but if she had said she was going and had closed up her flat then she would make every effort to get away. She was afraid some of them might go home and leave it for her to ring them all up if there was any chance of their getting off and that would mean muddles and in-competence and end by their not going at all. So she said:

'It can't be Charlie Troupe, the thing's absurd, he'd never do anything like that, he's an old friend of mine. About this beastly train I can't imagine why they are keeping us here like sheep in a market. An inspector was very nice and told me that the fog was lifting outside, so I don't suppose it will be too long now.'

'But, darling, in that case don't you think we ought to try and find Max at once?'

'I know, Julia, but Robert and Thomson have gone to look for him.'

'No, that's just it, they're hunting round for Angela. Don't you think we ought to send Edwards after him?'

Alex announced he could see Angela and then that she could see him. 'Can't you find her, there, behind that fat man, look she's waving, who's the individual with her?'

The individual with Miss Angela Crevy was her young man, Mr Robin Adams, who so objected to her going away with them, he hated them so much.

'There they all are,' Angela said to him, 'except I don't see Max.'

Yes, Mr Adams thought to himself, that was like Max, the offensive swine, it was like him not to turn up when this was his party so to speak, as he would be paying for them. It went against the grain to have men of his type paying for Angela. It was not her fault, she did not realize, but when she had been about a bit more she would be sorry she hadn't taken it in.

For a moment Mr Adams even felt jealous of Alex.

They had drawn nearer, they were all now waving to each other, or rather Angela was waving to them and they were all waving back. Looking at them Mr Adams thought what a bloody lot of swine they were. His one consolation was that he expected a most frightful display of affection when they were within speaking distance. He was not disappointed. Alex's voice came to them, high-pitched:

'Have you brought your bed with you, darling? I can't remember whether I told Mr Crump to pack mine, because we'll never get away from here,' and he added with intuition, 'Evelyna won't let us.'

Angela replied, 'but darling, didn't you pack a double bed for us then?' Her young man asked himself what could be in worse taste and then was heartened when he saw how badly they had taken it. Of course she did not know them well enough to say things of that kind he thought, and he was wrong. In their day they had made too many jokes in that strain, they were no longer amused, so they took it just as he had done for a different reason.

They were shaking hands and Angela told Claire she had seen her aunt, 'ages ago back there among all those people. I can't tell you what a time we've had trying to get to you, didn't we, Robin? It's such an enormous place, we couldn't find where to go and I got into such a fuss.'

A faint sound of cheering came from right away at the back of this station. Heads turned towards it and Julia could see a waiter who was looking out of one of the hotel windows and who seemed to be miles away, he looked so puny, joined by another at this window and both leaned out to watch something below them.

'What can it be?' she said under her breath, 'I do feel so nervous.'

She thought here was their party laughing and shrieking as though nobody was going travelling; and then no one but her seemed to mind where Max was; where could her charms be? Jemima said she had put them in the cabin trunk but she would look in her dressing case, they were more likely to be there.

Squatting down apart she opened this case. Everything was packed in different coloured tissue papers. They were her summer things and as she lifted and recognized them she called to mind where she had last worn each one with Max. She often went away weekends to house parties and it often happened that he was there. If she had no memory for words she could always tell what she had worn each time she met him. Turning over her clothes as they had been packed she was turning over days.

Her porter sighed. He had enjoyed what he had seen of her things.

Thinking she might have been upset by their talk of Embassy Richard and because he liked to sympathize, Alex came up and asked if she was sick to death of their discussing that silly business and postmarks and all that. He found, as he had not realized, there was so much noise she could not hear what he said. Or perhaps she was crying. Julia still kept her head turned so he could not see but when he repeated himself she said yes, it was ridiculous wasn't it? He craned round and saw she was not crying and then she knew he was looking for tears.

'Oh dear,' she said, 'there are so many – too many people, aren't there?'

Alex told her he thought there would soon be many more and that he found it bewildering.

So did Mr Hignam, pushing his way through crowds, only his word for it was appalling. He felt probably they had already found Angela for themselves, there ought to be dogs, he thought, to find people for them. Though he would be sorry for dogs in this crowd, it was a wretched business, damp and cold, everyone looked as if they had had enough. How anyone was going to get a train was obviously more than the railway people could imagine. He found himself by a bar and that was an idea. They could not expect you for ever to go round shouting Angela where are you? It was crowded but he would fight through and have one.

Max was already drinking in this bar. After ringing up Amabel he had wondered if it would not be possible for her to trace where he was through the Exchange, so he had paid his bill and left. Then he had not felt up to meeting the others yet, and in any case he did not mind where they were. His feeling was he must get across the Channel and it was better to go with people than alone.

Forcing his way through, meeting half resistance everywhere and that hot smell of tea, cups guarded by elbows and half-turned bodies with 'mind my tea,' Robert thrust on and on. When small he had found patches of bamboo in his parents' garden and it was his romance at that time to force through them; they grew so thick you could not see what temple might lie in ruins just beyond. It was so now, these bodies so thick they might have been a store of tailors' dummies, water heated. They were so stiff they might as well have been soft, swollen bamboos in groves only because he had once pushed through these, damp and warm.

His ruined temple then appeared, still keeping to whisky, seated on one of those chrysanthemums with chromium-plated stalks which Miss Fellowes had observed. And she was still here, not feeling so well again, all of her turned in on herself, thrusting her load of darkness.

Robert was not so pleased to see Max, but both were polite enough to say hullo. Robert asked him if he had seen Claire's aunt by chance. Max did not hear, so let it pass. Robert asked again, this time he put it this way, that Claire had sent him to find her aunt. There was too much noise, it did not reach Max. He shouted back, 'what will you have?'

'I've ordered, thanks.'

'I suppose they sent you to find me,' Max said and now that he had begun to talk it seemed easier to hear. Robert answered no, it was Claire's aunt who was lost. Oh, said Max, and was she coming too, and once again Robert thought how odd he was, it was practically his party and yet he did not seem to know who would be coming and appeared to be quite ready to have Claire's aunt along, although they meant to be away three weeks. He explained that she had only come to see them off. 'Don't know the party,' Max said.

Robert told him all the others were waiting by their luggage until such time as it could be registered and Max asked where Edwards was. Max then said perhaps they had both of them better get back to the girls. Robert told him he thought there was no hurry, no trains were running yet.

'I know, old boy, but we can't leave your wife and the girls on their own like that.'

'Well, Edwards is there and they've got their porters, they'll be all right.'

'They'll be all right of course, but what we don't want them to do is to go back home, we must get off to-day.'

Again Robert thought it was unlike Max to say that. No one had been sure that he would even get to the station and yet here he was anxious they should all go with him.

'Let's keep them waiting once in a way,' Robert said, 'and anyway I can't go back without finding her. Have you seen Alex? I was to find him too.' And then it struck him he had never been sent to find Claire's aunt, Evelyn had wanted him to get hold of Alex and Angela and Max, but she had 'said nothing about Miss Fellowes. Why then had he been looking for the aunt? At that moment he saw Miss Fellowes.

'But, good God, Max, there she is.' Max did not seem to hear and he was pleased, it would have been too difficult to explain.

'And, my God, there's Claire's nannie.'

'Have another, Robert?'

'No, thanks. I say Max, the old girl doesn't look any too good, does she?'

'I haven't made her out yet. Well, now you've found her we can get along.'

'You don't understand, I wasn't sent to find her, but I don't like the way she looks, old boy. Do you see her there?'

'Do you mean that woman with the parcel?'

'Yes, holding the whisky. Look here, Max, she's sitting all on a skew.'

'Why not go up and ask her.'

'I can't. I say, would you mind just keeping an eye on her and I'll be off and bring Claire along?'

Max agreed and ordered another drink. Both had forgotten the nannies who sat anxiously by in silence. And that man, who had spoken to Miss Fellowes earlier, kept his attention on her, one or two others watched and each time this man looked away from her he winked.

As Hignam made his way back Alexander's taxi driver arrived. He came up to Alex and said 'how now.' Then he described what streets they had been through on their way and what his clock showed when he had left his cab. He said it was larceny to bilk taxi drivers. Alex asked how he could think he was trying to get away without paying, no trains could or would leave that evening or afternoon and anyway, he had paid, he said. His porter was brought in to witness, he had seen no money pass, Alex's voice became more shrill. Evelyn said it did seem ridiculous to be expected to pay twice when taxis were now 9d for the first mile. Then Julia stopped it by saying all this was more than she could stand and begged Alex not to be difficult. His answer was to move with the taxi driver out of earshot, where they went on gesticulating, though it was obvious now that they were suddenly on the best of terms.

'It did seem so silly, didn't it?' Julia said. 'Don't you think, darlings?'

'Oh, I don't know, poor Alex, but they seem to be getting on very well together now,' said Evelyna, and then went on 'here's Robert coming, Claire.'

'Well,' said his wife, as he came up, bullying him at once, 'I suppose you didn't find them. Angela's been here for ages, and so has Alex.'

'I say, Claire, a most extraordinary thing happened,' Robert said and drew her aside. 'You know I went to find Alex and Max as you told me. I got to the bar and thought I would go in and have a drink. Well, I found Max in there having one too and the next thing I did was to ask him if he had seen your aunt.'

'But you idiotic old thing, that wasn't what you were sent to do. Nobody mentioned her.'

'Yes, you did, Claire. But wait a moment. The odd thing was that just after I'd asked Max about her I actually did see her there.'

'I don't see anything funny in it at all. You never could keep anything in your head. But you found Max anyway, although you don't seem to have been looking for him. Why are you always like this? Yesterday I asked you to put more coal on the fire and you passed me the egg.'

Robert thought no one would ever understand, it had been a shock to him, his mind had been full of the others and then he had blurted her name out and on that had seen her sitting there. Perhaps there was nothing in it but he wondered.

'Look here, she did not look at all well, there's something wrong, I think you ought to go and have a peek at her, I can't say I like the way she was. Why don't you and the others go along there? I left Max to keep his eye on things.'

'Don't be so ridiculous, she's resting that's all.'

'She had a glass of whisky.'

'Oh, Robert, darling, you do make me laugh. Who has ever heard of Auntie May being drunk or who could ever imagine such a thing?'

'I never said she was tight, all I said, or suggested rather, was that you should all go down there where Max is and that your aunt was very ill and needed you probably. I don't care. Where is Angela?'

'Oh, she's got a beau with her, they've wandered off. All right, darling, then I'll go but I don't want the others to know, do you understand, not a word to them. If Auntie May is ill I'll see to it. Now then you stay here.' ✓

'What shall I say about you?'

'I'll be back in ten minutes.'

Julia came up to Robert with Miss Henderson and said really he had not been very clever, they had found Alex and Angela all for themselves. She then asked him where Claire had gone. He said, oh, she had been called away and that he had found Max, he was in the bar now and, it slipped out so to speak, that was where Claire was going.

'Is that where he is then? Has Claire gone to fetch him?' asked Evelyna.

'No, there was something else, I really don't know where she was going.'

Julia said she thought they had better send Edwards for Max. Miss Henderson said Claire would come back and that now they had all found each other it would be madness to separate once more. Julia said again, but wouldn't it be better to send Edwards to fetch Max. At this Edwards broke in and said Mr Adey had told him to stay where he was and that he would be along himself directly.

Julia said: 'Oh, I think it's outrageous,' and all were embarrassed and fell silent.

At that three things happened. A large force of police filed in, followed by some of the crowd who had been waiting outside, Alex came back without his driver and the station master marked them as being Miss Wray's party and was bearing down on them. This force of police stamped in and their steps sounded ringing out as though they were on hollow ground. The crowd followed and lined up by where they had halted so you could only see the tops of their helmets. Alex said it was rather hard if they were all of them going to be arrested now, particularly after he had paid for his taxi. Miss Henderson said she thought they ought to give you receipts for payments of that kind and the station master said:

'Am I by any chance speaking to Miss Julia Wray?'

'Yes.'

'Miss Wray, your uncle rang me up to say we were to take particular care of you and your party. Now, I don't like to see you waiting about here in all this crowd, can I not persuade you to wait in the Hotel? It belongs to the Company and I am sure you will be very comfortable there.'

'That's very nice of you, yes, I think we should love to, but the only thing is we aren't all together yet you see, that is, the rest of our party hasn't all arrived.'

Alex interrupted, 'My dear Angela's just there and we know where Max is, I think it's a marvellous idea, we could have a fire.'

'But what about Max?' Evelyn said.

Alex became agitated at this, he felt he might be prevented from getting his comforts.

'Bother Max,' he said, 'what consideration has he shown us? Why he said he would wait for me at his flat' (this was not true) 'to come on to the station with me, but when I got there I found he was gone.'

Julia asked why they could not get into their train and be off. She spoke sharply for her. And then they all moved off without discussing that hotel any more, with the station master explaining how this fog had complicated things. Edwards came to them as they made their way and Alex brought Angela up with her young man. Edwards asked what he was to do and Julia said: 'You can wait for Mr Adey, Edwards, as he told you to.' Robert said he must go and tell Claire and he would let Max know as well, and that he would meet them in the hotel.

After Alex had fetched them and they were making their way back to the hotel, Robin said to Angela, he supposed they were now going to dance attendance on Max Adey who, although he was host, had not had the decency to turn up yet and was probably putting drinks down wherever he was. 'Well,' Angela said, 'and have you ever seen him drunk?' 'Of course I have, stinking drunk. My dear girl, what on earth d'you think?' 'I bet you haven't, no one ever has. And I suppose you're never tipsy either. I don't know why I have to listen to all this, I wish you'd go and have done with it. You are so tiresome, now go and give me some peace.' He went off fast, almost running, not trusting himself to speak. As she came up she told the

411

others self-consciously Robin had had to be off. They paid no attention and she found that Julia had returned to the question of why
they could not get into their train and go. After all she said this fog
was only twenty feet up, it was not down to ground level and the
station master, with that patience he was paid to have, explained
again how impossible it was to see one's hand in front of one's face
less than three hundred yards south of where they were now. And in
this way they got near to the hotel.

Before they went inside Evelyn took charge and sent Robert into
the bar to tell Max and Claire where they were going, with instructions that he himself was to come back at once if possible with
Max. When they got inside she told the station master she was sure
he was very busy and that now they were here they would be quite
all right. This was nerves on her part, there was no reason for getting rid of him. Speaking to Julia and not to Evelyna he replied that
he must just reserve a room for them, they would be guests of the
Company, it was far too crowded for them to stay in any of the
public rooms and he made off to that broad open window which had
RECEPTION lit up over it. One pale young man in morning clothes
was inside this window and twelve people were bothering him.

'But I thought Max was to be here, where on earth is he?' Julia
said. 'It's perfectly wicked, here we all are turning up to time and
not a sign of him, only that wretched Edwards.'

'Here he is now, darling,' Angela said and as he came up Mr
Adey said: 'There you all are,' as if it was they who had been lost
and were late.

Evelyna was so relieved she became snappy. She asked him where
on earth had he been and he said why here, of course, and Julia,
knowing how he disliked other people getting rooms and meals – if
he was in a party he would never let anyone else pay for whatever it
might be – told him the station master was getting rooms for them.

'Can't have that,' he said, and it was one of those things Julia
liked about Max, she thought it generous. She went forward with
him to the reception desk. The young man in morning clothes recognized Max and, 'why Mr Adey,' he said, 'are you in the station
master's party, what can I do for you?'

'I don't know anything about the station master, I want three
sitting rooms.'

'All on one floor, Mr Adey?'

'Of course not. No, two on one floor and one on the floor above.'

'I'm afraid they'll have to be with bedrooms, we don't have sitting rooms separate.'

'I know, I know. Be quick about it.'

In the meantime Julia had tried to explain to her station master that Max would not hear of the Company taking a room for them because he was like that, it was very kind of the station master, it wasn't that she was ungrateful, nor was Max being rude, it was most kind of him to have looked after them and she was sure he must be very busy and ought to get back. When she returned, Max was being given three keys.

'But, darling,' she said, 'whatever do we want with three rooms?'

'Claire's aunt,' he said, 'sick.'

'Oh no.'

'Doesn't want anyone to know.'

'How awful.'

'Just arranged for three men to carry her up the back way where she won't be seen.'

'What on earth is the matter with her, Max, is she bad?'

'Don't know; tight I should say. Look out, here's the others.'

As they came up, a hall porter was with them and when he saw it was Max he said to him:

'Same room, sir?'

'No; 95, 96 and 196 this time.'

Alex said so this was where he had been hiding, and, tactlessly, what had he wanted with a room before? Max lied again, he said he had had to see his lawyer.

Julia knew he was a liar, it was one of those things one had to put up with when one was with him. But it did seem to her unfair that he should go and spoil it all now that he was here. She had forgotten how much she had resented his not turning up in her pleasure at seeing him, and now he was telling them this fairy tale about his lawyer. People were cruel. But perhaps he had wanted to make his will. Anything might happen to any one of them, everything was so going wrong. As she looked about her, at the other travellers, she could get no comfort out of what she saw. Perhaps he was not lying, which was frightening enough, but if he was then why was he lying? And this time she could not look through her things for charms, they had been left behind with her porter.

She was in a long hall with hidden lighting and, for ornament, a vast chandelier with thousands of glass drops and rather dirty. It was full of people and those who had found seats, which were all of them too low, lay with blank faces as if exhausted and, if there was anything to hope for, as though they had lost hope. Most of them were enormously fat. One man there had a cigar in his mouth, and then she saw he had one glass eye, and in his hand he had a box of matches which now and again he would bring up to his cigar. Just as he was about to strike his match he looked round each time and let his hands drop back to his lap, his match not lighted. Those standing in groups talked low and were rather bent and there was a huge illuminated clock they all kept looking at. Almost every woman was having tea as if she owned the whole tray of it. Almost every man had a dispatch case filled with daily newspapers. She thought it was like an enormous doctor's waiting room and that it would be like that when they were all dead and waiting at the gates.

She saw Claire coming and rushed forward to meet her and cried:

'My darling, my darling, in this awful place I wondered whether we weren't all dead really.'

'Julia darling, it is such a bother. I've just come from Auntie May, Robert found her when he was looking for Max and she is not at all well. I don't want a soul to know. I'm very worried about her.'

'Claire, I am sorry. Can I do anything?'

'I think we must get her in here, don't you?'

'Of course we must. As a matter of fact I know Max has taken an extra room, well to tell you the truth he's taken three rooms, just like him.'

'Yes, he's been very good. He's arranged to have her taken in the back way, poor Auntie May, she can't walk, you see. But nobody must know. Of course, darling, I would be miserable keeping it from you but not a word to another soul, please. Max didn't say anything, did he?'

'No, not to me.'

'That's all right then. Darling, I must fly and see that her room is all ready,' and when she made off Julia went to where Max was waiting for her to make him swear he would not tell another soul because of Claire.

And now Claire, who had been stopped by Evelyna, was telling her about Miss Fellowes and was swearing her to secrecy. Alex thought something was going on so he came up and he was told on condition that he did not breathe it to anyone. So in the end there was only Miss Crevy and Robin, her young man, who did not know. He would not have cared if they had all become lepers (after going off he had made up his mind he ought to keep his eye on Angela in case she might want him; he was now trying to get in the back way so she could not know he was hanging around). Angela felt very much out of it all. She had noticed, and it was obvious they were keeping secrets from her. Now Robin was gone she felt she had been left on their hands and felt inclined to blame him for going off like that without saying good-bye.

Robert came in and stopped by Julia.

'Do you know about it?' he said.

'Yes, I do.'

'Well, they are just carrying her in now.'

'Robert, is she very ill, poor thing?'

'I don't know. It's such a bore for Claire.'

'Robert, what on earth are they doing to the doors?'

'Oh that? They are putting up steel shutters over the main entrance so they told me when I came in. I say, you know about Claire not wanting anyone to know about her Aunt May? Well, when we were small there was a bamboo patch in the kitchen garden and do you remember we used to imagine there was something out of the way in the middle of it they grew so thick? I was only thinking of it just now. Well, Claire was practically brought up with us, wasn't she, when we were small and when she was sent over to play with us you know we never told her about those bamboos. Curious, wasn't it?'

'But, my dear, they aren't going to shut us up in this awful place, surely? What do they want to put shutters up for and steel ones?'

'It's the fog, I believe. Last time there was bad fog and a lot of people were stuck here they made a rush for this place I believe to get something to eat. Good Lord! it doesn't make you nervous, does it?'

It did make Julia feel very nervous and she moved to Alex where he happened to be teasing Angela because he might be nervous too which would comfort her. People who weren't nervous were useless because they did not know what it meant, but however nervous he

415

was, and if he wasn't then Julia felt she would like to make him be, he would comfort because, after all, he was a man.

There was a crash.

'Good heavens,' Alex said, 'what's that?'

'It's the steel door,' Julia cried, 'they've shut it down and how ever Claire will get her—' and then she was silent as she expected Angela did not know. 'Oh, Alex dear,' she went on, 'we're shut in now, what shall we do, isn't it awful?'

He could think of nothing better to say than what do you know about that? There was a hush, everyone in this hall was looking towards that now impenetrable entrance, women held cups half-way to their lips, little fingers of their right hands stuck out pointing towards where that crash had come from. And it was this moment the individual who could not or would not light his cigar chose to light the match in such a way that every match in his box was lit and it exploded. He was so upset his cigar tumbled out of his mouth; it was his moment, everyone now looked at him.

'But how about my claustrophobia?' Alex asked. They all heard the man near them say to his companion, a woman, no, he would certainly do nothing of the kind. And Julia demanded to know about their luggage, was it to be left out there to be looted, for their porters would not protect it.

'It's all too disastrous,' Alex said and then when he saw Max, who had come up to them, 'my dear,' he said to him, 'hadn't we all better go home and start another day?'

'Can't get home in this fog. No, I've taken rooms here.'

'But, Max, we can't sleep here.'

'You won't have to, old boy. Trains will be running soon. Come along, Angela, let's all go up.'

'If it wasn't so ludicrous it would be quite comic,' Alex said to Julia as they followed. She said she could not go up in the lift, she never could go up in them, would he mind climbing with her? As they went up short flights from landing to landing on deep plush carpets with sofas covered in tartan on each landing, Miss Fellowes was being carried by two hotel porters up the back stairs. For every step Alex and Julia took Miss Fellowes was taken up one too, slumped on one of those chromium-plated seats, her parcel on her lap, followed by the two silent nannies and, coming last, that same man who had sat next her, he who winked.

Max got Angela into one of that pair of rooms he had reserved on one floor so that she could not see Miss Fellowes carried in as Claire seemed so keen on nobody knowing. He said Julia looked a bit down, he had better order drinks.

He telephoned and was just saying:

'Please send up cocktail things. No, I don't want a man, we'll make them ourselves. I want a shaker, some gin, a bottle of Cointreau and some limes. How much? Send up two of everything and about twelve limes. No, no, only one bottle of Cointreau. These people here are fools.' He was just saying this as Julia and Alex came in. Julia said:

'She's arrived, Max.'

'Who, darling?' Angela asked.

'Oh, no one. Wouldn't you like some tea, darling,' she said to Angela, 'it might do us all some good. Max, be an angel and tell them to send up some tea.' So he ordered tea and said they had better send up whisky and two syphons also. Angela, who did not know them well, wondered at how Julia ordered Max about, and at this room, and at the prodigious number of things he had just sent for and then heard him asking for flowers.

Angela said: 'Now Robin isn't here, because you know he is a relation of Embassy Dick's, do tell me, has anyone heard any more about it?'

Alex put her right about that. 'Embassy Richard, dear, not Embassy Dick,' he said.

'Nonsense, Alex, I think Embassy Dick is a perfectly good name for him and a much better one anyway,' said Julia. Max now made one of his observations. 'If he was a bird,' he said, 'he would not last long.' Julia asked him what on earth he meant and got no answer. Then Angela went on to say this Richard had met her mother and for no reason at all, that is to say he had no cause to bring it in to what they had been saying, he had told her mother he would not be able to go to that reception. Alex objected that Embassy Richard was always saying things of that kind, it proved nothing, and Julia wondered whether Angela was not inventing it all. 'But what I mean is,' Angela said, 'he made a point of his not being able to go. So don't you see someone who might have heard him and had got to know that he had not been invited saw their chance and sent that notice to the papers.'

'But surely, my dear, you don't mean to suggest that he sent the message himself.'

'Alex, what do you mean?'

'Look here, Angela, you seem to think that just because someone overheard him making his alibi about that party it proves that someone else must have sent the notice to the society columns. Well,' Alex went on and so lost track of his argument, 'surely that must be so. I mean no one has ever suggested that he sent the message himself.'

'So you said before, so I seem to remember,' Julia said, who loved arguments, 'but I don't see any reason for saying he didn't send it himself.'

Alex was very taken with this suggestion and complimented Julia on it; he said no one had ever thought of it or, at any rate, not in his hearing. Angela said but surely Embassy Richard wouldn't willingly have brought all that on himself to which Alex replied by asking how he could have known the Ambassador would disown him.

'The Ambassador knows him quite well, too.'

'All the more reason then, Angela dear,' Alex said, 'I expect he was fed up with him.'

'Poisonous chap,' said Max.

'Max, darling, don't be so aggravating, which one do you mean, the Ambassador or Richard?'

'Well, after all, Julia, why should he be called Embassy Richard if he wasn't?' Alex said.

Julia said she did not agree, she thought him very good-looking and didn't Angela think so too. Angela agreed and Alex said 'Oh, very fetching!'

'No, Alex, don't, you're spoiling the whole argument by attacking him. It's neither here nor there to say that he's awful, what we're talking about is whether he sent that notice himself.'

Max chose this moment to leave the room and again Angela felt she was out of it, that they were keeping things from her and, as she thought Alex had been tiresome with her over this argument, she decided she would rather go for him.

'Anyhow, Alex,' she said, 'I bet there's one thing you don't know.'

'I expect there are several.'

'And that is that the Prince Royal is a friend of Richard's and was frightfully angry with his Ambassador when he saw the letter he wrote.'

'I must say I can't see that makes the slightest difference. Anyway I did know about the Prince what d'you call him. You see, Angela, we were arguing about who could have sent the notice if Embassy Richard didn't sent it for himself. I can't see that it matters two hoots if the Prince Royal was cross.'

'I can,' said Julia, entering into it again. 'I think it's a score for Richard if the Ambassador's employer is cross with him for trying to score off Richard.'

'No,' and Alex was now speaking in his high voice he used when he was upset, 'that's not the point. The real point is that the Ambassador ticked off Embassy Richard in public by writing to the papers to say he had never invited him to his party. If the Prince Royal told his Ambassador off for doing it, it doesn't make any difference to the fact that Richard was shown up in public.'

'But Alex, dear, it does,' Julia said. 'If the Prince Royal did not approve, and the party was being given for him, then it means that Embassy Richard should have been invited all the time.'

'I don't see that it does, Julia. He may not have approved of the way his Ambassador did it. My whole point is that the Prince Royal never made his Ambassador write another letter to the papers saying that Richard should have been invited after all. D'you see?'

Angela said 'No, Alex, I don't.'

'Well, what I mean is that you and I may know the Prince Royal was tremendously angry and threw fits, if you like, when he read his Ambassador's letter but the thousands of people in the street who read their newspapers every morning would not hear about it. All that they know is that Embassy Richard regretted not being able to attend a party he was not invited to.'

'Oh, if that's it,' said Angela, 'then who cares about the people in the street and what they think about it.'

They were all silent trying to keep their tempers when Evelyn Henderson came in. They all told her at one time what they had said and what they had meant and when she had gathered what all this was about she said:

'But I don't understand your saying that the Ambassador knew Richard quite well. You know in that letter of his the newspapers printed he said he had never seen him in his life. And then for the matter of that, isn't the story of Embassy Richard's being a friend of the Prince Royal just the sort of thing Richard would put round to clear himself? Does anyone know, really know, that it's true?'

Angela said well, as a matter of fact, she did know for certain they were friends because her mother knew the Prince Royal well and he had told her so. Alex asked if that was before or after this business about the party and she replied that it was before. He was just about to say the Prince Royal might think very differently about Richard now and Angela was waiting for him – she was in that state she would have accused him of being rude whatever he said – when Alex saw signs of agitation in Evelyn Henderson and guessed she must have news of Miss Fellowes. So, in order to occupy her attention, he began to make peace with Angela while Evelyn drew Julia aside. In a minute these two went out together and Angela, when she saw it, realized how treacherous Alex really was.

When they were outside that room Miss Henderson said to Julia:

'My dear, you look very pale, are you all right?'

'Yes, I think so. I get so excited, up one moment, down the next, you know how it is,' and Miss Henderson when she heard this thought poor child, it is in love. She was three years older than Julia. 'Well,' she said, 'what I wanted to tell you and of course I didn't want the others in there to hear, is that poor Claire's aunt is very ill, I'm sure of it.'

'Oh dear!'

'Yes. Robert has gone to try and find a doctor. I expect there'll be one stuck in this beastly hotel same as we are. But there's more than that. I'm rather unhappy in my own mind about it. She had a parcel of sorts and as we were getting her on the bed it fell down and came open and there was a pigeon of all things inside.'

'A dead pigeon? Perhaps she was taking it back for her supper.'

'No, it was all wet.'

'Oh, Evelyna, how disgusting! But how could it be wet?'

'That's what I asked myself. But Claire's old nannie, who has been keeping an eye on her tells me she saw Claire's Auntie May washing it in the "Ladies".'

'Well, I think that's rather sweet.'

'I'm not so sure about that, my darling Julie, and I'd rather you did not say anything to Claire about that part of it. I don't think she knows and she is so upset already, I don't want her worried any more.'

'Yes, if you say so, but I don't see anything so very awful in it.'

'Good heavens, do you see what I see, those poor old dears are crying. Why,' Evelyn said, hurrying up to where those two nannies sat in tears on a settee, 'it is being a tiresome difficult day for us all, isn't it?' she said to them. 'Now, wouldn't you like a nice cup of tea?'

They made noises which could be taken to mean yes and Julia explained to Miss Henderson how Max had already ordered tea so that it would be easy to carry two cups along to them without Angela knowing. As they moved off down the corridor Evelyn said she did not like the way they were crying, did Julia think Miss Fellowes had donè anything? Julia said something or other in reply. She was now struck by how extraordinary it was their being here in this corridor with the South of France, where they were going, waiting for them at the end of their journey. They had all, except for Angela Crevy, been in the same party twelve months ago to the same place, so fantastically different from this. One day would be so fine you wondered if it could be true, the next it rained like anywhere else. But when it was fine you sat on the terrace for dinner looking over a sea of milk with a sky fainting into dusk with the most delicate blushes – Oh! she cried in her heart, if only we could be there now. Indeed, this promise of where they were going lay back of all their minds or feelings, common to all of them. If they did not mention it, it was why they were in this hotel and there was not one of them, except of course for Miss Fellowes and the nannies, who did not every now and again most secretly revert to it.

As for Miss Fellowes, she was fighting. Lying inanimate where they had laid her she waged war with storms of darkness which rolled up over her in a series, like tides summoned by a moon. What made her fight was the one thought that she must not be ill in front of these young people. She did not know how ill she was.

Those nannies, like the chorus in Greek plays, knew Miss Fellowes was very ill. Their profession had been for forty years to ward illness off in others and their small talk had been of sudden strokes, slow cancers, general paralysis, consumption, diabetes and of chills, rheumatism, lumbago, chicken pox, scarlet fever, vaccination and the common cold. They had therefore an unfailing instinct for dis-

421

aster. By exaggeration, and Fate they found rightly was most often exaggerated, they could foretell from one chilblain on a little toe the gangrene that would mean first that toe coming off, then that leg below the knee, next the upper leg and finally an end so dreadful that it had to be whispered behind hands.

Robert Hignam appeared, asked how his aunt by marriage was and said he thought they would be able to find a doctor for her. Julia said how sorry she felt for Claire, and Robert said yes, it was rather a bore for her. He went on:

'You know, a most extraordinary thing happened about Claire's aunt. You know, Evelyn, you wanted me to go and find Angela and Max. Well, when I found myself outside the bar down there I went in and came up against Max. D'you know the first thing I asked him was whether he had seen Claire's aunt although no one had ever asked me to find her? As a matter of fact Max did not know her by sight but as soon as I'd finished telling him, there she was in a chair, large as life and ill at that.'

'I knew all along I'd forgotten something,' Julia said, but almost to herself and in so low a voice they did not catch it, 'there's Thomson outside now still looking for the others and he's probably looking for us now as well.'

Evelyn told Robert it could never be thought-transference as if anyone had been thinking of Miss Fellowes they could not have known she was ill. He said it had made him feel rather uncomfortable and she said she did not see how it made him feel that. 'That's all very well,' he said, 'but wouldn't you if for no reason at all you began asking after someone you had no reason to think of?'

Evelyn was very practical. 'But that's just it, Robert,' she said, 'you had cause to think of her because you had probably seen her unconsciously as you came in, though you did not realize it at the time, and that is what made you ask after her.'

And now Julia, who had been worrying about Thomson, got to that pitch like when a vessel is being filled it gets so full the water spills over. Julia broke in, saying but what about Thomson, he was sent out with you Robert, what's happened to him?

'Half a tick, Julia. No, look here, Evelyn, if I had seen her subconsciously as you say I would not have been so surprised when I did realize she was there.'

'But how do you know?'

'Oh, bother you two and your questions,' said Julia. 'What am I to do about Thomson? Now that they have put that steel door down over the hotel he won't be able to find us or anyone.'

Miss Henderson suggested he might have gone back to their luggage.

'Robert, I wonder if you will do something for me,' Julia said. 'Could you go to the station master, no, of course you can't get outside. But you could telephone to him, couldn't you, and say it's for me, and ask him to send someone out to look for Thomson and tell him that he must go back at once to where the luggage is and tell him to see my porter does not put it in the cloakroom if we are a long time. I told my porter that he must not put it in the cloakroom whatever happened, I don't trust these places, but you know what these porters are. Robert, will you do that for me?'

'Yes, only too glad to. But I say, Julia, you know that station master must be a pretty busy man, what with the fog and everything. What do you think?'

'He'll be glad to do it because of my uncle. It would be ever so sweet of you, my dear.'

Miss Fellowes, in her room, felt she was on a shore wedged between two rocks, soft and hard. Out beyond a grey sea with, above, a darker sky, she would notice small clouds where sea joined sky and these clouds coming far away together into a darker mass would rush across from that horizon towards where she was held down. As this cumulus advanced the sea below would rise, most menacing and capped with foam, and as it came nearer she could hear the shrieking wind in throbbing through her ears. She would try not to turn her eyes down to where rising waves broke over rocks as the nearer that black mass advanced so fast the sea rose and ate up what little was left between her and those wild waters. Each time this scene was repeated she felt so frightened, and then it was menacing and she throbbed unbearably, it was all forced into her head; it was so menacing she thought each time the pressure was such her eyes would be forced out of her head to let her blood out. And then when she thought she must be overwhelmed, or break, this storm would go back and those waters and her blood recede, that moon would go out above her head, and a sweet tide washed down from scalp to toes and she could rest.

'My dear Mr Hinham,' the station master said to Robert, for he had not caught his name, 'My dear sir, there are now, we estimate, thirty thousand people in the station. The last time we had a count, on the August Bank Holiday of last year, we found that when they really began coming in, nine hundred and sixty-five persons could enter this station by the various subways each minute. So supposing I sent a man out to look for the individual Thomson, and he did not find him in ten minutes, there would be forty thousand people to choose from. A needle in a – a needle in a—' and he was searching for some better word, 'a haystack,' he said at last, at a loss.

'I know,' said Robert.

'So you see, sir, I'm afraid we can't,' the station master said, and quickly rang off before his temper got the better of him.

Miss Crevy asked Alex where everyone had got to, and he said he could not think where they could be. She asked him outright if anything had happened to anybody, and then, because this question seemed awkward, especially as whatever it was that had happened was obviously being kept from her, she lost her grip and fell further into it by asking him did he know what had become of her Robin. She knew she had been thinking of him without realizing it, all this time.

'But he's gone, Angela.'

'Oh, yes, of course, he had to go away.'

To tide over her embarrassment Alex suggested they might mix the cocktails now.

'But Max isn't here,' she said.

'That doesn't matter. He won't mind.'

Because of all that had gone before, she said:

'But it's rude to drink other people's cocktails before they come in. You wouldn't go into someone else's house . . .' and she stopped there, realizing, of course, he probably would if he knew them well enough. She felt miserable. Alex had been so tiresome about Embassy Richard – she must remember to call him by his proper name – and they were all conspiring together to keep something or other from her and then she had shown about Rob, everyone now would think they were engaged. And it was really so rude to start on his drinks without Max being there.

As for Alex he was frantic that she had been asked on their party. People one hardly knew were always putting one in false positions.

It would have been too offensive, though so tempting, to reply that naturally one could go into someone's house and drink their drink, not champagne, of course, but why not gin and lime juice, everyone else did. And besides, it was a question of how well you knew the person, it was intolerable that he should be put wrong because she did not know Max well. It was true that people used not to do it, but when one was in the schoolroom one did not suck one's fingers after jam; on account of one's sisters' governess one wiped them, but one sucked them now, one was grown up.

'I'm sorry, I'm afraid I'm being tiresome,' she said. 'But this journey is being so long, isn't it? I think I'm going out for a minute.'

'Oh, don't go,' was all he could think of saying, and she all but said try and stop me if you can, I could knock you down, but she did no more than look away as she went by him.

When she went out into that corridor she had made up her mind she must go home. She felt she had only been invited so they could humiliate her; not that Max would ever do such things, it was the others. Then she saw the nannies, who were still crying. Poor ducks, she thought, have they been vile to them too, how really beastly, poor old things and one of them Claire's nanny. She went up and said,

'There, there, it will be quite all right.'

But they would not cry in front of a stranger, and she was surprised and rather hurt to find their tears were drying up, and in two moments she saw they would be putting their handkerchiefs away. Even their nannies, she thought, even their nannies are in league to make one feel out of it. At that instant the man who had been with Miss Fellowes in the bar, and had spoken to her and watched her, and who had followed when she had been carried up, reappeared walking slowly up the corridor. His head was bent forward. He stared at those nannies when he was close to them. He stopped and then, for the first time, he looked at her.

'Ah, they carried 'er up here. Terrible bad she was then, I reckon.'

There was a long silence. He went on:

'On one of them stools with backs to 'em there was in the bar.'

Alex had come out after Angela. It upset him to see this man. He spoke in his high voice he had when he was upset.

'What are you doing here?' he said.

'What's that to you, my lad?'

'Why don't you go away? These are private rooms here.'

'Aye, but the corridor's public,' this man returned, and without any warning he had used Yorkshire accent where previously he had been speaking in Brummagem. This sudden change did his trick as it had so often done before and Alex, losing his nerve, asked him in to have a drink. He thought he might be the hotel detective.

'What'll you have?'

'I don't mind,' this man said, speaking this time in an educated voice.

'I'm afraid everything must seem very odd to you,' said Alex, 'I mean there seems to be so much going on, but you see we are all going on a party together abroad, and now here we are stuck in this hotel on account of fog.'

It was difficult for Alex. He had come out after Angela because he could never stand things being left in what he called false positions. He was friendly by nature and if he could not help feeling annoyed with Miss Crevy and having digs at her, particularly when she tried to put him in the wrong as he now felt she was continually trying to do, he did not want her to bear him a grudge. It was as much this particularity of his which led him to entertain the mystery man as it was his feeling that he might make trouble for Miss Fellowes if he was not kept amused. While he busily talked with this little man he kept on despairing of ever getting things straight with Angela.

Miss Crevy stood outside with those two nannies, who were also standing up now. She was not so anxious to get home. She was wondering what could be going on that they would not tell her. Then Claire came out with a man who was too obviously the hotel doctor. He looked at Angela with suspicion, and walking down that corridor he said to Claire, quietly:

'What relation is the lady I have just examined to you?'

'She is my aunt.'

'I see, I see.'

'What are we to do?' Claire asked him. 'It really is such a bore poor Auntie May getting like this, and it seems quite impossible to get her out of here. It was extraordinarily lucky that we were able to get hold of you. But, of course, it is too tiresome for her, I can't think of anything worse, can you, than being ill in a hotel bedroom? It was so lucky I did go where they told me I'd find her, because I could see at once she was very ill. What do you think of her?'

'Has she been drinking any stimulants, within the last hour shall we say?'

'Why, yes, I think someone said she had.'

'Well, I don't think you need worry about her. It would be a good thing if she could get some sleep. Keep her warm, of course. Oh, yes, it will pass off. Perhaps I might see your husband, wasn't it, for a moment?'

When Robert Hignam came out this doctor drew him aside and said that would be ten and sixpence, please. Claire sent those nannies in to watch Miss Fellowes telling them there was nothing to worry over in her condition, which they did not believe, and she told Julia who was there, too, that it was nothing, and they could go back to that other room and have a drink. Max had come back after trying unsuccessfully to get an ambulance to take Miss Fellowes home (it appeared the streets were so choked with traffic that no communication was possible) and Robert having paid the doctor they all, with Angela, came into the room where Alex was pouring drinks.

As they came in, Robert was explaining to Julia how impossible it was for any search to be made for Thomson. She said:

'Good heavens, who's that?'

They saw facing them that little man, with his glass of whisky, and in the other hand a shabby bowler hat. His tie was thin, as thin as him, and his collar clean and stiff, and so was he; his clothes were black, and his face white with pale, blue eyes. Compared to them he looked like another escaped poisoner, and as if he was looking out for victims. Alex, in the silence this man had made with his appearance, asked him loudly if he would have another drink, and this time he nodded, as though he did not want to speak until he could make up his mind which accent would do his trick best this time.

After she had glanced at Max and seen that he did not seem to care either way about the little man being there, Julia decided it was best to ignore him.

'But are you sure you gave my name?' she said to Robert.

'Yes, I did, and he said he felt you would understand.'

'But what about poor Thomson's tea? He is most frightfully particular about that.'

'Well, after all, he can get some for himself,' and Robert thought it was absurd. Julia would say nothing of keeping Thomson up for something or other until three in the morning, why start this game about tea?

Angela said to Max:

'Darling, who is that man?'

'Don't know.'

'But then why is Alex giving him drinks?'

'Don't care, do you?'

'Max, darling, is there any chance of going home do you think? I mean, it does seem to be rather hopeless hanging about here.'

'No chance at all. I couldn't even get an ambulance for Claire's aunt.'

'What, is she ill?'

'Didn't you know?'

'Yes, darling, didn't you know?' Claire said. 'But the doctor says there is nothing the matter with her really. Rest would put her right, he said.'

Alex was overjoyed, and said why, that was splendid, loudly, and that little man did not seem pleased, gulped down his drink and left them, saying, in Brummagem, she had been cruel bad when he seen her last.

'Who on earth was that, Alex?'

'My dear Julia, I'm perfectly sure it was the hotel detective.'

'But why?'

'Why? But don't you see that if this Miss Fellowes had been really bad, and he had found out he would have insisted on having her moved.'

'I don't see at all.'

'They won't have people, well, people who are very bad in hotels.'

Claire asked who had said her Aunt May was very bad, and Alex could only say his little man had. Angela said 'Oh, well, if you will believe what he said,' and Julia took that up and said she thought Alex had been perfectly right. Angela, trying to be malicious and yet not rude, said she was horrified to hear Miss Fellowes had been ill, and that she had only remarked to Robin Adams when they met her how she had not seemed right. Alex wanted to ask Miss Crevy where Mr Adams was, but he did not dare, and Claire said yes, she knew, but she thought it so awful of people to saddle others with their family troubles, Max had been perfectly sweet to put her aunt in a room of her own, but it did seem so unfair that all the rest of

428

them should be bothered by it. 'So I didn't tell you,' she said to Angela, and in so doing, gave herself away, for she had at first seemed surprised that Miss Crevy did not know. And Miss Crevy, thinking to withdraw and be nice, said well, poor Miss Fellowes could not help herself feeling ill could she, and, sensing that she must have said the wrong thing, she added that whenever she felt ill she consoled herself with those sentiments.

'But, darling, why did you think he was a hotel detective?' Julia said to Alex.

'Because he had a bowler hat, of course,' said Claire. 'If Alex will go to so many films where they are the only people who do wear bowlers, of course, that's how he gets it into his head. No, you needn't be embarrassed, I know exactly how it was, you couldn't have told how ill she was, and I think it was perfectly sweet of you to have looked after this man like you did, and like that angel Evelyna is looking after Auntie May this moment. And that reminds me that I must go back and relieve poor Evelyn, I shan't be long,' and with that she left. Alex felt better but not entirely justified so he asked Julia why she was so certain it could not have been a detective. Julia, however, had seen Max put his arm round Angela Crevy and draw her to the window where they now stood looking down at crowds beneath. Alex did not find that Julia was giving him her attention.

Angela said to Max, speaking confidentially, that she was having a marvellous time, even if it was a bit overwhelming occasionally. He said he was glad. She went on that it would be so marvellous to be really off, that is, in their train and on their way, with the sun waiting for them where they were going, and that she adored going in boats, other people hated Channel crossings, but for her they were more fun than all the rest of her journey. He squeezed her in reply.

'Max, darling, where's our tea?' Julia asked.

He apologized and, going to the telephone, he got on to the management. When he had finished, and they had finally apologized this voice said:

'Oh, Mr Adey, a lady has been ringing up to ask if you put a call through to her.'

'Well?'

'We said that you had not done so '

Max said right and putting his arm round Julia this time he led her to the window. Looking down she saw the whole of that station below them, lit now by electricity, and covered from end to end by one mass of people. 'Oh, my dear!' she said, 'poor Thomson.' As those people smoked below, or it might have been the damp off their clothes evaporating rather than their cigarettes, it did seem like November sun striking through mist rising off water. Or, so she thought, like those illustrations you saw in weekly papers, of corpuscles in blood, for here and there a narrow stream of people shoved and moved in lines three deep and where they did this they were like veins. She wondered if this were what you saw when you stood on your wedding day, a Queen, on your balcony looking at subjects massed below.

'It's like being a Queen,' she told Max. He squeezed her.

'You didn't do anything about Edwards, did you?' she said and he did not reply.

She saw the electric trains drawn up in lines with no one on their platforms, everyone was locked out behind barriers and she thought, too, how wonderful it would be when they had arrived.

Alex came up and said what they saw now was like a view from the gibbet and she exclaimed against that. And Miss Fellowes wearily faced another tide of illness. Aching all over she watched helpless while that cloud rushed across to where she was wedged and again the sea below rose with it, most menacing and capped with foam and as it came nearer she heard again the shrieking wind in throbbing through her ears. In terror she watched the seas rise to get at her, so menacing her blood throbbed unbearably, and again it was all forced into her head but this had happened so often she felt she had experienced the worst of it. But now with a roll of drums and then a most frightful crash lightning came out of that cloud and played upon the sea, and this was repeated, and then again, each time nearer till she knew she was worse than she had ever been. One last crash which she knew to be unbearable and she burst and exploded into complete insensibility. She vomited.

'Come away for a minute,' Max said to Julia. As they went off and passed that door it opened and Claire came out with Evelyna. Both of them were smiling and said she would do better now, now she had done what the doctor said.

\*

As she walked down that corridor with Max, and he still had his arm round her, she wondered so faintly she hardly knew she had it in her mind where he could be taking her and all the while she was telling him about her charms, her mood softening and made expansive by his having taken her away.

Max was dark and excessively handsome, one of those rich young men who when still younger had been taken up by an older woman, richer than himself. Money always goes to money, the poor always marry someone poorer than themselves, but it is only the rich who rule worlds such as we describe and no small part of Max's attraction lay in his having started so well with someone even richer than himself.

It was generally believed that he had lived with this rich lady, there was hardly anyone who would not have sworn this was the case, and indeed they were on such terms that both were glad to admit they had. As it happened they had on no occasion had anything to do with each other.

It follows that, having begun so well, Max had by now become extraordinarily smart in every sense and his reputation was that he went to bed with every girl. Through being so rich he certainly had more chances. He took them and, of serious offers accepted, his most recent had been Amabel.

Max therefore was reckoned to be of importance, he was well known, he moved in circles made up of people older than himself, and there was no girl of his own age like Julia, Claire Hignam or Miss Crevy – even Evelyna Henderson although she was hardly in it – who did not feel something when they were on his arm, particularly when he was so good-looking. Again one of his attractions was that they all thought they could stop him drinking, not that he ever got drunk because he had not yet lost his head for drink, but they were all sure that if they married him they could make him into something quite wonderful, and that they could get him away from all those other women, or so many of them as were not rather friends of their own. It was for this therefore she made out it meant something to be going on this trip, that it was fun to be walking down this corridor, getting him away from the others, or that was all she would admit she found about him who was more than anyone to her.

'So I went back, darling, and I asked my darling Jemima where could she have put my charms,' Julia said, leaning on him a little, 'and she promised me faithfully they were in my cabin trunk. Are you like that, have you anything you don't like to travel without? Not toothbrushes or sponges I mean, but things you can't use, like mascots.' At this they came to some stairs and the lift.

'Where on earth are you taking me?' she said.

'Got some tea for you in a special room.'

People were going up and down so he took his arm off her as they came up and rang for the lift. She had forgotten, through being with him, her dislike of going in these. As they got out on the next floor she was thinking no one else would have bothered to spare her walking up one flight of stairs.

'Yes, so then I had to simply fly back, in a taxi this time, as I was terrified I was going to miss you all. You know I've never never done anything so eerie as walking through the Park in the dark when it was only four o'clock or whatever time it was. The extraordinary part was the birds who had gone to sleep as they thought it was night and then were woken up by the car lights so they muttered in their sleep, the darlings, just like Jemima tells me I do when she pulls the blinds. I got so frightened. And then do you know I imagined what I should say to you if I met you walking alone there. But that was silly and then I remembered about my charms and went back to the house like I told you.'

They came to the room he had reserved.

'Oh, tea, tea!' she cried as she went in and clapped her hands, 'tea and crumpets, how divine of you, darling, and so grand, just for us two. You know I think I will take my hat off,' and doing this she wandered round looking at pictures on the walls.

One of these was of Nero fiddling while Rome burned, on a marble terrace. He stood to his violin and eight fat women reclined on mattresses in front while behind was what was evidently a great conflagration.

'Nero and his wives,' she said and passed on.

Another was one of those reproductions of French eighteenth-century paintings which showed a large bed with covers turned back and half in, half out of it a fat girl with fat legs sticking out of her nightdress and one man menacing and another disappearing behind curtains.

'Here's a to-do,' she said.

Another was of a church, obviously in Scotland, and snow and sheep, at the back of a bleak mountain, fir trees in the middle distance and you could see church bells were ringing, they were at an angle in the belfry.

'Oh, do look, Max darling, come here. Isn't that like the church at Barshottie which you took last winter, do you remember?' And then as he put his arm round her again she said: 'No, don't do that, it's too hot in here. Let's have some tea or my crumpets will be cold.'

· When she was pouring him out his tea she asked him if he had heard anything about Embassy Richard. Speaking slowly in his rather low voice he said he understood that there had been a girl this man had wanted to see at that party. She wanted to know who that might be but he would not tell her although she pressed him; she approved of his not giving this girl's name away, it proved to her that he was safe.

'But Max, my dear,' she said, 'surely the point is that Embassy Richard didn't go to the party. Some people think he sent that notice to the papers himself saying he could not attend, and if he did that then he can't have meant to go.'

'All I know is he's head over heels in love with this girl,' Mr Adey said, 'and he was not invited and she was, and he meant to go whether he got his invitation or not.'

'But my dear how absolutely thrilling; then why didn't he go?'

'What I heard was that Charlie Troupe, who knew of this, rang him up to say his girl was not going after all but would be at the Beavis's dance.'

'I see. All the same, Max, he had only to ring up his friend to see if she was going or not.'

'No, he had had a row with her.'

'Then if what you say is right it does look like Charlie Troupe after all, I mean.it does seem as though it was Charlie Troupe who sent that notice out. But if you won't tell me the name of the girl I shall still go on believing that Richard did it himself.'

'Believe it or not, it's true that he didn't and I call it a dirty trick to play.'

'When he was in love, you mean,' she said. 'But that's just the time people do play dirty tricks,' and at this she looked very knowledgeable.

'On each other, yes, but it's not playing the game for a third person to do it.'

'Perhaps Charlie Troupe was in love with her himself. If you would only tell me her name I'd know.'

'I don't hold any brief for Charlie Troupe or Embassy Richard but I think it was a low-down trick,' he said.

'People do play awful tricks on each other when they are in love, don't they, Max? I can't understand why people can't go on just being ordinary to each other even if they are in love.' She became quite serious. 'After all, it's the most marvellous thing that can happen to a person, to two people, there's no point in making it all beastly. You know that thing of making up to someone else so as to make the one you really mind about more mad about you, well, I think that's simply too awful, and very dangerous after all.'

He laughed and asked her if she did that after all, and she laughed and said now he was asking questions. She went on, 'perhaps that girl friend of Embassy Richard's was trying to hot him up with Charlie Troupe, that would fit in with your idea that it was Charlie Troupe who sent the notice out, but if she was, then I think she deserves everything she gets. Why don't you like Embassy Richard?'

'I don't know, but look at his name. Always crawling round Embassies. And you can see him any night there isn't one of those grander shows on, crawling round night clubs with older women old enough to be his grandmother.'

At this she thought how odd it was that people always seemed to dislike in others just what they were always doing themselves, for Max went everywhere at night with older women. Then, to get this conversation back to herself, however indirectly, she said:

'But perhaps Charlie Troupe is only going about like that to make some girl jealous.'

'Not Charlie Troupe.'

'I don't know,' she said, 'don't you be too sure. What do we know about anyone?' said she, thinking of herself.

'Not Charlie Troupe.'

'Oh, all right. In fact I'm very glad. I think it's perfectly horrible and very wrong to walk out with a third person just because you are in love with another. It's not playing fair. After all, it's the most marvellous thing that can happen to anyone, or at any rate that's what they say,' she said to cover her tracks, 'and to make a point of making the real person jealous is simply beastly,' she said with great sincerity.

Meanwhile Mr Robin Adams, Miss Angela Crevy's young man, sat in a bar downstairs in this hotel and wondered angrily how Angela could go with these revolting people. Here they were engaged, even if it was not yet in the papers he had her word for it, she would not take his ring but she had said she would be engaged to him when she came back from this trip of theirs, so they must be engaged. And then in spite of it she would insist on going off although she knew he did not approve, although she knew it gave him pain, agony in fact; it was perfectly damnable and made him miserable, it was so unfair. At this moment Robert Hignam hit him hard between the shoulders.

'Robin, old boy, I didn't know you were here,' he said. 'Have you got sick of them upstairs too? Well, I don't mind telling you I've been sent on so many damn messages, fatigues and things, I said to myself it's time you took a rest and went downstairs and got yourself a drink. Not that old Max hasn't seen to the liquid refreshment, there's plenty of that up there – a small Worthington, please miss – but I should be sent off on some message or other for certain the moment I settled down. It's Claire's aunt, you know. Came to see us off and the doctor here says she's tight or so he gave me to believe, and charged me ten-and-six. That's all tommy rot, you understand, there's something more wrong with her than just that, but I'm not telling the girls; one doesn't want them to get upset. But I must tell you,' he went on, thinking poor old Robin seemed a bit glum about something, 'the most extraordinary thing happened about Claire's aunt. I'd been sent off to see whether I couldn't find Angela and you and someone else, I forget which of them it was, and I was finding it pretty dry work so I dropped into the bar outside there. Mind you, no one had said a word to me about Claire's aunt but d'you know the first thing I asked Max – I found him sitting there having one before me – was whether he had seen the old lady. And the next thing was I was her sitting right in the corner and looking pretty queer, too, I can tell you. Bit of an extraordinary thing, wasn't it?'

'Funny thing,' Mr Adams said and he had not listened.

'Yes, that's what the doctor said,' Miss Evelyn Henderson was telling Alex, 'and now, between ourselves, she has been vomiting so if what the doctor says is right she ought to be getting better.'

'Well, that's splendid.'

'Yes, but I'm not so sure that doctor knew what he was talking about. Don't go and tell anyone, but she was such a bad colour.'

'Evelyn, my dear,' Alex said, 'don't put your opinion against the doctor's, it's perfectly fatal. If he said what was wrong with her as he did then that's what is the matter, never mind what you or I think. I'm not sure that I agree with you, in any case it's quite likely she had one too many, probably she felt tired and let it get the better of her.'

He mixed himself another drink.

'Now don't you go and get drunk too,' she said. 'I can't have two drunks on my hands.'

He laughed and then, because she had rather annoyed him, he made this suggestion:

'Why don't you let Claire look after her? After all she is her niece.'

'My dear, Claire couldn't look after a sick cat. As it is I don't know what I should have done if it hadn't been for her old nanny and the friend. They have been simply wonderful. Of course it was they who put me on the track of it and I didn't have a chance of taking that doctor aside, but I don't think they are satisfied either.'

'What do you mean?'

'No, I should not have said that. I think you are quite right that I should take what the doctor said,' she said to close the subject.

'Well,' said Alex, 'I have been doing my bit too. A most extraordinary individual blew in here a short time back and I took him for the hotel detective. I thought he was trying to nose out something about this Miss Fellowes. So I buckled to and began plying him with drinks and the others have been chaffing me about it.'

'I think you were quite right, perfectly right. It would be dreadful if there was a scandal. Now I must go back. I don't mean a scandal, that's not the right word, a fuss. Now I must go back in there. You go and talk to Angela, she's sitting all alone,' and with that Miss Henderson went off.

Upstairs Max and Julia had finished their tea and, in an interval of silence, she had gone over to the window and was looking down on that crowd below. As he came over to join her she said well anyway, those police over there would protect their luggage, as they were drawn up in front of the Registration Hall. And as she watched she saw this crowd was in some way different. It could not be larger as there was no room, but in one section under her window it seemed to be swaying like branches rock in a light wind and, paying greater attention, she seemed to hear a continuous murmur coming from it. When she noticed heads everywhere turned towards that section just below she flung her window up. Max said: 'Don't go and let all that in,' and she heard them chanting beneath: "WE WANT TRAINS, WE WANT TRAINS.' Also that raw air came in, harsh with fog and from somewhere a smell of cooking, there was a shriek from somewhere in the crowd, it was all on a vast scale and not far above her was that vault of glass which was blue now instead of green, now that she was closer to it. She had forgotten what it was to be outside, what it smelled and felt like, and she had not realized what this crowd was, just seeing it through glass. It went on chanting WE WANT TRAINS, WE WANT TRAINS from that one section which surged to and fro and again that same woman shrieked, two or three men were shouting against the chant but she could not distinguish words. She thought how strange it was when hundreds of people turned their heads all in one direction, their faces so much lighter than their dark hats, lozenges, lozenges, lozenges.

The management had shut the steel doors down because when once before another fog had come as thick as this hundreds and hundreds of the crowd, unable to get home by train or bus, had pushed into this hotel and quietly clamoured for rooms, beds, meals, and more and more had pressed quietly, peaceably in until, although they had been most well behaved, by weight of numbers they had smashed everything, furniture, lounges, reception offices, the two bars, doors. Fifty-two had been injured and compensated and one of them was a little Tommy Tucker, now in a school for cripples, only fourteen years of age, and to be supported all his life at the railway company's expense by order of a High Court Judge.

'It's terrifying,' Julia said, 'I didn't know there were so many people in the world.'

'Do shut the window, Julia.'

'But why? Max, there's a poor woman down there where that end of the crowd's swaying. Did you hear her call? Couldn't you do something about it?'

He leaned out of the window.

'Couldn't get down there I'm afraid, doors are shut,' he said.

At that she closed this window and said he was quite right and that it was silly of her to suggest it. 'After all,' she said, 'one must not hear too many cries for help in this world. If my uncle answered every begging letter he received he would have nothing left in no time.' It was extraordinary how quiet their room became once that window was shut. 'What do you do with your appeals and things?' He answered that everything was in the hands of his secretary. He decided with his accountants, who managed his affairs for him, what he would set aside for charities during the year and then he told his secretary which ones he wanted to support and his accountants had to approve the actual amount before it was paid. He explained this rather disjointedly and gave her to understand that it was his secretary who really decided everything for him.

'And your accountants, or whatever you call them, decide how much it is to be?'

'That's right.'

'Then do you actually spend less than you receive?'

'I don't know.'

'But you must know.'

'No, I don't. You see my accountants report to my trustees.'

'Then don't your trustees tell you?'

'They made a bit of a stink years ago when they said I'd spent too much. It was then they fixed up this system. They haven't said anything since so I suppose it's all right. Will you have a cocktail or something?'

She refused. She began to feel rather uncomfortable in this closed room. He asked if she would mind his sending for some whisky and telephoned down for it.

'Ask them if there is any chance of there being some trains running soon.' He reported that they said not for another hour or two, although this fog seemed to be lifting along the coast. She wondered what she had better do, whether her best plan was not to ring up her uncle to say they were all stuck in this hotel, whether it would not be safer supposing he found out they had spent hours penned up alone in here. But then, she argued, it was not as if they were not in a party and no one knew she was up here with Max. And if her uncle told her to come back home then she might not catch their train if it did in the end go off rather unexpectedly. How frightfully rich Max must be. No, it would be better if she stayed where she was, she was not going to miss this trip for anything. She had been

438

looking forward to it for weeks. And besides she wondered, she wondered what he was going to do now that he had her all alone. It made the whole trip so much more exciting to begin with a whole three weeks before them to get everything right in.

'Cheer up,' Alex said to Miss Crevy, going up to where she sat alone in that room downstairs, 'don't look so glum, Angela.'

'Do I?' she said, and she put up her hands to rearrange her hair. 'Yes, I suppose I do feel low.' In actual fact she felt so low she could not be angry with him any more, though she did still resent him.

'Are you sure,' he said, 'that you won't have anything to drink?' When she refused he went on that this kind of breakdown in the arrangements was typical of all travelling with Max. 'Have you ever been on a trip with him before?' She said she had, which he was pretty certain was a lie. He went on:

'I remember last year, when we were going to the same place we are going now, there was the most frightful business in Paris because all our sleepers weren't together. He had reserved the whole of one coach and when we all got to the train he found they had put us all over it. He made a great row and for some time he threatened not to take the train. Of course, they said he could do exactly as he liked but that he would have to pay for those sleepers in any case and there weren't any others for four days the trains were so full. Well, you know it didn't matter in the least to us where we were, they were single sleepers anyway, but he wouldn't have it and we all stood there thinking perhaps we would never go after all.'

'It was rather sweet of him.'

'Yes,' said Alex, 'it was.' Alex was anxious to be on good terms with everyone and did not want to remember that Miss Crevy had got on his nerves. 'Yes, in many ways he is too good a host, that was why he was so anxious no one should know about Claire's aunt,' he said, embroidering, 'so that no one should be bothered about anyone else being ill. D'you know,' he said, 'I've been thinking it over and I think you were quite right about Embassy Richard, that he didn't send that notice out himself.'

'All I said was,' Angela said rather wearily, 'he had told my mother that he was not going to the party.'

'That's just it, so I don't think that he could have sent the notice out himself in view of what you have just told me. I quite forget what I said at the time but it's obvious you were right about that and that I was wrong,' he said, ignoring altogether that he had originally agreed with her on this point although he had then rather lost track of his argument. But he was anxious to be friends.

'Oh, don't let's talk about that, Alex. But then what happened about the sleepers, did you go in the end?'

'Good heavens, yes, of course we went. They compromised by putting some of us together. Oh, yes, one always goes but it's a certainty something perfectly appalling crops up like this fog or the business about sleepers or any one of the hundreds of things that turn up when he travels. I'm not saying that one isn't exceedingly comfortable, but it's definitely wearing.'

He thought to himself that she was not posing to be such an expert on travelling with Max after all. Perhaps she had been once to Scotland with him.

'Have you ever been to Barshottie?'

'No,' she said, 'why do you ask?'

Miss Fellowes was better. She was having a perfectly serene dream that she was riding home, on an evening after hunting, on an antelope between rows of giant cabbages. Earth and sky were inverted, her ceiling was an indeterminate ridge and furrow barely lit by crescent moons in the azure sky she rode on.

In the sitting-room next to where she lay dreaming watched by those two nannies, Claire and Evelyn discussed Angela's looks, which they admired, and her clothes, of which they did not think so much.

'But, darling,' said Claire, 'why do you think Max asked her?'

'Why, for that matter, did he ask us?'

'Oh, but Evelyna, we've all known him for ages.'

'Yes, but surely to goodness he can get to know someone else. I think we're all unfair to him.'

'How do you mean?'

'Well, my dear, of course we're all hoping he'll get engaged to Julia and I don't know if it's because of that but I do think we seem to be getting almost proprietary about him. After all, Claire, he's independent enough now with all these creatures he goes about with at night. He's been most good to me taking me about when I couldn't possibly have afforded to go alone and I can't question who he asks besides.'

'I can't either,' Claire said, 'but I can't help wondering. And anyway,' she said, rising in her own defence, 'I don't think because Robert and I and you are asked that's any reason why we shouldn't discuss him.'

'I know just what you mean but we seem to be doing it all the time nowadays. Not with Julia though, she never talks about him now. Has she said anything to you about him lately?'

'No, Julia is most frightfully close about herself,' Claire said. 'She's never so much as breathed a word to me ever, has she to you?'

'No, not a word.'

'Then you mean what I mean, that she doesn't discuss him now because she minds?'

'Well, of course she does. We knew she did months ago.'

'I know, but it is too divine, isn't it?' Claire said and then described how Julia had suddenly said to her about how hopeless Max was, when they were sitting outside together on their luggage.

'Still,' said Evelyn, 'that's just what people do do.'

'What?'

'Talk about their affairs when they are really upset about them.'

'Well, Evelyn my dear, she did sort of let it out to me when we were sitting there as I've just told you.'

'I didn't mean that. What I meant was really having it out. And that she has never done with any of us.'

'Julia's not the same as everyone, that's why she is so sweet.'

'Well, Claire, I think we are all the same about things like that, and she's never really had it out with any of us.'

If Julia had wondered where Max was taking her as they went upstairs together Max, for his part, had wondered where she was taking him. With this difference however, that, if she had done no more than ask herself what room he was taking her to, he had asked himself whether he was going to fall for her. Again, while she had wondered so faintly she hardly knew she had it in her mind or, in other words, had hardly expressed to herself what she was thinking, he was much further from putting his feelings into words, as it was not until he felt sure of anything that he knew what he was thinking of. When he thought, he was only conscious of uneasy feelings and he only knew that he had been what he did not even call thinking when his feelings hurt him. When he was sure then he felt it must at once be put to music, which was his way of saying words.

This is not to say that Max was one of those men with ungovernable actions in that sense in which one speaks of men with ungovernable tempers, always breaking out into rages. He was not so often sure he was in love with anyone that he was always assaulting girls. But when he was sure then he felt he had to do something.

Julia, of course, he had been continually meeting for eighteen months. He had brought her along when they had been abroad before, though he had not seen much of her then, but since that time he had met her again and again at houses where he happened to be staying and when they had been a great deal more together than with the other guests.

'Tell me about your toys,' he said.

'My toys, what do you mean? Oh, you're trying to say my charms. No, I certainly won't if you call them my toys.'

'Your charms,' he said.

'Well, if you swear you won't laugh I might.' She was most anxious to tell him because she naturally wanted to talk about herself.

'I won't laugh,' he said.

'I don't know how I first got them,' she said, for she was not going to tell anyone ever that it was her mother, of course, who had given them to her and who had died when she was two years old. Here she broke off to ask him if he had overheard Robert Hignam telling her about that patch of bamboos they had played round as children. 'He is so silly, as if I should ever forget,' she said. 'We were brought up together.' She went on to say what Robert had never known was that one of her charms, the wooden pistol, had been buried plumb in the middle of the bamboo patch. In consequence, and no one had ever known of it, these bamboos, or probably they had been overgrown artichokes, had taken on a great importance in her mind because of this secret buried in them. And she asked Max if he did not think it often was the case that certain things people remembered about when they were children were important to them only because they were far more important to someone else.

She explained that each time they went through those artichokes pretending they were explorers in jungles, she was excited because she knew she had buried her pistol there and because the others did not know. She felt her excitement had made their game more secret

442

and that it was the secrecy which was what Robert remembered of it. 'So that it was my having hidden the pistol there which made the whole thing for him. He'll never know,' she said.

So her wooden pistol was stained and had rather crumbled away, after she had dug it up, but she had it still, nothing would ever part her from it. The egg she described as being hollow, painted outside with rings of red and yellow, half the size of duck's eggs, and it had inside three little ivory elephants. 'You'll never believe about my egg,' she said, 'and I've never told another soul,' which was a lie. But she did tell him, and it was like this. When she had been no more than four years old she had been out with her nanny for their afternoon's walk. She was carrying a huge golfing umbrella she could not be happy without at that particular time, quartered in red and yellow silk. Her nanny had opened it for her and she was so very small she had had to carry it with both hands to the handle as it spread above her head. Now she also had with her the wooden egg with elephants inside in one of her pockets and as she happened to be walking on a bank a sudden gust of wind had taken hold of her umbrella and, as she had not let go, had carried her for what, at this length of time, she now considered to be great distances, as far as from cliffs into the sea, but what, as it actually happened, had been no more than three or four feet and into a puddle. 'And I said "Nanny, if I hadn't my egg in my pocket I should have been drowned."' Julia could now see herself swaying down 10,000 feet tied to a red and yellow parachute. 'So you see,' she said, 'I can't ever leave it behind now, can I?'

'Yes, I must have looked a sight with my skinny legs,' and as these were now one of her best features she stretched them out under his nose, 'sailing away under my umbrella with the nanny waving so I shouldn't get frightened and let go. I was such a shrimp in those days.'

'I bet you never were,' he said.

'I was.'

'And what about your top?'

'What about my top? Who told you about my top?'

'Nobody.'

'Who told you? I've never said a word about it to anyone.'

'You must have done or I should not have known,' he said uneasily.

Who could have told him? Claire surely wouldn't have. People you trusted talked about you behind your back and ruined everything. He must have been laughing at her all the time she was on about her charms.

'Oh, Max,' she said, 'you are so tiresome.' And then, to cover up her tracks, 'First you wouldn't tell me who Embassy Richard's girl was and now you won't say who told you about me. Who is it?'

He made as if to sit on the arm of her chair.

'No,' she said, 'and if you won't come out with it then you can't expect me to go on filling you up with things to laugh at me about.'

'But I was not laughing.'

'Very well then, what toys did you have when you were a little boy?'

He thought this was an unlucky business. Rather shamefacedly he said:

'I had a Teddy Bear.'

'All little boys have Teddy Bears.'

'Well I say, Julia, I can't help that, can I?'

'What else did you have? What did you have you are ashamed of now?'

'But Julia really, what is there to be ashamed of in a wooden egg?'

'Who said I was ashamed? Don't be so ridiculous. Go on now, what did you have?'

He lied and said: 'I had a doll as well.'

'I don't believe it. What sort of a doll?'

'Well, it was dressed up, a girl, in an Eton blue frock.'

'Did you?' she said beginning to smile at last. 'And did you take her to bed with you?'

'Of course. I wouldn't sleep without it.'

'How sweet,' she said ironically, 'how perfectly sweet. And are you ashamed of her now?'

'No, why should I be?'

'No,' she said, calming down, 'there's no reason why one should be, is there?' After all, when one was little one was just like other little boys and girls. But she could not get over someone having told him. Had they been laughing at her over it? Or had he been asking people about her?

'How did you get to know?' she said.

'Someone told me.'

'Yes, I know, but how? I mean people don't just tell things like that.'

He took the plunge into another lie.

'Well, if you must know,' he said, 'I asked them.'

'Oh, you did, did you? So then you know.'

'Know what?'

'The story of my top.'

'No, I don't. All I was told was that you had one – "like Julia who keeps a top" – they said.'

She left over thinking out whether he had really asked after her until she was alone.

'Oh, is that all you know? Then would you like to hear? You swear you aren't laughing.'

'I swear.'

'How much would you like to know?'

Again he came over as if to sit on the arm of her chair.

'If you do that,' she said getting up, 'I shan't be able to tell you about my top.'

He thought bother her top.

'And it's most frightfully important.'

'Do tell me.'

'Do you really want to know? Then I'll tell you. There's no story at all about my top. I've just always had it, that's all.'

He advanced on her as if to kiss her.

'No, no,' she said, 'it's too early in the day yet for that sort of thing,' and as he still came forward she began to step back.

'No, Max, I'm not going to start a chase round this squalid room.' And as he came up to her she brought her hands smack together as though she were bringing him out of a trance. 'Go back and sit in your chair,' she said, 'mix yourself another drink if you like, but you aren't going to muss me up now.' He did as he was told and she was pleased she could make him do as she told him. Then she wondered if he wasn't angry, which he was. So she came over to where he was sitting, and, his hands taken up with pouring out his drink, she kissed his cheek and then sat down opposite.

There was a silence and then he exclaimed:

'By God, I wonder if they have sent up those flowers.' He went to telephone and got on to Alex at last and asked him. Alex said yes the flowers had arrived.

'Are they all right? I mean are they decent ones?' Alex said they were and Julia wondered, when he put down the receiver and went over to the window, that he had not asked Alex to have them sent up to her.

In the meantime Hignam had persuaded Robin Adams that he would do better to come upstairs and see what had become of the others. Against his better judgment Mr Adams had agreed. As he had not been able to leave this hotel owing to those steel doors having been shut down, he considered he might as well be with Angela if he could not get away from their bloody party. He might be able to be of service to her yet.

Now both Julia and Angela had kissed their young men when these had been cross, when Mr Adams had made off down in the station and when Max had stopped chasing Julia to sit in his chair.

People, in their relations with one another, are continually doing similar things but never for similar reasons.

All this party had known each other for some time, except Max and Angela. Max had taken them up and they had got to know Angela through him. When Max had asked her she had insisted on going although her parents had objected that she did not know them well. Now that she was with them she was not enjoying it because she found she was without what she would call one supporter among them.

For when Angela had kissed Mr Adams she had not wanted him to stay, it had been no more than a peck, but now she had seen more of their party she wished she had kissed him harder, and she was beginning to blame him. He had been extremely tiresome and he had deserved it when she had sent him off. But she felt now that she had never deserved it when he had gone.

As for Julia she had kissed Max to keep him sweet so to speak, and so, in one way, had Miss Crevy kissed her young man. But what lay behind Julia's peck was this three weeks they both had in front of them, it would never do to start too fast and furious. Angela had no such motive because Mr Adams was not coming with them.

Angela then was more than missing her young man. Accordingly when he was led by Robert Hignam into this room where she was sitting she was glad to see him. And Alex was very glad to see him. He had been made more and more nervous by Miss Crevy because he could see she was getting in a state. He called out what would he have to drink and Angela said to him:

'Where have you been all this time?'

Now that he did see her again Mr Adams was so thankful he could find nothing to say. He thought she looked so much more lovely than ever, almost as though he had expected to find she had been assaulted by those others with her clothes torn and her hair hanging down as he put it, although she wore it short. It was then her mood so swiftly changed that it began to seem too tiresome the way he stood there saying nothing when he should have come back long ago. Unfortunately for him he was so taken up with his feeling of how madly beautiful she was that he feared he would give himself away if he went anywhere near her. She felt she could never forgive him if he stayed away, but he went over to Alex and Robert Hignam and mixed himself a drink, turning his back.

If Julia's fears had left her earlier when Max arrived in the lounge downstairs and, at the first sign of him, she had forgotten how angry she had been at his not turning up before, Angela was now the reverse of comforted when she saw Mr Adams, even if she had been longing for him to come back. Anyway she thought it monstrous that he should stand as he did with his back to her. She said:

'Isn't someone going to ask me what I'd like to drink?' and she put emphasis on the someone. This brought them all over to her side apologizing and carrying the tray with everything on it. When Mr Adams apologized he tried pathetically enough to make his voice sound as though he were saying in so many words how sorry he was that he had ever gone and even, by the tone of it, how unlucky she was to have one such as he so full of her. But his putting himself in the wrong only made her feel more sure that she was right and he might as well have said it to his glass for she proceeded to ignore him.

Her answer was to begin making up to Alex. She called him darling, which was of no significance except that she had never done so before, and he did not at once tumble to it that her smiles and friendliness for him, which like any other girl she could turn on at will so that it poured pleasantly out in the way water will do out of taps, had no significance either. Still it was very different from how she had been when they were alone together and as he could not

447

bear people being as cross and hurt with him as she had seemed to be he was both surprised and pleased.

'And, darling,' she said to Alex, 'do you know what is on the other side of that door there?'

He went to see. 'Beds!' he cried.

'Yes, twin beds. But I brought my own sheets.'

He was still pleased even if this last remark embarrassed him as much as it had done when, at first sight of him down in the station she had called out had he brought his bed. Then he wondered if this change of manner did not come from her wanting to annoy this Robin Adams or to make him jealous. He said she thought of everything and went on,

'But it's really rather early for that sort of thing, isn't it? There's no close season, I know that, but we've got the whole night before us, if you know what I mean.'

'Alex, darling, how can you speak like that? It's the most pansy thing I ever heard you say. And in any case,' she went on, 'it wouldn't be very nice in a sleeper, would it?' Alex passed this off by saying he had given up all idea of their getting a train that evening. As for Mr Adams he had been so tormented when he saw her again by such a crawling frenzy of love for her that he had not been fit to hear what was going on. This now, however, began to percolate through to him as when clouds curtain an August day that has been enormously still and soft with elms swooning in the haze; and as hot days can become ominous and dark so soon he began to dread what she might make him hear.

Alex said well come along then, knowing that she would never commit herself in front of those others. He suspected that she was only trying to distress this poor creature Adams and was curious to see how she would get out of going into that bedroom with him. He was sure she would never do it and yet she would only make herself look ridiculous now if she did not go. She said he didn't seem very keen, it was hardly flattering to her she said and he thought of answering this by asking her why didn't she try one of the others then, but he refrained, he was afraid this would be too awkward for her. All he did say was that she would soon see who was being flattered once the door was locked on them.

This surprised her into saying, 'Oh, I don't think I'd allow you to do that.' Her pretence was wearing rather thin he thought and decided to drive her further into a corner. He asked why on earth not and was enormously touched when she explained that she would never let him lock the door because of course she would not mind being caught with him. He suspected she was only playing him up and he knew it was fatuous but he could not help being flattered. He tried to appear cross in order to hide this and so as to lead her on.

'You mean it would not matter if you were caught with me, either to you or anyone else,' he said. Robert Hignam interrupted:

'Don't let that worry you. I'll stand on guard and if I whistle three times, what, you'll know someone is coming.'

Mr Adams walked to the window and wondered, as he tried not to hear, if he was going to be sick.

'But I don't mind,' she said, 'you old silly,' using one of Claire's expressions to her husband, 'don't you understand I don't mind if anyone did find us? Has no one ever made a proposal to you?'

This word proposal seemed to him to have a fatal ring and rather in desperation he said well, all right, come on then. 'Well, all right, come on then,' she echoed, 'that's a fine way to put it. Well, hold the door open for me.'

'Where on earth is Max?' said Mr Adams, turning round from his window. Alex and Robert Hignam were disgusted to see his face had gone white.

'Now, look here, Angela,' Alex said, determined now to escape, 'what about that hotel detective?'

Robert Hignam led Mr Adams away to have a drink in the other corner.

'I must say you don't seem very gallant,' she said and thought poor Robin had looked awful, but he must learn his lesson and it was too late to turn back now, she would look silly if she did.

'Alex,' she said, 'Alex,' and jerked her head towards that other room she stood outside by the open door. He saw now those others were not watching, that she only wanted to say something in private and he felt proportionately foolish for ever having imagined she meant a rough and tumble. He hurried in and she shut them in and said:

'Now you must go straight out into the corridor by that other door over there and don't come back.'

'You aren't going to do something awful, are you?' he said,

because after all he did not know her well enough to say he would stand for no further baiting of Mr Adams.

'Now, Alex, run along now at once,' and he did go, feeling outraged at having been so used. The moment he had shut the door she clapped her hands twice. Mr Adams, of course, was in her room at once, slamming the door behind him so Robert Hignam could not follow. He found her sitting in front of the glass, powdering her face, and apparently calm as calm.

'What?' he said, 'what?'

'What do you mean?' she said.

'Was that you slapping someone's face?' he said and he was panting hard.

'Who slapped whose face? I didn't hear anyone,' she said.

'I heard it twice,' he said and his knees were trembling.

She burst into tears, her face screwed up and got red and she held her handkerchief to her nose and sniffled as if that was where her tears were coming from.

'Oh, my God,' he said and then his knees went so that he thought he would sink to the floor, where he had been standing.

Speaking through her handkerchief, her voice going up and down and interrupted by sobs, grunts and once she choked, she was saying :

'You've been so beastly to me. Going away when you did. As if I was nothing to you. And all these beastly people being beastly to me. How do you expect me to love you? How could you go like that? Oh, I do feel so miserable.' At this point she got hiccups. 'How could you? I feel I could die. I feel so miserable.'

He began moving towards her, saying darling, darling. By this time they neither of them knew what they were doing.

When Alex came back through the corridor into this sitting room where they had all been, Robert Hignam became facetious which was his way of hiding curiosity.

'I say, old boy, that was a bit sudden, wasn't it, what did you do to the girl?'

Alex hated him for it. He said if he could only strangle her now he would, 'and you too,' he thought of saying.

'But come on, what did you do to the poor girl to make her fetch you one like that?'

450

'Nothing, you poor fool, nothing at all. Oh, all right, laugh, yes, but can't you see all she was doing was playing me up to make her boy friend.'

Robert felt somehow he had been put in the wrong, but he was not going to stop for that, he wanted to get down to it. 'Right,' he said, 'right, I'd spotted that. As a matter of fact, if I'd been you I doubt if I'd have gone in the first place.'

'Afraid of Claire coming in I suppose.'

'Here, lay off. But all's well that ends well I expect, isn't it?' he said, nodding to the bedroom door and getting to it.

'You silly idiot, Bob, she's probably putting him through a hoop in some fabulous way.'

'I don't know, he's probably got all he wanted by now, but I wouldn't stand for her slapping me for it.' He waited till he saw there was no more to come and then he said he wondered what the others were doing.

Claire was sitting telephoning in the room outside Miss Fellowes' bedroom with Evelyn Henderson telephoning too; for some reason this room had two telephones. The door between had been cruelly left open so that her aunt, if her condition was so she could hear, could do so. Both Claire and Evelyn then were speaking at one and the same time and Claire was saying:

'Yes, Mrs Knight, she is sleeping now.' Mrs Knight was maid to Miss Fellowes. 'I don't think you need worry too much about her. No, you would never be able to get here, I shouldn't come along if I were you. No, Mrs Knight, you mustn't. For one thing the traffic simply isn't running, you would never get here, and then if you did you would never be able to get in, we are simply in a state of siege you know, yes, no one's allowed in or out. Yes, nanny and her friend are with us, they have been angels. Of course, I had a terrible time getting her up here, she had to be carried.'

Miss Henderson was telephoning to a female friend.

'My dear,' she said, 'you would hardly believe it but you remember I told you I was going to the South of France, I'd been looking forward to it so much for such a long time. The fact is that with this fog no trains are running and I've a very good idea, though I've said nothing to the others about it, that we shan't get away at all. Well, the difficult part of it is that I've closed my little flat up you see and sent the woman who looks after me away on her own holiday. Mrs Jukes, yes. What's that? My dear, do you really mean it, that would be kind of you. May I really? It would only be for one night at the most. You will put me up, you're sure it won't be too much of a bother? My dear, that is too kind of you. Several extraordinary things have happened I can't tell you about now. What's that?'

Claire was saying:

'Now, Mrs Knight, you're not to worry like this. Of course I don't know what would have become of her if I hadn't been here. No, we don't know what the matter with her is yet. The doctor said a rest would put everything right and after all we must take what the doctors say, mustn't we? Of course, I have given her a hot water bottle. Well, it's her breathing, so short you know. Has she ever had anything of this kind before?'

Evelyna was still talking:

'I can't tell you the name now,' she said, almost whispering into the receiver, 'but the doctor says she is drunk. No, don't laugh because I think she is very ill indeed. It's not extremely nice. My dear, she had a pigeon, all wet, done up in brown paper. Well, yes wet. I think it's some sort of a sexual fit, don't you agree? With women of her age, yes, she is just that age, it so often is, don't you think? What I am so concerned about is whether it won't come out in another and more violent form, do you see what I mean?'

'No, Mrs Knight,' Claire was saying, 'of course it's all very unpleasant for me you know, there have been certain things that really have been – well I won't go on, no, I won't tell you now they would only bother you, but I've made arrangements to get an ambulance directly they can bring one round to send her back to you. Oh, not at all. Poor Auntie May. Good-bye.'

Her Auntie May was going over her row with that girl in the bar. Very white she lay still as death on her back and her lips moved, only she had no voice to speak with. Well, she was saying, if there's no one to serve me I might just as well not be here at all. And a voice spoke soundless in answer through her lips. It said everyone must wait their turn. She replied she had waited her turn and that people who had come after had been served first.

It might have been an argument with death. And so it went on, reproaches, insults, threats to report and curiously enough it was mixed up in her mind with thoughts of dying and she asked herself whom she could report death to. And another voice asked her why had she brought a pigeon, was it right to order whisky, did she think, when she was carrying such a parcel? And she did feel frightfully ill and weighed down, so under water, so gasping. It was coming on her again. And she argued why shouldn't she order whisky if they always had it when they were children, and as for the pigeon it was saving the street-cleaner trouble, when they died they were never left out to rot in the streets nowadays. But the voice asked why she had washed it and she felt like when she was very small and had a dirty dress. She said out loud so that she frightened those nannies. 'Oh, why can't you leave me alone?' She struggled to turn over on her side but when they both laid their hands to soothe her then she felt them to be angels' hands and had some rest.

But there was nothing of that kind for Mr Adams. As Alex had guessed, he was being put through the hoop. It was a malign comedy Miss Crevy was creating as she acted.

'But how could I tell,' he was saying and he was by her side now while she watched his back in a mirror behind him, 'how could I tell how much you minded?'

'If you had cared for me you would,' she said.

'You know I do.'

'But how do you show it, by going off just when I need you most?'

'Yes, but darling, you told me to go.'

'My dear,' she said, 'that was only because you had been so beastly to me.'

'I thought you wanted to go with these people and that you didn't want me.'

For one moment she thought she felt so she might burst into tears again and admit she did not want to go, but then it struck her that he would insist on her coming away if she said it. What she wanted to do was to make him properly sorry that she was going, so she said:

'How do you expect me to love you if you don't respect my feelings?'

He felt as though he was gazing into a prism, and he could see no end to it.

'But, my darling, I do, you must believe me, I do.'

'And how do you show it?' she asked. 'As soon as I'm a little bit upset you go off as if I was being difficult or something.'

'But you told me to go.'

'You'd been so rude about Claire Hignam's aunt.'

'I'm afraid I was very rude about her and I hope you will believe me when I say how very sorry I am if anything I said was rude about her.'

'I never wanted you to go, you see,' she said.

'Oh, God,' he said, reaching depths he had never known about before, 'I wish I was more worthy of you. When I think how wonderful you are from the top of your wonderful golden head to your toes.'

'Is it gold?' she said, putting her hands up to it.

'It is,' he said and coming to sit by her on the stool in front of that looking glass he lightly kissed the hair above her ear. As he did this he looked into the glass to see himself doing it because he was in that state when he thought it incredible that he should be so lucky to be kissing someone so marvellous. Unluckily for him she saw this in the mirror she had been watching his back in. She did not like it. She got up. She said:

'I won't have you watching yourself in the mirror when you're kissing me. It proves you don't love me and anyway no nice person does that.'

'Darling,' he said, 'are you being reasonable?'

'It's not a question of being reasonable. The fact is you despise me. You think I'm too easy, you treat me like a tart.'

He lost his temper. 'I won't have you say things like that,' he said, 'you torture me, I'm in such a condition now I don't know what I'm doing. And I've been like that for the past year.' Then it seemed monstrous to him that he should speak to her in anger. 'I don't mean it,' he said. 'I don't know what I'm saying.'

'Will you promise never to leave me again like that?'

'I promise.'

'Well then,' she said smiling directly at him, 'I expect I have been unreasonable as you call it.'

'You haven't,' he said stoutly.

'Yes, I expect I have. But you see it's different with women. I expect I have been being tiresome, but in some ways it was too much.'

He said: 'Do you know what I think is the matter with us, at all events I know it is with me?'

She thought now he is going to talk about getting engaged again.

'No,' she said, 'what is it?'

'You won't be angry with me.'

She knew then it must be what he was going to say.

'No,' she said, moving further away from him for safety's sake.

'I don't know how to say it. I bet you know what's coming too.'

She thought why couldn't he get on with it and then, looking at him, saw that fatuous smile on his face he always wore on these occasions.

'No,' she said.

'Well, really it's that I think we are in an unnatural relationship to each other. You know that I'm in love for ever with you. I know that you don't see this as I do but don't you think that if we could do away with this sort of being at a distance from each other, if we could only tell the world that we were in love by publishing our engagement, don't you feel that it would make things easier for us? I'm not saying this from my point of view. I can't help believing, even if I make you angry with me again, that you do care something for me or else,' and he hesitated here, 'well here goes, you would not have been as put out as you were when I went off.' He went on rather quickly, 'I must ask you to believe that I'd never have gone off when I did if I hadn't sincerely thought you wanted me to.' In his embarrassment he became even more formal again, 'I must ask you to believe that I wouldn't for anything in the world give you a second's unhappiness,' and he was going to add because I love you so, but he realized in time he was in such a state he might burst into tears if he said it, so, having lost his thread he wound up by saying, 'you must believe that.'

There was complete silence. He picked up his argument again.

'I do feel this, I know that if only we were married I could make you feel differently about me.'

'My dear,' she said, 'you've told me that before and I know who said it to you, it was your grandmother, wasn't it? In her generation everybody's marriages were arranged for them and as they were never allowed to be alone with a man for more than three minutes, of course the poor darlings fell for the first man they were left alone with.'

He said nothing at all.

'My dear, it is perfectly sweet of you and I think you are sweet

455

too, but you must give me time. You know what you and I both think about marriage, that it's the most serious thing one can do. Well, it's just simply that I can't be sure.'

He still said nothing. He was looking at the carpet. From her having to go on talking she became palpably insincere. She was also looking at the carpet. She said:

'You see, I might make you unhappy and you are much too sweet for anyone to risk doing that to. I believe if I saw anyone making you unhappy I would go and scratch their eyes out, yes I would. And so don't you see I can't, I mustn't be in a hurry; you do see, don't you?'

He got up and walked up and down once or twice and then he stopped and asked her did she know how Miss Fellowes was now. He still would not look at any more of her than her toes. She supposed she had been beastly to him again but why, she asked herself, must he choose this hotel room of all places to propose in, with beds slept in by hundreds of fat, middle-aged husbands and wives. And this particular time.

'They are being frightfully mysterious about her,' she said.

Almost paralysed by his misery he said:

'Are you sure you wouldn't like some tea?'

'Well, we can't very well, can we?' she said, 'Max isn't here. I got some for those two old nannies when I found them crying their eyes out outside about Miss Fellowes, but that was different. Do you know I'm inclined to agree with you that she is being a thorough old nuisance. And then Alex, as I thought, very rudely sent for the drinks there were in that other room, but that's his affair. I don't see very well how we can order tea, do you, without Max?'

'But I'll pay for it on a separate bill.'

'You don't know what he's like, he'd never let you and all these others trade on that, I think it's too disgusting.'

There was another silence.

'Darling,' she said, 'don't take all this too tragically. After all I'm only going away for three weeks, and I'm hoping by that time I'll have been able to make up my mind. You do understand?' And as he stood still with his back turned to her she came up and, rather awkwardly, took him by one finger of his sweating hand.

Amabel's flat had been decorated by the same people Max had his flat done by, her furniture was like his, his walls like hers, their chair coverings were alike and even their ash trays were the same. There were in London at this time more than one hundred rooms identical with these. Even what few books there were bore the same titles and these were dummies. But if one said here are two rooms alike in every way so their two owners must have similar tastes like twins, one stood no greater chance of being right than if one were to argue their two minds, their hearts even must beat as one when their books, even if they were only bindings, bore identical titles.

In this way Max and Amabel and their friends baffled that class of person who will judge people by what they read or by the colour of their walls. One had to see that other gross of rooms and know who lived in them to realize how fashionable this style of decoration was, how right for those who were so fashionable, and rich of course, themselves.

If people then who see much of each other come to do their rooms up the same, all one can say is they are like household servants in a prince's service, all in his livery. But in the same way that some footmen will prefer to wear livery because there can then be no question of their having to provide clothes so, by going to the same decorator, these people avoided any sort of trouble over what might bother them, such as doing up their rooms themselves, and by so doing they proclaimed their service to the kind of way they lived or rather to the kind of way they passed their time.

They avoided all discussions on taste and were not encumbered by possessions; what they had was theirs in law but was never personal to them. If their houses were burned down they had only to go to the same man they all thought best to get another built, if they lost anything or even if it was mislaid the few shops they went to would be glad to lend whatever it might be, up to elephants or rhinos, until what had been missed could be replaced.

This role applied to everything they had except themselves, being so rich they could not be bought, so they laid more store than most on mutual relationships. Rich people cling together because the less well off embarrass them and there are not so many available who are rich for one rich man who drops out to be easily replaced.

Again, as between Amabel and Max, as indeed between all of them, there was more, there was her power over him as we shall see which she valued not least because both were so rich, there was also and most important that she found him altogether attractive. Also she did not see why she need let these girls who were after his money have it all their own way while he was paying for them.

She had not taken long to find out where Max was in hiding. When she rang up the airport she had not used her own name to ask if he was there, so they made no difficulty about telling her they had not seen him. She knew with all this fog he would be waiting his first chance to be off and, as she knew him, that he would be entertaining his party, so she began ringing every Terminus Hotel. If he had already been out of England she might not have followed, but now she realized he must be delayed, she really did not see why he should go without her. And this feeling grew until she made out she could not do without him, until, as she thought it over, knowing he was still there, she realized she was lost alone or so it seemed. In this way, where other women might have given him up and consoled themselves, blaming him for his lies, and might have sat down to make up their minds they would let him go because they could not trust him, she found out where he was at once without any trouble and went there.

She told her maid to pack and follow on while she set out on foot. She would save twenty minutes by walking.

She saw nothing of what she passed by, not the crowds of people who had lost their way or those who, faced by such beauty suddenly looming up on them through darkness, had fingered their ties, stepped exaggeratedly to one side, or turned and followed mumbling to themselves.

While she was on her way Angela, still holding on to his finger, had told Adams they must go back or what would those others think of them and still holding on because she felt almost sorry, as she was telling herself it was not his fault, it was the effect she had on him, she led him back. She dropped his finger once they were fairly back in this room. Adams thought to himself these two must know how it is with me, blast them, and that he did not care. He saw, and he thought that proved it, how Alex did not look at either of them, whereas Angela, who had also noticed this, thought it must be that Alex disapproved of what she might have done. She did not care.

Adams went off to mix himself a drink. That's it, she thought to herself, they say they're heartbroken and then they go and drink it off. In any case why take drinks from Max when he says he can't stand him and when he says he won't have anything to do with him. She decided it was selfishness and said to Alex:

'Well and what's happened?'

'Nothing. We've been here, that's all.'

Hignam just looked from Adams to Miss Crevy and from Miss Angela Crevy back to Adams.

'Oh, dear,' she said and sat down. She looked at her Adams and kept her eyes on him. She began to feel hopeless and asked herself if she had not treated him badly. Usually when she was watching him he knew at once and would look up in hopes her eyes might give him that encouragement they had now and which he had never yet seen, but this time he was too low, doubled up with cramp, he was drowning in his depth. He watched his glass, afraid to show his eyes, and she watched, offering what he wanted. In a moment she looked away, blaming him for not knowing how she felt.

She wondered if they could have heard what had been said and then thought it would have been impossible so long as Alex had not listened through the keyhole, but then she said to herself he would never have done that with Robert Hignam there. Or did men do such things? It was into this strangling silence that Amabel arrived.

She was lovely and when she opened the door and came in they looked up and knew again how beautiful she was.

'Hullo,' she said, 'at last I've found you.'

Robert Hignam was very much surprised to see her. He knew from his wife that Max, if he came at all, would come alone. Alex was surprised for he expected Max would leave her behind. Mr Adams, when he was introduced by Angela, who barely knew her, had no idea of any complication, to him she was no more than another member of this lot he despised and hated. He did not even admire her. So that when she asked, as she did at once, what Max had done with himself, it was he who answered that he was upstairs with Julia. No one could imagine how he knew.

'I supposed so,' she said, giving an appearance of just being late and that she had not bothered to hurry. Alex and Robert Hignam then rushed in, chattering to entertain her and she took this easily, charmingly, though she was rather silent. She made one think she was so used to it all, that it was sweet of them and she liked it, but that she knew a thing worth two of that. They grew almost boisterous offering her chairs and cups of tea and anything they could think of. When they had begun to die down she drew Miss Angela Crevy on one side.

She began to make secrets which was her way when she did not know how things would turn out. Whispering so those others could not hear, she said how nice it was to see Angela. This was very flattering and she went on that Angela must be a dear and do something for her and come to her rescue. She could not be left alone with Max, even for one moment, he had such a temper and would be so cross at her for being late.

Angela warmed to her and said she ought not to fuss, which Amabel had not thought of doing, and that Max had been most frightfully late himself. They had only really found him when they had left the station to come into this hotel she said, and Amabel explained this by claiming that Max had been telephoning her to make haste. If it hadn't been for the fog, she said, tenderly smiling, she might have missed their train. And Angela believed her when she said all she had been was late and at once assumed she had always been coming. Indeed she had come to think this was another thing the others had been keeping from her.

Amabel by now had had enough of Miss Crevy. 'Alex dear,' she called out, 'come and talk to me. It's so lovely to see you and I did get into such a state when I thought I was going to miss you. I was so very late.' He said again he was so glad to see her, and he was glad, but he could not think what it meant her being here and was placidly apprehensive.

'My dear,' Amabel went on at him, 'I wonder if you would ring down and order me a bath.'

'How splendid,' he said, 'of course.'

'I got so dirty coming along. My maid will be up in a minute. Of course it will have to have a room with it and then you can come and talk to me through the door.'

It was at this point Mr Adams left them again, unnoticed now by all, unsung.

'Though,' she said, talking a lot for her, 'it would be funny if my bathroom was on the corridor and you had to talk from it in front of everyone.'

'I couldn't,' he said, 'it is prowling with detectives. Is that the office? Mr Adey wants another room with a bath, one of his guests here wants to have one.'

When Angela heard him order yet another thing in Max's name she looked guiltily round to see whether Adams had heard. She was relieved to find he was gone for she would have felt worse if it had been said in front of him. On her own as she was now it was different, she did not mind so much, for she did not know any of them at all well; when she had seen Max it had been at night in night clubs when he had usually been with Amabel. And she was so young that having Amabel with them was more exciting for her than Max alone could ever be. Amabel had her own position in London, shop girls in Northern England knew her name and what she looked like from photographs in illustrated weekly papers, in Hyderabad the colony knew the colour of her walls. So that to be with her was for Angela as much as it might be for a director of the Zoo to be taking his okapi for walks in leading strings for other zoologists to see or, as she herself would have put it, it was being grand with grand people. And if she had been nervous once she was not so any more for she felt Amabel would put them right now that she was here, she would see that Max did not abandon them. She was someone. And Amabel had asked her help so she was in league with her now. In fact her one criticism was that she thought the others were too squalid. Alex dragged them all down the most; it was absurd he could not be natural even about ordering things. It was too much he should make them embarrassed about something elementary and she almost made up her mind to say she would pay herself next time.

'But what about your bath salts?' Alex said just as Claire and Evelyna came in from where they had been telephoning.

'Have I packed mine?' said Claire, alive to every danger, 'how enchanting to see you darling,' she said to Amabel, wondering why she was here. 'Do they let bath salts through the customs free? Is it true there's alcohol in them to freshen up one's skin?' Amabel explained she was going to have a bath, she was asking Alex to ring up her maid to bring her crystals, and Robert Hignam offered her a drink which she refused. She never drank spirits and very little wine, she was serious about her complexion.

Now even Miss Crevy began to notice how more than strained they had become. Alex's voice cracked when Amabel's maid could not understand about her bath salts; he kept on saying yes she is going to have a bath. Evelyn had only just greeted her and this feeling was intensified when Claire began to explain about her Auntie May and how she was so ill.

'We have had the doctor, Robert did you pay him, what does one do about hotel doctors, Amabel, do you know, or do they put it on the bill?' She looked round and saw her husband was not listening, he was staring at Amabel. 'Yes,' she went on, 'it really is too strange, Evelyn and I can't make her out at all, it's so unlike her.' And then, more embarrassing still, she realized Amabel was not listening.

'So here we are, my dears,' she said at large, 'stuck here without...' – our host she was about to say and then thought better of it, it was better not to mention him, it always was. 'Without any chance to get away,' she made it into and then bit her lip; put that way Amabel might take it they were all here to escape her which of course in one sense they were, but then what could it matter when people were as rude as Amabel.

But it was not rudeness, not positively that in her case. It is true she did not bother but then she did not expect it of others so that it was almost flattering when she did take notice. At any rate Alex was pleasantly surprised when he had put back the receiver to find Amabel thanking him before he had time to let her know her maid was coming round directly. He did not see she had done this to stop the others knowing. But he did get as far as to feel bewildered; for while he had been sure Amabel would not be coming with them he could not be certain. When she had come in so naturally he had been almost ready to believe Max had changed his plans again as only rich people can and do. Now in his conversation with her maid he had found out she had only just made up her mind to come otherwise she would have had her things packed some time ago or anyway have given orders. It might have been that Max telephoned her but that was not likely if Julia had been with him all this time. So he was embarrassed to know what he should do, whether or no he should get word to Max that Amabel was here, as it seemed likely Amabel had come unknown to Max.

And Alex had that shock when one's thought is answered by someone present, so much so he wondered if, without knowing, he had let what he was thinking out. For what he had almost decided was to let things well alone, he had all but made up his mind he did not know enough to interfere by tipping Max the wink. But when he had been thanked for telephoning, and by her, it was so like gratitude for keeping other's secrets and for not doing what he could and should, he had no alternative but to decide that he must warn him.

As for Amabel, she was not going to bother about the others, excepting Alex. Miss Crevy would have been surprised to learn Amabel had spoken to her only to make secrets and because she guessed the other girls would be against her coming, so that it seemed policy to make one friend at once. Also she wanted to make sure she would not be left alone with Max before she had found out how things were. Miss Crevy would have been surprised as well to learn that Amabel classed her equally with the others and lower, and with contempt as being more out for a free trip abroad because she could less afford to go if she was not taken. Amabel was a money snob. So that Amabel's silence, which Angela in her ignorance might call poise, was no more than wariness coloured by distaste for her own sex. She was here to manage Max and was not going to bother with anyone else but Alex.

At the same time no one can be sure they know what others are thinking any more than anyone can say where someone is when they are asleep. And if behind that blank face and closed eyelids and a faint smile on closed lips they are wandering it may be in Tartary, it is their stillness which makes it all possible to one's wildest dreams.

In her silence and in seeming unapproachable, although he realized it might be studied, and Alex admired her so much he was almost jealous of her, it seemed to him she was not unlike ground so high, so remote it had never been broken and that her outward beauty lay in that if any man had marked her with intimacy as one treads on snow, then that trace which would be left could not fail to invest him, whoever he might be, with some part of those unvulgar heights so covered, not so much of that last field of snow before any summit as of a high memory unvisited, and kept.

He realized she always worked on him by being there and this woke him to how embarrassed they all were except for Angela and Amabel. Again he offered chairs and drinks for Claire and Evelyn but he was alone in it this time, Robert was too wary to make any move when he saw his wife was fussed.

'Where on earth have you been, darlings?' Amabel said to them as though they were at fault, and Claire, who no longer wanted to talk about Auntie May in front of her, said 'Oh, just outside.'

Evelyn Henderson, who was in fact the least well off of all, said to herself why does this woman always make me feel like a schoolgirl.

If people vary at all then it can only be in the impressions they leave on others' minds, and if their turns of phrases are similar and if their rooms are done up by the same firm and, when they are women, if they go to the same shops, what is it makes them different, Evelyna asked herself and then gave the answer: money. Amabel sat there without saying anything; not, so it seemed to Evelyn, because there was anything special about her but because, by being rich or, better still, through having piled up riches in presents from young men, or both, the newspapers had picked her out and now there was no getting away from it, Amabel had grown to be like some beauty spot in Wales. Whether it was pretty or suited to all tastes people would come distances to see it and be satisfied when it lay before them. Amabel had been sanctified, so she thought, by constant printed references as though it was of general concern what she looked like or how beautiful she might be. But then there was no question of beauty here, Evelyn thought, because there were no features, and it could not be called poise, and then she became offensive in her thoughts of her. But Amabel had that azure glance of fame and was secure.

She said: 'How on earth did Max ever come to take this awful room?' This was another way to ignore Claire and Evelyn, to talk to them without any mention of what they had been saying and Evelyn, when she found herself agreeing, as she did almost automatically, despised herself for playing up to her. It was a question of prestige, she thought. When you come on a famous view you feel bound to praise it as you do with some famous beauty when you see one. 'And I agree with what any well-known lovely says because she is so handsome,' she said to herself, 'it's not as if I was pretending she was not as beautiful as all that. I have to go and publicly agree with everything she says because she has said it. Really it's craven.'

Angela, who had by now forgotten Mr Adams she was so excited at being, so she thought, in league with Amabel, tried to put in her word for Max as though she had been confided in and was a party to their intimate affairs.

'Oh, no, poor Max,' she said, 'it's not his fault, every room is like this; of course, I don't know but I expect so.'

'Well then,' said Amabel, 'I bet you had to order drinks,' and

Alex laughed. 'When shall I ever,' she went on, 'be able to teach him how to make people comfortable,' and then was silent.

Claire, who did not care for silences, she thought them unnatural, took up what Amabel had said about this room. While she went rattling on, blaming the directors for allowing decorations such as these and saying she could not think what Julia's uncle was about in letting them do such things, Amabel wondered again how Max would be and what he had on with Julia. She had expected to find him with these others and when she had opened the door she had been braced up to meet him. She was like someone who opens his front door expecting to step out into a gale of wind and then stays bent although he finds he has no wind to lean against, although it is still whining in the chimney and rattling windows. She knew well she could deal with Max but he was always escaping. It was while he was not there that she felt anxious and that was one reason why she had made up her mind to come along.

Mrs Hignam was still talking. 'It is a perfectly ridiculous price to ask for rooms of this kind when you can get something really comfortable for only double at any of the best hotels. I can't understand it,' she said and was going on when Amabel, although she had already been told once, expressed what she was feeling:

'Where has Max got to? I've been here fifteen minutes,' she said.

Claire thought this was too rude and that anyway they were all sick of this endless thing between Amabel and Max. She would have nothing more to do with it. 'Let's go back,' she said to Evelyn and when they were outside she said 'Well, surely the poor man can call five minutes of his time his own.' As they went into Miss Fellowes' room she began to elaborate on this theme. Unaware of her aunt who had long been unaware of them and of those nannies whose training made them seem deaf and dumb at moments her voice rose and fell like a celluloid ball on the water-jet men shoot at and miss at fairs. When it fell through lack of breath Evelyn, like any paid attendant, put that ball back with an encouraging word and Claire was off again.

No one answered Amabel and now that he was alone with Angela and her again and that her last remark reminded him he had not yet got word to Max that she was here, he suddenly felt more strongly than ever before how these girls were a different species and were quite definitely hostile. As he looked at them both, exquisitely

465

dressed, Angela smoking and watching her smoke rings, Amabel looking at her nails like you and I gaze into crystals, as he looked at them waiting it struck him again how women always seemed to expect things, and for that matter, events even, to be brought to them for their pleasure, in white cotton gloves on plates. He determined he would do nothing, if Max had been in his place he would not have done anything or even have thought of it, and then it was too much for these two girls to expect. For he now thought Amabel had only been late as she had so often been before. He did not see why he should get Max for her. It was easier to believe her maid had been mistaken or that she had forgotten her orders to pack the things. In this way he showed how he had been taken in by Amabel, whose wish it was that she should not show haste. In this way also he showed again how impossible it is to tell what others are thinking or what, in ordinary life, brings people to do what they are doing. So he sat quiet, said nothing, and watched the bubbles in his glass.

Through those lidded windows, the curtains so thick and heavy they seemed made of plaster on stage sets, there faintly whispered through to them in waves of sound as in summer when you are coming on a waterfall through woods and it is still unseen or, in summer, breathless in the meadows an aeroplane high up drones alternately loud then soft and low it is so high, what were shouted protests or cheering or just a hubbub of that crowd away below, all this gently came in and passed them by. All three wondered and dreaded a little perhaps in their different ways but no one said anything, there was nothing to say.

Max and Julia, come to an end of talk and speeches, of his saying yes and of her saying no, had moved again to their window upstairs which they had opened and now they were leaning out. The crowds were singing.

Looking down then on thousands of Smiths, thousands of Alberts, hundreds of Marys, woven tight as any office carpet or, more elegantly made, the holy Kaaba soon to set out for Mecca, with some kind of design made out of bookstalls and kiosks seen from above and through one part of that crowd having turned towards those who were singing, thus lightening the dark mass with their pale lozenged faces; observing how this design moved and was alive where in a few lanes or areas people swayed forward or back like a pattern writhing; coughing as fog caught their two throats or perhaps it was smoke from those below who had put on cigarettes or pipes, because tobacco smoke was coming up in drifts; leaning out then, so secure, from their window up above and left by their argument on terms of companionship unalloyed, Julia and Max could not but feel infinitely remote, although at the same time Julia could not fail to be remotely excited at themselves.

When earlier on she had asked him to go down when she had heard someone scream, the crowd was now too great, indeed it was so thick it was plain they could never get out of their hotel to go home if they wanted and she was glad, everything she felt now would come right between them if only it was not hurried, and that promise of the birds which had flown under the arch she stood on would be fulfilled if only, as seemed likely, she could see sea-gulls that night on their crossing. What that promise could be she had no idea, and she did not let herself think of what she wanted, her feeling was just what she had when in a hot bath so exactly right she could not bear to wonder even. In fact she did not want anything different from how things were now this instant. She certainly did not want him to go down and get in the crowd, although its thousands of troubles and its discomfort put new heart into her.

'You're not to go down there, even if I ask you,' she said rather loud to him. 'No one's to go down there, I tell you.'

'What about your servant?'

'Oh, him! Bother him!'

For where she had at one time been nervous and had clutched at straws to fuss over, she now wanted things to stay as they were and, if put to it, she would have insisted she had asked Robert to ring the station master only so as to tease him. Also whatever there is in crowds had reached into her, for these thousands below were now working up a kind of boisterous good humour. If they had been angry individually at first at the delay, and at not being able to get in or out, they were now like sheep with golden tenor voices, so she was thinking, happily singing their troubles away and being good companions. What she could not tell was that those who were singing were Welshmen up for a match, and what they sang in Welsh was of the rape of a Druid's silly daughter under one of Snowdon's wilder mountains. She thought only they knew what it meant, but it sounded light-hearted.

Also she felt encouraged and felt safe because they could not by any chance get up from below; she had seen those doors bolted, and through being above them by reason of Max having bought their room and by having money, she saw in what lay below her an example of her own way of living because they were underneath and kept there.

'Aren't you glad you aren't down there?' she said, and he replied he wondered how it was going to be possible to get them out.

'Have you ever been in a great crowd?' she said, because she had this feeling she must exchange and share with him.

Down below Amabel broke into their silence by saying:

'Well, and what about my bath, if you please?'

Alex said: 'Good Lord, yes, haven't they done anything about it yet?' apologized, and telephoned down while Angela dutifully made comments on how impossible it was to get things done in hotels. Alex was told there was a bath to their room, it was through the bedroom and he passed this news on, and also that her maid was coming.

When she came in she said at once, as though she was alone with Amabel: 'Oh, Madam, I had such a time, you would hardly credit it, Madam, but we got here in the car although one man did get up on the running-boards. Oh, Moddom, you can't have any idea of what it's like. Do you think it's the revolution, Madam, and I have your bath-salts unpacked and your bath is ready for you now.'

'Shall I come with you and watch you have it?' Angela asked her, but Amabel was not having that.

'Darling,' she said, 'look, I've something I must say to Alex.'

As they went out and Angela was left, wishing once more her Adams was back with her again, she wondered if Amabel was going to let him see her in her bath. But surely not in front of her maid, she thought, without noticing how this would make it better in one sense, even if it could not make it right. After all, she knew them so little, she only knew Amabel as being very smart, but she had not bargained to let Alex see her in her own bath, or any other young man like that, or any man at all, and she hoped she would not have to, not for Max or anyone; it could not be expected of her. And how could Alex make compliments on how Amabel looked in a bath with her maid standing by handing her sponges, or would he make no compliments because it had happened so often before and was so ordinary? She made up her mind she would show what she thought by not going in when Amabel sent for her, and in any case she felt she never would be able to if Alex was there; she could not be by the bath in front of Alex, looking into his eyes it would be as if they had done murder, or so it seemed to her it would be to look into his eyes laid upon the woman's nakedness.

Actually most elaborate precautions were taken, and of this Angela knew nothing because she could not bring herself to go and see. Alex had to stand far away when her maid came out, which she did so continually that Amabel might have been in the way of being brought to bed. He saw nothing of her and did not even hear her well.

Amabel giggled. 'She thinks we are in here together,' she said, as if she could dream of it, with Alex of all men.

'I know,' he said back through her door. And he for his part imagined her where she lay, pink with warmth and wrapped round with steam so comfortable she would be more animated now, more cheerful. Aromatic steam as well from her bath salts so that if her maid had been a negress then Amabel's eyes might have shone like two humming birds in the tropic airs she glistened in.

'Oh, Toddy,' she said to her maid, 'you have brought the right bath-salts.'

'What's that?' he shouted.

She kicked her legs and splashed and sent fountains of water up among the wreaths of sweet steam, and her hands with rings still on her fingers were water-lilies done in rubies.

'Do you take your rings off,' he shouted, 'when you have your bath?'

'Why?' she said.

'I was wondering what you looked like.'

'Sweet of you,' she shouted back, and she would have been offended if he had not said something of that kind. She did not think it sweet of him at all.

'Did they make you wear a nightdress in your bath when you were at school?'

She laughed and said he must not shout so loud or Angela would know he was not in with her. Her maid, stifling, wondered if it would not bring her asthma on again.

Auntie May's room was next door and Claire said to Evelyn,

Amabel was keeping Alex hanging on. Even those who went to bed with her never were allowed to see her with no clothes on, because someone quite early in her life had carved his initials low on her back with an electric-light wire, or so Embassy Richard had told her.

'D'you think Angela Crevy ever's met him?'

'No I don't,' Evelyn said to her. 'She's trying to be one of us.'

At this poor Auntie May shifted slightly in her bed.

'My dear, what are we to do with her?' Evelyn put a finger to her lips, but Claire went on. 'I don't care,' she said, 'she must get well, it's too absurd her being ill here, letting that idiot doctor say fantastic things about her, even if they might be true. Why are the old allowed to go about alone; they ought to make a law about it. What would have happened to her if we had not been there and Max, he is so perfectly sweet, hadn't taken this room? But it's unfair to him if she doesn't get well soon or get over it, whichever it is, or both,' she said.

And Auntie May, half-way round from another spell of what had come over her and struck her down into nightmares and exhaustion and wandering so that she had been diagnosed as tight, and tight she was with dreams spoke up from mists which wrapped her round not sweet and warm. She mistook her niece for another barmaid, and said in a high wavering voice:

'I'm surprised at you, surprised I am,' she said, 'you should be glad I came in and gave you custom, a customer I came in, that's what you are here for, here for,' she said, and was silent. 'I shall complain,' she said, trying to raise herself on her arm, and Claire leaned forward and said: 'Hush, auntie, you don't know what you are saying.' This silenced her again.

'Claire, d'you suppose she heard us?'

'What on earth do you mean? My dear, she is raving. Oh, why did she come to be such a worry to us, isn't it a shame?'

'You mean she thought she was talking to a waitress,' Evelyn said. 'But you know it is so dangerous to speak in front of people when they are ill, you think they can't hear, but one can never tell. I remember my mother telling me when Grannie died the nurse said she had only so long to live, ten hours, or whatever it was then, and she said, "Don't," just like that. And that was after she had lain there like a log for two days and nights.'

'Well then,' Claire whispered, 'don't talk in front of her.'

'Oh,' said Evelyn, also in whispers now, 'but she is not going to die, is she?'

'My dear, don't you of all people go and let me down. I've trouble enough on my hands now in all conscience without – oh well,' she said, 'I'm sorry, it's not easy just now, is it? And where's that wretched husband of mine, why doesn't he do something?'

'But surely that's just it,' said Evelyn, 'there's nothing to do.'

Thomson, who was still looking after Julia's luggage where it had been left until it could be registered, felt he must stretch his legs again. He said to her porter: 'Jack, I'll be back,' and came out from behind her barricade of trunks to find Edwards sitting on one of Max's suit-cases.

'Mr Adey, I believe,' he said, and raised his hat.

'Mr Livingstone, I presume, Miss Wray,' said Edwards. They both of them laughed. Thomson sat down on yet another pigskin case and said what game was it this they were playing? and he got his answer, hide and seek. Oranges and lemons he suggested was more likely, but no, said Edwards, sardines was all the rage now not blind bloody man's buff, which was kept for Dartmoor Sunday afternoons. Both laughed again.

'Well,' Thomson said, 'it was a funny game whatever it was, and even if it had not got a name, it was more like drivers waiting outside shops or at dances.' He asked if Edwards had had his tea. Neither had so much as tasted it this afternoon. Edwards had some chocolate in bars which he called iron rations, but he explained he did not want to touch that, not knowing but what they might be here all night when they might want something more urgent, for even if it had been three hours or more since their dinner it might be long night before they saw supper. Thomson said he was not going to wait all that long time, and Edwards asked him why he did not go along and see if he could get himself something. Thomson explained it did not taste like it should if he had his tea alone, he liked company with it, and why didn't Edwards come along and see what they could find? But Edwards considered they would find every tea place full. Also he would not leave this dressing-case of his.

'Then what's in it?'

'It's fitted.'

'What, gold and silver stoppers and all that? Come on, it's insured and chances are he'd like a new one.'

'Go on if you like and pick up some bird, alive or dead, Thomson, and get yourself your cup o' tea if you feel like it.'

'What d'you mean, alive or dead?'

'Not but you'll find everything full and more than full out there. There's trouble enough to get in without trying for a cup o' tea. Alive or dead? I meant nothing.'

'Not wrapped up in brown paper you didn't?'

'What's that?'

'Oh, nothing. This is a rum thing this party. And they call it pleasure, eh?'

'I don't know. It's not their business if fog comes down like it's done, they can't be accountable for that.'

'No, but then why stay here or in that hotel, why not go back and sit down to a nice tea while you wait?'

'It's plain to see you haven't been outside, my lad, not lately. You couldn't get back now if you tried.'

'Oh, look at those blue eyes,' Thomson said, and Mr Adey's porter lifted his heavy head. Round one massive up-ended cabin trunk a girl was looking. 'Lovely blue eyes, and I like that nose.'

Edwards said: 'Now then, don't let's have anything like that here.'

'Anything?' said Thomson. 'Did you 'ear what that rude man called it, a lovely kiss?' he said, still sitting where he did. 'What a thing to call it. Listen, if that gentleman with the luggage will drop off again like he 'as been doing this last thirty minutes and my pal here turns his dirty disapproving face, will you give us a kiss, darling? There's none could see with these bags and things.'

'I like your cheek,' she said scornfully. 'Here,' she said, 'if you want one,' and crept round and kissed him on his mouth. Not believing his luck he put his arms round her and the porter said, 'God bless me,' when a voice over that barricade began calling: 'Emily, where are you, Emily?' and he let her go, and off she went.

'God bless 'er little 'eart,' the porter said, smacking his lips. He called out to his mate, having to shout it there was so much noise: 'Come up out of the bloody ground, and gave him a great bloody kiss when he asked her.'

'Poor Thomson,' Julia said just then to Max, putting on her hat

472

again, 'd'you think he's all right, and what about his tea?'

'We ought to go down,' he said.

'Yes, the others will be wondering what's become of us.' And what had become of both of them, she asked herself, suddenly despairing; nothing, alas!

'Oh, Max,' she said, 'everything is going to be all right, isn't it?'

'All right?'

'Do you see, I'm wondering about this journey. All the fog and all that,' she said, leading him off.

'You do think our train will run, don't you?' she went on.

'It'll have to.'

'I know,' she said, 'but things don't always go right because they have to. I wonder if I ought to ring my uncle and let him know what's become of us,' she said, because she was not and could not be sure Max would come to anything in the South of France. 'D'you think I'd better. Max darling, do say something. What do you think?'

He looked at the telephone and considered and at last he told her he saw no point in doing so. And now she remembered those two birds which had flown under the arch she had been on when she had started, and now she forgot they were sea-gulls and thought they had been doves and so was comforted.

'Good heavens! Come along, what will they think?' she said brightening. 'We must get on down.'

'Well,' said Thomson, 'and what do you think of that Emily? Emily,' he cried in a falsetto voice echoing the old lady who had called her back, but not so loud that she could hear. 'Where are you Emily, my lovey-dove?'

'Disgusting, I call it.'

'And what's disgusting? Lord, what's in a kiss? It don't mean nothing to her, nor anything to me, but it did make an amount of difference when I hadn't 'ad my tea.'

'You do meet some funny ones about these days,' Edwards said to the porter. 'Still thinking along of his tea and look what he's just got.'

'No,' said Thomson. 'No, it's fellow feeling, that's what I like about it. Without so much as a by your leave when she sees some-one hankering after a bit of comfort, God bless 'er, she gives it him, not like some little bitches I could name,' he darkly said, looking up and over to where their hotel room would be. Their porter tapped his forehead. 'It's been too much for 'im,' he cried at large, 'too much by a long chalk. So it is for most of these young fellers, carried away by it,' he said.

'Waiting about in basements, with no light and in the damp and dark,' Mr Thomson muttered to himself, and if he and that girl had been alone together, in between kisses he would have pitied both of them clinging together on dim whirling waters.

'Well, there you are,' said Julia as she came in and before she could see who was there and in such a tone she might as well have been asking where had they all been all this time. 'Why it's you, Angela, my dear,' she said. 'Where are the others?'

'Alex is helping Amabel, actually, in her bath,' Miss Crevy said, and wished she had a periscope to see that bomb explode. But if it went off it did so out of sight, for Julia did no more than turn to Max, though she did this in the direction her heart had turned over when she heard.

'How did she get there?' he said, and he felt shocked.

'She walked, she told me, and she got here in front of her maid who came in the car.'

'Is Toddy here then?'

'Oh, Max,' said Miss Crevy, 'who ever heard of Amabel travelling without her maid?'

So she is coming after all, Julia thought, maid and all and six cabin trunks full of every kind of lovely dress. But how unfair, she thought, how vile of her when she knew Max did not want her, how low to pursue him in this way. She also noticed Miss Crevy seemed quick in using her Christian name and wondered if they mightn't somehow be in league. But it was going to ruin their entire trip her coming, and she went over in her mind when she heard him say he had asked Amabel.

She had been wearing her blue dress and the new shoes and they had gone on together alone somewhere to dance and she had been nervous about whether he would have too much to drink perhaps, but anyway it had been fun and lots of people there and then Embassy Richard had come up. How absurd of Angela to call him Embassy Dick like any bird; she was too free the way she made out she knew people. Perhaps that was why Max had seemed so much against him, but when Richard had come up he had said something

474

jokingly about his knowing someone Max was going to leave behind and who would be simply furious at being left. And that was all, come to think of it, and she had taken it to mean Amabel, but she might be wrong, there might be someone else. What could it mean?

'I didn't know Amabel was coming,' she said, meaning why had he not told her.

'She was most awfully upset she was so late,' Miss Crevy told Max, 'she told me to say to you how dreadfully sorry she was, and of course she would have missed the train if it hadn't been for this fog. But you see it was just that, the fog's so thick she simply could not get here, so she says you mustn't be too hard on her, please, she could not really help herself.'

Julia said, well anyway they had all got here in time, and that she had no maid to pack for her. 'In fact,' she said, because this news had upset her so she had to speak about herself, 'Jemima the old thing who packs for me, you can't call her a maid really, never can learn to put in my charms. You know,' she said to Angela very seriously, 'I simply can't go anywhere without them, the most frightful things have happened if I haven't brought them, and not to me only, but to everyone who was with me too. So you see it makes me most terribly nervous. You see I don't know to this minute whether I have them with me or not, and nervous not only for myself but for all of you, my poor darlings.'

Miss Crevy did not take this well as she could not understand the calm with which they seemed to accept, not Amabel's presence, which she thought natural, but the fact that Alex was in there with her. It made her furious they should make so little of it, and she burst out:

'Oh, no, but I think it's disgusting his being in there helping with her bath.'

This was so sudden it made Julia forget about her charms.

'My dear,' she said, 'what do you mean, helping?' And Angela who, as soon as she began to explain, felt in some way she was weakening her argument, had to say she did not know how he was helping, and at that she laughed, but he was in there and he ought not to in front of all of them.

'He is not,' said Max. Miss Crevy looked to see if he was jealous, but saw that he simply did not believe her.

'But I tell you I heard them.'

'My dear, what did you hear about them?' Julia said.

Feeling in some way she was making her argument still weaker Miss Crevy explained how Amabel had asked him in front of her not half an hour ago.

'She did not,' said Max, and Miss Crevy said no more. If they did not believe her then let them find out for themselves and then, rather late, it came over her that she had not seen for herself, it was possible Alex was still in the bedroom and she felt foolish until she thought, well anyway if he wasn't in there now he soon would be.

On this Julia left them. She thought Miss Crevy an impossible girl and went to find Claire and Evelyn to tell them and ask after Miss Fellowes. This would be her way of apologizing for having gone off with Max. And Max, who wanted time to face up to this news began to make it by asking Angela if she had all she wanted. She would hardly answer him.

When Julia went into that bedroom where Miss Fellowes lay, she said to Evelyn and Claire, 'Well there you are,' in such tones she might have been telling them how hard it had been for her to find them, and as though she were saying she had been looking for them all that time she had been upstairs with Max. She asked after Miss Fellowes and they replied, all this in whispers, and then so soon as she decently could she said would they not leave Miss Fellowes to those nannies, she had something she must tell them. Both wondered if she were going to announce her engagement, but it seemed she was more angry than pleased, and for one moment Claire wondered if that idiot Robert, her idiotic husband, had tried to pounce on her.

When those nannies had been got in and they themselves were in the corridor outside, Julia began on Angela. 'Children,' she went on, using this word because Evelyn who was older than any of them always used it when she wanted their attention, 'what do you think of Angela Crevy? And do you know what she has just accused my darling Alex of? Why of being with Amabel in her bath.' At this Claire and Evelyn registered disgust. 'Oh, my darlings,' she went on, 'isn't it too despairing, why must Max out of pure good nature ask people like her to come with his oldest friends who have known each other for ages?' 'I know,' they both murmured back. 'And Amabel, what is she doing, and anyway, why can't that great ninny Angela see she is trying to set us by the ears?'

'Isn't that just what I was saying to you?' Claire said to Evelyn.

'Yes, we were,' said Evelyn.

At this they stood all three facing each other with serious faces, when Robert turned the corner and came down that corridor towards them.

'What's this?' he says, 'in a committee meeting?' He smells faintly of whisky.

'Go away,' says Claire to him, 'we're busy. Run along now,' she said, and as he went and was just opening the door to go in to Max and Angela, and as they stayed silent so that Max should not hear anything through that open door, the man who had followed Miss Fellowes and whom Alex had taken for a detective also came round that same corner and made after Robert. Julia whispered: 'Oh dear, who's this? What can he want?' she said as he went in after Mr Hignam, 'or is it another friend of Max's we have to do with?'

Max, when he saw Hignam, thought it would be best to find out what he could about Amabel rather than pretend he had always known she would be coming, for there was no knowing what she might have said while she was alone with them, so he asked him, 'What's this about Amabel?' Miss Crevy took this to mean that Max had believed her when she had, so she thought, told on Alex. But Mr Hignam had no time to reply that he knew nothing before that false detective was on to him. Putting his head inside he said, 'I want you,' in educated accents this time.

'Yes,' said Robert, taken aback. 'Well, what for? Right you are, I'll come outside,' he said.

They walked up that corridor where his wife and those two others could not hear them and then Mr Hignam asked again what might be wanted of him.

'How is she?'

'How's who? My aunt, you mean? I say, who are you?'

'She were mortal bad I reckon when I see her took upstairs,' this strange man said, speaking now in Brummagem. 'Now don't misunderstand me,' he said. 'I don't mean any harm, just a civil inquiry, that's all. You see I was sitting nigh her when she was taken bad,' and by now he was speaking ordinarily, 'and I think I'll just ask after her.'

'She's better, thank you,' Robert answered, and began to see how he could use this man.

'Well, 'ere's a to-do if you like with this fog and none being able to get off to their own fireside like with no trains running on account of it. But I'm right glad to 'ear from you as she's better. Of course it's different for the likes of you as can afford it, and thank God for it, I say. I'm not one of those as 'olds there ought only to be the poor and no rich in this world, but it's different for you so it is as can take rooms and be a bit comfortable like instead of 'aving to stand like cattle waiting to be butchered in that yard beneath. Not but what I thought,' he said going back to Miss Fellowes, 'she looked terrible ill down there in that tea-room where I was just getting a bit of comfort down inside me. I remember it now,' he said, smacking his lips.

'What did she have down there?'

'Why, bless my soul, not more than one small whisky on account of 'ow strange she was feeling, I'll be bound. The properest lady that ever stepped,' he added. 'I felt sorry for her, that I did; aye and I thought to myself, my lad, I thought, you can go and ask after her, you know a real lady when you sees one. She's a goner.'

'She's what?'

'Oh, aye, she's a goner. She's your aunt, you said. Yes, I don't give her long.'

'You know better than the doctor then.'

'Aye she's a goner.'

'Look here, you doing anything just now, what? I mean if I slipped you ten bob, could you get outside?'

'What for?'

'Ten bob.'

'No, what d'you want me to do?' he said in his educated voice again.

'Only to go out and find Miss Julia Wray's man who's called Thomson and ask him if her luggage is all right. He ought to be with it down in that place where it's registered.'

After some difficulty Robert got him off and went back to be with Angela and Max. Before he could reach their room Julia called out to him and asked who had that man been and what did he want. Robert answered he had sent him out to find Thomson as she seemed so upset about her luggage, and as he said it he showed how pleased he was; he thought he was killing two birds with one stone. And as he went in and Angela began to ask him this same question,

Julia said how perfectly sweet of Robert, and then added to herself, but not that man, couldn't he have gone himself, not that man of all men? She looked so distracted, Claire said to her: 'Now, darling, don't get in a fuss.'

When Mr Hignam had explained, Angela said: 'But you can't treat him like that, he's the hotel detective.'

'He's not.'

'But, Robert, I tell you he is,' she said, using his Christian name for the first time. 'Alex found that out when he came in before, and I was here.'

'He isn't one.'

This she could take from Max but not from Robert. 'How do you know he isn't one?' she said, going white under her make-up. All of a sudden she was so angry she began to tremble from her toes up.

And Amabel was just drying hers on a towel. The walls were made of looking-glass, and were clouded over with steam; from them her body was reflected in a faint pink mass. She leaned over and traced her name Amabel in that steam and that pink mass loomed up to meet her in the flesh and looked through bright at her through the letters of her name. She bent down to look at her eyes in the A her name began with, and as she gazed at them steam or her breath dulled her reflection and the blue her eyes were went out or faded.

She rubbed with the palm of her hand, and now she could see all her face. She always thought it more beautiful than anything she had ever seen, and when she looked at herself it was as though the two of them would never meet again, it was to bid farewell; and at the last she always smiled, and she did so this time as it was clouding over, tenderly smiled as you might say good-bye, my darling darling.

Angela's raised voice came through to her.

'She sounds cross,' she said to Alex, and he replied she was cross by nature, she did such dreadful things. 'It was too intolerable,' he told her, 'there was this young man of hers, he had gone before you came, and she left him outside and made me come in where I am now, sent me out again into that corridor and then clapped her hands as though she was slapping my face.'

'Oh, no!'

'Yes, it's true.'

'Alex, my dear, how very funny. Wasn't it a bit hard on you?' she said to humour him, and went on drying herself. Her bath-towel was huge and she slowly rubbed every inch of herself with it as though she were polishing. She was gradually changing colour, where she was dry was going back to white; for instance, her face was dead white but her neck was red. She was polishing her shoulders now and her neck was paling from red into pink and then suddenly it would go white. And all this time she dried herself she moved her toes as if she was moulding something.

When Alex came to an end she had not properly heard what he had been saying so she said something almost under her breath, or so low that he in his turn should not catch what she had said, but so that it would be enough to tell him she was listening.

As she went over herself with her towel it was plain that she loved her own shape and skin. When she dried her breasts she wiped them with as much care as she would puppies after she had given them their bath, smiling all the time. But her stomach she wiped unsmiling upwards to make it thin. When she came to dry her legs she hissed like grooms do. And as she got herself dry that steam began to go off the mirror walls so that as she got white again more and more of herself began to be reflected.

She stood out as though so much health, such abundance and happiness should have never clothes to hide it. Indeed she looked as though she were alone in the world she was so good, and so good that she looked mild, which she was not.

She put out her tongue and carefully examined this. Then she smiled herself good-bye again and began to powder all over her.

'What on earth are you doing?' he said. 'I don't believe you listened to a word I said.'

'Is Max out there, d'you suppose?'

'I don't know. Shall I go and find him?'

'No, of course not. Let him find me.'

'As you are? In or out of your bath?'

'No such luck for him,' she said, and laughed. She began whistling.

Max said he would ask Alex what he thought this man had been, it seemed to him a natural excuse to see what they were doing. Going in he found Alex wearily leaning his shoulder against the shut door of that bathroom.

'Hullo, old boy!'

'Amabel,' said Max.

'Why, hullo, darling,' she said. 'I'm having a bath.'

'Good,' he said.

Angela came in. 'Alex,' she said, 'didn't you say that man was the hotel detective?'

'What man?'

'The man you gave a drink to.'

'I thought he might be, but I shouldn't think so.'

He could not have been, for now that he was trying to get out of this hotel, and it was like trying to get out of one world into another, no one in authority seemed to know him. If they let people out they said then they would have to allow them in, they had experienced that before when everything had been broken up, no, he could not go outside. Then he asked them what right they had to keep him in, and they told him it was to protect their own property. He had said he must go out, and then each of those officials had left him.

In the lounge where he was now it was even fuller than it had been. Every seat was occupied and people sat about on their bags as they had done outside when there had been room to sit down. One wall had windows high up along it which looked out over the station, and on their outside ledges were perched young men, mostly amusing themselves at the guests inside. These youths were putting out their yellow tongues at one old lady seated by him, and while he thought how he could get out he watched her shake her paper at them. As he always interfered he told her not to bother, and in this he was right, as she encouraged them by showing temper. But she would not listen. 'Go away,' she said, and once she had said that began mouthing soundlessly, go away, articulating with her lips at those youths behind glass. They caught on to this and mouthed back through the shut window, only what they brought soundless out were obscenities. He could read their lips, but she never knew. He said to her, 'Now don't you go and throw something at them, ma'am, it would not be proper in someone in your position and you might never know what you got back.' 'Go away,' she said out loud again.

Although all those windows had been shut there was a continual dull roar came through them from outside, and this noise sat upon those within like clouds upon a mountain so they were obscured and levelled and, as though they had been airmen, in danger of running fatally into earth. Clouds also, if they are banked up, will so occupy the sky as to dwarf what is beneath and this low roar, which was only conversation in that multitude without, lay over them in such a pall, like night coming on and there is no light when one must see, that these people here were obscured by it and were dimmed into anxious Roman numerals.

Not putting this into words he did feel relieved when he got into a passage where it was emptier, though three people lay at full length against one wall. Seeing another stranger come out of one door to go into another, 'Hi, Charlie,' he shouted, not knowing his name, and stopped him. These three sleepers moaned in their darkness. 'Charlie,' he went on, coming up to him, 'any way out of 'ere?' 'No, lad, it's all shut up.' 'But say you or me wanted to get out?' 'He'd slip out of a window,' this other stranger said and went off.

'Have you looked outside?' Julia said to Evelyn upstairs.

'How d'you mean, outside?'

'Why at all those millions down below,' she said, and led them past where Angela was sitting by the curtains. 'Look at that, darlings,' she said almost tearfully, for what had exhilarated her not so long ago was forbidding now. She frowned.

Max came back to be with them, unseeing. Now that he had heard Amabel and that he knew she was in her bath undressed, it seemed to him that when they had been together she had warmed him every side. When he opened his eyes close beside her in the flat she had blotted out the light, only where her eye would be he could see dazzle, all the rest of her mountain face had been that dark acreage against him. He had lain in the shadow of it under softly beaten wings of her breathing, and his thoughts, hatching up out of sleep, had bundled back into the other darkness of her plumes. So being entirely delivered over he had lain still, he remembered, because he had been told by that dazzle her eyelids were not down so that she lay still awake.

He wanted her.

So this stranger on his mission went into rooms at a venture, tried windows and found them locked, and then went out again until he came to one room where two maids leant out of an open casement towards their knight standing on his friend's shoulder from the station floor ten foot beneath. His bowler hat lay next his friend's feet and in a cross neatly on the crown of it lay his pair of gloves.

Through this open window noise of all those outside smote him in one vast confused hum like numbers of aeroplanes flying by and against which these two maids' shrill female voices, screeching to make themselves appreciated by their white-collared boy, were like urgent wheels that had not been oiled. Interfering again he came forward and he said, 'Save us, young fellow. Don't you go and fall down or you might be hurt.'

'It's her eyes enfold me and uphold me,' was his gallant answer.

'Did you hear that?' she screeched, and her friend leaned further out and said:

'Which one, which eyes?'

'Now don't make me choose,' he said, reaching up with one arm, his other hand sucking to the wall. 'Hold me,' he said, 'hold me.' One of them stretched her dainty dirty fingers down and he caught her wrist. 'Now,' he said, 'where would you be if I jumped off his shoulder?' These two screamed now like rats smelling food when they have been starved in empty milk-churns. 'Listen,' this stranger interrupted, 'that's murder,' leaning out himself. 'What's murder?' was his answer, and the other said he could not stand Ed's weight much longer. They redoubled their shrieks, they were famished and had not been so charmed for ages.

'She'd fall slap on her 'ead and break 'er neck,' he said pondering, when the one who was being held broke off her shrieks to say, well it was her neck, wasn't it?

'I'll jump off and then I'll knock his block off for him,' he murmured and scrambled out, hung at arm's length, while Ed said, mind my gloves and hat, dropped lightly for his age, and began ploughing his way through. He had forgotten them at once.

To push through this crowd was like trying to get through bamboo or artichokes grown thick together or thousands of tailors' dummies stored warm on a warehouse floor.

'What targets,' one by him remarked, 'what targets for a bomb.'

Max leaned his forehead against a shut window tormented by his dreams of Amabel, daydreams brought on by her voice, by her being so near, by her choosing to be undressed behind that door and because she used another voice when she wore no clothes, she mocked.

He was in that state when she no longer haunted him all day, but it came back at night and when, if thinking about her while she was not there did not make him as desperate as he had once been when first he knew her he still had that same feeling come over him at times and all the more, very often, when they had just met again.

Five months ago, when his love had been first conceived, he had been maddened by his thoughts of her when she was away, they had boiled all over him and then when she came back they would simmer down again to his happiness. But now he was cooling off he still had returns of that old feeling made worse because he resented her still having that command.

She still swayed him like water moves a trailing weed, and froth and some little dirt collects round, and sometimes when he first heard her voice again and when as now she used that private tone, then it was as if his tide had turned and helpless he was turned back, delivered up to move to her tune and trail back the way he had come helpless, delivered over, benighted.

And as does, in moonlight in cold deep-shadowed other day, push him out of his burrow and kick the old buck to death so when they saw him down, these girls and Amabel, coming out as she now did, all set upon him he was so absurd.

'Look round, darling,' Amabel said as cruel as could be, 'I'm here, not floating around outside.' Angel, he said to himself, angel and knew how fatuous it was and could not help himself. When he did turn round to say how do you do, like Robin Adams he could not bring himself to look at her and this made him seem ashamed.

'Hamlet,' said Julia, and then all three girls laughed.

'Well, my darlings, and what shall we do?' she went on and laughed twice, for Max had turned his back again, he looked so like any boy at school, 'here we are, three lovely girls all mewed up and can't get out. What d'you say?'

Amabel smiled at his back as though she was taken up with thinking all of him over. She held a bone paper knife against her cheek, along her nose now and then across her forehead. She thought these three bits prettiest in her face.

Angela said how lovely her dressing gown and bent down to stroke it and Amabel murmured Embassy Richard had given it her. So all three of them laughed again, and Amabel said, 'I'm so bored, darling.' They were in league against him and watched his back like cats over offal or as if they thought his heart might fall out at their feet feebly smiling and stuck all over with darts or safety pins.

Miss Crevy asked where Alex had got to and Julia said, why didn't she know he was up to his old tricks with Toddy, how he adored her, for as soon as Amabel looked another way he would always be after her maid.

'Is she so very pretty then?'

Julia laughed and explained she was ever so old and besides hadn't Angela seen her in here already and Amabel sat on, quite still and quiet, looking at his back.

'Lot of people down there,' he said at last.

Julia thought she would take him in hand. 'Max, why don't you turn round and entertain us?' she said and smiled at Amabel who smiled back. 'You do look such a silly standing there as if they'd made you dunce or put you in coventry or something.'

But this shot went too near home. Amabel said again and this time more kindly, 'I'm so bored, darling,' for she did not care to let them go too far with him.

He turned round and again could not bring himself to raise his eyes. He said:

'There's nothing for it,' and at that he saw her feet which were bare in sandals and looked fantastic on that cheap carpet. Her toes were pink and quite perfect for him, so much so they had no character at all and he thought they were unreal. The nails glittered.

'Are you going to go out like that?' he said.

'I might.'

He still looked at her toes and while she watched his face she began to move them one after another. He quickly dared one look at her face to see what she was driving at and what he saw, remembered beauty, turned his heart to stone so tight that he smiled into her jewelled eyes like any Fido asking for his bone. Now she was back he was delivered up for punishment, only wanting to be slaves again. She looked hard at him. 'Oh, God,' he said and turned away again.

Julia laughed. 'Max,' she said, 'we're here, this way, and not out there. Oh, d'you remember,' she went on, 'that time we were out at Svengalo's when the mad waiter, that one who never finished re-arranging one's knives and forks, began to lose his trousers, they simply began to slip down like petticoats and he never knew? It was Embassy Richard had unbuttoned him and he had no idea, d'you

485

all remember how Max got up and went out on us, because he couldn't take it, and there we were left to blush?'

'Oh, no!' said Angela, who had not been with them.

'Amabel, d'you remember it?' Julia went on, 'and then we never saw that mad waiter again, Svengalo sacked him for not minding his trousers, so they all use safety pins now, the other waiters. Richard said Svengalo does too, he'd tried the other night. Come back to us, Max darling.'

As he made no reply she went on:

'And do you remember that time I fainted and you took me outside and that drunk made a pass at me when you had stretched me out? Shall I ever let you forget how you left me at once after I was better and went right away? And didn't come back. Defenceless, mind you, or almost, against that gorilla and he was so beastly drunk he didn't know what he was doing except when he picked on me. Why do you go away, Max?'

'Yes,' Amabel said, 'why do you leave us?' and all he could find to say was well he was here, wasn't he, speaking with his back still turned to them.

'But then what on earth happened to you?' Angela said.

'Oh, well, you see there were others in our party, there always are,' Julia said and she looked at Angela gravely, 'but wasn't it beastly of him, Am?' she said, turning to her, but Amabel was looking at her toes. 'And then there was that time when he walked out on you, Am, and I said you can't do that, go back. D'you remember? It was that night we went out by car to bathe and the farmer thought we had no clothes on. And when life's so short.'

'Did you say that then, darling?' Amabel said and smiled sweetly up at her.

'But what are you thinking of, darling, it was Mr Hignam, no less, said it to Claire of course, though what he can have meant I can't imagine.' She smiled as sweetly back.

'When was this, do tell me?' Angela said.

'Not for your ears, darling,' and while she said this Amabel kept her eyes on Julia. She began to move her toes again.

'But why, my dear, what's this?' said Julia, because nothing had happened then or she would have remembered. But she saw how Amabel did not know this, or did not mean to see it.

'Well, really,' Julia said, 'well, well.'

Max had turned round. He looked at each in turn.

'Hey,' he said, 'what's this?'

'That night when we went to bathe,' said Amabel.

'Which one?'

'When the farmer thought Julia had no clothes on.'

'Yes.'

'And you wondered too.'

'I wondered?'

'Oh no, he didn't,' Julia said and laughed quite differently.

'By God Max,' Amabel said, 'the way you go on with my friends,' she said, although Max had first introduced Julia to her and they had never become friends.

'No, darling, really, I had on my flesh-coloured suit.'

'I don't remember anything.'

'Well, if you don't remember,' Amabel said to him, 'I should think you were tight. Anyway, by the way you went on in my car afterwards you would be.'

'You think I have to get tight to . . .' he said and broke off and this made Amabel laugh. It seemed to her she had sufficiently established her claim over him, so she laughed again.

And Julia laughed to save her face and lastly Angela laughed to keep in with them.

'Oh, you know what I mean,' he said.

'We know,' Miss Crevy said.

'Oh, do you, darling?' said Amabel and getting up she stepped forward and kissed him and then stayed by, leaving her face close to his. He found her hair was still damp and this tortured him for something he remembered of her once and then it came over him she meant to put him through it before the others. And then because he had realized this it put him right, he felt he had seen through her little game and anyway he thought with glee what were they doing but fighting over him so that he grinned with confidence right into her mouth. She gave way at once, half opened her jaws and sat down again. He could see her pink tongue. She looked tired and older. He laughed.

'You think I have . . .' he said and laughed once more.

'Why not?' said Julia and turned away, thinking this was disgusting.

'Why not what?' he said.

'Oh, get tight or anything.'

'Who said anything about getting tight?' for he had already forgotten anyone had spoken about getting drunk he felt so relieved. As if he had escaped, as indeed he had back into slavery again or as if his punishment was over, while it was just preparing. And now Julia was caught back into her old misery, so much so she felt she could not bear it and must get out of here so she went outside to find Claire and Evelyn.

'Why don't you tell me about all these thrilling parties and things? What happened with Farmer Bangs?' Miss Crevy said.

'Oh, nothing.'

'No, Max, it was obviously something thrilling.'

'We went out to bathe.'

'Well?'

'And Am said we ought to go back.'

'Well?' she said and got no reply; he was looking at Amabel.

'Yes?' she said.

'You know how it is.'

'That's just what I don't know.'

He was the one who laughed now. He laughed and said:

'Then you'd better learn.'

'Not knowing isn't the same as not having learned.'

'What is it then?'

'Isn't he extraordinary?' she said to Amabel, but got no help from her, she was looking at her toes. 'My dear Max,' she went on, 'even if I do know all the answers it doesn't mean I know what went on that evening.'

'You can guess then.'

This was rude but she was not going to give in to any of them again, not even to Max.

'But what did the farmer say?' she said and had no answer.

'Oh, come on,' she said and stamped her foot.

'Oh, what did he say?' she said again.

'Darling,' said Amabel turning to her, 'he said them that are asked no questions won't be told no lies.' Max laughed and said it wasn't him so much, it was his dog. And at this, although she had not been gone more than three minutes, Julia came back to them. 'My dear,' she said to Max, ignoring those others, 'I'm afraid Claire's Auntie May is rather bad.'

'Rather bad you say?' he repeated after her, not having taken this in.

'Yes, rather bad I said, though I think it's worse than that.'

'I can't help it,' he said. 'She's got a room, hasn't she?' and Amabel asked him if Claire's aunt was coming on their party too, and he laughed and said he did not know.

'How can you stand there and laugh, Max darling, really,' Julia said, not because she was worried about how ill the old thing might be but so as to get him out of this room, no matter how.

'I say,' he said, rising, 'that's bad.'

'I thought you ought to know.'

He stood quiet. Amabel was looking at Julia. 'Poor Claire,' she said, 'what a shame.'

'What about a doctor?'

'Oh, they had one in hours ago, Max.'

'What did he say?' Angela said, getting finally in on this story at last. And Julia, realizing, felt she ought to explain, and while she was explaining thought she would pass over what the doctor really said about Miss Fellowes, they would only laugh when they heard and Max would pay no more attention. 'Well, you see, Angela darling, Claire did not want anyone to know, you know how people are that way. Anyway,' she said, lying, 'I believe this aunt of hers asked Claire not to say one word to anyone; you see she felt she had been trouble enough already, Max had been perfectly sweet and taken her a room. She did not want to be any more bother, did she, because after all we are supposed to be going off on our holiday, aren't we? But still, Max, my dear, there it is and I thought you ought to know. As a matter of fact the doctor was very worried about her.'

'What did he do?' said Max.

'What did he do?' she echoed, 'why, what do doctors do? Of course he got his fee, Robert paid him, but you know what they are; he went away again; she might die for all he cared.'

'Where is Robert?' he said. He could not bear it if anyone in any party of his paid for anything.

'Downstairs in the bar. Why?' she said.

'Can't have that, you know.'

'Oh, Max, you are sweet!' she said, 'but really, after all, it is his own aunt and she was not in our party; really she's got nothing to do with you.'

Amabel asked herself why then come to bother him about this old trout, and then told herself she knew.

'Can't have it,' he said cheerfully, as people do when they are living up to their own characters.

'Darling,' said Amabel, 'don't be so like yourself.'

'I wish you would help,' Julia said and then thought why not put it on to Claire. 'Poor Claire,' she went on, 'she is so worried.'

'What's that crack for?' he said to Amabel.

'What crack?'

'Don't be so like yourself or something?'

'Oh, nothing,' she said and smiled up at him as if he enormously amused her.

'Well, if that's all,' he said still looking at her, 'then I'd better go see what can be done.'

'But I mean,' said Angela, and they all turned surprised for they had forgotten her, 'I mean would Claire like that? I thought she wanted nobody to know,' she said with malice.

'Claire's upset, poor darling, it's horrible for her,' Julia explained and at this moment Alex came back in again.

'There's no one anywhere like your Toddy,' he said to Amabel and looked tremendously pleased. 'The things I've found out about you, you'll never be able to be quite the same to me again with all I've got on you now. Really Am, it's fantastic, you can't imagine, I mean it makes coming and all this waiting worth while. Not of course that it isn't heaven our all being here together and all that, only there is so little to do, but have baths and gossip. Why, what's the matter, it's nothing I've said or done is it? You all look as if you'd been at one of my uncle Joe's board meetings.'

'It's about Claire's aunt, this Miss Fellowes. She's very ill.'

'I know all about it, Julia, you told me ages ago and tried to be frightfully mysterious about it.'

'I'm very worried about her.'

'I'll bet you aren't really,' he said, 'and if she's going to die, even, what difference—'

'Oh, no, Alex,' she said.

'—does it make to you?' he went on, and she said 'Alex, no, no,' again. 'Well,' he said, 'we've all got to come to it some time, though why it should be here of all places I can't imagine.' While he was talking Miss Crevy looked at him with loathing. 'Oh, I know,' he went on, 'I know she's not so bad as all that but I don't care anyhow and I advise everyone to feel the same. Otherwise I shall go home,' he said, blushing with anger all of a sudden, 'yes, and I shall advise everyone to do the same. We all fuss too much.'

'Really, Alex,' said Julia and was staggered, 'what has come over you? I don't think you are being very polite, are you?'

'When is he ever?' said Miss Crevy.

'Yes,' he said, quickly recovering himself, 'like the cornet player said at the Salvation Army meeting, "I'll give you one more 'oly 'oly 'oly and then I'm off 'ome."'

They did not know what to make of this so Max said 'Good for you, Alex,' and Amabel said to him, 'Darling, tell me something very nice.' At this Alex smiled, sat on the arm of her chair and turned round to look into her face. She smiled sideways at him and as always when she smiled so far as he was concerned it was so brilliant it made him shy. She then reached out and with one long vermilion finger-nail she began to scratch gently at one of his knuckles, for she liked making him shy, he who was not supposed to care about girls. He thought how much cleaner her wrist was than his hand it lay across and how much stronger it looked than you would expect, but then of course she was probably extremely powerful and he always had thought women were more powerful than men. And so, as she scratched gently she began to gain power over him and he felt himself slipping away she did it so well, just right, so that if he had been her pussy cat he would have purred. He was going to shut down his eyes and give himself over to sleep, it was stretching up over him from his hand when he lazily thought he must look ridiculous and this at once went through him as if he was being rung up so that he hung up on her, drawing away out of reach. For two minutes she went on gently scratching at the chair arm. It was embarrassment on his part, he was afraid he would be made to look foolish and she knew this very well. She went on smiling at him without any change of expression and still sideways, almost as though what she had begun with him she had put over on herself as well.

The others went on talking, Max was quite forthcoming now, and as no one paid them any attention he thought what a pity, and this was what she meant him to feel, why if he was left on a desert island with this girl he would only count what nuts there might be on those spreading awkward palms for fear monkeys should see him. Not looking at her he put his hand out again and having won she laughed and only patted it once and then turned to those others again. He laughed and said:

'I missed my chance.'

She turned back to him for an instant and he saw from her eyes she was not bothering any more about him. When she did not smile her eyes were not so blue but now she smiled, patted him once again, and finally left him though he had only to stretch out to take hold of her dressing-gown and she was wearing nothing underneath.

'I always do,' he said, but she did not come back so he tried one last time, 'miss my chance,' he said, but it was no good and he gave up trying. He did not see that she had kept him with them, not knowing whether he really meant to go home. Her purpose was to keep them round her to show herself off in front of Max.

'No,' Max was saying, 'particularly now that Claire has her aunt down with something I don't see how we can go home. No need for you others to stay, of course; and for the matter of that there's nothing to be done about her, is there? But I ought to stay.'

'But, Max,' said Julia, 'as Evelyn said while we were outside, it's all very well talking of going home, but they won't keep the train waiting when they do send it off just for us to come and catch it. If anyone goes they'll miss it.'

'I'm sorry, everybody, it was my idea about waiting at home,' Alex said, 'but I was in a filthy mood. I didn't mean it.'

'What I mean is,' said Max, 'I could have you rung up if you all went back to my flat. They would let me know when they were going to send our train off in time to get you here.' And as he said this he was well aware that Julia's uncle was a director of this line but he liked better to make out they would do all this for him. However, Julia agreed with Evelyn, and felt so strongly about it she almost made a scene. She said if they once left they would never get back again and she described how much thicker it was the way she had come than it really had been and made so much fuss they had to give in largely out of a loyalty all felt to her moods, all that is except Miss Crevy. When she had had her way she said why didn't they get Claire and Evelyn to leave Miss Fellowes and come along to join them, surely they could risk that, she could not be so bad those old nannies could not see to her. Max approved of this and went to fetch them.

'Will anyone have a drink?' said Alex, 'I fancy it would do us all some good,' but no one answered and now that Max was no longer with them Angela and Julia had nothing to say, nor had Amabel. He wondered how often this had happened to him before and marvelled again that anyone should be so run after as Max, though never so run after in such an awful room before. Places alter circumstances, he thought, and there was little amusing in being ignored in these surroundings, armchairs that were too deep with too narrow backs and covered in modified plush, that is plush with the pile shaved off so that those chairs were to him like so many clean-shaven port drinkers.

Clean-shaven port drinkers enough, he went on, mixing his drink, one for each girl, that is three chairs but only Amabel sitting on those gouty knees, that sodden lap; and then public house lace curtains to guard them in from fog and how many naked bodies on sentry go underneath adequately, inadequately dressed. Here he pointed his moral. That is what it is to be rich, he thought, if you are held up, if you have to wait then you can do it after a bath in your dressing-gown and if you have to die then not as any bird tumbling dead from its branch down for the foxes, light and stiff, but here in bed, here inside, with doctors to tell you it is all right and with relations to ask if it hurts. Again no standing, no being pressed together, no worry since it did not matter if one went or stayed, no fellow feeling, true, and once more sounds came up from outside to make him think they were singing, no community singing he said to himself, not that even if it did mean fellow feeling. And in this room, as always, it seemed to him there was a sort of bond between the sexes and with these people no more than that, only dull antagonism otherwise. But not in this room he said to himself again, not with that awful central light, that desk at which no one had ever done more than pay bills or write their dentist, no, no, not here, not thus. Never again, he swore, but not aloud, never again in this world because it was too boring and he had done it so many times before.

It was all the fault of these girls. It had been such fun in old days when they had just gone and no one had minded what happened. They had been there to enjoy themselves and they had been friends but if you were girls and went on a party then it seemed to him you thought only of how you were doing, of how much it looked to others you were enjoying yourself and worse than that of how much

493

whoever might be with you could give you reasons for enjoying it. Or, in other words, you competed with each other in how well you were doing well and doing well was getting off with the rich man in the party. Whoever he might be such treatment was bad for him. Max was not what he had been. No one could have people fighting over him and stay himself. It was not Amabel's fault, she was all right even if she did use him, it was these desperate inexperienced bitches, he thought, who never banded together but fought everyone and themselves and were like camels, they could go on for days without one sup of encouragement. Under their humps they had tanks of self-confidence so that they could cross any desert area of arid prickly pear without one compliment, or dewdrop as they called it in his family, to uphold them. So bad for the desert, he said to himself, developing his argument and this made him laugh aloud.

'What are you laughing about?' said Julia, who felt out of whatever Max was doing with himself outside.

'Oh, nothing,' he said.

'I do hate people who go away, darling,' she said to Amabel, 'not physically I mean,' she said, catching herself up, 'but when they are in a room and then they go and leave one.' But while Amabel had been ready to take this up where Max was concerned, Alex did not exist for her any more and her answer was to send him for her nail things with another smile just as brilliantly blue as when she had been thinking of him. And now, when for the moment he was gone, silence fell over them with lifeless wings.

While he was away, which was not for long, no one spoke. Amabel looked at her nails from which she was going to take one coloured varnish to put on another. Julia fidgeted with the cuff of what she was wearing and Miss Crevy examined her face in a mirror out of her bag like any jeweller with a precious stone, and it was indeed without price, but it had its ticket and this had Marriage written on it.

When he came back and gave Amabel what she wanted he was struck again by how glum they seemed. He said into their silence, 'and to think this is supposed to be the happiest time of our lives.' Julia did not understand. 'Why now exactly?' she said from far away. 'Well, we're young,' he said, 'we'll never be young again you see.' 'Why aren't you happy then?' she said, as though she was on an ivory tower. 'That's not the point,' said he, his eyes on Amabel, 'but I'm so bored.' 'Aren't we all?' she said and because she thought this sort of conversation silly Miss Crevy broke in by asking Amabel what kind of nail polish she used. Already the acetone she had filled this room with its smell of peardrops like a terrible desert blossom. He coughed, it stifled him.

'I was wondering if I wouldn't make them darker,' she said, 'like the sloe gin Max gives me out shooting.'

'What's that?' said Angela.

'It's more like port, isn't it?' Julia said to show she had been out with him too. 'Oh, do you remember?' she asked, though as she did it now it was almost automatic as though it was her part she had to play to evoke good times, alone, on top of this ivory tower with his dreaming world beneath, sleeping beauty, all of them folded so she imagined into their thoughts of him. 'Amabel,' she said, 'd'you remember that time it was corked?' But she said it so low, so quietly this time that no one followed her. Memory is a winding lane and as she went up it, waving them to follow, the first bend in it hid her from them and she was left to pick her flowers alone.

Memory is a winding lane with high banks on which flowers grow and here she wandered in a nostalgic summer evening in deep soundlessness.

Angela went back to her mirror and began touching the tips of her eyelashes with her fingers' ends. Alex picked up a newspaper and behind it picked his nose.

Night was coming up and it came out of the sea. Over harbours, up the river, by factories, bringing lights in windows and lamps on the streets until it met this fog where it lay and poured more darkness in.

Fog burdened with night began to roll into this station striking cold through thin leather up into their feet where in thousands they stood and waited. Coils of it reached down like women's long hair reached down and caught their throats and veiled here and there what they could see, like lovers' glances. A hundred cold suns switched on above found out these coils where, before the night joined in, they had been smudges and looking up at two of them above was like she was looking down at you from under long strands hanging down from her forehead only that light was cold and these curls tore at your lungs.

It was not comfortable and there were signs that this long wait was beginning to fray tempers. At first there had been patient jokes and then some community singing but nice as these had been and as everyone had felt in taking all this nicely, it was beginning to wear thin until only those who were getting off with girls could say they were enjoying themselves. They searched round and about picking and choosing. 'I hope you don't mind my speaking to you,' they would say or 'I don't know when we shall get back, do you?' or 'I say this is very unconventional my speaking to you like this,' although they had wifey and the couple of kids at home. These girls, and many of them had been chosen for their looks where they worked, were so sick and tired, and this kind of approach was so much more reason for tiredness, they turned away with no words to answer them, disgusted.

There was nothing wonderful or strange in what they saw. For any of these people, night ended once a night and was only remembered by some of them for a person the moon that certain night had shone on in their arms, those loving arms. And when fog was joined to night who was there to dream of that cruel oblivion of sight it made when they had in mind chintz curtains waiting to be drawn across shut windows.

Again, being in it, how was it possible for them to view themselves as part of that vast assembly for even when they had tried singing they had only heard those next them; it was impossible to tell if all had joined except when, perhaps at the end of a verse, one section made themselves heard as they were late and had not yet finished. Then everyone knew everyone was singing but this feeling did not last and soon they did not agree about songs, that section would be going on while another sang one of their own. Then no one sang at all.

So crowded together they were beginning to be pressed against each other, so close that every breath had been inside another past that lipstick or those cracked lips, those even teeth, loose dentures, down into other lungs, so weary, so desolate and cold it silenced them.

Then one section had begun to chant 'we want our train' over and over again and at first everyone had laughed and joined in and then had failed, there were no trains. And so, having tried everything, desolation overtook them.

They were like ruins in the wet, places that is where life has been, palaces, abbeys, cathedrals, throne rooms, pantries, cast aside and tumbled down with no immediate life and with what used to be in them lost rather than hidden now the roof has fallen in. Ruins that is not of their suburban homes for they had hearts, and feelings to dream, and hearts to make up what they did not like into other things. But ruins, for life in such circumstances was only possible because it would not last, only endurable because it had broken down and as it lasted and became more desolate and wet so, as it seemed more likely to be permanent, at least for an evening, they grew restive.

Where ruins lie, masses of stone grown over with ivy unidentifiable with the mortar fallen away so that stone lies on stone loose and propped up or crumbling down in mass then as a wind starts up at dusk and stirs the ivy leaves and rain follows slanting down, so deserted no living thing seeks what little shelter there may be, it is all brought so low, then movements of impatience began to flow across all these people and as ivy leaves turn one way in the wind they themselves surged a little here and there in their blind search behind bowler hats and hats for trains.

But at one point no movement showed where, like any churchyard, gravestone luggage waited with mourners, its servants and owners, squatted in between. Here Thomson, still without his tea, had not forgotten yet that kiss she had blessed him with and went rambling on, both aloud and in his mind, how he could not bear that she had been called away. Every now and again he would get up to look over the monuments about, but she was no longer with those other mourners who glared back at him for intruding on their lives in the little rooms their luggage made them. Indeed one old lady had gone so far as to get her 'Primus' out and was making tea as though playing at Indians in second childhood and Thomson was telling Edwards he was sure this was his girl's party and how if that old creature had not been there he might have had his tea and kisses too. Edwards asked him to beware, saying so much imagination must be bad for anyone, let alone somebody as crazy as he seemed to be.

'Only crazy for what I haven't got,' he said, 'like any drowning, starving man.'

'Drowning are you now? I'd have sworn you was like any little schoolboy with his first sweetheart, his pretty honeypot.'

'All right, but it's natural, isn't it, same as it is to want a cup of tea.' He went on that if someone were to come now and offer him half a dollar for this luggage he would accept if it did mean his job, or he would for a cup of tea even. Edwards said now he was back harping on it, 'your jew's harp,' he went on, straining his fancy, 'always wanting more than what you have.'

But Thomson's trouble was sex. He could not hold that kiss she had given him as it might be an apple in his hand to turn over while he made up his mind to bite, he was like any starving creature who wanted one more apple and this made him restless. And this was why, though he did not know it, he went on about his tea. He always had a cup of tea if his mind ran for too long on girls, that is when he had no girl ready to his hand.

'It's not my tea so much,' he said, expressing this.

'You want the moon,' said Edwards.

Meantime Robert Hignam's man, who had so frightened Julia, was making his way from one grieving mourner to another or, as they sat abandoned, cast away each by his headstone, they were like the dead resurrected in their clothes under this cold veiled light and in an antiseptic air. He dodged about asking any man he saw if he was Miss Julia Wray's, so much as to say, 'I be the grave-digger, would I bury you again?'

When he found Thomson he tried to persuade him to hand the luggage over so that he could get it into the hotel because he wanted to be clever and do more than Robert had required. Thomson asked who had sent him and when he heard it was Hignam he said he could not take orders from any but Miss Wray. Edwards said who was he anyway, he might be Arsene Lupin easy, and what did he take them for?

'Well, as you might say, the orders did come from that young lady.'

'Tell us,' said Thomson and Edwards could not understand how he could go on talking with this man who might be anybody, 'what's going on in there?' he said, nodding over to where they were sitting quarrelling up above behind lace curtains.

'She's a goner.'

'Who's a goner?'

'Why that young lady's aunt.'

'Don't talk so silly,' Edwards said.

'As sure as I'm here,' he answered.

'Have you seen her?'

'Of course I've seen her,' he said, speaking in educated tones again. 'She was taken bad in the buffet and they had to carry her upstairs.'

'And what about a doctor?'

'Ah,' he said, 'they've had the doctor to her, but he's no doctor, I've not been around all these years without I know about that hotel doctor. He's killed any number of them,' he said, 'when they've been carried in,' and as he talked of death his speech relapsed into some dialect of his own, 'any bloody number of 'em,' he went on, 'as've been took bad on the bloody Continent and 'ave said well if they were going to be sick they'd be sick in their own native land and so left it too late, appendicitis and all,' he said.

'Not bloody likely,' said Edwards, any talk of death making him swear.

'It's the bloody truth.'

'Well then,' said Edwards, 'if anything was to come to her, it's unpack for you and me, my lad,' he said to Thomson.

At this a huge wild roar broke from the crowd. They were beginning to adjust that board indicating times of trains which had stood all of two hours behind where it had reached when first the fog came down.

'Wild animals,' Edwards said.

'Won't do her any good,' said Hignam's man.

'Well, that's a shocking thing,' Thomson said, 'if anything were to happen to Miss Fellowes, why my young lady wouldn't half take on, you know, soft 'earted.'

'Death's a bloody awful thing,' said Edwards, 'but it isn't as easy as all that, it takes time to die. She couldn't have been well enough to come all that way here if she was going to die this minute. Depend upon it she's all right, or will be.'

'Well,' said Thomson, 'I reckon if what he says is right it will put paid to this party, they'll all be off 'ome and we'll get no thanks for it.'

Edwards remarked Miss Fellowes had been acting very extra-ordinary before, very extraordinary, but that did not mean anything except she had come over queer.

'And shall I take these things?' this strange man said.

'Where's a copper?'

'Who are you talking to, young feller?'

'Go on and get off,' said Edwards, 'we've had enough of you and now you've bloody well upset me with your talk. Who'd you think is going to give you his luggage, now get on, go off.'

He went and Thomson said some people did have strange ideas. Now who would imagine he would try to go through all that mob with valuable luggage, just so as Miss Julia could see it was still there, when she hadn't even said she wanted to. But it did seem this man knew something about them and it was rotten about Miss Fellowes. If she was ill why they'd none of them start, they'd put it off as sure as anything.

Edwards said not to be too sure, she was no relation of theirs, meaning Mr Adey's and Miss Wray's. He'd known worse happen without his gentleman turning back.

'Well, it wouldn't be right, not to start like that, not with that behind you,' said Thomson. 'And if she did die why you'd never be the same, none of them would, not for three days at all events.'

'And I thought you wanted your tea so bad you'd have given all this away for sixpence.'

'Oh, that was different,' said Thomson, meaning his Emily.

'But then would you go, you,' he went on, 'if anything of that kind was to happen?'

'No, I would not,' said Edwards, 'but then they're different.'

'It's all the old same, excuse me,' Thomson said, 'death's death, if you understand me.'

'Let's get this straight. No one except that loony said she was going to die, did they?'

'Well, it's the same if she was really bad, they'd never go.'

'Mr Adey would.'

'And my young lady wouldn't.'

'Don't you be so sure, my lad. I fancy she'd follow him all over, or she'd like to.'

'I won't speak about that if you don't mind,' said Thomson, 'I don't hold with following what anyone's after or saying this or that about them. What they do is none of my concern. No, I don't like it,' he said and probably did not know what he really meant. Anyway they both of them dropped it.

But this was what Claire was talking about with Evelyn. Max was in her bedroom with those two old nannies and they were standing in the corridor outside.

'What do you think?' Claire said to her.

'I know,' said Evelyn, 'it's very worrying isn't it?'

'What would you do?'

'I don't know.'

'You see what so upsets me is when one of them in there says, and I don't know which of the old things it was, mine or the other, did you hear it, she said "oh no, dearie, why you couldn't go now, not with your own aunt lying there." When she calls me dearie it makes me feel like a street woman. And that when the doctor said it was nothing, or anyway if it wasn't nothing that it wasn't serious. Evelyn, my dear, when anyone is as drunk as that they sleep it off, don't they, I mean they don't lie there unconscious and after all she has passed out now hasn't she, that is she lies there breathing in that awful way she's not asleep is she? I don't know, if we could get hold of another doctor he might be able to tell us something, but then I don't want to seem nasty and I hate to say it but supposing he said she was very bad, well then, it would not help her if we went or stayed, would it? Oh, can you tell me why that idiot Robert doesn't do something?'

Evelyn did not reply. Claire seemed to ponder for a moment. 'D'you think it would do any good if we tried to make her sick again?'

'Oh, no, I shouldn't.'

'Well, after all, that's what the doctor said was the matter, didn't he? But then it's so impossible, Evelyn darling, why I've known Auntie May all my life, she couldn't be like this because of that. And I couldn't tell my own nanny about what the doctor said about mother's sister, could I? You do agree, don't you?'

'Of course.'

'But then you see I can't help feeling they may be right. After all, what could that doctor know about poor Auntie May, he may have just said to himself here's another old lady who likes port too much. And we can't get her out of here, and any minute just because Julia's uncle or guardian is a director of the railway they may come and tell us we must go. D'you think I ought to stay behind and perhaps come on afterwards?'

'Well, she lives alone, doesn't she, I mean she hasn't got anybody.'

'Those nannies could look after her, they've got absolutely nothing to do, you know, they are pensioned off, mine just lives at home, at number nine I mean and drinks tea all day. Besides she nursed me through several very serious illnesses and with all that experience and being so fond of the family she would be better than any trained nurse, they never care whether you live or die.'

'You mean there's no one else to look after her.'

'No, there's absolutely no one. There's her maid and I don't know why we didn't make her come round when it first started, you remember I rang her up telling her to stay away. I can't imagine why but of course she has fits, no, absolutely everyone else is dead and mother's abroad as you know. It's rather touching, that's why she came to see us off really, it's her only link. No, but it's not touching actually because she goes and gets ill. Oh, Evelyn, it's so unfair, isn't it?'

And as she said this surprisingly she began to cry, not sobbing or that free flow out of a contorted face, but it was as though some miracle had occurred, as though tears were gently one by one rolling down graven image features which had stayed dry under cover for centuries, carved out of hard wood, so that these tears threatened to crack a polished surface it looked so unused to being wetted, only creamed.

'Oh, my dear,' said Evelyn, 'you mustn't let yourself get upset about this business and besides I think you've been perfectly wonderful about it all the way through, you've hardly left her for an instant.'

'It's not that,' she said, and she spoke as though she were not crying, her tears seemed to be quite separate from her, only a phenomenon, 'it's that I feel the whole thing is so unfair. I do know Julia is rather counting on having me with her this trip and now that Amabel has dropped out of the sky I do deeply feel I can't let her down.' This was untrue. She went on and as people will when they have just lied she began to speak out genuinely for once what she did really feel. 'What I'm so afraid of is that doctor had no idea what he was talking about, that Aunt May is very bad and that I ought to get her to hospital and I am doing nothing about it. I ought not to be here,' she said, 'but you know how it is, I thought it was just a faint and that she would come round and that after a bit of rest she would be able to go home. One thing you can be quite sure of is that she's not drunk, poor darling, she probably felt it coming over her whatever it is and took something to keep it off.' Her tears had stopped now. 'But then you see,' she went on, 'there's no way of getting her out of here though if she was really bad of course the hotel would manage it somehow you know how they are.'

'Don't.'

'Well, there's no blinking it you know, they would if they thought she was going to die.'

'Then oughtn't we to send for her maid whatever her name is?'

'Yes, if she could get in. And then she has fits.'

'Good heavens, we don't want two on our hands.'

'She probably had one when I rang up an hour ago. I don't know what to do,' she said. 'Sorry for crying,' and she began to powder her nose.

'I think what we are both afraid of,' said Evelyn, 'is that parcel she had and what was inside it. She never belonged to any societies for animals, did she? She never kept pigeons herself I mean?'

'Of course not. Besides she used to shoot.'

'You know I have absolute faith in searching out whatever it is that is really worrying one underneath what seems on the surface to be the matter with anything if you understand me, Claire, my dear. And I know in my case it was her having picked that pigeon up somewhere and then seeming so ill. She can't have bought it or she would have had it delivered, unless she got it off a barrow, but then they don't sell them on barrows. D'you see what I mean? But if she just found it dead and picked it up what did she want it for, it was so dirty? I'm sure that's what's been worrying us, but when you come to think of it, darling, there's nothing in it, is there? What is it after all? Now if it had been a goose or some other bird. No, that isn't so I don't suppose it would have been any less odd. Anyway it is definitely not a thing to worry about.'

At this moment Max came out of her room.

'She's better,' he said.

'Max, dear,' said Claire, 'you've been too sweet about it all, getting her this lovely room and everything, I don't know how to thank you, it's been too kind of you.'

'Nonsense,' he said, 'bad business. Where's Robert?'

'Oh, my dear,' she said, 'don't ask me that. Where do you suppose, in the Bar I should think.' At this Amabel appeared in a fur coat and drew him away, and as Claire hurried back in with Evelyn she said to herself how like a man to come out as if he had settled everything and made her better just by going in.

She was better, but they could not help feeling that she was improving only to get worse. She lay fretful and conscious, propped up in bed.

'Why am I here?' she said.

'Oh, Auntie May, you are ever so much better, aren't you? Now you mustn't lie there worrying, just relax?'

'Where am I?'

'Now don't bother your head about anything, you're quite all right and now you are going to have a nice long rest.'

'What happened to me?'

'You mustn't bother your head about anything like that. Nothing happened to you really, you just fainted. Now lie back and get back your strength.'

'Excuse me,' she said, and her one eye you could see looked agitated, 'no, child I never fainted, I never have.'

'Oh, Auntie May, how could you be so naughty, you'll upset yourself in a minute, do be careful after all. You've made us all quite anxious, well not that exactly,' she said, because those two old nannies had shaken their heads at this, 'but, of course, we were all distressed, shall we say you were not feeling quite the thing?' she said and went rambling on while her aunt, who had given up wondering and had given up listening and whose only feeling was of exhaustion as though she had been pounded for days, had enough strength left to know she had always disliked Claire, just as she had never got on with her mother.

When they were in that room upstairs where Julia had asked him not to muss her about, Amabel's first words were 'kiss me' and this more than anything showed the difference between these two girls, not so much in temperament as in their relations with him.

After some time she drew back and powdered her nose. He walked round and round where she was sitting as though she were a river and a bridge off which he felt impelled to jump to drown.

'Be quiet,' she said, 'sit back.'

He stood in front of her and she fixed him with her eyes which drew him like the glint a hundred feet beneath and called on him to throw himself over. He had always been drugged by heights and turned away experiencing that longing and demand to see again as they feel who want to jump when they look down. Her eyes were expressionless and brilliant.

'Darling,' she said at last, 'you didn't really mean to do that to me.'

'I was mad.'

'I thought you of all people couldn't mean it.'

'I didn't.'

'Didn't what?' she said, feeling her way.

'Mean it,' he said.

They spoke slowly in soft voices and both of them now kept entirely still.

'When you rang up I knew it wasn't you speaking somehow, you sounded different. Why do we have to be like this to each other?'

'I'm the only one,' he said, 'I was mad.'

'But why?'

'I don't know. Mad. Mad.'

'Don't go on telling me you were mad,' and here she raised her voice, 'no one's mad these days! What was it?'

'This awful weather. Felt I had to get away,' he mumbled.

'I'm sorry. But then what came between us to make you speak the way you did?'

'I don't know. I don't.'

'And you knew what my doctor said, I told you. If you didn't want me to come you'd only to say so. That's been the wonderful thing about us.'

'I did want you to.'

'We've had that pact from the very beginning, if one of us wanted to go away you could or I could without saying a word. What made you ring up like that?'

'But I swear I wanted you to come.'

'And then to lie to me like you did,' she said, even softer. 'To say just that you wouldn't come out to-night after you'd said you would. I'm not sure now what you did really say you upset me so.'

'I was in an awful state,' he said.

'Just when the doctor told me I ought to get away from this frightful weather and everything else. But all I want to do is understand. Darling, what made you do it?'

'I don't know.'

'Well, we're both of us free, we can do as we want but what did make you do it?'

'Am, darling,' he said, 'don't you think you could come along,' he said, not knowing her things were packed. 'Do, darling, now, if it isn't too much. I always meant you to come.'

'But, dear,' she said, 'what am I to believe? There's your voice over that beastly phone I wish it had never been invented, saying first that you would meet me to-night when you knew you were going and then again within twenty minutes saying you wouldn't be there.'

'The first time I didn't know whether I was going or not.'

'Didn't you? But then was it nice to invite me when you didn't know if you would turn up? Oh, Max, when you think of what our evenings have been.'

'I know.'

'I sometimes wonder if you ever have known at all.'

'I'm hopeless.'

'But why,' she said, and pulled at her handkerchief, 'if you would only tell me so I could understand.'

There was a pause. She was looking over her shoulder away from him. He had been dazed but he hated tears, he never found them genuine and as he thought she might be going to cry he spoke more sharply, taking the initiative.

'Look, darling,' he said, 'it's this way. Come away with me now. Your maid can pack and follow on by aeroplane if she doesn't catch the train. Forget what I've been and let's have our lovely times over again. Darling, couldn't we?'

'What,' she said, still looking away but not crying, 'with all these other people, whoever they are?'

'Well, it's a bit awkward about them. We could leave them somewhere. It's really Evelyn Henderson. She's a very old friend and she's terribly badly off. I fixed it so they could all go for her really, whether I went or not.'

She turned round, caught his eyes in the glare of hers and stamped.

'Don't you dare,' she said and gasped. 'Don't you dare,' she said in a small voice she was so angry, 'try and put that over on me. It's Julia Wray and I've known it all along.'

'Julia? What do you mean?'

'What do I mean? You are mad if you think I'll swallow that,' and she laughed and spoke naturally. It was when she had herself under control that she could rule him.

'There's nothing about Julia. ... I say ...' he said and could not finish. He was under her command.

'Well, we had the arrangement,' she said in her hard tone of voice, 'we're both free,' she was absolutely certain of him now, 'we can both do as we like.'

'Oh, no!'

'Yes, I know when I'm not wanted.'

'You are. You're the point of the whole trip.'

'You see I've come to know I can't trust a single thing you say. Max, my dear, you're hopeless and I don't know why I'm here. Try and think what you're saying.'

'How d'you mean?'

'Don't play the innocent. The telephone.'

'I tell you I was mad.'

'But you weren't, you'd thought it out.'

He began to think, to slip out of her control and be impatient. He showed it by not looking away when they met each other's eyes. As soon as she saw this she smiled at him. It was wonderfully done. She smiled in just the way she had done when first they became intimate, in such a way that she might have been talking to him almost under her breath when they had nothing, nothing between them.

He kissed her again. This time when she drew back she laughed.

'How much do you really want me to come?' she said.

He laughed.

'No, go on, how much, tell me, you must, how much,' she said, as Julia had about her top. He looked at her, she was radiantly smiling, and again he felt lost and given over before her moods.

He went to kiss her again and she laughed and said no, no, not before he had told her.

'You know how much,' he said and looked so expectant as to be idiotic.

'More than to go fishing,' she said, calling on another afternoon.

'Yes.'

'Even when the wind or whatever it was was just right.'

'Of course.'

'No,' she said and looked at him as though he meant everything to her, 'you remember, don't you, even if you had been waiting for whatever you have to wait for fishing even for weeks?'

'I do.'

'Do you? No, you mustn't kiss me again, I haven't nearly finished. More than Ascot week, more than going to bed or staying up and, d'you remember, on that hill when you didn't want to go home?'

'Don't.'

'Very well. What were we talking about before? Oh, blast you, why do you make me feel so sad?' she said and she made her eyes cloud over.

'Darling.'

'All right, I'm not going to be tiresome or anything like that, but I can't think what I was doing when I fell for you,' and she made way before him, making herself small.

'I do,' he said, 'because there's nobody like you.'

'Isn't there?'

'Nobody like you.'

'Is that all?' she said in her small voice. He laughed and kissed her again. This time she did not kiss him back but handed herself over.

When he found she had nothing on underneath she stopped him at once.

'No,' she said, 'hands off, I've just had my bath, I've just had my bath I tell you.'

He got up and began walking round and round where she sat again. She had so wound him up that in his feeling for her as it was now he was thrown back on his grievance.

'What were you doing last night?' he said.

'How d'you mean?'

'When I rang up.'

'Oh, then! Well, I did pop out for a moment,' she said, looking long at her face in her glass.

'Who with?'

'We went to that cocktail club round the corner.'

'Who's we?'

'No, let me finish,' she said, putting more red on her lips. Her face blushed in spots where he had kissed her. 'You've made such a mess of my face. Here, hold this,' she said and gave him her mirror. His hand shook so he was no use to her. 'Darling, you mustn't get upset about little things like that. It was only Richard and you know what he is.'

'Embassy Richard?'

'Yes.'

'Why him?'

'Why not, darling?'

'When I rang up you said Marjorie was with you.'

'No, I didn't. You said you couldn't get on to me.'

'I meant afterwards.'

'Oh, then! I didn't want to tell you, that's all.'

'It would take more than him to upset me,' he said.

'Then what's the matter with you now?' she said sweetly.

'Nothing's the matter.'

'I can't understand you these days at all. Here, give me back my mirror. What shall I do?' she said, 'it is in a mess,' tilting and turning her face from side to side.

'Well, what about it?'

'About Richard you mean? Why, nothing. By the way, he said he was coming on your train.'

'You didn't invite him by any chance?'

'How could I? I'm not coming, you know, you didn't invite me. It's absurd, I can't just get packed like that at a moment's notice.'

'Then I shan't go,' he said, turning away and going back to the window.

She did not take much notice of this. 'But, darling,' she said, 'you can't just leave them like that when you asked them.'

'I can. I've given old Evelyn the tickets. It's arranged.'

'But you can't, they're your guests. You mustn't be so independent. I won't let you. Think what they'll say.'

'I don't care.'

'Oh, yes, you do, you must care. The whole thing's absurd,' and, forgetting she had just said she was not coming, 'it's absurd,' she said, 'you say we can't go because Richard is in the hotel and travelling on the same train.'

They did not either of them notice the slip she had made.

'How d'you know?' he said, turning round.

'I don't know,' she said, looking at him, 'only he said he would be here and when he says he will be somewhere, I believe him more than when you tell me the same thing.'

'You've seen him?'

'Max, darling, don't be so ridiculous. I haven't set eyes on him since last night. He might be in Timbuctoo for all I care and anyway I don't know, darling. I must say, my dear, you don't seem very upset at my not coming.'

'If you don't come, then I don't.'

'Why must you be like this? I tell you you can't behave like that. You'll never be able to get anyone to go abroad with you again.'

'I don't care.' There was a pause. 'In any case,' he said, 'I wasn't going to go.'

'Then why did you say what you did when you rang me up the last time?'

'Because,' he said, finding it at last, 'because I saw with all this fog I might be with them for hours as the trains weren't running. I had to see them off, you know.' He came up to her smiling.

'No, keep away,' she said, 'I've got to think this out.' He's such an awful liar, she thought, but already everything seemed different. 'No, I don't believe it,' she said and began to hope.

'It's true,' he said and then she knew he was lying and did not care. All she wanted from him was something reasonable like a password which would take her along without humiliation past frontiers and into that smiling country their journey together would open in their hearts as she hoped, the promised land. Not of marriage but of any kind of happiness, not for ever but while it lasted. She knew better than to want too much of any situation and marriage she had never wanted, though often imagined, after the first three weeks. It would have been better with almost anyone else but there it was, he fascinated her and so it was for her to fascinate him.

'Well then, supposing I did,' she said.

'You really are going to come?'

'I might.'

'That's good.'

'Is that all you are going to say about it?'

'It's marvellous,' he said. They kissed again. Some little time later it was he who drew away.

'Where's Embassy Richard going?'

She lay back irritated that he had left her.

'How should I know?'

'I suppose that party business was too much for him. London's getting too hot to hold him,' he said.

'You know if I'm really going to go away with you you've got to be nice to me,' she said.

'What d'you mean?'

'No tricks with the other girls, mind, or I'll be off home again.'

'If you do,' he said, 'I'll go back with you.'

'I shan't let you.'

'I know more than to let you go off alone.'

'That's being too silly for words,' she said. 'Why did you stop kissing me like that? And anyway, how many of those others have you kissed up here this afternoon?'

'Now it's you are being ridiculous.'

'Not as I know you, my dear. Oh, well, go on then and kiss them. Who cares?'

'I don't kiss them.'

'I suppose I'm being tiresome again, darling, am I? Never mind. Let's have a rest. No, don't kiss me again, please not, give my complexion a rest. Sit down here. I'll put my head on your shoulder and have a sleep.' She yawned and settled herself down, shifted round a little, shut her eyes, breathed deeply twice and went off at once. She always could whenever she wanted.

As he sat there he realized he did not know if she was going to come or not. And if she did come out he did not know if she would stay or when she would get it into her head to start home which she might at any time. He realized without putting it into words he did not even know if he was glad she was going to come or sorry she was going to stay at home, he only knew that now she was here he would probably have to be with her wherever she made up her mind to be.

She lay on his shoulder in this ugly room, folded up with almost imperceptible breathing like seagulls settled on the water cock over gentle waves. Looking at her head and body, richer far than her rare fur coat, holding as he did to these skins which enfolded what ruled him, her arms and shoulders, everything, looking down on her face which ever since he had first seen it had been his library, his gallery, his palace, and his wooded fields he began at last to feel content and almost that he owned her.

Lying in his arms, her long eyelashes down along her cheeks, her hair tumbled and waved, her hands drifted to rest like white doves drowned on peat water, he marvelled again he should ever dream of leaving her who seemed to him then his reason for living as he made himself breathe with her breathing as he always did when she was in his arms to try and be more with her.

It was so luxurious he nodded, perhaps it was also what she had put on her hair, very likely it may have been her sleep reaching out over him, but anyway he felt so right he slipped into it too and dropped off on those outspread wings into her sleep with his, like two soft evenings meeting.

They slept and then a huge wild roar broke from the crowd outside. They were beginning to adjust that board indicating times of trains which had stood all of two hours behind where it had reached when first the fog came down. This woke him so that he started and this in turn woke her.

Like someone who is lost she did not know where she had been and in the same way neither of them knew how long they had been asleep so that when, after stretching and asking him where she might be, she found she was in this hotel she thought they had slept much longer than they had. She told him they must get down to join the others. She laughed. 'They would never believe if we told them we had been asleep wrapped up in our clothes like babes in the wood,' she said.

He wondered what it would be like to have Julia here in his arms to sleep on his shoulder for if he had only slept five minutes it was as though he had travelled miles. His sleep had made him forget the urgency of what Amabel had been.

'Yes,' he said, 'we've got to go.'

'What's the hurry?' she said, noticing at once how he had changed, 'they've waited all this time they can wait a bit longer.'

But now he had become silent again and paid no attention to her. He smoothed down his clothes and straightened his tie while she lay back watching him. When he was done he came up to her politely smiling, took hold of her wrists and pulled her up. He did not kiss her, even when her coat fell open.

'There are times I hate you,' she said.

Alex had been left alone again with Miss Crevy when Amabel had changed into her fur coat to lie in wait for Max to take him off upstairs. If all this delay had tried the crowd beneath he now found it intolerable and he suspected she was doing no more than bide her time until Max should come back to take a look at her again. He found that when Max was not there to look she lost interest and would hardly bother to answer him when he complained of how he felt. And when people paid no attention to his feelings this made him talk of these the more, so much so it was like a man whose hand trembles trying to pour red wine into a jug, he misses it and that wine falling on the table, shows red no more but is like water.

Pouring himself out as he did then, and faster because he was missing and more wildly he was so upset her jug was dry he got to such a pitch he stopped, humiliated, and wondered if she had even noticed, if he had even splashed some in. She gave no sign so that when Claire and Evelyn came back he began at once on them but this time he went further, he emptied all he had at once, and then more than he really had in mind. He tried to make Claire agree to give up the idea of going at any rate for today and, aiming better this time, went for her through her aunt.

'I must say, darling,' he said, 'I don't see very well how you can leave her even if she is much better as you say.'

'I'm not the only one to say so,' she explained, 'Evelyn, you thought her ever so much better, didn't you, darling?'

'Really she's almost all right to look after herself. As a matter of fact' Evelyn said, and here she knew she was lying, 'you said didn't you, darling, that you thought it silly of thinking to stay behind for her.' Now Miss Henderson had never said this. It was true she had nearly said it. It was true she very much wanted to go today and that she was afraid if Claire had to stay that she would make her stay with her to have company when she was able to travel. You could make Robert Hignam do some things, he would carry messages, but they knew he would never stay behind because his wife had to. But Evelyn had never actually said it, at least she did not

513

think she had because she had been too conscientious, too genuinely sorry for Miss Fellowes. Now Claire held the cup out for her to drink it was too much and she said 'Yes, darling.'

'Well, you know best,' he said, 'though I must say this, I'd think twice myself of leaving her to the tender mercies of those two old ghouls. And anyway, her companion or her nurse, or whatever she is, has fits, hasn't she?'

'My dear, what on earth has that to do with it?'

'Nothing I know. I remember calling on her once, I can't imagine why, and she practically had one on the doormat in front of me. I was just drawing a deep breath to scream for help when your aunt came out and whisked her away.'

'How awkward for you,' Miss Crevy said.

'Yes, wasn't it? But you see what I feel about all this is that it's too insane to stay here and the only thing to do is to go back home, unpack all over again and forget until to-morrow morning that we ever thought of going abroad to-day.'

'But, good heavens!' Evelyna said, 'what about the tickets?'

'Well, if Max wants us to come he can send us some more. We might just as well face it,' he said, 'we shall never see either of them again this evening, they're making whatever it is up upstairs and it will take hours. It's hopeless now, I know it is. And then half the suburbs are stranded down below. As things are now and with the government we have to-day, don't laugh, it's a serious thing, they are bound to evacuate them before they run our boat train.'

'Alex,' said Evelyn, 'you're being absurd.'

'But are you comfortable here?' he said, 'have you ever in your life known such a frightful afternoon? We ought to be at Calais by now you know. And by the way, where's Julia?'

'She's upstairs with Max, isn't she?' said Miss Crevy.

'No,' she said, 'Amabel's with him.'

'Well, couldn't they both be there?'

'Not possibly,' he said.

'Well, all I know is Am went in there,' she said, pointing to that bedroom door, 'and I know she's still there.'

'She went in to change into her fur coat and then they both went up. Evelyn and I saw them,' said Claire. 'I don't know where Julia can have got to.'

'I don't care where anyone is,' Alex said, 'what I want is to go home.'

'Then why don't you go?' Miss Crevy said.

'I can't, can I? Here are all you girls with no one to look after you, Robert is always in the bar; I can't possibly go,' he said, and smiled, amused. 'What would you do without me?'

'Really, Alex,' Claire said, 'you must be more careful. Why are you in such a state? And that's no reason for you to be rude.'

'I'm sorry if I was, but don't you see there's no point in just one of us having enough and going off, we want to make a gesture and all go home and enjoy ourselves for a bit after the frightful time we've had.'

Miss Crevy said: 'You mean no one would miss you if you went alone.'

'If you like, if you like,' said he. 'No, what I want is that we should make a demonstration.'

'And what's the use of that?' Miss Henderson said, and turning out an enormous handbag she began counting over their tickets and reservations.

'You've got the tickets?' he said. 'Why didn't you tell me? Why then the whole thing's simple, all we've got to do is to take them with us wherever we go to have a party, because we must have one to make up for all this, and make them come to us instead of waiting endlessly for them.'

'I can't do it,' said Claire. 'I couldn't go away and leave my poor Auntie May.'

'Really, Claire, that's fabulous,' he said. 'First you want to leave her behind when she's got no one but you and a maid who has fits, and then when it's a question of our all dropping her home you say you couldn't leave her.'

'Alex, you're being impossible, darling.'

'No, but why not do as I say and we'll all take her back.'

'She's too ill to be moved,' Miss Henderson said.

'Well, then leave her here then as you said at first. I take back what I said about those two old ghouls though they do sit like vultures round the dying—'

'Alex!'

'All right, I'm sorry—'

'No, Alex, it's not enough.'

'All right—'

'Not enough to just say you're sorry every time.'

'Well then,' he said, raising his voice. 'What do you want to do?'

'Where is Robert?' said Claire.

'What we want is,' said Miss Crevy, 'is for you to leave us alone.'

'Even so you can't want to stay here.'

'I don't know why not.'

'Oh come on,' he said to Claire, 'it's a bad business all round, but don't let's suffer it in silence or in this sort of discomfort.'

'I'm sorry, Alex, but I can't do anything.'

'Evelyn,' he said, about to appeal to Miss Henderson when Julia came in looking rather mad.

'My dears,' she said panting, 'they've broken in below, isn't it too awful?'

Alex laughed. 'It would be too late,' he said. Everyone else asked questions together.

'Why, all those people outside, of course,' said Julia, 'and they're all drunk, naturally. But what are we to do?'

'Who told you?'

'That man your Robert sent to find Thomson, Claire.'

'Oh, my dear, I shouldn't believe anything he said.'

'No, well he did seem rather odd about it and there you are. But what are we to do? Where's Max? Someone ought to tell him. Oh, what are we to do?'

'Now, Julia,' Alex said, 'there's nothing to get all worked up about—'

'No, darling, there really isn't,' said Claire, and he went on:

'There's nothing to do, they won't come and kill us in our beds because we aren't in bed.'

She turned away and stamped her foot at this, and Evelyn said: 'Now, Alex—'

'No, seriously,' he said, 'they'll stay down by the bar if any have got in and they'll be got out of it in no time.'

'Oh, but then they'll come up here and be dirty and violent,' and she hung her handkerchief over her lips and spoke through it like she was talking into the next room through a curtain. 'They'll probably try and kiss us or something.'

'I'd like to see them try,' said Miss Crevy.

'Now, Julia,' Alex said, 'you aren't in Marseilles or Singapore. You know an English crowd is the best behaved in the world. You'll be quite all right here.'

She turned round. She was beside herself.

'Where's Max?' she said. 'I must see him.'

'And where's Robert?' Claire said, afraid for Julia.

'Max is upstairs with Amabel, darling.'

'Oh no, Alex, how revolting,' she said, and gave herself away. She blushed with rage. 'You mean to say she's taken him upstairs just when this has happened.'

'Oh, Julia my dear, do listen to me,' Alex said. 'Don't let it all run away with you.'

'I don't know what you mean,' she said, and became quiet with anger.

'It's this,' he said, changing his ground. 'Please don't think these people are violent or anything, because they aren't.'

'And how d'you know?'

'Because they never are, they never have been in hundreds of years. Besides, if they have broken in as you say, well here we are inside and we can't hear a word. I mean, if they were breaking in down below we should hear shouts and everything. Robert would have come up to warn us. Really, you know, I don't think it can have happened. What I do say is it all proves we should never have stayed when we saw how bad this fog was.' He spoke to them all. 'That's all I've been getting at,' he said, 'and anyway it's obvious we can't get out now if we wanted to.'

'Oh, why not?' said Julia.

'But, darling,' Evelyn said, 'for the very reason that all these people haven't got in, because it is all so locked up that not a soul can get in or out.'

'Then how did that horrible man do it when Robert sent him to get hold of Thomson?'

'He's the house detective.'

'No, he isn't,' said Miss Crevy.

'And how d'you know?' he said.

'I don't,' said she, 'but there aren't any in this country.'

'You go into a young man's room in any English hotel and you'll soon see.'

'Don't be so personal, Alex. Really, what we've had to put up

517

with from you this afternoon,' Claire said, 'and coming on top of everything else, it's too much.'

'Look what we've all had to put up with,' he said. 'Oh, don't let's squabble.'

'You mean to say,' said Claire, 'you don't think there's any chance of getting my Auntie May out of here any more? But then what's to happen to her if she has a turn for the worse? Oh, where is that idiotic Robert? Look here, Alex, I wonder if you would mind so terribly going down and bringing him back up here, you'll know where to find him, and he's simply got to do something about my aunt. Really, I've done enough, haven't I, Evelyn? Would you mind, Alex?'

'No,' he said, 'of course not, it's a good idea,' and hurried out.

Claire began to explain him away to Miss Crevy. 'I'm afraid you'll think him very odd, but he's had such a miserable time at home for so many years that we're all used to his being extra-ordinary so that doesn't surprise us a bit now, does it, darling?' she said to Julia to try and stop her thinking about herself. 'Yes,' she went on, 'his mother died when he was ten and he was simply devoted to her,' and here she began to speak like the older woman she was to become, 'and then his father went mad and it took a long time or something, anyway it was absolutely exhausting whatever it was, and he has to go down and see him once every month wherever it is he's locked away. Then he has a sister that no one in the world has ever seen; she's got something the matter with her, too, and he's got very little money and he's perfectly marvellous about it, always paying out for them all the whole time, so that a trip like this means so much to him.'

Miss Crevy was touched. 'I didn't know,' she said.

'Yes, so we all make rather special allowances for him,' she went on, 'don't we, darling?' she said to Julia. 'It's all so miserable for him really, he hasn't had a chance.'

'Why did we let him go? We'll never get him back.'

'Now, Julia, do be a dear and don't fuss.'

'But I am fussing. I'm fussing madly about my things. They'll run through my trunks and steal everything, and you know I can't travel without my charms.'

'Well then my dear,' said Evelyn Henderson, 'what would you like to do? Do you want to go or stay? You can't very well get out there and sit on your bags in all that crowd, and besides you would get so cold. Now settle down, darling, and wait till Alex comes back with Robert.'

'Oh, I know,' she said. 'I know I'm being tiresome, but I can't help it, you see, things get too much for me, and it's so unfair of Max, who ought to be arranging everything for us, going away like this just when we want him most. That's why it suddenly seemed so fatal to let Alex go, we must have a man about in case those sorts of things happen.'

'That's why I sent for Robert,' said Claire. 'I don't want to say anything behind his back that I wouldn't say to his face, but you know, Alex has been through so much and he's not one of those people who are made more useful by having had frightful things happen to them. In fact it always seems to me to have made him most frightfully selfish, as if after all those awful things he could only think of his own comfort.'

'Yes, that's very true,' said Evelyn.

'You know I think people so often go like that,' Claire went on, 'not that men are much use anyway, my God, no. Who is it has to get the cook out of the house when she's drunk, may I ask? But you have to have them around,' she said to Julia, 'but at the same time I don't count Alex as one of them, he's been through too much till somehow he's got nothing left.'

Angela said it must have been rather awful for him, but perhaps he was one of those people who never had very much to start with.

'Oh, no,' said Claire, too briskly, 'he's a dear and a very great friend of mine. In many ways you can absolutely rely on him; no, I can't really have a word against Alex. I know he complains, but he never really bothers one if you get what I mean. He's not much use at a time like this, but then who would be with us stuck the way we are, and my aunt in the condition she's in. Evelyn, my dear, don't you think we ought to go back to see how she's getting on, though sometimes I feel as though we bring back luck with us every time we go into that room. What d'you say?'

'Shall I go?' said Evelyn.

'Oh no, darling, I can't leave you to do all my duties. It's sweet of you,' she said, and they went out together.

Julia thought how selfish everyone is, they go on bothering about their aunts and don't give one thought to how others are feeling.

They were all the same, but Max was the worst, it was too low to be making love upstairs in the same room he had tried to pounce on her when they all wanted him and when there were thousands of things waiting which only he could settle. At this Miss Crevy, whom Julia was always forgetting as though she did not properly exist, spoke up and said:

'Would you like me to come down with you to see if we can do anything about your things?'

This seemed to Julia the sweetest thing she had ever heard, to offer to brave those frantic drinking hordes of awful people all because someone was upset about their charms and all the more because this angelic angel could not know about them or what they meant to her or about her and how miserable she got. She was made better at once for, like delicate plants must be watered every so often so Julia must have sympathy every now and then, as Alex must have someone to listen to him, and once she had it was all right for another little while. So Julia refused but so warmly Miss Crevy was surprised into thinking she could only be engaged to Max who, she now realized, must be upstairs with Amabel.

It was at this moment that Max came in with Amabel, so that Julia knew she would almost at once forget about her charms now he was back, and all her worries.

When he was in the room she could even stand apart and watch herself, she grew so confident. She thought he looked terrific, but when she had taken in Amabel's new looks and her brilliant eyes, she thought she was most like a cat that has just had its mouse coming among other cats who had only had the smell.

He was why she changed so she would forget what she had been six minutes back, he it was who nagged at her feelings when he was not there, and when he came in again worked her up so she had soon to go out though not for long, it was his fault, but then she knew it to be hers for being like she was about him, oh, who would be this kind of a girl, she thought.

Before anyone had spoken the telephone rang and while Max said 'what's this,' and went to answer it, Amabel arranged herself where she had been sitting before.

'Yes,' he said into it, 'yes, she's here. No, shall I take a message?' and he turned to look at Julia, so that she knew they were ringing her up. She went across to be at hand. 'You mean now?' he asked. 'I see. You understand this is my party, mind,' he said, 'it is Mr Adey speaking. Yes, we'll be ready,' and he rang off.

He put his arm through Julia's and pressed his elbow tight against it and this to her was as though he knew everything and that he was sorry for anything he might have done and that anyway it was all right. It was like sugar and water fed to plants in a last emergency and was what she had been ordered. 'Well,' he said, as though it was as easy as anything, 'we've got to get ready to go, they've just rung me up.'

I can't bear it, Julia said to herself, it's too wonderful, it's too much. If we go now everything will come right, but if only we go now this instant minute, it must be at once, oh, please.

Angela said 'goody' and Julia thought of a difficulty. 'But how on earth?' she cried and he said gently, 'by the lift.' Amabel sat on as though she had not heard as people do who know it will all be the same wherever they may be and who have maids to look after them.

'Oh, you don't understand,' said Julia off her balance and wildly excited, 'you can't, no one can go, they've broken in below you see, d'you mean they really want us to be off?'

'I say,' Angela said, 'my luggage is in the cloakroom.'

Max said he would see to that and Julia began. She rambled, not pronouncing what she was saying very well and looking sideways at the carpet while she now pressed his arm hard with hers. She wanted to know what she was to do about Thomson and when their train would go, did she have time to get ready, and again how would they get out as Max had not heard about the crowds that had broken in and hadn't they better ring her uncle up to find out if it was safe? Max took no notice of her except he said once he would look after it and gradually Julia began to run down and as she did so happiness came back to her, budding out of her fingers and her cheeks and hair like new landscapes open with a change of season after frost. She felt she was living again and with that feeling she wondered if she had not been rather ridiculous perhaps. She said Evelyn and Claire ought to be told and with that she suddenly left them and ran out, and looking back in through the door she said, 'but we haven't to go just at once, have we?' and then was gone again.

Radiantly happy she rushed into that room Miss Fellowes lay in and thinking that she would be unconscious, burst out saying, 'children we are to go, they've telephoned to say it's all over, isn't it wonderful and we're to get ready, darlings, just think.'

But Miss Fellowes, who was sitting up in bed, took this to mean that they were at last ready to remove her.

'My dear,' she said, 'I'm very glad to hear it, I feel I've been here long enough, though Claire will insist on saying I ought to stay the night.'

Julia had not seen Miss Fellowes when she came in so that it was a shock to hear her voice and more than a shock to see her propped up in bed exhausted. She looked as if she had been travelling.

Julia had never thought of her as being old. She had been brought up with Claire and so had always known Miss Fellowes who had in consequence seemed ageless to her in that her appearance had not altered much in all those years. And now she saw her all at once as very old and for the last time that day she heard the authentic threatening knock of doom she listened for so much when things were not going right. But it was impossible for anything to upset her now they were really going.

'Why, Auntie Fellowes,' she said, 'I never saw you and there you are sitting up in bed. Why you see,' she rushed on, 'it's for us, our train is going to run after all, isn't it wonderful?'

'Darling,' said Claire, 'I was telling Auntie May she really must be good and stay here for a while, at least until she gets her strength.'

'But I feel quite well now, Claire, quite well.'

'You must be careful, darling, really.'

'Now, darling Aunt Fellowes,' Julia said, 'you mustn't get in a fuss.'

She was about to say she was in no fuss and that all she asked, and it was reasonable enough, was to be allowed to get better in the comforts of her home, when she realized it would be better to let them think they were having their own way like Daisy had when they put her in that asylum. She had kept on telling them how glad she was to be there until they had pronounced her sane and let her go. She could remember now Daisy saying they would have put her in the strait-jacket if she had resisted, so she determined to say nothing but unfortunately she was so weak she began to cry. She began to shake also. Claire kissed her and said she was to rest and not to worry and took those other two girls out with her again.

They stood outside in the corridor and Julia, who was unaffected, she was so excited at their going away, said she was sorry, she had no idea she would be able to hear anything, she had thought she would still be unconscious.

'Well, it was rather a pity, darling,' Claire said, 'and just when I was telling her we could not move her out or get her doctor in.'

'She's ill,' Julia said, 'and she'll just have to get used to the idea. When one's ill one's ill and there's an end of it, one has to stay there till one gets better.'

'I was thinking,' Claire said, 'you know I don't think I can come, not now anyway, I can't leave her like that. I'd never forgive myself if anything happened to her.'

'Darling, you can't speak like that,' said Julia quite serene. 'If you don't come then I won't either, I couldn't go without you when our party's in the state it's in.' She spoke gaily, certain that Claire did not mean what she said.

'But, my dear, Max would never forgive me if I was the cause of your not going just because I had an aunt who was taken ill on the platform. My dear, he'd never speak to me again. She's been enough nuisance to him already, you can't mean to say you'd let her break the whole thing up.'

'Well, if you don't go, I won't.'

'But look, I shall be coming on in a few days, to-morrow probably.'

'No, Claire my dear, no Claire no Julia. Besides,' she said, more serious, 'you know what the doctor said, there's nothing really the matter with her, is there? Why don't you let her go home if that is what she really wants?'

'Why here's that idiotic Robert,' Claire said. As he came up to them foolishly smiling, she said:

'Have you been drinking?'

'Yes.'

'Are you drunk?'

'No, of course I'm not.'

'There's no of course about it as I know you,' she said, examining him.

Julia explained. 'It's too awful, Robert dear,' she said. 'I've gone and upset your aunt. You see the great news is that we've been told to get ready to go at last and I rushed into her room and told them

523

and she thought it was meant for her and was so disappointed when Claire told her she couldn't be moved yet, poor darling,' she said cheerfully.

'What are we to do about her?' Claire said to Robert.

'I don't know.'

'Then why don't you know?' Claire was always much harder on him when others were present. When they were alone she was another person and knowing this made her easier for him to bear.

'She's not my aunt,' he said and laughed.

'She is, aren't we married? Oh, now my darlings, you see what I have to put up with.'

'Well, what do you want to do?' he said shrewdly.

'You wouldn't think it very awful if I left her now, would you?' Claire began. 'You see she has Nanny and her friend to look after her and she does seem so much better at last. Of course she is awfully weak and it was rather naughty of Julia to come in like that and upset her, but really when all's said and done I think she is getting to the age,' Miss Fellowes was fifty-one, 'when it's better for them to do what they want when they are ill. D'you remember what the doctor said when your father died, but of course she's not as bad as that, only she does worry me so, I'm afraid she's not so well really. Robert, think now, what d'you say about it? You don't think it would be very awful of me, really?'

'Of course not,' he said and he had only been waiting to agree with whatever it was she wanted. 'Of course not,' he said.

Now it was settled they should go and that Claire would come with them in spite of Miss Fellowes, Julia went back to Max expecting to find them getting ready. Amabel had gone to dress but those others had opened the windows and were leaning out. She went behind Max and said, 'Don't move, it's me,' and willed her leg where it touched his to tell him she was glad.

Looking down they could see which platforms had already been opened, for at the gates a thin line of people were being extruded through in twos and threes to spread out on those emptier platforms. Separated there they became people again and were no longer menaces as they had been in one mass when singing or all of their faces turning one way to a laugh or a scream. She could even smile at them, they were so like sheep herded to be fold-driven, for they were safe now, they could be shepherded into pens and journey back to food, home, warmth and sleep. Again, if they had broken in below, which she was ready now to disbelieve, they would slowly begin to drain away again, their tide had turned and when they raised one last cheer as the first train went out she swallowed she was so afraid she was going to cry. Dear good English people, she thought, who never make trouble no matter how bad it is, come what may no matter.

Max turned away when he had seen enough, and probably because she had given up watching and had been looking at the back of his head and had been loving him, so because she had been feeling for him when he should have been loving her without her having to do one thing about it, then she began to try and worry at him again.

'Well,' she said, 'here we all are, why don't we go?'

'Am's not ready yet,' he said.

'Then hadn't you better tell her to hurry up. They won't keep our train back for us while we dress, you know.' He said they had told him there was not that much hurry and put his arm through Julia's once more.

'But how,' she said, 'how on earth when we do go do we get through all those people there are still down there, can you tell me that?'

'They said they would take us along this floor through the hotel and then the office till we can get down by a lift on to the place they keep for visiting big noises, where they receive them you see.'

'Oh, Max, as though they held receptions for noises,' she said, but he did not laugh, he never laughed at himself. Besides he had just surprised himself regretting that Amabel was coming with them.

When she had first come in it was guilt had made him so worked up about her but this feeling had gone when he saw how she was working on him until he had begun to feel his influence over her and had become indifferent, so that he did not care if she went or stayed. Finally, back to Julia as he was now and with Angela Crevy in reserve he would much rather Amabel stayed behind. Besides there was Embassy Richard. He could not stand him.

'Where's Embassy Richard?' he said. 'Has anyone seen the man?'

They all exclaimed at this and Alex, who had come back when he found Robert Hignam, turned round from his window where he had been leaning out.

'Richard?' he said, 'where?'

'Someone said so. I haven't seen him.'

'Why then,' said Alex, 'we can ask him straight out if he did write that letter.'

'And d'you suppose he'd really tell you?' said Miss Crevy.

'No, I know,' he said because he now wanted to be amiable, he thought he had gone rather far before, 'I suppose he wouldn't.'

And so everything now hung on Amabel, as it had done earlier when she was not there for even then she had remote control over Max so that he might have been some sort of a Queen Bee. At first he had hidden himself from them because he could not but feel guilty about her and then when they had found him he had still been hiding; his fun such as it was at that time had been stolen as he had known she would find him out. Now that she had found him he wanted fun and no longer cared how he got it, but one cannot break into houses when in the station cell and she had the key. So he wondered if he could get Richard to come along with them to keep her occupied. And now she came back in again.

'Where is he?' he said. 'I'd better find him,' and he left Julia to telephone.

'But, darling,' she said, following, 'I thought you hated him.'

'No, good chap, Richard.'

He made enquries and was told which room he was in. He asked to be put through.

'What on earth are you up to now?' Amabel said, and Julia knew at once by her voice there had been trouble. She moved away from him slightly, hoping they would have a row and so as not to distract his attention from how tiresome she hoped Amabel would be.

'I'm going to get him along.'

'But have you thought at all? I mean does anyone want him?' she said.

'Oh, rather, lots of questions for him, ask Alex.'

'Is that you, Richard?' he said, 'I say, come along and have a drink. Come on,' and he gave their room number.

'You aren't really going to ask him about that letter are you?' Miss Crevy said to Alex. 'It may embarrass him terribly, you know.'

'It may,' Alex said, 'but he'd rather we did, I think.'

'But it's not something to be proud of, is it? I'd have said he would hate it. Isn't it rather hitting a man when he's down?' and she said this in such a way, stressing the word 'man', that made it sound as though everyone kicked, bit, and hit women when they were down.

'Oh, I agree with you, it is,' Alex said, 'but you see he'll enjoy it, he'd be sorry if we didn't, but if you like we won't say anything, we'll let him start it on his own. He enjoys it you see. I'll bet you he'll bring it up himself within five minutes.'

'Then I think it's revolting.'

'Darling,' Julia said to her, still hoping Max and Amabel would quarrel about him, 'it's because like when one is shy about something one simply can't stop talking about it. And besides he wants everyone he meets to tell him it's all right.'

'Well,' Max said to Amabel, as though she had been speaking for Angela Crevy, 'here he is now, we'll see,' and at that he came in.

Mr Richard Cumberland was not unlike Alex and when he spoke his manner was much the same. He said, 'Why, hullo, my old dears,' and shook hands all round. If he could he took each hand in one of his, if only one was offered, then he took hold with both hands. He did not shake, he pressed as though to make secrets he would never keep, as though to embrace each private thought you had and to let you know he shared it with you and would share it again with anyone he met. As against this, when he spoke it was never to less than three people. It may have been tact, or that he was circumspect, but he paid no attention to Amabel.

'You've all heard about my little bit of trouble,' he said, 'well the town's too hot to hold me now. You know I put that thing in all the papers about my not being able to come to something or other, well they all made such a fuss you'd never believe so I thought it was time for little Richard to say good-bye for now and here I am.'

'What a pity,' Alex said, 'what a pity.'

'You don't sound very glad all of you to see me.'

'My dear, I couldn't be more pleased in every way, you must know that, only we had such arguments about who did send that announcement to the papers and I said all through it had been you so . . .'

'Oh no Alex, excuse me you never did,' Miss Crevy said, 'just the opposite really, you know. You always said someone else had sent it.'

'There you are,' Alex said to him, 'it's been like this the whole time and there you've been not three minutes away, my dear, and we never know.'

'I say, Richard,' said Max, 'where are you aiming for?'

'Why?' he said, smiling round at all of them.

'Why don't you come with us?'

'D'you all really mean it?' he said, 'well, yes, I might.'

'That's fixed then,' said Max and fixed it was.

So for anything in the world, it seemed to Julia, it was most like that afternoon when Miss Fellowes had said let's take the child to a matinee, when she had never yet gone to the theatre, it was so wonderful to see Max planning as he must be doing, to keep Amabel occupied with someone for herself. So like when you were small and they brought children over to play with you and you wanted to play on your own then someone, as they hardly ever did, came along and took them off so you could do what you wanted. And as she hoped this party would be, if she could get a hold of Max, it would be as though she could take him back into her life from where it had started and show it to him for them to share in a much more exciting thing of their own, artichokes, pigeons and all, she thought and laughed aloud.

'But weren't you going anywhere?' Amabel said to Richard, only she looked at Max.

'I can go where I was going afterwards,' he said to all of them and smiled.

London,
• 1931–1938